Nov 13/74

MURDER ON BOARD

Recent Mystery Novels by Agatha Christie

Agatha Christie

MURDER ON BOARD

INCLUDING

THE MYSTERY OF THE BLUE TRAIN

WHAT MRS. McGILLICUDDY SAW!

DEATH IN THE AIR

Dodd, Mead & Company

New York

Contents

The Mystery
of the Blue Train

Dedicated to

TWO DISTINGUISHED MEMBERS
OF THE O. F. D.

CARLOTTA *and* PETER

1

The Man with the White Hair

It was close on midnight when a man crossed the Place de la Concorde. In spite of the handsome fur coat which garbed his meager form, there was something essentially weak and paltry about him.

A little man with a face like a rat. A man, one would say, who could never play a conspicuous part, or rise to prominence in any sphere. And yet, in leaping to such a conclusion, an onlooker would have been wrong. For this man, negligible and inconspicuous as he seemed, played a prominent part in the destiny of the world. In an empire where rats ruled, he was the king of the rats.

Even now, an embassy awaited his return. But he had business to do first—business of which the embassy was not officially cognizant. His face gleamed white and sharp in the moonlight.

He came to the Seine, crossed it, and entered one of the less reputable quarters of Paris. Here he stopped before a tall, dilapidated house and made his way up to an apartment on the fourth floor. He had barely time to knock before the door was opened by a woman who had evidently been awaiting his arrival. She gave him no greeting, but helped him off with his overcoat and then led the way into the tawdrily furnished sitting room. The electric light was shaded with dirty pink festoons, and it softened, but could not disguise, the girl's face with its mask of crude paint. Could not disguise, either, the broad Mongolian cast of her countenance. There was no doubt of Olga Demiroff's profession, nor of her nationality.

"All is well, little one?"

"All is well, Boris Ivanovitch."

He nodded, murmuring: "I do not think I have been followed."

But there was anxiety in his tone. He went to the window, drawing the curtains aside slightly, and peering carefully out. He started away violently.

"There are two men—on the opposite pavement. It looks to me—" He broke off and began gnawing at his nails—a habit he had when anxious.

The Russian girl was shaking her head with a slow, reassuring action.

"They were here before you came."

"All the same, it looks to me as though they were watching this house."

"Possibly," she admitted indifferently.

"But then—"

"What of it? Even if they *know*—it will not be *you* they will follow from here."

A thin, cruel smile came to his lips.

"No," he admitted, "that is true."

He mused for a minute or two and then observed.

"This damned American—he can look after himself as well as anybody."

"I suppose so."

He went again to the window.

"Tough customers," he muttered, with a chuckle. "Known to the police, I fear. Well, well, I wish Brother Apache good hunting."

Olga Demiroff shook her head.

"If the American is the kind of man they say he is, it will take more than a couple of cowardly apaches to get the better of him." She paused. "I wonder—"

"Well?"

"Nothing. Only twice this evening a man has passed along this street—a man with white hair."

"What of it?"

"This. As he passed those two men, he dropped his glove. One of them picked it up and returned it to him. A threadbare device."

"You mean—that the white-haired man is—their employer?"

"Something of the kind."

The Russian looked alarmed and uneasy.

"You are sure—the parcel is safe? It has not been tampered with? There has been too much talk . . . much too much talk."

He gnawed his nails again.

"Judge for yourself."

She bent to the fireplace, deftly removing the coals. Underneath, from among the crumpled balls of newspaper, she selected from the very middle an oblong package wrapped round with grimy newspaper, and handed it to the man.

"Ingenious," he said, with a nod of approval.

"The apartment has been searched twice. The mattress on my bed was ripped open."

"It is as I said," he muttered. "There has been too much talk. This haggling over the price—it was a mistake."

He had unwrapped the newspaper. Inside was a small brown paper parcel. This in turn he unwrapped, verified the contents, and quickly wrapped it up once more. As he did so, an electric bell rang sharply.

"The American is punctual," said Olga, with a glance at the clock.

She left the room. In a minute she returned ushering in a stranger, a big, broad-shouldered man whose transatlantic origin was evident. His keen glance went from one to the other.

"Monsieur Krassnine?" he inquired politely.

"I am he," said Boris. "I must apologize for—for the unconventionality of this meeting place. But secrecy is urgent. I—I cannot afford to be connected with this business in any way."

"Is that so?" said the American politely.

"I have your word, have I not, that no details of this transaction will be made public? That is one of the conditions of—sale."

The American nodded.

"That has already been agreed upon," he said indifferently. "Now, perhaps, you will produce the goods."

"You have the money—in notes?"

"Yes," replied the other.

He did not, however, make any attempt to produce it. After a moment's hesitation, Krassnine gestured towards the small parcel on the table.

The American took it up and unrolled the wrapping paper. The contents he took over to a small electric lamp and submitted them to a very thorough examination. Satisfied, he drew from his pocket a thick leather wallet and extracted from it a wad of notes. These he handed to the Russian, who counted them carefully.

"All right?"

"I thank you, monsieur. Everything is correct."

"Ah!" said the other. He slipped the brown paper parcel negligently into his pocket. He bowed to Olga. "Good evening, made-moiselle. Good evening, Monsieur Krassnine."

He went out, shutting the door behind him. The eyes of the two in the room met. The man passed his tongue over his dry lips.

"I wonder—will he ever get back to his hotel?" he muttered.

By common accord, they both turned to the window. They were just in time to see the American emerge into the street below. He turned to the left and marched along at a good pace without once turning his head. Two shadows stole from a doorway and followed noiselessly. Pursuers and pursued vanished into the night. Olga Demiroff spoke.

"He will get back safely," she said. "You need not fear—or hope—whichever it is."

"Why do you think he will be safe?" asked Krassnine curiously.

"A man who has made as much money as he has could not possibly be a fool," said Olga. "And talking of money—"

She looked significantly at Krassnine.

"Eh?"

"My share, Boris Ivanovitch."

With some reluctance, Krassnine handed over two of the notes. She nodded her thanks, with a complete lack of emotion, and tucked them away in her stocking.

"That is good," she remarked, with satisfaction.

He looked at her curiously.

"You have no regrets, Olga Vassilovna?"

"Regrets? For what?"

"For what has been in your keeping. There are women—most women, I believe, who go mad over such things."

She nodded reflectively.

"Yes, you speak truth there. Most women have that madness. I—have not. I wonder now—" She broke off.

"Well?" asked the other curiously.

"The American will be safe with them—yes, I am sure of that. But afterwards—"

"Eh? What are you thinking of?"

"He will give them, of course, to some woman," said Olga thoughtfully. "I wonder what will happen then. . . ."

She shook herself impatiently and went over to the window. Suddenly she uttered an exclamation and called to her companion.

"See, he is going down the street now—the man I mean."

They both gazed down together. A slim, elegant figure was progressing along at a leisurely pace. He wore an opera hat and a cloak. As he passed a street lamp, the light illumined a thatch of thick white hair.

2

Monsieur le Marquis

THE man with the white hair continued on his course, unhurried, and seemingly indifferent to his surroundings. He took a side turning to the right and another one to the left. Now and then he hummed a little air to himself.

Suddenly he stopped dead and listened intently. He had heard a certain sound. It might have been the bursting of a tire or it might have been—a shot. A curious smile played round his lips for a minute. Then he resumed his leisurely walk.

On turning a corner he came upon a scene of some activity. A representative of the law was making notes in a pocketbook, and one or two late passers-by had collected on the spot. To one of these the man with the white hair made a polite request for information.

"Something has been happening, yes?"

"*Mais oui*, monsieur. Two apaches set upon an elderly American gentleman."

"They did him no injury?"

"No, indeed." The man laughed. "The American, he had a revolver in his pocket, and before they could attack him, he fired shots so closely round them that they took alarm and fled. The police, as usual, arrived too late."

"Ah!" said the inquirer.

He displayed no emotion of any kind.

Placidly and unconcernedly he resumed his nocturnal strolling. Presently he crossed the Seine and came in to the richer areas of the city. It was some twenty minutes later that he came to a stop before a certain house in a quiet but aristocratic thoroughfare.

The shop, for shop it was, was a restrained and unpretentious one. D. Papopolous, dealer in antiques, was so known to fame that he needed no advertisement, and indeed most of his business was not done over a counter. Monsieur Papopolous had a very handsome apartment of his own overlooking the Champs Élysées, and it might reasonably be supposed that he would have been found there and not at his place of business at such an hour, but the man with the white hair seemed confident of success as he pressed the obscurely placed bell, having first given a quick glance up and down the deserted street.

His confidence was not misplaced. The door opened and a man stood in the aperture. He wore gold rings in his ears and was of a swarthy cast of countenance.

"Good evening," said the stranger. "Your master is within?"

"The master is here, but he does not see chance visitors at this time of night," growled the other.

"I think he will see me. Tell him that his friend Monsieur le Marquis is here."

The man opened the door a little wider and allowed the visitor to enter.

The man who gave his name as Monsieur le Marquis had shielded his face with his hand as he spoke. When the manservant returned with the information that Monsieur Papopolous would be pleased to receive the visitor a further change had taken place in the stranger's appearance. The manservant must have been very unobservant or very well trained, for he betrayed no surprise at the small black satin mask which hid the other's features. Leading the way to a door at the end of the hall, he opened it and announced in a respectful murmur: "Monsieur le Marquis."

The figure which rose to receive this strange guest was an imposing one. There was something venerable and patriarchal about Monsieur Papopolous. He had a high domed forehead and a beautiful white beard. His manner had in it something ecclesiastical and benign.

"My dear friend," said Monsieur Papopolous.

He spoke in French and his tones were rich and unctuous.

"I must apologize," said the visitor, "for the lateness of the hour."

"Not at all. Not at all," said Monsieur Papopolous—"an interesting time of night. You have had, perhaps, an interesting evening?"

"Not personally," said Monsieur le Marquis.

"Not personally," repeated Monsieur Papopolous, "no, no, of course not. And there is news, eh?"

He cast a sharp glance sideways at the other, a glance that was not ecclesiastical or benign in the least.

"There is no news. The attempt failed. I hardly expected anything else."

"Quite so," said Monsieur Papopolous; "anything crude—"

He waved his hand to express his intense distaste for crudity in any form. There was indeed nothing crude about Monsieur Papopolous nor about the goods he handled. He was well known in most European courts, and kings called him Demetrius in a friendly manner. He had the reputation for the most exquisite discretion. That, together with the nobility of his aspect, had carried him through several very questionable transactions.

"The direct attack—" said Monsieur Papopolous. He shook his head. "It answers sometimes—but very seldom."

The other shrugged his shoulders.

"It saves time," he remarked, "and to fail costs nothing—or next to nothing. The other plan—will not fail."

"Ah," said Monsieur Papopolous, looking at him keenly.

The other nodded slowly.

"I have great confidence in your—er—reputation," said the antique dealer.

Monsieur le Marquis smiled gently.

"I think I may say," he murmured, "that your confidence will not be misplaced."

"You have unique opportunities," said the other, with a note of envy in his voice.

"I make them," said Monsieur le Marquis.

He rose and took up the cloak which he had thrown carelessly on the back of a chair.

"I will keep you informed, Monsieur Papopolous, through the usual channels, but there must be no hitch in your arrangements."

Monsieur Papopolous was pained.

"There is *never* a hitch in my arrangements," he complained.

The other smiled, and without any further word of adieu he left the room, closing the door behind him.

Monsieur Papopolous remained in thought for a moment stroking his venerable white beard, and then moved across to a second door which opened inwards. As he turned the handle, a young woman, who only too clearly had been leaning against it with her ear to the keyhole, stumbled headlong into the room. Monsieur Papopolous displayed neither surprise nor concern. It was evidently all quite natural to him.

"Well, Zia?" he asked.

"I did not hear him go," explained Zia.

She was a handsome young woman, built on Junoesque lines, with dark flashing eyes and such a general air of resemblance to Monsieur Papopolous that it was easy to see they were father and daughter.

"It is annoying," she continued vexedly, "that one cannot see through a keyhole and hear through it at the same time."

"It has often annoyed me," said Monsieur Papopolous, with great simplicity.

"So that is Monsieur le Marquis," said Zia slowly. "Does he always wear a mask, Father?"

"Always."

There was a pause.

"It is the rubies, I suppose?" asked Zia.

Her father nodded.

"What do you think, my little one?" he inquired, with a hint of amusement in his beady black eyes.

"Of Monsieur le Marquis?"

"Yes."

"I think," said Zia slowly, "that it is a very rare thing to find a well-bred Englishman who speaks French as well as that."

"Ah!" said Monsieur Papopolous. "So that is what you think."

As usual, he did not commit himself, but he regarded Zia with benign approval.

"I thought, too," said Zia, "that his head was an odd shape."

"Massive," said her father—"a trifle massive. But then that effect is always created by a wig."

They both looked at each other and smiled.

3

Heart of Fire

RUFUS VAN ALDIN passed through the revolving doors of the Savoy, and walked to the reception desk. The desk clerk smiled a respectful greeting.

"Pleased to see you back again, Mr. Van Aldin," he said.

The American millionaire nodded his head in a casual greeting.

"Everything all right?" he asked.

"Yes, sir. Major Knighton is upstairs in the suite now."

Van Aldin nodded again.

"Any mail?" he vouchsafed.

"They have all been sent up, Mr. Van Aldin. Oh! Wait a minute."

He dived into a pigeonhole, and produced a letter.

"Just come this minute," he explained.

Rufus Van Aldin took the letter from him, and as he saw the handwriting, a woman's flowing hand, his face was suddenly transformed. The harsh contours of it softened, and the hard line of his mouth relaxed. He looked a different man. He walked across to the lift with the letter in his hand and the smile still on his lips.

In the drawing room of his suite, a young man was sitting at a desk nimbly sorting correspondence with the ease born of long practice. He sprang up as Van Aldin entered.

"Hallo, Knighton!"

"Glad to see you back, sir. Had a good time?"

"So-so!" said the millionaire unemotionally. "Paris is rather a one-horse city nowadays. Still—I got what I went over for."

He smiled to himself rather grimly.

"You usually do, I believe," said the secretary, laughing.

"That's so," agreed the other.

He spoke in a matter-of-fact manner, as one stating a well-known fact. Throwing off his heavy overcoat, he advanced to the desk.

"Anything urgent?"

"I don't think so, sir. Mostly the usual stuff. I have not quite finished sorting it out."

Van Aldin nodded briefly. He was a man who seldom expressed either blame or praise. His methods with those he employed were simple; he gave them a fair trial and dismissed promptly those who were inefficient. His selections of people were unconventional. Knighton, for instance, he had met casually at a Swiss resort two months previously. He had approved of the fellow, looked up his war record, and found in it the explanation of the limp with which he walked. Knighton had made no secret of the fact that he was looking for a job, and indeed diffidently asked the millionaire if he knew of any available post. Van Aldin remembered, with a grim smile of amusement, the young man's complete astonishment when he had been offered the post of secretary to the great man himself.

"But—but I have no experience of business," he had stammered.

"That doesn't matter," Van Aldin had replied. "I have got three secretaries already to attend to that kind of thing. But I am likely to be in England for the next six months, and I want an Englishman who—well, knows the ropes—and can attend to the social side of things for me."

So far, Van Aldin had found his judgment confirmed. Knighton had proved quick, intelligent, and resourceful, and he had a distinct charm of manner.

The secretary indicated three or four letters placed by themselves on the top of the desk.

"It might perhaps be as well, sir, if you glanced at these," he suggested. "The top one is about the Colton agreement—"

But Rufus Van Aldin held up a protesting hand.

"I am not going to look at a darned thing tonight," he declared. "They can all wait till the morning. Except this one," he added, looking down at the letter he held in his hand. And again that strange transforming smile stole over his face.

Richard Knighton smiled sympathetically.

"Mrs. Kettering?" he murmured. "She rang up yesterday and today. She seems very anxious to see you at once, sir."

"Does she, now!"

The smile faded from the millionaire's face. He ripped open the envelope which he held in his hand and took out the enclosed sheet. As he read it his face darkened, his mouth set grimly in the line which Wall Street knew so well, and his brows knit themselves ominously. Knighton turned tactfully away, and went on opening letters and sorting them. A muttered oath escaped the millionaire, and his clenched fist hit the table sharply.

"I'll not stand for this," he muttered to himself. "Poor little girl, it's a good thing she has her old father behind her."

He walked up and down the room for some minutes, his brows drawn together in a scowl. Knighton still bent assiduously over the desk. Suddenly Van Aldin came to an abrupt halt. He took up his overcoat from the chair where he had thrown it.

"Are you going out again, sir?"

"Yes; I'm going round to see my daughter."

"If Colton's people ring up—"

"Tell them to go to the devil," said Van Aldin.

"Very well," said the secretary unemotionally.

Van Aldin had his overcoat on by now. Cramming his hat upon his head, he went towards the door. He paused with his hand upon the handle.

"You are a good fellow, Knighton," he said. "You don't worry me when I am rattled."

Knighton smiled a little, but made no reply.

"Ruth is my only child," said Van Aldin, "and there is no one on this earth who knows quite what she means to me."

A faint smile irradiated his face. He slipped his hand into his pocket.

"Care to see something, Knighton?"

He came back towards the secretary.

From his pocket he drew out a parcel carelessly wrapped in brown paper. He tossed off the wrapping and disclosed a big, shabby, red velvet case. In the center of it were some twisted initials surmounted by a crown. He snapped the case open, and the secretary drew in his breath sharply. Against the slightly dingy white of the interior, the stones glowed like blood.

"My God, sir!" said Knighton. "Are they—are they real?"

Van Aldin laughed a quiet little cackle of amusement.

"I don't wonder at your asking that. Among these rubies are the three largest in the world. Catherine of Russia wore them, Knighton. That center one there is known as Heart of Fire. It's perfect—not a flaw in it."

"But," the secretary murmured, "they must be worth a fortune."

"Four or five hundred thousand dollars," said Van Aldin nonchalantly, "and that is apart from the historical interest."

"And you carry them about—like that, loose in your pocket?"

Van Aldin laughed amusedly.

"I guess so. You see, they are my little present for Ruthie."

The secretary smiled discreetly.

"I can understand now Mrs. Kettering's anxiety over the telephone," he murmured.

But Van Aldin shook his head. The hard look returned to his face.

"You are wrong there," he said. "She doesn't know about these; they are my little surprise for her."

He shut the case, and began slowly to wrap it up again.

"It's a hard thing, Knighton," he said, "how little one can do for those one loves. I can buy a good portion of the earth for Ruth, if it would be any use to her, but it isn't. I can hang these things round her neck and give her a moment or two's pleasure, maybe, but—"

He shook his head.

"When a woman is not happy in her home—"

He left the sentence unfinished. The secretary nodded discreetly. He knew, none better, the reputation of the Honorable Derek Kettering. Van Aldin sighed. Slipping the parcel back in his coat pocket, he nodded to Knighton and left the room.

4

In Curzon Street

The Honorable Mrs. Derek Kettering lived in Curzon Street. The butler who opened the door recognized Rufus Van Aldin at once and permitted himself a discreet smile of greeting. He led the way upstairs to the big double drawing room on the first floor.

A woman who was sitting by the window started up with a cry.

"Why, Dad, if that isn't too good for anything! I've been telephoning Major Knighton all day to try and get hold of you, but he couldn't say for sure when you were expected back."

Ruth Kettering was twenty-eight years of age. Without being beautiful, or in the real sense of the word even pretty, she was striking-looking because of her coloring. Van Aldin had been called Carrots and Ginger in his time, and Ruth's hair was almost pure auburn. With it went dark eyes and very black lashes—the effect somewhat enhanced by art. She was tall and slender, and moved well. At a careless glance it was the face of a Raphael Madonna. Only if one looked closely did one perceive the same line of jaw and chin as in Van Aldin's face, bespeaking the same hardness and determination. It suited the man, but suited the woman less well. From her childhood upward Ruth Van Aldin had been accustomed to having her own way, and anyone who had ever stood up against her soon realized that Rufus Van Aldin's daughter never gave in.

"Knighton told me you'd phoned him," said Van Aldin. "I only got back from Paris half an hour ago. What's all this about Derek?"

Ruth Kettering flushed angrily.

"It's unspeakable. It's beyond all limits," she cried. "He—he doesn't seem to listen to anything I say."

There was bewilderment as well as anger in her voice.

"He'll listen to me," said the millionaire grimly.

Ruth went on.

"I've hardly seen him for the last month. He goes about everywhere with that woman."

"With what woman?"

"Mirelle. She dances at the Parthenon, you know."

Van Aldin nodded.

"I was down at Leconbury last week. I—I spoke to Lord Leconbury. He was awfully sweet to me, sympathized entirely. He said he'd give Derek a good talking-to."

"Ah!" said Van Aldin.

"What do you mean by 'Ah,' Dad?"

"Just what you think I mean, Ruthie. Poor old Leconbury is a washout. Of course he sympathized with you, of course he tried to soothe you down. Having got his son and heir married to the daughter of one of the richest men in the States, he naturally doesn't want to mess the thing up. But he's got one foot in the grave already, everyone knows that, and anything he may say will cut darned little ice with Derek."

"Can't *you* do anything, Dad?" urged Ruth, after a minute or two.

"I might," said the millionaire. He waited a second reflectively, and then went on. "There are several things I might do, but there's only one that will be any real good. How much pluck have you got, Ruthie?"

She stared at him. He nodded back at her.

"I mean just what I say. Have you got the grit to admit to all the world that you've made a mistake? There's only one way out of this mess, Ruthie. Cut your losses and start afresh."

"You mean—"

"Divorce."

"Divorce!"

Van Aldin smiled dryly.

"You say that word, Ruth, as though you'd never heard it before. And yet your friends are doing it all round you every day."

"Oh! I know that. But—"

She stopped, biting her lip. Her father nodded comprehendingly.

"I know, Ruth. You're like me, you can't bear to let go. But I've learned, and you've got to learn, that there are times when it's the only way. I might find ways of whistling Derek back to you, but it would all come to the same in the end. He's no good, Ruth; he's rotten through and through. And mind you, I blame myself for ever letting you marry him. But you were kind of set on having him, and he seemed in earnest about turning over a new leaf—and well, I'd crossed you once, honey . . ."

He did not look at her as he said the last words. Had he done so, he might have seen the swift color that came up in her face.

"You did," she said in a hard voice.

"I was too darned soft-hearted to do it a second time. I can't tell you how I wish I had, though. You've led a poor kind of life for the last few years, Ruth."

"It has not been very—agreeable," agreed Mrs. Kettering.

"That's why I say to you that this thing has got to stop!" He brought his hand down with a bang on the table. "You may have a hankering after the fellow still. Cut it out. Face facts. Derek Kettering married you for your money. That's all there is to it. Get rid of him, Ruth."

Ruth Kettering looked down at the ground for some moments, then she said, without raising her head:

"Supposing he doesn't consent?"

Van Aldin looked at her in astonishment.

"He won't have a say in the matter."

She flushed and bit her lip.

"No—no—of course not. I only meant—"

She stopped. Her father eyed her keenly.

"What did you mean?"

"I meant—" She paused, choosing her words carefully. "He mayn't take it lying down."

The millionaire's chin shot out grimly.

"You mean he'll fight the case? Let him! But, as a matter of fact, you're wrong. He won't fight. Any solicitor he consults will tell him he hasn't a leg to stand upon."

"You don't think"—she hesitated—"I mean—out of sheer spite against me—he might, try to make it awkward?"

Her father looked at her in some astonishment.

"Fight the case, you mean?"

He shook his head.

"Very unlikely. You see, he would have to have something to go upon."

Mrs. Kettering did not answer. Van Aldin looked at her sharply.

"Come, Ruth, out with it. There's something troubling you—what is it?"

"Nothing, nothing at all."

But her voice was unconvincing.

"You are dreading the publicity, eh? Is that it? You leave it to me. I'll put the whole thing through so smoothly that there will be no fuss at all."

"Very well, Dad, if you really think it's the best thing to be done."

"Got a fancy for the fellow still, Ruth? Is that it?"

"No."

The word came with no uncertain emphasis. Van Aldin seemed satisfied. He patted his daughter on the shoulder.

"It will be all right, little girl. Don't you worry any. Now let's forget all about this. I have brought you a present from Paris."

"For me? Something very nice?"

"I hope you'll think so," said Van Aldin, smiling.

He took the parcel from his coat pocket and handed it to her. She unwrapped it eagerly, and snapped open the case. A long-drawn "Oh!" came from her lips. Ruth Kettering loved jewels—always had done so.

"Dad, how—how wonderful!"

"Rather in a class by themselves, aren't they?" said the millionaire, with satisfaction. "You like them, eh?"

"Like them? Dad, they're unique. How did you get hold of them?"

Van Aldin smiled.

"Ah! That's my secret. They had to be bought privately, of course. They are rather well known. See that big stone in the middle? You have heard of it, maybe; that's the historic 'Heart of Fire.' "

"Heart of Fire!" repeated Mrs. Kettering.

She had taken the stones from the case and was holding them against her breast. The millionaire watched her. He was thinking of the series of women who had worn the jewels. The heartaches, the despairs, the jealousies. "Heart of Fire," like all famous stones, had left behind it a trail of tragedy and violence. Held in Ruth Kettering's assured hand, it seemed to lose its potency of evil. With her cool, equable poise, this woman of the western world seemed a negation to tragedy or heart-burnings. Ruth returned the stones to their case; then, jumping up, she flung her arms round her father's neck.

"Thank you, thank you, thank you, Dad! They are wonderful! You do give me the most marvelous presents always."

"That's all right," said Van Aldin, patting her shoulder. "You are all I have, you know, Ruthie."

"You will stay to dinner, won't you, Father?"

"I don't think so. You were going out, weren't you?"

"Yes, but I can easily put that off. Nothing very exciting."

"No," said Van Aldin. "Keep your engagement. I have got a good deal to attend to. See you tomorrow, my dear. Perhaps if I phone you, we can meet at Galbraiths'?"

Messrs. Galbraith, Galbraith, Cuthbertson, & Galbraith were Van Aldin's London solicitors.

"Very well, Dad." She hesitated. "I suppose it—this—won't keep me from going to the Riviera?"

"When are you off?"

"On the fourteenth."

"Oh, that will be all right. These things take a long time to mature. By the way, Ruth, I shouldn't take those rubies abroad if I were you. Leave them at the bank."

Mrs. Kettering nodded.

"We don't want to have you robbed and murdered for the sake of 'Heart of Fire,'" said the millionaire jocosely.

"And yet you carried it about in your pocket loose," retorted his daughter, smiling.

"Yes—"

Something, some hesitation, caught her attention.

"What is it, Dad?"

"Nothing." He smiled. "Thinking of a little adventure of mine in Paris."

"An adventure?"

"Yes, the night I bought these things."

He made a gesture towards the jewel case.

"Oh, do tell me."

"Nothing to tell, Ruthie. Some apache fellows got a bit fresh and I shot at them and they got off. That's all."

She looked at him with some pride.

"You're a tough proposition, Dad."

"You bet I am, Ruthie."

He kissed her affectionately and departed. On arriving back at the Savoy, he gave a curt order to Knighton.

"Get hold of a man called Goby; you'll find his address in my private book. He's to be here tomorrow morning at half-past nine."

"Yes, sir."

"I also want to see Mr. Kettering. Run him to earth for me if you can. Try his club—at any rate, get hold of him somehow, and arrange for me to see him here tomorrow morning. Better make it latish, about twelve. His sort aren't early risers."

The secretary nodded in comprehension of these instructions. Van Aldin gave himself into the hands of his valet. His bath was prepared, and as he lay luxuriating in the hot water, his mind went back over the conversation with his daughter. On the whole he was well satisfied. His keen mind had long since accepted the fact that divorce was the only possible way out. Ruth had agreed to the proposed solution with more readiness than he had hoped for. Yet, in spite of her acquiescence, he was left with a vague sense of uneasiness. Something about her manner, he felt, had not been quite natural. He frowned to himself.

"Maybe I'm fanciful," he muttered, "and yet—I bet there's something she has not told me."

5

A Useful Gentleman

RUFUS VAN ALDIN had just finished the sparse breakfast of coffee and dry toast, which was all he ever allowed himself, when Knighton entered the room.

"Mr. Goby is below, sir, waiting to see you."

The millionaire glanced at the clock. It was just half-past nine.

"All right," he said curtly. "He can come up."

A minute or two later, Mr. Goby entered the room. He was a small, elderly man, shabbily dressed, with eyes that looked carefully all round the room, and never at the person he was addressing.

"Good morning, Goby," said the millionaire. "Take a chair."

"Thank you, Mr. Van Aldin."

Mr. Goby sat down with his hands on his knees, and gazed earnestly at the radiator.

"I have got a job for you."

"Yes, Mr. Van Aldin?"

"My daughter is married to the Honorable Derek Kettering, as you may perhaps know."

Mr. Goby transferred his gaze from the radiator to the left-hand drawer of the desk, and permitted a deprecating smile to pass over his face. Mr. Goby knew a great many things, but he always hated to admit the fact.

"By my advice, she is about to file a petition for divorce. That, of course, is a solicitor's business. But, for private reasons, I want the fullest and most complete information."

Mr. Goby looked at the cornice and murmured:

"About Mr. Kettering?"

"About Mr. Kettering."

"Very good, sir."

Mr. Goby rose to his feet.

"When will you have it ready for me?"

"Are you in a hurry, sir?"

"I'm always in a hurry," said the millionaire.

Mr. Goby smiled understandingly at the fender.

"Shall we say two o'clock this afternoon, sir?" he asked.

"Excellent," approved the other. "Good morning, Goby."

"Good morning, Mr. Van Aldin."

"That's a very useful man," said the millionaire as Goby went out and his secretary came in. "In his own line he's a specialist."

"What is his line?"

"Information. Give him twenty-four hours and he would lay the private life of the Archbishop of Canterbury bare for you."

"A useful sort of chap," said Knighton, with a smile.

"He has been useful to me once or twice," said Van Aldin. "Now then, Knighton, I'm ready for work."

The next few hours saw a vast quantity of business rapidly transacted. It was half-past twelve when the telephone bell rang, and Mr. Van Aldin was informed that Mr. Kettering had called. Knighton looked at Van Aldin, and interpreted his brief nod.

"Ask Mr. Kettering to come up, please."

The secretary gathered up his papers and departed. He and the visitor passed each other in the doorway, and Derek Kettering stood aside to let the other go out. Then he came in, shutting the door behind him.

"Good morning, sir. You are very anxious to see me, I hear."

The lazy voice with its slightly ironic inflection roused memories in Van Aldin. There was charm in it—there had always been charm in it. He looked piercingly at his son-in-law. Derek Kettering was thirty-four, lean of build, with a dark, narrow face, which had even now something indescribably boyish in it.

"Come in," said Van Aldin curtly. "Sit down."

Kettering flung himself lightly into an armchair. He looked at his father-in-law with a kind of tolerant amusement.

"Not seen you for a long time, sir," he remarked pleasantly. "About two years, I should say. Seen Ruth yet?"

"I saw her last night," said Van Aldin.

"Looking very fit, isn't she?" said the other lightly.

"I didn't know you had had much opportunity of judging," said Van Aldin dryly.

Derek Kettering raised his eyebrows.

"Oh, we sometimes meet at the same night club, you know," he said airily.

"I am not going to beat about the bush," Van Aldin said curtly. "I have advised Ruth to file a petition for divorce."

Derek Kettering seemed unmoved.

"How drastic!" he murmured. "Do you mind if I smoke, sir?"

He lit a cigarette, and puffed out a cloud of smoke as he added nonchalantly:

"And what did Ruth say?"

"Ruth proposes to take my advice," said her father.

"Does she really?"

"Is that all you have got to say?" demanded Van Aldin sharply.

Kettering flicked his ash into the grate.

"I think, you know," he said, with a detached air, "that she's making a great mistake."

"From your point of view she doubtless is," said Van Aldin grimly.

"Oh, come now," said the other; "don't let's be personal. I really wasn't thinking of myself at the moment. I was thinking of Ruth. You know my poor old Governor really can't last much longer; all the doctors say so. Ruth had better give it a couple more years, then I shall be Lord Leconbury, and she can be châtelaine of Leconbury, which is what she married me for."

"I won't have any of your darned impudence," roared Van Aldin.

Derek Kettering smiled at him quite unmoved.

"I agree with you. It's an obsolete idea," he said. "There's nothing in a title nowadays. Still, Leconbury is a very fine old place, and, after all, we are one of the oldest families in England. It will be very annoying for Ruth if she divorces me to find me marrying again, and some other woman queening it at Leconbury instead of her."

"I am serious, young man," said Van Aldin.

"Oh, so am I," said Kettering. "I am in very low water financially; it will put me in a nasty hole if Ruth divorces me, and, after all, if she has stood it for ten years, why not stand it a little longer? I give you my word of honor that the old man can't possibly last out another eighteen months, and, as I said before, it's a pity Ruth shouldn't get what she married me for."

"You suggest that my daughter married you for your title and position?"

Derek Kettering laughed a laugh that was not all amusement.

"You don't think it was a question of a love match?" he asked.

"I know," said Van Aldin slowly, "that you spoke very differently in Paris ten years ago."

"Did I? Perhaps I did. Ruth was very beautiful, you know—rather like an angel or a saint, or something that had stepped down from a niche in a church. I had fine ideas, I remember, of turning over a new leaf, of settling down and living up to the highest traditions of English home life with a beautiful wife who loved me."

He laughed again, rather more discordantly.

"But you don't believe that, I suppose?" he said.

"I have no doubt at all that you married Ruth for her money," said Van Aldin unemotionally.

"And that she married me for love?" asked the other ironically.

"Certainly," said Van Aldin.

Derek Kettering stared at him for a minute or two, then he nodded reflectively.

"I see you believe that," he said. "So did I at the time. I can assure you, my dear father-in-law, I was very soon undeceived."

"I don't know what you are getting at," said Van Aldin, "and I don't care. You have treated Ruth darned badly."

"Oh, I have," agreed Kettering lightly, "but she's tough, you know. She's your daughter. Underneath the pink-and-white softness of her she's as hard as granite. You have always been known as a hard man, so I have been told, but Ruth is harder than you are. You, at any rate, love one person better than yourself. Ruth never has and never will."

"That is enough," said Van Aldin. "I asked you here so that I could tell you fair and square what I meant to do. My girl has got to have some happiness, and remember this, I am behind her."

Derek Kettering got up and stood by the mantelpiece. He tossed away his cigarette. When he spoke, his voice was very quiet.

"What exactly do you mean by that, I wonder?" he said.

"I mean," said Van Aldin, "that you had better not try to defend the case."

"Oh," said Kettering. "Is that a threat?"

"You can take it any way you please," said Van Aldin.

Kettering drew a chair up to the table. He sat down fronting the millionaire.

"And supposing," he said softly, "that, just for argument's sake, I did defend the case?"

Van Aldin shrugged his shoulders.

"You have not got a leg to stand upon, you young fool. Ask your solicitors, they will soon tell you. Your conduct has been notorious, the talk of London."

"Ruth has been kicking up a row about Mirelle, I suppose. Very foolish of her. I don't interfere with her friends."

"What do you mean?" said Van Aldin sharply.

Derek Kettering laughed.

"I see you don't know everything, sir," he said. "You are, perhaps naturally, prejudiced."

He took up his hat and stick and moved towards the door.

"Giving advice is not much in my line." He delivered his final thrust. "But, in this case, I should advise most strongly perfect frankness between father and daughter."

He passed quickly out of the room and shut the door behind him just as the millionaire sprang up.

"Now, what the hell did he mean by that?" said Van Aldin as he sank back into his chair again.

All his uneasiness returned in full force. There was something here that he had not yet got to the bottom of. The telephone was by his elbow; he seized it, and asked for the number of his daughter's house.

"Hallo! Hallo! Is that Mayfair 81907? Mrs. Kettering in? Oh, she's out, is she? Yes, out to lunch. What time will she be in? You don't know? Oh, very good; no, there's no message."

He slammed the receiver down again angrily. At two o'clock he was pacing the floor of his room waiting expectantly for Goby. The latter was ushered in at ten minutes past two.

"Well?" barked the millionaire sharply.

But little Mr. Goby was not to be hurried. He sat down at the table, produced a very shabby pocketbook, and proceeded to read from it in a monotonous voice. The millionaire listened attentively, with an increasing satisfaction. Goby came to a full stop, and looked attentively at the wastepaper basket.

"Um!" said Van Aldin. "That seems pretty definite. The case will go through like winking. The hotel evidence is all right, I suppose?"

"Cast iron," said Mr. Goby, and looked malevolently at a gilt armchair.

"And financially he's in very low water. He's trying to raise a loan now, you say? Has already raised practically all he can upon his expectations from his father. Once the news of the divorce gets about, he won't be able to raise another cent, and not only that, his obligations can be bought up and pressure can be put upon him from that quarter. We have got him, Goby; we have got him in a cleft stick."

He hit the table a bang with his fist. His face was grim and triumphant.

"The information," said Mr. Goby in a thin voice, "seems satisfactory."

"I have got to go round to Curzon Street now," said the millionaire. "I am much obliged to you, Goby. You are the goods all right."

A pale smile of gratification showed itself on the little man's face. "Thank you, Mr. Van Aldin," he said; "I try to do my best."

Van Aldin did not go direct to Curzon Street. He went first to the City, where he had two interviews which added to his satisfaction. From there he took the tube to Down Street. As he was walking along Curzon Street, a figure came out of No. 160, and turned up the street towards him, so that they passed each other on the pavement. For a moment, the millionaire had fancied it might be Derek Kettering himself; the height and build were not unlike. But as they came face to face, he saw that the man was a stranger to him. At least—no, not a stranger; his face awoke some call of recognition in the millionaire's mind, and it was associated definitely with something unpleasant. He cudgeled his brains in vain, but the thing eluded him. He went on, shaking his head irritably. He hated to be baffled.

Ruth Kettering was clearly expecting him. She ran to him and kissed him when he entered.

"Well, Dad, how are things going?"

"Very well," said Van Aldin; "but I have got a word or two to say to you, Ruth."

Almost insensibly he felt the change in her; something shrewd and watchful replaced the impulsiveness of her greeting. She sat down in a big armchair.

"Well, Dad?" she asked. "What is it?"

"I saw your husband this morning," said Van Aldin.

"You saw Derek?"

"I did. He said a lot of things, most of which were darned cheek. Just as he was leaving, he said something that I didn't understand. He advised me to be sure that there was perfect frankness between father and daughter. What did he mean by that, Ruthie?"

Mrs. Kettering moved a little in her chair.

"I—I don't know, Dad. How should I?"

"Of course you know," said Van Aldin. "He said something else, about his having his friends and not interfering with yours. What did he mean by that?"

"I don't know," said Ruth Kettering again.

Van Aldin sat down. His mouth set itself in a grim line.

"See here, Ruth. I am not going into this with my eyes closed. I am not at all sure that that husband of yours doesn't mean to make trouble. Now, he can't do it, I am sure of that. I have got the means to silence him, to shut his mouth for good and all, but I have got to know if there's any need to use those means. What did he mean by your having your own friends?"

Mrs. Kettering shrugged her shoulders.

"I have got lots of friends," she said uncertainly. "I don't know what he meant, I am sure."

"You do," said Van Aldin.

He was speaking now as he might have spoken to a business adversary.

"I will put it plainer. Who is the man?"

"What man?"

"*The* man. That's what Derek was driving at. Some special man who is a friend of yours. You needn't worry, honey, I know there is nothing in it, but we have got to look at everything as it might appear to the court. They can twist these things about a good deal, you know. I want to know who the man is, and just how friendly you have been with him."

Ruth didn't answer. Her hands were kneading themselves together in intense nervous absorption.

"Come, honey," said Van Aldin in a softer voice. "Don't be afraid of your old dad. I was not too harsh, was I, even that time in Paris? By gosh!"

He stopped, thunderstruck.

"That's who it was," he murmured to himself. "I thought I knew his face."

"What are you talking about, Dad? I don't understand."

The millionaire strode across to her and took her firmly by the wrist.

"See here, Ruth, have you been seeing that fellow again?"

"What fellow?"

"The one we had all that fuss about years ago. You know who I mean well enough."

"You mean"—she hesitated—"you mean the Comte de la Roche?"

"Comte de la Roche!" snorted Van Aldin. "I told you at the time that the man was no better than a swindler. You had entangled yourself with him then very deeply, but I got you out of his clutches."

"Yes, you did," said Ruth bitterly. "And I married Derek Kettering."

"You wanted to," said the millionaire sharply.

She shrugged her shoulders.

"And now," said Van Aldin slowly, "you have been seeing him again—after all I told you. He has been in the house today. I met him outside, and couldn't place him for the moment."

Ruth Kettering had recovered her composure.

"I want to tell you one thing, Dad; you are wrong about Armand —the Comte de la Roche, I mean. Oh, I know there were several regrettable incidents in his youth—he has told me about them; but —well, he has cared for me always. It broke his heart when you parted us in Paris, and now—"

She was interrupted by the snort of indignation her father gave.

"So you fell for that stuff, did you? You, a daughter of mine! My God!"

He threw up his hands.

"That women can be such darned fools!"

6

Mirelle

DEREK KETTERING emerged from Van Aldin's suite so precipitantly that he collided with a lady passing across the corridor. He apologized, and she accepted his apologies with a smiling reassurance and passed on, leaving with him a pleasant impression of a soothing personality and rather fine gray eyes.

For all his nonchalance, his interview with his father-in-law had shaken him more than he cared to show. He had a solitary lunch, and after it, frowning to himself a little, he went around to the sumptuous flat that housed the lady known as Mirelle. A trim Frenchwoman received him with smiles.

"But enter then, monsieur. Madame reposes herself."

He was ushered into the long room with its Eastern setting which he knew so well. Mirelle was lying on the divan, supported by an incredible number of cushions, all in varying shades of amber, to harmonize with the yellow ocher of her complexion. The dancer was a beautifully made woman, and if her face, beneath its mask of yellow, was in truth somewhat haggard, it had a bizarre charm of its own, and her orange lips smiled invitingly at Derek Kettering.

He kissed her, and flung himself into a chair.

"What have you been doing with yourself? Just got up, I suppose?"

The orange mouth widened into a long smile.

"No," said the dancer. "I have been at work."

She flung out a long, pale hand towards the piano, which was littered with untidy music scores.

"Ambrose has been here. He has been playing me the new opera."

Kettering nodded without paying much attention. He was profoundly uninterested in Claud Ambrose and the latter's operatic setting of Ibsen's *Peer Gynt*. So was Mirelle, for that matter, regarding it merely as a unique opportunity for her own presentation as Anitra.

"It is a marvelous dance," she murmured. "I shall put all the passion of the desert into it. I shall dance hung over with jewels—ah! and, by the way, *mon ami,* there is a pearl that I saw yesterday in Bond Street—a black pearl."

She paused, looking at him invitingly.

"My dear girl," said Kettering, "it's no use talking of black pearls to me. At the present minute, as far as I am concerned, the fat is in the fire."

She was quick to respond to his tone. She sat up, her big black eyes widening.

"What is that you say, Dereek? What has happened?"

"My esteemed father-in-law," said Kettering, "is preparing to go off the deep end."

"Eh?"

"In other words, he wants Ruth to divorce me."

"How stupid!" said Mirelle. "Why should she want to divorce you?"

Derek Kettering grinned.

"Mainly because of you, *chérie!*" he said.

Mirelle shrugged her shoulders.

"That is foolish," she observed in a matter-of-fact voice.

"Very foolish," agreed Derek.

"What are you going to do about it?" demanded Mirelle.

"My dear girl, what can I do? On the one side, the man with unlimited money; on the other side, the man with unlimited debts. There is no question as to who will come out on top."

"They are extraordinary, these Americans," commented Mirelle. "It is not as though your wife were fond of you."

"Well," said Derek, "what are we going to do about it?"

She looked at him inquiringly. He came over and took both her hands in his.

"Are you going to stick to me?"

"What do you mean? After—"

"Yes," said Kettering. "After, when the creditors come down like wolves on the fold. I am damned fond of you, Mirelle. Are you going to let me down?"

She pulled her hands away from him.

"You know I adore you, Dereek."

He caught the note of evasion in her voice.

"So that's that, is it? The rats will leave the sinking ship."

"Ah, Dereek!"

"Out with it," he said violently. "You will fling me over. Is that it?"

She shrugged her shoulders.

"I am fond of you, *mon ami*—indeed I am fond of you. You are very charming—*un beau garçon,* but *ce n'est pas pratique.*"

"You are a rich man's luxury, eh? Is that it?"

"If you like to put it that way."

She leaned back on the cushions, her head flung back.

"All the same, I am fond of you, Dereek."

He went over to the window and stood there some time looking out, with his back to her. Presently the dancer raised herself on her elbow and stared at him curiously.

"What are you thinking of, *mon ami?*"

He grinned at her over his shoulder, a curious grin that made her vaguely uneasy.

"As it happened, I was thinking of a woman, my dear."

"A woman, eh?"

Mirelle pounced on something that she could understand.

"You are thinking of some other woman, is that it?"

"Oh, you needn't worry; it is purely a fancy portrait. 'Portrait of a lady with gray eyes.'"

Mirelle said sharply, "When did you meet her?"

Derek Kettering laughed, and his laughter had a mocking, ironical sound.

"I ran into the lady in the corridor of the Savoy Hotel."

"Well! What did she say?"

"As far as I can remember, I said, 'I beg your pardon,' and she said, 'It doesn't matter,' or words to that effect."

"And then?" persisted the dancer.

Kettering shrugged his shoulders.

"And then—nothing. That was the end of the incident."

"I don't understand a word of what you are talking about," declared the dancer.

"Portrait of a lady with gray eyes," murmured Derek reflectively. "Just as well I am never likely to meet her again."

"Why?"

"She might bring me bad luck. Women do."

Mirelle slipped quickly from her couch, and came across to him, laying one long, snakelike arm round his neck.

"You are foolish, Dereek," she murmured. "You are very foolish. You are *beau garçon,* and I adore you, but I am not made to be poor —no, decidedly I am not made to be poor. Now listen to me; everything is very simple. You must make it up with your wife."

"I am afraid that's not going to be actually in the sphere of practical politics," said Derek dryly.

"How do you say? I do not understand."

"Van Aldin, my dear, is not taking any. He is the kind of man who makes up his mind and sticks to it."

"I have heard of him," nodded the dancer. "He is very rich, is he not? Almost the richest man in America. A few days ago, in Paris, he bought the most wonderful ruby in the world—'Heart of Fire' it is called."

Kettering did not answer. The dancer went on musingly:

"It is a wonderful stone—a stone that should belong to a woman like me. I love jewels, Dereek; they say something to me. Ah! To wear a ruby like 'Heart of Fire.'"

She gave a little sigh, and then became practical once more.

"You don't understand these thing, Dereek; you are only a man. Van Aldin will give these rubies to his daughter, I suppose. Is she his only child?"

"Yes."

"Then when he dies, she will inherit all his money. She will be a rich woman."

"She is a rich woman already," said Kettering dryly. "He settled a couple of millions on her at her marriage."

"A couple of million! But that is immense. And if she died suddenly, eh? That would all come to you?"

"As things stand at present," said Kettering slowly, "it would. As far as I know she has not made a will."

"*Mon Dieu!*" said the dancer. "If she were to die, what a solution that would be."

There was a moment's pause, and then Derek Kettering laughed outright.

"I like your simple, practical mind, Mirelle, but I am afraid what you desire won't come to pass. My wife is an extremely healthy person."

"*Eh bien!*" said Mirelle. "There are accidents."

He looked at her sharply but did not answer.

She went on.

"But you are right, *mon ami,* we must not dwell on possibilities. See now, my little Dereek, there must be no more talk of this divorce. Your wife must give up the idea."

"And if she won't?"

The dancer's eyes widened to slits.

"I think she will, my friend. She is one of those who would not like the publicity. There are one or two pretty stories that she would not like her friends to read in the newspapers."

"What do you mean?" asked Kettering sharply.

Mirelle laughed, her head thrown back.

"*Parbleu!* I mean the gentleman who calls himself the Comte de la Roche. I know all about him. I am Parisienne, you remember. He was her lover before she married you, was he not?"

Kettering took her sharply by the shoulders.

"That is a damned lie," he said, "and please remember that, after all, you are speaking of my wife."

Mirelle was a little sobered.

"You are extraordinary, you English," she complained. "All the same, I dare say that you may be right. The Americans are so cold, are they not? But you will permit me to say, *mon ami,* that she was in love with him before she married you, and her father stepped in and sent the Comte about his business. And the little mademoiselle, she wept many tears! But she obeyed. Still, you must know as well as I do, Dereek, that it is a very different story now. She sees him nearly every day, and on the fourteenth she goes to Paris to meet him."

"How do you know all this?" demanded Kettering.

"Me? I have friends in Paris, my dear Dereek, who know the Comte intimately. It is all arranged. She is going to the Riviera, so she says, but in reality the Comte meets her in Paris and—who knows! Yes, yes, you can take my word for it, it is all arranged."

Derek Kettering stood motionless.

"You see," purred the dancer, "if you are clever, you have her in the hollow of your hand. You can make things very awkward for her."

"Oh, for God's sake be quiet," cried Kettering. "Shut your cursed mouth!"

Mirelle flung herself down again on the divan with a laugh. Kettering caught up his hat and coat and left the flat, banging the door violently. And still the dancer sat on the divan and laughed softly to herself. She was not displeased with her work.

7

Letters

Mrs. Samuel Harfield presents her compliments to Miss Katherine Grey and wishes to point out that under the circumstances Miss Grey may not be aware—

Mrs. Harfield, having written so far fluently, came to a dead stop, held up by what has proved an insuperable difficulty to many other people—namely, the difficulty of expressing oneself fluently in the third person.

After a minute or two of hesitation, Mrs. Harfield tore up the sheet of notepaper and started afresh.

Dear Miss Grey—Whilst fully appreciating the adequate way you discharged your duties to my Cousin Emma (whose recent death has indeed been a severe blow to us all), I cannot but feel—

Again Mrs. Harfield came to a stop. Once more the letter was consigned to the wastepaper basket. It was not until four false starts had been made that Mrs. Harfield at last produced an epistle that satisfied her. It was duly sealed and stamped and addressed to Miss Katherine Grey, Little Crampton, St. Mary Mead, Kent, and it lay beside that lady's plate on the following morning at breakfast time in company with a more important-looking communication in a long blue envelope.

Katherine Grey opened Mrs. Harfield's letter first. The finished production ran as follows:

Dear Miss Grey—My husband and I wish to express our thanks to you for your services to my poor cousin, Emma. Her death has been a great blow to us, though we were, of course, aware that her mind has been failing for some time past. I understand that her latter testamentary dispositions have been of a most peculiar character, and they would not hold good, of course, in any court of law. I have no doubt that, with your usual good sense, you have already realized this fact. If these matters can be arranged privately it is always so much better, my husband says. We shall be pleased to recommend you most highly for a similar post and hope that you will also accept a small present. Believe me, dear Miss Grey, yours cordially, MARY ANNE HARFIELD.

Katherine Grey read the letter through, smiled a little, and read it a second time. Her face as she laid the letter down after the second reading was distinctly amused. Then she took up the second letter. After one brief perusal she laid it down and stared very straight in front of her. This time she did not smile. Indeed, it would have been hard for anyone watching her to guess what emotions lay behind that quiet, reflective gaze.

Katherine Grey was thirty-three. She came of good family, but her father had lost all his money, and Katherine had had to work for her living from an early age. She had been just twenty-three when she had come to old Mrs. Harfield as companion.

It was generally recognized that old Mrs. Harfield was "difficult." Companions came and went with startling rapidity. They arrived full of hope and they usually left in tears. But from the moment Katherine Grey set foot in Little Crampton, ten years ago, perfect peace had reigned. No one knows how these things come about. Snake charmers, they say, are born, not made. Katherine Grey was born with the power of managing old ladies, dogs, and small boys, and she did it without any apparent sense of strain.

At twenty-three she had been a quiet girl with beautiful eyes. At thirty-three she was a quiet woman with those same gray eyes, shining steadily out on the world with a kind of happy serenity that nothing could shake. Moreover, she had been born with, and still possessed, a sense of humor.

As she sat at the breakfast table, staring in front of her, there was a ring at the bell, accompanied by a very energetic rat-a-tat-tat at the knocker. In another minute the little maidservant opened the door and announced rather breathlessly:

"Dr. Harrison."

The big, middle-aged doctor came bustling in with the energy and breeziness that had been foreshadowed by his onslaught on the knocker.

"Good morning, Miss Grey."

"Good morning, Dr. Harrison."

"I dropped in early," began the doctor, "in case you should have heard from one of those Harfield cousins. Mrs. Samuel, she calls herself—a perfectly poisonous person."

Without a word, Katherine picked up Mrs. Harfield's letter from the table and gave it to him. With a good deal of amusement she watched his perusal of it, the drawing together of the bushy eyebrows, the snorts and grunts of violent disapproval. He dashed it down again on the table.

"Perfectly monstrous," he fumed. "Don't you let it worry you, my dear. They're talking through their hat. Mrs. Harfield's intellect was as good as yours or mine, and you won't get anyone to say the contrary. They wouldn't have a leg to stand upon, and they know it. All that talk of taking it into court is pure bluff. Hence this attempt to get round you in a hole-and-corner way. And look here, my dear, don't let them get round you with soft soap either. Don't get fancying it's your duty to hand over the cash, or any tomfoolery of conscientious scruples."

"I'm afraid it hasn't occurred to me to have scruples," said Katherine. "All these people are distant relatives of Mrs. Harfield's husband, and they never came near her or took any notice of her in her lifetime."

"You're a sensible woman," said the doctor. "I know, none better, that you've had a hard life of it for the last ten years. You're fully entitled to enjoy the old lady's savings, such as they were."

Katherine smiled thoughtfully.

"Such as they were," she repeated. "You've no idea of the amount, Doctor?"

"Well—enough to bring in five hundred a year or so, I suppose."

Katherine nodded.

"That's what I thought," she said. "Now read this."

She handed him the letter she had taken from the long blue envelope. The doctor read and uttered an exclamation of utter astonishment.

"Impossible," he muttered. "Impossible."

"She was one of the original shareholders in Mortaulds. Forty years ago she must have had an income of eight or ten thousand a year. She has never, I am sure, spent more than four hundred a year. She was always terribly careful about money. I always believed that she was obliged to be careful about every penny."

"And all the time the income has accumulated at compound interest. My dear, you're going to be a very rich woman."

Katherine Grey nodded.

"Yes," she said, "I am."

She spoke in a detached, impersonal tone, as though she were looking at the situation from outside.

"Well," said the doctor, preparing to depart, "you have all my congratulations." He flicked Mrs. Samuel Harfield's letter with his thumb. "Don't worry about that woman and her odious letter."

"It really isn't an odious letter," said Miss Grey tolerantly. "Under the circumstances, I think it's really quite a natural thing to do."

"I have the gravest suspicions of you sometimes," said the doctor.

"Why?"

"The things that you find perfectly natural."

Katherine Grey laughed.

Dr. Harrison retailed the great news to his wife at lunchtime. She was very excited about it.

"Fancy old Mrs. Harfield—with all that money. I'm glad she left it to Katherine Grey. That girl's a saint."

The doctor made a wry face.

"Saints I always imagine must have been difficult people. Katherine Grey is too human for a saint."

"She's a saint with a sense of humor," said the doctor's wife, twinkling. "And, though I don't suppose you've ever noticed the fact, she's extremely good-looking."

"Katherine Grey?" The doctor was honestly surprised. "She's got very nice eyes, I know."

"Oh, you men!" cried his wife. "Blind as bats. Katherine's got all the makings of a beauty in her. All she wants is clothes!"

"Clothes? What's wrong with her clothes? She always looks very nice."

Mrs. Harrison gave an exasperated sigh, and the doctor rose preparatory to starting on his rounds.

"You might look in on her, Polly," he suggested.

"I'm going to," said Mrs. Harrison promptly.

She made her call about three o'clock.

"My dear, I'm so glad," she said warmly, as she squeezed Katherine's hand. "And everyone in the village will be glad too."

"It's very nice of you to come and tell me," said Katherine. "I hoped you would come in because I wanted to ask about Johnnie."

"Oh! Johnnie. Well—"

Johnnie was Mrs. Harrison's youngest son. In another minute she was off, retailing a long history in which Johnnie's adenoids and tonsils bulked largely. Katherine listened sympathetically. Habits die hard. Listening had been her portion for ten years now. "My dear, I wonder if I ever told you about that naval ball at Portsmouth? When Lord Charles admired my gown?" And composedly, kindly, Katherine would reply: "I rather think you have, Mrs. Harfield, but I've forgotten about it. Won't you tell it me again?" And then the old lady would start off full swing, with numerous details. And half of Katherine's mind would be listening, saying the right things mechanically when the old lady paused. . . .

Now, with that same curious feeling of duality to which she was accustomed, she listened to Mrs. Harrison.

At the end of half an hour, the latter recalled herself suddenly.

"I've been talking about myself all this time," she exclaimed. "And I came here to talk about you and your plans."

"I don't know that I've got any yet."

"My dear—you're not going to stay on *here*."

Katherine smiled at the horror in the other's tone.

"No; I think I want to travel. I've never seen much of the world, you know."

"I should think not. It must have been an awful life for you cooped up here all these years."

"I don't know," said Katherine. "It gave me a lot of freedom."

She caught the other's gasp, and reddened a little.

"It must sound foolish—saying that. Of course, I hadn't much freedom in the downright physical sense—"

"I should think not," breathed Mrs. Harrison, remembering that Katherine had seldom had that useful thing as a "day off."

"But, in a way, being tied physically gives you lots of scope mentally. You're always free to think. I've had a lovely feeling always of mental freedom."

Mrs. Harrison shook her head.

"I can't understand that."

"Oh! You would if you'd been in my place. But, all the same, I feel I want a change. I want—well, I want things to happen. Oh! Not to me—I don't mean that. But to be in the midst of things, exciting things—even if I'm only the looker-on. You know, things don't happen in St. Mary Mead."

"They don't indeed," said Mrs. Harrison, with fervor.

"I shall go to London first," said Katherine. "I have to see the solicitors, anyway. After that, I shall go abroad, I think."

"Very nice."

"But, of course, first of all—"

"Yes?"

"I must get some clothes."

"Exactly what I said to Arthur this morning," cried the doctor's wife. "You know, Katherine, you could look possibly positively beautiful if you tried."

Miss Grey laughed unaffectedly.

"Oh! I don't think you could ever make a beauty out of me," she said sincerely. "But I shall enjoy having some really good clothes. I'm afraid I'm talking about myself an awful lot."

Mrs. Harrison looked at her shrewdly.

"It must be quite a novel experience for you," she said dryly.

Katherine went to say good-by to old Miss Viner before leaving the village. Miss Viner was two years older than Mrs. Harfield, and her mind was mainly taken up with her own success in outliving her dead friend.

"You wouldn't have thought I'd have outlasted Jane Harfield, would you?" she demanded triumphantly of Katherine. "We were at school together, she and I. And here we are, she taken, and I left. Who would have thought it?"

"You've always eaten brown bread for supper, haven't you?" murmured Katherine mechanically.

"Fancy your remembering that, my dear. Yes; if Jane Harfield had had a slice of brown bread every evening and taken a little stimulant with her meals she might be here today."

The old lady paused, nodding her head triumphantly; then added in sudden remembrance:

"And so you've come into a lot of money, I hear? Well, well. Take care of it. And you're going up to London to have a good time? Don't think you'll get married, though, my dear, because you won't. You're not the kind to attract the men. And, besides, you're getting on. How old are you now?"

"Thirty-three," Katherine told her.

"Well," remarked Miss Viner doubtfully, "that's not so very bad. You've lost your first freshness, of course."

"I'm afraid so," said Katherine, much entertained.

"But you're a very nice girl," said Miss Viner kindly. "And I'm sure there's many a man might do worse than take you for a wife instead of one of these flibbertigibbets running about nowadays showing more of their legs than the Creator ever intended them to. Good-by, my dear, and I hope you'll enjoy yourself, but things are seldom what they seem in this life."

Heartened by these prophecies, Katherine took her departure. Half the village came to see her off at the station, including the little maid of all work, Alice, who brought a stiff wired nosegay and cried openly.

"There ain't a many like her," sobbed Alice when the train had finally departed. "I'm sure when Charlie went back on me with that girl from the dairy, nobody could have been kinder than Miss Grey was, and though particular about the brasses and the dust, she was always one to notice when you'd give a thing an extra rub. Cut myself in little pieces for her, I would, any day. A real lady, that's what I call her."

Such was Katherine's departure from St. Mary Mead.

8

Lady Tamplin Writes a Letter

"WELL," said Lady Tamplin, "well."

She laid down the continental *Daily Mail* and stared out across the blue waters of the Mediterranean. A branch of golden mimosa, hanging just above her head, made an effective frame for a very charming picture. A golden-haired, blue-eyed lady in a very becoming negligee. That the golden hair owed something to art, as did the pink-and-white complexion, was undeniable, but the blue of the eyes was Nature's gift, and at forty-four Lady Tamplin could still rank as a beauty.

Charming as she looked, Lady Tamplin was, for once, not thinking of herself. That is to say, she was not thinking of her appearance. She was intent on graver matters.

Lady Tamplin was a well-known figure on the Riviera, and her parties at the Villa Marguerite were justly celebrated. She was a woman of considerable experience, and had had four husbands. The first had been merely an indiscretion, and so was seldom referred to by the lady. He had had the good sense to die with commendable promptitude, and his widow thereupon espoused a rich manufacturer of buttons. He too had departed for another sphere after three years of married life—it was said after a congenial evening with some boon companions. After him came Viscount Tamplin, who had placed Rosalie securely on those heights where she wished to tread. She had retained her title when she married for a fourth time. This fourth venture had been undertaken for pure pleasure. Mr. Charles Evans, an extremely good-looking young man of twenty-seven, with delightful manners, a keen love of sport, and an appreciation of this world's goods, had no money of his own whatsoever.

Lady Tamplin was very pleased and satisfied with life generally, but she had occasional faint preoccupations about money. The button manufacturer had left his widow a considerable fortune, but, as Lady Tamplin was wont to say, "what with one thing and another—" (one thing being the depreciation of stocks owing to the war, and the other the extravagances of the late Lord Tamplin). She was still comfortably off. But to be merely comfortably off is hardly satisfactory to one of Rosalie Tamplin's temperament.

So, on this particular January morning, she opened her blue eyes extremely wide as she read a certain item of news and uttered that noncommittal monosyllable "Well." The only other occupant of the balcony was her daughter, the Hon. Lenox Tamplin. A daughter such as Lenox was a sad thorn in Lady Tamplin's side, a girl with no kind of tact, who actually looked older than her age, and whose peculiar sardonic form of humor was, to say the least of it, uncomfortable.

"Darling," said Lady Tamplin, "just fancy."

"What is it?"

Lady Tamplin picked up the *Daily Mail*, handed it to her daughter, and indicated with an agitated forefinger the paragraph of interest.

Lenox read it without any of the signs of agitation shown by her mother. She handed back the paper.

"What about it?" she asked. "It is the sort of thing that is always happening. Cheese-paring old women are always dying in villages and leaving fortunes of millions to their humble companions."

"Yes, dear, I know," said her mother, "and I dare say the fortune is not anything like as large as they say it is; newspapers are so inaccurate. But even if you cut it down by half—"

"Well," said Lenox, "it has not been left to us."

"Not exactly, dear," said Lady Tamplin; "but this girl, this Katherine Grey, is actually a cousin of mine. One of the Worcestershire Greys, the Edgeworth lot. My very own cousin! Fancy!"

"Ah-ha," said Lenox.

"And I was wondering—" said her mother.

"What there was in it for us," finished Lenox, with that sideways smile that her mother always found difficult to understand.

"Oh, darling," said Lady Tamplin, on a faint note of reproach.

It was very faint, because Rosalie Tamplin was used to her daughter's outspokenness and to what she called Lenox's uncomfortable way of putting things.

"I was wondering," said Lady Tamplin, again drawing her artistically penciled brows together, "whether—oh, good morning, Chubby darling. Are you going to play tennis? How nice!"

Chubby, thus addressed, smiled kindly at her, remarked perfunctorily, "How topping you look in that peach-colored thing," and drifted past them and down the steps.

"The dear thing," said Lady Tamplin, looking affectionately after her husband. "Let me see, what was I saying? Ah!" She switched her mind back to business once more. "I was wondering—"

"Oh, for God's sake get on with it. That is the third time you have said that."

"Well, dear," said Lady Tamplin, "I was thinking that it would be very nice if I wrote to dear Katherine and suggested that she should pay us a little visit out here. Naturally, she is quite out of touch with society. It would be nicer for her to be launched by one of her own people. An advantage for her and an advantage for us."

"How much do you think you would get her to cough up?" asked Lenox.

Her mother looked at her reproachfully and murmured:

"We should have to come to some financial arrangement, of course. What with one thing and another—the war—your poor father—"

"And Chubby now," said Lenox. "He is an expensive luxury, if you like."

"She was a nice girl as I remember her," murmured Lady Tamplin, pursuing her own line of thought—"quiet, never wanted to shove herself forward, not a beauty, and never a manhunter."

"She will leave Chubby alone, then?" said Lenox.

Lady Tamplin looked at her in protest. "Chubby would never—" she began.

"No," said Lenox, "I don't believe he would; he knows a jolly sight too well which way his bread is buttered."

"Darling," said Lady Tamplin, "you have such a coarse way of putting things."

"Sorry," said Lenox.

Lady Tamplin gathered up the *Daily Mail* and her negligee, a vanity bag, and various odd letters.

"I shall write to dear Katherine at once," she said, "and remind her of the dear old days at Edgeworth."

She went into the house, a light of purpose shining in her eyes.

Unlike Mrs. Samuel Harfield, correspondence flowed easily from her pen. She covered four sheets without pause or effort, and on re-reading it found no occasion to alter a word.

Katherine received it on the morning of her arrival in London. Whether she read between the lines of it or not is another matter. She put it in her handbag and started out to keep the appointment she had made with Mrs. Harfield's lawyers.

The firm was an old-established one in Lincoln's Inn Fields, and after a few minutes' delay Katherine was shown into the presence of the senior partner, a kindly, elderly man with shrewd blue eyes and a fatherly manner.

They discussed Mrs. Harfield's will and various legal matters for some minutes, then Katherine handed the lawyer Mrs. Samuel's letter.

"I had better show you this, I suppose," she said, "though it is really rather ridiculous."

He read it with a slight smile.

"Rather a crude attempt, Miss Grey. I need hardly tell you, I suppose, that these people have no claim of any kind upon the estate, and if they endeavor to contest the will no court will uphold them."

"I thought as much."

"Human nature is not always very wise. In Mrs. Samuel Harfield's place, I should have been more inclined to make an appeal to your generosity."

"That is one of the things I wanted to speak to you about. I should like a certain sum to go to these people."

"There is no obligation."

"I know that."

"And they will not take it in the spirit it is meant. They will probably regard it as an attempt to pay them off, though they will not refuse it on that account."

"I can see that, and it can't be helped."

"I should advise you, Miss Grey, to put that idea out of your head."

Katherine shook her head. "You are quite right, I know, but I should like it done all the same."

"They will grab at the money and abuse you all the more afterwards."

"Well," said Katherine, "let them if they like. We all have our own ways of enjoying ourselves. They were, after all, Mrs. Harfield's only relatives, and though they despised her as a poor relation and paid no attention to her when she was alive, it seems to me unfair that they should be cut off with nothing."

She carried her point, though the lawyer was still unwilling, and she presently went out into the streets of London with a comfortable assurance that she could spend money freely and make what plans she liked for the future. Her first action was to visit the establishment of a famous dressmaker.

A slim, elderly Frenchwoman, rather like a dreaming duchess, received her, and Katherine spoke with a certain naiveté.

"I want, if I may, to put myself in your hands. I have been very poor all my life and know nothing about clothes, but now I have come into some money and want to look really well-dressed."

The Frenchwoman was charmed. She had an artist's temperament, which had been soured earlier in the morning by a visit from an Argentine meat queen, who had insisted on having those models least suited to her flamboyant type of beauty. She scrutinized Katherine with keen, clever eyes. "Yes—yes, it will be a pleasure. Mademoiselle has a very good figure; for her the simple lines will be best. She is also *très anglaise*. Some people it would offend them if I said that, but Mademoiselle, no. *Une belle Anglaise,* there is no style more delightful."

The demeanor of a dreaming duchess was suddenly put off. She screamed out direction to various mannequins. "Clothilde, Virginie, quickly, my little ones, the little *tailleur gris clair* and the *robe de soirée 'soupir d'automne.'* Marcelle, my child, the little mimosa suit of crêpe de chine."

It was a charming morning. Marcelle, Clothilde, Virginie, bored and scornful, passed slowly round, squirming and wriggling in the time-honored fashion of mannequins. The Duchess stood by Katherine and made entries in a small notebook.

"An excellent choice, mademoiselle. Mademoiselle has great *goût.* Yes, indeed. Mademoiselle cannot do better than those little suits if she is going to the Riviera, as I suppose, this winter."

"Let me see that evening dress once more," said Katherine—"the pinky mauve one."

Virginie appeared, circling slowly.

"That is the prettiest of all," said Katherine, as she surveyed the exquisite draperies of mauve and gray and blue. "What do you call it?"

"*Soupir d'automne;* yes, yes, that is truly the dress of Mademoiselle."

What was there in these words that came back to Katherine with a faint feeling of sadness after she had left the dressmaking establishment.

"'*Soupir d'automne; that is truly the dress of Mademoiselle.*'" Autumn, yes, it was autumn for her. She who had never known spring or summer, and would never know them now. Something she had lost never could be given to her again. These years of servitude in St. Mary Mead—and all the while life passing by.

"I am an idiot," said Katherine. "I am an idiot. What do I want? Why, I was more contented a month ago than I am now."

She drew out from her handbag the letter she had received that morning from Lady Tamplin. Katherine was no fool. She understood the nuances of that letter as well as anybody and the reason of Lady Tamplin's sudden show of affection towards a long-forgotten cousin was not lost upon her. It was for profit and not for pleasure that Lady Tamplin was so anxious for the company of her dear cousin. Well, why not? There would be profit on both sides.

"I will go," said Katherine.

She was walking down Piccadilly at the moment, and turned into Cook's to clinch the matter then and there. She had to wait for a few minutes. The man with whom the clerk was engaged was also going to the Riviera. Everyone, she felt, was going. Well, for the first time in her life, she, too, would be doing what "everybody did."

The man in front of her turned abruptly, and she stepped into his place. She made her demand to the clerk, but at the same time half of her mind was busy with something else. That man's face—in some vague way it was familiar to her. Where had she seen him before? Suddenly she remembered. It was in the Savoy outside her room that morning. She had collided with him in the passage. Rather an odd coincidence that she should run into him twice in a day. She glanced over her shoulder, rendered uneasy by something, she knew not what. The man was standing in the doorway looking back at her. A cold shiver passed over Katherine; she had a haunting sense of tragedy, of doom impending. . . .

Then she shook the impression from her with her usual good sense and turned her whole attention to what the clerk was saying.

9

An Offer Refused

IT was rarely that Derek Kettering allowed his temper to get the better of him. An easy-going insouciance was his chief characteristic, and it had stood him in good stead in more than one tight corner. Even now, by the time he had left Mirelle's flat, he had cooled down. He had need of coolness. The corner he was in now was a tighter one than he had ever been in before, and unforeseen factors had arisen with which, for the moment, he did not know how to deal.

He strolled along deep in thought. His brow was furrowed, and there was none of the easy, jaunty manner which sat so well upon him. Various possibilities floated through his mind. It might have been said of Derek Kettering that he was less of a fool than he looked. He saw several roads that he might take—one in particular. If he shrank from it, it was for the moment only. Desperate ills need desperate remedies. He had gauged his father-in-law correctly. A war between Derek Kettering and Rufus Van Aldin could end only one way. Derek damned money and the power of money vehemently to himself. He walked up St. James's Street, across Piccadilly, and strolled along it in the direction of Piccadilly Circus. As he passed the offices of Messrs. Thomas Cook & Sons, his footsteps slackened. He walked on, however, still turning the matter over in his mind. Finally, he gave a brief nod of his head, turned sharply—so sharply as to collide with a couple of pedestrians who were following in his footsteps, and went back the way he had come. This time he did not pass Cook's, but went in. The office was comparatively empty, and he got attended to at once.

"I want to go to Nice next week. Will you give me particulars?"

"What date, sir?"

"The fourteenth. What is the best train?"

"Well, of course, the best train is what they call the Blue Train. You avoid the tiresome customs business at Calais."

Derek nodded. He knew all this, none better.

"The fourteenth," murmured the clerk; "that is rather soon. The Blue Train is nearly always all booked up."

"See if there is a berth left," said Derek. "If there is not—" He left the sentence unfinished, with a curious smile on his face.

The clerk disappeared for a few minutes, and presently returned. "That is all right, sir; still three berths left. I will book you one of them. What name?"

"Pavett," said Derek. He gave the address of his rooms in Jermyn Street.

The clerk nodded, finished writing it down, wished Derek good morning politely, and turned his attention to the next client.

"I want to go to Nice—on the fourteenth. Isn't there a train called the Blue Train?"

Derek looked round sharply.

Coincidence—a strange coincidence. He remembered his own half-whimsical words to Mirelle, *"Portrait of a lady with gray eyes. I don't suppose I shall ever see her again."* But he *had* seen her again, and, what was more, she proposed to travel to the Riviera on the same day as he did.

Just for a moment a shiver passed over him; in some ways he was superstitious. He had said, half laughingly, that this woman might bring him bad luck. Suppose—suppose that should prove to be true. From the doorway he looked back at her as she stood talking to the clerk. For once his memory had not played him false. A lady—a lady in every sense of the word. Not very young, not singularly beautiful. But with something—gray eyes that might perhaps see too much. He knew as he went out of the door that in some way he was afraid of this woman. He had a sense of fatality.

He went back to his rooms in Jermyn Street and summoned his man.

"Take this check, Pavett, cash it first thing in the morning, and go around to Cook's in Piccadilly. They will have some tickets there booked in your name, pay for them, and bring them back."

"Very good, sir."

Pavett withdrew.

Derek strolled over to a side table and picked up a handful of letters. They were of a type only too familiar. Bills, small bills and

large bills, one and all pressing for payment. The tone of the demands was still polite. Derek knew how soon that polite tone would
change if—if certain news became public property.

He flung himself moodily into a large, leather-covered chair. A
damned hole—that was what he was in. Yes, a damned hole! And
ways of getting out of that damned hole were not too promising.

Pavett appeared with a discreet cough.

"A gentleman to see you—sir—Major Knighton."

"Knighton, eh?"

Derek sat up, frowned, became suddenly alert. He said in a softer
tone, almost to himself: "Knighton—I wonder what is in the wind
now?"

"Shall I—er—show him in, sir?"

His master nodded. When Knighton entered the room, he found
a charming and genial host awaiting him.

"Very good of you to look me up," said Derek.

Knighton was nervous.

The other's keen eyes noticed that at once. The errand on which
the secretary had come was clearly distasteful to him. He replied
almost mechanically to Derek's easy flow of conversation. He declined a drink, and, if anything, his manner became stiffer than before. Derek appeared at last to notice it.

"Well," he said cheerfully, "what does my esteemed father-in-law
want with me? You have come on his business, I take it?"

Knighton did not smile in reply.

"I have, yes," he said carefully. "I—I wish Mr. Van Aldin had
chosen someone else."

Derek raised his eyebrows in mock dismay.

"Is it as bad as all that? I am not very thin-skinned, I can assure
you, Knighton."

"No," said Knighton; "but this—"

He paused.

Derek eyed him keenly.

"Go on, out with it," he said kindly. "I can imagine my dear father-
in-law's errands might not always be pleasant ones."

Knighton cleared his throat. He spoke formally in tones that he
strove to render free of embarrassment.

"I am directed by Mr. Van Aldin to make you a definite offer."

"An offer?" For a moment Derek showed his surprise. Knighton's opening words were clearly not what he had expected. He offered a cigarette to Knighton, lit one himself, and sank back in his chair, murmuring in a slightly sardonic voice:

"An offer? That sounds rather interesting."

"Shall I go on?"

"Please. You must forgive my surprise, but it seems to me that my dear father-in-law has rather climbed down since our chat this morning. And climbing down is not what one associates with strong men, Napoleons of finance, et cetera. It shows—I think it shows that he finds his position weaker than he thought it."

Knighton listened politely to the easy, mocking voice, but no sign of any kind showed itself on his rather stolid countenance. He waited until Derek had finished, and then he said quietly:

"I will state the proposition in the fewest possible words."

"Go on."

Knighton did not look at the other. His voice was curt and matter-of-fact.

"The matter is simply this. Mrs. Kettering, as you know, is about to file a petition for divorce. If the case goes undefended you will receive one hundred thousand on the day that the decree is made absolute."

Derek, in the act of lighting his cigarette, suddenly stopped dead.

"A hundred thousand!" he said sharply. "Dollars?"

"Pounds."

There was dead silence for at least two minutes. Kettering had his brows together thinking. A hundred thousand pounds. It meant Mirelle and a continuance of his pleasant, carefree life. It meant that Van Aldin knew something. Van Aldin did not pay for nothing. He got up and stood by the chimney piece.

"And in the event of my refusing his handsome offer?" he asked, with a cold, ironical politeness.

Knighton made a deprecating gesture.

"I can assure you, Mr. Kettering," he said earnestly, "that it is with the utmost unwillingness that I came here with this message."

"That's all right," said Kettering. "Don't distress yourself; it's not your fault. Now then—I asked you a question. Will you answer it?"

Knighton also rose. He spoke more reluctantly than before.

"In the event of your refusing this proposition," he said, "Mr. Van Aldin wished me to tell you in plain words that he proposes to break you. Just that."

Kettering raised his eyebrows, but he retained his light, amused manner.

"Well, well!" he said. "I suppose he can do it. I certainly should not be able to put up much of a fight against America's man of millions. A hundred thousand! If you are going to bribe a man, there is nothing like doing it thoroughly. Supposing I were to tell you that for two hundred thousand I'd do what he wanted, what then?"

"I would take your message back to Mr. Van Aldin," said Knighton unemotionally. "Is that your answer?"

"No," said Derek; "funnily enough it is not. You can go back to my father-in-law and tell him to take himself and his bribes to hell. Is that clear?"

"Perfectly," said Knighton. He got up, hesitated, and then flushed. "I—you will allow me to say, Mr. Kettering, that I am glad you have answered as you have."

Derek did not reply. When the other had left the room, he remained for a minute or two lost in thought. A curious smile came to his lips.

"And that is that," he said softly.

10

On the Blue Train

"DAD!"

Mrs. Kettering started violently. Her nerves were not completely under control this morning. Very perfectly dressed in a long mink coat and a little hat of Chinese lacquer red, she had been walking along the crowded platform of Victoria deep in thought, and her father's sudden appearance and hearty greeting had an unlooked-for effect upon her.

"Why, Ruth, how you jumped!"

"I didn't expect to see you, I suppose, Dad. You said good-by to me last night and said you had a conference this morning."

"So I have," said Van Aldin, "but you are more to me than any number of darned conferences. I came to take a last look at you, since I am not going to see you for some time."

"That is very sweet of you, Dad. I wish you were coming too."

"What would you say if I did?"

The remark was merely a joking one. He was surprised to see the quick color flame in Ruth's cheeks. For a moment he almost thought he saw dismay flash out of her eyes. She laughed uncertainly and nervously.

"Just for a moment I really thought you meant it," she said.

"Would you have been pleased?"

"Of course." She spoke with exaggerated emphasis.

"Well," said Van Aldin, "that's good."

"It isn't really for very long, Dad," continued Ruth; "you know, you are coming out next month."

"Ah!" said Van Aldin unemotionally. "Sometimes I guess I will go to one of these big guys in Harley Street and have him tell me that I need sunshine and change of air right away."

"Don't be so lazy," cried Ruth; "next month is ever so much nicer than this month out there. You have got all sorts of things you can't possibly leave just now."

"Well, that's so, I suppose," said Van Aldin, with a sigh. "You had better be getting on board this train of yours, Ruth. Where is your seat?"

Ruth Kettering looked vaguely up at the train. At the door of one of the Pullman cars a thin, tall woman dressed in black was standing—Ruth Kettering's maid. She drew aside as her mistress came up to her.

"I have put your dressing case under your seat, madam, in case you should need it. Shall I take the rugs, or will you require one?"

"No, no, I shan't want one. Better go and find your own seat now, Mason."

"Yes, madam."

The maid departed.

Van Aldin entered the Pullman car with Ruth. She found her seat, and Van Aldin deposited various papers and magazines on the table in front of her. The seat opposite to her was already taken, and the American gave a cursory glance at its occupant. He had a fleeting impression of attractive gray eyes and a neat traveling costume. He indulged in a little more desultory conversation with Ruth, the kind of talk peculiar to those seeing other people off by train.

Presently, as whistles blew, he glanced at his watch.

"I had best be clearing out of here. Good-by, my dear. Don't worry, I will attend to things."

"Oh, Father!"

He turned back sharply. There had been something in Ruth's voice, something so entirely foreign to her usual manner, that he was startled. It was almost a cry of despair. She had made an impulsive movement towards him, but in another minute she was mistress of herself once more.

"Till next month," she said cheerfully.

Two minutes later the train started.

Ruth sat very still, biting her underlip and trying hard to keep the unaccustomed tears from her eyes. She felt a sudden sense of horrible desolation. There was a wild longing upon her to jump out of the train and to go back before it was too late. She, so calm, so self-assured, for the first time in her life felt like a leaf swept by the wind. If her father knew—what would he say?

Madness! Yes, just that, madness! For the first time in her life she was swept away by emotion, swept away to the point of doing a thing which even she knew to be incredibly foolish and reckless. She was enough Van Aldin's daughter to realize her own folly, and level-headed enough to condemn her own action. But she was his daughter in another sense also. She had that same iron determination that would have what it wanted, and once it had made up its mind would not be balked. From her cradle she had been self-willed; the very circumstances of her life had developed that self-will in her. It drove her now remorselessly. Well, the die was cast. She must go through with it now.

She looked up, and her eyes met those of the woman sitting opposite. She had a sudden fancy that in some way this other woman had read her mind. She saw in those gray eyes understanding and —yes—compassion.

It was only a fleeting impression. The faces of both women hardened to well-bred impassiveness. Mrs. Kettering took up a magazine, and Katherine Grey looked out of the window and watched a seemingly endless vista of depressing streets and suburban houses.

Ruth found an increasing difficulty in fixing her mind on the printed page in front of her. In spite of herself, a thousand apprehensions preyed on her mind. What a fool she had been! What a fool she was! Like all cool and self-sufficient people, when she did lose her self-control she lost it thoroughly. It was too late. . . . Was it too late? Oh, for someone to speak to, for someone to advise her. She had never before had such a wish; she would have scorned the idea of relying on any judgment other than her own, but now—what was the matter with her? Panic. Yes, that would describe it best— panic. She, Ruth Kettering, was completely and utterly panic-stricken.

She stole a covert glance at the figure opposite. If only she knew someone like that, some nice, cool, calm, sympathetic creature. That was the sort of person one could talk to. But you can't, of course, confide in a stranger. And Ruth smiled to herself a little at the idea. She picked up the magazine again. Really, she must control herself. After all, she had thought all this out. She had decided of her own free will. What happiness had she ever had in her life up to now? She said to herself restlessly: "Why shouldn't I be happy? No one will ever know."

It seemed no time before Dover was reached. Ruth was a good

sailor. She disliked the cold, and was glad to reach the shelter of the private cabin she had telegraphed for. Although she would not have admitted the fact, Ruth was in some ways superstitious. She was of the order of people to whom coincidence appeals. After disembarking at Calais and settling herself down with her maid in her double compartment in the Blue Train, she went along to the luncheon car. It was with a little shock of surprise that she found herself set down to a small table with, opposite her, the same woman who had been her *vis-à-vis* in the Pullman. A faint smile came to the lips of both women.

"This is quite a coincidence," said Mrs. Kettering.

"I know," said Katherine; "it is odd the way things happen."

A flying attendant shot up to them with the wonderful velocity always displayed by the Compagnie Internationale des Wagons-Lits and deposited two cups of soup. By the time the omelette succeeded the soup they were chatting together in friendly fashion.

"It will be heavenly to get into the sunshine," sighed Ruth.

"I am sure it will be a wonderful feeling."

"You know the Riviera well?"

"No; this is my first visit."

"Fancy that."

"You go every year, I expect?"

"Practically. January and February in London are horrible."

"I have always lived in the country. They are not very inspiring months there either. Mostly mud."

"What made you suddenly decide to travel?"

"Money," said Katherine. "For ten years I have been a paid companion with just enough money of my own to buy myself strong country shoes; now I have been left what seems to me a fortune, though I dare say it would not seem so to you."

"Now I wonder why you say that—that it would not seem so to me."

Katherine laughed. "I don't really know. I suppose one forms impressions without thinking of it. I put you down in my own mind as one of the very rich of the earth. It was just an impression. I dare say I am wrong."

"No," said Ruth, "you are not wrong." She had suddenly become very grave. "I wish you would tell me what other impressions you formed about me?"

"I—"

Ruth swept on, disregarding the other's embarrassment.

"Oh, please, don't be conventional. I want to know. As we left Victoria I looked across at you, and I had the sort of feeling that you—well, understood what was going on in my mind."

"I can assure you I am not a mind reader," said Katherine, smiling.

"No; but will you tell me, please, just what you thought." Ruth's eagerness was so intense and so sincere that she carried her point.

"I will tell you if you like, but you must not think me impertinent. I thought that for some reason you were in great distress of mind, and I was sorry for you."

"You are right. You are quite right. I am in terrible trouble. I—I should like to tell you something about it, if I may."

"Oh, dear," Katherine thought to herself, "how extraordinarily alike the world seems to be everywhere! People were always telling me things in St. Mary Mead, and it is just the same thing here, and I don't really want to hear anybody's troubles!"

She replied politely:

"Do tell me."

They were just finishing their lunch. Ruth gulped down her coffee, rose from her seat, and quite oblivious of the fact that Katherine had not begun to sip her coffee, said: "Come to my compartment with me."

They were two single compartments with a communicating door between them. In the second of them a thin maid, whom Katherine had noticed at Victoria, was sitting very upright on the seat, clutching a big scarlet morocco case with the initials R. V. K. on it. Mrs. Kettering pulled the communicating door to and sank down on the seat. Katherine sat down beside her.

"I am in trouble and I don't know what to do. There is a man whom I am fond of—very fond of indeed. We cared for each other when we were young, and we were thrust apart most brutally and unjustly. Now we have come together again."

"Yes?"

"I—I am going to meet him now. Oh! I dare say you think it is all wrong, but you don't know the circumstances. My husband is impossible. He has treated me disgracefully."

"Yes," said Katherine again.

"What I feel so badly about is this. I have deceived my father— it was he who came to see me off at Victoria today. He wishes me to divorce my husband, and, of course, he has no idea—that I am going to meet this other man. He would think it extraordinarily foolish."

"Well, don't you think it is?"

"I—I suppose it is."

Ruth Kettering looked down at her hands; they were shaking violently.

"But I can't draw back now."

"Why not?"

"I—it is all arranged, and it would break his heart."

"Don't you believe it," said Katherine robustly; "hearts are pretty tough."

"He will think I have no courage, no strength of purpose."

"It seems to me an awfully silly thing that you are going to do," said Katherine. "I think you realize that yourself."

Ruth Kettering buried her face in her hands. "I don't know—I don't know. Ever since I left Victoria I have had a horrible feeling of something—something that is coming to me very soon—that I can't escape."

She clutched convulsively at Katherine's hand.

"You must think I am mad talking to you like this, but I tell you I know something horrible is going to happen."

"Don't think it," said Katherine; "try to pull yourself together. You could send your father a wire from Paris, if you like, and he would come to you at once."

The other brightened.

"Yes, I could do that. Dear old Dad. It is queer—but I never knew until today how terribly fond of him I am." She sat up and dried her eyes with a handkerchief. "I have been very foolish. Thank you so much for letting me talk to you. I don't know why I got into such a queer, hysterical state."

She got up. "I am quite all right now. I suppose, really, I just needed someone to talk to. I can't think now why I have been making such an absolute fool of myself."

Katherine got up too.

"I am so glad you feel better," she said, trying to make her voice sound as conventional as possible. She was only too well aware that the aftermath of confidences is embarrassment. She added tactfully:

"I must be going back to my own compartment."

She emerged into the corridor at the same time as the maid was also coming out from the next door. The latter looked towards Katherine, over her shoulder, and an expression of intense surprise showed itself on her face. Katherine turned also, but by that time whoever it was who had aroused the maid's interest had retreated into his or her compartment, and the corridor was empty. Katherine walked down it to regain her own place, which was in the next coach. As she passed the end compartment, the door opened and a woman's face looked out for a moment and then pulled the door to sharply. It was a face not easily forgotten, as Katherine was to know when she saw it again. A beautiful face, oval and dark, very heavily made up in a bizarre fashion. Katherine had a feeling that she had seen it before somewhere.

She regained her own compartment without other adventure and sat for some time thinking of the confidence which had just been made to her. She wondered idly who the woman in the mink coat might be, wondered also how the end of her story would turn out.

"If I have stopped anyone from making an idiot of themselves, I suppose I have done good work," she thought to herself. "But who knows? That is the kind of woman who is hard-headed and egotistical all her life, and it might be good for her to do the other sort of thing for a change. Oh, well—I don't suppose I shall ever see her again. She certainly won't want to see *me* again. That is the worst of letting people tell you things. They never do."

She hoped that she would not be given the same place at dinner. She reflected, not without humor, that it might be awkward for both of them. Leaning back with her head against a cushion, she felt tired and vaguely depressed. They had reached Paris, and the slow journey round the *ceinture*, with its interminable stops and waits, was very wearisome. When they arrived at the Gare de Lyon she was glad to get out and walk up and down the platform. The keen cold air was refreshing after the steam-heated train. She observed with a smile that her friend of the mink coat was solving the possible awkwardness of the dinner problem in her own way. A dinner basket was being handed up and received through the window by the maid.

When the train started once more, and dinner was announced by a violent ringing of bells, Katherine went along to it much relieved in mind. Her *vis-à-vis* tonight was of an entirely different kind—a small man, distinctly foreign in appearance, with a rigidly waxed mustache and an egg-shaped head which he carried rather on one side. Katherine had taken in a book to dinner with her. She found the little man's eyes fixed upon it with a kind of twinkling amusement.

"I see, madame, that you have a *roman policier*. You are fond of such things?"

"They amuse me," Katherine admitted.

The little man nodded with the air of complete understanding.

"They have a good sale always, so I am told. Now why is that, eh, mademoiselle? I ask it of you as a student of human nature—why should that be?"

Katherine felt more and more amused.

"Perhaps they give one the illusion of living an exciting life," she suggested.

He nodded gravely.

"Yes; there is something in that."

"Of course, one knows that such things don't really happen," Katherine was continuing, but he interrupted her sharply.

"Sometimes, mademoiselle! Sometimes! I who speak to you—they have happened to *me*."

She threw him a quick, interested glance.

"Someday, who knows, *you* might be in the thick of things," he went on. "It is all chance."

"I don't think it is likely," said Katherine. "Nothing of that kind ever happens to me."

He leaned forward.

"Would you like it to?"

The question startled her, and she drew in her breath sharply.

"It is my fancy, perhaps," said the little man, as he dexterously polished one of the forks, "but I think that you have a yearning in you for interesting happenings. *Eh bien,* mademoiselle, all through my life I have observed one thing—'All one wants one gets!' Who knows?" His face screwed itself up comically. "You may get more than you bargain for."

"Is that a prophecy?" asked Katherine, smiling as she rose from the table.

The little man shook his head.

"I never prophesy," he declared pompously. "It is true that I have the habit of being always right—but I do not boast of it. Good night, mademoiselle, and may you sleep well."

Katherine went back along the train amused and entertained by her little neighbor. She passed the open door of her friend's compartment and saw the conductor making up the bed. The lady in the mink coat was standing looking out of the window. The second compartment, as Katherine saw through the communicating door, was empty, with rugs and bags heaped up on the seat. The maid was not there.

Katherine found her own bed prepared, and since she was tired, she went to bed and switched off her light about half-past nine.

She woke with a sudden start; how much time had passed, she did not know. Glancing at her watch, she found that it had stopped. A feeling of intense uneasiness pervaded her and grew stronger moment by moment. At last she got up, threw her dressing gown round her shoulders, and stepped out into the corridor. The whole train seemed wrapped in slumber. Katherine let down the window and sat by it for some minutes, drinking in the cool night air and trying vainly to calm her uneasy fears. She presently decided that she would go along to the end and ask the conductor for the right time so that she could set her watch. She found, however, that his little chair was vacant. She hesitated for a moment and then walked through into the next coach. She looked down the long, dim line of the corridor and saw, to her surprise, that a man was standing with his hand on the door of the compartment occupied by the lady in the mink coat. That is to say, she thought it was the compartment. Probably, however, she was mistaken. He stood there for a moment or two with his back to her, seeming uncertain and hesitating in his attitude. Then he slowly turned, and with an odd feeling of fatality, Katherine recognized him as the same man whom she had noticed twice before—once in the corridor of the Savoy Hotel and once in Cook's offices. Then he opened the door of the compartment and passed in, drawing it to behind him.

An idea flashed across Katherine's mind. Could this be the man of whom the other woman had spoken—the man she was journeying to meet?

Then Katherine told herself that she was romancing. In all probability she had mistaken the compartment.

She went back to her own carriage. Five minutes later the train slackened speed. There was the long plaintive hiss of the Westinghouse brake, and a few minutes later the train came to a stop at Lyons.

11

Murder

KATHERINE wakened the next morning to brilliant sunshine. She went along to breakfast early, but met none of her acquaintances of the day before. When she returned to her compartment, it had just been restored to its daytime appearance by the conductor, a dark man with a drooping mustache and melancholy face.

"Madame is fortunate," he said; "the sun shines. It is always a great disappointment to passengers when they arrive on a gray morning."

"I should have been disappointed, certainly," said Katherine.

The man prepared to depart.

"We are rather late, madame," he said. "I will let you know just before we get to Nice."

Katherine nodded. She sat by the window, entranced by the sunlit panorama. The palm trees, the deep blue of the sea, the bright yellow mimosa came with all the charm of novelty to the woman who for fourteen years had known only the drab winters of England.

When they arrived at Cannes, Katherine got out and walked up and down the platform. She was curious about the lady in the mink coat, and looked up at the windows of her compartment. The blinds were still drawn down—the only ones to be so on the whole train. Katherine wondered a little, and when she reentered the train, she passed along the corridor and noticed that these two compartments were still shuttered and closed. The lady of the mink coat was clearly no early riser.

Presently the conductor came to her and told her that in a few minutes the train would arrive at Nice. Katherine handed him a tip; the man thanked her, but still lingered. There was something odd about him. Katherine, who had at first wondered whether the tip had not been big enough, was now convinced that something far more serious was amiss. His face was of a sickly pallor, he was shaking all over, and looked as if he had been frightened out of his life. He was eyeing her in a curious manner. Presently he said abruptly: "Madame will excuse me, but is she expecting friends to meet her at Nice?"

"Probably," said Katherine. "Why?"

But the man merely shook his head and murmured something that Katherine could not catch and moved away, not reappearing until the train came to rest at the station, when he started handing her belongings down from the window.

Katherine stood for a moment or two on the platform rather at a loss, but a fair young man with an ingenuous face came up to her and said rather hesitatingly:

"Miss Grey, is it not?"

Katherine said that it was, and the young man beamed upon her seraphically and murmured:

"I am Chubby, you know—Lady Tamplin's husband. I expect she mentioned me, but perhaps she forgot. Have you got your *billet de bagages*? I lost mine when I came out this year, and you would not believe the fuss they made about it. Regular French red tape!"

Katherine produced it, and was just about to move off beside him when a very gentle and insidious voice murmured in her ear:

"A little moment, madame, if you please."

Katherine turned to behold an individual who made up for insignificance of stature by a large quantity of gold lace and uniform. The individual explained. "There were certain formalities. Madame would perhaps be so kind as to accompany him. The regulations of the police—" He threw up his arms. "Absurd, doubtless, but there it was."

Mr. Chubby Evans listened with a very imperfect comprehension, his French being of a limited order.

"So like the French," murmured Mr. Evans. He was one of those staunch patriotic Britons who, having made a portion of a foreign country their own, strongly resent the original inhabitants of it. "Always up to some silly dodge or other. They've never tackled people on the station before, though. This is something quite new. I suppose you'll have to go."

Katherine departed with her guide. Somewhat to her surprise, he led her towards a siding where a coach of the departed train had been shunted. He invited her to mount into this, and, preceding her down the corridor, held aside the door of one of the compartments. In it was a pompous-looking official personage, and with him a nondescript being who appeared to be a clerk. The pompous-looking personage rose politely, bowed to Katherine, and said:

"You will excuse me, madame, but there are certain formalities to be complied with. Madame speaks French, I trust?"

"Sufficiently, I think, monsieur," replied Katherine in that language.

"That is good. Pray be seated, madame. I am Monsieur Caux, the Commissary of Police." He blew out his chest importantly, and Katherine tried to look sufficiently impressed.

"You wish to see my passport?" she inquired. "Here it is."

The Commissary eyed her keenly and gave a little grunt.

"Thank you, madame," he said, taking the passport from her. He cleared his throat. "But what I really desire is a little information."

"Information?"

The Commissary nodded his head slowly.

"About a lady who has been a fellow passenger of yours. You lunched with her yesterday."

"I am afraid I can't tell you anything about her. We fell into conversation over our meal, but she is a complete stranger to me. I have never seen her before."

"And yet," said the Commissary sharply, "you returned to her compartment with her after lunch and sat talking for some time?"

"Yes," said Katherine; "that is true."

The Commissary seemed to expect her to say something more. He looked at her encouragingly.

"Yes, madame?"

"Well, monsieur?" said Katherine.

"You can, perhaps, give me some kind of idea of that conversation?"

"I could," said Katherine, "but at the moment I see no reason to do so."

In somewhat British fashion she felt annoyed. This foreign official seemed to her impertinent.

"No reason?" cried the Commissary. "Oh yes, madame, I can assure you that there *is* a reason."

"Then perhaps you will give it to me."

The Commissary rubbed his chin thoughtfully for a minute or two without speaking.

"Madame," he said at last, "the reason is very simple. The lady in question was found dead in her compartment this morning."

"Dead!" gasped Katherine. "What was it—heart failure?"

"No," said the Commissary in a reflective, dreamy voice. "No— she was murdered."

"Murdered!" cried Katherine.

"So you see, madame, why we are anxious for any information we can possibly get."

"But surely her maid—"

"The maid has disappeared."

"Oh!" Katherine paused to assemble her thoughts.

"Since the conductor had seen you talking with her in her compartment, he quite naturally reported the fact to the police, and that is why, madame, we have detained you, in the hope of gaining some information."

"I am very sorry," said Katherine; "I don't even know her name."

"Her name is Kettering. That we know from her passport and from the labels on her luggage. If we—"

There was a knock on the compartment door. Monsieur Caux frowned. He opened it about six inches.

"What is the matter?" he said peremptorily. "I cannot be disturbed."

The egg-shaped head of Katherine's dinner acquaintance showed itself in the aperture. On his face was a beaming smile.

"My name," he said, "is Hercule Poirot."

"Not," the Commissary stammered, "not *the* Hercule Poirot?"

"The same," said Mr. Poirot. "I remember meeting you once, Monsieur Caux, at the Sûreté in Paris, though doubtless you have forgotten me?"

"Not at all, monsieur, not at all," declared the Commissary heartily. "But enter, I pray of you. You know of this—"

"Yes, I know," said Hercule Poirot. "I came to see if I might be of any assistance?"

"We should be flattered," replied the Commissary promptly. "Let me present you, Mr. Poirot, to"—he consulted the passport he still held in his hand—"to Madame—er—Mademoiselle Grey."

Poirot smiled across at Katherine.

"It is strange, is it not," he murmured, "that my words should have come true so quickly?"

"Mademoiselle, alas! can tell us very little," said the Commissary.

"I have been explaining," said Katherine, "that this poor lady was a complete stranger to me."

Poirot nodded.

"But she talked to you, did she not?" he said gently. "You formed an impression—is it not so?"

"Yes," said Katherine thoughtfully. "I suppose I did."

"And that impression was—"

"Yes, mademoiselle"—the Commissary jerked himself forward—"let us by all means have your impressions."

Katherine sat turning the whole thing over in her mind. She felt in a way as if she were betraying a confidence, but with that ugly word "Murder" ringing in her ears she dared not keep anything back. Too much might hang upon it. So, as nearly as she could, she repeated word for word the conversation she had had with the dead woman.

"That is interesting," said the Commissary, glancing at the other. "Eh, Monsieur Poirot, that is interesting? Whether it has anything to do with the crime—" He left the sentence unfinished.

"I suppose it could not be suicide," said Katherine, rather doubtfully.

"No," said the Commissary, "it could not be suicide. She was strangled with a length of black cord."

"Oh!" Katherine shivered. Monsieur Caux spread out his hands apologetically. "It is not nice—no. I think that our train robbers are more brutal than they are in your country."

"It is horrible."

"Yes, yes"—he was soothing and apologetic—"but you have great courage, mademoiselle. At once, as soon as I saw you, I said to myself, 'Mademoiselle has great courage.' That is why I am going to ask you to do something more—something distressing, but I assure you very necessary."

Katherine looked at him apprehensively.

He spread out his hands apologetically.

"I am going to ask you, mademoiselle, to be so good as to accompany me to the next compartment."

"Must I?" asked Katherine in a low voice.

"Someone must identify her," said the Commissary, "and since the maid has disappeared"—he coughed significantly—"you appear to be the person who has seen most of her since she joined the train."

"Very well," said Katherine quietly; "if it is necessary—"

She rose. Poirot gave her a little nod of approval.

"Mademoiselle is sensible," he said. "May I accompany you, Monsieur Caux?"

"Enchanted, my dear Monsieur Poirot."

They went out into the corridor, and Monsieur Caux unlocked the door of the dead woman's compartment. The blinds on the far side had been drawn halfway up to admit light. The dead woman lay on the berth to their left, in so natural a posture that one could have thought her asleep. The bedclothes were drawn up over her, and her head was turned to the wall, so that only the red auburn curls showed. Very gently Monsieur Caux laid a hand on her shoulder and turned the body back so that the face came into view. Katherine flinched a little and dug her nails into her palms. A heavy blow had disfigured the features almost beyond recognition. Poirot gave a sharp exclamation.

"When was that done, I wonder?" he demanded. "Before death or after?"

"The doctor says after," said Monsieur Caux.

"Strange," said Poirot, drawing his brows together. He turned to Katherine. "Be brave, mademoiselle; look at her well. Are you sure that this is the woman you talked to in the train yesterday?"

Katherine had good nerves. She steeled herself to look long and earnestly at the recumbent figure. Then she leaned forward and took up the dead woman's hand.

"I am quite sure," she replied at length. "The face is too disfigured to recognize, but the build and carriage and hair are exact, and besides I noticed *this*"—she pointed to a tiny mole on the dead woman's wrist—"while I was talking to her."

"*Bon*," approved Poirot. "You are an excellent witness, mademoiselle. There is, then, no question as to the identity, but it is strange, all the same." He frowned down on the dead woman in perplexity.

Monsieur Caux shrugged his shoulders.

"The murderer was carried away by rage, doubtless," he suggested.

"If she had been struck down, it would have been comprehensible," mused Poirot, "but the man who strangled her slipped up behind and caught her unawares. A little choke—a little gurgle—that is all that would be heard, and then afterwards—that smashing blow on her face. Now why? Did he hope that if the face were unrecognizable she might not be identified? Or did he hate her so much that he could not resist striking that blow even after she was dead?"

Katherine shuddered, and he turned at once to her kindly.

"You must not let me distress you, mademoiselle," he said. "To you this is all very new and terrible. To me, alas! it is an old story. One moment, I pray of you both."

They stood against the door watching him as he went quickly round the compartment. He noted the dead woman's clothes neatly folded on the end of the berth, the big fur coat that hung from a hook, and the little red lacquer hat tossed up on the rack. Then he passed through into the adjoining compartment, that in which Katherine had seen the maid sitting. Here the berth had not been made up. Three or four rugs were piled loosely on the seat; there was a hatbox and a couple of suitcases. He turned suddenly to Katherine.

"You were in here yesterday," he said. "Do you see anything changed, anything missing?"

Katherine looked carefully round both compartments.

"Yes," she said, "there is something missing—a scarlet morocco case. It had the initials 'R. V. K.' on it. It might have been a small dressing case or a big jewel case. When I saw it, the maid was holding it."

"Ah!" said Poirot.

"But, surely," said Katherine. "I—of course, I don't know anything about such things, but surely it is plain enough, if the maid and the jewel case are missing?"

"You mean that it was the maid who was the thief? No, mademoiselle; there is a very good reason against that."

"What?"

"The maid was left behind in Paris."

He turned to Poirot.

"I should like you to hear the conductor's story yourself," he murmured confidentially. "It is very suggestive."

"Mademoiselle would doubtless like to hear it also," said Poirot. "You do not object, Monsieur le Commissaire?"

"No," said the Commissary, who clearly did object very much. "No, certainly, Monsieur Poirot, if you say so. You have finished here?"

"I think so. One little minute."

He had been turning over the rugs, and now he took one to the window and looked at it, picking something off it with his fingers.

"What is it?" demanded Monsieur Caux sharply.

"Four auburn hairs." He bent over the dead woman. "Yes, they are from the head of Madame."

"And what of it? Do you attach importance to them?"

Poirot let the rug drop back on the seat.

"What is important? What is not? One cannot say at this stage. But we must note each little fact carefully."

They went back again into the first compartment, and in a minute or two the conductor of the carriage arrived to be questioned.

"Your name is Pierre Michel?" said the Commissary.

"Yes, Monsieur le Commissaire."

"I should like you to repeat to this gentleman"—he indicated Poirot—"the story that you told me as to what happened in Paris."

"Very good, Monsieur le Commissaire. It was after we had left the Gare de Lyon I came along to make the beds, thinking that Madame would be at dinner, but she had a dinner basket in her compartment. She said to me that she had been obliged to leave her maid behind in Paris, so that I only need make up one berth. She took her dinner basket into the adjoining compartment, and sat there while I made up the bed; then she told me that she did not wish to be wakened early in the morning, that she liked to sleep on. I told her I quite understood, and she wished me 'good night.'"

"You yourself did not go into the adjoining compartment?"

"No, monsieur."

"Then you did not happen to notice if a scarlet morocco case was among the luggage there?"

"No, monsieur, I did not."

"Would it have been possible for a man to have been concealed in the adjoining compartment?"

The conductor reflected.

"The door was half open," he said. "If a man had stood behind that door I should not have been able to see him, but he would, of course, have been perfectly visible to Madame when she went in there."

"Quite so," said Poirot. "Is there anything more you have to tell us?"

"I think that is all, monsieur. I can remember nothing else."

"And now this morning?" prompted Poirot.

"As Madame had ordered, I did not disturb her. It was not until just before Cannes that I ventured to knock at the door. Getting no reply, I opened it. The lady appeared to be in her bed asleep. I took her by the shoulder to rouse her, and then—"

"And then you saw what had happened," volunteered Poirot. *"Très bien.* I think I know all I want to know."

"I hope, Monsieur le Commissaire, it is not that I have been guilty of any negligence," said the man piteously. "Such an affair to happen on the Blue Train! It is horrible."

"Console yourself," said the Commissary. "Everything will be done to keep the affair as quiet as possible, if only in the interests of justice. I cannot think you have been guilty of any negligence."

"And Monsieur le Commissaire will report as much to the company?"

"But certainly, but certainly," said Monsieur Caux impatiently. "That will do now."

The conductor withdrew.

"According to the medical evidence," said the Commissary, "the lady was probably dead before the train reached Lyons. Who then was the murderer? From Mademoiselle's story, it seems clear that somewhere on her journey she was to meet this man of whom she spoke. Her action in getting rid of the maid seems significant. Did the man join the train at Paris, and did she conceal him in the adjoining compartment? If so, they may have quarreled, and he may have killed her in a fit of rage. That is one possibility. The other, and the more likely to my mind, is that her assailant was a train robber traveling on the train; that he stole along the corridor unseen by the conductor, killed her, and went off with the red morocco case, which doubtless contained jewels of some value. In all probability he left the train at Lyons, and we have already telegraphed to the station there for full particulars of anyone seen leaving the train."

"Or he might have come on to Nice," suggested Poirot.

"He might," agreed the Commissary, "but that would be a very bold course."

Poirot let a minute or two go by before speaking, and then he said:

"In the latter case you think the man was an ordinary train robber?"

The Commissary shrugged his shoulders.

"It depends. We must get hold of the maid. It is possible that she has the red morocco case with her. If so, then the man of whom she spoke to Mademoiselle may be concerned in the case, and the affair is a crime of passion. I myself think the solution of a train robber is the more probable. These bandits have become very bold of late."

Poirot looked suddenly across to Katherine.

"And you, mademoiselle," he said, "you heard and saw nothing during the night?"

"Nothing," said Katherine.

Poirot turned to the Commissary.

"We need detain Mademoiselle no longer, I think," he suggested. The latter nodded.

"She will leave us her address?" he said.

Katherine gave him the name of Lady Tamplin's villa. Poirot made her a little bow.

"You permit that I see you again, mademoiselle?" he said. "Or have you so many friends that your time will be all taken up?"

"On the contrary," said Katherine, "I shall have plenty of leisure, and I shall be very pleased to see you again."

"Excellent," said Poirot, and gave her a little friendly nod. "This shall be a *'roman policier'* à nous. We will investigate this affair together."

12

At the Villa Marguerite

"THEN you were really in the thick of it all!" said Lady Tamplin enviously. "My dear, how thrilling!" She opened her china blue eyes very wide and gave a little sigh.

"A real murder," said Mr. Evans gloatingly.

"Of course Chubby had no idea of anything of the kind," went on Lady Tamplin; "he simply could *not* imagine why the police wanted you. My dear, what an opportunity! I think, you know— yes, I certainly think something might be made out of this."

A calculating look rather marred the ingenuousness of the blue eyes.

Katherine felt slightly uncomfortable. They were just finishing lunch, and she looked in turn at the three people sitting round the table. Lady Tamplin, full of practical schemes; Mr. Evans, beaming with naive appreciation, and Lenox with a queer crooked smile on her dark face.

"Marvelous luck," murmured Chubby; "I wish I could have gone along with you—and seen—all the exhibits."

His tone was wistful and childlike.

Katherine said nothing. The police had laid no injunctions of secrecy upon her, and it was clearly impossible to suppress the bare facts or try to keep them from her hostess. But she did rather wish it had been possible to do so.

"Yes," said Lady Tamplin, coming suddenly out of her reverie, "I do think something might be done. A little account, you know, cleverly written up. An eyewitness, a feminine touch: '*How I chatted with the dead woman, little thinking—*' that sort of thing, you know."

"Rot!" said Lenox.

"You have no idea," said Lady Tamplin in a soft, wistful voice, "what newspapers will pay for a little titbit! Written, of course, by someone of really unimpeachable social position. You would not like to do it yourself, I dare say, Katherine dear, but just give me the bare bones of it, and *I* will manage the whole thing for you. Mr. de Haviland is a special friend of mine. We have a little understanding together. A most delightful man—not at all reporterish. How does the idea strike you, Katherine?"

"I would much prefer to do nothing of the kind," said Katherine bluntly.

Lady Tamplin was rather disconcerted at this uncompromising refusal. She sighed and turned to the elucidation of further details.

"A very striking-looking woman, you said? I wonder now who she could have been. You didn't hear her name?"

"It was mentioned," Katherine admitted, "but I can't remember it. You see, I was rather upset."

"I should think so," said Mr. Evans; "it must have been a beastly shock."

It is to be doubted whether, even if Katherine had remembered the name, she would have admitted the fact. Lady Tamplin's remorseless cross-examination was making her restive. Lenox, who was observant in her own way, noticed this, and offered to take Katherine upstairs to see her room. She left her there, remarking kindly before she went: "You mustn't mind Mother; she would make a few pennies' profit out of her dying grandmother if she could."

Lenox went down again to find her mother and her stepfather discussing the newcomer.

"Presentable," said Lady Tamplin, "quite presentable. Her clothes are all right. That gray thing is the same model that Gladys Cooper wore in *Palm Trees in Egypt.*"

"Have you noticed her eyes—what?" interposed Mr. Evans.

"Never mind her eyes, Chubby," said Lady Tamplin tartly; "we are discussing the things that really matter."

"Oh, quite," said Mr. Evans, and retired into his shell.

"She doesn't seem to me very—malleable," said Lady Tamplin, rather hesitating to choose the right word.

"She has all the instincts of a lady, as they say in books," said Lenox, with a grin.

"Narrow-minded," murmured Lady Tamplin. "Inevitable under the circumstances, I suppose."

"I expect you will do your best to broaden her," said Lenox, with a grin, "but you will have your work cut out. Just now, you noticed, she stuck down her forefeet and laid back her ears and refused to budge."

"Anyway," said Lady Tamplin hopefully, "she doesn't look to me at all mean. Some people, when they come into money, seem to attach undue importance to it."

"Oh, you'll easily touch her for what you want," said Lenox; "and, after all, that is all that matters, isn't it? That is what she is here for."

"She is my own cousin," said Lady Tamplin, with dignity.

"Cousin, eh?" said Mr. Evans, waking up again. "I suppose I call her Katherine, don't I?"

"It is of no importance at all what you call her, Chubby," said Lady Tamplin.

"Good," said Mr. Evans; "then I will. Do you suppose she plays tennis?" he added hopefully.

"Of course not," said Lady Tamplin. "She has been a companion, I tell you. Companions don't play tennis—or golf. They might possibly play golf-croquet, but I have always understood that they wind wool and wash dogs most of the day."

"O God!" said Mr. Evans. "Do they really?"

Lenox drifted upstairs again to Katherine's room. "Can I help you?" she asked rather perfunctorily.

On Katherine's disclaimer, Lenox sat on the edge of the bed and stared thoughtfully at her guest.

"Why did you come?" she said at last. "To us, I mean. We're not your sort."

"Oh, I am anxious to get into society."

"Don't be an ass," said Lenox promptly, detecting the flicker of a smile. "You know what I mean well enough. You are not a bit what I thought you would be. I say, you *have* got some decent clothes." She sighed. "Clothes are no good to me. I was born awkward. It's a pity, because I love them."

"I love them too," said Katherine, "but it has not been much use my loving them up to now. Do you think this is nice?"

She and Lenox discussed several models with artistic fervor.

"I like you," said Lenox suddenly. "I came up to warn you not to be taken in by Mother, but I think now that there is no need to do that. You are frightfully sincere and upright and all those queer things, but you are not a fool. Oh, hell! What is it now?"

Lady Tamplin's voice was calling plaintively from the hall:

"Lenox, Derek has just rung up. He wants to come to dinner to-night. Will it be all right? I mean, we haven't got anything awkward, like quails, have we?"

Lenox reassured her and came back into Katherine's room. Her face looked brighter and less sullen.

"I'm glad old Derek is coming," she said; "you'll like him."

"Who is Derek?"

"He is Lord Leconbury's son, married a rich American woman. Women are simply potty about him."

"Why?"

"Oh, the usual reason—very good-looking and a regular bad lot. Everyone goes off their head about him."

"Do you?"

"Sometimes I do," said Lenox, "and sometimes I think I would like to marry a nice curate and live in the country and grow things in frames." She paused a minute, and then added, "An Irish curate would be best, and then I should hunt."

After a minute or two she reverted to her former theme. "There is something queer about Derek. All that family are a bit potty— mad gamblers, you know. In the old days they used to gamble away their wives and their estates, and did most reckless things just for the love of it. Derek would have made a perfect highwayman— debonair and gay, just the right manner." She moved to the door. "Well, come down when you feel like it."

Left alone, Katherine gave herself up to thought. Just at present she felt thoroughly ill at ease and jarred by her surroundings. The shock of the discovery in the train and the reception of the news by her new friends jarred upon her susceptibilities. She thought long and earnestly about the murdered woman. She had been sorry for Ruth, but she could not honestly say that she had liked her. She had divined only too well the ruthless egoism that was the keynote of her personality, and it repelled her.

She had been amused and a trifle hurt by the other's cool dismissal of her when she had served her turn. That she had come to some decision, Katherine was quite certain, but she wondered now what that decision had been. Whatever it was, death had stepped in and made all decisions meaningless. Strange that it should have been so, and that a brutal crime should have been the ending of that fateful journey. But suddenly Katherine remembered a small fact that she ought, perhaps, to have told the police—a fact that had for the moment escaped her memory. Was it of any real importance? She had certainly thought that she had seen a man going into that particular compartment, but she realized that she might easily have been mistaken. It might have been the compartment next door, and certainly the man in question could be no train robber. She recalled him very clearly as she had seen him on those two previous occasions—once at the Savoy and once at Cook's office. No, doubtless she had been mistaken. He had not gone into the dead woman's compartment, and it was perhaps as well that she had said nothing to the police. She might have done incalculable harm by doing so.

She went down to join the others on the terrace outside. Through the branches of mimosa, she looked out over the blue of the Mediterranean, and, while listening with half an ear to Lady Tamplin's chatter, she was glad that she had come. This was better than St. Mary Mead.

That evening she put on the mauvy pink dress that went by the name of *soupir d'automne*, and after smiling at her reflection in the mirror, went downstairs with, for the first time in her life, a faint feeling of shyness.

Most of Lady Tamplin's guests had arrived, and since noise was the essential of Lady Tamplin's parties, the din was already terrific. Chubby rushed up to Katherine, pressed a cocktail upon her, and took her under his wing.

"Oh, here you are, Derek," cried Lady Tamplin, as the door opened to admit the last comer. "Now at last we can have something to eat. I am starving."

Katherine looked across the room. She was startled. So this—was Derek, and she realized that she was not surprised. She had always known that she would someday meet the man whom she had seen three times by such a curious chain of coincidences. She thought, too, that he recognized her. He paused abruptly in what he was saying to Lady Tamplin, and went on again as though with an effort. They all went in to dinner, and Katherine found that he was placed beside her. He turned to her at once with a vivid smile.

"I knew I was going to meet you soon," he remarked, "but I never dreamed that it would be here. It had to be, you know. Once at the Savoy and once at Cook's—never twice without three times. Don't say you can't remember me or never noticed me. I insist upon your pretending that you noticed me, anyway."

"Oh, I did," said Katherine; "but this is not the third time. It is the fourth. I saw you on the Blue Train."

"On the Blue Train!" Something undefinable came over his manner; she could not have said just what it was. It was as though he had received a check, a setback. Then he said carelessly:

"What was the rumpus this morning? Somebody had died, hadn't they?"

"Yes," said Katherine slowly; "somebody had died."

"You shouldn't die on a train," remarked Derek flippantly. "I believe it causes all sorts of legal and international complications, and it gives the train an excuse for being even later than usual."

"Mr. Kettering?" A stout American lady, who was sitting opposite, leaned forward and spoke to him with the deliberate intonation of her race. "Mr. Kettering, I do believe you have forgotten me, and I thought you such a perfectly lovely man."

Derek leaned forward, answering her, and Katherine sat almost dazed.

Kettering! That was the name, of course! She remembered it now —but what a strange, ironical situation! Here was this man whom she had seen go into his wife's compartment last night, who had left her alive and well, and now he was sitting at dinner, quite unconscious of the fate that had befallen her. Of that there was no doubt. He did not know.

A servant was leaning over Derek, handing him a note and murmuring in his ear. With a word of excuse to Lady Tamplin, he broke it open, and an expression of utter astonishment came over his face as he read; then he looked at his hostess.

"This is most extraordinary. I say, Rosalie, I am afraid I will have to leave you. The Prefect of Police wants to see me at once. I can't think what about."

"Your sins have found you out," remarked Lenox.

"They must have," said Derek; "probably some idiotic nonsense, but I suppose I shall have to push off to the Prefecture. How dare the old boy rout me out from dinner? It ought to be something deadly serious to justify that," and he laughed as he pushed back his chair and rose to leave the room.

13

Van Aldin Gets a Telegram

On the afternoon of the 15th February a thick yellow fog had settled down on London. Rufus Van Aldin was in his suite at the Savoy and was making the most of the atmospheric conditions by working double time. Knighton was overjoyed. He had found it difficult of late to get his employer to concentrate on the matters in hand. When he had ventured to urge certain courses, Van Aldin had put him off with a curt word. But now Van Aldin seemed to be throwing himself into work with redoubled energy, and the secretary made the most of his opportunities. Always tactful, he plied the spur so unobtrusively that Van Aldin never suspected it.

Yet in the middle of this absorption in business matters, one little fact lay at the back of Van Aldin's mind. A chance remark of Knighton's, uttered by the secretary in all unconsciousness, had given rise to it. It now festered unseen, gradually reaching further and further forward into Van Aldin's consciousness, until at last, in spite of himself, he had to yield to its insistence.

He listened to what Knighton was saying with his usual air of keen attention, but in reality not one word of it penetrated his mind. He nodded automatically, however, and the secretary turned to some other paper. As he was sorting them out, his employer spoke:

"Do you mind telling me that over again, Knighton?"

For a moment Knighton was at a loss.

"You mean about this, sir?" He held up a closely written company report.

"No, no," said Van Aldin; "what you told me about seeing Ruth's maid in Paris last night. I can't make it out. You must have been mistaken."

"I can't have been mistaken, sir; I actually spoke to her."

"Well, tell me the whole thing again."

Knighton complied.

"I had fixed up the deal with Bartheimers," he explained, "and had gone back to the Ritz to pick up my traps preparatory to having dinner and catching the nine o'clock train from the Gare du Nord. At the reception desk I saw a woman whom I was quite sure was Mrs. Kettering's maid. I went up to her and asked if Mrs. Kettering was staying there."

"Yes, yes," said Van Aldin. "Of course. Naturally. And she told you that Ruth had gone on to the Riviera and had sent her to the Ritz to await further orders there?"

"Exactly that, sir."

"It is very odd," said Van Aldin. "Very odd, indeed, unless the woman had been impertinent or something of that kind."

"In that case," objected Knighton, "surely Mrs. Kettering would have paid her down a sum of money, and told her to go back to England. She would hardly have sent her to the Ritz."

"No," muttered the millionaire; "that's true."

He was about to say something further, but checked himself. He was fond of Knighton and liked and trusted him, but he could hardly discuss his daughter's private affairs with his secretary. He had already felt hurt by Ruth's lack of frankness, and this chance information which had come to him did nothing to allay his misgivings.

Why had Ruth got rid of her maid in Paris? What possible object or motive could she have had in so doing?

He reflected for a moment or two on the curious combination of chance. How should it have occurred to Ruth, except as the wildest coincidence, that the first person that the maid should run across in Paris should be her father's secretary? Ah, but that was the way things happened. That was the way things got found out.

He winced at the last phrase; it had arisen with complete naturalness to his mind. Was there then "something to be found out"? He hated to put this question to himself; he had no doubt of the answer. The answer was—he was sure of it—Armand de la Roche.

It was bitter to Van Aldin that a daughter of his should be gulled by such a man, yet he was forced to admit that she was in good company—that other well-bred and intelligent women had succumbed just as easily to the Count's fascination. Men saw through him, women did not.

He sought now for a phrase that would allay any suspicion that his secretary might have felt.

"Ruth is always changing her mind about things at a moment's notice," he remarked, and then he added in a would-be careless tone: "The maid didn't give any—er—reason for this change of plan?"

Knighton was careful to make his voice as natural as possible as he replied:

"She said, sir, that Mrs. Kettering had met a friend unexpectedly."

"Is that so?"

The secretary's practiced ears caught the note of strain underlying the seemingly casual tone.

"Oh, I see. Man or woman?"

"I think she said a man, sir."

Van Aldin nodded. His worst fears were being realized. He rose from his chair and began pacing up and down the room, a habit of his when agitated. Unable to contain his feelings any longer, he burst forth:

"There is one thing no man can do, and that is to get a woman to listen to reason. Somehow or other, they don't seem to have any kind of *sense*. Talk of woman's instinct—why, it is well known all the world over that a woman is the surest mark for any rascally swindler. Not one in ten of them knows a scoundrel when she meets one; they can be preyed on by any good-looking fellow with a soft side to his tongue. If I had my way—"

He was interrupted. A page boy entered with a telegram. Van Aldin tore it open, and his face went a sudden chalky white. He caught hold of the back of a chair to steady himself, and waved the page boy from the room.

"What's the matter, sir?"

Knighton had risen in concern.

"Ruth!" said Van Aldin hoarsely.

"Mrs. Kettering?"

"Killed!"

"An accident to the train?"

Van Aldin shook his head.

"No. From this it seems she has been robbed as well. They don't use the word, Knighton, but my poor girl has been murdered."

"Oh, my God, sir!"

Van Aldin tapped the telegram with his forefinger.

"This is from the police at Nice. I must go out there by the first train."

Knighton was efficient as ever. He glanced at the clock.

"Five o'clock from Victoria, sir."

"That's right. You will come with me, Knighton. Tell my man, Archer, and pack your own things. See to everything here. I want to go round to Curzon Street."

The telephone rang sharply, and the secretary lifted the receiver.

"Yes; who is it?"

Then to Van Aldin.

"Mr. Goby, sir."

"Goby? I can't see him now. No—wait, we have plenty of time. Tell them to send him up."

Van Aldin was a strong man. Already he had recovered that iron calm of his. Few people would have noticed anything amiss in his greeting to Mr. Goby.

"I am pressed for time, Goby. Got anything important to tell me?"

Mr. Goby coughed.

"The movements of Mr. Kettering, sir. You wished them reported to you."

"Yes—well?"

"Mr. Kettering, sir, left London for the Riviera yesterday morning."

"What?"

Something in his voice must have startled Mr. Goby. That worthy gentleman departed from his usual practice of never looking at the person to whom he was talking, and stole a fleeting glance at the millionaire.

"What train did he go on?" demanded Van Aldin.

"The Blue Train, sir."

Mr. Goby coughed again and spoke to the clock on the mantelpiece.

"Mademoiselle Mirelle, the dancer from the Parthenon, went by the same train."

14

Ada Mason's Story

"I CANNOT repeat to you often enough, monsieur, our horror, our consternation, and the deep sympathy we feel for you."

Thus Monsieur Carrège, the Juge d'Instruction, addressed Van Aldin. Monsieur Caux, the Commissary, made sympathetic noises in his throat. Van Aldin brushed away horror, consternation, and sympathy with an abrupt gesture. The scene was the Examining Magistrate's room at Nice. Besides Monsieur Carrège, the Commissary, and Van Aldin, there was a further person in the room. It was that person who now spoke.

"Monsieur Van Aldin," he said, "desires action—swift action."

"Ah!" cried the Commissary, "I have not yet presented you. Monsieur Van Aldin, this is Monsieur Hercule Poirot; you have doubtless heard of him. Although he has retired from his profession for some years now, his name is still a household word as one of the greatest living detectives."

"Pleased to meet you, Monsieur Poirot," said Van Aldin, falling back mechanically on a formula that he had discarded some years ago. "You have retired from your profession?"

"That is so, monsieur. Now I enjoy the world."

The little man made a grandiloquent gesture.

"Monsieur Poirot happened to be traveling on the Blue Train," explained the Commissary, "and he has been so kind as to assist us out of his vast experience."

The millionaire looked at Poirot keenly. Then he said unexpectedly:

"I am a very rich man, Monsieur Poirot. It is usually said that a rich man labors under the belief that he can buy everything and everyone. That is not true. I am a big man in my way, and one big man can ask a favor from another big man."

Poirot nodded a quick appreciation.

"That is very well said, Monsieur Van Aldin. I place myself entirely at your service."

"Thank you," said Van Aldin. "I can only say call upon me at any time, and you will not find me ungrateful. And now, gentlemen, to business."

"I propose," said Monsieur Carrège, "to interrogate the maid, Ada Mason. You have her here, I understand?"

"Yes," said Van Aldin. "We picked her up in Paris in passing through. She was very upset to hear of her mistress's death, but she tells her story coherently enough."

"We will have her in, then," said Monsieur Carrège.

He rang the bell on his desk, and in a few minutes Ada Mason entered the room.

She was very neatly dressed in black, and the tip of her nose was red. She had exchanged her gray traveling gloves for a pair of black suede ones. She cast a look round the Examining Magistrate's office in some trepidation, and seemed relieved at the presence of her mistress's father. The Examining Magistrate prided himself on his geniality of manner, and did his best to put her at her ease. He was helped in this by Poirot, who acted as interpreter, and whose friendly manner was reassuring to the Englishwoman.

"Your name is Ada Mason; is that right?"

"Ada Beatrice I was christened, sir," said Mason primly.

"Just so. And we can understand, Mason, that this has all been very distressing."

"Oh, indeed it has, sir. I have been with many ladies and always given satisfaction, I hope, and I never dreamed of anything of this kind happening in any situation where I was."

"No, no," said Monsieur Carrège.

"Naturally I have read of such things, of course, in the Sunday papers. And then I always have understood that those foreign trains—" She suddenly checked her flow, remembering that the gentlemen who were speaking to her were of the same nationality as the trains.

"Now let us talk this affair over," said Monsieur Carrège. "There was, I understand, no question of your staying in Paris when you started from London?"

"Oh no, sir. We were to go straight through to Nice."

"Have you ever been abroad with your mistress before?"

"No, sir. I had only been with her two months, you see."

"Did she seem quite as usual when starting on this journey?"

"She was worried-like and a bit upset, and she was rather irritable and difficult to please."

Monsieur Carrège nodded.

"Now then, Mason, what was the first you heard of your stopping in Paris?"

"It was at the place they call the Gare de Lyon, sir. My mistress was thinking of getting out and walking up and down the platform. She was just going out into the corridor when she gave a sudden exclamation, and came back into her compartment with a gentleman. She shut the door between her carriage and mine, so that I didn't see or hear anything, till she suddenly opened it again and told me that she had changed her plans. She gave me some money and told me to get out and go to the Ritz. They knew her well there, she said, and would give me a room. I was to wait there until I heard from her; she would wire me what she wanted me to do. I had just time to get my things together and jump out of the train before it started off. It was a rush."

"While Mrs. Kettering was telling you this, where was the gentleman?"

"He was standing in the other compartment, sir, looking out of the window."

"Can you describe him to us?"

"Well, you see, sir, I hardly saw him. He had his back to me most of the time. He was a tall gentleman and dark; that's all I can say. He was dressed very like any other gentleman in a dark blue overcoat and a gray hat."

"Was he one of the passengers on the train?"

"I don't think so, sir; I took it that he had come to the station to see Mrs. Kettering in passing through. Of course he might have been one of the passengers; I never thought of that."

Mason seemed a little flurried by the suggestion.

"Ah!" Monsieur Carrège passed lightly to another subject. "Your mistress later requested the conductor not to rouse her early in the morning. Was that a likely thing for her to do, do you think?"

"Oh yes, sir. The mistress never ate any breakfast and she didn't sleep well at nights, so that she liked sleeping on in the morning."

Again Monsieur Carrège passed to another subject.

"Among the luggage there was a scarlet morocco case, was there not?" he asked. "Your mistress's jewel case?"

"Yes, sir."

"Did you take that case to the Ritz?"

"*Me* take the mistress's jewel case to the Ritz! Oh no, indeed, sir." Mason's tones were horrified.

"You left it behind you in the carriage?"

"Yes, sir."

"Had your mistress many jewels with her, do you know?"

"A fair amount, sir; made me a bit uneasy sometimes, I can tell you, with those nasty tales you hear of being robbed in foreign countries. They were insured, I know, but all the same it seemed a frightful risk. Why, the rubies alone, the mistress told me, were worth several hundred thousand pounds."

"The rubies! What rubies?" barked Van Aldin suddenly.

Mason turned to him.

"I think it was you who gave them to her, sir, not very long ago."

"My God!" cried Van Aldin. "You don't say she had those rubies with her? I told her to leave them at the bank."

Mason gave once more the discreet cough which was apparently part of her stock-in-trade as a lady's maid. This time it expressed a good deal. It expressed far more clearly than words could have done that Mason's mistress had been a lady who took her own way.

"Ruth must have been mad," muttered Van Aldin. "What on earth could have possessed her?"

Monsieur Carrège in turn gave vent to a cough, again a cough of significance. It riveted Van Aldin's attention on him.

"For the moment," said Monsieur Carrège, addressing Mason, "I think that is all. If you will go into the next room, mademoiselle, they will read over to you the questions and answers, and you will sign accordingly."

Mason went out escorted by the clerk, and Van Aldin said immediately to the Magistrate:

"Well?"

Monsieur Carrège opened a drawer in his desk, took out a letter, and handed it across to Van Aldin.

"This was found in Madame's handbag."

Chère Amie [the letter ran]—I will obey you; I will be prudent, discreet—all those things that a lover most hates. Paris would perhaps have been unwise, but the Isles d'Or are far away from the world, and you may be assured that nothing will leak out. It is like you and your divine sympathy to be so interested in the work on famous jewels that I am writing. It will, indeed, be an extraordinary privilege to actually see and handle these historic rubies. I am devoting a special passage to "Heart of Fire." My wonderful one! Soon I will make up to you for all those sad years of separation and emptiness. Your ever-adoring,

ARMAND.

15

The Comte de la Roche

VAN ALDIN read the letter through in silence. His face turned a
dull angry crimson. The men watching him saw the veins start out
on his forehead, and his big hands clench themselves unconsciously. He handed back the letter without a word. Monsieur Carrège was looking with close attention at his desk, Monsieur Caux's
eyes were fixed upon the ceiling, and Monsieur Hercule Poirot was
tenderly brushing a speck of dust from his coat sleeve. With the
greatest tact they none of them looked at Van Aldin.

It was Monsieur Carrège, mindful of his status and his duties,
who tackled the unpleasant subject.

"Perhaps, monsieur," he murmured, "you are aware by whom—
er—this letter was written?"

"Yes, I know," said Van Aldin heavily.

"Ah?" said the Magistrate inquiringly.

"A scoundrel who calls himself the Comte de la Roche."

There was a pause; then Monsieur Poirot leaned forward, straightened a ruler on the judge's desk, and addressed the millionaire
directly.

"Monsieur Van Aldin, we are all sensible, deeply sensible, of the
pain it must give you to speak of these matters, but believe me,
monsieur, it is not the time for concealments. If justice is to be
done, we must know everything. If you will reflect a little minute
you will realize the truth of that clearly for yourself."

Van Aldin was silent for a moment or two, then almost reluctantly he nodded his head in agreement.

"You are quite right, Monsieur Poirot," he said. "Painful as it is,
I have no right to keep anything back."

The Commissary gave a sigh of relief, and the Examining Magistrate leaned back in his chair and adjusted a pince-nez on his long thin nose.

"Perhaps you will tell us in your own words, Monsieur Van Aldin," he said, "all that you know of this gentleman."

"It began eleven or twelve years ago—in Paris. My daughter was a young girl then, full of foolish, romantic notions, like all young girls are. Unknown to me, she made the acquaintance of this Comte de la Roche. You have heard of him, perhaps?"

The Commissary and Poirot nodded in assent.

"He calls himself the Comte de la Roche," continued Van Aldin, "but I doubt if he has any right to the title."

"You would not have found his name in the *Almanac de Gotha*," agreed the Commissary.

"I discovered as much," said Van Aldin. "The man was a good-looking, plausible scoundrel, with a fatal fascination for women. Ruth was infatuated with him, but I soon put a stop to the whole affair. The man was no better than a common swindler."

"You are quite right," said the Commissary. "The Comte de la Roche is well known to us. If it were possible, we should have laid him by the heels before now, but *ma foi!* it is not easy; the fellow is cunning, his affairs are always conducted with ladies of high social position. If he obtains money from them under false pretenses or as the fruit of blackmail, *eh bien!* naturally they will not prosecute. To look foolish in the eyes of the world, oh no, that would never do, and he has an extraordinary power over women."

"That is so," said the millionaire heavily. "Well, as I told you, I broke the affair up pretty sharply. I told Ruth exactly what he was, and she had, perforce, to believe me. About a year afterwards, she met her present husband and married him. As far as I knew, that was the end of the matter; but only a week ago, I discovered, to my amazement, that my daughter had resumed her acquaintance with the Comte de la Roche. She had been meeting him frequently in London and Paris. I remonstrated with her on her imprudence, for I may tell you gentlemen, that, on my insistence, she was preparing to bring a suit for divorce against her husband."

"That is interesting," murmured Poirot softly, his eyes on the ceiling.

Van Aldin looked at him sharply, and then went on.

"I pointed out to her the folly of continuing to see the Comte under the circumstances. I thought she agreed with me."

The Examining Magistrate coughed delicately.

"But according to this letter—" he began, and then stopped.

Van Aldin's jaw set itself squarely.

"I know. It's no good mincing matters. However unpleasant, we have got to face facts. It seems clear that Ruth had arranged to go to Paris and meet de la Roche there. After my warnings to her, however, she must have written to the Count suggesting a change of rendezvous."

"The Isles d'Or," said the Commissary thoughtfully, "are situated just opposite Hyères, a remote and idyllic spot."

Van Aldin nodded.

"My God! How could Ruth be such a fool?" he exclaimed bitterly. "All this talk about writing a book on jewels! Why, he must have been after the rubies from the first."

"There are some very famous rubies," said Poirot, "originally part of the crown jewels of Russia; they are unique in character, and their value is almost fabulous. There has been a rumor that they have lately passed into the possession of an American. Are we right in concluding, monsieur, that you were the purchaser?"

"Yes," said Van Aldin. "They came into my possession in Paris about ten days ago."

"Pardon me, monsieur, but you have been negotiating for their purchase for some time?"

"A little over two months. Why?"

"These things become known," said Poirot. "There is always a pretty formidable crowd on the track of jewels such as these."

A spasm distorted the other's face.

"I remember," he said brokenly, "a joke I made to Ruth when I gave them to her. I told her not to take them to the Riviera with her, as I could not afford to have her robbed and murdered for the sake of the jewels. My God! the things one says—never dreaming or knowing they will come true."

There was a sympathetic silence, and then Poirot spoke in a detached manner.

"Let us arrange our facts with order and precision. According to our present theory, this is how they run. The Comte de la Roche knows of your purchase of these jewels. By an easy stratagem he induces Madame Kettering to bring the stones with her. He, then, is the man Mason saw in the train at Paris."

The other three nodded in agreement.

"Madame is surprised to see him, but she deals with the situation promptly. Mason is got out of the way; a dinner basket is ordered. We know from the conductor that he made up the berth for the first compartment, but he did not go into the second compartment, and that a man could quite well have been concealed from him. So far the Comte could have been hidden to a marvel. No one knows of his presence on the train except Madame; he has been careful that the maid did not see his face. All that she could say is that he was tall and dark. It is all most conveniently vague. They are alone—and the train rushes through the night. There would be no outcry, no struggle, for the man is, so she thinks, her lover."

He turned gently to Van Aldin.

"Death, monsieur, must have been almost instantaneous. We will pass over that quickly. The Comte takes the jewel case which lies ready to his hand. Shortly afterwards the train draws into Lyons."

Monsieur Carrège nodded his approval.

"Precisely. The conductor without descends. It would be easy for our man to leave the train unseen; it would be easy to catch a train back to Paris or anywhere he pleases. And the crime would be put down as an ordinary train robbery. But for the letter found in Madame's bag, the Comte would not have been mentioned."

"It was an oversight on his part not to search that bag," declared the Commissary.

"Without doubt he thought she had destroyed that letter. It was—pardon me, monsieur—it was an indiscretion of the first water to keep it."

"And yet," murmured Poirot, "it was an indiscretion the Comte might have foreseen."

"You mean?"

"I mean we are all agreed on one point, and that is that the Comte de la Roche knows one subject *à fond:* Women. How was it that, knowing women as he does, he did not foresee that Madame would have kept that letter?"

"Yes—yes," said the Examining Magistrate doubtfully, "there is something in what you say. But at such times, you understand, a man is not master of himself. He does not reason calmly. *Mon Dieu!*" he added, with feeling, "if our criminals kept their heads and acted with intelligence, how should we capture them?"

Poirot smiled to himself.

"It seems to me a clear case," said the other, "but a difficult one to prove. The Comte is a slippery customer, and unless the maid can identify him—"

"Which is most unlikely," said Poirot.

"True, true." The Examining Magistrate rubbed his chin. "It is going to be difficult."

"If he did indeed commit the crime—" began Poirot. Monsieur Caux interrupted.

"If—you say *if?*"

"Yes, Monsieur le Juge, I say *if.*"

The other looked at him sharply. "You are right," he said at last, "we go too fast. It is possible that the Comte may have an alibi. Then we should look foolish."

"*Ah, ça par exemple,*" replied Poirot, "that is of no importance whatever. Naturally, if he committed the crime he will have an alibi. A man with the Comte's experience does not neglect to take precautions. No, I said *if* for a very different reason."

"And what was that?"

Poirot wagged an emphatic forefinger. "The psychology."

"Eh?" said the Commissary.

"The psychology is at fault. The Comte is a scoundrel—yes. The Comte is a swindler—yes. The Comte preys upon women—yes. He proposes to steal Madame's jewels—again yes. Is he the kind of man to commit murder? I say *no!* A man of the type of the Comte is always a coward; he takes no risks. He plays the safe, the mean, what the English call the low-down game; but murder, a hundred times no!" He shook his head in a dissatisfied manner.

The Examining Magistrate, however, did not seem disposed to agree with him.

"The day always comes when such gentry lose their heads and go too far," he observed sagely. "Doubtless that is the case here. Without wishing to disagree with you, Monsieur Poirot—"

"It was only an opinion," Poirot hastened to explain. "The case is, of course, in your hands, and you will do what seems fit to you."

"I am satisfied in my own mind that the Comte de la Roche is the man we need to get hold of," said Monsieur Carrège. "You agree with me, Monsieur le Commissaire?"

"Perfectly."

"And you, Monsieur Van Aldin?"

"Yes," said the millionaire. "Yes; the man is a thorough-paced villain, no doubt about it."

"It will be difficult to lay hands on him, I am afraid," said the Magistrate, "but we will do our best. Telegraphed instructions shall go out at once."

"Permit me to assist you," said Poirot. "There need be no difficulty."

"Eh?"

The others stared at him. The little man smiled beamingly back at them.

"It is my business to know things," he explained. "The Comte is a man of intelligence. He is at present at a villa he has leased, the Villa Marina at Antibes."

16

Poirot Discusses the Case

EVERYBODY looked respectfully at Poirot. Undoubtedly the little man had scored heavily. The Commissary laughed—on a rather hollow note.

"You teach us all our business," he cried. "Monsieur Poirot knows more than the police."

Poirot gazed complacently at the ceiling, adopting a mock-modest air.

"What will you; it is my little hobby," he murmured, "to know things. Naturally I have the time to indulge it. I am not overburdened with affairs."

"Ah!" said the Commissary, shaking his head portentously. "As for me—"

He made an exaggerated gesture to represent the cares that lay on his shoulders.

Poirot turned suddenly to Van Aldin.

"You agree, monsieur, with this view? You feel certain that the Comte de la Roche is the murderer?"

"Why, it would seem so—yes, certainly."

Something guarded in the answer made the Examining Magistrate look at the American curiously. Van Aldin seemed aware of his scrutiny and made an effort as though to shake off some preoccupation.

"What about my son-in-law?" he asked. "You have acquainted him with the news? He is in Nice, I understand."

"Certainly, monsieur." The Commissary hesitated, and then murmured very discreetly: "You are doubtless aware, Monsieur Van Aldin, that Monsieur Kettering was also one of the passengers on the Blue Train that night?"

The millionaire nodded.

"Heard it just before I left London," he vouchsafed laconically.

"He tells us," continued the Commissary, "that he had no idea his wife was traveling on the train."

"I bet he hadn't," said Van Aldin grimly. "It would have been rather a nasty shock to him if he'd come across her on it."

The three men looked at him questioningly.

"I'm not going to mince matters," said Van Aldin savagely. "No one knows what my poor girl has had to put up with. Derek Kettering wasn't alone. He had a lady with him."

"Ah?"

"Mirelle—the dancer."

Monsieur Carrège and the Commissary looked at each other and nodded as though confirming some previous conversation. Monsieur Carrège leaned back in his chair, joined his hands, and fixed his eyes on the ceiling.

"Ah!" he murmured again. "One wondered." He coughed. "One has heard rumors."

"The lady," said Monsieur Caux, "is very notorious."

"And also," murmured Poirot softly, "very expensive."

Van Aldin had gone very red in the face. He leaned forward and hit the table a bang with his fist.

"See here," he cried, "my son-in-law is a damned scoundrel!"

He glared at them, looking from one face to another.

"Oh, I know," he went on. "Good looks and a charming, easy manner. It took me in once upon a time. I suppose he pretended to be brokenhearted when you broke the news to him—that is, if he didn't know it already."

"Oh, it came as a complete surprise to him. He was overwhelmed."

"Darned young hypocrite," said Van Aldin. "Simulated great grief, I suppose?"

"N-no," said the Commissary cautiously. "I would not quite say that—eh, Monsieur Carrège?"

The Magistrate brought the tips of his fingers together, and half closed his eyes.

"Shock, bewilderment, horror—these things, yes," he declared judicially. "Great sorrow—no—I should not say that."

Hercule Poirot spoke once more.

"Permit me to ask, Monsieur Van Aldin, does Monsieur Kettering benefit by the death of his wife?"

"He benefits to the tune of a couple of millions," said Van Aldin.

"Dollars?"

"Pounds. I settled that sum on Ruth absolutely on her marriage. She made no will and leaves no children, so the money will go to her husband."

"Whom she was on the point of divorcing," murmured Poirot. "Ah, yes—*précisément*."

The Commissary turned and looked sharply at him.

"Do you mean—" he began.

"I mean nothing," said Poirot. "I arrange the facts, that is all."

Van Aldin stared at him with awakening interest.

The little man rose to his feet.

"I do not think I can be of any further service to you, Monsieur le Juge," he said politely, bowing to Monsieur Carrège. "You will keep me informed of the course of events? It will be a kindness."

"But certainly—most certainly."

Van Aldin rose also.

"You don't want me any more at present?"

"No, monsieur; we have all the information we need for the moment."

"Then I will walk a little way with Monsieur Poirot. That is, if he does not object?"

"Enchanted, monsieur," said the little man, with a bow.

Van Aldin lighted a large cigar, having first offered one to Poirot, who declined it and lit one of his own tiny cigarettes. A man of great strength of character, Van Aldin already appeared to be his everyday, normal self once more. After strolling along for a minute or two in silence, the millionaire spoke:

"I take it, Monsieur Poirot, that you no longer exercise your profession?"

"That is so, monsieur. I enjoy the world."

"Yet you are assisting the police in this affair?"

"Monsieur, if a doctor walks along the street and an accident happens, does he say, 'I have retired from my profession, I will continue my walk,' when there is someone bleeding to death at his feet? If I had been already in Nice, and the police had sent to me and asked me to assist them, I should have refused. But this affair, the good God thrust it upon me."

"You were on the spot," said Van Aldin thoughtfully. "You examined the compartment, did you not?"

Poirot nodded.

"Doubtless you found things that were, shall we say, suggestive to you?"

"Perhaps," said Poirot.

"I hope you see what I am leading up to?" said Van Aldin. "It seems to me that the case against this Comte de la Roche is perfectly clear, but I am not a fool. I have been watching you for this last hour or so, and I realize that for some reason of your own you don't agree with that theory?"

Poirot shrugged his shoulders.

"I may be wrong."

"So we come to the favor I want to ask you. Will you act in this matter for me?"

"For you personally?"

"That was my meaning."

Poirot was silent for a moment or two. Then he said:

"You realize what you are asking?"

"I guess so," said Van Aldin.

"Very well," said Poirot. "I accept. But in that case, I must have frank answers to my questions."

"Why, certainly. That is understood."

Poirot's manner changed. He became suddenly brusque and businesslike.

"This question of a divorce," he said. "It was you who advised your daughter to bring the suit?"

"Yes."

"When?"

"About ten days ago. I had had a letter from her complaining of her husband's behavior, and I put it to her very strongly that divorce was the only remedy."

"In what way did she complain of his behavior?"

"He was being seen about with a *very* notorious lady—the one we have been speaking of—Mirelle."

"The dancer. Ah-ha! And Madame Kettering objected? Was she very devoted to her husband?"

"I would not say that," said Van Aldin, hesitating a little.

"It was not her heart that suffered, it was her pride—is that what you would say?"

"Yes, I suppose you might put it like that."

"I gather that the marriage had not been a happy one from the beginning?"

"Derek Kettering is rotten to the core," said Van Aldin. "He is incapable of making any woman happy."

"He is, as you say in England, a bad lot. That is right, is it not?"

Van Aldin nodded.

"*Très bien!* You advise Madame to seek a divorce, she agrees; you consult your solicitors. When does Monsieur Kettering get news of what is in the wind?"

"I sent for him myself, and explained the course of action I proposed to take."

"And what did he say?" murmured Poirot softly.

Van Aldin's face darkened at the remembrance.

"He was infernally impudent."

"Excuse the question, monsieur, but did he refer to the Comte de la Roche?"

"Not by name," growled the other unwillingly, "but he showed himself cognizant of the affair."

"What, if I may ask, was Monsieur Kettering's financial position at the time?"

"How do you suppose I should know that?" asked Van Aldin, after a very brief hesitation.

"It seemed likely to me that you would inform yourself on that point."

"Well—you are quite right, I did. I discovered that Kettering was on the rocks."

"And now he has inherited two million pounds! *La vie*—it is a strange thing, is it not?"

Van Aldin looked at him sharply.

"What do you mean?"

"I moralize," said Poirot. "I reflect, I speak the philosophy. But to return to where we were. Surely Monsieur Kettering did not propose to allow himself to be divorced without making a fight for it?"

Van Aldin did not answer for a minute or two, then he said:

"I don't exactly know what his intentions were."

"Did you hold any further communications with him?"

Again a slight pause, then Van Aldin said:

"No."

Poirot stopped dead, took off his hat, and held out his hand.

"I must wish you good day, monsieur. I can do nothing for you."

"What are you getting at?" demanded Van Aldin angrily.

"If you do not tell me the truth, I can do nothing."

"I don't know what you mean."

"I think you do. You may rest assured, Monsieur Van Aldin, that I know how to be discreet."

"Very well, then," said the millionaire. "I'll admit that I was not speaking the truth just now. I *did* have further communication with my son-in-law."

"Yes?"

"To be exact, I sent my secretary, Major Knighton, to see him, with instructions to offer him the sum of one hundred thousand pounds in cash if the divorce went through undefended."

"A pretty sum of money," said Poirot appreciatively; "and the answer of Monsieur your son-in-law?"

"He sent back word that I could go to hell," replied the millionaire succinctly.

"Ah!" said Poirot.

He betrayed no emotion of any kind. At the moment he was engaged in methodically recording facts.

"Monsieur Kettering has told the police that he neither saw nor spoke to his wife on the journey from England. Are you inclined to believe that statement, monsieur?"

"Yes, I am," said Van Aldin. "He would take particular pains to keep out of her way, I should say."

"Why?"

"Because he had got that woman with him."

"Mirelle?"

"Yes."

"How did you come to know that fact?"

"A man of mine, whom I had put on to watch him, reported to me that they had both left by that train."

"I see," said Poirot. "In that case, as you said before, he would not be likely to attempt to hold any communication with Madame Kettering."

The little man fell silent for some time. Van Aldin did not interrupt his meditation.

17

An Aristocratic Gentleman

"You have been to the Riviera before, Georges?" said Poirot to his valet the following morning.

George was an intensely English, rather wooden-faced individual.

"Yes, sir. I was here two years ago when I was in the service of Lord Edward Frampton."

"And today," murmured his master, "you are here with Hercule Poirot. How one mounts in the world!"

The valet made no reply to this observation. After a suitable pause he asked:

"The brown lounge suit, sir? The wind is somewhat chilly today."

"There is a grease spot on the waistcoat," objected Poirot. "A *morceau* of *Fillet de sole à la Jeanette* alighted there when I was lunching at the Ritz last Tuesday."

"There is no spot there now, sir," said George reproachfully. "I have removed it."

"*Très bien!*" said Poirot. "I am pleased with you, Georges."

"Thank you, sir."

There was a pause, and then Poirot murmured dreamily:

"Supposing, my good Georges, that you had been born in the same social sphere as your late master, Lord Edward Frampton—that, penniless yourself, you had married an extremely wealthy wife, but that that wife proposed to divorce you, with excellent reasons, what would you do about it?"

"I should endeavor, sir," replied George, "to make her change her mind."

"By peaceful or by forcible methods?"

George looked shocked.

"You will excuse me, sir," he said, "but a gentleman of the aristocracy would not behave like a Whitechapel coster. He would not do anything low."

"Would he not, Georges? I wonder now. Well, perhaps you are right."

There was a knock on the door. George went to it and opened it a discreet inch or two. A low murmured colloquy went on, and then the valet returned to Poirot.

"A note, sir."

Poirot took it. It was from Monsieur Caux, the Commissary of Police.

"We are about to interrogate the Comte de la Roche. The Juge d'Instruction begs that you will be present."

"Quickly, my suit, Georges! I must hasten myself."

A quarter of an hour later, spick and span in his brown suit, Poirot entered the Examining Magistrate's room. Monsieur Caux was already there, and both he and Monsieur Carrège greeted Poirot with polite *empressement*.

"The affair is somewhat discouraging," murmured Monsieur Caux. "It appears that the Comte arrived in Nice the day before the murder."

"If that is true, it will settle your affair nicely for you," responded Poirot.

Monsieur Carrège cleared his throat.

"We must not accept this alibi without very cautious inquiry," he declared. He struck the bell upon the table with his hand.

In another minute a tall dark man, exquisitely dressed, with a somewhat haughty cast of countenance, entered the room. So very aristocratic-looking was the Count, that it would have seemed sheer heresy even to whisper that his father had been an obscure corn chandler in Nantes—which, as a matter of fact, was the case. Looking at him, one would have been prepared to swear that innumerable ancestors of his must have perished by the guillotine in the French Revolution.

"I am here, gentlemen," said the Count haughtily. "May I ask why you wish to see me?"

"Pray be seated, Monsieur le Comte," said the Examining Magistrate politely. "It is the affair of the death of Madame Kettering that we are investigating."

"The death of Madame Kettering? I do not understand."

"You were—ahem!—acquainted with the lady, I believe, Monsieur le Comte?"

"Certainly I was acquainted with her. What has that to do with the matter?"

Sticking an eyeglass in his eye, he looked coldly round the room, his glance resting longest on Poirot, who was gazing at him with a kind of simple, innocent admiration which was most pleasing to the Count's vanity. Monsieur Carrège leaned back in his chair and cleared his throat.

"You do not perhaps know, Monsieur le Comte"—he paused— "that Madame Kettering was murdered?"

"Murdered? *Mon Dieu,* how terrible!"

The surprise and the sorrow were excellently done—so well done, indeed, as to seem wholly natural.

"Madame Kettering was strangled between Paris and Lyons," continued Monsieur Carrège, "and her jewels were stolen."

"It is iniquitous!" cried the Count warmly. "The police should do something about these train bandits. Nowadays no one is safe."

"In Madame's handbag," continued the Judge, "we found a letter to her from you. She had, it seemed, arranged to meet you?"

The Count shrugged his shoulders and spread out his hands.

"Of what use are concealments," he said frankly. "We are all men of the world. Privately and between ourselves, I admit the affair."

"You met her in Paris and traveled down with her, I believe?" said Monsieur Carrège.

"That was the original arrangement, but by Madame's wish it was changed. I was to meet her at Hyères."

"You did not meet her on the train at the Gare de Lyon on the evening of the fourteenth?"

"On the contrary, I arrived in Nice on the morning of that day, so what you suggest is impossible."

"Quite so, quite so," said Monsieur Carrège. "As a matter of form, you would perhaps give me an account of your movements during the evening and night of the fourteenth."

The Count reflected for a minute.

"I dined in Monte Carlo at the Café de Paris. Afterwards I went to the Le Sporting. I won a few thousand francs." He shrugged his shoulders. "I returned home at perhaps one o'clock."

"Pardon me, monsieur, but how did you return home?"

"In my own two-seater car."

"No one was with you?"

"No one."

"You could produce witnesses in support of this statement?"

"Doubtless many of my friends saw me there that evening. I dined alone."

"Your servant admitted you on your return to your villa?"

"I let myself in with my own latchkey."

"Ah!" murmured the Magistrate.

Again he struck the bell on the table with his hand. The door opened, and a messenger appeared.

"Bring in the maid, Mason," said Monsieur Carrège.

"Very good, Monsieur le Juge."

Ada Mason was brought in.

"Will you be so good, mademoiselle, as to look at this gentleman. To the best of your ability, was it he who entered your mistress's compartment in Paris?"

The woman looked long and searchingly at the Count, who was, Poirot fancied, rather uneasy under this scrutiny.

"I could not say, sir, I am sure," said Mason at last. "It might be and again it might not. Seeing as how I only saw his back, it's hard to say. I rather think it *was* the gentleman."

"But you are not sure?"

"No-o," said Mason unwillingly; "n-no, I am not sure."

"You have seen this gentleman before in Curzon Street?"

Mason shook her head.

"I should not be likely to see any visitors that come to Curzon Street," she explained, "unless they were staying in the house."

"Very well, that will do," said the Examining Magistrate sharply. Evidently he was disappointed.

"One moment," said Poirot. "There is a question I would like to put to Mademoiselle, if I may?"

"Certainly, Monsieur Poirot—certainly, by all means."

Poirot addressed himself to the maid.

"What happened to the tickets?"

"The tickets, sir?"

"Yes; the tickets from London to Nice. Did you or your mistress have them?"

"The mistress had her own Pullman ticket, sir; the others were in my charge."

"What happened to them?"

"I gave them to the conductor on the French train, sir; he said it was usual. I hope I did right, sir?"

"Oh, quite right, quite right. A mere matter of detail."

Both Monsieur Caux and the Examining Magistrate looked at him curiously. Mason stood uncertainly for a minute or two, and then the Magistrate gave her a brief nod of dismissal, and she went out. Poirot scribbled something on a scrap of paper and handed it across to Monsieur Carrège. The latter read it and his brow cleared.

"Well, gentlemen," demanded the Count haughtily, "am I to be detained further?"

"Assuredly not, assuredly not," Monsieur Carrège hastened to say, with a great deal of amiability. "Everything is now cleared up as regards your own position in this affair. Naturally, in view of Madame's letter, we were bound to question you."

The Count rose, picked up his handsome stick from the corner, and, with rather a curt bow, left the room.

"And that is that," said Monsieur Carrège. "You were quite right, Monsieur Poirot—much better to let him feel he is not suspected. Two of my men will shadow him night and day, and at the same time we will go into the question of the alibi. It seems to me rather —er—a fluid one."

"Possibly," agreed Poirot thoughtfully.

"I asked Monsieur Kettering to come here this morning," continued the Magistrate, "though really I doubt if we have much to ask him, but there are one or two suspicious circumstances—" He paused, rubbing his nose.

"Such as?" asked Poirot.

"Well"—the Magistrate coughed—"this lady with whom he is said to be traveling—Mademoiselle Mirelle. She is staying at one hotel and he at another. That strikes me—er—as rather odd."

"It looks," said Monsieur Caux, "as though they were being careful."

"Exactly," said Monsieur Carrège triumphantly; "and what should they have to be careful about?"

"An excess of caution is suspicious, eh?" said Poirot.

"*Précisément.*"

"We might, I think," murmured Poirot, "ask Monsieur Kettering one or two questions."

The Magistrate gave instructions. A moment or two later, Derek Kettering, debonair as ever, entered the room.

"Good morning, monsieur," said the Judge politely.

"Good morning," said Derek Kettering curtly. "You sent for me. Has anything fresh turned up?"

"Pray sit down, monsieur."

Derek took a seat and flung his hat and stick on the table.

"Well?" he asked impatiently.

"We have, so far, no fresh data," said Monsieur Carrège cautiously.

"That's very interesting," said Derek dryly. "Did you send for me here in order to tell me that?"

"We naturally thought, monsieur, that you would like to be informed of the progress of the case," said the Magistrate severely.

"Even if the progress was nonexistent?"

"We also wished to ask you a few questions."

"Ask away."

"You are quite sure that you neither saw nor spoke with your wife on the train?"

"I've answered that already. I did not."

"You had, no doubt, your reasons."

Derek stared at him suspiciously.

"I—did—not—know—she—was—on—the—train," he explained, spacing his words elaborately, as though to someone dull of intellect.

"That is what you say, yes," murmured Monsieur Carrège.

A frown suffused Derek's face.

"I should like to know what you're driving at. Do you know what I think, Monsieur Carrège?"

"What do you think, monsieur?"

"I think the French police are vastly overrated. Surely you must have some data as to these gangs of train robbers. It's outrageous that such a thing could happen on a *train de luxe* like that, and that the French police should be helpless to deal with the matter."

"We are dealing with it, monsieur, never fear."

"Madame Kettering, I understand, did not leave a will," interposed Poirot suddenly. His fingertips were joined together, and he was looking intently at the ceiling.

"I don't think she ever made one," said Kettering. "Why?"

"It is a very pretty little fortune that you inherit there," said Poirot—"a very pretty little fortune."

Although his eyes were still on the ceiling, he managed to see the dark flush that rose to Derek Kettering's face.

"What do you mean, and who are you?"

Poirot gently uncrossed his knees, withdrew his gaze from the ceiling, and looked the young man full in the face.

"My name is Hercule Poirot," he said quietly, "and I am probably the greatest detective in the world. You are quite sure that you did not see or speak to your wife on that train?"

"What are you getting at? Do you—do you mean to insinuate that I—I killed her?"

He laughed suddenly.

"I mustn't lose my temper; it's too palpably absurd. Why, if I killed her I should have had no need to steal her jewels, would I?"

"That is true," murmured Poirot, with a rather crestfallen air. "I did not think of that."

"If ever there were a clear case of murder and robbery, this is it," said Derek Kettering. "Poor Ruth, it was those damned rubies did for her. It must have got about she had them with her. There has been murder done for those same stones before now, I believe."

Poirot sat up suddenly in his chair. A very faint green light glowed in his eyes. He looked extraordinarily like a sleek, well-fed cat.

"One more question, Monsieur Kettering," he said. "Will you give me the date when you last saw your wife?"

"Let me see," Kettering reflected. "It must have been—yes, over three weeks ago. I am afraid I can't give you the date exactly."

"No matter," said Poirot dryly; "that is all I wanted to know."

"Well," said Derek Kettering impatiently, "anything further?"

He looked towards Monsieur Carrège. The latter sought inspiration from Poirot, and received it in a very faint shake of the head.

"No, Monsieur Kettering," he said politely; "no, I do not think we need trouble you any further. I wish you good morning."

"Good morning," said Kettering. He went out, banging the door behind him.

Poirot leaned forward and spoke sharply, as soon as the young man was out of the room.

"Tell me," he said peremptorily, "when did you speak of these rubies to Monsieur Kettering?"

"I have not spoken of them," said Monsieur Carrège. "It was only yesterday afternoon that we learned about them from Monsieur Van Aldin."

"Yes; but there was a mention of them in the Comte's letter."

Monsieur Carrège looked pained.

"Naturally I did not speak of that letter to Monsieur Kettering," he said in a shocked voice. "It would have been most indiscreet at the present juncture of affairs."

Poirot leaned forward and tapped the table.

"*Then how did he know about them?*" he demanded softly. "Madame could not have told him, for he has not seen her for three weeks. It seems unlikely that either Monsieur Van Aldin or his secretary would have mentioned them; their interviews with him have been on entirely different lines, and there has not been any hint or reference to them in the newspapers."

He got up and took his hat and stick.

"And yet," he murmured to himself, "our gentleman knows all about them. I wonder now, yes, I wonder!"

18

Derek Lunches

DEREK KETTERING went straight to the Negresco, where he ordered a couple of cocktails and disposed of them rapidly; then he stared moodily out over the dazzling blue sea. He noted the passers-by mechanically—a damned dull crowd, badly dressed, and painfully uninteresting; one hardly ever saw anything worthwhile nowadays. Then he corrected this last impression rapidly, as a woman placed herself at a table a little distance away from him. She was wearing a marvelous confection of orange and black, with a little hat that shaded her face. He ordered a third cocktail; again he stared out to sea, and then suddenly he started. A well-known perfume assailed his nostrils, and he looked up to see the orange-and-black lady standing beside him. He saw her face now, and recognized her. It was Mirelle. She was smiling that insolent, seductive smile he knew so well.

"Dereek!" she murmured. "You are pleased to see me, no?"

She dropped into a seat the other side of the table.

"But welcome me, then, stupid one," she mocked.

"This is an unexpected pleasure," said Derek. "When did you leave London?"

She shrugged her shoulders.

"A day or two ago."

"And the Parthenon?"

"I have, how do you say it?—given them the chuck!"

"Really?"

"You are not very amiable, Dereek."

"Do you expect me to be?"

Mirelle lit a cigarette and puffed at it for a few minutes before saying:

"You think, perhaps, that it is not prudent so soon?"

Derek stared at her, then he shrugged his shoulders and remarked formally:

"You are lunching here?"

"*Mais oui.* I am lunching with you."

"I am extremely sorry," said Derek. "I have a very important engagement."

"*Mon Dieu!* But you men are like children," exclaimed the dancer. "But yes, it is the spoilt child that you act to me, ever since that day in London when you flung yourself out of my flat, you sulk. Ah! *mais c'est inouï!*"

"My dear girl," said Derek, "I really don't know what you are talking about. We agreed in London that rats desert a sinking ship, that is all that there is to be said."

In spite of his careless words, his face looked haggard and strained. Mirelle leaned forward suddenly.

"You cannot deceive me," she murmured. "I know—I know what you have done for me."

He looked up at her sharply. Some undercurrent in her voice arrested his attention. She nodded her head at him.

"Ah! Have no fear; I am discreet. You are magnificent! You have a superb courage, but, all the same, it was I who gave you the idea that day, when I said to you in London that accidents sometimes happened. And you are not in danger? The police do not suspect you?"

"What the devil—"

"Hush!"

She held up a slim olive hand with one big emerald on the little finger.

"You are right; I should not have spoken so in a public place. We will not speak of the matter again, but our troubles are ended; our life together will be wonderful—wonderful!"

Derek laughed suddenly—a harsh, disagreeable laugh.

"So the rats come back, do they? Two million makes a difference —of course it does. I ought to have known that." He laughed again. "You will help me to spend that two million, won't you, Mirelle? You know how, no woman better." He laughed again.

"Hush!" cried the dancer. "What is the matter with you, Dereek? See—people are turning to stare at you."

"Me? I will tell you what is the matter. I have finished with you, Mirelle. Do you hear? Finished!"

Mirelle did not take it as he expected her to do. She looked at him for a minute or two, and then she smiled softly.

"But what a child! You are angry—you are sore, and all because I am practical. Did I not always tell you that I adored you?"

She leaned forward.

"But I know you, Dereek. Look at me—see, it is Mirelle who speaks to you. You cannot live without her, you know it. I loved you before, I will love you a hundred times more now. I will make life wonderful for you—but wonderful. There is no one like Mirelle."

Her eyes burned into his. She saw him grow pale and draw in his breath, and she smiled to herself contentedly. She knew her own magic and power over men.

"That is settled," she said softly, and gave a little laugh. "And now, Dereek, will you give me lunch?"

"No."

He drew in his breath sharply and rose to his feet.

"I am sorry, but I told you—I have got an engagement."

"You are lunching with someone else? Bah! I don't believe it."

"I am lunching with that lady over there."

He crossed abruptly to where a lady in white had just come up the steps. He addressed her a little breathlessly.

"Miss Grey, will you—will you have lunch with me? You met me at Lady Tamplin's, if you remember."

Katherine looked at him for a minute or two with those thoughtful gray eyes that said so much.

"Thank you," she said, after a moment's pause; "I should like to very much."

19

An Unexpected Visitor

THE Comte de la Roche had just finished *déjeuner,* consisting of an *omelette fines herbes,* an *entrecôte Bearnaise,* and a *Savarin au Rhum.* Wiping his fine black mustache delicately with his table napkin, the Comte rose from the table. He passed through the salon of the villa, noting with appreciation the few *objets d'art* which were carelessly scattered about. The Louis XV snuffbox, the satin shoe worn by Marie Antoinette, and the other historic trifles were part of the Comte's *mise en scène.* They were, he would explain to his fair visitors, heirlooms in his family. Passing through onto the terrace, the Comte looked out on the Mediterranean with an unseeing eye. He was in no mood for appreciating the beauties of scenery. A fully matured scheme had been rudely brought to naught, and his plans had to be cast afresh. Stretching himself out in a basket chair, a cigarette held between his white fingers, the Comte pondered deeply.

Presently Hippolyte, his manservant, brought out coffee and a choice of liqueurs. The Comte selected some very fine old brandy.

As the manservant was preparing to depart, the Comte arrested him with a slight gesture. Hippolyte stood respectfully to attention. His countenance was hardly a prepossessing one, but the correctitude of his demeanor went far to obliterate the fact. He was now the picture of respectful attention.

"It is possible," said the Comte, "that in the course of the next few days various strangers may come to the house. They will endeavor to scrape acquaintance with you and with Marie. They will probably ask you various questions concerning me."

"Yes, Monsieur le Comte."

"Perhaps this has already happened?"

"No, Monsieur le Comte."

"There have been no strangers about the place? You are certain?"

"There has been no one, Monsieur le Comte."

"That is well," said the Comte dryly; "nevertheless they will come—I am sure of it. They will ask questions."

Hippolyte looked at his master in intelligent anticipation.

The Comte spoke slowly, without looking at Hippolyte.

"As you know, I arrived here last Tuesday morning. If the police or any other inquirer should question you, do not forget that fact. I arrived on Tuesday, the fourteenth—not Wednesday, the fifteenth. You understand?"

"Perfectly, Monsieur le Comte."

"In an affair where a lady is concerned, it is always necessary to be discreet. I feel certain, Hippolyte, that you can be discreet."

"I can be discreet, monsieur."

"And Marie?"

"Marie also. I will answer for her."

"That is well then," murmured the Comte.

When Hippolyte had withdrawn, the Comte sipped his black coffee with a reflective air. Occasionally he frowned, once he shook his head slightly, twice he nodded it. Into the midst of these cogitations came Hippolyte once more.

"A lady, monsieur."

"A lady?"

The Comte was surprised. Not that a visit from a lady was an unusual thing at the Villa Marina, but at this particular moment the Comte could not think who the lady was likely to be.

"She is, I think, a lady not known to Monsieur," murmured the valet helpfully.

The Comte was more and more intrigued.

"Show her out here, Hippolyte," he commanded.

A moment later a marvelous vision in orange and black stepped out on the terrace, accompanied by a strong perfume of exotic blossoms.

"Monsieur le Comte de la Roche?"

"At your service, mademoiselle," said the Comte, bowing.

"My name is Mirelle. You may have heard of me."

"Ah, indeed, mademoiselle, but who has not been enchanted by the dancing of Mademoiselle Mirelle? Exquisite!"

The dancer acknowledged this compliment with a brief mechanical smile.

"My descent upon you is unceremonious," she began.

"But seat yourself, I beg of you, mademoiselle," cried the Comte, bringing forward a chair.

Behind the gallantry of his manner he was observing her narrowly. There were very few things that the Comte did not know about women. True, his experience had not lain much in ladies of Mirelle's class, who were themselves predatory. He and the dancer were, in a sense, birds of a feather. His arts, the Comte knew, would be thrown away on Mirelle. She was a Parisienne, and a shrewd one. Nevertheless, there was one thing that the Comte could recognize infallibly when he saw it. He knew at once that he was in the presence of a very angry woman, and an angry woman, as the Comte was well aware, always says more than is prudent, and is occasionally a source of profit to a level-headed gentleman who keeps cool.

"It is most amiable of you, mademoiselle, to honor my poor abode thus."

"We have mutual friends in Paris," said Mirelle. "I have heard of you from them, but I come to see you today for another reason. I have heard of you since I came to Nice—in a different way, you understand."

"Ah?" said the Comte softly.

"I will be brutal," continued the dancer; "nevertheless, believe that I have your welfare at heart. They are saying in Nice, Monsieur le Comte, that you are the murderer of the English lady, Madame Kettering."

"I! The murderer of Madame Kettering? Bah! But how absurd!"

He spoke more languidly than indignantly, knowing that he would thus provoke her further.

"But yes," she insisted; "it is as I tell you."

"It amuses people to talk," murmured the Comte indifferently. "It would be beneath me to take such wild accusations seriously."

"You do not understand." Mirelle bent forward, her dark eyes flashing. "It is not the idle talk of those in the streets. It is the police."

"The police—ah?"

The Comte sat up, alert once more.

Mirelle nodded her head vigorously several times.

"Yes, yes. You comprehend me—I have friends everywhere. The Prefect himself—" She left the sentence unfinished, with an eloquent shrug of the shoulders.

"Who is not indiscreet where a beautiful woman is concerned?" murmured the Count politely.

"The police believe that you killed Madame Kettering. But they are wrong."

"Certainly they are wrong," agreed the Comte easily.

"You say that, but you do not know the truth. I do."

The Comte looked at her curiously.

"You know who killed Madame Kettering? Is that what you would say, mademoiselle?"

Mirelle nodded vehemently.

"Yes."

"Who was it?" asked the Comte sharply.

"Her husband." She bent nearer to the Comte, speaking in a low voice that vibrated with anger and excitement. "It was her husband who killed her."

The Comte leaned back in his chair. His face was a mask.

"Let me ask you, mademoiselle—how do you know this?"

"How do I know it?" Mirelle sprang to her feet, with a laugh. "He boasted of it beforehand. He was ruined, bankrupt, dishonored. Only the death of his wife could save him. He told me so. He traveled on the same train—but she was not to know it. Why was that, I ask you? So that he might creep upon her in the night— Ah!"—she shut her eyes—"I can see it happening. . . ."

The Count coughed.

"Perhaps—perhaps," he murmured. "But surely, mademoiselle, in that case he would not steal the jewels?"

"The jewels!" breathed Mirelle. "The jewels. Ah! Those rubies . . ."

Her eyes grew misty, a faraway light in them. The Comte looked at her curiously, wondering for the hundredth time at the magical influence of precious stones on the female sex. He recalled her to practical matters.

"What do you want me to do, mademoiselle?"

Mirelle became alert and businesslike once more.

"Surely it is simple. You will go to the police. You will say to them that Monsieur Kettering committed this crime."

"And if they do not believe me? If they ask for proof?" He was eyeing her closely.

Mirelle laughed softly, and drew her orange-and-black wrap closer round her.

"Send them to me, Monsieur le Comte," she said softly; "I will give them the proof they want."

Upon that she was gone, an impetuous whirlwind, her errand accomplished.

The Comte looked after her, his eyebrows delicately raised.

"She is in a fury," he murmured. "What has happened now to upset her? But she shows her hand too plainly. Does she really believe that Mr. Kettering killed his wife? She would like me to believe it. She would even like the police to believe it."

He smiled to himself. He had no intention whatsoever of going to the police. He saw various other possibilities; to judge by his smile, an agreeable vista of them.

Presently, however, his brow clouded. According to Mirelle, he was suspected by the police. That might be true or it might not. An angry woman of the type of the dancer was not likely to bother about the strict veracity of her statements. On the other hand, she might easily have obtained—inside information. In that case—his mouth set grimly—in that case he must take certain precautions.

He went into the house and questioned Hippolyte closely once more as to whether any strangers had been to the house. The valet was positive in his assurances that this was not the case. The Comte went up to his bedroom and crossed over to an old bureau that stood against the wall. He let down the lid of this, and his delicate fingers sought for a spring at the back of one of the pigeonholes. A secret drawer flew out; in it was a small brown paper package. The Comte took this out and weighed it in his hand carefully for a minute or two. Raising his hand to his head, with a slight grimace he pulled out a single hair. This he placed on the lip of the drawer and shut it carefully. Still carrying the small parcel in his hand, he went downstairs and out of the house to the garage, where stood a scarlet two-seater car. Ten minutes later he had taken the road for Monte Carlo.

He spent a few hours at the casino, then sauntered out into the town. Presently he reentered the car and drove off in the direction of Mentone. Earlier in the afternoon he had noticed an inconspicuous gray car some little distance behind him. He noticed it again now. He smiled to himself. The road was climbing steadily upwards. The Comte's foot pressed hard on the accelerator. The little red car had been specially built to the Comte's design, and had a far more powerful engine than would have been suspected from its appearance. It shot ahead.

Presently he looked back and smiled; the gray car was following behind. Smothered in dust, the little red car leaped along the road. It was traveling now at a dangerous pace, but the Comte was a first-class driver. Now they were going downhill, twisting and curving unceasingly. Presently the car slackened speed, and finally came to a standstill before a Bureau de Poste. The Comte jumped out, lifted the lid of the tool chest, extracted the small brown paper parcel and hurried into the post office. Two minutes later he was driving once more in the direction of Mentone. When the gray car arrived there, the Comte was drinking English five o'clock tea on the terrace of one of the hotels.

Later, he drove back to Monte Carlo, dined there, and reached home once more at eleven o'clock. Hippolyte came out to meet him with a disturbed face.

"Ah! Monsieur le Comte has arrived. Monsieur le Comte did not telephone me, by any chance?"

The Comte shook his head.

"And yet at three o'clock I received a summons from Monsieur le Comte to present myself to him at Nice, at the Negresco."

"Really," said the Comte; "and you went?"

"Certainly, monsieur, but at the Negresco they knew nothing of Monsieur le Comte. He had not been there."

"Ah," said the Comte, "doubtless at that hour Marie was out doing her afternoon marketing?"

"That is so, Monsieur le Comte."

"Ah, well," said the Comte, "it is of no importance. A mistake."

He went upstairs, smiling to himself.

Once within his own room, he bolted his door and looked sharply round. Everything seemed as usual. He opened various drawers and cupboards. Then he nodded to himself. Things had been replaced almost exactly as he had left them, but not quite. It was evident that a very thorough search had been made.

He went over to the bureau and pressed the hidden spring. The drawer flew open, but the hair was no longer where he had placed it. He nodded his head several times.

"They are excellent, our French police," he murmured to himself—"excellent. Nothing escapes them."

20

Katherine Makes a Friend

ON the following morning Katherine and Lenox were sitting on the terrace of the Villa Marguerite. Something in the nature of a friendship was springing up between them, despite the difference in age. But for Lenox, Katherine would have found life at the Villa Marguerite quite intolerable. The Kettering case was the topic of the moment. Lady Tamplin frankly exploited her guest's connection with the affair for all it was worth. The most persistent rebuffs that Katherine could administer quite failed to pierce Lady Tamplin's self-esteem. Lenox adopted a detached attitude, seemingly amused at her mother's maneuvers, and yet with a sympathetic understanding of Katherine's feelings. The situation was not helped by Chubby, whose naive delight was unquenchable, and who introduced Katherine to all and sundry as:

"This is Miss Grey. You know that Blue Train business? She was in it up to the ears! Had a long talk with Ruth Kettering a few hours before the murder! Bit of luck for her, eh?"

A few remarks of this kind had provoked Katherine that morning to an unusually tart rejoinder, and when they were alone together Lenox observed in her slow drawl:

"Not used to exploitation, are you? You have a lot to learn, Katherine."

"I am sorry I lost my temper. I don't, as a rule."

"It is about time you learned to blow off steam. Chubby is only an ass; there is no harm in him. Mother, of course, is trying, but you can lose your temper with her until kingdom come, and it won't make any impression. She will open large, sad blue eyes at you and not care a bit."

Katherine made no reply to this filial observation, and Lenox presently went on:

"I am rather like Chubby. I delight in a good murder, and besides —well, knowing Derek makes a difference."

Katherine nodded.

"So you lunched with him yesterday," pursued Lenox reflectively. "Do you like him, Katherine?"

Katherine considered for a minute or two.

"I don't know," she said very slowly.

"He is very attractive."

"Yes, he is attractive."

"What don't you like about him?"

Katherine did not reply to the question, or at any rate not directly. "He spoke of his wife's death," she said. "He said he would not pretend that it had been anything but a bit of most marvelous luck for him."

"And that shocked you, I suppose," said Lenox. She paused, and then added in rather a queer tone of voice: "He likes you, Katherine."

"He gave me a very good lunch," said Katherine, smiling.

Lenox refused to be sidetracked.

"I saw it the night he came here," she said thoughtfully. "The way he looked at you; and you are not his usual type—just the opposite. Well, I suppose it is like religion—you get it at a certain age."

"Mademoiselle is wanted at the telephone," said Marie, appearing at the window of the salon. "Monsieur Hercule Poirot desires to speak with her."

"More blood and thunder. Go on, Katherine; go and dally with your detective."

Monsieur Hercule Poirot's voice came neat and precise in its intonation to Katherine's ear.

"That is Mademoiselle Grey who speaks? *Bon.* Mademoiselle, I have a word for you from Monsieur Van Aldin, the father of Madame Kettering. He wishes very much to speak with you, either at the Villa Marguerite or at his hotel, whichever you prefer."

Katherine reflected for a moment, but she decided that for Van Aldin to come to the Villa Marguerite would be both painful and unnecessary. Lady Tamplin would have hailed his advent with far too much delight. She never lost a chance of cultivating millionaires. She told Poirot that she would much rather come to Nice.

"Excellent, mademoiselle. I will call for you myself in an auto. Shall we say in about three-quarters of an hour?"

Punctually to the moment Poirot appeared. Katherine was waiting for him, and they drove off at once.

"Well, mademoiselle, how goes it?"

She looked at his twinkling eyes, and was confirmed in her first impression that there was something very attractive about Monsieur Hercule Poirot.

"This is our own *roman policier*, is it not?" said Poirot. "I made you the promise that we should study it together. And me, I always keep my promises."

"You are too kind," murmured Katherine.

"Ah, you mock yourself at me; but do you want to hear the developments of the case, or do you not?"

Katherine admitted that she did, and Poirot proceeded to sketch for her a thumbnail portrait of the Comte de la Roche.

"You think he killed her," said Katherine thoughtfully.

"That is the theory," said Poirot guardedly.

"Do you yourself believe that?"

"I did not say so. And you, mademoiselle, what do you think?" Katherine shook her head.

"How should I know? I don't know anything about those things, but I should say that—"

"Yes," said Poirot encouragingly.

"Well—from what you say the Count does not sound the kind of man who would actually kill anybody."

"Ah! Very good," cried Poirot, "you agree with me; that is just what I have said." He looked at her sharply. "But tell me, you have met Mr. Derek Kettering?"

"I met him at Lady Tamplin's, and I lunched with him yesterday."

"A *mauvais sujet*," said Poirot, shaking his head; "but *les femmes* —they like that, eh?"

He twinkled at Katherine and she laughed.

"He is the kind of man one would notice anywhere," continued Poirot. "Doubtless you observed him on the Blue Train?"

"Yes, I noticed him."

"In the restaurant car?"

"No. I didn't notice him at meals at all. I only saw him once— going into his wife's compartment."

Poirot nodded. "A strange business," he murmured. "I believe you said you were awake, mademoiselle, and looked out of your window at Lyons? You saw no tall dark man such as the Comte de la Roche leave the train?"

Katherine shook her head. "I don't think I saw anyone at all," she said. "There was a youngish lad in a cap and overcoat who got out, but I don't think he was leaving the train, only walking up and down the platform. There was a fat Frenchman with a beard, in pajamas and an overcoat, who wanted a cup of coffee. Otherwise, I think there were only the train attendants."

Poirot nodded his head several times. "It is like this, you see," he confided, "the Comte de la Roche has an alibi. An alibi, it is a very pestilential thing, and always open to the gravest suspicion. But here we are!"

They went straight up to Van Aldin's suite, where they found Knighton. Poirot introduced him to Katherine. After a few common-places had been exchanged, Knighton said, "I will tell Mr. Van Aldin that Miss Grey is here."

He went through a second door into an adjoining room. There was a low murmur of voices, and then Van Aldin came into the room and advanced towards Katherine with outstretched hand, giving her at the same time a shrewd and penetrating glance.

"I am pleased to meet you, Miss Grey," he said simply. "I have been wanting very badly to hear what you can tell me about Ruth."

The quiet simplicity of the millionaire's manner appealed to Katherine strongly. She felt herself in the presence of a very genuine grief, the more real for its absence of outward sign.

He drew forward a chair.

"Sit here, will you, and just tell me all about it."

Poirot and Knighton retired discreetly into the other room, and Katherine and Van Aldin were left alone together. She found no difficulty in her task. Quite simply and naturally she related her conversation with Ruth Kettering, word for word as nearly as she could. He listened in silence, leaning back in his chair, with one hand shading his eyes. When she had finished, he said quietly:

"Thank you, my dear."

They both sat silent for a minute or two. Katherine felt that words of sympathy would be out of place. When the millionaire spoke, it was in a different tone:

"I am very grateful to you, Miss Grey. I think you did something to ease my poor Ruth's mind in the last hours of her life. Now I want to ask you something. You know—Monsieur Poirot will have told you—about the scoundrel that my poor girl had got herself mixed up with. He was the man of whom she spoke to you—the man she was going to meet. In your judgment, do you think she might have changed her mind after her conversation with you? Do you think she meant to go back on her word?"

"I can't honestly tell you. She had certainly come to some decision, and seemed more cheerful in consequence of it."

"She gave you no idea where she intended to meet the skunk—whether in Paris or at Hyères?"

Katherine shook her head.

"She said nothing as to that."

"Ah!" said Van Aldin thoughtfully. "And that is the important point. Well, time will show."

He got up and opened the door of the adjoining room. Poirot and Knighton came back.

Katherine declined the millionaire's invitation to lunch, and Knighton went down with her and saw her into the waiting car. He returned to find Poirot and Van Aldin deep in conversation.

"If we only knew," said the millionaire thoughtfully, "what decision Ruth came to. It might have been any of half a dozen. She might have meant to leave the train at Paris and cable to me. She may have meant to have gone on to the south of France and have an explanation with the Count there. We are in the dark—absolutely in the dark. But we have the maid's word for it that she was both startled and dismayed at the Count's appearance at the station in Paris. That was clearly not part of the preconceived plan. You agree with me, Knighton?"

The secretary started. "I beg your pardon, Mr. Van Aldin. I was not listening."

"Daydreaming, eh?" said Van Aldin. "That's not like you. I believe that girl has bowled you over."

Knighton blushed.

"She is a remarkably nice girl," said Van Aldin thoughtfully, "very nice. Did you happen to notice her eyes?"

"Any man," said Knighton, "would be bound to notice her eyes."

21

At the Tennis

SEVERAL days had elapsed. Katherine had been for a walk by herself one morning, and came back to find Lenox grinning at her expectantly.

"Your young man has been ringing you up, Katherine!"

"Who do you call my young man?"

"A new one—Rufus Van Aldin's secretary. You seem to have made rather an impression there. You are becoming a serious breaker of hearts, Katherine. First Derek Kettering, and now this young Knighton. The funny thing is, that I remember him quite well. He was in Mother's war hospital that she ran out here. I was only a kid of about eight at the time."

"Was he badly wounded?"

"Shot in the leg, if I remember rightly—rather a nasty business. I think the doctors messed it up a bit. They said he wouldn't limp or anything, but when he left here, he was still completely dot and go one."

Lady Tamplin came out and joined them.

"Have you been telling Katherine about Major Knighton?" she asked. "Such a dear fellow! Just at first I didn't remember him—one had so many—but now it all comes back."

"He was a bit too unimportant to be remembered before," said Lenox. "Now that he is a secretary to an American millionaire, it is a very different matter."

"Darling!" said Lady Tamplin in her vague reproachful voice.

"What did Major Knighton ring up about?" inquired Katherine.

"He asked if you would like to go to the tennis this afternoon. If so, he would call for you in a car. Mother and I accepted for you with *empressement*. While you dally with a millionaire's secretary, you might give me a chance with the millionaire, Katherine. He is about sixty, I suppose, so that he will be looking about for a nice sweet young thing like me."

"I should like to meet Mr. Van Aldin," said Lady Tamplin earnestly; "one has heard so much of him. Those fine rugged figures of the Western world"—she broke off—"so fascinating," she murmured.

"Major Knighton was very particular to say it was Mr. Van Aldin's invitation," said Lenox. "He said it so often that I began to smell a rat. You and Knighton would make a very nice pair, Katherine. Bless you, my children!"

Katherine laughed and went upstairs to change her clothes.

Knighton arrived soon after lunch and endured manfully Lady Tamplin's transports of recognition.

When they were driving together towards Cannes, he remarked to Katherine: "Lady Tamplin has changed wonderfully little."

"In manner or appearance?"

"Both. She must be, I suppose, well over forty, but she is a remarkably beautiful woman still."

"She is," agreed Katherine.

"I am very glad that you could come today," went on Knighton. "Monsieur Poirot is going to be there also. What an extraordinary little man he is. Do you know him well, Miss Grey?"

Katherine shook her head. "I met him on the train on the way here. I was reading a detective novel, and I happened to say something about such things not happening in real life. Of course, I had no idea of who he was."

"He is a very remarkable person," said Knighton slowly, "and has done some very remarkable things. He has a kind of genius for going to the root of the matter, and right up to the end no one has any idea of what he is really thinking. I remember I was staying at a house in Yorkshire, and Lady Clanravon's jewels were stolen. It seemed at first to be a simple robbery, but it completely baffled the local police. I wanted them to call in Hercule Poirot, and said he was the only man who could help them, but they pinned their faith to Scotland Yard."

"And what happened?" said Katherine curiously.

"The jewels were never recovered," said Knighton dryly.

"You really do believe in him?"

"I do indeed. The Comte de la Roche is a pretty wily customer. He has wriggled out of most things. But I think he has met his match in Hercule Poirot."

"The Comte de la Roche," said Katherine thoughtfully; "so you really think he did it?"

"Of course." Knighton looked at her in astonishment. "Don't you?"

"Oh yes," said Katherine hastily; "that is, I mean, if it was not just an ordinary train robbery."

"It might be, of course," agreed the other, "but it seems to me that the Comte de la Roche fits into this business particularly well."

"And yet he has an alibi."

"Oh, alibis!" Knighton laughed and his face broke into his attractive boyish smile.

"You confess that you read detective stories, Miss Grey. You must know that anyone who has a perfect alibi is always open to grave suspicion."

"Do you think that real life is like that?" asked Katherine, smiling.

"Why not? Fiction is founded on fact."

"But is rather superior to it," suggested Katherine.

"Perhaps. Anyway, if I was a criminal, I should not like to have Hercule Poirot on my track."

"No more should I," said Katherine, and laughed.

They were met on arrival by Poirot. As the day was warm, he was attired in a white duck suit, with a white camellia in his buttonhole.

"*Bon jour*, mademoiselle," said Poirot. "I look very English, do I not?"

"You look wonderful," said Katherine tactfully.

"You mock yourself at me," said Poirot genially, "but no matter. Papa Poirot, he always laughs the last."

"Where is Mr. Van Aldin?" asked Knighton.

"He will meet us at our seats. To tell you the truth, my friend, he is not too well pleased with me. Oh, those Americans—the repose, the calm, they know it not! Mr. Van Aldin, he would that I fly myself in the pursuit of criminals through all the byways of Nice."

"I should have thought myself that it would not have been a bad plan," observed Knighton.

"You are wrong," said Poirot; "in these matters one needs not energy but finesse. At the tennis one meets everyone. That is so important. Ah, there is Mr. Kettering."

Derek came abruptly up to them. He looked reckless and angry, as though something had arisen to upset him. He and Knighton greeted each other with some frigidity. Poirot alone seemed unconscious of any sense of strain, and chatted pleasantly in a laudable attempt to put everyone at their ease. He paid little compliments.

"It is amazing, Monsieur Kettering, how well you speak the French," he observed—"so well that you could be taken for a Frenchman if you chose. That is a very rare accomplishment among Englishmen."

"I wish I did," said Katherine. "I am only too well aware that my French is of a painfully British order."

They reached their seats and sat down, and almost immediately Knighton perceived his employer signaling to him from the other end of the court, and went off to speak to him.

"Me, I approve of that young man," said Poirot, sending a beaming smile after the departing secretary; "and you, mademoiselle?"

"I like him very much."

"And you, Monsieur Kettering?"

Some quick rejoinder was springing to Derek's lips, but he checked it as though something in the little Belgian's twinkling eyes had made him suddenly alert. He spoke carefully, choosing his words.

"Knighton is a very good fellow," he said.

Just for a moment Katherine fancied that Poirot looked disappointed.

"He is a great admirer of yours, Monsieur Poirot," she said, and she related some of the things that Knighton had said. It amused her to see the little man plume himself like a bird, thrusting out his chest, and assuming an air of mock modesty that would have deceived no one.

"That reminds me, mademoiselle," he said suddenly, "I have a little matter of business I have to speak to you about. When you were sitting talking to that poor lady in the train, I think you must have dropped a cigarette case."

Katherine looked rather astonished. "I don't think so," she said. Poirot drew from his pocket a cigarette case of soft blue leather, with the initial "K" on it in gold.

"No, that is not mine," Katherine said.

"Ah, a thousand apologies. It was doubtless Madame's own. 'K,' of course, stands for Kettering. We were doubtful, because she had another cigarette case in her bag, and it seemed odd that she should have two." He turned to Derek suddenly. "You do not know, I suppose, whether this was your wife's case or not?"

Derek seemed momentarily taken aback. He stammered a little in his reply: "I—I don't know. I suppose so."

"It is not yours by any chance?"

"Certainly not. If it were mine, it would hardly have been in my wife's possession."

Poirot looked more ingenuous and childlike than ever.

"I thought perhaps you might have dropped it when you were in your wife's compartment," he explained guilelessly.

"I never was there. I have already told the police that a dozen times."

"A thousand pardons," said Poirot, with his most apologetic air. "It was Mademoiselle here who mentioned having seen you going in."

He stopped with an air of embarrassment.

Katherine looked at Derek. His face had gone rather white, but perhaps that was her fancy. His laugh, when it came, was natural enough.

"You made a mistake, Miss Grey," he said easily. "From what the police have told me, I gather that my own compartment was only a door or two away from that of my wife's—though I never suspected the fact at the time. You must have seen me going into my own compartment." He got up quickly as he saw Van Aldin and Knighton approaching.

"I'm going to leave you now," he announced. "I can't stand my father-in-law at any price."

Van Aldin greeted Katherine very courteously, but was clearly in a bad humor.

"You seem fond of watching tennis, Monsieur Poirot," he growled.

"It is a pleasure to me, yes," cried Poirot placidly.

"It is as well you are in France," said Van Aldin. "We are made of sterner stuff in the States. Business comes before pleasure there."

Poirot did not take offense; indeed, he smiled gently and confidingly at the irate millionaire.

"Do not enrage yourself, I beg of you. Everyone has his own methods. Me, I have always found it a delightful and pleasing idea to combine business and pleasure together."

He glanced at the other two. They were deep in conversation, absorbed in each other. Poirot nodded his head in satisfaction, and then leaned towards the millionaire, lowering his voice as he did so.

"It is not only for pleasure that I am here, Monsieur Van Aldin. Observe just opposite us that tall old man—the one with the yellow face and the venerable beard."

"Well, what of him?"

"That," Poirot said, "is Monsieur Papopolous."

"A Greek, eh?"

"As you say—a Greek. He is a dealer in antiques of world-wide reputation. He has a small shop in Paris, and he is suspected by the police of being something more."

"What?"

"A receiver of stolen goods, especially jewels. There is nothing as to the re-cutting and re-setting of gems that he does not know. He deals with the highest in Europe and with the lowest of the riff-raff of the underworld."

Van Aldin was looking at Poirot with suddenly awakened attention.

"Well?" he demanded, a new note in his voice.

"I ask myself," said Poirot, "I, Hercule Poirot"—he thumped himself dramatically on the chest—"ask myself *why is Monsieur Papopolous suddenly come to Nice?*"

Van Aldin was impressed. For a moment he had doubted Poirot and suspected the little man of being past his job, a *poseur* only. Now, in a moment, he switched back to his original opinion. He looked straight at the little detective.

"I must apologize to you, Monsieur Poirot."

Poirot waved the apology aside with an extravagant gesture.

"Bah!" he cried. "All that is of no importance. Now listen, Monsieur Van Aldin; I have news for you."

The millionaire looked sharply at him, all his interest aroused.

Poirot nodded.

"It is as I say. You will be interested. As you know, Monsieur Van Aldin, the Comte de la Roche has been under surveillance ever since his interview with the Juge d'Instruction. The day after that, during his absence, the Villa Marina was searched by the police."

"Well," said Van Aldin, "did they find anything? I bet they didn't."

Poirot made him a little bow.

"Your acumen is not at fault, Monsieur Van Aldin. They found nothing of an incriminating nature. It was not to be expected that they would. The Comte de la Roche, as your expressive idiom has it, was not born on the preceding day. He is an astute gentleman with great experience."

"Well, go on," growled Van Aldin.

"It may be, of course, that the Comte had nothing of a compromising nature to conceal. But we must not neglect the possibility. If, then, he has something to conceal, where is it? Not in his house—the police searched thoroughly. Not on his person, for he knows that he is liable to arrest at any minute. There remains—his car. As I say, he was under surveillance. He was followed on that day to Monte Carlo. From there he went by road to Mentone, driving himself. His car is a very powerful one, it outdistanced his pursuers, and for about a quarter of an hour they completely lost sight of him."

"And during that time you think he concealed something by the roadside?" asked Van Aldin, keenly interested.

"By the roadside, no. *Ça n'est pas pratique.* But listen now—me, I have made a little suggestion to Monsieur Carrège. He is graciously pleased to approve of it. In each Bureau de Poste in the neighborhood it has been seen to that there is someone who knows the Comte de la Roche by sight. Because, you see, messieurs, the best way of hiding a thing is by sending it away by the post."

"Well?" demanded Van Aldin; his face was keenly alight with interest and expectation.

"Well—*voilà!*" With a dramatic flourish Poirot drew out from his pocket a loosely wrapped brown paper package from which the string had been removed.

"During that quarter of an hour's interval, our good gentleman mailed this."

"The address?" asked the other sharply.

Poirot nodded his head.

"Might have told us something, but unfortunately it does not. The package was addressed to one of these little newspaper shops in Paris where letters and parcels are kept until called for on payment of a small commission."

"Yes, but what is inside?" demanded Van Aldin impatiently.

Poirot unwrapped the brown paper and disclosed a square cardboard box. He looked round him.

"It is a good moment," he said quietly. "All eyes are on the tennis. Look, monsieur!"

He lifted the lid of the box for the fraction of a second. An exclamation of utter astonishment came from the millionaire. His face turned as white as chalk.

"My God!" he breathed. "The rubies."

He sat for a minute as though dazed. Poirot restored the box to his pocket and beamed placidly. Then suddenly the millionaire seemed to come out of his trance; he leaned across to Poirot and wrung his hand so heartily that the little man winced with pain.

"This is great," said Van Aldin. "Great! You are the goods, Monsieur Poirot. Once and for all, you are the goods."

"It is nothing," said Poirot modestly. "Order, method, being prepared for eventualities beforehand—that is all there is to it."

"And now, I suppose, the Comte de la Roche has been arrested?" continued Van Aldin eagerly.

"No," said Poirot.

A look of utter astonishment came over Van Aldin's face.

"But why? What more do you want?"

"The Comte's alibi is still unshaken."

"But that is nonsense."

"Yes," said Poirot; "I rather think it is nonsense, but unfortunately we have to prove it so."

"In the meantime he will slip through your fingers."

Poirot shook his head very energetically.

"No," he said, "he will not do that. The one thing the Comte cannot afford to sacrifice is his social position. At all costs he must stop and brazen it out."

Van Aldin was still dissatisfied.

"But I don't see—"

Poirot raised a hand. "Grant me a little moment, monsieur. Me, I have a little idea. Many people have mocked themselves at the little ideas of Hercule Poirot—and they have been wrong."

"Well," said Van Aldin, "go ahead. What is this little idea?"

Poirot paused for a moment and then he said:

"I will call upon you at your hotel at eleven o'clock tomorrow morning. Until then, say nothing to anyone."

22

Monsieur Papopolous Breakfasts

MONSIEUR PAPOPOLOUS was at breakfast. Opposite him sat his daughter, Zia.

There was a knock at the sitting-room door, and a chasseur entered with a card which he brought to Mr. Papopolous. The latter scrutinized it, raised his eyebrows, and passed it over to his daughter.

"Ah!" said Monsieur Papopolous, scratching his left ear thoughtfully. "Hercule Poirot. I wonder now."

Father and daughter looked at each other.

"I saw him yesterday at the tennis," said Monsieur Papopolous. "Zia, I hardly like this."

"He was very useful to you once," his daughter reminded him.

"That is true," acknowledged Monsieur Papopolous; "also he has retired from active work, so I hear."

These interchanges between father and daughter had passed in their own language. Now Monsieur Papopolous turned to the chasseur and said in French:

"Faites monter ce monsieur."

A few minutes later Hercule Poirot, exquisitely attired and swinging a cane with a jaunty air, entered the room.

"My dear Monsieur Papopolous."

"My dear Monsieur Poirot."

"And Mademoiselle Zia." Poirot swept her a low bow.

"You will excuse us going on with our breakfast," said Monsieur Papopolous, pouring himself out another cup of coffee. "Your call is —ahem!—a little early."

"It is scandalous," said Poirot, "but see you, I am pressed."

"Ah!" murmured Monsieur Papopolous. "You are on an affair then?"

"A very serious affair," said Poirot: "the death of Madame Kettering."

"Let me see," Monsieur Papopolous looked innocently up at the ceiling, "that was the lady who died on the Blue Train, was it not? I saw a mention of it in the papers, but there was no suggestion of foul play."

"In the interests of justice," said Poirot, "it was thought best to suppress that fact."

There was a pause.

"And in what way can I assist you, Monsieur Poirot?" asked the dealer politely.

"*Voilà*," said Poirot, "I shall come to the point." He took from his pocket the same box that he had displayed at Cannes, and, opening it, he took out the rubies and pushed them across the table to Papopolous.

Although Poirot was watching him narrowly, not a muscle of the old man's face moved. He took up the jewels and examined them with a kind of detached interest, then he looked across at the detective inquiringly:

"Superb, are they not?" asked Poirot.

"Quite excellent," said Monsieur Papopolous.

"How much should you say they are worth?"

The Greek's face quivered a little.

"Is it really necessary to tell you, Monsieur Poirot?" he asked.

"You are shrewd, Monsieur Papopolous. No, it is not. They are not, for instance, worth five hundred thousand dollars."

Papopolous laughed, and Poirot joined with him.

"As an imitation," said Papopolous, handing them back to Poirot, "they are, as I said, quite excellent. Would it be indiscreet to ask, Monsieur Poirot, where you came across them?"

"Not at all," said Poirot; "I have no objection to telling an old friend like yourself. They were in the possession of the Comte de la Roche."

Monsieur Papopolous' eyebrows lifted themselves eloquently.

"In-deed," he murmured.

Poirot leaned forward and assumed his most innocent and beguiling air.

"Monsieur Papopolous," he said, "I am going to lay my cards upon the table. The original of these jewels was stolen from Madame Kettering on the Blue Train. Now I will say to you first this: *I am not concerned with the recovery of these jewels. That is the affair of the police.* I am working not for the police but for Monsieur Van Aldin. I want to lay hands on the man who killed Madame Kettering. I am interested in the jewels only in so far as they may lead me to the man. You understand?"

The last two words were uttered with great significance. Monsieur Papopolous, his face quite unmoved, said quietly:

"Go on."

"It seems to me probable, monsieur, that the jewels will change hands in Nice—may already have done so."

"Ah!" said Monsieur Papopolous.

He sipped his coffee reflectively, and looked a shade more noble and patriarchal than usual.

"I say to myself," continued Poirot, with animation, "what good fortune! My old friend, Monsieur Papopolous, is in Nice. He will aid me."

"And how do you think I can aid you?" inquired Monsieur Papopolous coldly.

"I said to myself, without doubt Monsieur Papopolous is in Nice on business."

"Not at all," said Monsieur Papopolous, "I am here for my health —by the doctor's orders."

He coughed hollowly.

"I am desolated to hear it," replied Poirot, with somewhat insincere sympathy. "But to continue. When a Russian grand duke, an Austrian archduchess, or an Italian prince wish to dispose of their family jewels—to whom do they go? To Monsieur Papopolous, is it not? He who is famous all over the world for the discretion with which he arranges these things."

The other bowed.

"You flatter me."

"It is a great thing, discretion," mused Poirot, and was rewarded by the fleeting smile which passed across the Greek's face. "I, too, can be discreet."

The eyes of the two men met.

Then Poirot went on speaking very slowly, and obviously picking his words with care.

"I say to myself, this: if these jewels have changed hands in Nice, Monsieur Papopolous would have heard of it. He has knowledge of all that passes in the jewel world."

"Ah!" said Monsieur Papopolous, and helped himself to a *croissant*.

"The police, you understand," said Monsieur Poirot, "do not enter into the matter. It is a personal affair."

"One hears rumors," admitted Monsieur Papopolous cautiously.

"Such as?" prompted Poirot.

"Is there any reason why I should pass them on?"

"Yes," said Poirot, "I think there is. You may remember, Monsieur Papopolous, that seventeen years ago there was a certain article in your hands, left there as security by a very—er—prominent person. It was in your keeping and it unaccountably disappeared. You were, if I may use the English expression, in the soup."

His eyes came gently round to the girl. She had pushed her cup and plate aside, and with both elbows on the table and her chin resting on her hands was listening eagerly. Still keeping an eye on her, he went on:

"I am in Paris at the time. You send for me. You place yourself in my hands. If I restore to you that—article, you say I shall earn your undying gratitude. *Eh bien!* I did restore it to you."

A long sigh came from Monsieur Papopolous.

"It was the most unpleasant moment of my career," he murmured.

"Seventeen years is a long time," said Poirot thoughtfully, "but I believe that I am right in saying, monsieur, that your race does not forget."

There was a silence, and then the old man drew himself up proudly.

"You are right, Monsieur Poirot," he said quietly. "As you say, our race does not forget."

"You will aid me then?"

"As regards the jewels, monsieur, I can do nothing."

The old man, as Poirot had done just now, picked his words carefully.

"I know nothing. I have heard nothing. But I can perhaps do you a good turn—that is, if you are interested in racing."

"Under certain circumstances I might be," said Poirot, eyeing him steadily.

"There is a horse running at Longchamps that would, I think, repay attention. I cannot say for certain, you understand; this news passed through so many hands."

He stopped, fixing Poirot with his eye, as though to make sure that the latter was comprehending him.

"Perfectly, perfectly," said Poirot, nodding.

"The name of the horse," said Monsieur Papopolous, leaning back and joining the tips of his fingers together, "is the Marquis. I think, but I am not sure, that it is an English horse, eh, Zia?"

"I think so too," said the girl.

Poirot got up briskly.

"I thank you, monsieur," he said. "It is a great thing to have what the English call a tip from the stable. Au revoir, monsieur, and many thanks."

He turned to the girl.

"Au revoir, Mademoiselle Zia. It seems to me but yesterday that I saw you in Paris. One would say that two years had passed at most."

"There is a difference between sixteen and thirty-three," said Zia ruefully.

"Not in your case," declared Poirot gallantly. "You and your father will perhaps dine with me one night."

"We shall be delighted," replied Zia.

"Then we will arrange it," declared Poirot, "and now—*je me sauve*."

Poirot walked along the street humming a little tune to himself. He twirled his stick with a jaunty air, once or twice he smiled to himself quietly. He turned into the first Bureau de Poste he came to and sent off a telegram. He took some time in wording it, but it was in code and he had to call upon his memory. It purported to deal with a missing scarfpin, and was addressed to Inspector Japp, Scotland Yard.

Decoded, it was short and to the point. *"Wire me everything known about man whose soubriquet is the Marquis."*

23

A New Theory

It was exactly eleven o'clock when Poirot presented himself at Van Aldin's hotel. He found the millionaire alone.

"You are punctual, Monsieur Poirot," he said, with a smile, as he rose to greet the detective.

"I am always punctual," said Poirot. "The exactitude—always do I observe it. Without order and method—"

He broke off. "Ah, but it is possible that I have said these things to you before. Let us come at once to the object of my visit."

"Your little idea?"

"Yes, my little idea." Poirot smiled.

"First of all, monsieur, I should like to interview once more the maid, Ada Mason. She is here?"

"Yes, she's here."

"Ah!"

Van Aldin looked at him curiously. He rang the bell, and a messenger was dispatched to find Mason.

Poirot greeted her with his usual politeness.

"Good afternoon, mademoiselle," he said cheerfully. "Be seated, will you not, if Monsieur permits."

"Yes, yes, sit down, my girl," said Van Aldin.

"Thank you, sir," said Mason primly, and she sat down on the extreme edge of a chair. She looked bonier and more acid than ever.

"I have come to ask you yet more questions," said Poirot. "We must get to the bottom of this affair. Always I return to the question of the man in the train. You have been shown the Comte de la Roche. You say that it is possible he was the man, but you are not sure."

"As I told you, sir, I never saw the gentleman's face. That is what makes it so difficult."

Poirot beamed and nodded.

"Precisely, exactly. I comprehend well the difficulty. Now, mademoiselle, you have been in the service of Madame Kettering two months, you say. During that time, how often did you see your master?"

Mason reflected a minute or two, and then said:

"Only twice, sir."

"And was that near to, or far away?"

"Well once, sir, he came to Curzon Street. I was upstairs, and I looked over the banisters and saw him in the hall below. I was a bit curious-like, you understand, knowing the way things—er—were." Mason finished up with her discreet cough.

"And the other time?"

"I was in the park, sir, with Annie—one of the housemaids, sir, and she pointed out the master to me walking with a foreign lady."

Again Poirot nodded.

"Now listen, Mason, this man whom you saw in the carriage talking to your mistress at the Gare de Lyon, how do you know it was not your master?"

"The master, sir? Oh, I don't think it could have been."

"But you are not sure," Poirot persisted.

"Well—I never thought of it, sir."

Mason was clearly upset at the idea.

"You have heard that your master was also on the train. What more natural than that it should be he who came along the corridor."

"But the gentleman who was talking to the mistress must have come from outside, sir. He was dressed for the street. In an overcoat and soft hat."

"Just so, mademoiselle, but reflect a minute. The train has just arrived at the Gare de Lyon. Many of the passengers promenade themselves upon the quay. Your mistress was about to do so, and for that purpose had doubtless put on her fur coat, eh?"

"Yes, sir," agreed Mason.

"Your master, then, does the same. The train is heated, but outside in the station it is cold. He puts on his overcoat and his hat and he walks along beside the train, and looking up at the lighted windows he suddenly sees Madame Kettering. Until then he has had no idea that she was on the train. Naturally, he mounts the carriage and goes to her compartment. She gives an exclamation of surprise at seeing him and quickly shuts the door between the two compartments since it is possible that their conversation may be of a private nature."

He leaned back in his chair and watched the suggestion slowly take effect. No one knew better than Hercule Poirot that the type to which Mason belongs cannot be hurried. He must give her time to get rid of her own preconceived ideas. At the end of three minutes she spoke:

"Well, of course, sir, it might be so. I never thought of it that way. The master is tall and dark, and just about that build. It was seeing the hat and coat that made me say it was a gentleman from outside. Yes, it might have been the master. I would not like to say either way, I am sure."

"Thank you very much, mademoiselle. I shall not require you any further. Ah, just one thing more." He took from his pocket the cigarette case he had already shown to Katherine. "Is that your mistress's case?" he said to Mason.

"No, sir, it is not the mistress's—at least—"

She looked suddenly startled. An idea was clearly working its way to the forefront of her mind.

"Yes," said Poirot encouragingly.

"I think, sir—I can't be sure, but I think—it is a case that the mistress bought to give to the master."

"Ah," said Poirot in a noncommittal manner.

"But whether she ever did give it to him or not, I can't say, of course."

"Precisely," said Poirot, "precisely. That is all, I think, mademoiselle. I wish you good afternoon."

Ada Mason retired discreetly, closing the door noiselessly behind her.

Poirot looked across at Van Aldin, a faint smile upon his face. The millionaire looked thunderstruck.

"You think—you think it was Derek?" he queried. "But—everything points the other way. Why, the Count has actually been caught red-handed with the jewels on him."

"No."

"But you told me—"

"What did I tell you?"

"That story about the jewels. You showed them to me."

"No."

Van Aldin stared at him.

"You mean to say you didn't show them to me?"

"No."

"Yesterday—at the tennis?"

"No."

"Are you crazy, Monsieur Poirot, or am I?"

"Neither of us is crazy," said the detective. "You ask me a question; I answer it. You say have I not shown you the jewels yesterday? I reply—no. What I showed you, Monsieur Van Aldin, was a first-class imitation hardly to be distinguished except by an expert from the real ones."

24

Poirot Gives Advice

It took the millionaire some few minutes to take the thing in. He stared at Poirot as though dumbfounded. The little Belgian nodded at him gently.

"Yes," he said, "it alters the position, does it not?"

"Imitation!"

He leaned forward.

"All along, Monsieur Poirot, you have had this idea? All along this is what you have been driving at? You never believed that the Comte de la Roche was the murderer?"

"I have had doubts," said Poirot quietly. "I said as much to you. Robbery with violence and murder"—he shook his head energetically—"no, it is difficult to picture. It does not harmonize with the personality of the Comte de la Roche."

"But you believe that he meant to steal the rubies?"

"Certainly. There is no doubt as to that. See, I will recount to you the affair as I see it. The Comte knew of the rubies and he laid his plans accordingly. He made up a romantic story of a book he was writing, so as to induce your daughter to bring them with her. He provided himself with an exact duplicate. It is clear, is it not, that substitution is what he was after. Madame, your daughter, was not an expert on jewels. It would probably be a long time before she discovered what had occurred. When she did so—well—I do not think she would prosecute the Comte. Too much would come out. He would have in his possession various letters of hers. Oh yes, a very safe scheme from the Comte's point of view—one that he has probably carried out before."

"It seems clear enough, yes," said Van Aldin musingly.

"It accords with the personality of the Comte de la Roche," said Poirot.

"Yes, but now—" Van Aldin looked searchingly at the other. "What actually happened? Tell me that, Monsieur Poirot."

Poirot shrugged his shoulders.

"It is quite simple," he said; "someone stepped in ahead of the Comte."

There was a long pause.

Van Aldin seemed to be turning things over in his mind. When he spoke, it was without beating about the bush.

"How long have you suspected my son-in-law, Monsieur Poirot?"

"From the very first. He had the motive and the opportunity. Everyone took for granted that the man in Madame's compartment in Paris was the Comte de la Roche. I thought so, too. Then you happened to mention that you had once mistaken the Comte for your son-in-law. That told me that they were of the same height and build, and alike in coloring. It put some curious ideas in my head. The maid had only been with your daughter a short time. It was unlikely that she would know Mr. Kettering well by sight, since he had not been living in Curzon Street; also the man was careful to keep his face turned away."

"You believe he—murdered her," said Van Aldin hoarsely.

Poirot raised a hand quickly.

"No, no, I did not say that—but it is a possibility—a very strong possibility. He was in a tight corner, a very tight corner, threatened with ruin. This was the one way out."

"But why take the jewels?"

"To make the crime appear an ordinary one committed by train robbers. Otherwise suspicion might have fallen on him straight-away."

"If that is so, what has he done with the rubies?"

"That remains to be seen. There are several possibilities. There is a man in Nice who may be able to help, the man I pointed out at the tennis."

He rose to his feet and Van Aldin rose also and laid his hand on the little man's shoulder. His voice when he spoke was harsh with emotion.

"Find Ruth's murderer for me," he said, "that is all I ask."

Poirot drew himself up.

"Leave it in the hands of Hercule Poirot," he said superbly; "have no fears. I will discover the truth."

He brushed a speck of fluff from his hat, smiled reassuringly at the millionaire, and left the room. Nevertheless, as he went down the stairs some of the confidence faded from his face.

"It is all very well," he murmured to himself, "but there are difficulties. Yes, there are great difficulties." As he was passing out of the hotel, he came to a sudden halt. A car had drawn up in front of the door. In it was Katherine Grey, and Derek Kettering was standing beside it talking to her earnestly. A minute or two later the car drove off and Derek remained standing on the pavement looking after it. The expression on his face was an odd one. He gave a sudden impatient gesture of the shoulders, sighed deeply, and turned to find Hercule Poirot standing at his elbow. In spite of himself he started. The two men looked at each other. Poirot steadily and unwaveringly and Derek with a kind of lighthearted defiance. There was a sneer behind the easy mockery of his tone when he spoke, raising his eyebrows slightly as he did so.

"Rather a dear, isn't she?" he asked easily.

His manner was perfectly natural.

"Yes," said Poirot thoughtfully, "that describes Mademoiselle Katherine very well. It is very English, that phrase there, and Mademoiselle Katherine, she also is very English."

Derek remained perfectly still without answering.

"And yet she is *sympathique*, is it not so?"

"Yes," said Derek; "there are not many like her."

He spoke softly, almost as though to himself. Poirot nodded significantly. Then he leaned towards the other and spoke in a different tone, a quiet, grave tone that was new to Derek Kettering.

"You will pardon an old man, monsieur, if he says to you something that you may consider impertinent. There is one of your English proverbs that I would quote to you. It says that 'it is well to be off with the old love, before being on with the new.'"

Kettering turned on him angrily.

"What the devil do you mean?"

"You enrage yourself at me," said Poirot placidly. "I expected as much. As to what I mean—I mean, monsieur, that there is a second car with a lady in it. If you turn your head you will see her."

Derek spun round. His face darkened with anger.

"Mirelle, damn her!" he muttered. "I will soon—"

Poirot arrested the movement he was about to make.

"Is it wise what you are about to do there?" he asked warningly. His eyes shone softly with a green light in them. But Derek was past noticing the warning signs. In his anger he was completely off his guard.

"I have broken with her utterly, and she knows it," cried Derek angrily.

"You have broken with her, yes, but has *she* broken with you?"

Derek gave a sudden harsh laugh.

"She won't break with two million pounds if she can help it," he murmured brutally; "trust Mirelle for that."

Poirot raised his eyebrows.

"You have the outlook cynical," he murmured.

"Have I?" There was no mirth in his sudden wide smile. "I have lived in the world long enough, Monsieur Poirot, to know that all women are pretty much alike." His face softened suddenly. "All save one."

He met Poirot's gaze defiantly. A look of alertness crept into his eyes, then faded again. "That one," he said, and jerked his head in the direction of Cap Martin.

"Ah!" said Poirot.

This quiescence was well calculated to provoke the impetuous temperament of the other.

"I know what you are going to say," said Derek rapidly, "the kind of life I have led, the fact that I am not worthy of her. You will say that I have no right to think even of such a thing. You will say that it is not a case of giving a dog a bad name—I know that it is not decent to be speaking like this with my wife dead only a few days, and murdered at that."

He paused for breath, and Poirot took advantage of the pause to remark in his plaintive tone:

"But, indeed, I have not said anything at all."

"But you will."

"Eh?" said Poirot.

"You will say that I have no earthly chance of marrying Katherine."

"No," said Poirot, "I would not say that. Your reputation is bad, yes, but with women—never does that deter them. If you were a man of excellent character, of strict morality, who had done nothing that he should not do, and—possibly everything that he should do—*eh bien!* then I should have grave doubts of your success. Moral worth, you understand, it is not romantic. It is appreciated, however, by widows."

Derek Kettering stared at him, then he swung round on his heel and went up to the waiting car.

Poirot looked after him with some interest. He saw the lovely vision lean out of the car and speak.

Derek Kettering did not stop. He lifted his hat and passed straight on.

"Ça y est," said Monsieur Hercule Poirot, "it is time, I think, that I return *chez moi*."

He found the imperturbable George pressing trousers.

"A pleasant day, Georges, somewhat fatiguing, but not without interest," he said.

George received these remarks in his usual wooden fashion.

"Indeed, sir."

"The personality of a criminal, Georges, is an interesting matter. Many murderers are men of great personal charm."

"I always heard, sir, that Dr. Crippen was a pleasant-spoken gentleman. And yet he cut up his wife like so much mincemeat."

"Your instances are always apt, Georges."

The valet did not reply, and at that moment the telephone rang. Poirot took up the receiver.

"'Allo—'allo—yes, yes, it is Hercule Poirot who speaks."

"This is Knighton. Will you hold the line a minute, Monsieur Poirot? Mr. Van Aldin would like to speak to you."

There was a moment's pause, then the millionaire's voice came through.

"Is that you, Monsieur Poirot? I just wanted to tell you that Mason came to me now of her own accord. She has been thinking it over, and she says that she is almost certain that the man at Paris was Derek Kettering. There was something familiar about him at the time, she says, but at the minute she could not place it. She seems pretty certain now."

"Ah," said Poirot, "thank you, Monsieur Van Aldin. That advances us."

He replaced the receiver and stood for a minute or two with a very curious smile on his face. George had to speak to him twice before obtaining an answer.

"Eh?" said Poirot. "What is that that you say to me?"

"Are you lunching here, sir, or are you going out?"

"Neither," said Poirot, "I shall go to bed and take a *tisane*. The expected has happened, and when the expected happens, it always causes me emotion."

25

Defiance

As Derek Kettering passed the car, Mirelle leaned out.

"Dereek—I must speak to you for a moment—"

But, lifting his hat, Derek passed straight on without stopping.

When he got back to his hotel, the concierge detached himself from his wooden pen and accosted him.

"A gentleman is waiting to see you, monsieur."

"Who is it?" asked Derek.

"He did not give me his name, monsieur, but he said his business with you was important, and that he would wait."

"Where is he?"

"In the little salon, monsieur. He preferred it to the lounge he said, as being more private."

Derek nodded, and turned his steps in that direction.

The small salon was empty except for the visitor, who rose and bowed with easy foreign grace as Derek entered. As it chanced, Derek had only seen the Comte de la Roche once, but found no difficulty in recognizing that aristocratic nobleman, and he frowned angrily. Of all the consummate impertinence!

"The Comte de la Roche, is it not?" he said. "I am afraid you have wasted your time in coming here."

"I hope not," said the Comte agreeably. His white teeth glittered.

The Comte's charm of manner was usually wasted on his own sex. All men, without exception, disliked him heartily. Derek Kettering was already conscious of a distinct longing to kick the Count bodily out of the room. It was only the realization that scandal would be unfortunate just at present that restrained him. He marveled anew that Ruth could have cared, as she certainly had, for this fellow. A bounder, and worse than a bounder. He looked with distaste at the Count's exquisitely manicured hands.

"I called," said the Comte, "on a little matter of business. It would be advisable, I think, for you to listen to me."

Again Derek felt strongly tempted to kick him out, but again he refrained. The hint of a threat was not lost upon him, but he interpreted it in his own way. There were various reasons why it would be better to hear what the Comte had to say.

He sat down and drummed impatiently with his fingers on the table.

"Well," he said sharply, "what is it?"

It was not the Comte's way to come out into the open at once.

"Allow me, monsieur, to offer you my condolences on your recent bereavement."

"If I have any impertinence from you," said Derek quietly, "you go out by that window."

He nodded his head towards the window beside the Comte, and the latter moved uneasily.

"I will send my friends to you, monsieur, if that is what you desire," he said haughtily.

Derek laughed.

"A duel, eh? My dear Count, I don't take you seriously enough for that. But I should take a good deal of pleasure in kicking you down the Promenade des Anglais."

The Comte was not at all anxious to take offense. He merely raised his eyebrows and murmured:

"The English are barbarians."

"Well," said Derek, "what is it you have to say to me?"

"I will be frank," said the Comte, "I will come immediately to the point. That will suit us both, will it not?"

Again he smiled in his agreeable fashion.

"Go on," said Derek curtly.

The Comte looked at the ceiling, joined the tips of his fingers together, and murmured softly:

"You have come into a lot of money, monsieur."

"What the devil has that got to do with you?"

The Comte drew himself up.

"Monsieur, my name is tarnished! I am suspected—accused—of foul crime."

"The accusation does not come from me," said Derek coldly; "as an interested party I have not expressed any opinion."

"I am innocent," said the Comte, "I swear before heaven"—he raised his hand to heaven—"that I am innocent."

"Monsieur Carrège is, I believe, the Juge d'Instruction in charge of the case," hinted Derek politely.

The Comte took no notice.

"Not only am I unjustly suspected of a crime that I did not commit, but I am also in serious need of money."

He coughed softly and suggestively.

Derek rose to his feet.

"I was waiting for that," he said softly; "you blackmailing brute! I will not give you a penny. My wife is dead, and no scandal that you can make can touch her now. She wrote you foolish letters, I dare say. If I were to buy them from you for a round sum at this minute, I am pretty certain that you would manage to keep one or two back; and I will tell you this, Monsieur de la Roche, blackmailing is an ugly word both in England and in France. That is my answer to you. Good afternoon."

"One moment"—the Comte stretched out a hand as Derek was turning to leave the room. "You are mistaken, monsieur. You are completely mistaken. I am, I hope, a 'gentleman.'" Derek laughed. "Any letters that a lady might write to me I should hold sacred." He flung back his head with a beautiful air of nobility. "The proposition that I was putting before you was of quite a different nature. I am, as I said, extremely short of money, and my conscience might impel me to go to the police with certain information."

Derek came slowly back into the room.

"What do you mean?"

The Comte's agreeable smile flashed forth once more.

"Surely it is not necessary to go into details," he purred. "Seek whom the crime benefits, they say, don't they? As I said just now, you have come into a lot of money lately."

Derek laughed.

"If that is all—" he said contemptuously.

But the Comte was shaking his head.

"But it is not all, my dear sir. I should not come to you unless I had much more precise and detailed information than that. It is not agreeable, monsieur, to be arrested and tried for murder."

Derek came close up to him. His face expressed such furious anger that involuntarily the Comte drew back a pace or two.

"Are you threatening *me?*" the young man demanded angrily.

"You shall hear nothing more of the matter," the Comte assured him.

"Of all the colossal bluffs that I have ever struck—"

The Comte raised a white hand.

"You are wrong. It is not a bluff. To convince you I will tell you this. My information was obtained from a certain lady. It is she who holds the irrefutable proof that you committed the murder."

"She? Who?"

"Mademoiselle Mirelle."

Derek drew back as though struck.

"Mirelle," he muttered.

The Comte was quick to press what he took to be his advantage.

"A bagatelle of one hundred thousand francs," he said. "I ask no more."

"Eh?" said Derek absently.

"I was saying, monsieur, that a bagatelle of one hundred thousand francs would satisfy my—conscience."

Derek seemed to re-collect himself. He looked earnestly at the Comte.

"You would like my answer now?"

"If you please, monsieur."

"Then here it is. You can go to the devil. See?"

Leaving the Comte too astonished to speak, Derek turned on his heel and swung out of the room.

Once out of the hotel he hailed a taxi and drove to Mirelle's hotel. On inquiring, he learned that the dancer had just come in. Derek gave the concierge his card.

"Take this up to Mademoiselle and ask if she will see me."

A very brief interval elapsed, and then Derek was bidden to follow a chasseur.

A wave of exotic perfume assailed Derek's nostrils as he stepped over the threshold of the dancer's apartments. The room was filled with carnations, orchids, and mimosa. Mirelle was standing by the window in a peignoir of foamy lace.

She came towards him, her hands outstretched.

"Dereek—you have come to me. I knew you would."

He put aside the clinging arms and looked down on her sternly.

"Why did you send the Comte de la Roche to me?"

She looked at him in astonishment, which he took to be genuine.

"I? Send the Comte de la Roche to you? But for what?"

"Apparently—for blackmail," said Derek grimly.

Again she stared. Then suddenly she smiled and nodded her head.

"Of course. It was to be expected. It is what he would do, *ce type là*. I might have known it. No, indeed, Dereek, I did not send him."

He looked at her piercingly, as though seeking to read her mind.

"I will tell you," said Mirelle. "I am ashamed, but I will tell you. The other day, you comprehend, I was mad with rage, quite mad—" she made an eloquent gesture. "My temperament, it is not a patient one. I want to be revenged on you, and so I go to the Comte de la Roche, and I tell him to go to the police and say so and so, and so and so. But have no fear, Dereek. Not completely did I lose my head; the proof rests with me alone. The police can do nothing without my word, you understand? And now—now?"

She nestled up close to him, looking up at him with melting eyes.

He thrust her roughly away from him. She stood there, her breast heaving, her eyes narrowing to a catlike slit.

"Be careful, Dereek, be very careful. You have come back to me, have you not?"

"I shall never come back to you," said Derek steadily.

"Ah!"

More than ever the dancer looked like a cat. Her eyelids flickered.

"So there is another woman? The one with whom you lunched that day. Eh! Am I right?"

"I intend to ask that lady to marry me. You might as well know."

"That prim Englishwoman! Do you think that I will support that for one moment? Ah, no." Her beautiful lithe body quivered. "Listen, Dereek, do you remember that conversation we had in London? You said the only thing that could save you was the death of your wife. You regretted that she was so healthy. Then the idea of an accident came to your brain. And more than an accident."

"I suppose," said Derek contemptuously, "that it was this conversation that you repeated to the Comte de la Roche."

Mirelle laughed.

"Am I a fool? Could the police do anything with a vague story like that? See—I will give you a last chance. You shall give up this

Englishwoman. You shall return to me. And then, *chéri*, never, never will I breathe—"

"Breathe what?"

She laughed softly. "You thought no one saw you—"

"What do you mean?"

"As I say, you thought no one saw you—but *I* saw you, Dereek, *mon ami; I saw you coming out of the compartment of Madame your wife just before the train got into Lyons that night. And* I know more than that. I know that when you came out of her compartment she was dead."

He stared at her. Then, like a man in a dream he turned very slowly and went out of the room, swaying slightly as he walked.

26

A Warning

"And so it is," said Poirot, "that we are the good friends and have no secrets from each other."

Katherine turned her head to look at him. There was something in his voice, some undercurrent of seriousness, which she had not heard before.

They were sitting in the gardens of Monte Carlo. Katherine had come over with her friends, and they had run into Knighton and Poirot almost immediately on arrival. Lady Tamplin had seized upon Knighton and had overwhelmed him with reminiscences, most of which Katherine had a faint suspicion were invented. They had moved away together, Lady Tamplin with her hand on the young man's arm. Knighton had thrown a couple of glances back over his shoulder, and Poirot's eyes twinkled a little as he saw them.

"Of course we are friends," said Katherine.

"From the beginning we have been sympathetic to each other," mused Poirot.

"When you told me that a *roman policier* occurs in real life."

"And I was right, was I not?" he challenged her, with an emphatic forefinger. "Here we are, plunged in the middle of one. That is natural for me—it is my *métier*—but for you it is different. Yes," he added in a reflective tone, "for you it is different."

She looked sharply at him. It was as though he were warning her, pointing out to her some menace that she had not seen.

"Why do you say that I am in the middle of it? It is true that I had that conversation with Mrs. Kettering just before she died, but now—now all that is over. I am not connected with the case any more."

"Ah, mademoiselle, mademoiselle, can we ever say, 'I have finished with this or that'?"

Katherine turned defiantly round to face him.

"What is it?" she asked. "You are trying to tell me something—to convey it to me rather. But I am not clever at taking hints. I would much rather that you said anything you have to say straight out."

Poirot looked at her sadly. *"Ah, mais c'est Anglais ça,"* he murmured, "everything in black and white, everything clear-cut and well-defined. But life, it is not like that, mademoiselle. There are the things that are not yet, but which cast their shadow before."

He dabbed his brow with a very large silk pocket handkerchief and murmured:

"Ah, but it is that I become poetical. Let us, as you say, speak only of facts. And, speaking of facts, tell me what you think of Major Knighton."

"I like him very much indeed," said Katherine warmly; "he is quite delightful."

Poirot sighed.

"What is the matter?" asked Katherine.

"You reply so heartily," said Poirot. "If you had said in an indifferent voice, 'Oh, quite nice,' *eh bien,* do you know I should have been better pleased."

Katherine did not answer. She felt slightly uncomfortable. Poirot went on dreamily:

"And yet, who knows? With *les femmes,* they have so many ways of concealing what they feel—and heartiness is perhaps as good a way as any other."

He sighed.

"I don't see—" began Katherine.

He interrupted her.

"You do not see why I am being so impertinent, mademoiselle? I am an old man, and now and then—not very often—I come across someone whose welfare is dear to me. We are friends, mademoiselle. You have said so yourself. And it is just this—I should like to see you happy."

Katherine stared very straight in front of her. She had a cretonne sunshade with her, and with its point she traced little designs in the gravel at her feet.

"I have asked you a question about Major Knighton, now I will ask you another. Do you like Mr. Derek Kettering?"

"I hardly know him," said Katherine.

"That is not an answer, that."

"I think it is."

He looked at her, struck by something in her tone. Then he nodded his head gravely and slowly.

"Perhaps you are right, mademoiselle. See you, I who speak to you have seen much of the world, and I know that there are two things which are true. A good man may be ruined by his love for a bad woman—but the other way holds good also. A bad man may equally be ruined by his love for a good woman."

Katherine looked up sharply.

"When you say ruined—"

"I mean from his point of view. One must be wholehearted in crime as in everything else."

"You are trying to warn me," said Katherine in a low voice. "Against whom?"

"I cannot look into your heart, mademoiselle; I do not think you would let me if I could. I will just say this. There are men who have a strange fascination for women."

"The Comte de la Roche," said Katherine, with a smile.

"There are others—more dangerous than the Comte de la Roche. They have qualities that appeal—recklessness, daring, audacity. You are fascinated, mademoiselle; I see that, but I think that it is no more than that. I hope so. This man of whom I speak, the emotion he feels is genuine enough, but all the same—"

"Yes?"

He got up and stood looking down at her. Then he spoke in a low, distinct voice:

"You could, perhaps, love a thief, mademoiselle, *but not a murderer.*"

He wheeled sharply away on that and left her sitting there.

He heard the little gasp she gave and paid no attention. He had said what he meant to say. He left her there to digest that last unmistakable phrase.

Derek Kettering, coming out of the casino into the sunshine, saw her sitting alone on the bench and joined her.

"I have been gambling," he said, with a light laugh, "gambling unsuccessfully. I have lost everything—everything, that is, that I have with me."

Katherine looked at him with a troubled face. She was aware at once of something new in his manner, some hidden excitement that betrayed itself in a hundred different infinitesimal signs.

"I should think you were always a gambler. The spirit of gambling appeals to you."

"Every day and in every way a gambler? You are about right. Don't *you* find something stimulating in it? To risk all on one throw—there is nothing like it."

Calm and stolid as she believed herself to be, Katherine felt a faint answering thrill.

"I want to talk to you," went on Derek, "and who knows when I may have another opportunity? There is an idea going about that I murdered my wife—no, please don't interrupt. It is absurd, of course." He paused for a minute or two, then went on, speaking more deliberately. "In dealing with the police and local authorities here I have had to pretend to—well—a certain decency. I prefer not to pretend with you. I meant to marry money. I was on the lookout for money when I first met Ruth Van Aldin. She had the look of a slim Madonna about her, and I—well—I made all sorts of good resolutions—and was bitterly disillusioned. My wife was in love with another man when she married me. She never cared for me in the least. Oh, I am not complaining; the thing was a perfectly respectable bargain. She wanted Leconbury and I wanted money. The trouble arose simply through Ruth's American blood. Without caring a pin for me, she would have liked me to be continually dancing attendance. Time and again she as good as told me that she had bought me and that I belonged to her. The result was that I behaved abominably to her. My father-in-law will tell you that, and he is quite right. At the time of Ruth's death, I was faced with absolute disaster." He laughed suddenly. "One *is* faced with absolute disaster when one is up against a man like Rufus Van Aldin."

"And then?" asked Katherine in a low voice.

"And then," Derek shrugged his shoulders, "Ruth was murdered —very providentially."

He laughed, and the sound of his laugh hurt Katherine. She winced.

"Yes," said Derek, "that wasn't in very good taste. But it is quite true. Now I am going to tell you something more. From the very first moment I saw you I knew you were the only woman in the world for me. I was—afraid of you. I thought you might bring me bad luck."

"Bad luck?" said Katherine sharply.

He stared at her. "Why do you repeat it like that? What have you got in your mind?"

"I was thinking of things that people have said to me."

Derek grinned suddenly. "They will say a lot to you about me, my dear, and most of it will be true. Yes, and worse things too—things that I shall never tell you. I have been a gambler always—and I have taken some long odds. I shan't confess to you now or at any other time. The past is done with. There is one thing I do wish you to believe. I swear to you solemnly that I did not kill my wife."

He said the words earnestly enough, yet there was somehow a theatrical touch about them. He met her troubled gaze and went on:

"I know. I lied the other day. It *was* my wife's compartment I went into."

"Ah," said Katherine.

"It's difficult to explain just why I went in, but I'll try. I did it on an impulse. You see, I was more or less spying on my wife. I kept out of sight on the train. Mirelle had told me that my wife was meeting the Comte de la Roche in Paris. Well, as far as I had seen, that was not so. I felt ashamed, and I thought suddenly that it would be a good thing to have it out with her once and for all, so I pushed open the door and went in."

He paused.

"Yes," said Katherine gently.

"Ruth was lying on the bunk asleep—her face was turned away from me—I could only see the back of her head. I could have waked her up, of course. But suddenly I felt a reaction. What, after all, was there to say that we hadn't both of us said a hundred times before? She looked so peaceful lying there. I left the compartment as quietly as I could."

"Why lie about it to the police?" asked Katherine.

"Because I'm not a complete fool. I've realized from the beginning that, from the point of view of motive, I'm the ideal murderer. If I once admitted that I had been in her compartment just before she was murdered, I'd do for myself once and for all."

"I see."

Did she see? She could not have told herself. She was feeling the magnetic attraction of Derek's personality, but there was something in her that resisted, that held back . . .

"Katherine—"

"I—"

"You know that I care for you. Do—do you care for me?"

"I—I don't know."

Weakness there. Either she knew or she did not know. If—if only—

She cast a look round desperately as though seeking something that would help her. A soft color rose in her cheeks as a tall fair man with a limp came hurrying along the path towards them—Major Knighton.

There was relief and an unexpected warmth in her voice as she greeted him.

Derek stood up scowling, his face black as a thundercloud.

"Lady Tamplin having a flutter?" he said easily. "I must join her and give her the benefit of my system."

He swung round on his heel and left them together. Katherine sat down again. Her heart was beating rapidly and unevenly, but as she sat there talking commonplaces to the quiet, rather shy man beside her, her self-command came back.

Then she realized with a shock that Knighton also was laying bare his heart, much as Derek had done, but in a very different manner.

He was shy and stammering. The words came haltingly, with no eloquence to back them.

"From the first moment I saw you—I—I ought not to have spoken so soon—but Mr. Van Aldin may leave here any day, and I might not have another chance. I know you can't care for me so soon—that is impossible. I dare say it is presumption anyway on my part. I have private means, but not very much—no, please don't answer now. I know what your answer would be. But in case I went away suddenly I just wanted you to know—that I care."

She was shaken—touched. His manner was so gentle and appealing.

"There's one thing more. I just wanted to say that if—if you are ever in trouble, anything that I can do—"

He took her hand in his, held it tightly for a minute, then dropped it and walked rapidly away towards the casino without looking back.

Katherine sat perfectly still, looking after him. Derek Kettering— Richard Knighton—two men so different—so very different. There was something kind about Knighton, kind and trustworthy. As to Derek—

Then suddenly Katherine had a very curious sensation. She felt that she was no longer sitting alone on the seat in the casino gardens, but that someone was standing beside her, and that that someone was the dead woman, Ruth Kettering. She had a further impression that Ruth wanted—badly—to tell her something. The impression was so curious, so vivid, that it could not be driven away. She felt absolutely certain that the spirit of Ruth Kettering was trying to convey something of vital importance to her. The impression faded. Katherine got up, trembling a little. What was it that Ruth Kettering had wanted so badly to say?

27

Interview with Mirelle

WHEN Knighton left Katherine he went in search of Hercule Poirot, whom he found in the Rooms, jauntily placing the minimum stake on the even numbers. As Knighton joined him, the number thirty-three turned up, and Poirot's stake was swept away.

"Bad luck!" said Knighton. "Are you going to stake again?"

Poirot shook his head.

"Not at present."

"Do you feel the fascination of gambling?" asked Knighton curiously.

"Not at roulette."

Knighton shot a swift glance at him. His own face became troubled. He spoke haltingly, with a touch of deference.

"I wonder, are you busy, Monsieur Poirot? There is something I would like to ask you about."

"I am at your disposal. Shall we go outside? It is pleasant in the sunshine."

They strolled out together, and Knighton drew a deep breath.

"I love the Riviera," he said. "I came here first twelve years ago, during the war, when I was sent to Lady Tamplin's hospital. It was like paradise, coming from Flanders to this."

"It must have been," said Poirot.

"How long ago the war seems now!" mused Knighton.

They walked on in silence for some little way.

"You have something on your mind?" said Poirot.

Knighton looked at him in some surprise.

"You are quite right," he confessed. "I don't know how you knew it, though."

"It showed itself only too plainly," said Poirot dryly.

"I did not know that I was so transparent."

"It is my business to observe the physiognomy," the little man explained, with dignity.

"I will tell you, Monsieur Poirot. You have heard of this dancer woman—Mirelle?"

"She who is the *chère amie* of Monsieur Derek Kettering?"

"Yes, that is the one; and, knowing this, you will understand that Monsieur Van Aldin is naturally prejudiced against her. She wrote to him, asking for an interview. He told me to dictate a curt refusal, which of course I did. This morning she came to the hotel and sent up her card, saying that it was urgent and vital that she should see Mr. Van Aldin at once."

"You interest me," said Poirot.

"Mr. Van Aldin was furious. He told me what message to send down to her. I ventured to disagree with him. It seemed to me both likely and probable that this woman Mirelle might give us valuable information. We know that she was on the Blue Train, and she may have seen or heard something that it might be vital for us to know. Don't you agree with me, Monsieur Poirot?"

"I do," said Poirot dryly. "Monsieur Van Aldin, if I may say so, behaved exceedingly foolishly."

"I am glad you take that view of the matter," said the secretary. "Now I am going to tell you something, Monsieur Poirot. So strongly did I feel the unwisdom of Mr. Van Aldin's attitude that I went down privately and had an interview with the lady."

"*Eh bien?*"

"The difficulty was that she insisted on seeing Mr. Van Aldin himself. I softened his message as much as I possibly could. In fact—to be candid—I gave it in a very different form. I said that Mr. Van Aldin was too busy to see her at present, but that she might make any communication she wished to me. That, however, she could not bring herself to do, and she left without saying anything further. But I have a strong impression, Monsieur Poirot, that that woman knows something."

"This is serious," said Poirot quietly. "You know where she is staying?"

"Yes." Knighton mentioned the name of the hotel.

"Good," said Poirot; "we will go there immediately."

The secretary looked doubtful.

"And Mr. Van Aldin?" he queried doubtfully.

"Monsieur Van Aldin is an obstinate man," said Poirot dryly. "I do not argue with obstinate men. I act in spite of them. We will go and see the lady immediately. I will tell her that you are empowered by Monsieur Van Aldin to act for him, and you will guard yourself well from contradicting me."

Knighton still looked slightly doubtful, but Poirot took no notice of his hesitation.

At the hotel, they were told that Mademoiselle was in, and Poirot sent up both his and Knighton's cards, with "From Mr. Van Aldin" penciled upon them.

Word came down that Mademoiselle Mirelle would receive them.

When they were ushered into the dancer's apartments, Poirot immediately took the lead.

"Mademoiselle," he murmured, bowing very low, "we are here on behalf of Monsieur Van Aldin."

"Ah! And why did he not come himself?"

"He is indisposed," said Poirot mendaciously; "the Riviera throat, it has him in its grip, but me, I am empowered to act for him, as is Major Knighton, his secretary. Unless, of course, Mademoiselle would prefer to wait a fortnight or so."

If there was one thing of which Poirot was tolerably certain, it was that to a temperament such as Mirelle's the mere word "wait" was anathema.

"*Eh bien,* I will speak, messieurs," she cried. "I have been patient. I have held my hand. And for what? That I should be insulted! Yes, insulted! Ah! Does he think to treat Mirelle like that? To throw her off like an old glove. I tell you never has a man tired of me. Always it is I who tire of them."

She paced up and down the room, her slender body trembling with rage. A small table impeded her free passage and she flung it from her into a corner, where it splintered against the wall.

"That is what I will do to him," she cried, "and that!"

Picking up a glass bowl filled with lilies, she flung it into the grate, where it smashed into a hundred pieces.

Knighton was looking at her with cold British disapproval. He felt embarrassed and ill at ease. Poirot, on the other hand, with twinkling eyes was thoroughly enjoying the scene.

"Ah, it is magnificent!" he cried. "It can be seen—Madame has a temperament."

"I am an artist," said Mirelle; "every artist has a temperament. I told Dereek to beware, and he would not listen." She whirled round on Poirot suddenly. "It is true, is it not, that he wants to marry that English miss?"

Poirot coughed.

"*On m'a dit,*" he murmured, "that he adores her passionately."

Mirelle came towards them.

"He murdered his wife," she screamed. "There—now you have it! He told me beforehand that he meant to do it. He had got to an impasse—zut! he took the easiest way out."

"You say that Monsieur Kettering murdered his wife."

"Yes, yes, yes. Have I not told you so?"

"The police," murmured Poirot, "will need proof of that—er—statement."

"I tell you I saw him come out of her compartment that night on the train."

"When?" asked Poirot sharply.

"Just before the train reached Lyons."

"You will swear to that, mademoiselle?"

It was a different Poirot who spoke now, sharp and decisive.

"Yes."

There was a moment's silence. Mirelle was panting, and her eyes, half defiant, half frightened, went from the face of one man to the other.

"This is a serious matter, mademoiselle," said the detective. "You realize how serious?"

"Certainly I do."

"That is well," said Poirot. "Then you understand, mademoiselle, that no time must be lost. You will, perhaps, accompany us immediately to the office of the Examining Magistrate."

Mirelle was taken aback. She hesitated, but, as Poirot had foreseen, she had no loophole for escape.

"Very well," she muttered. "I will fetch a coat."

Left alone together, Poirot and Knighton exchanged glances.

"It is necessary to act while—how do you say it?—the iron is hot," murmured Poirot. "She is temperamental; in an hour's time, maybe, she will repent, and she will wish to draw back. We must prevent that at all costs."

Mirelle reappeared, wrapped in a sand-colored velvet wrap trimmed with leopard skin. She looked not altogether unlike a leopardess, tawny and dangerous. Her eyes still flashed with anger and determination.

They found Monsieur Caux and the Examining Magistrate together. A few brief introductory words from Poirot, and Mademoiselle Mirelle was courteously entreated to tell her tale. This she did in much the same words as she had done to Knighton and Poirot, though with far more soberness of manner.

"This is an extraordinary story, mademoiselle," said Monsieur Carrège slowly. He leaned back in his chair, adjusted his pince-nez, and looked keenly and searchingly at the dancer through them.

"You wish us to believe Monsieur Kettering actually boasted of the crime to you beforehand?"

"Yes, yes. She was too healthy, he said. If she were to die it must be an accident—he would arrange it all."

"You are aware, mademoiselle," said Monsieur Carrège sternly, "that you are making yourself out to be an accessory before the fact?"

"Me? But not the least in the world, monsieur. Not for a moment did I take that statement seriously. Ah no, indeed! I know men, monsieur; they say many wild things. It would be an odd state of affairs if one were to take all they said *au pied de la lettre*."

The Examining Magistrate raised his eyebrows.

"We are to take it, then, that you regarded Monsieur Kettering's threats as mere idle words? May I ask, mademoiselle, what made you throw up your engagements in London and come out to the Riviera?"

Mirelle looked at him with melting black eyes.

"I wished to be with the man I loved," she said simply. "Was it so unnatural?"

Poirot interpolated a question gently.

"Was it, then, at Monsieur Kettering's wish that you accompanied him to Nice?"

Mirelle seemed to find a little difficulty in answering this. She hesitated perceptibly before she spoke. When she did, it was with a haughty indifference of manner.

"In such matters I please myself, monsieur," she said.

That the answer was not an answer at all was noted by all three men. They said nothing.

"When were you first convinced that Monsieur Kettering had murdered his wife?"

"As I tell you, monsieur, I saw Monsieur Kettering come out of his wife's compartment just before the train drew into Lyons. There was a look on his face—ah! at the moment I could not understand it—a look haunted and terrible. I shall never forget it."

Her voice rose shrilly, and she flung out her arms in an extravagant gesture.

"Quite so," said Monsieur Carrège.

"Afterwards, when I found that Madame Kettering was dead when the train left Lyons, then—then I knew!"

"And still—you did not go to the police, mademoiselle," said the Commissary mildly.

Mirelle glanced at him superbly; she was clearly enjoying herself in the role she was playing.

"Shall I betray my lover?" she asked. "Ah no; do not ask a woman to do that."

"Yet now—" hinted Monsieur Caux.

"Now it is different. He has betrayed me! Shall I suffer that in silence . . . ?"

The Examining Magistrate checked her.

"Quite so, quite so," he murmured soothingly. "And now, Mademoiselle, perhaps you will read over the statement of what you have told us, see that it is correct, and sign it."

Mirelle wasted no time on the document.

"Yes, yes," she said, "it is correct." She rose to her feet. "You require me no longer, messieurs?"

"At present, no, mademoiselle."

"And Dereek will be arrested?"

"At once, mademoiselle."

Mirelle laughed cruelly and drew her fur draperies closer about her.

"He should have thought of this before he insulted me," she cried.

"There is one little matter"—Poirot coughed apologetically—"just a matter of detail."

"Yes?"

"What makes you think Madame Kettering was dead when the train left Lyons?"

Mirelle stared.

"But she *was* dead."

"Was she?"

"Yes, of course. I—"

She came to an abrupt stop. Poirot was regarding her intently, and he saw the wary look that came into her eyes.

"I have been told so. Everybody says so."

"Oh," said Poirot, "I was not aware that the fact had been mentioned outside the Examining Magistrate's office."

Mirelle appeared somewhat discomposed.

"One hears those things," she said vaguely; "they get about. Somebody told me. I can't remember who it was."

She moved to the door. Monsieur Caux sprang forward to open it for her, and as he did so, Poirot's voice rose gently once more.

"And the jewels? Pardon, mademoiselle. Can you tell me anything about those?"

"The jewels? What jewels?"

"The rubies of Catherine the Great. Since you hear so much, you must have heard of them."

"I know nothing about any jewels," said Mirelle sharply.

She went out, closing the door behind her. Monsieur Caux came back to his chair; the Examining Magistrate sighed.

"What a fury!" he said. "But *diablement chic,* I wonder if she is telling the truth? I think so."

"There is *some* truth in her story, certainly," said Poirot. "We have confirmation of it from Miss Grey. She was looking down the corridor a short time before the train reached Lyons and she saw Monsieur Kettering go into his wife's compartment."

"The case against him seems quite clear," said the Commissary, sighing. "It is a thousand pities," he murmured.

"How do you mean?" asked Poirot.

"It has been the ambition of my life to lay the Comte de la Roche by the heels. This time, *ma foi,* I thought we had got him. This other —it is not nearly so satisfactory."

Monsieur Carrège rubbed his nose.

"If anything goes wrong," he observed cautiously, "it will be most awkward. Monsieur Kettering is of the aristocracy. It will get into the newspapers. If we have made a mistake—" He shrugged his shoulders forebodingly.

"The jewels now," said the Commissary, "what do you think he has done with them?"

"He took them for a plant, of course," said Monsieur Carrège; "they must have been a great inconvenience to him and very awkward to dispose of."

Poirot smiled.

"I have an idea of my own about the jewels. Tell me, messieurs, what do you know of a man called the Marquis?"

The Commissary leaned forward excitedly.

"The Marquis," he said, "the Marquis? Do you think he is mixed up in this affair, Monsieur Poirot?"

"I ask you what you know of him."

The Commissary made an expressive grimace.

"Not as much as we should like to," he observed ruefully. "He works behind the scenes, you understand. He has underlings who do his dirty work for him. But he is someone high up. That we are sure of. He does not come from the criminal classes."

"A Frenchman?"

"Y-es. At least we believe so. But we are not sure. He has worked in France, in England, in America. There was a series of robberies in Switzerland last autumn which were laid at his door. By all accounts he is a *grand seigneur*, speaking French and English with equal perfection and his origin is a mystery."

Poirot nodded and rose to take his departure.

"Can you tell us nothing more, Monsieur Poirot?" urged the Commissary.

"At present, no," said Poirot, "but I may have news awaiting me at my hotel."

Monsieur Carrège looked uncomfortable. "If the Marquis is concerned in this—" he began, and then stopped.

"It upsets our ideas," complained Monsieur Caux.

"It does not upset mine," said Poirot. "On the contrary, I think it agrees with them very well. Au revoir, messieurs; if news of any importance comes to me, I will communicate it to you immediately."

He walked back to his hotel with a grave face. In his absence a telegram had come to him. Taking a paper cutter from his pocket, he slit it open. It was a long telegram, and he read it over twice before slowly putting it in his pocket. Upstairs, George was awaiting his master.

"I am fatigued, Georges, much fatigued. Will you order for me a small pot of chocolate?"

The chocolate was duly ordered and brought, and George set it at the little table at his master's elbow. As he was preparing to retire, Poirot spoke:

"I believe, Georges, that you have a good knowledge of the English aristocracy?" murmured Poirot.

George smiled apologetically.

"I think that I might say that I have, sir," he replied.

"I suppose that it is your opinion, Georges, that criminals are invariably drawn from the lower orders."

"Not always, sir. There was great trouble with one of the Duke of Devize's younger sons. He left Eton under a cloud, and after that he caused great anxiety on several occasions. The police would not accept the view that it was kleptomania. A very clever young gentleman, sir, but vicious through and through, if you take my meaning. His Grace shipped him to Australia, and I hear he was convicted out there under another name. Very odd, sir, but there it is. The young gentleman, I need hardly say, was not in want financially."

Poirot nodded his head slowly.

"Love of excitement," he murmured, "and a little kink in the brain somewhere. I wonder now—"

He drew out the telegram from his pocket and read it again.

"Then there was Lady Mary Fox's daughter," continued the valet in a mood of reminiscence. "Swindled tradespeople something shocking, she did. Very worrying to the best families, if I may say so, and there are many other queer cases I could mention."

"You have a wide experience, Georges," murmured Poirot. "I often wonder, having lived so exclusively with titled families, that you demean yourself by coming as a valet to me. I put it down to love of excitement on your part."

"Not exactly, sir," said George. "I happened to see in *Society Snippets* that you had been received at Buckingham Palace. That was just when I was looking for a new situation. His Majesty, so it said, had been most gracious and friendly and thought very highly of your abilities."

"Ah," said Poirot, "one always likes to know the reason for things."

He remained in thought for a few moments and then said:

"You rang up Mademoiselle Papopolous?"

"Yes, sir; she and her father will be pleased to dine with you to-night."

"Ah," said Poirot thoughtfully. He drank off his chocolate, set the cup and saucer neatly in the middle of the tray, and spoke gently, more to himself than to the valet.

"The squirrel, my good Georges, collects nuts. He stores them up in the autumn so that they may be of advantage to him later. To make a success of humanity, Georges, we must profit by the lessons of those below us in the animal kingdom. I have always done so. I have been the cat, watching at the mouse hole. I have been the good dog following up the scent, and not taking my nose from the trail. And also, my good Georges, I have been the squirrel. I have stored away the little fact here, the little fact there. I go now to my store and I take out one particular nut, a nut that I stored away—let me see, seventeen years ago. You follow me, Georges?"

"I should hardly have thought, sir," said George, "that nuts would have kept so long as that, though I know one can do wonders with preserving bottles."

Poirot looked at him and smiled.

28

Poirot Plays the Squirrel

POIROT started to keep his dinner appointment with a margin of three-quarters of an hour to spare. He had an object in this. The car took him, not straight to Monte Carlo, but to Lady Tamplin's house at Cap Martin, where he asked for Miss Grey. The ladies were dressing and Poirot was shown into a small salon to wait, and here, after a lapse of three or four minutes, Lenox Tamplin came to him.

"Katherine is not quite ready yet," she said. "Can I give her a message, or would you rather wait until she comes down?"

Poirot looked at her thoughtfully. He was a minute or two in replying, as though something of great weight hung upon his decision. Apparently the answer to such a simple question mattered.

"No," he said at last, "no, I do not think it is necessary that I should wait to see Mademoiselle Katherine. I think, perhaps, that it is better that I should not. These things are sometimes difficult."

Lenox waited politely, her eyebrows slightly raised.

"I have a piece of news," continued Poirot. "You will, perhaps, tell your friend. Monsieur Kettering was arrested tonight for the murder of his wife."

"You want me to tell Katherine that?" asked Lenox. She breathed rather hard, as though she had been running; her face, Poirot thought, looked white and strained—rather noticeably so.

"If you please, mademoiselle."

"Why?" said Lenox. "Do you think Katherine will be upset? Do you think she cares?"

"I don't know, mademoiselle," said Poirot. "See, I admit it frankly. As a rule I know everything, but in this case, I—well, I do not. You, perhaps, know better than I do."

"Yes," said Lenox, "I know—but I am not going to tell you all the same."

She paused for a minute or two, her dark brows drawn together in a frown.

"You believe he did it?" she said abruptly.

Poirot shrugged his shoulders.

"The police say so."

"Ah," said Lenox, "hedging, are you? So there is something to hedge about."

Again she was silent, frowning. Poirot said gently:

"You have known Derek Kettering a long time, have you not?"

"Off and on ever since I was a kid," said Lenox gruffly.

Poirot nodded his head several times without speaking.

With one of her brusque movements Lenox drew forward a chair and sat down on it, her elbows on the table and her face supported by her hands. Sitting thus, she looked directly across the table at Poirot.

"What have they got to go on?" she demanded. "Motive, I suppose. Probably came into money at her death."

"He came into two million."

"And if she had not died he would have been ruined?"

"Yes."

"But there must have been more than that," persisted Lenox. "He traveled by the same train, I know, but—that would not be enough to go on by itself."

"A cigarette case with the letter 'K' on it which did not belong to Mrs. Kettering was found in her carriage, and he was seen by two people entering and leaving the compartment just before the train got into Lyons."

"What two people?"

"Your friend Miss Grey was one of them. The other was Mademoiselle Mirelle, the dancer."

"And he, Derek, what has he got to say about it?" demanded Lenox sharply.

"He denies having entered his wife's compartment at all," said Poirot.

"Fool!" said Lenox crisply, frowning. "Just before Lyons, you say? Does nobody know when—when she died?"

"The doctors' evidence necessarily cannot be very definite," said Poirot; "they are inclined to think that death was unlikely to have occurred after leaving Lyons. And we know this much, that a few moments after leaving Lyons Mrs. Kettering was dead."

"How do you know that?"

Poirot was smiling rather oddly to himself.

"Someone else went into her compartment and found her dead."

"And they did not rouse the train?"

"No."

"Why was that?"

"Doubtless they had their reasons."

Lenox looked at him sharply.

"Do you know the reason?"

"I think so—yes."

Lenox sat still, turning things over in her mind. Poirot watched her in silence. At last she looked up. A soft color had come into her cheeks and her eyes were shining.

"You think someone on the train must have killed her, but that need not be so at all. What is to stop anyone swinging themselves onto the train when it stopped at Lyons? They could go straight to her compartment, strangle her, and take the rubies and drop off the train again without anyone being the wiser. She may have been actually killed while the train was in Lyons station. Then she would have been alive when Derek went in, and dead when the other person found her."

Poirot leaned back in his chair. He drew a deep breath. He looked across at the girl and nodded his head three times, then he heaved a sigh.

"Mademoiselle," he said, "what you have said there is very just—very true. I was struggling in darkness, and you have shown me a light. There was a point that puzzled me and you have made it plain."

He got up.

"And Derek?" said Lenox.

"Who knows?" said Poirot, with a shrug of his shoulders. "But I will tell you this, mademoiselle. I am not satisfied; no, I, Hercule Poirot, am not yet satisfied. It may be that this very night I shall learn something more. At least, I go to try."

"You are meeting someone?"

"Yes."

"Someone who knows something?"

"Someone who might know something. In these matters one must leave no stone unturned. Au revoir, mademoiselle."

Lenox accompanied him to the door.

"Have I—helped?" she asked.

Poirot's face softened as he looked up at her standing on the doorstep above him.

"Yes, mademoiselle, you have helped. If things are very dark, always remember that."

When the car had driven off, he relapsed into a frowning absorption, but in his eyes was that faint green light which was always the precursor of the triumph to be.

He was a few minutes late at the rendezvous, and found that Monsieur Papopolous and his daughter had arrived before him. His apologies were abject, and he outdid himself in politeness and small attentions. The Greek was looking particularly benign and noble this evening, a sorrowful patriarch of blameless life. Zia was looking handsome and good-humored. The dinner was a pleasant one. Poirot was his best and most sparkling self. He told anecdotes, he made jokes, he paid graceful compliments to Zia Papopolous, and he told many interesting incidents of his career. The menu was a carefully selected one, and the wine was excellent.

At the close of dinner Monsieur Papopolous inquired politely:

"And the tip I gave you? You have had your little flutter on the horse?"

"I am in communication with—er—my bookmaker," replied Poirot.

The eyes of the two men met.

"A well-known horse, eh?"

"No," said Poirot; "it is what our friends, the English, call a dark horse."

"Ah!" said Monsieur Papopolous thoughtfully.

"Now we must step across to the casino and have our little flutter at the roulette table," cried Poirot gaily.

At the casino the party separated, Poirot devoting himself solely to Zia, while Papopolous himself drifted away.

Poirot was not fortunate, but Zia had a run of good luck, and had soon won a few thousand francs.

"It would be as well," she observed dryly to Poirot, "if I stopped now."

Poirot's eyes twinkled.

"Superb!" he exclaimed. "You are the daughter of your father, Mademoiselle Zia. To know when to stop. Ah! That is the art."

He looked round the rooms.

"I cannot see your father anywhere about," he remarked carelessly. "I will fetch your cloak for you, mademoiselle, and we will go out in the gardens."

He did not, however, go straight to the cloakroom. His sharp eyes had seen but a little while before the departure of Monsieur Papopolous. He was anxious to know what had become of the wily Greek. He ran him to earth unexpectedly in the big entrance hall. He was standing by one of the pillars, talking to a lady who had just arrived. The lady was Mirelle.

Poirot sidled unostentatiously round the room. He arrived at the other side of the pillar, and unnoticed by the two who were talking together in an animated fashion—or rather, that is to say, the dancer was talking, Papopolous contributing an occasional monosyllable and a good many expressive gestures.

"I tell you I must have time," the dancer was saying. "If you give me time, I will get the money."

"To wait"—the Greek shrugged his shoulders—"it is awkward."

"Only a very little while," pleaded the other. "Ah! But you must! A week—ten days—that is all I ask. You can be sure of your affair. The money will be forthcoming."

Papopolous shifted a little and looked round him uneasily—to find Poirot almost at his elbow with a beaming innocent face.

"*Ah! Vous voilà*, Monsieur Papopolous. I have been looking for you. It is permitted that I take Mademoiselle Zia for a little turn in the gardens? Good evening, mademoiselle." He bowed very low to Mirelle. "A thousand pardons that I did not see you immediately."

The dancer accepted his greetings rather impatiently. She was clearly annoyed at the interruption of her tête-à-tête. Poirot was quick to take the hint. Papopolous had already murmured: "Certainly—but certainly," and Poirot withdrew forthwith.

He fetched Zia's cloak, and together they strolled out into the gardens.

"This is where the suicides take place," said Zia.

Poirot shrugged his shoulders. "So it is said. Men are foolish, are they not, mademoiselle? To eat, to drink, to breathe the good air, it is a very pleasant thing, mademoiselle. One is foolish to leave all that simply because one has no money—or because the heart aches. *L'amour*, it causes many fatalities, does it not?"

Zia laughed.

"You should not laugh at love, mademoiselle," said Poirot, shaking an energetic forefinger at her. "You who are young and beautiful."

"Hardly that," said Zia; "you forget that I am thirty-three, Monsieur Poirot. I am frank with you, because it is no good being otherwise. As you told my father, it is exactly seventeen years since you aided us in Paris that time."

"When I look at you, it seems much less," said Poirot gallantly. "You were then very much as you are now, mademoiselle, a little thinner, a little paler, a little more serious. Sixteen years old and fresh from your pension. Not quite the *petite pensionnaire*, not quite a woman. You were very delicious, very charming, Mademoiselle Zia; others thought so too, without doubt."

"At sixteen," said Zia, "one is simple and a little fool."

"That may be," said Poirot, "yes, that well may be. At sixteen one is credulous, is one not? One believes what one is told."

If he saw the quick sideways glance that the girl shot at him, he pretended not to have done so. He continued dreamily: "It was a curious affair that, altogether. Your father, mademoiselle, has never understood the true inwardness of it."

"No?"

"When he asked me for details, for explanations, I said to him thus: 'Without scandal, I have got back for you that which was lost. You must ask no questions.' Do you know, mademoiselle, why I said these things?"

"I have no idea," said the girl coldly.

"It was because I had a soft spot in my heart for a little *pensionnaire*, so pale, so thin, so serious."

"I don't understand what you are talking about," cried Zia angrily.

"Do you not, mademoiselle? Have you forgotten Antonio Pirezzio?"

He heard the quick intake of her breath—almost a gasp.

"He came to work as an assistant in the shop, but not thus could he have got hold of what he wanted. An assistant can lift his eyes to his master's daughter, can he not? If he is young and handsome with a glib tongue. And since they cannot make love all the time, they must occasionally talk of things that interest them both—such as that very interesting thing which was temporarily in Monsieur Papopolous' possession. And since, as you say, mademoiselle, the young are foolish and credulous, it was easy to believe him and to give him a sight of that particular thing, to show him where it was kept. And afterwards when it is gone—when the unbelievable catastrophe has happened. Alas! The poor little *pensionnaire*. What a terrible position she is in. She is frightened, the poor little one. To speak or not to speak? And then there comes along that excellent fellow, Hercule Poirot. Almost a miracle it must have been, the way things arranged themselves. The priceless heirlooms are restored and there are no awkward questions."

Zia turned on him fiercely.

"You have known all the time? Who told you? Was it—was it Antonio?"

Poirot shook his head.

"No one told me," he said quietly. "I guessed. It was a good guess, was it not, mademoiselle? You see, unless you are good at guessing, it is not much use being a detective."

The girl walked along beside him for some minutes in silence. Then she said in a hard voice:

"Well, what are you going to do about it? Are you going to tell my father?"

"No," said Poirot sharply. "Certainly not."

She looked at him curiously.

"You want something from me?"

"I want your help, mademoiselle."

"What makes you think that I can help you?"

"I do not think so. I only hope so."

"And if I do not help you, then—you will tell my father?"

"But no, but no! Debarrass yourself of that idea, mademoiselle. I am not a blackmailer. I do not hold your secret over your head and threaten you with it."

"If I refuse to help you—" began the girl slowly.

"Then you refuse, and that is that."

"Then why—" She stopped.

"Listen, and I will tell you why. Women, mademoiselle, are generous. If they can render a service to one who has rendered a service to them, they will do it. I was generous once to you, mademoiselle. When I might have spoken, I held my tongue."

There was another silence; then the girl said, "My father gave you a hint the other day."

"It was very kind of him."

"I do not think," said Zia slowly, "that there is anything that I can add to that."

If Poirot was disappointed, he did not show it. Not a muscle of his face changed.

"*Eh bien!*" he said cheerfully. "Then we must talk of other things."

And he proceeded to chat gaily. The girl was *distraite*, however, and her answers were mechanical and not always to the point. It was when they were approaching the casino once more that she seemed to come to a decision.

"Monsieur Poirot?"

"Yes, mademoiselle?"

"I—I should like to help you if I could."

"You are very amiable, mademoiselle—very amiable."

Again there was a pause. Poirot did not press her. He was quite content to wait and let her take her own time.

"Ah bah," said Zia, "after all, why should I not tell you? My father is cautious—always cautious in everything he says. But I know that with you it is not necessary. You have told us it is only the murderer you seek, and that you are not concerned over the jewels. I believe you. You were quite right when you guessed that we were in Nice because of the rubies. They have been handed over here according to plan. My father has them now. He gave you a hint the other day as to who our mysterious client was."

"The Marquis?" murmured Poirot softly.

"Yes, the Marquis."

"Have you ever seen the Marquis, Mademoiselle Zia?"

"Once," said the girl. "But not very well," she added. "It was through a keyhole."

"That always presents difficulties," said Poirot sympathetically, "but all the same you saw him. You would know him again?"

Zia shook her head.

"He wore a mask," she explained.

"Young or old?"

"He had white hair. It may have been a wig, it may not. It fitted very well. But I do not think he was old. His walk was young, and so was his voice."

"His voice?" said Poirot thoughtfully. "Ah, his voice! Would you know it again, Mademoiselle Zia?"

"I might," said the girl.

"You were interested in him, eh? It was that that took you to the keyhole."

Zia nodded.

"Yes, yes. I was curious. One had heard so much—he is not the ordinary thief—he is more like a figure of history or romance."

"Yes," said Poirot thoughtfully, "yes; perhaps so."

"But it is not this that I meant to tell you," said Zia. "It was just one other little fact that I thought might be—well—useful to you."

"Yes?" said Poirot encouragingly.

"The rubies, as I say, were handed over to my father here at Nice. I did not see the person who handed them over, but—"

"Yes?"

"I know one thing. *It was a woman.*"

29

A Letter from Home

DEAR KATHERINE—Living among grand friends as you are doing now, I don't suppose you will care to hear any of our news; but as I always thought you were a sensible girl, perhaps you are a trifle less swollen-headed than I suppose. Everything goes on much the same here. There was great trouble about the new curate, who is scandalously high. In my view, he is neither more nor less than a Roman. Everybody has spoken to the Vicar about it, but you know what the Vicar is—all Christian charity and no proper spirit. I have had a lot of trouble with maids lately. That girl Annie was no good—skirts up to her knees and wouldn't wear sensible woollen stockings. Not one of them can bear being spoken to. I have had a lot of pain with my rheumatism one way and another, and Dr. Harris persuaded me to go and see a London specialist—a waste of three guineas and a railway fare, as I told him; but by waiting until Wednesday I managed to get a cheap return. The London doctor pulled a long face and talked all round about and never straight out, until I said to him, "I'm a plain woman, Doctor, and I like things to be plainly stated. Is it cancer, or is it not?" And then, of course, he had to say it was. They say a year with care, and not too much pain, though I am sure I can bear pain as well as any other Christian woman. Life seems rather lonely at times, with most of my friends dead or gone before. I wish you were in St. Mary Mead, my dear, and that is a fact. If you hadn't come into this money and gone off into grand society, I would have offered you double the salary poor Jane gave you to come and look after me; but there—there's no good wanting what we can't get. However, if things should go ill with you—and that is always possible. I have heard no end of tales of bogus noblemen marrying girls and getting hold of their money and then leaving them at the church door. I dare say you are too sensible for anything of the kind to happen to you, but one never knows; and never having had much attention of any kind, it might easily go to your head now. So just in case, my dear, remember there is always a home for you here; and though a plain-spoken woman I am a warmhearted one too.—Your affectionate old friend,

AMELIA VINER.

P.S.—I saw a mention of you in the paper with your cousin, Viscountess Tamplin, and I cut it out and put it with my cuttings. I prayed for you on Sunday that you might be kept from pride and vainglory.

Katherine read this characteristic epistle through twice, then she laid it down and stared out of her bedroom window across the blue waters of the Mediterranean. She felt a curious lump in her throat. A sudden wave of longing for St. Mary Mead swept over her. So full of familiar, everyday, stupid little things—and yet—home. She felt very inclined to lay her head down on her arms and indulge in a real good cry.

Lenox, coming in at the moment, saved her.

"Hello, Katherine," said Lenox. "I say—what is the matter?"

"Nothing," said Katherine, grabbing up Miss Viner's letter and thrusting it into her handbag.

"You looked rather queer," said Lenox. "I say—I hope you don't mind—I rang up your detective friend, Monsieur Poirot, and asked him to lunch with us in Nice. I said you wanted to see him, as I thought he might not come for me."

"Did you want to see him then?" asked Katherine.

"Yes," said Lenox. "I have rather lost my heart to him. I never met a man before whose eyes were really green like a cat's."

"All right," said Katherine. She spoke listlessly. The last few days had been trying. Derek Kettering's arrest had been the topic of the hour, and the Blue Train Mystery had been thrashed out from every conceivable standpoint.

"I have ordered the car," said Lenox, "and I have told Mother some lie or other—unfortunately I can't remember exactly what; but it won't matter, as she never remembers. If she knew where we were going, she would want to come too, to pump Monsieur Poirot."

The two girls arrived at the Negresco to find Poirot waiting.

He was full of Gallic politeness, and showered so many compliments upon the two girls that they were soon helpless with laughter; yet for all that, the meal was not a gay one. Katherine was dreamy and distracted, and Lenox made bursts of conversation, interspersed by silences. As they were sitting on the terrace sipping their coffee, she suddenly attacked Poirot bluntly.

"How are things going? You know what I mean?"

Poirot shrugged his shoulders. "They take their course," he said.

"And you are just letting them take their course?"

He looked at Lenox a little sadly.

"You are young, mademoiselle, but there are three things that cannot be hurried—*le bon Dieu*, Nature, and old people."

"Nonsense!" said Lenox. "You are not old."

"Ah, it is pretty what you say there."

"Here is Major Knighton," said Lenox.

Katherine looked round quickly and then turned back again.

"He is with Mr. Van Aldin," continued Lenox. "There is something I want to ask Major Knighton about. I won't be a minute."

Left alone together, Poirot bent forward and murmured to Katherine:

"You are *distraite*, mademoiselle; your thoughts, they are far away, are they not?"

"Just as far as England, no farther."

Guided by a sudden impulse, she took the letter she had received that morning and handed it across to him to read.

"That is the first word that has come to me from my old life; somehow or other—it hurts."

He read it through and then handed it back to her. "So you are going back to St. Mary Mead?" he said slowly.

"No, I am not," said Katherine; "why should I?"

"Ah," said Poirot, "it is my mistake. You will excuse me one little minute."

He strolled across to where Lenox Tamplin was talking to Van Aldin and Knighton. The American looked old and haggard. He greeted Poirot with a curt nod but without any other sign of animation.

As he turned to reply to some observation made by Lenox, Poirot drew Knighton aside.

"Monsieur Van Aldin looks ill," he said.

"Do you wonder?" asked Knighton. "The scandal of Derek Kettering's arrest has about put the lid on things, as far as he is concerned. He is even regretting that he asked you to find out the truth."

"He should go back to England," said Poirot.

"We are going the day after tomorrow."

"That is good news," said Poirot.

He hesitated, and looked across the terrace to where Katherine was sitting.

"I wish," he murmured, "that you could tell Miss Grey that."

"Tell her what?"

"That you—I mean that Monsieur Van Aldin is returning to England."

Knighton looked a little puzzled, but he readily crossed the terrace and joined Katherine.

Poirot saw him go with a satisfied nod of the head, and then joined Lenox and the American. After a minute or two they joined the others. Conversation was general for a few minutes, then the millionaire and his secretary departed. Poirot also prepared to take his departure.

"A thousand thanks for your hospitality, mesdemoiselles," he cried; "it has been a most charming luncheon. *Ma foi,* I needed it!" He swelled out his chest and thumped it. "I am now a lion—a giant. Ah, Mademoiselle Katherine, you have not seen me as I can be. You have seen the gentle, the calm Hercule Poirot; but there is another Hercule Poirot. I go now to bully, to threaten, to strike terror into the hearts of those who listen to me."

He looked at them in a self-satisfied way, and they both appeared to be duly impressed, though Lenox was biting her underlip, and the corners of Katherine's mouth had a suspicious twitch.

"And I shall do it," he said gravely. "Oh yes, I shall succeed."

He had gone but a few steps when Katherine's voice made him turn.

"Monsieur Poirot, I—I want to tell you. I think you were right in what you said. I am going back to England almost immediately."

Poirot stared at her very hard, and under the directness of his scrutiny she blushed.

"I see," he said gravely.

"I don't believe you do," said Katherine.

"I know more than you think, mademoiselle," he said quietly.

He left her, with an odd little smile upon his lips. Entering a waiting car, he drove to Antibes.

Hippolyte, the Comte de la Roche's wooden-faced manservant, was busy at the Villa Marina polishing his master's beautiful cut table glass. The Comte de la Roche himself had gone to Monte Carlo for the day. Chancing to look out of the window, Hippolyte espied a visitor walking briskly up to the hall door, a visitor of so uncommon a type that Hippolyte, experienced as he was, had some difficulty in placing him. Calling to his wife Marie, who was busy in the kitchen, he drew her attention to what he called *ce type là*.

"It is not the police again?" said Marie anxiously.

"Look for yourself," said Hippolyte.

Marie looked.

"Certainly not the police," she declared. "I am glad."

"They have not really worried us much," said Hippolyte. "In fact, but for Monsieur le Comte's warning, I should never have guessed that stranger at the wineshop to be what he was."

The hall bell pealed and Hippolyte, in a grave and decorous manner, went to open the door.

"Monsieur le Comte, I regret to say, is not at home."

The little man with the large mustaches beamed placidly.

"I know that," he replied. "You are Hippolyte Flavelle, are you not?"

"Yes, monsieur, that is my name."

"And you have a wife, Marie Flavelle?"

"Yes, monsieur, but—"

"I desire to see you both," said the stranger, and he stepped nimbly past Hippolyte into the hall.

"Your wife is doubtless in the kitchen," he said. "I will go there."

Before Hippolyte could recover his breath, the other had selected the right door at the back of the hall and passed along the passage and into the kitchen, where Marie paused open-mouthed to stare at him.

"*Voilà*," said the stranger, and sank into a wooden armchair; "I am Hercule Poirot."

"Yes, monsieur?"

"You do not know the name?"

"I have never heard it," said Hippolyte.

"Permit me to say that you have been badly educated. It is the name of one of the great ones of this world."

He sighed and folded his hands across his chest.

Hippolyte and Marie were staring at him uneasily. They were at a loss what to make of this unexpected and extremely strange visitor.

"Monsieur desires—" murmured Hippolyte mechanically.

"I desire to know why you have lied to the police."

"Monsieur!" cried Hippolyte. "I—lied to the police? Never have I done such a thing."

Monsieur Poirot shook his head.

"You are wrong," he said; "you have done it on several occasions. Let me see." He took a small notebook from his pocket and consulted it. "Ah, yes; on seven occasions at least. I will recite them to you."

In a gentle unemotional voice he proceeded to outline the seven occasions.

Hippolyte was taken aback.

"But it is not of these past lapses that I wish to speak," continued Poirot, "only, my dear friend, do not get into the habit of thinking yourself too clever. I come now to the particular lie in which I am concerned—your statement that the Comte de la Roche arrived at this villa on the morning of 14th January."

"But that was no lie, monsieur; that was the truth. Monsieur le Comte arrived here on the morning of Tuesday, the fourteenth. That is so, Marie, is it not?"

Marie assented eagerly.

"Ah, yes, that is quite right. I remember it perfectly."

"Ah," said Poirot, "and what did you give your good master for *déjeuner* that day?"

"I—" Marie paused, trying to collect herself.

"Odd," said Poirot, "how one remembers some things—and forgets others."

He leaned forward and struck the table a blow with his fist; his eyes flashed with anger.

"Yes, yes, it is as I say. You tell your lies and you think nobody knows. But there are two people who know. Yes—two people. One is *le bon Dieu*—"

He raised a hand to heaven, and then settling himself back in his chair and shutting his eyelids, he murmured comfortably:

"And the other is Hercule Poirot."

"I assure you, monsieur, you are completely mistaken. Monsieur le Comte left Paris on Monday night—"

"True," said Poirot—"by the Rapide. I do not know where he broke his journey. Perhaps you do not know that. What I do know is that he arrived here on Wednesday morning, and not on Tuesday morning."

"Monsieur is mistaken," said Marie stolidly.

Poirot rose to his feet.

"Then the law must take its course," he murmured. "A pity."

"What do you mean, monsieur?" asked Marie, with a shade of uneasiness.

"You will be arrested and held as accomplices concerned in the murder of Mrs. Kettering, the English lady who was killed."

"Murder!"

The man's face had gone chalk-white, his knees knocked together. Marie dropped the rolling pin and began to weep.

"But it is impossible—impossible. I thought—"

"Since you stick to your story, there is nothing to be said. I think you are both foolish."

He was turning towards the door when an agitated voice arrested him.

"Monsieur, monsieur, just a little moment. I—I had no idea that it was anything of this kind. I—I thought it was just a matter concerning a lady. There have been little awkwardnesses with the police over ladies before. But murder—that is very different."

"I have no patience with you," cried Poirot. He turned round on them and angrily shook his fist in Hippolyte's face. "Am I to stop here all day, arguing with a couple of imbeciles thus? It is the truth I want. If you will not give it to me, that is your lookout. *For the last time, when did Monsieur le Comte arrive at the Villa Marina— Tuesday morning or Wednesday morning?*"

"Wednesday," gasped the man, and behind him Marie nodded confirmation.

Poirot regarded them for a minute or two, then inclined his head gravely.

"You are wise, my children," he said quietly. "Very nearly you were in serious trouble."

He left the Villa Marina, smiling to himself.

"One guess confirmed," he murmured to himself. "Shall I take a chance on the other?"

It was six o'clock when the card of Monsieur Hercule Poirot was brought up to Mirelle. She stared at it for a moment or two, and then nodded. When Poirot entered, he found her walking up and down the room feverishly. She turned on him furiously.

"Well?" she cried. "Well? What is it now? Have you not tortured me enough, all of you? Have you not made me betray my poor Dereek? What more do you want?"

"Just one little question, mademoiselle. After the train left Lyons, when you entered Mrs. Kettering's compartment—"

"What is that?"

Poirot looked at her with an air of mild reproach and began again.

"I say when you entered Mrs. Kettering's compartment—"

"I never did."

"And found her—"

"I never did.

"Ah, sacré!"

He turned on her in a rage and shouted at her, so that she cowered back before him.

"Will you lie to me? I tell you I know what happened as well as though I had been there. You went into her compartment and you found her dead. I tell you I know it. To lie to me is dangerous. Be careful, Mademoiselle Mirelle."

Her eyes wavered beneath his gaze and fell.

"I—I didn't—" she began uncertainly and stopped.

"There is only one thing about which I wonder," said Poirot. "I wonder, mademoiselle, if you found what you were looking for or whether—"

"Whether what?"

"Or whether someone else had been before you."

"I will answer no more questions," screamed the dancer. She tore herself away from Poirot's restraining hand, and flinging herself down on the floor in a frenzy, she screamed and sobbed. A frightened maid came rushing in.

Hercule Poirot shrugged his shoulders, raised his eyebrows, and quietly left the room.

But he seemed satisfied.

30

Miss Viner Gives Judgment

KATHERINE looked out of Miss Viner's bedroom window. It was raining, not violently, but with a quiet, well-bred persistence. The window looked out on a strip of front garden with a path down to the gate and neat little flower beds on either side, where later roses and pinks and blue hyacinths would bloom.

Miss Viner was lying in a large Victorian bedstead. A tray with the remains of breakfast had been pushed to one side and she was busy opening her correspondence and making various caustic comments upon it.

Katherine had an open letter in her hand and was reading it through for the second time. It was dated from the Ritz Hotel, Paris.

> CHÈRE MADEMOISELLE KATHERINE [it began]—I trust that you are in good health and that the return to the English winter has not proved too depressing. Me, I prosecute my inquiries with the utmost diligence. Do not think that it is the holiday that I take here. Very shortly I shall be in England, and I hope then to have the pleasure of meeting you once more. It shall be so, shall it not? On arrival in London I shall write to you. You remember that we are the colleagues in this affair? But indeed I think you know that very well.
>
> Be assured, mademoiselle, of my most respectful and devoted sentiments.
>
> HERCULE POIROT.

Katherine frowned slightly. It was as though something in the letter puzzled and intrigued her.

"A choir boys' picnic indeed," came from Miss Viner. "Tommy Saunders and Albert Dykes ought to be left behind, and I shan't subscribe to it unless they are. What those two boys think they are doing in church on Sundays, I don't know. Tommy sang, 'O God, make speed to save us,' and never opened his lips again, and if Albert Dykes wasn't sucking a mint humbug, my nose is not what it is and always has been."

"I know, they are awful," agreed Katherine.

She opened her second letter, and a sudden flush came to her cheeks. Miss Viner's voice in the room seemed to recede into the far distance.

When she came back to a sense of her surroundings, Miss Viner was bringing a long speech to a triumphant termination.

"And I said to her, 'Not at all. As it happens, Miss Grey is Lady Tamplin's own cousin.' What do you think of that?"

"Were you fighting my battles for me? That was very sweet of you."

"You can put it that way if you like. There is nothing to me in a title. Vicar's wife or no vicar's wife, that woman is a cat. Hinting you had bought your way into society."

"Perhaps she was not so very far wrong."

"And look at you," continued Miss Viner. "Have you come back a stuck-up fine lady, as well you might have done? No, there you are, as sensible as ever you were, with a pair of good balbriggan stockings on and sensible shoes. I spoke to Ellen about it only yesterday. 'Ellen,' I said, 'you look at Miss Grey. She has been hobnobbing with some of the greatest in the land, and does she go about as you do with skirts up to her knees and silk stockings that ladder when you look at them, and the most ridiculous shoes that ever I set eyes on?'"

Katherine smiled a little to herself; it had apparently been worthwhile to conform to Miss Viner's prejudices. The old lady went on with increasing gusto.

"It has been a great relief to me that you have not had your head turned. Only the other day I was looking for my cuttings. I have several about Lady Tamplin and her war hospital and what not, but I cannot lay my hand upon them. I wish you would look, my dear; your eyesight is better than mine. They are all in a box in the bureau drawer."

Katherine glanced down at the letter in her hand and was about to speak, but checked herself, and going over to the bureau found the box of cuttings and began to look over them. Since her return to St. Mary Mead her heart had gone out to Miss Viner in admiration of the old woman's stoicism and pluck. She felt that there was little she could do for her old friend, but she knew from experience how much those seemingly small trifles meant to old people.

"Here is one," she said presently. "'Viscountess Tamplin, who is running her villa at Nice as an officers' hospital, has just been the victim of a sensational robbery, her jewels having been stolen. Among them were some very famous emeralds, heirlooms of the Tamplin family.'"

"Probably paste," said Miss Viner; "a lot of these society women's jewels are."

"Here is another," said Katherine. "A picture of her, 'A charming camera study of Viscountess Tamplin with her little daughter Lenox.'"

"Let me look," said Miss Viner. "You can't see much of the child's face, can you? But I dare say that is just as well. Things go by contraries in this world and beautiful mothers have hideous children. I dare say the photographer realized that to take the back of the child's head was the best thing he could do for her."

Katherine laughed.

"'One of the smartest hostesses on the Riviera this season is Viscountess Tamplin, who has a villa at Cap Martin. Her cousin, Miss Grey, who recently inherited a vast fortune in a most romantic manner, is staying with her there.'"

"That is the one I wanted," said Miss Viner. "I expect there has been a picture of you in one of the papers that I have missed; you know the kind of thing. Mrs. Somebody or other Jones-Williams, at the something or other Point-to-Point, usually carrying a shooting stick and having one foot lifted up in the air. It must be a trial to some of them to see what they look like."

Katherine did not answer. She was smoothing out the cutting with her finger, and her face had a puzzled, worried look. Then she drew the second letter out of its envelope and mastered its contents once more. She turned to her friend.

"Miss Viner? I wonder—there is a friend of mine, someone I met on the Riviera, who wants very much to come down and see me here?"

"A man," said Miss Viner.

"Yes."

"Who is he?"

"He is secretary to Mr. Van Aldin, the American millionaire."

"What is his name?"

"Knighton. Major Knighton."

"Hm—secretary to a millionaire. And wants to come down here. Now, Katherine, I am going to say something to you for your own good. You are a nice girl and a sensible girl, and though you have your head screwed on the right way about most things, every woman makes a fool of herself once in her life. Ten to one what this man is after is your money."

With a gesture she arrested Katherine's reply. "I have been waiting for something of this kind. What is a secretary to a millionaire? Nine times out of ten it is a young man who likes living soft. A young man with nice manners and a taste for luxury and no brains and no enterprise, and if there is anything that is a softer job than being a secretary to a millionaire, it is marrying a rich woman for her money. I am not saying that you might not be some man's fancy. But you are not young, and though you have a very good complexion you are not a beauty, and what I say to you is, don't make a fool of yourself; but if you are determined to do so, do see that your money is properly tied up on yourself. There, now I have finished. What have you got to say?"

"Nothing," said Katherine; "but would you mind if he did come down to see me?"

"I wash my hands of it," said Miss Viner. "I have done my duty, and whatever happens now is on your own head. Would you like him to lunch or to dinner? I dare say Ellen could manage dinner— that is, if she didn't lose her head."

"Lunch would be very nice," said Katherine. "It is awfully kind of you, Miss Viner. He asked me to ring him up, so I will do so and say that we shall be pleased if he will lunch with us. He will motor down from town."

"Ellen does a steak with grilled tomatoes pretty fairly," said Miss Viner. "She doesn't do it well, but she does it better than anything else. It is no good having a tart because she is heavy-handed with pastry; but her little castle puddings are not bad, and I dare say you could find a nice piece of Stilton at Abbot's. I have always heard that gentlemen like a nice piece of Stilton, and there is a good deal of father's wine left, a bottle of sparkling Moselle, perhaps."

"Oh no, Miss Viner; that is really not necessary."

"Nonsense, my child. No gentleman is happy unless he drinks something with his meal. There is some good pre-war whisky if you think he would prefer that. Now do as I say and don't argue. The key of the wine cellar is in the third drawer down in the dressing table, in the second pair of stockings on the left-hand side."

Katherine went obediently to the spot indicated.

"The second pair, now mind," said Miss Viner. "The first pair has my diamond earrings and my filigree brooch in it."

"Oh," said Katherine, rather taken aback, "wouldn't you like them put in your jewel case?"

Miss Viner gave vent to a terrific and prolonged snort.

"No, indeed! I have much too much sense for that sort of thing, thank you. Dear, dear, I well remember how my poor father had a safe built in downstairs. Pleased as Punch he was with it, and he said to my mother, 'Now, Mary, you bring me your jewels in their case every night and I will lock them away for you.' My mother was a very tactful woman, and she knew that gentlemen like having their own way, and she brought him the jewel case locked up just as he said.

"And one night burglars broke in, and of course—naturally—the first thing they went for was the safe! It would be, with my father talking up and down the village and bragging about it until you might have thought he kept all King Solomon's diamonds there. They made a clean sweep, got the tankards, the silver cups, and the presentation gold plate that my father had had presented to him, *and* the jewel case."

She sighed reminiscently. "My father was in a great state over my mother's jewels. There was the Venetian set and some very fine cameos, and some pale pink corals, and two diamond rings with quite large stones in them. And then, of course, she had to tell him that, being a sensible woman, she had kept her jewelry rolled up in a pair of corsets, and there it was still as safe as anything."

"And the jewel case had been quite empty?"

"Oh no, dear," said Miss Viner, "it would have been too light a weight then. My mother was a very intelligent woman; she saw to that. She kept her buttons in the jewel case, and a very handy place it was. Boot buttons in the top tray, trouser buttons in the second tray, and assorted buttons below. Curiously enough, my father was quite annoyed with her. He said he didn't like deceit. But I mustn't go chattering on; you want to go and ring up your friend, and mind you choose a nice piece of steak, and tell Ellen she is not to have holes in her stockings when she waits at lunch."

"Is her name Ellen or Helen, Miss Viner? I thought—"

Miss Viner closed her eyes.

"I can sound my h's, dear, as well as anyone, but Helen is *not* a suitable name for a servant. I don't know what the mothers in the lower classes are coming to nowadays."

The rain had cleared away when Knighton arrived at the cottage. The pale fitful sunshine shone down on it and burnished Katherine's head as she stood in the doorway to welcome him. He came up to her quickly, almost boyishly.

"I say, I hope you don't mind. I simply had to see you again soon. I hope the friend you are staying with does not mind."

"Come in and make friends with her," said Katherine. "She can be most alarming, but you will soon find that she has the softest heart in the world."

Miss Viner was enthroned majestically in the drawing room, wearing a complete set of the cameos which had been so providentially preserved in the family. She greeted Knighton with dignity and an austere politeness which would have damped many men. Knighton, however, had a charm of manner which was not easily set aside, and after about ten minutes Miss Viner thawed perceptibly. Luncheon was a merry meal, and Ellen, or Helen, in a new pair of silk stockings devoid of ladders, performed prodigies of waiting. Afterwards, Katherine and Knighton went for a walk and they came back to have tea tête-à-tête, since Miss Viner had gone to lie down.

When the car had finally driven off, Katherine went slowly upstairs. A voice called her and she went into Miss Viner's bedroom.

"Friend gone?"

"Yes. Thank you so much for letting me ask him down."

"No need to thank me. Do you think I am the sort of old curmudgeon who never will do anything for anybody?"

"I think you are a dear," said Katherine affectionately.

"Humph," said Miss Viner, mollified.

As Katherine was leaving the room, she called her back.

"Katherine?"

"Yes."

"I was wrong about that young man of yours. A man when he is making up to anybody can be cordial and gallant and full of little attentions and altogether charming. But when a man is really in love, he can't help looking like a sheep. Now, whenever that young man looked at you, he looked like a sheep. I take back all I said this morning. It is genuine."

31

Mr. Aarons Lunches

"Ah!" said Mr. Joseph Aarons appreciatively.

He took a long draught from his tankard, set it down with a sigh, wiped the froth from his lips, and beamed across the table at his host, Monsieur Hercule Poirot.

"Give me," said Mr. Aarons, "a good Porterhouse steak and a tankard of something worth drinking, and anyone can have your French fallals and whatnots, your ordoovers and your omelettes and your little bits of quail. Give me," he reiterated, "a Porterhouse steak."

Poirot, who had just complied with this request, smiled sympathetically.

"Not that there is much wrong with a steak and kidney pudding," continued Mr. Aarons. "Apple tart? Yes, I will take apple tart, thank you, miss, and a jug of cream."

The meal proceeded. Finally, with a long sigh, Mr. Aarons laid down his spoon and fork preparatory to toying with some cheese before turning his mind to other matters.

"There was a little matter of business I think you said, Monsieur Poirot," he remarked. "Anything I can do to help you I am sure I shall be most happy."

"That is very kind of you," said Poirot. "I said to myself, 'If you want to know anything about the dramatic profession, there is one person who knows all that is to be known and that is my old friend, Mr. Joseph Aarons.'"

"And you don't say far wrong," said Mr. Aarons complacently; "whether it is past, present, or future, Joe Aarons is the man to come to."

"*Précisément.* Now I want to ask you, Monsieur Aarons, what you know about a young woman called Kidd."

"Kidd? Kitty Kidd?"

"Kitty Kidd."

"Pretty smart, she was. Male impersonator, song and a dance—
That one?"

"That is the one."

"*Very* smart, she was. Made a good income. Never out of an engagement. Male impersonation mostly, but, as a matter of fact, you
could not touch her as a character actress."

"So I have heard," said Poirot; "but she has not been appearing
lately, has she?"

"No. Dropped right out of things. Went over to France and took
up with some swell nobleman there. She quitted the stage then for
good and all, I guess."

"How long ago was that?"

"Let me see. Three years ago. And she has been a loss—let me
tell you that."

"She was clever?"

"Clever as a cartload of monkeys."

"You don't know the name of the man she became friends with
in Paris?"

"He was a swell, I know that. A count—or was it a marquis? Now
I come to think of it, I believe it was a marquis."

"And you know nothing about her since?"

"Nothing. Never even run across her accidentally like. I bet she
is tooling it round some of these foreign resorts. Being a marquise
to the life. You couldn't put one over on Kitty. She would give as
good as she got any day."

"I see," said Poirot thoughtfully.

"I am sorry I can't tell you more, Monsieur Poirot," said the other.
"I would like to be of use to you if I could. You did me a good
turn once."

"Ah, but we are quits on that; you, too, did me a good turn."

"One good turn deserves another. Ha, ha!" said Mr. Aarons.

"Your profession must be a very interesting one," said Poirot.

"So-so," said Mr. Aarons noncommittally. "Taking the rough with
the smooth, it is all right. I don't do so badly at it, all things considered, but you have to keep your eyes skinned. Never know
what the public will jump for next."

"Dancing has come very much to the fore in the last few years,"
murmured Poirot reflectively.

"*I* never saw anything in this Russian ballet, but people like it. Too highbrow for me."

"I met one dancer out on the Riviera—Mademoiselle Mirelle."

"Mirelle? She is hot stuff, by all accounts. There is always money going to back her—though, so far as that goes, the girl can dance; I have seen her, and I know what I am talking about. I never had much to do with her myself, but I hear she is a terror to deal with. Tempers and tantrums all the time."

"Yes," said Poirot thoughtfully; "yes, so I should imagine."

"Temperament!" said Mr. Aarons. "Temperament! That is what they call it themselves. My missus was a dancer before she married me, but I am thankful to say she never had any temperament. You don't want temperament in the home, Monsieur Poirot."

"I agree with you, my friend; it is out of place there."

"A woman should be calm and sympathetic, and a good cook," said Mr. Aarons.

"Mirelle has not been long before the public, has she?" asked Poirot.

"About two and a half years, that is all," said Mr. Aarons. "Some French duke started her. I hear now that she has taken up with the ex-Prime Minister of Greece. These are the chaps who manage to put money away quietly."

"That is news to me," said Poirot.

"Oh, she's not one to let the grass grow under her feet. They say that young Kettering murdered his wife on her account. I don't know, I am sure. Anyway, he is in prison, and she had to look round for herself, and pretty smart she has been about it. They say she is wearing a ruby the size of a pigeon's egg—not that I have ever seen a pigeon's egg myself, but that is what they always call it in works of fiction."

"A ruby the size of a pigeon's egg!" said Poirot. His eyes were green and catlike. "How interesting!"

"I had it from a friend of mine," said Mr. Aarons. "But, for all I know, it may be colored glass. They are all the same, these women —they never stop telling tall stories about their jewels. Mirelle goes about bragging that it has got a curse on it. 'Heart of Fire,' I think she calls it."

"But if I remember rightly," said Poirot, "the ruby that is named 'Heart of Fire' is the center stone in a necklace."

"There you are! Didn't I tell you there is no end to the lies women will tell about their jewelry? This is a single stone, hung on a platinum chain round her neck; but, as I said before, ten to one it is a bit of colored glass."

"No," said Poirot gently; "no—somehow I do not think it is colored glass."

32

Katherine and Poirot Compare Notes

"You have changed, mademoiselle," said Poirot suddenly. He and Katherine were seated opposite each other at a small table at the Savoy.

"Yes, you have changed," he continued.

"In what way?"

"Mademoiselle, these nuances are difficult to express."

"I am older."

"Yes, you are older. And by that I do not mean that the wrinkles and the crow's-feet are coming. When I first saw you, mademoiselle, you were a looker-on at life. You had the quiet, amused look of one who sits back in the stalls and watches the play."

"And now?"

"Now, you no longer watch. It is an absurd thing, perhaps, that I say here, but you have the wary look of a fighter who is playing a difficult game."

"My old lady is difficult sometimes," said Katherine, with a smile; "but I can assure you that I don't engage in deadly contests with her. You must go down and see her someday, Monsieur Poirot. I think you are one of the people who would appreciate her pluck and her spirit."

There was a silence while the waiter deftly served them with chicken *en casserole*. When he had departed, Poirot said:

"You have heard me speak of my friend Hastings?—he who said that I was a human oyster. *Eh bien,* mademoiselle, I have met my match in you. You, far more than I, play a lone hand."

"Nonsense," said Katherine lightly.

"Never does Hercule Poirot talk nonsense. It is as I say."

Again there was a silence. Poirot broke it by inquiring:

"Have you seen any of our Riviera friends since you have been back, mademoiselle?"

"I have seen something of Major Knighton."

"A-ha! Is that so?"

Something in Poirot's twinkling eyes made Katherine lower hers.

"So Mr. Van Aldin remains in London?"

"Yes."

"I must try to see him tomorrow or the next day."

"You have news for him?"

"What makes you think that?"

"I—wondered, that is all."

Poirot looked across at her with twinkling eyes.

"And now, mademoiselle, there is much that you wish to ask me, I can see that. And why not? Is not the affair of the Blue Train our own *roman policier?*"

"Yes, there are things I should like to ask you."

"Eh bien?"

Katherine looked up with a sudden air of resolution.

"What were you doing in Paris, Monsieur Poirot?"

Poirot smiled slightly.

"I made a call at the Russian Embassy."

"Oh."

"I see that that tells you nothing. But I will not be a human oyster. No, I will lay my cards on the table, which is assuredly a thing that oysters do not do. You suspect, do you not, that I am not satisfied with the case against Derek Kettering?"

"That is what I have been wondering. I thought, in Nice, that you had finished with the case."

"You do not say all that you mean, mademoiselle. But I admit everything. It was I—my researches—which placed Derek Kettering where he is now. But for me the Examining Magistrate would still be vainly trying to fasten the crime on the Comte de la Roche. *Eh bien*, mademoiselle, what I have done I do not regret. I have only one duty—to discover the truth, and that way led straight to Mr. Kettering. But did it end there? The police say yes, but I, Hercule Poirot, am not satisfied."

He broke off suddenly. "Tell me, mademoiselle, have you heard from Mademoiselle Lenox lately?"

"One very short, scrappy letter. She is, I think, annoyed with me for coming back to England."

Poirot nodded.

"I had an interview with her the night that Monsieur Kettering was arrested. It was an interesting interview in more ways than one."

Again he fell silent, and Katherine did not interrupt his train of thought.

"Mademoiselle," he said at last, "I am now on delicate ground, yet I will say this to you. There is, I think, someone who loves Monsieur Kettering—correct me if I am wrong—and for her sake—well—for her sake I hope that I am right and the police are wrong. You know who that someone is?"

There was a pause, then Katherine said:

"Yes—I think I know."

Poirot leaned across the table towards her.

"I am not satisfied, mademoiselle; no, I am not satisfied. The facts, the main facts, led straight to Monsieur Kettering. But there is one thing that has been left out of account."

"And what is that?"

"The disfigured face of the victim. I have asked myself, mademoiselle, a hundred times, 'Was Derek Kettering the kind of man who would deal that smashing blow after having committed the murder?' What end would it serve? What purpose would it accomplish? Was it a likely action for one of Monsieur Kettering's temperament? And, mademoiselle, the answer to these questions is profoundly unsatisfactory. Again and again I go back to that one point—'why?' And the only things I have to help me to a solution of the problem are these."

He whipped out his pocketbook and extracted something from it which he held between his finger and thumb.

"Do you remember, mademoiselle? You saw me take these hairs from the rug in the railway carriage."

Katherine leaned forward, scrutinizing the hairs keenly.

Poirot nodded his head slowly several times.

"They suggest nothing to you, I see that, mademoiselle. And yet— I think somehow that you see a good deal."

"I have had ideas," said Katherine slowly, "curious ideas. That is why I ask you what you were doing in Paris, Monsieur Poirot."

"When I wrote to you—"

"From the Ritz?"

A curious smile came over Poirot's face.

"Yes, as you say, from the Ritz. I am a luxurious person some-times—when a millionaire pays."

"The Russian Embassy," said Katherine, frowning. "No, I don't see where that comes in."

"It does not come in directly, mademoiselle. I went there to get certain information. I saw a particular personage and I threatened him—yes, mademoiselle, I, Hercule Poirot, threatened him."

"With the police?"

"No," said Poirot dryly, "with the press—a much more deadly weapon."

He looked at Katherine and she smiled at him, just shaking her head.

"Are you not just turning back into an oyster again, Monsieur Poirot?"

"No, no! I do not wish to make mysteries. See, I will tell you everything. I suspect this man of being the active party in the sale of the jewels of Monsieur Van Aldin. I tax him with it, and in the end I get the whole story out of him. I learn where the jewels were handed over, and I learn, too, of the man who paced up and down outside in the street—a man with a venerable head of white hair, but who walked with the light, springy step of a young man—and I give that man a name in my own mind—the name of 'Monsieur le Marquis.'"

"And now you have come to London to see Mr. Van Aldin?"

"Not entirely for that reason. I had other work to do. Since I have been in London I have seen two more people—a theatrical agent and a Harley Street doctor. From each of them I have got certain information. Put these things together, mademoiselle, and see if you can make of them the same as I do."

"I?"

"Yes, you. I will tell you one thing, mademoiselle. There has been a doubt all along in my mind as to whether the robbery and the murder were done by the same person. For a long time I was not sure—"

"And now?"

"And now I *know*."

There was a silence. Then Katherine lifted her head. Her eyes were shining.

"I am not clever like you, Monsieur Poirot. Half the things that you have been telling me don't seem to me to point anywhere at all. The ideas that came to me came from such an entirely different angle—"

"Ah, but that is always so," said Poirot quietly. "A mirror shows the truth, but everyone stands in a different place for looking into the mirror."

"My ideas may be absurd—they may be entirely different from yours, but—"

"Yes?"

"Tell me, does this help you at all?"

He took a newspaper cutting from her outstretched hand. He read it and, looking up, he nodded gravely.

"As I told you, mademoiselle, one stands at a different angle for looking into the mirror, but it is the same mirror and the same things are reflected there."

Katherine got up. "I must rush," she said. "I have only just time to catch my train. Monsieur Poirot—"

"Yes, mademoiselle?"

"It—it mustn't be much longer, you understand. I—I can't go on much longer."

There was a break in her voice.

He patted her hand reassuringly.

"Courage, mademoiselle, you must not fail now; the end is very near."

33

A New Theory

"Monsieur Poirot wants to see you, sir."

"Damn the fellow!" said Van Aldin.

Knighton remained sympathetically silent.

Van Aldin got up from his chair and paced up and down.

"I suppose you have seen the cursed newspapers this morning?"

"I have glanced at them, sir."

"Still at it hammer and tongs?"

"I am afraid so, sir."

The millionaire sat down again and pressed his hand to his forehead.

"If I had had an idea of this," he groaned. "I wish to God I had never got that little Belgian to ferret out the truth. Find Ruth's murderer—that was all I thought about."

"You wouldn't have liked your son-in-law to go scot-free?"

Van Aldin sighed.

"I would have preferred to take the law into my own hands."

"I don't think that would have been a very wise proceeding, sir."

"All the same—are you sure the fellow wants to see me?"

"Yes, Mr. Van Aldin. He is very urgent about it."

"Then I suppose he will have to. He can come along this morning if he likes."

It was a very fresh and debonair Poirot who was ushered in. He did not seem to see any lack of cordiality in the millionaire's manner, and chatted pleasantly about various trifles. He was in London, he explained, to see his doctor. He mentioned the name of an eminent surgeon.

"No, no, *pas la guerre*—a memory of my days in the police force, a bullet of a rascally apache."

He touched his left shoulder and winced realistically.

"I always consider you a lucky man, Monsieur Van Aldin; you are not like our popular idea of American millionaires, martyrs to the dyspepsia."

"I am pretty tough," said Van Aldin. "I lead a very simple life, you know; plain fare and not too much of it."

"You have seen something of Miss Grey, have you not?" inquired Poirot, innocently turning to the secretary.

"I—yes; once or twice," said Knighton.

He blushed slightly and Van Aldin exclaimed in surprise:

"Funny you never mentioned to me that you had seen her, Knighton?"

"I didn't think you would be interested, sir."

"I like that girl very much," said Van Aldin.

"It is a thousand pities that she should have buried herself once more in St. Mary Mead," said Poirot.

"It is very fine of her," said Knighton hotly. "There are very few people who would bury themselves down there to look after a cantankerous old woman who has no earthly claim on her."

"I am silent," said Poirot, his eyes twinkling a little; "but all the same I say it is a pity. And now, messieurs, let us come to business."

Both the other men looked at him in some surprise.

"You must not be shocked or alarmed at what I am about to say. Supposing, Monsieur Van Aldin, that, after all, Monsieur Derek Kettering did not murder his wife?"

"What?"

Both men stared at him in blank surprise.

"Supposing, I say, that Monsieur Kettering did not murder his wife?"

"Are you mad, Monsieur Poirot?"

It was Van Aldin who spoke.

"No," said Poirot, "I am not mad. I am eccentric, perhaps—at least certain people say so; but as regards my profession, I am very much, as one says, 'all there.' I ask you, Monsieur Van Aldin, whether you would be glad or sorry if what I tell you should be the case?"

Van Aldin stared at him.

"Naturally I should be glad," he said at last. "Is this an exercise in suppositions, Monsieur Poirot, or are there any facts behind it?"

Poirot looked at the ceiling.

"There is an off chance," he said quietly, "that it might be the

Comte de la Roche after all. At least I have succeeded in upsetting his alibi."

"How did you manage that?"

Poirot shrugged his shoulders modestly.

"I have my own methods. The exercise of a little tact, a little cleverness—and the thing is done."

"But the rubies," said Van Aldin, "these rubies that the Count had in his possession were false."

"And clearly he would not have committed the crime except for the rubies. But you are overlooking one point, Monsieur Van Aldin. Where the rubies were concerned, someone might have been before him."

"But this is an entirely new theory," cried Knighton.

"Do you really believe all this rigmarole, Monsieur Poirot?" demanded the millionaire.

"The thing is not proved," said Poirot quietly. "It is as yet only a theory, but I tell you this, Monsieur Van Aldin, the facts are worth investigating. You must come out with me to the south of France and go into the case on the spot."

"You really think this is necessary—that I should go, I mean."

"I thought it would be what you yourself would wish," said Poirot.

There was a hint of reproach in his tone which was not lost upon the other.

"Yes, yes, of course," he said. "When do you wish to start, Monsieur Poirot?"

"You are very busy at present, sir," murmured Knighton.

But the millionaire had now made up his mind, and he waved the other's objections aside.

"I guess this business comes first," he said. "All right, Monsieur Poirot, tomorrow. What train?"

"We will go, I think, by the Blue Train," said Poirot, and he smiled.

34

The Blue Train Again

"THE MILLIONAIRE'S TRAIN," as it is sometimes called, swung round a curve of line at what seemed a dangerous speed. Van Aldin, Knighton, and Poirot sat together in silence. Knighton and Van Aldin had two compartments connecting with each other, as Ruth Kettering and her maid had had on the fateful journey. Poirot's own compartment was further along the coach.

The journey was a painful one for Van Aldin, recalling as it did the most agonizing memories. Poirot and Knighton conversed occasionally in low tones without disturbing him.

When, however, the train had completed its slow journey round the *ceinture* and reached the Gare de Lyon, Poirot became suddenly galvanized into activity. Van Aldin realized that part of his object in traveling by the train had been to attempt to reconstruct the crime. Poirot himself acted every part. He was in turn the maid, hurriedly shut into her own compartment, Mrs. Kettering, recognizing her husband with surprise and a trace of anxiety, and Derek Kettering discovering that his wife was traveling on the train. He tested various possibilities, such as the best way for a person to conceal himself in the second compartment.

Then suddenly an idea seemed to strike him. He clutched at Van Aldin's arm.

"*Mon Dieu*, but that is something I have not thought of! We must break our journey in Paris. Quick, quick, let us alight at once."

Seizing suitcases, he hurried from the train. Van Aldin and Knighton, bewildered but obedient, followed him. Van Aldin having once formed his opinion of Poirot's ability was slow to part from it. At the barrier they were held up. Their tickets were in charge of the conductor of the train, a fact which all three of them had forgotten.

Poirot's explanations were rapid, fluent, and impassioned, but they produced no effect upon the stolid-faced official.

"Let us get quit of this," said Van Aldin abruptly. "I gather you are in a hurry, Monsieur Poirot. For God's sake, pay the fares from Calais and let us get right on with whatever you have got in your mind."

But Poirot's flood of language had suddenly stopped dead, and he had the appearance of a man turned to stone. His arm, still outflung in an impassioned gesture, remained there as though stricken with paralysis.

"I have been an imbecile," he said simply. "*Ma foi*, I lose my head nowadays. Let us return and continue our journey quietly. With reasonable luck the train will not have gone."

They were only just in time, the train moving off as Knighton, the last of the three, swung himself and his suitcase on board.

The conductor remonstrated with them feelingly, and assisted them to carry their luggage back to their compartments. Van Aldin said nothing, but he was clearly disgusted at Poirot's extraordinary conduct. Alone with Knighton for a moment or two, he remarked:

"This is a wild-goose chase. The man has lost his grip on things. He has got brains up to a point, but any man who loses his head and scuttles round like a frightened rabbit is no earthly darned good."

Poirot came to them in a moment or two, full of abject apologies and clearly so crestfallen that harsh words would have been superfluous. Van Aldin received his apologies gravely, but managed to restrain himself from making acid comments.

They had dinner on the train, and afterwards, somewhat to the surprise of the other two, Poirot suggested that they should all three sit up in Van Aldin's compartment.

The millionaire looked at him curiously.

"Is there anything that you are keeping back from us, Monsieur Poirot?"

"I?" Poirot opened his eyes in innocent surprise. "But what an idea."

Van Aldin did not answer, but he was not satisfied. The conductor was told that he need not make up the beds. Any surprise he might have felt was obliterated by the largeness of the tip which Van Aldin handed to him. The three men sat in silence. Poirot fidgeted and seemed restless. Presently he turned to the secretary.

"Major Knighton, is the door of your compartment bolted? The door into the corridor, I mean."

"Yes; I bolted it myself just now."

"Are you sure?" said Poirot.

"I will go and make sure, if you like," said Knighton, smiling.

"No, no, do not derange yourself. I will see for myself."

He passed through the connecting door and returned in a second or two, nodding his head.

"Yes, yes, it is as you said. You must pardon an old man's fussy ways."

He closed the connecting door and resumed his place in the right-hand corner.

The hours passed. The three men dozed fitfully, waking with uncomfortable starts. Probably never before had three people booked berths on the most luxurious train available, then declined to avail themselves of the accommodation they had paid for. Every now and then Poirot glanced at his watch, and then nodded his head and composed himself to slumber once more. On one occasion he rose from his seat and opened the connecting door, peered sharply into the adjoining compartment, and then returned to his seat, shaking his head.

"What is the matter?" whispered Knighton. "You are expecting something to happen, aren't you?"

"I have the nerves," confessed Poirot. "I am like the cat upon the hot tiles. Every little noise it makes me jump."

Knighton yawned.

"Of all the darned uncomfortable journeys," he murmured. "I suppose you know what you are playing at, Monsieur Poirot."

He composed himself to sleep as best he could. Both he and Van Aldin had succumbed to slumber, when Poirot, glancing for the fourteenth time at his watch, leaned across and tapped the millionaire on the shoulder.

"Eh? What is it?"

"In five or ten minutes, monsieur, we shall arrive at Lyons."

"My God!" Van Aldin's face looked white and haggard in the dim light. "Then it must have been about this time that poor Ruth was killed."

He sat staring straight in front of him. His lips twitched a little, his mind reverting back to the terrible tragedy that had saddened his life.

There was the usual long screaming sigh of the brake, and the train slackened speed and drew into Lyons. Van Aldin let down the window and leaned out.

"If it wasn't Derek—if your new theory is correct, it is here that the man left the train?" he asked over his shoulder.

Rather to his surprise Poirot shook his head.

"No," he said thoughtfully, "no *man* left the train, but I think—yes, I think, a *woman* may have done so."

Knighton gave a gasp.

"A woman?" demanded Van Aldin sharply.

"Yes, a woman," said Poirot, nodding his head. "You may not remember, Monsieur Van Aldin, but Miss Grey in her evidence mentioned that a youth in a cap and overcoat descended onto the platform ostensibly to stretch his legs. Me, I think that that youth was most probably a woman."

"But who was she?"

Van Aldin's face expressed incredulity, but Poirot replied seriously and categorically:

"Her name—or the name under which she was known for many years—is Kitty Kidd, but you, Monsieur Van Aldin, knew her by another name—*that of Ada Mason.*"

Knighton sprang to his feet.

"What?" he cried.

Poirot swung round to him.

"Ah!—before I forget it." He whipped something from a pocket and held it out.

"Permit me to offer you a cigarette—out of your own cigarette case. It was careless of you to drop it when you boarded the train on the *ceinture* at Paris."

Knighton stood staring at him as though stupefied. Then he made a movement, but Poirot flung up his hand in a warning gesture.

"No, don't move," he said in a silky voice; "the door into the next compartment is open, and you are being covered from there this minute. I unbolted the door into the corridor when we left Paris, and our friends the police were told to take their places there. As I expect you know, the French police want you rather urgently, Major Knighton—or shall we say—Monsieur le Marquis?"

35

Explanations

"Explanations?"

Poirot smiled. He was sitting opposite the millionaire at a luncheon table in the latter's private suite at the Negresco. Facing him was a relieved but very puzzled man. Poirot leaned back in his chair, lit one of his tiny cigarettes, and stared reflectively at the ceiling.

"Yes, I will give you explanations. It began with the one point that puzzled me. You know what that point was? *The disfigured face.* It is not an uncommon thing to find when investigating a crime and it rouses an immediate question, the question of identity. That naturally was the first thing that occurred to me. Was the dead woman really Mrs. Kettering? But that line led me nowhere, for Miss Grey's evidence was positive and very reliable, so I put that idea aside. The dead woman *was* Ruth Kettering."

"When did you first begin to suspect the maid?"

"Not for some time, but one peculiar little point drew my attention to her. The cigarette case found in the railway carriage and which she told us was one which Mrs. Kettering had given to her husband. Now that was, on the face of it, most improbable, seeing the terms that they were on. It awakened a doubt in my mind as to the general veracity of Ada Mason's statements. There was the rather suspicious fact to be taken into consideration, that she had only been with her mistress for two months. Certainly it did not seem as if she could have had anything to do with the crime since she had been left behind in Paris and Mrs. Kettering had been seen alive by several people afterwards, but—"

Poirot leaned forward. He raised an emphatic forefinger and wagged it with intense emphasis at Van Aldin.

"But I am a good detective. I suspect. There is nobody and nothing that I do not suspect. I believe nothing that I am told. I say to myself: how do we know that Ada Mason was left behind in Paris? And at first the answer to that question seemed completely satisfactory. There was the evidence of your secretary, Major Knighton, a complete outsider whose testimony might be supposed to be entirely impartial, and there was the dead woman's own words to the conductor on the train. But I put the latter point aside for the moment, because a very curious idea—an idea perhaps fantastic and impossible—was growing up in my mind. If by any outside chance it happened to be true, that particular piece of testimony was worthless.

"I concentrated on the chief stumbling-block to my theory, Major Knighton's statement that he saw Ada Mason at the Ritz after the Blue Train had left Paris. That seemed conclusive enough, but yet, on examining the facts carefully, I noted two things. First, that by a curious coincidence he, too, had been exactly two months in your service. Secondly, his initial letter was the same—'K.' Supposing—just supposing—that it was *his* cigarette case which had been found in the carriage. Then, if Ada Mason and he were working together, and she recognized it when we showed it to her, would she not act precisely as she had done? At first, taken aback, she quickly evolved a plausible theory that would agree with Mr. Kettering's guilt. *Bien entendu*, that was not the original idea. The Comte de la Roche was to be the scapegoat, though Ada Mason would not make her recognition of him too certain, in case he should be able to prove an alibi. Now, if you will cast your mind back to that time, you will remember a significant thing that happened. I suggested to Ada Mason that the man she had seen was not the Comte de la Roche, but Derek Kettering. She seemed uncertain at the time, but after I had got back to my hotel you rang me up and told me that she had come to you and said that, on thinking it over, she was now quite convinced that the man in question *was* Mr. Kettering. I had been expecting something of the kind. There could be but one explanation of this sudden certainty on her part. After my leaving your hotel, she had had time to consult with somebody, and had received instructions which she acted upon. Who had given her these instructions? Major Knighton. And there was another very small point, which might mean nothing or might mean a great deal. In casual conversation Knighton had talked of a jewel robbery in Yorkshire in a house where he was staying. Perhaps a mere coincidence —perhaps another small link in the chain."

"But there is one thing I do not understand, Monsieur Poirot. I guess I must be dense or I would have seen it before now. Who was the man in the train at Paris? Derek Kettering or the Comte de la Roche?"

"That is the simplicity of the whole thing. *There was no man.* Ah—*mille tonnerres!*—do you not see the cleverness of it all? Whose word have we for it that there ever was a man there? Only Ada Mason's. And we believe in Ada Mason because of Knighton's evidence that she was left behind in Paris."

"But Ruth herself told the conductor that she had left her maid behind there," demurred Van Aldin.

"Ah! I am coming to that. We have Mrs. Kettering's own evidence there, but, on the other hand, we have not really got her evidence, because, Monsieur Van Aldin, a dead woman cannot give evidence. It is not *her* evidence, but the evidence of the conductor of the train—a very different affair altogether."

"So you think the man was lying?"

"No, no, not at all. He spoke what he thought to be the truth. But the woman who told him that she had left her maid in Paris was not Mrs. Kettering."

Van Aldin stared at him.

"Monsieur Van Aldin, Ruth Kettering was dead before the train arrived at the Gare de Lyon. It was Ada Mason, dressed in her mistress's very distinctive clothing, who purchased a dinner basket and who made that very necessary statement to the conductor."

"Impossible!"

"No, no, Monsieur Van Aldin; not impossible. *Les femmes,* they look so much alike nowadays that one identifies them more by their clothing than by their faces. Ada Mason was the same height as your daughter. Dressed in that very sumptuous fur coat and the little red lacquer hat jammed down over her eyes, with just a bunch of auburn curls showing over each ear, it was no wonder that the conductor was deceived. He had not previously spoken to Mrs. Kettering, you remember. True, he had seen the maid just for a moment when she handed him the tickets, but his impression had been merely that of a gaunt, black-clad female. If he had been an unusually intelligent man, he might have gone so far as to say that mistress and maid were not unlike, but it is extremely unlikely that he would even think that. And remember, Ada Mason, or Kitty Kidd, was an actress, able to change her appearance and tone of voice at a moment's notice. No, no; there was no danger of his recognizing the maid in the mistress's clothing, but there *was* the danger that when he came to discover the body he might realize it was not the woman he had talked to the night before. And now we see the reason for the disfigured face. The chief danger that Ada Mason ran was that Katherine Grey might visit her compartment after the train left Paris, and she provided against that difficulty by ordering a dinner basket and by locking herself in her compartment."

"But who killed Ruth—and when?"

"First, bear it in mind that the crime was planned and undertaken by the two of them—Knighton and Ada Mason, working together. Knighton was in Paris that day on your business. He boarded the train somewhere on its way round the *ceinture*. Mrs. Kettering would be surprised, but she would be quite unsuspicious. Perhaps he draws her attention to something out the window, and as she turns to look he slips the cord round her neck—and the whole thing is over in a second or two. The door of the compartment is locked, and he and Ada Mason set to work. They strip off the dead woman's outer clothes. Mason and Knighton roll the body up in a rug and put it on the seat in the adjoining compartment among the bags and suitcases. Knighton drops off the train, taking the jewel case containing the rubies with him. Since the crime is not supposed to have been committed until nearly twelve hours later, he is perfectly safe, and his evidence and the supposed Mrs. Kettering's words to the conductor will provide a perfect alibi for his accomplice.

"At the Gare de Lyon Ada Mason gets a dinner basket, and shutting herself into the toilet compartment she quickly changes into her mistress's clothes, adjusts two false bunches of auburn curls, and generally makes up to resemble her as closely as possible. When the conductor comes to make up the bed, she tells him the prepared story about having left her maid behind in Paris; and while he is making up the berth, she stands looking out of the window, so that her back is towards the corridor and people passing along there. That was a wise precaution, because, as we know, Miss Grey was one of those passing, and she, among others, was willing to swear that Mrs. Kettering was still alive at that hour."

"Go on," said Van Aldin.

"Before getting to Lyons, Ada Mason arranged her mistress's body in the bunk, folded up the dead woman's clothes neatly on the end of it, and herself changed into a man's clothes and prepared to leave the train. When Derek Kettering entered his wife's compartment, and, as he thought, saw her asleep in her berth, the scene had been set, and Ada Mason was hidden in the next compartment waiting for the moment to leave the train unobserved. As soon as the conductor had swung himself down onto the platform at Lyons, she follows, slouching along as though just taking a breath of air. At a moment when she is unobserved, she hurriedly crosses to the other platform and takes the first train back to Paris and the Ritz Hotel. Her name has been registered there as taking a room the night before by one of Knighton's female accomplices. She has nothing to do but wait there placidly for your arrival. The jewels are not, and never have been, in her possession. No suspicion attaches to him, and, as your secretary, he brings them to Nice without the least fear of discovery. Their delivery there to Monsieur Papopolous is already arranged for and they are entrusted to Mason at the last moment to hand over to the Greek. Altogether a very neatly planned coup, as one would expect from a master of the game such as the Marquis."

"And you honestly mean that Richard Knighton is a well-known criminal, who has been at this business for years?"

Poirot nodded.

"One of the chief assets of the gentleman called the Marquis was his plausible, ingratiating manner. You fell a victim to his charm, Monsieur Van Aldin, when you engaged him as a secretary on such a slight acquaintanceship."

"I could have sworn that he never angled for the post," cried the millionaire.

"It was very astutely done—so astutely done that it deceived a man whose knowledge of other men is as great as yours is."

"I looked up his antecedents too. The fellow's record was excellent."

"Yes, yes; that was part of the game. As Richard Knighton his life was quite free from reproach. He was well-born, well-connected, did honorable service in the war, and seemed altogether above suspicion; but when I came to glean information about the mysterious Marquis, I found many points of similarity. Knighton spoke French like a Frenchman, he had been in America, France, and England at much the same time as the Marquis was operating. The Marquis was last heard of as engineering various jewel robberies in Switzerland, and it was in Switzerland that you had come across Major Knighton; and it was at precisely that time that the first rumors were going round of your being in treaty for the famous rubies."

"But why murder?" murmured Van Aldin brokenly. "Surely a clever thief could have stolen the jewels without running his head into a noose."

Poirot shook his head. "This is not the first murder that lies to the Marquis's charge. He is a killer by instinct; he believes, too, in leaving no evidence behind him. Dead men and women tell no tales.

"The Marquis had an intense passion for famous and historical jewels. He laid his plans far beforehand by installing himself as your secretary and getting his accomplice to obtain the situation of maid with your daughter, for whom he guessed the jewels were destined. And, though this was his matured and carefully thought-out plan, he did not scruple to attempt a short-cut by hiring a couple of apaches to waylay you in Paris on the night you bought the jewels. That plan failed, which hardly surprised him, I think. This plan was, so he thought, completely safe. No possible suspicion could attach to Richard Knighton. But like all great men—and the Marquis was a great man—he had his weaknesses. He fell genuinely in love with Miss Grey, and suspecting her liking for Derek Kettering, he could not resist the temptation to saddle him with the crime when the opportunity presented itself. And now, Monsieur Van Aldin, I am going to tell you something very curious. Miss Grey is not a fanciful woman by any means, yet she firmly believes that she felt your daughter's presence beside her one day in the casino gardens at Monte Carlo, just after she had been having a long talk with Knighton. She was convinced, she says, that the dead woman was urgently trying to tell her something, and it suddenly came to her that what the dead woman was trying to say was that Knighton was her murderer! The idea seemed so fantastic at the time that Miss Grey spoke of it to no one. But she was so convinced of its truth that she acted on it—wild as it seemed. She did not discourage Knighton's advances, and she pretended to him that she was convinced of Derek Kettering's guilt."

"Extraordinary," said Van Aldin.

"Yes, it is very strange. One cannot explain these things. Oh, by the way, there is one little point that baffled me considerably. Your secretary has a decided limp—the result of a wound that he received in the war. Now the Marquis most decidedly did not limp. That was a stumbling-block. But Miss Lenox Tamplin happened to mention one day that Knighton's limp had been a surprise to the surgeons who had been in charge of the case in her mother's hospital. That suggested camouflage. When I was in London I went to the surgeon in question, and I got several technical details from him which confirmed me in that belief. I mentioned the name of that surgeon in Knighton's hearing the day before yesterday. The natural thing would have been for Knighton to mention that he had been attended by him during the war, but he said nothing—and that little point, if nothing else, gave me the last final assurance that my theory of the crime was correct. Miss Grey, too, provided me with a cutting, showing that there had been a robbery at Lady Tamplin's hospital during the time that Knighton had been there. She realized that I was on the same track as herself when I wrote to her from the Ritz in Paris.

"I had some trouble in my inquiries there, but I got what I wanted—evidence that Ada Mason arrived on the morning after the crime and not on the evening of the day before."

There was a long silence, then the millionaire stretched out a hand to Poirot across the table.

"I guess you know what this means to me, Monsieur Poirot," he said huskily. "I am sending you round a check in the morning, but no check in the world will express what I feel about what you have done for me. You are the goods, Monsieur Poirot. Every time, you are the goods."

Poirot rose to his feet; his chest swelled.

"I am only Hercule Poirot," he said modestly, "yet, as you say, in my own way I am a big man, even as you also are a big man. I am glad and happy to have been of service to you. Now I go to repair the damages caused by travel. Alas! my excellent Georges is not with me."

In the lounge of the hotel he encountered a friend—the venerable Monsieur Papopolous, his daughter Zia beside him.

"I thought you had left Nice, Monsieur Poirot," murmured the Greek as he took the detective's affectionately proffered hand.

"Business compelled me to return, my dear Monsieur Papopolous."

"Business?"

"Yes, business. And talking of business, I hope your health is better, my dear friend?"

"Much better. In fact, we are returning to Paris tomorrow."

"I am enchanted to hear such good news. You have not completely ruined the Greek ex-Minister, I hope."

"I?"

"I understand you sold him a very wonderful ruby which—strictly *entre nous*—is being worn by Mademoiselle Mirelle, the dancer?"

"Yes," murmured Monsieur Papopolous; "yes, that is so."

"A ruby not unlike the famous 'Heart of Fire.'"

"It has points of resemblance, certainly," said the Greek casually.

"You have a wonderful hand with jewels, Monsieur Papopolous. I congratulate you. Mademoiselle Zia, I am desolate that you are returning to Paris so speedily. I had hoped to see some more of you now that my business is accomplished."

"Would one be indiscreet if one asked what that business was?" asked Monsieur Papopolous.

"Not at all, not at all. I have just succeeded in laying the Marquis by the heels."

A faraway look came over Monsieur Papopolous' noble countenance.

"The Marquis?" he murmured. "Now why does that seem familiar to me? No—I cannot recall it."

"You would not, I am sure," said Poirot. "I refer to a very notable criminal and jewel robber. He has just been arrested for the murder of the English lady, Madame Kettering."

"Indeed? How interesting these things are!"

A polite exchange of farewells followed, and when Poirot was out of earshot, Monsieur Papopolous turned to his daughter.

"Zia," he said, with feeling, "that man is the devil!"

"I like him."

"I like him myself," admitted Monsieur Papopolous. "But he is the devil, all the same."

36

By the Sea

THE mimosa was nearly over. The scent of it in the air was faintly unpleasant. There were pink geraniums twining along the balustrade of Lady Tamplin's villa, and masses of carnations below sent up a sweet, heavy perfume. The Mediterranean was at its bluest. Poirot sat on the terrace with Lenox Tamplin. He had just finished telling her the same story he had told to Van Aldin two days before. Lenox had listened to him with absorbed attention, her brows knitted and her eyes somber.

When he had finished, she said simply:

"And Derek?"

"He was released yesterday."

"And he has gone—where?"

"He left Nice last night."

"For St. Mary Mead?"

"Yes, for St. Mary Mead."

There was a pause.

"I was wrong about Katherine," said Lenox. "I thought she did not care."

"She is very reserved. She trusts no one."

"She might have trusted me," said Lenox, with a shade of bitterness.

"Yes," said Poirot gravely, "she might have trusted you. But Mademoiselle Katherine has spent a great deal of her life listening, and those who have listened do not find it easy to talk; they keep their sorrows and joys to themselves and tell no one."

"I was a fool," said Lenox; "I thought she really cared for Knighton. I ought to have known better. I suppose I thought so because—well, I hoped so."

Poirot took her hand and gave it a little friendly squeeze. "Courage, mademoiselle," he said gently.

Lenox looked very straight out across the sea, and her face, in its ugly rigidity, had for the moment a tragic beauty.

"Oh, well," she said at last, "it would not have done. I am too young for Derek; he is like a kid that has never grown up. He wants the Madonna touch."

There was a long silence, then Lenox turned to him quickly and impulsively. "But I *did* help, Monsieur Poirot—at any rate I did help."

"Yes, mademoiselle. It was you who gave me the first inkling of the truth when you said that the person who committed the crime need not have been on the train at all. Before that, I could not see how the thing had been done."

Lenox drew a deep breath.

"I am glad," she said; "at any rate—that is something."

From far behind them there came a long-drawn-out scream of an engine's whistle.

"That is that damned Blue Train," said Lenox. "Trains are relentless things, aren't they, Monsieur Poirot? People are murdered and die, but they go on just the same. I am talking nonsense, but you know what I mean."

"Yes, yes, I know. Life is like a train, mademoiselle. It goes on. And it is a good thing that that is so."

"Why?"

"Because the train gets to its journey's end at last, and there is a proverb about that in your language, mademoiselle."

"'Journeys end in lovers meeting.'" Lenox laughed. "That is not going to be true for me."

"Yes—yes, it is true. You are young, younger than you yourself know. Trust the train, mademoiselle, for it is *le bon Dieu* who drives it."

The whistle of the engine came again.

"Trust the train, mademoiselle," murmured Poirot again. "And trust Hercule Poirot. He knows."

What Mrs. McGillicuddy Saw!

1

Mrs. McGillicuddy panted along the platform in the wake of the porter carrying her suitcase. Mrs. McGillicuddy was short and stout, the porter was tall and free-striding. In addition, Mrs. McGillicuddy was burdened with a large quantity of parcels; the result of a day's Christmas shopping. The race was, therefore, an uneven one, and the porter turned the corner at the end of the platform while Mrs. McGillicuddy was still coming up the straight.

No. 1 platform was not at the moment unduly crowded, since a train had just gone out; but, in the no man's land beyond, a milling crowd was rushing in several directions at once, to and from undergrounds, left-luggage offices, tea rooms, inquiry offices, indicator boards and the two outlets, Arrival and Departure, to the outside world.

Mrs. McGillicuddy and her parcels were buffeted to and fro, but she arrived eventually at the entrance to No. 3 platform, and deposited one parcel at her feet while she searched her bag for the ticket that would enable her to pass the stern, uniformed guardian at the gate.

At that moment, a voice, raucous yet refined, burst into speech over her head.

"The train standing at Platform Three," the voice told her, "is the four fifty-four for Brackhampton, Milchester, Waverton, Carvil Junction, Roxeter and stations to Chadmouth. Passengers for Brackhampton and Milchester travel at the rear of the train. Passengers for Vanequay change at Roxeter." The voice shut itself off with a click, and then reopened conversation by announcing the arrival at Platform 9 of the 4:35 from Birmingham and Wolverhampton.

Mrs. McGillicuddy found her ticket and presented it. The man clipped it, murmured: "On the right—rear portion."

Mrs. McGillicuddy padded up the platform and found her porter, looking bored and staring into space, outside the door of a third-class carriage.

"Here you are, lady."

"I'm traveling first class," said Mrs. McGillicuddy.

"You didn't say so," grumbled the porter. His eye swept her masculine-looking pepper-and-salt tweed coat disparagingly.

Mrs. McGillicuddy who had said so, did not argue the point. She was sadly out of breath.

The porter retrieved the suitcase and marched with it to the adjoining coach where Mrs. McGillicuddy was installed in solitary splendor. The 4:54 was not much patronized, the first-class clientele preferring either the faster morning express or the 6:40 with dining cars. Mrs. McGillicuddy handed the porter his tip which he received with disappointment, clearly considering it more applicable to third-class than to first-class travel. Mrs. McGillicuddy, though prepared to spend money on comfortable travel after a night journey from the North and a day's feverish shopping, was at no time an extravagant tipper.

She settled herself back on the plush cushions with a sigh and opened a magazine. Five minutes later, whistles blew and the train started. The magazine slipped from Mrs. McGillicuddy's hand, her head dropped sideways, three minutes later she was asleep. She slept for thirty-five minutes and awoke refreshed. Resettling her hat which had slipped askew, she sat up and looked out of the window at what she could see of the flying countryside. It was quite dark now, a dreary, misty December day—Christmas was only five days ahead. London had been dark and dreary; the country was no less so, though occasionally rendered cheerful with its constant clusters of lights as the train flashed through towns and stations.

"Serving last tea now," said an attendant, whisking open the corridor door like a jinni. Mrs. McGillicuddy had already partaken of tea at a large department store. She was for the moment amply nourished. The attendant went on down the corridor uttering his monotonous cry. With a pleased expression, Mrs. McGillicuddy looked up at the rack where her various parcels reposed. The face towels had been excellent value and just what Margaret wanted, the space gun for Robby and the rabbit for Jean were highly satisfactory, and that evening coatee was just the thing she herself wanted, warm but dressy. The pullover for Hector, too . . . her mind dwelt with approval on the soundness of her purchases.

Her satisfied gaze returned to the window, a train traveling in the opposite direction rushed by with a screech, making the windows rattle and causing her to start. The train clattered over points and passed through a station.

Then it began suddenly to slow down, presumably in obedience to a signal. For some minutes it crawled along, then stopped, presently it began to move forward again. Another up train passed them, though with less vehemence than the first one. The train gathered speed again. At that moment another train, also on a down line, swerved inward toward them, for a moment with almost alarming effect. For a time the two trains ran parallel, now one gaining a little, now the other. Mrs. McGillicuddy looked from her window through the windows of the parallel carriages. Most of the blinds were down, but occasionally the occupants of the carriages were visible. The other train was not very full and there were many empty carriages.

At the moment when the two trains gave the illusion of being stationary, a blind in one of the carriages flew up with a snap. Mrs. McGillicuddy looked into the lighted first-class carriage that was only a few feet away.

Then she drew her breath in with a gasp and half rose to her feet.

Standing with his back to the window and to her was a man. His hands were round the throat of a woman who faced him, and he was slowly, remorselessly, strangling her. Her eyes were starting from their sockets, her face was purple and congested. As Mrs. McGillicuddy watched, fascinated, the end came, the body went limp and crumpled in the man's hands.

At the same moment, Mrs. McGillicuddy's train slowed down again and the other began to gain speed. It passed forward and a moment or two later it had vanished from sight.

Almost automatically Mrs. McGillicuddy's hand went up to the communication cord, then paused, irresolute. After all, what use would it be ringing the cord of the train in which she was traveling? The horror of what she had seen at such close quarters and the unusual circumstances made her feel paralyzed. Some immediate action was necessary—but what?

The door of her compartment was drawn back and a ticket collector said, "Ticket, please."

Mrs. McGillicuddy turned to him with vehemence.

"A woman has been strangled," she said. "In a train that has just passed. I saw it."

The ticket collector looked at her doubtfully.

"I beg your pardon, madam?"

"A man strangled a woman! In a train. I saw it—through there." She pointed to the window.

The ticket collector looked extremely doubtful.

"Strangled?" he said disbelievingly.

"Yes, strangled! I saw it, I tell you. You must do something at once!"

The ticket collector coughed apologetically.

"You don't think, madam, that you may have had a little nap and —er—" he broke off tactfully.

"I have had a nap, but if you think this was a dream, you're quite wrong. I saw it, I tell you."

The ticket collector's eyes dropped to the open magazine lying on the seat. On the exposed page was a girl being strangled while a man with a revolver threatened the pair from an open doorway.

He said persuasively: "Now don't you think, madam, that you'd been reading an exciting story, and that you just dropped off, and awaking a little confused—"

Mrs. McGillicuddy interrupted him.

"I saw it," she said. "I was as wide awake as you are. And I looked out of the window into the window of the train alongside, and a man was strangling a woman. And what I want to know is, what are you going to do about it?"

"Well—madam—"

"You're going to do something, I suppose?"

The ticket collector sighed reluctantly and glanced at his watch.

"We shall be in Brackhampton in exactly seven minutes. I'll report what you've told me. In what direction was the train you mention going?"

"This direction, of course. You don't suppose I'd have been able to see all this if a train had flashed past going in the other direction?"

The ticket collector looked as though he thought Mrs. McGillicuddy was quite capable of seeing anything anywhere as the fancy took her. But he remained polite.

"You can rely on me, madam," he said. "I will report your statement. Perhaps I might have your name and address—just in case—"

Mrs. McGillicuddy gave him the address where she would be staying for the next few days and her permanent address in Scotland, and he wrote them down. Then he withdrew with the air of a man who has done his duty and dealt successfully with a tiresome member of the traveling public.

Mrs. McGillicuddy remained frowning and vaguely unsatisfied. Would the ticket collector really report her statement? Or had he just been soothing her down? There were, she supposed vaguely, a lot of elderly women traveling around, fully convinced that they had unmasked Communist plots, were in danger of being murdered, saw flying saucers and secret spaceships, and reported murders that had never taken place. If the man dismissed her as one of those . . .

The train was slowing down now, passing over points, and running through the bright lights of a large town.

Mrs. McGillicuddy opened her handbag, pulled out a receipted bill which was all she could find, wrote a rapid note on the back of it with her ball-point pen, put it into a spare envelope that she fortunately happened to have, stuck the envelope down and wrote on it.

The train drew slowly into a crowded platform. The usual ubiquitous voice was intoning:

"The train now arriving at Platform One is the five thirty-eight for Milchester, Waverton, Roxeter and stations to Chadmouth. Passengers for Market Basing take the train now waiting at Number Three platform. Number One Bay for stopping train to Carbury."

Mrs. McGillicuddy looked anxiously along the platform. So many passengers and so few porters. Ah, there was one! She hailed him authoritatively.

"Porter! Please take this at once to the stationmaster's office."

She handed him the envelope and with it a shilling.

Then, with a sigh, she leaned back. Well, she had done what she could. Her mind lingered with an instant's regret on the shilling. Sixpence would really have been enough . . .

Her mind went back to the scene she had witnessed. Horrible, quite horrible. She was a strong-nerved woman, but she shivered. What a strange—what a fantastic thing to happen to her, Elspeth McGillicuddy. If the blind of the carriage had not happened to fly up . . . But that, of course, was Providence.

Providence had willed that she, Elspeth McGillicuddy, should be a witness of the crime. Her lips set grimly.

Voices shouted, whistles blew, doors were banged shut. The 5:38 drew slowly out of Brackhampton Station. An hour and five minutes later it stopped at Milchester.

Mrs. McGillicuddy collected her parcels and her suitcase and got out. She peered up and down the platform. Her mind reiterated its former judgment: not enough porters. Such porters as there were seemed to be engaged with mailbags and luggage vans. Passengers nowadays seemed always expected to carry their own cases. Well, she couldn't carry her suitcase and her umbrella and all her parcels. She would have to wait. In due course she secured a porter.

"Taxi?"

"There will be something to meet me, I expect."

Outside Milchester Station, a taxi driver who had been watching the exit came forward. He spoke in a soft local voice.

"Is it Mrs. McGillicuddy? For St. Mary Mead?"

Mrs. McGillicuddy acknowledged her identity. The porter was recompensed, adequately if not handsomely. The car, with Mrs. McGillicuddy, her suitcase and her parcels, drove off into the night. It was a nine-mile drive. Sitting bolt upright in the car, Mrs. McGillicuddy was unable to relax. Her feelings yearned for expression. At last the taxi drove along the familiar village street and finally drew up at its destination; Mrs. McGillicuddy got out and walked up the brick path to the door. The driver deposited the cases inside as the door was opened by an elderly maid. Mrs. McGillicuddy passed straight through the hall to where, at the open sitting-room door, her hostess awaited her: an elderly, frail old lady.

"Elspeth!"

"Jane!"

They kissed, and without preamble or circumlocution, Mrs. McGillicuddy burst into speech.

"Oh, Jane!" she wailed. "I've just seen a murder!"

2

TRUE to the precepts handed down to her by her mother and grand-mother—to wit: that a true lady can neither be shocked nor surprised—Miss Marple merely raised her eyebrows and shook her head, as she said:

"Most distressing for you, Elspeth, and surely most unusual. I think you had better tell me about it at once."

That was exactly what Mrs. McGillicuddy wanted to do. Allowing her hostess to draw her nearer to the fire, she sat down, pulled off her gloves and plunged into a vivid narrative.

Miss Marple listened with close attention. When Mrs. McGillicuddy at last paused for breath, Miss Marple spoke with decision.

"The best thing, I think, my dear, is for you to go upstairs and take off your hat and have a wash. Then we will have supper—during which we will not discuss this at all. After supper we can go into the matter thoroughly and discuss it from every aspect."

Mrs. McGillicuddy concurred with this suggestion. The two ladies had supper, discussing as they ate various aspects of life as lived in the village of St. Mary Mead. Miss Marple commented on the general distrust of the new organist, related the recent scandal about the chemist's wife, and touched on the hostility between the schoolmistress and the Village Institute. They then discussed Miss Marple's and Mrs. McGillicuddy's gardens.

"Peonies," said Miss Marple as she rose from table, "are most unaccountable. Either they do—or they don't do. But if they do establish themselves, they are with you for life, so to speak, and really most beautiful varieties nowadays."

They settled themselves by the fire again, and Miss Marple brought out two old Waterford glasses from a corner cupboard, and from another cupboard produced a bottle.

"No coffee tonight for you, Elspeth," she said. "You are already overexcited—and no wonder!—and probably would not sleep. I prescribe a glass of my cowslip wine, and later, perhaps, a cup of camomile tea."

Mrs. McGillicuddy acquiescing in these arrangements, Miss Marple poured out the wine.

"Jane," said Mrs. McGillicuddy, as she took an appreciative sip, "you don't think, do you, that I dreamed it, or imagined it?"

"Certainly not," said Miss Marple with warmth.

Mrs. McGillicuddy heaved a sigh of relief.

"That ticket collector," she said, "he thought so. Quite polite, but all the same—"

"I think, Elspeth, that that was quite natural under the circumstances. It sounded—and indeed was—a most unlikely story. And you were a complete stranger to him. No, I have no doubt at all that you saw what you've told me you saw. It's very extraordinary —but not at all impossible. I recollect myself being interested, when a train ran parallel to one in which I was traveling, to notice what a vivid and intimate picture one got of what was going on in one or two of the carriages. A little girl, I remember once, was playing with a teddy bear and suddenly she threw it deliberately at a fat man who was asleep in the corner, and he bounced up and looked most indignant, and the other passengers looked so amused. I saw them all quite vividly. I could have described afterward exactly what they looked like and what they had on."

Mrs. McGillicuddy nodded gratefully.

"That's just how it was."

"The man had his back to you, you say. So you didn't see his face?"

"No."

"And the woman, you can describe her? Young? Old?"

"Youngish. Between thirty and thirty-five, I should think. I couldn't say closer than that."

"Good-looking?"

"That again, I couldn't say. Her face, you see, was all contorted and—"

Miss Marple said quickly:

"Yes, yes, I quite understand. How was she dressed?"

"She had on a fur coat of some kind, a palish fur. No hat. Her hair was blonde."

"And there was nothing distinctive that you can remember about the man?"

Mrs. McGillicuddy took a little time to think carefully before she replied.

"He was tallish—and dark, I think. He had a heavy coat on so that I couldn't judge his build very well." She added despondently, "It's not really very much to go on."

"It's something," said Miss Marple. She paused before saying: "You feel quite sure, in your own mind, that the girl was—dead?"

"She was dead, I'm sure of it. Her tongue came out and—I'd rather not talk about it . . ."

"Of course not. Of course not," said Miss Marple quickly. "We shall know more, I expect, in the morning."

"In the morning?"

"I should imagine it will be in the morning papers. After this man had attacked and killed her, he would have a body on his hands. What would he do? Presumably he would leave the train quickly at the first station—by the way, can you remember if it was a corridor carriage?"

"No, it was not."

"That seems to point to a train that was not going far afield. It would almost certainly stop at Brackhampton. Let us say he leaves the train at Brackhampton, perhaps arranging the body in a corner seat, with the face hidden by the fur collar to delay discovery. Yes— I think that that is what he would do. But of course it will be discovered before very long—and I should imagine that the news of a murdered woman discovered on a train would be almost certain to be in the morning papers. We shall see."

II

But it was not in the morning papers.

Miss Marple and Mrs. McGillicuddy, after making sure of this, finished their breakfast in silence. Both were reflecting.

After breakfast, they took a turn round the garden. But this, usually an absorbing pastime, was today somewhat halfhearted. Miss Marple did indeed call attention to some new and rare species she had acquired for her rock garden but did so in an almost absent-minded manner. And Mrs. McGillicuddy did not, as was customary, counterattack with a list of her own recent acquisitions.

"The garden is not looking at all as it should," said Miss Marple, but still speaking absent-mindedly. "Doctor Haydock has absolutely forbidden me to do any stooping or kneeling—and really, what can you do if you don't stoop or kneel? There's old Edwards, of course —but so opinionated. And all this jobbing gets them into bad habits, lots of cups of tea and so much pottering—not any real work."

"Oh I know," said Mrs. McGillicuddy. "Of course there's no question of my being forbidden to stoop, but really, especially after meals—and having put on weight"—she looked down at her ample proportions—"it does bring on heartburn."

There was a silence and then Mrs. McGillicuddy planted her feet sturdily, stood still, and turned on her friend.

"Well?" she said.

It was a small, insignificant word but it acquired full significance from Mrs. McGillicuddy's tone, and Miss Marple understood its meaning perfectly.

"I know," she said.

The two ladies looked at each other.

"I think," said Miss Marple, "we might walk down to the police station and talk to Sergeant Cornish. He's intelligent and patient, and I know him very well and he knows me. I think he'll listen—and pass the information on to the proper quarter."

Accordingly some three quarters of an hour later, Miss Marple and Mrs. McGillicuddy were talking to a fresh-faced, grave man between thirty and forty who listened attentively to what they had to say.

Frank Cornish received Miss Marple with cordiality and even deference. He set chairs for the two ladies and said: "Now, what can we do for you, Miss Marple?"

Miss Marple said: "I would like you, please, to listen to my friend Mrs. McGillicuddy's story."

And Sergeant Cornish had listened. At the close of the recital he remained silent for a moment or two.

Then he said:

"That's a very extraordinary story." His eyes, without seeming to do so, had sized Mrs. McGillicuddy up while she was telling it.

On the whole, he was favorably impressed. A sensible woman, able to tell a story clearly; not, so far as he could judge, an over-imaginative or a hysterical woman. Moreover, Miss Marple, so it seemed, believed in the accuracy of her friend's story and he knew all about Miss Marple. Everybody in St. Mary Mead knew Miss Marple; fluffy and dithery in appearance, but inwardly as sharp and as shrewd as they make them.

He cleared his throat and spoke.

"Of course," he said, "you may have been mistaken—I'm not saying you were, mind—but you may have been. There's a lot of horseplay goes on. It mayn't have been serious or fatal."

"I know what I saw," said Mrs. McGillicuddy grimly.

"And you won't budge from it," thought Frank Cornish, "and I'd say that likely or unlikely, you may be right."

Aloud he said: "You reported it to the railway officials, and you've come and reported it to me. That's the proper procedure and you may rely on me to have inquiries instituted."

He stopped. Miss Marple nodded her head gently, satisfied. Mrs. McGillicuddy was not quite so satisfied, but she did not say anything. Sergeant Cornish addressed Miss Marple, not so much because he wanted her ideas, as because he wanted to hear what she would say.

"Granted the facts are as reported," he said. "What do you think has happened to the body?"

"There seem to be only two possibilities," said Miss Marple without hesitation. "The more likely one, of course, is that the body was left in the train, but that seems improbable now, for it would have been found sometime last night by another traveler or by the railway staff at the train's ultimate destination."

Frank Cornish nodded.

"The only other course open to the murderer would be to push the body out of the train on to the line. It must, I suppose, be still on the track somewhere as yet undiscovered—though that does seem a little unlikely. But there would be, as far as I can see, no other way of dealing with it."

"You read about bodies being put in trunks," said Mrs. McGillicuddy, "but no one travels with trunks nowadays, only suitcases, and you couldn't get a body into a suitcase."

"Yes," said Cornish. "I agree with you both. The body, if there is a body, ought to have been discovered by now, or will be very soon. I'll let you know any developments there are—though I daresay you'll read about them in the papers. There's the possibility, of course, that the woman, though savagely attacked, was not actually dead. She may have been able to leave the train on her own feet."

"Hardly without assistance," said Miss Marple. "And if so, it will have been noticed. A man, supporting a woman whom he says is ill."

"Yes, it will have been noticed," said Cornish. "Or if a woman was found unconscious or ill in a carriage and was removed to a hospital, that, too, will be on record. I think you may rest assured that you'll hear about it all in a very short time."

But that day passed and the next day. On that evening Miss Marple received a note from Sergeant Cornish.

In regard to the matter on which you consulted me, full inquiries have been made, with no result. No woman's body has been found. No hospital has administered treatment to a woman such as you describe, and no case of a woman suffering from shock or taken ill, or leaving a station supported by a man has been observed. You may take it that the fullest inquiries have been made. I suggest that your friend may have witnessed a scene such as she described but that it was much less serious than she supposed.

"LESS SERIOUS? Fiddlesticks!" said Mrs. McGillicuddy. "It was murder!"

She looked defiantly at Miss Marple and Miss Marple looked back at her.

"Go on, Jane," said Mrs. McGillicuddy. "Say it was all a mistake! Say I imagined the whole thing! That's what you think now, isn't it?"

"Anyone can be mistaken," Miss Marple pointed out gently. "Anybody, Elspeth, even you. I think we must bear that in mind. But I still think, you know, that you were most probably not mistaken. You use glasses for reading, but you've got very good far sight—and what you saw impressed you very powerfully. You were definitely suffering from shock when you arrived here."

"It's a thing I shall never forget," said Mrs. McGillicuddy with a shudder. "The trouble is, I don't see what I can do about it!"

"I don't think," said Miss Marple thoughtfully, "that there's anything more you can do about it." (If Mrs. McGillicuddy had been alert to the tones of her friend's voice, she might have noticed a very faint stress laid on the *you.*) "You've reported what you saw—to the railway people and to the police. No, there's nothing more you can do."

"That's a relief, in a way," said Mrs. McGillicuddy, "because, as you know, I'm going out to Ceylon immediately after Christmas to stay with Roderick and I certainly do not want to put that visit off—I've been looking forward to it so much. Though of course I would put it off if I thought it was my duty," she added conscientiously.

"I'm sure you would, Elspeth, but as I say, I consider you've done everything you possibly could do."

"It's up to the police," said Mrs. McGillicuddy. "And if the police choose to be stupid—"

Miss Marple shook her head decisively.

"Oh no," she said, "the police aren't stupid. And that makes it interesting, doesn't it?"

Mrs. McGillicuddy looked at her without comprehension and Miss Marple reaffirmed her judgment of her friend as a woman of excellent principles and no imagination.

"One wants to know," said Miss Marple, "what really happened."

"She was killed."

"Yes, but who killed her, and why, and what happened to her body? Where is it now?"

"That's the business of the police to find out."

"Exactly! And they haven't found out. That means, doesn't it, that the man was clever—very clever. I can't imagine, you know," said Miss Marple knitting her brows, "how he disposed of it. You kill a woman in a fit of passion—it must have been unpremeditated; you'd never choose to kill a woman in such circumstances just a few minutes before running into a big station. No, it must have been a quarrel—jealousy—something of that kind. You strangle her—and there you are, as I say, with a dead body on your hands and on the point of running into a station. What could you do except as I said at first, prop the body up in a corner as though asleep, hiding the face, and then yourself leave the train as quickly as possible. I don't see any other possibility. And yet there must have been one . . ."

Miss Marple lost herself in thought.

Mrs. McGillicuddy spoke to her twice before Miss Marple answered.

"You're getting deaf, Jane."

"Just a little, perhaps. People do not seem to me to enunciate their words as clearly as they used to do. But it wasn't that I didn't hear you. I'm afraid I wasn't paying attention."

"I just asked about the trains to London tomorrow. Would the afternoon be all right? I'm going to Margaret's and she isn't expecting me before teatime."

"I wonder, Elspeth, if you would mind going up by the twelve-fifteen? We could have an early lunch."

"Of course and—"

Miss Marple went on, drowning her friend's words:

"And I wonder, too, if Margaret would mind if you didn't arrive for tea—if you arrived about seven, perhaps?"

Mrs. McGillicuddy looked at her friend curiously.

"What's on your mind, Jane?"

"I suggest, Elspeth, that I should travel up to London with you, and that we should travel down again as far as Brackhampton in the train you traveled by the other day. You would then return to London from Brackhampton and I would come on here as you did. I, of course, would pay the fares." Miss Marple stressed this point firmly.

Mrs. McGillicuddy ignored the financial aspect.

"What on earth do you expect, Jane?" she asked. "Another murder?"

"Certainly not," said Miss Marple shocked. "But I confess I should like to see for myself, under your guidance, the—the—really it is most difficult to find the correct term—the terrain of the crime."

So accordingly on the following day Miss Marple and Mrs. McGillicuddy found themselves in two opposite corners of a first-class carriage speeding out of London by the 4:54 from Paddington. Paddington had been even more crowded than on the preceding Friday, as there were now only two days to go before Christmas, but the 4:54 was comparatively peaceful—at any rate in the rear portion.

On this occasion no train drew level with them, or they with another train. At intervals trains flashed past them toward London. On two occasions trains flashed past them the other way going at high speed. At intervals Mrs. McGillicuddy consulted her watch doubtfully.

"It's hard to tell just when— We'd passed through a station I know . . ." But they were continually passing through stations.

"We're due in Brackhampton in five minutes," said Miss Marple.

A ticket collector appeared in the doorway. Miss Marple raised her eyes interrogatively. Mrs. McGillicuddy shook her head. It was not the same ticket collector. He clipped their tickets and passed on, staggering just a little as the train swung round a long curve. It slackened speed as it did so.

"I expect we're coming into Brackhampton," said Mrs. McGillicuddy.

"We're getting into the outskirts, I think," said Miss Marple.

There were lights flashing past outside, buildings, an occasional glimpse of streets and trams. Their speed slackened further. They began crossing points.

"We'll be there in a minute," said Mrs. McGillicuddy, "and I can't really see this journey has been any good at all. Has it suggested anything to you, Jane?"

"I'm afraid not," said Miss Marple in a rather doubtful voice.

"A sad waste of good money," said Mrs. McGillicuddy but with less disapproval than she would have used had she been paying for herself. Miss Marple had been quite adamant on that point.

"All the same," said Miss Marple, "one likes to see with one's own eyes where a thing happened. This train's just a few minutes late. Was yours on time on Friday?"

"I think so. I didn't really notice."

The train drew slowly into the busy length of Brackhampton Station. The loud-speaker announced hoarsely, doors opened and shut, people got in and out, milled up and down the platform. It was a busy, crowded scene.

Easy, thought Miss Marple, for a murderer to merge into that crowd, to leave the station in the midst of that pressing mass of people, or even to select another carriage and go on in the train to wherever its ultimate destination might be. Easy to be one male passenger among many. But not so easy to make a body vanish into thin air. That body must be somewhere.

Mrs. McGillicuddy had descended. She spoke now from the platform, through the open window.

"Now take care of yourself, Jane," she said. "Don't catch a chill. It's a nasty treacherous time of year, and you're not so young as you were."

"I know," said Miss Marple.

"And don't let's worry ourselves any more over all this. We've done what we could."

Miss Marple nodded and said:

"Don't stand about in the cold, Elspeth. Or you'll be the one to catch a chill. Go and get yourself a good hot cup of tea in the refreshment room. You've got time, twelve minutes before your train back to town."

"I think perhaps I will. Good-by, Jane."

"Good-by, Elspeth. A happy Christmas to you. I hope you find Margaret well. Enjoy yourself in Ceylon, and give my love to dear Roderick—if he remembers me at all which I doubt."

"Of course he remembers you—very well. You helped him in some way when he was at school—something to do with money that was disappearing from a locker. He's never forgotten it."

"Oh, that!" said Miss Marple.

Mrs. McGillicuddy turned away, a whistle blew, the train began to move. Miss Marple watched the sturdy thick-set body of her friend recede. Elspeth could go to Ceylon with a clear conscience—she had done her duty and was freed from further obligation.

Miss Marple did not lean back as the train gathered speed. Instead she sat upright and devoted herself seriously to thought. Though in speech Miss Marple was woolly and diffuse, in mind she was clear and sharp. She had a problem to solve, the problem of her own future conduct; and, perhaps strangely, it presented itself to her as it had to Mrs. McGillicuddy, as a question of duty.

Mrs. McGillicuddy had said that they had both done all that they could do. It was true of Mrs. McGillicuddy, but about herself Miss Marple did not feel so sure.

It was a question, sometimes, of using one's special gifts. But perhaps that was conceited. After all, what could she do? Her friend's words came back to her, "You're not so young as you were . . ."

Dispassionately, like a general planning a campaign, or an accountant assessing a business, Miss Marple weighed up and set down in her mind the facts for and against further enterprise. On the credit side were the following:

1) *My long experience of life and human nature.*
2) *Sir Henry Clithering and his nephew (now at Scotland Yard, I believe), who was so very nice in the Little Paddocks case.*
3) *My nephew Raymond's second boy, David, who is, I am almost sure, in British Railways.*
4) *Griselda's boy Leonard who is so very knowledgeable about maps.*

Miss Marple reviewed these assets and approved them. They were all very necessary to reinforce the weaknesses on the debit side—in particular her own bodily weakness.

"It's not," thought Miss Marple, "as though I could go here, there and everywhere, making inquiries and finding out things."

Yes, that was the chief objection, her own age and weakness. Although, for her age, her health was good, yet she was old. And if Doctor Haydock had strictly forbidden her to do practical gardening he would hardly approve of her starting out to track down a murderer. For that, in effect, was what she was planning to do—and it was there that her loophole lay. For if heretofore murder had, so to speak, been forced upon her, in this case it would be that she herself set out deliberately to seek it. And she was not sure that she wanted to do so. She was old—old and tired. She felt at this moment, at the end of a tiring day, a great reluctance to enter upon any project at all. She wanted nothing at all but to reach home and sit by the fire with a nice tray of supper, and go to bed, and potter about the next day just snipping off a few things in the garden, tidying up in a very mild way, without stooping, without exerting herself.

"I'm too old for any more adventures," said Miss Marple to herself, watching absently out of the window the curving line of an embankment.

A curve.

Very faintly something stirred in her mind. Just after the ticket collector had clipped their tickets . . .

It suggested an idea. Only an idea. An entirely different idea. . . .

A little pink flush came into Miss Marple's face. Suddenly she did not feel tired at all!

"I'll write to David tomorrow morning," she said to herself.

And at the same time another valuable asset flashed through her mind.

"Of course. My faithful Florence!"

II

Miss Marple set about her plan of campaign methodically and making due allowance for the Christmas season which was a definitely retarding factor.

She wrote to her great nephew, David West, combining Christmas wishes with an urgent request for information.

Fortunately she was invited, as on previous years, to the vicarage for Christmas dinner, and here she was able to tackle young Leonard, home for the Christmas season, about maps.

Maps of all kinds were Leonard's passion. The reason for the old lady's inquiry about a large-scale map of a particular area did not rouse his curiosity. He discoursed on maps generally with fluency, and wrote down for her exactly what would suit her purpose best.

In fact, he did better. He actually found that he had such a map among his collection and he lent it to her, Miss Marple promising to take great care of it and return it in due course.

III

"Maps," said his mother Griselda who still, although she had a grown-up son, looked strangely young and blooming to be inhabiting the shabby old vicarage. "What does she want with maps? I mean, what does she want them for?"

"I don't know," said young Leonard, "I don't think she said exactly."

"I wonder now . . ." said Griselda. "It seems very fishy to me. At her age the old pet ought to give up that sort of thing."

Leonard asked what sort of thing, and Griselda said elusively: "Oh, poking her nose into things. Why maps, I wonder?"

In due course Miss Marple received a letter from her great-nephew David West. It ran affectionately:

> "Dear Aunt Jane. Now what are you up to? I've got the information you wanted. There are only two trains that can possibly apply—the 4:33 and the 5 o'clock. The former is a slow train and stops at Haling Broadway, Barwell Heath, Brackhampton and then stations to Market Basing. The 5 o'clock is the Welsh express for Cardiff, Newport and Swansea. The former might be overtaken somewhere by the 4:54, although it is due in Brackhampton five minutes earlier and the latter passes the 4:54 just before Brackhampton.
>
> In all this do I smell some village scandal of a fruity character? Did you, returning from a shopping spree in town by the 4:54, observe in a passing train the mayor's wife being embraced by the sanitary inspector? But why does it matter which train it was? A weekend at Porthcawl, perhaps? Thank you for the pullover. Just what I wanted.
>
> How's the garden? Not very active this time of year, I should imagine.
>
> Yours ever,
David."

Miss Marple smiled a little, then considered the information thus presented to her. Mrs. McGillicuddy had said definitely that the carriage had not been a corridor one. Therefore—not the Swansea express. The 4:33 was indicated.

Also some more traveling seemed unavoidable. Miss Marple sighed, but made her plans.

She went up to London as before on the 12:15, but this time returned not by the 4:54, but by the 4:33 as far as Brackhampton. The journey was uneventful, but she registered certain details. The train was not crowded—4:33 was before the evening rush hour. Of the first-class carriages only one had an occupant—a very old gentleman reading the *New Statesman*. Miss Marple traveled in an empty compartment and at the two stops, Haling Broadway and Barwell Heath, leaned out of the window to observe passengers entering and leaving the train. A small number of third-class passengers got in at Haling Broadway. At Barwell Heath several third-class passengers got out. Nobody entered or left a first-class carriage except the old gentleman carrying his *New Statesman*.

As the train neared Brackhampton, sweeping around a curve of line, Miss Marple rose to her feet and stood experimentally with her back to the window over which she had drawn down the blind.

Yes, she decided, the impetus of the sudden curving of the line and the slackening of speed did throw one off one's balance back against the window and the blind might, in consequence, very easily fly up. She peered out into the night. It was lighter than it had been when Mrs. McGillicuddy had made the same journey—only just dark, but there was little to see. For observation she must make a daylight journey.

On the next day she went up by the early-morning train, purchased four linen pillowcases (tut-tutting at the price!) so as to combine investigation with the provision of household necessities, and returned by a train leaving Paddington at 12:15. Again she was alone in a first-class carriage. "This taxation," thought Miss Marple, "that's what it is. No one can afford to travel first class except businessmen in the rush hours. I suppose because they can charge it to expenses."

About a quarter of an hour before the train was due at Brackhampton, Miss Marple got out the map with which Leonard had supplied her and began to observe the countryside. She had studied the map very carefully beforehand, and after noting the name of a station they passed through, she was soon able to identify where she was just as the train began to slacken for a curve. It was a very considerable curve, indeed. Miss Marple, her nose glued to the window, studied the ground beneath her (the train was running on a fairly high embankment) with close attention. She divided her attention between the country outside and her map until the train finally ran into Brackhampton.

That night she wrote and posted a letter addressed to Miss Florence Hill, 4 Madison Road, Brackhampton. On the following morning, going to the county library, she studied a *Brackhampton Directory and Gazeteer,* and a county history.

Nothing so far had contradicted the very faint and sketchy idea that had come to her. What she had imagined was possible. She would go no farther than that.

But the next step involved action—a good deal of action—the kind of action for which she, herself, was physically unfit. If her theory were to be definitely proved or disproved, she must at this point have help from some other person. The question was—who? Miss Marple reviewed various names and possibilities, rejecting them all with a vexed shake of the head. The intelligent people, on whose intelligence she could rely, were all far too busy. Not only had they all got jobs of varying importance, their leisure hours were usually apportioned long beforehand. The unintelligent who had time on their hands, were simply, Miss Marple decided, no good.

She pondered in growing vexation and perplexity.

Then suddenly her forehead cleared. She ejaculated aloud a name.

"Of course!" said Miss Marple. "Lucy Eyelesbarrow!"

4

THE NAME of Lucy Eyelesbarrow had already made itself felt in certain circles.

Lucy Eyelesbarrow was thirty-two. She had taken a First in mathematics at Oxford, was acknowledged to have a brilliant mind and was confidently expected to take up a distinguished academic career.

But Lucy Eyelesbarrow, in addition to scholarly brilliance, had a core of good, sound common sense. She could not fail to observe that a life of academic distinction was singularly ill rewarded. She had no desire whatever to teach and she took pleasure in contacts with minds much less brilliant than her own. In short, she had a taste for people, all sorts of people—and not the same people the whole time. She also, quite frankly, liked money. To gain money one must exploit shortage.

Lucy Eyelesbarrow hit at once upon a very serious shortage—the shortage of any kind of skilled domestic labor. To the amazement of her friends and fellow scholars, Lucy Eyelesbarrow entered the field of domestic labor.

Her success was immediate and assured. By now, after a lapse of some years, she was known all over the British Isles. It was quite customary for wives to say joyfully to husbands, "It will be all right. I can go with you to the States. *I've got Lucy Eyelesbarrow!*" The point of Lucy Eyelesbarrow was that once she came into a house, all worry, anxiety and hard work went out of it. Lucy Eyelesbarrow did everything, saw to everything, arranged everything. She was unbelievably competent in every conceivable sphere. She looked after elderly parents, accepted the care of young children, nursed the sickly, cooked divinely, got on well with any old crusted servants there might happen to be (there usually weren't), was tactful

with impossible people, soothed habitual drunkards, was wonderful
with dogs. Best of all she never minded what she did. She scrubbed
the kitchen floor, dug in the garden, cleaned up dog messes and
carried coals!

One of her rules was never to accept an engagement for any long
length of time. A fortnight was her usual period—a month at most
under exceptional circumstances. For that fortnight you had to pay
the earth! But, during that fortnight, your life was heaven. You could
relax completely, go abroad, stay at home, do as you pleased,
secure that all was going well on the home front in Lucy Eyelesbarrow's capable hands.

Naturally the demand for her services was enormous. She could
have booked herself up if she chose for about three years ahead.
She had been offered enormous sums to go as a permanency. But
Lucy had no intention of being a permanency, nor would she book
herself for more than six months ahead. And within that period,
unknown to her clamoring clients, she always kept certain free
periods which enabled her either to take a short luxurious holiday
(since she spent nothing otherwise and was handsomely paid and
kept) or to accept any position at short notice that happened to
take her fancy, either by reason of its character, or because she
"liked the people." Since she was not at liberty to pick and choose
among the vociferous claimants for her services, she went very
largely by personal liking. Mere riches would not buy you the services of Lucy Eyelesbarrow. She could pick and choose and she did
pick and choose. She enjoyed her life very much and found in it a
continual source of entertainment.

Lucy Eyelesbarrow read and reread the letter from Miss Marple.
She had made Miss Marple's acquaintance two years ago when her
services had been retained by Raymond West, the novelist, to go
and look after his old aunt who was recovering from pneumonia.
Lucy had accepted the job and had gone down to St. Mary Mead.
She had liked Miss Marple very much. As for Miss Marple, once
she had caught a glimpse out of her bedroom window of Lucy
Eyelesbarrow really trenching for sweet peas in the proper way, she
had leaned back on her pillows with a sigh of relief, eaten the tempt-
ing little meals that Lucy Eyelesbarrow brought to her, and listened,
agreeably surprised, to the tales told by her elderly irascible maidservant of how "I taught that Miss Eyelesbarrow a crochet pattern

what she'd never heard of! Proper grateful she was." And had surprised her doctor by the rapidity of her convalescence.

Miss Marple wrote asking if Miss Eyelesbarrow could undertake a certain task for her—rather an unusual one. Perhaps Miss Eyelesbarrow could arrange a meeting at which they could discuss the matter.

Lucy Eyelesbarrow frowned for a moment or two as she considered. She was in reality fully booked up. But the word unusual, and her recollection of Miss Marple's personality, carried the day and she rang up Miss Marple straightaway explaining that she could not come down to St. Mary Mead as she was at the moment working, but that she was free from two to four on the following afternoon and could meet Miss Marple anywhere in London. She suggested her own club, a rather nondescript establishment which had the advantage of having several small, dark writing rooms which were usually empty.

Miss Marple accepted the suggestion and on the following day the meeting took place.

Greetings were exchanged; Lucy Eyelesbarrow led her guest to the gloomiest of the writing rooms, and said: "I'm afraid I'm rather booked up just at present, but perhaps you'll tell me what it is you want me to undertake?"

"It's very simple, really," said Miss Marple. "Unusual, but simple. I want you to find a body."

For a moment the suspicion crossed Lucy's mind that Miss Marple was mentally unhinged, but she rejected the idea. Miss Marple was eminently sane. She meant exactly what she had said.

"What kind of a body?" asked Lucy Eyelesbarrow with admirable composure.

"A woman's body," said Miss Marple. "The body of a woman who was murdered—strangled actually—in a train."

Lucy's eyebrows rose slightly.

"Well, that's certainly unusual. Tell me about it."

Miss Marple told her. Lucy Eyelesbarrow listened attentively, without interrupting. At the end she said:

"It all depends on what your friend saw—or thought she saw—?"

She left the sentence unfinished with a question in it.

"Elspeth McGillicuddy doesn't imagine things," said Miss Marple. "That's why I'm relying on what she said. If it had been Dorothy Cartwright, now, it would have been quite a different matter. Dorothy always has a good story and quite often believes it herself, and there is usually a kind of basis of truth but certainly no more. But Elspeth is the kind of woman who finds it very hard to make herself believe that anything at all extraordinary or out of the way could happen. She's most unsuggestible, rather like granite."

"I see," said Lucy thoughtfully. "Well, let's accept it all. Where do I come in?"

"I was very much impressed by you," said Miss Marple, "and you see I haven't got the physical strength nowadays to get about and do things."

"You want me to make inquiries? That sort of thing? But won't the police have done all that? Or do you think they have been just slack?"

"Oh no," said Miss Marple. "They haven't been slack. It's just that I've got a theory about the woman's body. It's got to be some-where. If it wasn't found in the train, then it must have been pushed or thrown out of the train—but it hasn't been discovered anywhere on the line. So I traveled down the same way to see if there was anywhere where the body could have been thrown off the train and yet wouldn't have been found on the line—and there was. The railway line makes a big curve before getting into Brackhampton, on the edge of a high embankment. If a body were thrown out there, when the train was leaning at an angle, I think it would pitch right down the embankment."

"But surely it would still be found—even there?"

"Oh yes. It would have to be taken away. But we'll come to that presently. Here's the place—on this map."

Lucy bent to study where Miss Marple's finger pointed.

"It is right in the outskirts of Brackhampton now," said Miss Marple, "but originally it was a country house with extensive park and grounds and it's still there, untouched—ringed round now with building estates and small suburban houses. It's called Rutherford Hall. It was built by a man called Crackenthorpe, a very rich manufac-turer, in 1884. The original Crackenthorpe's son, an elderly man, is living there still with, I understand, a daughter. The railway en-circles quite half of the property."

"And you want me to do—what?"

Miss Marple replied promptly.

"I want you to get a post there. Everyone is crying out for effi-cient domestic help. I should not imagine it would be difficult."

"No, I don't suppose it would be difficult."

"I understand that Mr. Crackenthorpe is said locally to be somewhat of a miser. If you accept a low salary, I will make it up to the proper figure which should, I think, be rather more than the current rate."

"Because of the difficulty?"

"Not the difficulty so much as the danger. It might, you know, be dangerous. It's only right to warn you of that."

"I don't know," said Lucy pensively, "that the idea of danger would deter me."

"I didn't think it would," said Miss Marple. "You're not that kind of person."

"I dare say you thought it might even attract me? I've encountered very little danger in my life. But do you really believe it might be dangerous?"

"Somebody," Miss Marple pointed out, "has committed a very successful crime. There has been no hue and cry, no real suspicion. Two elderly ladies have told a rather improbable story, the police have investigated it and found nothing in it. So everything is nice and quiet. I don't think that this somebody, whoever he may be, will care about the matter being raked up—especially if you are successful."

"What do I look for exactly?"

"Any signs along the embankment, a scrap of clothing, broken bushes—that kind of thing."

Lucy nodded.

"And then?"

"I shall be quite close at hand," said Miss Marple. "An old maidservant of mine, my faithful Florence, lives in Brackhampton. She has looked after her old parents for years. They are now both dead, and she takes in lodgers—all most respectable people. She has arranged for me to have rooms with her. She will look after me most devotedly, and I feel I should like to be close at hand. I would suggest that you mention you have an elderly aunt living in the neighborhood, and that you want a post within easy distance of her, and also that you stipulate for a reasonable amount of spare time so that you can go and see her often."

Again Lucy nodded.

"I was going to Taormina the day after tomorrow," she said. "The holiday can wait. But I can only promise three weeks. After that, I am booked up."

"Three weeks should be ample," said Miss Marple. "If we can't find out anything in three weeks, we might as well give up the whole thing as a mare's nest."

Miss Marple departed, and Lucy, after a moment's reflection, rang up a registry office in Brackhampton, the manageress of which she knew very well. She explained her desire for a post in the neighborhood so as to be near her "aunt." After turning down, with a little difficulty and a good deal of ingenuity, several more desirable places, Rutherford Hall was mentioned.

"That sounds exactly what I want," said Lucy firmly.

The registry office rang up Miss Crackenthorpe, Miss Crackenthorpe rang up Lucy.

Two days later Lucy left London en route for Rutherford Hall.

II

Driving her own small car, Lucy Eyelesbarrow turned through an imposing pair of vast iron gates. Just inside them was what had originally been a small lodge which now seemed completely derelict, whether through war damage or merely through neglect, it was difficult to be sure. A long, winding drive led through large gloomy clumps of rhododendrons up to the house. Lucy caught her breath in a slight gasp when she saw the house which was a kind of miniature Windsor Castle. The stone steps in front of the door could have done with attention and the gravel sweep was green with neglected weeds.

She pulled an old-fashioned wrought-iron bell, and its clamor sounded echoing away inside. A slatternly woman, wiping her hands on her apron, opened the door and looked at her suspiciously.

"Expected, aren't you?" she said. "Miss Somethingbarrow, she told me."

"Quite right," said Lucy.

The house was desperately cold inside. Her guide led her along a dark hall and opened a door on the right. Rather to Lucy's surprise, it was quite a pleasant sitting room, with books and chintz-covered chairs.

"I'll tell Her," said the woman, and went away shutting the door after having given Lucy a look of profound disfavor.

After a few minutes the door opened again. From the first moment Lucy decided that she liked Emma Crackenthorpe.

She was a middle-aged woman with no very outstanding characteristics, neither good looking nor plain, sensibly dressed in tweeds and pullover, with dark hair swept back from her forehead, steady hazel eyes and a very pleasant voice.

She said: "Miss Eyelesbarrow?" and held out her hand.

Then she looked doubtful.

"I wonder," she said, "if this post is really what you're looking for? I don't want a housekeeper, you know, to supervise things. I want someone to do the work."

Lucy said that that was what most people needed.

Emma Crackenthorpe said apologetically:

"So many people, you know, seem to think that just a little light dusting will answer the case, but I can do all the light dusting myself."

"I quite understand," said Lucy. "You want cooking and washing up, and housework and stoking the boiler. That's all right. That's what I do. I'm not at all afraid of work."

"It's a big house, I'm afraid, and inconvenient. Of course we only live in a portion of it—my father and myself, that is. He is rather an invalid. We live quite quietly, and there is an Aga stove. I have several brothers, but they are not here very often. Two women come in, a Mrs. Kidder in the morning and Mrs. Hart three days a week, to do brasses and things like that. You have your own car?"

"Yes. It can stand out in the open if there's nowhere to put it. It's used to it."

"Oh, there are any amount of old stables. There's no trouble about that." She frowned a moment, then said, "Eyelesbarrow—rather an unusual name. Some friends of mine were telling me about a Lucy Eyelesbarrow—the Kennedys?"

"Yes. I was with them in North Devon when Mrs. Kennedy was having a baby."

Emma Crackenthorpe smiled.

"I know they said they'd never had such a wonderful time as when you were there seeing to everything. But I had the idea that you were terribly expensive. The sum I mentioned—"

"That's quite all right," said Lucy. "I want particularly, you see, to be near Brackhampton. I have an elderly aunt in a critical state of health and I want to be within easy distance of her. That's why the salary is a secondary consideration. I can't afford to do nothing. If I could be sure of having some time off most days?"

"Oh, of course. Every afternoon, till six, if you like?"

"That seems perfect."

Miss Crackenthorpe hesitated a moment before saying: "My father is elderly and a little—difficult—sometimes. He is very keen on economy, and he says things sometimes that upset people. I wouldn't like—"

Lucy broke in quickly.

"I'm quite used to elderly people of all kinds," she said. "I always manage to get on well with them."

Emma Crackenthorpe looked relieved.

"Trouble with father!" diagnosed Lucy. "I bet he's an old tartar."

She was apportioned a large, gloomy bedroom which a small electric heater did its inadequate best to warm, and was shown round the house, a vast uncomfortable mansion. As they passed a door in the hall a voice roared out:

"That you, Emma? Got the new girl there? Bring her in. I want to look at her."

Emma flushed, glanced at Lucy apologetically.

The two women entered the room. It was richly upholstered in dark velvet, the narrow windows let in very little light, and it was full of heavy mahogany Victorian furniture.

Old Mr. Crackenthorpe was stretched out in an invalid's chair, a silverheaded stick by his side.

He was a big gaunt man, his flesh hanging in loose folds. He had a face rather like a bulldog, with a pugnacious chin. He had thick, dark hair flecked with gray, and small suspicious eyes.

"Let's have a look at you, young lady."

Lucy advanced, composed and smiling.

"There's just one thing you'd better understand straight away. Just because we live in a big house doesn't mean we're rich. We're not rich. We live simply—do you hear?—simply! No good coming here with a lot of highfalutin ideas. Cod's as good a fish as turbot any day and don't you forget it. I don't stand for waste. I live here because my father built the house and I like it. After I'm dead they can sell it up if they want to—and I expect they will want to. No sense of family. This house is well built—it's solid, and we've got our own land round us. Keeps us private. It would bring in a lot for building land but not while I'm alive. You won't get me out of here until you take me out feet first."

He glared at Lucy.

"Your house is your castle," said Lucy.

"Laughing at me?"

"Of course not. I think it's very exciting to have a real country place all surrounded by town."

"Quite so. Can't see another house from here, can you? Fields with cows in them—right in the middle of Brackhampton. You hear the traffic a bit when the wind's that way, but otherwise it's still country."

He added, without pause or change of tone, to his daughter:

"Ring up that damnfool of a doctor. Tell him that last medicine's no good at all."

Lucy and Emma retired. He shouted after them:

"And don't let that damned woman who sniffs dust in here. She's disarranged all my books."

Lucy asked:

"Has Mr. Crackenthorpe been an invalid long?"

Emma said, rather evasively:

"Oh, for years now . . . This is the kitchen."

The kitchen was enormous. A vast kitchen range stood cold and neglected. An Aga stood demurely beside it.

Lucy asked times of meals and inspected the larder. Then she said cheerfully to Emma Crackenthorpe:

"I know everything now. Don't bother. Leave it all to me."

Emma Crackenthorpe heaved a sigh of relief as she went up to bed that night.

"The Kennedys were quite right," she said. "She's wonderful."

Lucy rose at six the next morning. She did the house, prepared vegetables, assembled, cooked and served breakfast. With Mrs. Kidder she made the beds and at eleven o'clock they sat down to strong tea and biscuits in the kitchen. Mollified by the fact that Lucy "had no airs about her" and also by the strength and sweetness of the tea, Mrs. Kidder relaxed into gossip. She was a small, spare woman with a sharp eye and tight lips.

"Regular old skinflint he is. What She has to put up with! All the same, She's not what I call downtrodden. Can hold her own all right when she has to. When the gentlemen come down She sees to it there's something decent to eat."

"The gentlemen?"

"Yes. Big family it was. The eldest, Mr. Edmund, he was killed in the war. Then there's Mr. Cedric, he lives abroad somewhere. He's not married. Paints pictures in foreign parts. Mr. Harold's in the City, lives in London—married an earl's daughter. Then there's Mr. Alfred, he's got a nice way with him, but he's a bit of a black sheep, been in trouble once or twice—and there's Miss Edith's husband, Mr. Bryan, ever so nice he is. She died some years ago, but he's always stayed one of the family. And there's Master Alexander, Miss Edith's little boy. He's at school, comes here for part of the holidays always; Miss Emma's terribly set on him."

Lucy digested all this information, continuing to press tea on her informant. Finally, reluctantly, Mrs. Kidder rose to her feet.

"Seem to have got along a treat we do, this morning," she said wonderingly. "Want me to give you a hand with the potatoes, dear?"

"They're already done."

"Well, you are a one for getting on with things! I might as well be getting along myself as there doesn't seem anything else to do."

Mrs. Kidder departed and Lucy, with time on her hands, scrubbed the kitchen table which she had been longing to do, but which she had put off so as not to offend Mrs. Kidder whose job it properly was. Then she cleaned the silver till it shone radiantly. She cooked lunch, cleared it away, washed up, and at two-thirty was ready to start exploration. She had set out the tea things ready on a tray, with sandwiches and bread and butter covered over with a damp napkin to keep them moist.

She strolled first round the gardens which would be the normal thing to do. The kitchen garden was sketchily cultivated with a few vegetables. The hothouses were in ruins. The paths everywhere were overgrown with weeds. A herbaceous border near the house was the only thing that showed free of weeds and in good condition and Lucy suspected that that had been Emma's hand. The gardener was a very old man, somewhat deaf, who was only making a show of working. Lucy spoke to him pleasantly. He lived in a cottage adjacent to the big stable yard.

Extending out from the stable yard, a back drive led through the park, which was fenced on either side of it, and under a railway arch into a small back lane.

Every few minutes a train thundered along the main line over the railway arch. Lucy watched the trains as they slackened speed going round the sharp curve that encircled the Crackenthorpe property. She passed under the railway arch and out into the lane. It seemed a little-used track. On the one side was the railway embankment, on the other was a high wall which enclosed some tall factory buildings. Lucy followed the lane until it came out into a street of small houses. She could hear a short distance away the busy hum of main-road traffic. She glanced at her watch. A woman came out of a house nearby and Lucy stopped her.

"Excuse me, can you tell me if there is a public telephone near here?"

"Post office just at the corner of the road."

Lucy thanked her and walked along until she came to the post office, which was a combination shop and post office. There was a telephone box at one side. Lucy went into it and made a call. She asked to speak to Miss Marple. A woman's voice spoke in a sharp bark.

"She's resting. And I'm not going to disturb her! She needs her rest—she's an old lady. Who shall I say called?"

"Miss Eyelesbarrow. There's no need to disturb her. Just tell her that I've arrived and everything is going on well and that I'll let her know when I've any news."

She replaced the receiver and made her way back to Rutherford Hall.

5

"I suppose it will be all right if I just practice a few iron shots in the park?" asked Lucy.

"Oh yes, certainly. Are you fond of golf?"

"I'm not much good, but I like to keep in practice. It's a more agreeable form of exercise than just going for a walk."

"Nowhere to walk outside this place," growled Mr. Cracken-thorpe. "Nothing but pavements and miserable little bandboxes of houses. Like to get hold of my land and build more of them. But they won't until I'm dead. And I'm not going to die to oblige anybody. I can tell you that! Not to oblige anybody!"

Emma Crackenthorpe said mildly:

"Now, Father."

"I know what they think—and what they're waiting for. All of 'em. Cedric, and that sly fox Harold with his smug face. As for Alfred I wonder he hasn't had a shot at bumping me off himself. Not sure he didn't, at Christmastime. That was a very odd turn I had. Puzzled old Quimper. He asked me a lot of discreet questions."

"Everyone gets these digestive upsets now and again, Father."

"All right, all right, say straight out that I ate too much! That's what you mean. And why did I eat too much? Because there was too much food on the table, far too much. Wasteful and extravagant. And that reminds me—you, young woman. Five potatoes you sent in for lunch—good-sized ones, too. Two potatoes are enough for anybody. So don't send in more than four in future. The extra one was wasted today."

"It wasn't wasted, Mr. Crackenthorpe. I've planned to use it in a Spanish omelet tonight."

"Urgh!" As Lucy went out of the room carrying the coffee tray she heard him say, "Slick young woman, that, always got all the answers. Cooks well, though—and she's a handsome kind of girl."

Lucy Eyelesbarrow took a light iron out of the set of golf clubs she had had the forethought to bring with her and strolled out into the park, climbing over the fencing.

She began playing a series of shots. After five minutes or so, a ball, apparently sliced, pitched on the side of the railway embankment. Lucy went up and began to hunt about for it. She looked back toward the house. It was a long way off and nobody was in the least interested in what she was doing. She continued to hunt for the ball. Now and then she played shots from the embankment down into the grass. During the afternoon she searched about a third of the embankment. Nothing. She played her ball back toward the house.

Then, on the next day, she came upon something. A thornbush growing about halfway up the bank had been snapped off. Bits of it lay scattered about. Lucy examined the tree itself. Impaled on one of the thorns was a torn scrap of fur. It was almost the same color as the wood, a pale brownish color. Lucy looked at it for a moment, then she took a pair of scissors out of her pocket and snipped it carefully in half. The half she had snipped off she put in an envelope which she had in her pocket. She came down the steep slope searching about for anything else. She looked carefully at the rough grass of the field. She thought she could distinguish a kind of track which someone had made walking through the long grass. But it was very faint—not nearly so clear as her own tracks were. It must have been made some time ago and it was too sketchy for her to be sure that it was not merely imagination on her part.

She began to hunt carefully down in the grass at the foot of the embankment just below the broken thornbush. Presently her search was rewarded. She found a powder compact, a small cheap enameled affair. She wrapped it in her handkerchief and put it in her pocket. She searched on but did not find anything more.

On the following afternoon, she got into her car and went to see her invalid aunt. Emma Crackenthorpe said kindly, "Don't hurry back. We shan't want you until dinnertime."

"Thank you, but I shall be back at six by the latest."

No. 4, Madison Road was a small drab house in a small drab street. It had very clean Nottingham lace curtains, a shining white doorstep and a well-polished brass door-handle. The door was opened by a tall, grim-looking woman, dressed in black with a large knob of iron-gray hair.

She eyed Lucy in suspicious appraisal as she showed her in to Miss Marple.

Miss Marple was occupying the back sitting room which looked out on to a small, tidy square of garden. It was aggressively clean with a lot of mats and doilies, a great many china ornaments, a rather big Jacobean suite and two ferns in pots. Miss Marple was sitting in a big chair by the fire busily engaged in crocheting.

Lucy came in and shut the door. She sat down in the chair facing Miss Marple.

"Well!" she said, "it looks as though you were right."

She produced her findings and gave the details of their discovery. A faint flush of achievement came into Miss Marple's cheeks.

"Perhaps one ought not to feel so," she said, "but it is rather gratifying to form a theory and get proof that it is correct!"

She fingered the small tuft of fur. "Elspeth said the woman was wearing a light-colored fur coat. I suppose the compact was in the pocket of the coat and fell out as the body rolled down the slope. It doesn't seem distinctive in any way, but it may help. You didn't take all the fur?"

"No, I left half of it on the thornbush."

Miss Marple nodded approval.

"Quite right. You are very intelligent, my dear. The police will want to check exactly."

"You are going to the police—with these things?"

"Well—not quite yet. . . ." Miss Marple considered. "It would be better, I think, to find the body first. Don't you?"

"Yes, but isn't that rather a tall order? I mean, granting that your estimate is correct. The murderer pushed the body out of the train, then presumably got out himself at Brackhampton and at some time —probably that same night—came along and removed the body. But what happened after that? He may have taken it anywhere."

"Not anywhere," said Miss Marple. "I don't think you've followed the thing to its logical conclusion, my dear Miss Eyelesbarrow."

"Do call me Lucy. Why not anywhere?"

"Because, if so, he might much more easily have killed the girl in some lonely spot and driven the body away from there. You haven't appreciated—"

Lucy interrupted.

"Are you saying—do you mean—that this was a premeditated crime?"

"I didn't think so at first," said Miss Marple. "One wouldn't—naturally. It seemed like a quarrel and a man losing control and strangling the girl and then being faced with the problem of disposing of his victim—a problem which he had to solve within a very few minutes. But it really is too much of a coincidence that he should kill the girl in a fit of passion, and then look out of the window and find the train was going round a curve exactly at a spot where he could tip the body out, and where he could be sure of finding his way later and removing it! If he'd just thrown her out there by chance, he'd have done no more about it, and the body would, long before now, have been found."

She paused. Lucy stared at her.

"You know," said Miss Marple thoughtfully, "it's really quite a clever way to have planned a crime—and I think it was very carefully planned. There's something so anonymous about a train. If he'd killed her in the place where she lived or was staying, somebody might have noticed him come or go. Or if he'd driven her out into the country somewhere, someone might have noticed the car and its number and make. But a train is full of strangers coming and going. In a non-corridor carriage, alone with her, it was quite easy—especially if you realize that he knew exactly what he was going to do next. He knew—he must have known—all about Rutherford Hall—its geographical position, I mean, its queer isolation: an island bounded by railway lines."

"It is exactly like that," said Lucy. "It's an anachronism out of the past. Bustling urban life goes on all around it, but doesn't touch it. The tradespeople deliver in the mornings and that's all."

"So we assume, as you said, that the murderer comes to Rutherford Hall that night. It is already dark when the body falls and no one is likely to discover it before the next day."

"No, indeed."

"The murderer would come—how? In a car? Which way?"

Lucy considered.

"There's a rough lane, alongside a factory wall. He'd probably come that way, turn in under the railway arch and along the back drive. Then he could climb the fence, go along at the foot of the embankment, find the body, and carry it back to the car."

"And then," continued Miss Marple, "he took it to some place he had already chosen beforehand. This was all thought out, you know. And I don't think, as I say, that he would take it away from Rutherford Hall, or if so, not very far. The obvious thing, I suppose, would be to bury it somewhere?" She looked inquiringly at Lucy.

"I suppose so," said Lucy considering. "But it wouldn't be quite as easy as it sounds."

Miss Marple agreed.

"He couldn't bury it in the park. Too hard work and very noticeable. Somewhere where the earth was turned already?"

"The kitchen garden, perhaps, but that's very close to the gardener's cottage. He's old and deaf—but still it might be risky."

"Is there a dog?"

"No."

"Then in a shed, perhaps, or an outhouse?"

"That would be simpler and quicker. There are a lot of unused old buildings: broken down pigsties, harness rooms, workshops that nobody ever goes near. Or he might perhaps have thrust it into a clump of rhododendrons or shrubs somewhere."

Miss Marple nodded.

"Yes, I think that's much more probable."

There was a knock on the door and the grim Florence came in with a tray.

"Nice for you to have a visitor," she said to Miss Marple, "I've made you my special scones you used to like."

"Florence always made the most delicious teacakes," said Miss Marple.

Florence, gratified, creased her features into a totally unexpected smile and left the room.

"I think, my dear," said Miss Marple, "we won't talk any more about murder during tea. Such an unpleasant subject!"

II

After tea Lucy rose.

"I'll be getting back," she said. "As I've already told you, there's no one actually living at Rutherford Hall who could be the man we're looking for. There's only an old man and a middle-aged woman, and an old, deaf gardener."

"I didn't say he was actually living there," said Miss Marple. "All

I mean is that he's someone who knows Rutherford Hall very well. But we can go into that after you've found the body."

"You seem to assume quite confidently that I shall find it," said Lucy. "I don't feel nearly so optimistic."

"I'm sure you will succeed, my dear Lucy. You are such an efficient person."

"In some ways, but I haven't had any experience in looking for bodies."

"I'm sure all it needs is a little common sense," said Miss Marple encouragingly.

Lucy looked at her, then laughed. Miss Marple smiled back at her.

Lucy set to work systematically the next afternoon.

She poked round outhouses, prodded the briars which wreathed the old pigsties, and was peering into the boiler room under the greenhouse when she heard a dry cough and turned to find old Hillman, the gardener, looking at her disapprovingly.

"You be careful you don't get a nasty fall, Miss," he warned her. "Them steps isn't safe, and you was up in the loft just now and the floor there ain't safe neither."

Lucy was careful to display no embarrassment.

"I expect you think I'm very nosy," she said cheerfully. "I was just wondering if something couldn't be made out of this place—growing mushrooms for the market, that sort of thing. Everything seems to have been let go terribly."

"That's the master, that is. Won't spend a penny. Ought to have two men and a boy here, I ought, to keep the place proper, but won't hear of it, he won't. Had all I could do to make him get a motor mower. Wanted me to mow all that front grass by hand, he did."

"But if the place could be made to pay—with some repairs?"

"Won't get a place like this to pay—too far gone. And he wouldn't care about that, anyway. Only cares about saving. Knows well enough what'll happen after he's gone—the young gentlemen'll sell up as fast as they can. Only waiting for him to pop off, they are. Going to come into a tidy lot of money when he dies, so I've heard."

"I suppose he's a very rich man?" said Lucy.

"Crackenthorpe's Fancies, that's what they are. The old gentleman started it, Mr. Crackenthorpe's father. A sharp one he was, by all accounts. Made his fortune and built this place. Hard as nails, they say, and never forgot an injury. But with all that, he was open-handed. Nothing of the miser about him. Disappointed in both his sons, so the story goes. Give 'em an education and brought 'em up to be gentlemen—Oxford and all. But they were too much of gentle-men to want to go into the business. The younger one married an actress and then smashed himself up in a car accident when he'd been drinking. The elder one, our one here, his father never fancied so much. Abroad a lot, he was, bought a lot of heathen statues and had them sent home. Wasn't so close with his money when he was young—come on him more in middle age, it did. No, they never did hit it off, him and his father, so I've heard."

Lucy digested this information with an air of polite interest. The old man leaned against the wall and prepared to go on with his saga. He much preferred talking to doing any work.

"Died afore the war, the old gentleman did. Terrible temper he had. Didn't do to give him any sauce, he wouldn't stand for it."

"And after he died, this Mr. Crackenthorpe came and lived here?"

"Him and his family, yes. Nigh to grown up they was by then."

"But surely— Oh, I see, you mean the 1914 war."

"No, I don't. Died in 1928, that's what I mean."

Lucy supposed that 1928 qualified as "before the war" though it was not the way she would have described it herself.

She said: "Well, I expect you'll be wanting to go on with your work. You mustn't let me keep you."

"Ar," said old Hillman without enthusiasm, "not much you can do this time of day. Light's too bad."

Lucy went back to the house, pausing to investigate a likely look-ing copse of birch and azalea on her way.

She found Emma Crackenthorpe standing in the hall reading a letter. The afternoon post had just been delivered.

"My nephew will be here tomorrow—with a school friend. Alex-ander's room is the one over the porch. The one next to it will do for James Stoddart-West. They'll use the bathroom just opposite."

"Yes, Miss Crackenthorpe. I'll see the rooms are prepared."

"They'll arrive in the morning before lunch." She hesitated. "I expect they'll be hungry."

"I bet they will," said Lucy. "Roast beef, do you think? And perhaps treacle tart?"

"Alexander's very fond of treacle tart."

The two boys arrived on the following morning. They both had well-brushed hair, suspiciously angelic faces, and perfect manners. Alexander Eastley had fair hair and blue eyes, Stoddart-West was dark and spectacled.

They discoursed gravely during lunch on events in the sporting world, with occasional references to the latest space fiction. Their manner was that of elderly professors discussing paleolithic implements. In comparison with them, Lucy felt quite young.

The sirloin of beef vanished in no time and every crumb of the treacle tart was consumed.

Mr. Crackenthorpe grumbled: "You two will eat me out of house and home."

Alexander gave him a blue-eyed reproving glance.

"We'll have bread and cheese if you can't afford meat, Grandfather."

"Afford it? I can afford it. I don't like waste."

"We haven't wasted any, sir," said Stoddart-West, looking down at his plate which bore clear testimony of that fact.

"You boys both eat twice as much as I do."

"We're at the body-building stage," Alexander explained. "We need a big intake of proteins."

The old man grunted.

As the two boys left the table, Lucy heard Alexander say apologetically to his friend:

"You mustn't pay any attention to my grandfather. He's on a diet or something and that makes him rather peculiar. He's terribly mean, too. I think it must be a complex of some kind."

Stoddart-West said comprehendingly:

"I had an aunt who kept thinking she was going bankrupt. Really, she had oodles of money. Pathological, the doctor said. Have you got that football, Alex?"

After she had cleared away and washed up lunch, Lucy went out. She could hear the boys calling out in the distance on the lawn. She herself went in the opposite direction, down the front drive and from there she struck across to some clumped masses of rhododendron bushes. She began to hunt carefully, holding back the leaves and peering inside. She moved from clump to clump systematically, and was raking inside with a golf club when the polite voice of Alexander Eastley made her start.

"Are you looking for something, Miss Eyelesbarrow?"

"A golf ball," said Lucy promptly. "Several golf balls, in fact. I've been practicing golf shots most afternoons and I've lost quite a lot of balls. I thought that today I really must find some of them."

"We'll help you," said Alexander obligingly.

"That's very kind of you. I thought you were playing football."

"One can't go on playing footer," explained Stoddart-West. "One gets too hot. Do you play a lot of golf?"

"I'm quite fond of it. I don't get much opportunity."

"I suppose you don't. You do the cooking here, don't you?"

"Yes."

"Did you cook the lunch today?"

"Yes. Was it all right?"

"Simply wizard," said Alexander. "We get awful meat at school, all dried up. I love beef that's pink and juicy inside. That treacle tart was pretty smashing, too."

"You must tell me what things you like best."

"Could we have apple meringue one day? It's my favorite thing."

"Of course."

Alexander sighed happily.

"There's a clock golf set under the stairs," he said. "We could fix it up on the lawn and do some putting. What about it, Stodders?"

"Good oh!" said Stoddart-West.

"He isn't really Australian," explained Alexander courteously. "But he's practicing talking that way in case his people take him out to see the Test Match next year."

Encouraged by Lucy, they went off to get the clock golf set. Later, as she returned to the house, she found them setting it out on the lawn and arguing about the position of the numbers.

"We don't want it like a clock," said Stoddart-West. "That's kid stuff. We want to make a course of it. Long holes and short ones. It's a pity the numbers are so rusty. You can hardly see them."

"They need a lick of white paint," said Lucy. "You might get some tomorrow and paint them."

"Good idea." Alexander's face lighted up. "I say, I believe there are some old pots of paint in the Long Barn—left there by the painters. Shall we see?"

"What's the Long Barn?" asked Lucy.

Alexander pointed to a long, stone building a little way from the house near the back drive.

"It's quite old," he said. "Grandfather calls it a Leak Barn and says it's Elizabethan, but that's just swank. It belonged to the farm that was here originally. My great-grandfather pulled it down and built this awful house instead."

He added: "A lot of grandfather's collection is in the barn. Things he had sent home from abroad when he was a young man. Most of them are pretty frightful, too. The Long Barn is used sometimes for whist drives and things like that. Women's Institute stuff. And Conservative Sales of Work. Come and see it."

Lucy accompanied them willingly.

There was a big oak, nail-studded door to the barn.

Alexander raised his hand and detached a key on a nail just under some ivy to the right hand of the top of the door. He turned it in the lock, pushed the door open and they went in.

At a first glance Lucy felt that she was in a singularly bad museum. The heads of two Roman emperors in marble glared at her out of bulging eyeballs, there was a huge sarcophagus of a decadent Greco-Roman period, a simpering Venus stood on a pedestal clutching her falling draperies. Besides these works of art, there were a couple of trestle tables, some stacked-up chairs, and sundry oddments such as a rusted hand mower, two buckets, a couple of moth-eaten car seats, and a green-painted, iron garden seat that had lost a leg.

"I think I saw the paint over here," said Alexander vaguely. He went to a corner and pulled aside a tattered curtain that shut it off.

They found a couple of paint pots and brushes; the latter dry and stiff.

"You really need some turpentine," said Lucy.

They could not, however, find any. The boys suggested bicycling off to get some, and Lucy urged them to do so. Painting the clock golf numbers would keep them amused for some time, she thought.

The boys went off, leaving her in the barn.

"This really could do with a clear up," she had murmured.

"I shouldn't bother," Alexander advised her. "It gets cleaned up if it's going to be used for anything, but it's practically never used this time of year."

"Do I hang the key up outside the door again? Is that where it's kept?"

"Yes. There's nothing to pinch here, you see. Nobody would want those awful marble things and anyway they weigh a ton."

Lucy agreed with him. She could hardly admire old Mr. Crackenthorpe's taste in art. He seemed to have an unerring instinct for selecting the worst specimen of any period.

She stood looking round her after the boys had gone. Her eyes came to rest on the sarcophagus and stayed there.

That sarcophagus. . . .

The air in the barn was faintly musty as though unaired for a long time. She went over to the sarcophagus. It had a heavy, close-fitting lid. Lucy looked at it speculatively.

Then she left the barn, went to the kitchen, found a heavy crowbar, and returned.

It was not an easy task but Lucy toiled doggedly.

Slowly the lid began to rise, pried up by the crowbar.

It rose sufficiently for Lucy to see what was inside.

6

A FEW MINUTES later Lucy, rather pale, left the barn, locked the door and put the key back on the nail.

She went rapidly to the stables, got out her car and drove down the back drive. She stopped at the post office at the end of the road. She went into the telephone box, put in the money and dialed.

"I want to speak to Miss Marple."

"She's resting, Miss. It's Miss Eyelesbarrow, isn't it?"

"Yes."

"I'm not going to disturb her and that's flat, Miss. She's an old lady and she needs her rest."

"You must disturb her. It's urgent."

"I'm not—"

"Please do what I say at once."

When she chose, Lucy's voice could be as incisive as steel. Florence knew authority when she heard it.

Presently Miss Marple's voice spoke.

"Yes, Lucy?"

Lucy drew a deep breath.

"You were quite right," she said. "I've found it."

"A woman's body?"

"Yes. A woman in a fur coat. It's in a stone sarcophagus in a kind of barn-*cum*-museum near the house. What do you want me to do? I ought to inform the police, I think."

"Yes. You must inform the police. At once."

"But what about the rest of it? About you? The first thing they'll want to know is why I was prying up a lid that weighs tons for apparently no reason. Do you want me to invent a reason? I can."

"No. I think, you know," said Miss Marple in her gentle serious voice, "that the only thing to do is to tell the exact truth."

"About you?"

"About everything."

A sudden grin split the whiteness of Lucy's face.

"That will be quite simple for me," she said. "But I imagine they'll find it quite hard to believe!"

She rang off, waited a moment, and then rang and got the police station.

"I have just discovered a dead body in a sarcophagus in the Long Barn at Rutherford Hall."

"What's that?"

Lucy repeated her statement and anticipating the next question gave her name.

She drove back, put the car away and entered the house.

She paused in the hall for a moment, thinking.

Then she gave a brief sharp nod of the head and went to the library where Miss Crackenthorpe was sitting helping her father to do the *Times* crossword.

"Can I speak to you a moment, Miss Crackenthorpe?"

Emma looked up, a shade of apprehension on her face. The apprehension was, Lucy thought, purely domestic. In such words do useful household staff announce their imminent departure.

"Well, speak up, girl, speak up," said old Mr. Crackenthorpe irritably.

Lucy said to Emma, "I'd like to speak to you alone, please."

"Nonsense," said Mr. Crackenthorpe. "You say straight out here what you've got to say."

"Just a moment, Father." Emma rose and went toward the door.

"All nonsense. It can wait," said the old man angrily.

"I'm afraid it can't wait," said Lucy.

Mr. Crackenthorpe said, "What impertinence!"

Emma came out into the hall. Lucy followed her and shut the door behind them.

"Yes?" said Emma, "what is it? If you think there's too much to do with the boys here, I can help you and—"

"It's not that at all," said Lucy. "I didn't want to speak before your father because I understand he is an invalid and it might give him a shock. You see, I've just discovered the body of a murdered woman in that big sarcophagus in the Long Barn."

Emma Crackenthorpe stared at her.

"In the sarcophagus? A murdered woman? It's impossible!"

"I'm afraid it's quite true. I've rung up the police. They will be here at any minute."

A slight flush came into Emma's cheek.

"You should have told me first—before notifying the police."

"I'm sorry," said Lucy.

"I didn't hear you ring up—" Emma's glance went to the telephone on the hall table.

"I rang up from the post office just down the road."

"But how extraordinary—why not from here?"

Lucy thought quickly.

"I was afraid the boys might be about—might hear—if I rang up from the hall here."

"I see . . . Yes—I see. They are coming—the police, I mean?"

"They're here now," said Lucy, as with a squeal of brakes a car drew up at the front door and the bell pealed through the house.

II

"I'm sorry, very sorry—to have asked this of you," said Inspector Bacon.

His hand under her arm, he led Emma Crackenthorpe out of the barn. Emma's face was very pale; she looked sick, but she walked firmly erect.

"I'm quite sure that I've never seen the woman before in my life."

"We're very grateful to you, Miss Crackenthorpe. That's all I wanted to know. Perhaps you'd like to lie down?"

"I must go to my father. I telephoned to Doctor Quimper as soon as I heard about this and he is with him now."

Doctor Quimper came out of the library as they crossed the hall. He was a tall, genial man, with a casual, offhand, cynical manner that his patients found very stimulating.

He and the Inspector nodded to each other.

"Miss Crackenthorpe has performed an unpleasant task very bravely," said Bacon.

"Well done, Emma," said the doctor, patting her on the shoulder. "You can take things. I've always known that. Your father's all right. Just go in and have a word with him, and then go into the dining room and get yourself a glass of brandy. That's a prescription."

Emma smiled at him gratefully and went into the library.

"That woman's the salt of the earth," said the doctor looking after her. "A thousand pities she's never married. The penalty of being the only female in a family of men. The other sister got clear, married at seventeen, I believe. This one's quite a handsome woman, really. She'd have been a success as a wife and mother."

"Too devoted to her father, I suppose," said Inspector Bacon.

"She's not really as devoted as all that—but she's got the instinct some women have to make their men folk happy. She sees that her father likes being an invalid, so she lets him be an invalid. She's the same with her brothers. Cedric feels he's a good painter, what's-his-name, Harold, knows how much she relies on his sound judgment—she lets Alfred shock her with his stories of his clever deals. Oh yes, she's a clever woman—no fool. Well, do you want me for anything? Want me to have a look at your corpse now Johnstone has done with it" (Johnstone was the police surgeon) "and see if it happens to be one of my medical mistakes?"

"I'd like you to have a look, yes, Doctor. We want to get her identified. I suppose it's impossible for old Mr. Crackenthorpe? Too much of a strain?"

"Strain? Fiddlesticks. He'd never forgive you or me if you didn't let him have a peep. He's all agog. Most exciting thing that's happened to him for fifteen years or so—and it won't cost him anything!"

"There's nothing really much wrong with him, then?"

"He's seventy-two," said the doctor. "That's all, really, that's the matter with him. He has odd rheumatic twinges—who doesn't? So he calls it arthritis. He has palpitations after meals—as well he may—he puts them down to 'heart.' But he can always do anything he wants to do! I've plenty of patients like that. The ones who are really ill usually insist desperately that they're perfectly well. Come on, let's go and see this body of yours. Unpleasant, I suppose?"

"Johnstone estimates she's been dead between a fortnight and three weeks."

"Quite unpleasant, then."

The doctor stood by the sarcophagus and looked down with frank curiosity, professionally unmoved by what he had named the "unpleasantness."

"Never seen her before. No patient of mine. I don't remember ever seeing her about in Brackhampton. She must have been quite good-looking once—hm— Somebody had it in for her all right."

They went out again into the air. Doctor Quimper glanced up at the building.

"Found in the—what do they call it?—the Long Barn—in a sarcophagus! Fantastic! Who found her?"

"Miss Lucy Eyelesbarrow."

"Oh, the latest lady help? What was she doing, poking about in sarcophagi?"

"That," said Inspector Bacon grimly, "is just what I am going to ask her. Now, about Mr. Crackenthorpe. Will you—?"

"I'll bring him along."

Mr. Crackenthorpe, muffled in scarves, came walking at a brisk pace, the doctor beside him.

"Disgraceful," he said. "Absolutely disgraceful! I brought back that sarcophagus from Florence in—let me see—it must have been in 1908—or was it 1909?"

"Steady now," the doctor warned him. "This isn't going to be nice, you know."

"No matter how ill I am, I've got to do my duty, haven't I?"

A very brief visit inside the Long Barn was, however, quite long enough. Mr. Crackenthorpe shuffled out into the air again with remarkable speed.

"Never saw her before in my life!" he said. "What's it mean? Absolutely disgraceful. It wasn't Florence—I remember now—it was Naples. A very fine specimen. And some fool of a woman has to come and get herself killed in it!"

He clutched at the folds of his overcoat on the left side.

"Too much for me . . . My heart . . . Where's Emma? Doctor. . . ."

Doctor Quimper took his arm.

"You'll be all right," he said. "I prescribe a little stimulant. Brandy."

They went back together toward the house.

"Sir. Please, sir."

Inspector Bacon turned. Two boys had arrived, breathless, on bicycles. Their faces were full of eager pleading.

"Please, sir, can we see the body?"

"No, you can't," said Inspector Bacon.

"Oh sir, please, sir. You never know. We might know who she was. Oh please, sir, do be a sport. It's not fair. Here's a murder, right in our own barn. It's the sort of chance that might never happen again. Do be a sport, sir."

"Who are you two?"

"I'm Alexander Eastley and this is my friend James Stoddart-West."

"Have you ever seen a blonde woman wearing a light-colored, dyed squirrel coat anywhere about the place?"

"Well—I can't remember exactly," said Alexander astutely. "If I were to have a look—"

"Take 'em in, Sanders," said Inspector Bacon to the constable who was standing by the barn door. "One's only young once!"

"Oh sir, thank you, sir." Both boys were vociferous. "It's very kind of you, sir."

Bacon turned away toward the house.

"And now," he said to himself grimly, "for Miss Lucy Eyelesbarrow!"

III

After leading the police to the Long Barn and giving a brief account of her actions, Lucy had retired into the background, but she was under no illusion that the police had finished with her.

She was preparing potatoes for chips that evening when word was brought to her that Inspector Bacon required her presence. Putting aside the large bowl of cold water and salt in which the chips were reposing, Lucy followed the policeman to where the Inspector awaited her. She sat down and awaited his questions composedly.

She gave her name, her address in London, and added of her own accord:

"I will give you some names and addresses of reference if you want to know all about me."

The names were very good ones. An Admiral of the Fleet, the provost of an Oxford college and a Dame of the British Empire. In spite of himself Inspector Bacon was impressed.

"Now, Miss Eyelesbarrow, you went into the Long Barn to find some paint—is that right? And after having found the paint you got a crowbar, forced up the lid of this sarcophagus and found the body. What were you looking for in the sarcophagus?"

"I was looking for a body," said Lucy.

"You were looking for a body—and you found one! Doesn't that seem to you a very extraordinary story?"

"Oh yes, it is an extraordinary story. Perhaps you will let me explain it to you."

"I certainly think you had better do so."

Lucy gave him a precise recital of the events which had led up to her sensational discovery.

The Inspector summed it up in an outraged voice.

"You were engaged by an elderly lady to obtain a post here and to search the house and grounds for a dead body? Is that right?"

"Yes."

"Who is this elderly lady?"

"Miss Jane Marple. She is at present living at 4 Madison Road."

The Inspector wrote it down.

"You expect me to believe this story?"

Lucy said gently:

"Not, perhaps, until after you have interviewed Miss Marple and got her confirmation of it."

"I shall interview her all right. She must be cracked."

Lucy forbore to point out that to be proved right is not really a proof of mental incapacity. Instead she said:

"What are you proposing to tell Miss Crackenthorpe? About me, I mean?"

"Why do you ask?"

"Well, as far as Miss Marple is concerned I've done my job. I've found the body she wanted found. But I'm still engaged by Miss Crackenthorpe, and there are two hungry boys in the house and probably some more of the family will soon be coming down after all this upset. She needs domestic help. If you go and tell her that I only took this post in order to hunt for dead bodies she'll probably throw me out. Otherwise I can get on with my job and be useful."

The Inspector looked hard at her.

"I'm not saying anything to anyone at present," he said. "I haven't verified your statement yet. For all I know you may be making the whole thing up."

Lucy rose.

"Thank you. Then I'll go back to the kitchen and get on with things."

7

"WE'D better have the Yard in on it; is that what you think, Bacon?"

The Chief Constable looked inquiringly at Inspector Bacon. The Inspector was a big solid man—his expression was that of one utterly disgusted with humanity.

"The woman wasn't a local, sir," he said. "There's some reason to believe—from her underclothing—that she might have been a foreigner. Of course," added Inspector Bacon hastily, "I'm not letting on about that yet awhile. We're keeping it up our sleeves until after the inquest."

The Chief Constable nodded.

"The inquest will be purely formal, I suppose?"

"Yes, sir. I've seen the coroner."

"And it's fixed for—when?"

"Tomorrow. I understand the other members of the Crackenthorpe family will be here for it. There's just a chance one of them might be able to identify her. They'll all be here."

He consulted a list he held in his hand.

"Harold Crackenthorpe, he's something in the City—quite an important figure, I understand. Alfred—don't quite know what he does. Cedric—that's the one who lives abroad. Paints!" The Inspector invested the word with its full quota of sinister significance. The Chief Constable smiled into his mustache.

"No reason, is there, to believe the Crackenthorpe family are connected with the crime in any way?" he asked.

"Not apart from the fact that the body was found on the premises," said Inspector Bacon. "And of course it's just possible that this artist member of the family might be able to identify her. What beats me is this extraordinary rigmarole about the train."

"Ah yes. You've been to see this old lady, this—er"—he glanced at the memorandum lying on his desk—"Miss Marple?"

"Yes, sir. And she's quite set and definite about the whole thing. Whether she's barmy or not, I don't know, but she sticks to her story —about what her friend saw and all the rest of it. As far as all that goes, I dare say it's just make believe—sort of thing old ladies do make up, like seeing flying saucers at the bottom of the garden, and Russian agents in the lending library. But it seems quite clear that she did engage this young woman, the lady help, and told her to look for a body—which the girl did."

"And found one," observed the Chief Constable. "Well, it's all a very remarkable story. Marple, Miss Jane Marple—the name seems familiar somehow. . . . Anyway, I'll get on to the Yard. I think you're right about its not being a local case—though we won't advertise the fact just yet. For the moment we'll tell the press as little as possible."

II

The inquest was a purely formal affair. No one came forward to identify the dead woman. Lucy was called to give evidence of finding the body and medical evidence was given as to the cause of death—strangulation. The proceedings were then adjourned.

It was a cold, blustery day when the Crackenthorpe family came out of the hall where the inquest had been held. There were five of them all told: Emma, Cedric, Harold, Alfred and Bryan Eastley, the husband of the dead daughter Edith. There was also Mr. Wimborne, the senior partner of the firm of solicitors who dealt with the Crackenthorpes' legal affairs. He had come down specially from London at great inconvenience to attend the inquest. They all stood for a moment on the pavement, shivering. Quite a crowd had assembled; the piquant details of the "Body in the Sarcophagus" had been fully reported in both the London and the local press.

A murmur went round: "That's them . . ."

Emma said sharply: "Let's get away."

The big hired Daimler drew up to the curb. Emma got in and motioned to Lucy. Mr. Wimborne, Cedric and Harold followed. Bryan Eastley said: "I'll take Alfred with me in my little bus." The chauffeur shut the door and the Daimler prepared to roll away.

"Oh, stop!" cried Emma. "There are the boys!"

The boys, in spite of aggrieved protests, had been left behind at Rutherford Hall, but they now appeared grinning from ear to ear.

"We came on our bicycles," said Stoddart-West. "The policeman was very kind and let us in at the back of the hall. I hope you don't mind, Miss Crackenthorpe," he added politely.

"She doesn't mind," said Cedric, answering for his sister. "You're only young once. Your first inquest, I expect?"

"It was rather disappointing," said Alexander. "All over so soon."

"We can't stay here talking," said Harold irritably. "There's quite a crowd. And all those men with cameras."

At a sign from him, the chauffeur pulled away from the curb. The boys waved cheerfully.

"All over so soon!" said Cedric. "That's what they think, the young innocents! It's just beginning."

"It's all very unfortunate. Most unfortunate," said Harold. "I suppose—"

He looked at Mr. Wimborne who compressed his thin lips and shook his head with distaste.

"I hope," he said sententiously, "that the whole matter will soon be cleared up satisfactorily. The police are very efficient. However, the whole thing, as Harold says, has been most unfortunate."

He looked, as he spoke, at Lucy, and there was distinct disapproval in his glance. "If it had not been for this young woman," his eyes seemed to say, "poking about where she had no business to be, none of this would have happened."

This sentiment, or one closely resembling it, was voiced by Harold Crackenthorpe.

"By the way—er—Miss er—er Eyelesbarrow, just what made you go looking in that sarcophagus?"

Lucy had already wondered just when this thought would occur to one of the family. She had known that the police would ask it first thing: what surprised her was that it seemed to have occurred to no one else until this moment.

Cedric, Emma, Harold and Mr. Wimborne all looked at her.

Her reply, for what it was worth, had naturally been prepared for some time.

"Really," she said in a hesitating voice, "I hardly know. . . . I did feel that the whole place needed a thorough clearing out and cleaning. And there was"—she hesitated—"a very peculiar and disagreeable smell—"

She had counted accurately on the immediate shrinking of everyone from the unpleasantness of this idea.

Mr. Wimborne murmured: "Yes, yes, of course . . . about three weeks the police surgeon said. I think, you know, we must all try and not let our minds dwell on this thing." He smiled encouragingly at Emma who had turned very pale. "Remember," he said, "this wretched young woman was nothing to do with any of us."

"Ah, but you can't be so sure of that, can you?" said Cedric.

Lucy Eyelesbarrow looked at him with some interest. She had already been intrigued by the rather startling differences between the three brothers. Cedric was a big man with a weather-beaten, rugged face, unkempt dark hair and a jocund manner. He had arrived from the airport unshaven, and though he had shaved in preparation for the inquest, he was still wearing the clothes in which he had arrived and which seemed to be the only ones he had: old gray-flannel trousers and a patched and rather threadbare baggy jacket. He looked the stage Bohemian to the life and proud of it.

His brother Harold, on the contrary, was the perfect picture of a city gentleman and a director of important companies. He was tall with a neat, erect carriage, had dark hair going slightly bald on the temples, a small black mustache, and was impeccably dressed in a dark, well-cut suit and a pearl-gray tie. He looked what he was, a shrewd and successful businessman.

He now said stiffly:

"Really, Cedric, that seems a most uncalled-for remark."

"Don't see why. She was in our barn after all. What did she come there for?"

Mr. Wimborne coughed and said:

"Possibly some—er—assignation. I understand that it was a matter of local knowledge that the key was kept outside on a nail."

His tone indicated outrage at the carelessness of such procedure. So clearly marked was this that Emma spoke apologetically.

"It started during the war. For the air-raid wardens. There was a little spirit stove and they made themselves hot cocoa. And afterward, since there was really nothing there anybody could have wanted to take, we went on leaving the key hanging up. It was convenient for the Women's Institute people. If we'd kept it in the house it might have been awkward—when there was no one at home to give it them when they wanted it to get the place ready. With only daily women and no resident servants . . ."

Her voice tailed away. She had spoken mechanically, giving a wordy explanation without interest, as though her mind was elsewhere.

Cedric gave her a quick, puzzled glance.

"You're worried, Sis. What's up?"

Harold spoke with exasperation:

"Really, Cedric, can you ask?"

"Yes, I do ask. Granted a strange young woman has got herself killed in the barn at Rutherford Hall (sounds like a Victorian melodrama) and granted it gave Emma a shock at the time—but Emma's always been a sensible girl—I don't see why she goes on being worried now. Dash it, one gets used to everything."

"Murder takes a little more getting used to by some people than it may in your case," said Harold acidly. "I dare say murders are two a penny in Majorca and—"

"Iviza, not Majorca."

"It's the same thing."

"Not at all—it's quite a different island."

Harold went on talking:

"My point is that though murder may be an everyday commonplace to you, living among hot-blooded Latin people, nevertheless in England we take such things seriously." He added with increasing irritation, "And really, Cedric, to appear at a public inquest in those clothes—"

"What's wrong with my clothes? They're comfortable."

"They're unsuitable."

"Well, anyway, they're the only clothes I've got with me. I didn't pack my wardrobe trunk when I came rushing home to stand in with the family over this business. I'm a painter and painters like to be comfortable in their clothes."

"So you're still trying to paint?"

"Look here, Harold, when you say trying to paint—"

Mr. Wimborne cleared his throat in an authoritative manner.

"This discussion is unprofitable," he said reprovingly. "I hope, my dear Emma, that you will tell me if there is any further way in which I can be of service to you before I return to town?"

The reproof had its effect. Emma Crackenthorpe said quickly:

"It was most kind of you to come down."

"Not at all. It was advisable that someone should be at the inquest to watch the proceedings on behalf of the family. I have arranged for an interview with the Inspector at the house. I have no doubt that, distressing as all this has been, the situation will soon be clarified. In my own mind, there seems little doubt as to what occurred. As Emma has told us, the key of the Long Barn was known locally to hang outside the door. It seems highly probable that the place was used in the winter months as a place of assignation by local couples. No doubt there was a quarrel and some young man lost control of himself. Horrified at what he had done, his eye lit on the sarcophagus and he realized that it would make an excellent place of concealment."

Lucy thought to herself, "Yes, it sounds most plausible. That's just what one might think."

Cedric said, "You say a local couple—but nobody's been able to identify the girl locally."

"It's early days yet. No doubt we shall get an identification before long. And it is possible, of course, that the man in question was a local resident, but that the girl came from elsewhere, perhaps from some other part of Brackhampton. Brackhampton's a big place—it's grown enormously in the last twenty years."

"If I were a girl coming to meet my young man, I'd not stand for being taken to a freezing-cold barn miles from anywhere," Cedric objected. "I'd stand out for a nice bit of cuddle in the cinema, wouldn't you, Miss Eyelesbarrow?"

"Do we need to go into all this?" Harold demanded plaintively.

And with the voicing of the question the car drew up before the front door of Rutherford Hall and they all got out.

8

On entering the library Mr. Wimborne blinked a little as his shrewd old eyes went past Inspector Bacon whom he had already met, to the fair-haired, good-looking man beyond him.

Inspector Bacon performed introductions.

"This is Detective Inspector Craddock of New Scotland Yard," he said.

"New Scotland Yard—hm." Mr. Wimborne's eyebrows rose.

Dermot Craddock, who had a pleasant manner, went easily into speech.

"We have been called in on the case, Mr. Wimborne," he said. "As you are representing the Crackenthorpe family, I feel it is only fair that we should give you a little confidential information."

Nobody could make a better show of presenting a very small portion of the truth and implying that it was the whole truth than young Inspector Craddock.

"Inspector Bacon will agree, I am sure," he added, glancing at his colleague.

Inspector Bacon agreed with all due solemnity and not at all as though the whole matter were prearranged.

"It's like this," said Craddock. "We have reason to believe, from information that has come into our possession, that the dead woman is not a native of these parts, that she actually traveled down here from London and that she had recently come from abroad. Probably—though we are not sure of that—from France."

Mr. Wimborne again raised his eyebrows.

"Indeed," he said. "Indeed?"

"That being the case," explained Inspector Bacon, "the Chief Constable felt that the Yard was better fitted to investigate the matter."

"I can only hope," said Mr. Wimborne, "that the case will be solved quickly. As you can no doubt appreciate, the whole business has been a source of much distress to the family. Although not personally concerned in any way, they are—"

He paused for a bare second, but Inspector Craddock filled the gap quickly.

"It's not a pleasant thing to find a murdered woman on your property. I couldn't agree with you more. Now I should like to have a brief interview with the various members of the family—"

"I really cannot see—"

"What they can tell me? Probably nothing of interest—but one never knows. I dare say I can get most of the information I want from you, sir. Information about this house and the family."

"And what can that possibly have to do with an unknown young woman coming from abroad and getting herself killed here?"

"Well, that's rather the point," said Craddock. "Why did she come here? Had she once had some connection with this house? Had she been, for instance, a servant here at one time? A lady's maid, for instance. Or did she come here to meet a former occupant of Rutherford Hall—"

Mr. Wimborne said coldly that Rutherford Hall had been occupied by the Crackenthorpes ever since Josiah Crackenthorpe built it in 1884.

"That's interesting in itself," said Craddock. "If you'd just give me a brief outline of the family history—"

Mr. Wimborne shrugged his shoulders.

"There is very little to tell. Josiah Crackenthorpe was a manufacturer of sweet and savory biscuits, relishes, pickles, etc. He accumulated a vast fortune. He built this house. Luther Crackenthorpe, his eldest son, lives here now."

"Any other sons?"

"One other son, Henry, who was killed in a motor accident in 1911."

"And the present Mr. Crackenthorpe has never thought of selling the house?"

"He is unable to do so," said the lawyer dryly. "By the terms of his father's will."

"Perhaps you'll tell me about the will?"

"Why should I?"

Inspector Craddock smiled.

"Because I can look it up myself if I want to at Somerset House."

Against his will, Mr. Wimborne gave a crabbed little smile.

"Quite right, Inspector. I was merely protesting that the information you ask for is quite irrelevant. As to Josiah Crackenthorpe's will, there is no mystery about it. He left his very considerable fortune in trust, the income from it to be paid to his son Luther for life, and after Luther's death the capital to be divided equally among Luther's children, Edmund, Cedric, Harold, Alfred, Emma and Edith. Edmund was killed in the war and Edith died four years ago, so that on Luther Crackenthorpe's decease the money will be divided among Cedric, Harold, Alfred, Emma and Edith's son Alexander Eastley."

"And the house?"

"That will go to Luther Crackenthorpe's eldest surviving son or his issue."

"Was Edmund Crackenthorpe married?"

"No."

"So the property will actually go—?"

"To the next son—Cedric."

"Mr. Luther Crackenthorpe himself cannot dispose of it?"

"No."

"And he has no control of the capital."

"No."

"Isn't that rather unusual? I suppose," said Inspector Craddock shrewdly, "that his father didn't like him."

"You suppose correctly," said Mr. Wimborne. "Old Josiah was disappointed that his eldest son showed no interest in the family business—or indeed in business of any kind. Luther spent his time traveling abroad and collecting *objets d'art*. Old Josiah was very unsympathetic to that kind of thing. So he left his money in trust for the next generation."

"But in the meantime the next generation have no income except what they make or what their father allows them, and their father has considerable capital but no power of disposal of it."

"Exactly. And what all this has to do with the murder of an unknown young woman of foreign origin I cannot imagine!"

"It doesn't seem to have anything to do with it," Inspector Craddock agreed promptly. "I just wanted to ascertain all the facts."

Mr. Wimborne looked at him sharply; then, seemingly satisfied with the result of his scrutiny, rose to his feet.

"I am proposing now to return to London," he said. "Unless there is anything further you wish to know?"

He looked from one man to the other.

"No, thank you, sir."

The sound of the gong rose fortissimo from the hall outside.

"Dear me," said Mr. Wimborne. "One of the boys, I think, must be performing."

Inspector Craddock raised his voice to be heard above the clamor, as he said:

"We'll leave the family to have lunch in peace, but Inspector Bacon and I would like to return after it—say at two-fifteen—and have a short interview with every member of the family."

"You think that is necessary?"

"Well—" Craddock shrugged his shoulders. "It's just an off chance. Somebody might remember something that would give us a clue to the woman's identity."

"I doubt it, Inspector. I doubt it very much. But I wish you good luck. As I said just now, the sooner this distasteful business is cleared up, the better for everybody."

Shaking his head, he went slowly out of the room.

II

Lucy had gone straight to the kitchen on getting back from the inquest, and was busy with preparations for lunch when Bryan Eastley put his head in.

"Can I give you a hand in any way?" he asked. "I'm handy about the house."

Lucy gave him a quick, slightly preoccupied glance. Bryan had arrived at the inquest direct in his small M.G. car and she had not as yet had much time to size him up.

What she saw was likeable enough. Eastley was an amiable-looking young man of thirty-odd with brown hair, rather plaintive blue eyes and an enormous fair mustache.

"The boys aren't back yet," he said, coming in and sitting on the end of the kitchen table. "It will take 'em another twenty minutes on their bikes."

Lucy smiled.

"They were certainly determined not to miss anything."

"Can't blame them. I mean to say—first inquest in their young lives and right in the family, so to speak."

"Do you mind getting off the table, Mr. Eastley? I want to put the baking dish down there."

Bryan obeyed.

"I say, that fat's corking hot. What are you going to put in it?"

"Yorkshire pudding."

"Good old Yorkshire. Roast beef of old England, is that the menu for today?"

"Yes."

"The funeral baked meats, in fact. Smells good," he sniffed appreciatively. "Do you mind my gassing away?"

"If you came in to help I'd rather you helped." She drew another pan from the oven. "Here—turn all these potatoes over so that they brown on the other side."

Bryan obeyed with alacrity.

"Have all these things been fizzling away in here while we've been at the inquest? Supposing they'd been all burned up."

"Most improbable. There's a regulating number on the oven."

"Kind of electric brain, eh what? Is that right?"

Lucy threw a swift look in his direction.

"Quite right. Now put the pan in the oven. Here, take the cloth. On the second shelf—I want the top one for the Yorkshire pudding."

Bryan obeyed, but not without uttering a shrill yelp.

"Burn yourself?"

"Just a bit. It doesn't matter. What a dangerous game cooking is!"

"I suppose you never do your own cooking?"

"As a matter of fact I do—quite often. But not this sort of thing. I can boil an egg, if I don't forget to look at the clock. And I can do eggs and bacon. And I can put a steak under the grill or open a tin of soup. I've got one of those little electric whatnots in my flat."

"You live in London?"

"If you call it living—yes."

His tone was despondent. He watched Lucy shoot in the dish with the Yorkshire pudding mixture.

"This is awfully jolly," he said, and sighed.

Her immediate preoccupations over, Lucy looked at him with more attention.

"What is—this kitchen?"

"Yes—reminds me of our kitchen at home—when I was a boy."

It struck Lucy that there was something strangely forlorn about Bryan Eastley. Looking closely at him, she realized that he was older than she had at first thought. He must be close on forty. It seemed difficult to think of him as Alexander's father. He reminded her of innumerable young pilots she had known during the war when she had been at the impressionable age of fourteen. She had gone on and grown up into a postwar world—but she felt as though Bryan had not gone on but had been overtaken in the passage of years. His next words confirmed this. He had subsided on to the kitchen table again.

"It's a difficult sort of world," he said, "isn't it? To get your bearings in, I mean. You see, one hasn't been trained for it."

Lucy recalled what she had heard from Emma.

"You were a fighter pilot, weren't you?" she said. "You've got a D.F.C."

"That's the sort of thing that puts you wrong. You've got a decoration and so people try to make it easy for you. Give you a job and all that. Very decent of them. But they're all white-collar jobs, and one simply isn't any good at that sort of thing. Sitting at a desk getting tangled up in figures. I've had ideas of my own, you know, tried out a wheeze or two. But you can't get the backing. Can't get the chaps to come in and put down the money. If I had a bit of capital—"

He brooded.

"You didn't know Edie, did you? My wife. No, of course you didn't. She was quite different from all this lot. Younger, for one thing. She was in the Air Force. She always said her old man was an Ebenezer Scrooge. He is, you know. Mean as hell over money. And it's not as though he could take it with him. It's got to be divided up when he dies. Edie's share will go to Alexander, of course. He won't be able to touch the capital until he's twenty-one, though."

"I'm sorry, but will you get off the table again. I want to dish up and make gravy."

At that moment Alexander and Stoddart-West arrived with rosy faces and very much out of breath.

"Hello, Bryan," said Alexander kindly to his father. "So this is where you've got to. I say, what a smashing piece of beef. Is there Yorkshire pudding?"

"Yes, there is."

"We have awful Yorkshire pudding at school—all damp and limp."

"Get out of my way," said Lucy. "I want to make the gravy."

"Make lots of gravy. Can we have two sauceboats full?"

"Yes."

"Good oh!" said Stoddart-West, pronouncing the words carefully.

"I don't like it pale," said Alexander anxiously.

"It won't be pale."

"She's a smashing cook," said Alexander to his father.

Lucy had a momentary impression that their roles were reversed. Alexander spoke like a kindly father to his son.

"Can we help you, Miss Eyelesbarrow?" asked Stoddart-West politely.

"Yes, you can. Alexander, go and sound the gong. James, will you carry this tray into the dining room? And will you take the joint in, Mr. Eastley? I'll bring the potatoes and the Yorkshire pudding."

"There's a Scotland Yard man here," said Alexander. "Do you think he will have lunch with us?"

"That depends on what your aunt arranges."

"I don't suppose Aunt Emma would mind. She's very hospitable. But I suppose Uncle Harold wouldn't like it. He's being very sticky over this murder." Alexander went out through the door with the tray, adding a little additional information over his shoulder. "Mr. Wimborne's in the library with the Scotland Yard men now. But he isn't staying to lunch. He said he had to get back to London. Come on, Stodders. Oh, he's gone to do the gong."

At that moment the gong took charge. Stoddart-West was an artist; he gave it everything he had and all further conversation was inhibited.

Bryan carried in the joint, Lucy followed with the vegetables—returned to the kitchen to get the two brimming sauceboats of gravy.

Mr. Wimborne was standing in the hall putting on his gloves as Emma came quickly down the stairs.

"Are you really sure you won't stop for lunch, Mr. Wimborne? It's all ready."

"No. I've an important appointment in London. There is a restaurant car on the train."

"It was very good of you to come down," said Emma gratefully.

The two police officers emerged from the library.

Mr. Wimborne took Emma's hand in his.

"There's nothing to worry about, my dear," he said. "This is Detective Inspector Craddock from New Scotland Yard who has come down to take charge of the case. He is coming back at two-fifteen to ask you for any facts that may assist him in his inquiry. But as I say, you have nothing to worry about." He looked toward Craddock. "I may repeat to Miss Crackenthorpe what you have told me?"

"Certainly, sir."

"Inspector Craddock has just told me that this almost certainly was not a local crime. The murdered woman is thought to have come from London and was probably a foreigner."

Emma Crackenthorpe said sharply, "A foreigner. Was she French?"

Mr. Wimborne had clearly meant his statement to be consoling. He looked slightly taken aback. Dermot Craddock's glance went quickly from him to Emma's face.

He wondered why she had leaped to the conclusion that the murdered woman was French, and why that thought disturbed her so much?

9

THE ONLY PEOPLE who really did justice to Lucy's excellent lunch were the two boys and Cedric Crackenthorpe, who appeared completely unaffected by the circumstances which had caused him to return to England. He seemed, indeed, to regard the whole thing as a rather good joke of a macabre nature.

This attitude, Lucy noted, was most unpalatable to his brother Harold. Harold seemed to take the murder as a kind of personal insult to the Crackenthorpe family and so great was his sense of outrage that he ate hardly any lunch. Emma looked worried and unhappy and also ate very little. Alfred seemed lost in a train of thought of his own and spoke very little. He was a good-looking man with a thin, dark face and eyes set rather too close together.

After lunch the police officers returned and politely asked if they could have a few words with Mr. Cedric Crackenthorpe.

Inspector Craddock was very pleasant and friendly.

"Sit down, Mr. Crackenthorpe. I understand you have just come back from the Balearics? You live out there?"

"Have done for the last six years. In Iviza. Suits me better than this dreary country."

"You get a good deal more sunshine than we do, I expect," said Inspector Craddock agreeably. "You were home not so very long ago, I understand—for Christmas, to be exact. What made it necessary for you to come back again so soon?"

Cedric grinned.

"Got a wire from Emma—my sister. We've never had a murder on the premises before. Didn't want to miss anything—so along I came."

"You are interested in criminology?"

"Oh, we needn't put it in such highbrow terms! I just like murders. Whodunnits and all that! With a whodunnit parked right on the family doorstep, it seemed the chance of a lifetime. Besides I thought poor old Em might need a spot of help—managing the old man and the police and all the rest of it."

"I see. It appealed to your sporting instincts and also to your family feelings. I've no doubt your sister will be very grateful to you—although her two other brothers have also come to be with her."

"But not to cheer and comfort," Cedric told him. "Harold is terrifically put out. It's not at all the thing for a city magnate to be mixed up with the murder of a questionable female."

Craddock's eyebrows rose gently.

"Was she—a questionable female?"

"Well, you're the authority on that point. Going by the facts, it seemed to me likely."

"I thought perhaps you might have been able to make a guess at who she was?"

"Come now, Inspector, you already know—or your colleagues will tell you—that I haven't been able to identify her."

"I said a guess, Mr. Crackenthorpe. You might never have seen the woman before, but you might have been able to make a guess at who she was—or who she might have been?"

Cedric shook his head.

"You're barking up the wrong tree. I've absolutely no idea. You're suggesting, I suppose, that she may have come to the Long Barn to keep an assignation with one of us? But we none of us live here—the only people in the house were a woman and an old man. You don't seriously believe that she came here to keep a date with my revered Pop?"

"Our point is—Inspector Bacon agrees with me—that the woman may once have had some association with this house. It may have been a considerable number of years ago. Cast your mind back, Mr. Crackenthorpe—"

Cedric thought a moment or two, then shook his head.

"We've had foreign help from time to time, like most people, but I can't think of any likely possibility. Better ask the others. They'd know more than I would."

"We shall do that, of course."

Craddock leaned back in his chair and went on:

"As you have heard at the inquest, the medical evidence cannot fix the time of death very accurately. Longer than two weeks, less than four—which brings it somewhere around Christmastime. You have told me you came home for Christmas. When did you arrive in England and when did you leave?"

Cedric reflected.

"Let me see . . . I flew. Got here on the Saturday before Christmas—that would be the twenty-first."

"You flew straight from Majorca?"

"Yes. Left at five in the morning and got here midday."

"And you left?"

"I flew back on the following Friday, the twenty-seventh."

"Thank you."

Cedric grinned.

"Leaves me well within the limit, unfortunately. But really, Inspector, strangling young women is not my favorite form of Christmas fun."

"I hope not, Mr. Crackenthorpe."

Inspector Bacon merely looked disapproving.

"There would be a remarkable absence of peace and good will about such an action, don't you agree?"

Cedric addressed this question to Inspector Bacon who merely grunted. Inspector Craddock said politely:

"Well, thank you, Mr. Crackenthorpe. That will be all."

"And what do you think of him?" Craddock asked as Cedric shut the door behind him.

Bacon grunted again.

"Cocky enough for anything," he said. "I don't care for the type, myself. A loose living lot, these artists, and very likely to be mixed up with a disreputable class of women."

Craddock smiled.

"I don't like the way he dresses, either," went on Bacon. "No respect—going to an inquest like that. Dirtiest pair of trousers I've seen in a long while. And did you see his tie? Looked as though it was made of colored string. If you ask me, he's the kind that would easily strangle a woman and make no bones about it."

"Well, he didn't strangle this one—if he didn't leave Majorca until the twenty-first. And that's a thing we can verify easily enough."

Bacon threw him a sharp glance.

"I notice that you're not tipping your hand yet about the actual date of the crime."

"No, we'll keep that dark for the present. I always like to have something up my sleeve in the early stages."

Bacon nodded in full agreement.

"Spring it on 'em when the time comes," he said. "That's the best plan."

"And now," said Craddock, "we'll see what our correct City gentleman has to say about it all."

Harold Crackenthorpe, thin-lipped, had very little to say about it. It was most distasteful—a very unfortunate incident. The newspapers, he was afraid— Reporters, he understood, had already been asking for interviews. All that sort of thing . . . Most regrettable . . .

Harold's staccato unfinished sentences ended. He leaned back in his chair with the expression of a man confronted with a very bad smell.

The Inspector's probing produced no result. No, he had no idea who the woman was or could be. Yes, he had been at Rutherford Hall for Christmas. He had been unable to come down until Christmas Eve, but had stayed on over the following weekend.

"That's that, then," said Inspector Craddock, without pressing his questions further. He had already made up his mind that Harold Crackenthorpe was not going to be helpful.

He passed on to Alfred, who came into the room with a nonchalance that seemed just a trifle overdone.

Craddock looked at Alfred Crackenthorpe with a faint feeling of recognition. Surely he had seen this particular member of the family somewhere before. Or had it been his picture in the paper? There was something discreditable attached to the memory. He asked Alfred his occupation and Alfred's answer was vague.

"I'm in insurance at the moment. Until recently I've been interested in putting a new type of talking machine on the market. Quite revolutionary. I did very well out of that, as a matter of fact."

Inspector Craddock looked appreciative, and no one could have had the least idea that he was noticing the superficially smart appearance of Alfred's suit and gauging correctly the low price it had cost. Cedric's clothes had been disreputable, almost threadbare, but they had been originally of good cut and excellent material. Here there was a cheap smartness that told its own tale. Craddock passed pleasantly on to his routine questions. Alfred seemed interested, even slightly amused.

"It's quite an idea, that the woman might once have had a job here. Not as a lady's maid; I doubt if my sister has ever had such a thing. I don't think anyone has nowadays. But of course there is a good deal of foreign domestic labor floating about. We've had Poles, and a temperamental German or two. As Emma definitely didn't recognize the woman, I think that washes your idea out, Inspector. Emma's got a very good memory for a face. No, if the woman came from London . . . What gives you the idea she came from London, by the way?"

He slipped the question in quite casually, but his eyes were sharp and interested.

Inspector Craddock smiled and shook his head.

Alfred looked at him keenly.

"Not telling, eh? Return ticket in her coat pocket, perhaps, is that it?"

"It could be, Mr. Crackenthorpe."

"Well, granting she came from London, perhaps the chap she came to meet had the idea that the Long Barn would be a nice place to do a quiet murder. He knows the setup here, evidently. I should go looking for him if I were you, Inspector."

"We are," said Inspector Craddock, and made the two little words sound quiet and confident.

He thanked Alfred and dismissed him.

"You know," he said to Bacon, "I've seen that chap somewhere before. . . ."

Inspector Bacon gave his verdict.

"Sharp customer," he said. "So sharp that he cuts himself sometimes."

II

"I don't suppose you want to see me," said Bryan Eastley apologetically, coming into the room and hesitating by the door. "I don't exactly belong to the family."

"Let me see, you are Mr. Bryan Eastley, the husband of Miss Edith Crackenthorpe, who died four years ago?"

"That's right."

"Well, it's very kind of you, Mr. Eastley, especially if you know something that you think could assist us in some way?"

"But I don't. Wish I did. Whole thing seems so ruddy peculiar, doesn't it? Coming along and meeting some fellow in that drafty old barn in the middle of winter. Wouldn't be my cup of tea!"

"It is certainly very perplexing," Inspector Craddock agreed.

"Is it true that she was a foreigner? Word seems to have got round to that effect."

"Does that fact suggest anything to you?" The Inspector looked at him sharply, but Bryan seemed amiably vacuous.

"No, it doesn't, as a matter of fact."

"Maybe she was French," said Inspector Bacon, with dark suspicion.

Bryan was roused to slight animation. A look of interest came into his blue eyes, and he tugged at his big, fair mustache.

"Really? Gay Paree?" He shook his head. "On the whole, it seems to make it even more unlikely, doesn't it? Messing about in the barn, I mean. You haven't had any other sarcophagus murders, have you? One of these fellows with an urge—or a complex? Thinks he's Caligula or someone like that?"

Inspector Craddock did not even trouble to reject this speculation. Instead, he asked in a casual manner:

"Nobody in the family got any French connections, or—or—relationships that you know of?"

Bryan said that the Crackenthorpes weren't a very gay lot.

"Harold's respectably married," he said. "Fish-faced woman, some impoverished peer's daughter. Don't think Alfred cares about women much—spends his life going in for shady deals which usually go wrong in the end. I dare say Cedric's got a few Spanish señoritas jumping through hoops for him in Iviza. Women rather fall for Cedric. Doesn't always shave and looks as though he never washes. Don't see why that should be attractive to women, but apparently it is—I say, I'm not being very helpful, am I?"

He grinned at them.

"Better get young Alexander on the job. He and James Stoddart-West are out hunting for clues in a big way. Bet you they turn up something."

Inspector Craddock said he hoped they would. Then he thanked Bryan Eastley and said he would like to speak to Miss Emma Crackenthorpe.

III

Inspector Craddock looked with more attention at Emma Crackenthorpe than he had done previously. He was still wondering about the expression that he had surprised on her face before lunch.

A quiet woman. Not stupid. Not brilliant, either. One of those comfortable, pleasant women whom men were inclined to take for granted, and who had the art of making a house into a home, giving it an atmosphere of restfulness and quiet harmony. Such, he thought, was Emma Crackenthorpe.

Women such as this were often underrated. Behind their quiet exterior they had force of character, they were to be reckoned with. Perhaps, Craddock thought, the clue to the mystery of the dead woman in the sarcophagus was hidden away in the recesses of Emma's mind.

While these thoughts were passing through his head, Craddock was asking various unimportant questions.

"I don't suppose there is much that you haven't already told Inspector Bacon," he said. "So I needn't worry you with many questions."

"Please ask me anything you like."

"As Mr. Wimborne told you, we have reached the conclusion that the dead woman was not a native of these parts. That may be a relief to you—Mr. Wimborne seemed to think it would be—but it makes it really more difficult for us. She's less easily identified."

"But didn't she have anything? A handbag? Papers?"

Craddock shook his head.

"No handbag, nothing in her pockets."

"You've no idea of her name—of where she came from—anything at all?"

Craddock thought to himself: She wants to know—she's very anxious to know—who the woman is. Has she felt like that all along, I wonder? Bacon didn't give me that impression—and he's a shrewd man. . . .

"We know nothing about her," he said. "That's why we hoped one of you could help us. Are you sure you can't? Even if you didn't recognize her, can you think of anyone she might be?"

He thought, but perhaps he imagined it, that there was a very slight pause before she answered.

"I've absolutely no idea," she said.

Imperceptibly, Inspector Craddock's manner changed. It was hardly noticeable except as a slight hardness in his voice.

"When Mr. Wimborne told you that the woman was a foreigner, why did you assume that she was French?"

Emma was not disconcerted. Her eyebrows rose slightly.

"Did I? Yes, I believe I did. I don't really know why, except that one always tends to think foreigners are French until one finds out what nationality they really are. Most foreigners in this country are French, aren't they?"

"Oh, I really wouldn't say that was so, Miss Crackenthorpe. Not nowadays. We have so many nationalities over here. Italians, Germans, Austrians, all the Scandinavian countries."

"Yes, I suppose you're right."

"You didn't have some special reason for thinking that this woman was likely to be French?"

She didn't hurry to deny it. She just thought a moment and then shook her head almost regretfully.

"No," she said. "I really don't think so."

Her glance met his placidly, without flinching.

Craddock looked toward Inspector Bacon. The latter leaned forward and presented a small, enamel powder compact.

"Do you recognize this, Miss Crackenthorpe?"

She took it and examined it.

"No. It's certainly not mine."

"You've no idea to whom it belonged?"

"No."

"Then I don't think we need worry you any more—for the present."

"Thank you."

She smiled briefly at them, got up, and left the room. Again he may have imagined it, but Craddock thought she moved rather quickly, as though a certain relief hurried her.

"Think she knows anything?" asked Bacon.

Inspector Craddock said ruefully:

"At a certain stage one is inclined to think everyone knows a little more than they are willing to tell you."

"They usually do, too," said Bacon out of the depth of his experience. "Only," he added, "it quite often isn't anything to do with the business in hand. It's some family peccadillo or some silly scrape that people are afraid is going to be dragged into the open."

"Yes, I know. Well, at least—"

But whatever Inspector Craddock had been about to say never got said, for the door was flung open and old Mr. Crackenthorpe shuffled in, in a high state of indignation.

"A pretty pass," he said. "Things have come to a pretty pass when Scotland Yard comes down and doesn't have the courtesy to talk to the head of the family first! Who's the master of this house, I'd like to know? Answer me that? Who's master here?"

"You are, of course, Mr. Crackenthorpe," said Craddock soothingly and rising as he spoke. "But we understood that you had already told Inspector Bacon all you knew, and that your health not being good, we must not make too many demands upon it. Doctor Quimper said—"

"I dare say. I dare say. I'm not a strong man. As for Doctor Quimper, he's a regular old woman—perfectly good doctor, understands my case—but inclined to wrap me up in cotton wool. Got a bee in his bonnet about food. Went on at me Christmastime when I had a bit of a turn. What did I eat? When? Who cooked it? Who served it? Fuss, fuss, fuss! But though I may have indifferent health, I'm well enough to give you all the help that's in my power. Murder in my own house, or at any rate in my own barn! Interesting building, that. Elizabethan. Local architect says not—but the fellow doesn't know what he's talking about. Not a day later than 1580— but that's not what we're talking about. What do you want to know? What's your present theory?"

"It's a little too early for theories, Mr. Crackenthorpe. We are still trying to find out who the woman was."

"Foreigner, you say?"

"We think so."

"Enemy agent?"

"Unlikely, I should say."

"You'd say! You'd say! They're everywhere, these people. Infiltrating! Why the Home Office lets them in beats me. Spying on industrial secrets, I'd bet. That's what she was doing."

"In Brackhampton?"

"Factories everywhere. One outside my own back gate."

Craddock shot an inquiring glance at Bacon who responded.

"Metal Boxes."

"How do you know that's what they're really making? Can't swallow all these fellows tell you. All right, if she wasn't a spy, who do you think she was? Think she was mixed up with one of my precious sons? It would be Alfred, if so. Not Harold, he's too careful. And Cedric doesn't condescend to live in this country. All right, then, she was Alfred's bit of skirt. And some violent fellow followed her down here, thinking she was coming to meet him, and did her in. How's that?"

Inspector Craddock said diplomatically that it was certainly a theory. But Mr. Alfred Crackenthorpe, he said, had not recognized her.

"Pah! Afraid, that's all! Alfred always was a coward. But he's a liar, remember, always was! Lie himself black in the face. None of my sons are any good. Crowd of vultures, waiting for me to die, that's their real occupation in life." He chuckled. "And they can wait. I won't die to oblige them! Well, if that's all I can do for you . . . I'm tired. Got to rest."

He shuffled out again.

"Alfred's bit of skirt?" said Bacon questioningly. "In my opinion the old man just made that up." He paused, hesitated. "I think, personally, Alfred's quite all right—perhaps a shifty customer in some ways, but not our present cup of tea. Mind you, I did just wonder about that Air Force chap."

"Bryan Eastley?"

"Yes. I've run into one or two of his type. They're what you might call adrift in the world—had danger and death and excitement too early in life. Now they find it tame. Tame and unsatisfactory. In a way, we've given them a raw deal. Though I don't really know what we could do about it. But there they are, all past and no future, so to speak. And they're the kind that don't mind taking chances. The ordinary fellow plays safe by instinct, it's not so much morality as prudence. But these fellows aren't afraid—playing safe isn't really in their vocabulary. If Eastley were mixed up with a woman and wanted to kill her—" He stopped, threw out a hand hopelessly. "But why should he want to kill her? And if you do kill a woman, why plant her in your father-in-law's sarcophagus? No, if you ask me, none of this lot had anything to do with the murder. If they had, they wouldn't have gone to all the trouble of planting the body on their own back doorstep, so to speak."

Craddock agreed that that hardly made sense.

"Anything more you want to do here?"

Craddock said there wasn't.

Bacon suggested coming back to Brackhampton and having a cup of tea, but Inspector Craddock said that he was going to call on an old acquaintance.

10

Miss Marple, sitting erect against a background of china dogs and presents from Margate, smiled approvingly at Inspector Dermot Craddock.

"I'm so glad," she said, "that you have been assigned to the case. I hoped you would be."

"When I got your letter," said Craddock, "I took it straight to the Assistant Commissioner. As it happened he had just heard from the Brackhampton people calling us in. They seemed to think it wasn't a local crime. The A.C. was very interested in what I had to tell him about you. He'd heard about you, I gather, from my uncle."

"Dear Sir Henry," murmured Miss Marple affectionately.

"He got me to tell him all about the Little Paddocks business. Do you want to hear what he said next?"

"Please tell me if it is not a breach of confidence."

"He said, 'Well, as this seems a completely cockeyed business, all thought up by a couple of old ladies who've turned out, against all probability, to be right, and since you already know one of these old ladies, I'm sending you down on the case.' So here I am! And now, my dear Miss Marple, where do we go from here? This is not, as you probably appreciate, an official visit. I haven't got my henchmen with me. I thought you and I might take down our back hair together first."

Miss Marple smiled at him.

"I'm sure," she said, "that no one who only knows you officially would ever guess that you could be so human, and better-looking than ever—don't blush. Now what, exactly, have you been told so far?"

"I've got everything, I think. Your friend Mrs. McGillicuddy's original statement to the police at St. Mary Mead, confirmation of her statement by the ticket collector and also the note to the stationmaster at Brackhampton. I may say that all the proper inquiries were made by the people concerned—the railway people and the police. But there's no doubt that you outsmarted them all by a most fantastic process of guesswork."

"Not guesswork," said Miss Marple. "And I had a great advantage. I knew Elspeth McGillicuddy. Nobody else did. There was no obvious confirmation of her story, and if there was no question of any woman being reported missing, then quite naturally they would think it was just an elderly lady imagining things—as elderly ladies often do, but not Elspeth McGillicuddy."

"Not Elspeth McGillicuddy," agreed the Inspector. "I'm looking forward to meeting her, you know. I wish she hadn't gone to Ceylon. We're arranging for her to be interviewed there, by the way."

"My own process of reasoning was not really original," said Miss Marple. "It's all in Mark Twain. The boy who found the horse. I just imagined where I would go if I were a horse and I went there and there was the horse."

"You imagined what you'd do if you were a cruel and cold-blooded murderer?" said Craddock, looking thoughtfully at Miss Marple's pink and white elderly fragility. "Really, your mind—"

"Like a sink, my nephew Raymond used to say," Miss Marple agreed, nodding her head briskly. "But as I always told him, sinks are necessary domestic equipment and actually very hygienic."

"Can you go a little further still, put yourself in the murderer's place, and tell me just where he is now?"

Miss Marple sighed.

"I wish I could. I've no idea—no idea at all. But he must be someone who has lived in, or knows all about Rutherford Hall."

"I agree. But that opens up a very wide field. Quite a succession of daily women have worked there. There's the Women's Institute, and the air-raid wardens before them. They all know the Long Barn and the sarcophagus and where the key was kept. The whole setup there is widely known locally. Anybody living roundabout might hit on it as a good spot for his purpose."

"Yes, indeed. I quite understand your difficulties."

Craddock said: "We'll never get anywhere until we identify the body."

"And that, too, may be difficult?"

"Oh, we'll get there—in the end. We're checking up on all the reported disappearances of a woman of that age and appearance. There's no one outstanding who fits the bill. The Medical Officer puts her down as about thirty-five, healthy, probably a married woman, has had at least one child. Her fur coat is a cheap one, purchased at a London store. Hundreds of such coats were sold in the last three months, about sixty per cent of them to blonde women. No salesgirl can recognize the photograph of the dead woman, or is likely to if the purchase were made just before Christmas. Her other clothes seem mainly of foreign manufacture, mostly purchased in Paris. There are no English laundry marks. We've communicated with Paris and they are checking up there for us. Sooner or later, of course, someone will come forward with a missing relative or lodger. It's just a matter of time."

"The compact wasn't any help?"

"Unfortunately, no. It's a type sold by the hundred in the rue de Rivoli, quite cheap. By the way, you ought to have turned that over to the police at once, you know, or rather Miss Eyelesbarrow should have done so."

Miss Marple shook her head.

"But at that moment there wasn't any question of a crime having been committed," she pointed out. "If a young lady, practicing golf shots, picks up an old compact of no particular value in the long grass, surely she doesn't rush straight off to the police with it?" Miss Marple paused, and then added firmly: "I thought it much wiser to find the body first."

Inspector Craddock was tickled.

"You don't seem to have ever had any doubts but that it would be found?"

"I was sure it would. Lucy Eyelesbarrow is a most efficient and intelligent person."

"I'll say she is! She scares the life out of me, she's so devastatingly efficient. No man will ever dare marry that girl."

"Now you know, I wouldn't say that. It would have to be a special type of man, of course." Miss Marple brooded on this thought a moment. "How is she getting on at Rutherford Hall?"

"They're completely dependent upon her as far as I can see. Eating out of her hand—literally as you might say. By the way, they know nothing about her connection with you. We've kept that dark."

"She has no connection now with me. She has done what I asked her to do."

"So she could hand in her notice and go if she wanted to?"

"Yes."

"But she stays on. Why?"

"She has not mentioned her reasons to me. She is a very intelligent girl. I suspect that she has become interested."

"In the problem? Or in the family?"

"It may be," said Miss Marple, "that it is rather difficult to separate the two."

Craddock looked hard at her.

"Have you got anything particular in mind?"

"Oh no—oh, dear me, no."

"I think you have."

Miss Marple shook her head.

Dermot Craddock sighed. "So all I can do is to 'prosecute my inquiries'—to put it in jargon. A policeman's life is a dull one!"

"You'll get results, I'm sure."

"Any ideas for me? More inspired guesswork?"

"I was thinking of things like theatrical companies," said Miss Marple rather vaguely. "Touring from place to place and perhaps not many home ties. One of those young women would be much less likely to be missed."

"Yes. Perhaps you've got something there. We'll pay special attention to that angle." He added, "What are you smiling about?"

"I was just thinking," said Miss Marple, "of Elspeth McGillicuddy's face when she hears we've found a body!"

II

"Well!" said Mrs. McGillicuddy. "Well!"

Words failed her. She looked across at the nicely spoken, pleasant young man who had called upon her with official credentials and then down at the photographs that he had handed her.

"That's her all right," she said. "Yes, that's her. Poor soul. Well, I must say I'm glad you've found her body. Nobody believed a word I said! The police or the railway people or anyone else. It's very galling not to be believed. At any rate, nobody could say I didn't do all I possibly could."

The nice young man made sympathetic and appreciative noises.

"Where did you say the body was found?"

"In a barn at a house called Rutherford Hall, just outside Brackhampton."

"Never heard of it. How did it get there, I wonder?"

The young man did not reply.

"Jane Marple found it, I suppose. Trust Jane."

"The body," said the young man, referring to some notes, "was found by a Miss Lucy Eyelesbarrow."

"Never heard of her either," said Mrs. McGillicuddy. "I still think Jane Marple had something to do with it."

"Anyway, Mrs. McGillicuddy, you definitely identify this picture as that of the woman whom you saw in a train?"

"Being strangled by a man. Yes, I do."

"Now, can you describe this man?"

"He was a tall man," said Mrs. McGillicuddy.

"Yes?"

"And dark."

"Yes?"

"That's all I can tell you," said Mrs. McGillicuddy. "He had his back to me. I didn't see his face."

"Would you be able to recognize him if you saw him?"

"Of course I shouldn't! He had his back to me. I never saw his face."

"You've no idea at all as to his age?"

Mrs. McGillicuddy considered.

"No—not really—I mean, I don't know. He wasn't, I'm almost sure, very young. His shoulders looked—well, set, if you know what I mean." The young man nodded. "Thirty and upward, I can't get closer than that. I wasn't really looking at him, you see. It was her —with those hands round her throat and her face—all blue. . . . You know, sometimes I dream of it even now."

"It must have been a very distressing experience," said the young man sympathetically.

He closed his notebook and said, "When are you returning to England?"

"Not for another three weeks. It isn't necessary, is it, for me?"

He quickly reassured her.

"Oh no. There's nothing you could do at present. Of course, if we make an arrest . . ."

It was left like that.

The mail brought a letter from Miss Marple to her friend. The writing was spiky and spidery and heavily underlined. Long practice made it easy for Mrs. McGillicuddy to decipher. Miss Marple wrote a very full account to her friend who devoured every word with great satisfaction.

She and Jane had shown them all right!

11

"I SIMPLY can't make you out," said Cedric Crackenthorpe.

He eased himself down on the decaying wall of a long-derelict pigsty and stared at Lucy Eyelesbarrow.

"What can't you make out?"

"What you're doing here."

"I'm earning my living."

"As a skivvy?" he spoke disparagingly.

"You're out of date," said Lucy. "Skivvy, indeed! I'm a household help, a professional domestician, or an answer to prayer, mainly the latter."

"You can't like all the things you have to do—cooking and making beds and whirring about with a Hoover cleaner and sinking your arms up to the elbows in greasy water."

Lucy laughed.

"Not the details, perhaps, but cooking satisfies my creative instincts, and there's something in me that really revels in clearing up mess."

"I live in a permanent mess," said Cedric. "I like it," he added defiantly.

"You look as though you did."

"My cottage in Iviza is run on simple straightforward lines. Three plates, two cups and saucers, a bed, a table and a couple of chairs. There's dust everywhere and smears of paint and chips of stone— I sculpt as well as paint—and nobody's allowed to touch a thing. I won't have a woman near the place."

"Not in any capacity?"

"Just what do you mean by that?"

"I was assuming that a man of such artistic tastes presumably had some kind of love life."

"My love life, as you call it, is my own business," said Cedric with dignity. "What I won't have is a woman in her tidying-up, interfering, bossing capacity!"

"How I'd love to have a go at your cottage," said Lucy. "It would be a challenge!"

"You won't get the opportunity."

"I suppose not."

Some bricks fell out of the pigsty. Cedric turned his head and looked into its nettle-ridden depths.

"Dear old Madge," he said. "I remember her well. A sow of most endearing disposition and a prolific mother. Seventeen in the last litter, I remember. We used to come here on fine afternoons and scratch Madge's back with a stick. She loved it."

"Why has this whole place been allowed to get into the state it's in? It can't only be the war?"

"You'd like to tidy this up, too, I suppose? What an interfering female you are. I quite see now why you would be the person to discover a body! You couldn't even leave a Greco-Roman sarcophagus alone." He paused and then went on. "No, it's not only the war. It's my father. What do you think of him, by the way?"

"I haven't had much time for thinking."

"Don't evade the issue. He's as mean as hell and in my opinion a bit crazy as well. Of course he hates all of us, except perhaps Emma. That's because of my grandfather's will."

Lucy looked inquiring.

"My grandfather was the man who mada-da-monitch. With the Crunchies and the Cracker Jacks and the Cozy Crisps. All the afternoon-tea delicacies, and then, being farsighted, he switched on very early to cheesies and canapés so that now we cash in on cocktail parties in a big way. Well, the time came when father intimated that he had a soul above Crunchies. He traveled in Italy and the Balkans and Greece and dabbled in art. My grandfather was peeved. He decided my father was no man of business and a rather poor judge of art (quite right in both cases), so left all his money in trust for his grandchildren. Father had the income for life, but he couldn't touch the capital. Do you know what he did? He stopped spending money. He came here and began to save. I'd say that by now he's accumulated nearly as big a fortune as my grandfather left. And in the meantime all of us, Harold, myself, Alfred and Emma haven't got a penny of grandfather's money. I'm a stony-broke painter. Harold went into business and is now a prominent man in the City—he's the one with the money-making touch, though I've heard rumors that he's in Queer Street lately. Alfred. Well, Alfred is usually known in the privacy of the family as Flash Alf."

"Why?"

"What a lot of things you want to know! The answer is that Alf is the black sheep of the family. He's not actually been to prison yet, but he's been very near it. He was in the Ministry of Supply during the war, but left it rather abruptly under questionable circumstances. And after that there were some dubious deals in tinned fruits, and trouble over eggs. Nothing in a big way—just a few doubtful deals on the side."

"Isn't it rather unwise to tell strangers all these things?"

"Why? Are you a police spy?"

"I might be."

"I don't think so. You were here slaving away before the police began to take an interest in us. I should say—"

He broke off as his sister Emma came through the door of the kitchen garden.

"Hullo, Em? You're looking very perturbed about something."

"I am. I want to talk to you, Cedric."

"I must get back to the house," said Lucy, tactfully.

"Don't go," said Cedric. "Murder has made you practically one of the family."

"I've got a lot to do," said Lucy. "I only came out to get some parsley."

She beat a rapid retreat to the kitchen garden. Cedric's eyes followed her.

"Good-looking girl," he said. "Who is she really?"

"Oh, she's quite well known," said Emma. "She's made a specialty of this kind of thing. But never mind Lucy Eyelesbarrow, Cedric. I'm terribly worried. Apparently the police think that this girl was a foreigner, perhaps French. Cedric, you don't think that she could possibly be—Martine?"

II

For a moment or two Cedric stared at her as though uncomprehending.

"Martine? But who on earth—oh, you mean Martine?"

"Yes. Do you think—"

"Why on earth should it be Martine?"

"Well, her sending that telegram was odd when you come to think of it. It must have been roughly about the same time. Do you think that she may, after all, have come down here and . . ."

"Nonsense. Why should Martine come down here and find her way into the Long Barn? What for? It seems wildly unlikely to me."

"You don't think, perhaps, that I ought to tell Inspector Bacon, or the other one?"

"Tell him what?"

"Well—about Martine. About her letter."

"Now don't you go complicating things, Sis, by bringing up a lot of irrelevant stuff that has nothing to do with all this. I was never very convinced about that letter from Martine, anyway."

"I was."

"You've always been good at believing impossible things before breakfast, old girl. My advice to you is, sit tight and keep your mouth shut. It's up to the police to identify their precious corpse. And I bet Harold would say the same."

"Oh, I know Harold would. And Alfred, also. But I'm worried, Cedric, I really am worried. I don't know what I ought to do."

"Nothing," said Cedric promptly. "You keep your mouth shut, Emma. Never go halfway to meet trouble, that's my motto."

Emma Crackenthorpe sighed. She went slowly back to the house, uneasy in her mind.

As she came into the drive, Doctor Quimper emerged from the house and opened the door of his battered Austin car. He paused when he saw her; then, leaving the car, he came toward her.

"Well, Emma," he said. "Your father's in splendid shape. Murder suits him. It's given him an interest in life. I must recommend it for more of my patients."

Emma smiled mechanically. Doctor Quimper was always quick to notice reactions.

"Anything particular the matter?" he asked.

Emma looked up at him. She had come to rely a lot on the kindliness and sympathy of the doctor. He had become a friend on whom to lean, not only a medical attendant. His calculated brusqueness did not deceive her; she knew the kindness that lay behind it.

"I am worried, yes," she admitted.

"Care to tell me? Don't, if you don't want to."

"I'd like to tell you. Some of it you know already. The point is I don't know what to do."

"I should say your judgment was usually most reliable. What's the trouble?"

"You remember—or perhaps you don't—what I once told you about my brother—the one who was killed in the war?"

"You mean about his having married, or wanting to marry, a French girl? Something of that kind?"

"Yes. Almost immediately after I got that letter, he was killed. We never heard anything of or about the girl. All we knew, actually, was her Christian name. We always expected her to write or to turn up, but she didn't. We never heard anything—until about a month ago, just before Christmas."

"I remember. You got a letter, didn't you?"

"Yes. Saying she was in England and would like to come and see us. It was all arranged and then, at the last minute, she sent a wire that she had to return unexpectedly to France."

"Well?"

"The police think that this woman who was killed—was French."

"They do, do they? She looked more of an English type to me, but one can't really judge. What's worrying you, then, is that just possibly the dead woman might be your brother's girl?"

"Yes."

"I think it's most unlikely," said Doctor Quimper, adding: "But all the same, I understand what you feel."

"I'm wondering if I ought not to tell the police about—about it all. Cedric and the others say it's quite unnecessary. What do you think?"

"Hm." Doctor Quimper pursed up his lips. He was silent for a moment or two, deep in thought. Then he said, almost unwillingly, "It's much simpler, of course, if you say nothing. I can understand what your brothers feel about it. All the same—"

"Yes?"

Quimper looked at her. His eyes had an affectionate twinkle in them.

"I'd go ahead and tell 'em," he said. "You'll go on worrying if you don't. I know you."

Emma flushed a little.

"Perhaps I'm foolish."

"You do what you want to do, my dear, and let the rest of the family go hang! I'd back your judgment against the lot of them any day."

12

"Girl! You, girl! Come in here."

Lucy turned her head, surprised. Old Mr. Crackenthorpe was beckoning to her fiercely from just inside a door.

"You want me, Mr. Crackenthorpe?"

"Don't talk so much. Come in here."

Lucy obeyed the imperative finger. Old Mr. Crackenthorpe took hold of her arm and pulled her inside the door and shut it.

"Want to show you something," he said.

Lucy looked round her. They were in a small room evidently designed to be used as a study, but equally evidently not used as such for a very long time. There were piles of dusty papers on the desk and cobwebs festooned from the corners of the ceiling. The air smelled damp and musty.

"Do you want me to clean this room?" she asked.

Old Mr. Crackenthorpe shook his head fiercely.

"No, you don't! I keep this room locked up. Emma would like to fiddle about in here, but I don't let her. It's my room. See these stones? They're geological specimens."

Lucy looked at a collection of twelve or fourteen lumps of rock, some polished and some rough.

"Lovely," she said kindly. "Most interesting."

"You're quite right. They are interesting. You're an intelligent girl. I don't show them to everybody. I'll show you some more things."

"It's very kind of you, but I ought really to get on with what I was doing. With six people in the house—"

"Eating me out of house and home. That's all they do when they come down here! Eat. They don't offer to pay for what they eat, either. Leeches! All waiting for me to die. Well, I'm not going to die just yet—I'm not going to die to please them. I'm a lot stronger than even Emma knows."

"I'm sure you are."

"I'm not so old, either. She makes out I'm an old man, treats me as an old man. You don't think I'm old, do you?"

"Of course not," said Lucy.

"Sensible girl. Take a look at this."

He indicated a large, faded chart which hung on the wall. It was, Lucy saw, a genealogical tree; some of it done so finely that one would have had to have a magnifying glass to read the names. The remote forbears, however, were written in large, proud capitals with crowns over the names.

"Descended from kings," said Mr. Crackenthorpe. "My mother's family tree, that is, not my father's. He was a vulgarian! Common old man! Didn't like me. I was a cut above him always. Took after my mother's side. Had a natural feeling for art and classical sculpture—he couldn't see anything in it, silly old fool. Don't remember my mother—died when I was two. Last of her family. They were sold up and she married my father. But you look there—Edward the Confessor—Ethelred the Unready—whole lot of them. And that was before the Normans came. Before the Normans—that's something, isn't it?"

"It is indeed."

"Now I'll show you something else." He guided her across the room to an enormous piece of dark oak furniture. Lucy was rather uneasily conscious of the strength of the fingers clutching her arm. There certainly seemed nothing feeble about old Mr. Crackenthorpe today. "See this? Came out of Lushington—that was my mother's people's place. Elizabethan, this is. Takes four men to move it. You don't know what I keep inside it, do you? Like me to show you?"

"Do show me," said Lucy politely.

"Curious, aren't you? All women are curious." He took a key from his pocket and unlocked the door of the lower cupboard. From this he took out a surprisingly new-looking cash box. This, again, he unlocked.

"Take a look here, my dear. Know what these are?"

He lifted out a small, paper-wrapped cylinder and pulled away the paper from one end. Gold coins trickled out into his palm.

"Look at these, young lady. Look at 'em, hold 'em, touch 'em. Know what they are? Bet you don't! You're too young. Sovereigns —that's what they are. Good, golden sovereigns. What we used before all these dirty bits of paper came into fashion. Worth a lot more than silly pieces of paper. Collected them a long time back. I've got other things in this box, too. Lots of things put away in here. All ready for the future. Emma doesn't know. Nobody knows. It's our secret, see, girl? D'you know why I'm telling you and showing you?"

"Why?"

"Because I don't want you to think I'm a played-out, sick old man. Lots of life in the old dog yet. My wife's been dead a long time. Always objecting to everything, she was. Didn't like the names I gave the children—good Saxon names. No interest in that family tree. I never paid any attention to what she said, though, and she was a poor-spirited creature—always gave in. Now you're a spirited filly—a very nice filly, indeed. I'll give you some advice. Don't throw yourself away on a young man. Young men are fools! You want to take care of your future. You wait—" His fingers pressed into Lucy's arm. He leaned to her ear. "I don't say more than that. Wait. Those silly fools think I'm going to die soon. I'm not. Shouldn't be surprised if I outlived the lot of them. And then we'll see! Oh yes, then we'll see. Harold's got no children. Cedric and Alfred aren't married. Emma—Emma will never marry now. She's a bit sweet on Quimper, but Quimper will never think of marrying Emma. There's Alexander, of course. Yes, there's Alexander. But, you know, I'm fond of Alexander. Yes, that's awkward. I'm fond of Alexander."

He paused for a moment, frowning, then said:

"Well, girl, what about it? What about it, eh?"

"Miss Eyelesbarrow . . ."

Emma's voice came faintly through the closed study door. Lucy seized gratefully at the opportunity.

"Miss Crackenthorpe's calling me. I must go. Thank you so much for all you have shown me."

"Don't forget . . . our secret . . ."

"I won't forget," said Lucy and hurried out into the hall, not quite certain as to whether she had or had not just received a conditional proposal of marriage.

II

Dermot Craddock sat at his desk in his room at New Scotland Yard. He was slumped sideways in an easy attitude and was talking into the telephone receiver which he held with one elbow propped up on the table. He was speaking in French, a language in which he was tolerably proficient.

"It was only an idea, you understand," he said.

"But decidedly it is an idea," said the voice at the other end, from the Prefecture in Paris. "Already I have set inquiries in motion in those circles. My agent reports that he has two or three promising lines of inquiry. Unless there is some family life or a lover, these women drop out of circulation very easily and no one troubles about them. They have gone on tour, or there is some new man—it is no one's business to ask. It is a pity that the photograph you sent me is so difficult for anyone to recognize. Strangulation, it does not improve the appearance. Still, that cannot be helped. I go now to study the latest reports of my agents on this matter. There will be, perhaps, something. *Au revoir, mon cher.*"

As Craddock reiterated the farewell politely, a slip of paper was placed before him on the desk. It read:

> Miss Emma Crackenthorpe
> To see Detective Inspector Craddock.
> Rutherford Hall case.

He replaced the receiver and said to the police constable:

"Bring Miss Crackenthorpe up."

As he waited, he leaned back in his chair, thinking.

So he had not been mistaken; there was something that Emma Crackenthorpe knew—not much, perhaps, but something. And she had decided to tell him.

He rose to his feet as she was shown in, shook hands, settled her in a chair and offered her a cigarette which she refused. Then there was a momentary pause. She was trying, he decided, to find just the words she wanted. He leaned forward.

"You have come to tell me something, Miss Crackenthorpe? Can I help you? You've been worried about something, haven't you? Some little thing, perhaps, that you feel probably has nothing to do with the case, but on the other hand just might be related to it.

You've come here to tell me about it, haven't you? It's to do, perhaps, with the identity of the dead woman. You think you know who she was?"

"No, no, not quite that. I think really it's most unlikely. But—"

"But there is some possibility that worries you. You'd better tell me about it, because we may be able to set your mind at rest."

Emma took a moment or two before speaking. Then she said:

"You have seen three of my brothers. I had another brother, Edmund, who was killed in the war. Shortly before he was killed, he wrote to me from France."

She opened her handbag and took out a worn and faded letter. She read from it:

"I hope this won't be a shock to you, Emmie, but I'm getting married—to a French girl. It's all been very sudden, but I know you'll be fond of Martine and look after her if anything happens to me. Will write you all the details in my next, by which time I shall be a married man! Break it gently to the old man, won't you? He'll probably go up in smoke."

Inspector Craddock held out a hand. Emma hesitated, then put the letter into it. She went on, speaking rapidly.

"Two days after receiving this letter, we had a telegram saying Edmund was missing, believed killed. Later he was definitely reported killed. It was just before Dunkirk and a time of great confusion. There was no Army record, as far as I could find out, of his having been married, but as I say, it was a confused time. I never heard anything from the girl. I tried, after the war, to make some inquiries, but I only knew her Christian name and that part of France had been occupied by the Germans and it was difficult to find out anything, without knowing the girl's surname and more about her. In the end I assumed that the marriage had never taken place and that the girl had probably married someone else before the end of the war, or might possibly herself have been killed."

Inspector Craddock nodded. Emma went on.

"Imagine my surprise to receive a letter, just about a month ago, signed *Martine Crackenthorpe*."

"You have it?"

Emma took it from her bag and handed it to him. Craddock read it with interest. It was written in a slanting French hand, an educated hand.

Dear Mademoiselle,

I hope it will not be a shock to you to get this letter. I do not even know if your brother Edmund told you that we were married. He said he was going to do so. He was killed only a few days after our marriage, and at the same time the Germans occupied our village. After the war ended, I decided that I would not write to you or approach you, though Edmund had told me to do so. But by then I had made a new life for myself, and it was not necessary. But now things have changed. For my son's sake I write this letter. He is your brother's son, you see, and I can no longer give him the advantages he ought to have. I am coming to England early next week. Will you let me know if I can come and see you? My address for letters is 126 Elvers Crescent, N. 10. I hope again this will not be the great shock to you.

I remain with assurance of my excellent sentiments,

Martine Crackenthorpe.

Craddock was silent for a moment or two. He reread the letter carefully before handing it back.

"What did you do on receipt of this letter, Miss Crackenthorpe?"

"My brother-in-law, Bryan Eastley, happened to be staying with me at the time and I talked to him about it. Then I rang up my brother Harold in London and consulted him about it. Harold was rather skeptical about the whole thing and advised extreme caution. We must, he said, go carefully into this woman's credentials."

Emma paused and then went on:

"That, of course, was only common sense and I quite agreed. But if this girl—woman—was really the Martine about whom Edmund had written to me, I felt that we must make her welcome. I wrote to the address she gave in her letter, inviting her to come down to Rutherford Hall and meet us. A few days later I received a telegram from London— *Very sorry forced to return to France unexpectedly. Martine.* There was no further letter or news of any kind."

"All this took place, when?"

Emma frowned.

"It was shortly before Christmas. I know, because I wanted to suggest her spending Christmas with us. But my father would not hear of it, so I suggested she should come down the weekend after Christmas while the family would still be there. I think the wire saying she was returning to France came actually a few days before Christmas."

"And you believe that this woman whose body was found in the sarcophagus might be this Martine?"

"No, of course I don't. But when you said she was probably a foreigner, well, I couldn't help wondering . . . if perhaps—"

Her voice died away.

Craddock spoke quickly and reassuringly.

"You did quite right to tell me about this. We'll look into it. I should say there is probably little doubt that the woman who wrote to you actually did go back to France and is there now, alive and well. On the other hand, there is a certain coincidence of dates, as you yourself have been clever enough to realize. As you heard at the inquest, the woman's death, according to the police surgeon's evidence, must have occurred about three to four weeks ago. Now don't worry, Miss Crackenthorpe, just leave it to us." He added casually, "You consulted Mr. Harold Crackenthorpe. What about your father and your other brothers?"

"I had to tell my father, of course. He got very worked up," she smiled faintly. "He was convinced it was a put-up thing to get money out of us. My father gets very excited about money. He believes, or pretends to believe, that he is a very poor man and that he must save every penny he can. I believe elderly people do get obsessions of that kind sometimes. It's not true, of course; he has a very large income and doesn't actually spend a quarter of it, or used not to until these days of high income tax. Certainly he has a large amount of savings put by." She paused and then went on. "I told my other two brothers also. Alfred seemed to consider it rather a joke, though he, too, thought it was almost certainly an imposture. Cedric just wasn't interested. He's inclined to be self-centered. Our idea was that the family would receive Martine, and that our lawyer, Mr. Wimborne, should also be asked to be present."

"What did Mr. Wimborne think about the matter?"

"We hadn't got as far as discussing the matter with him. We were on the point of doing so when Martine's telegram arrived."

"You have taken no further steps?"

"Yes. I wrote to the address in London with *Please forward* on the envelope, but I have had no reply of any kind."

"Rather a curious business. Hm . . ."

He looked at her sharply.

"What do you yourself think about it?"

"I don't know what to think."

"What were your reactions at the time? Did you think the letter was genuine, or did you agree with your father and brothers? What about your brother-in-law, by the way, what did he think?"

"Oh, Bryan thought that the letter was genuine."

"And you?"

"I wasn't sure."

"And what were your feelings about it, supposing that this girl really was your brother Edmund's widow?"

Emma's face softened.

"I was very fond of Edmund. He was my favorite brother. The letter seemed to me exactly the sort of letter that a girl like Martine would write under the circumstances. The course of events she described were entirely natural. I assumed that by the time the war ended she had either married again or was with some man who was protecting her and the child. Then, perhaps, this man had died or left her, and it then seemed right to her to apply to Edmund's family, as he himself had wanted her to do. The letter seemed genuine and natural to me, but of course, Harold pointed out that if it was written by an impostor, it would be written by some woman who had known Martine and who was in possession of all the facts, and so could write a thoroughly plausible letter. I had to admit the justice of that, but all the same—"

She stopped.

"You wanted it to be true?" said Craddock gently.

She looked at him gratefully.

"Yes, I wanted it to be true. I would be so glad if Edmund had left a son."

Craddock nodded.

"As you say, the letter, on the face of it, sounds genuine enough. What is surprising is the sequel; Martine Crackenthorpe's abrupt departure for Paris and the fact that you have never heard from her since. You had replied kindly to her, were prepared to welcome her. Why, even if she had to return to France, did she not write again? That is, presuming her to be the genuine article. If she were an impostor, of course, it's easier to explain. I thought perhaps that you might have consulted Mr. Wimborne, and that he might have instituted inquiries which alarmed the woman. That, you tell me, is not so. But it's still possible that one or other of your brothers may have done something of the kind. It's possible that this Martine may have had a background that would not stand investigation. She may have assumed that she would be dealing only with Edmund's affectionate sister, not with hardheaded, suspicious businessmen. She may have hoped to get sums of money out of you for the child—hardly a child now, a boy presumably of fifteen or sixteen—without many questions being asked. But instead she found she was going to run up against something quite different. After all, I should imagine that serious legal aspects would arise. If Edmund Crackenthorpe left a son, born in wedlock, he would be one of the heirs to your grandfather's estate?"

Emma nodded.

"Moreover, from what I have been told, he would in due course inherit Rutherford Hall and the land round it, very valuable building land, probably, by now."

Emma looked slightly startled.

"Yes, I hadn't thought of that."

"Well, I shouldn't worry," said Inspector Craddock. "You did quite right to come and tell me. I shall make inquiries, but it seems to me highly probable that there is no connection between the woman who wrote the letter—and who was probably trying to cash in on a swindle—and the woman whose body was found in the sarcophagus."

Emma rose with a sigh of relief.

"I'm so glad I've told you. You've been very kind."

Craddock accompanied her to the door.

Then he rang for Detective Sergeant Wetherall.

"Bob, I've got a job for you. Go to 126 Elvers Crescent, N. 10. Take photographs of the Rutherford Hall woman with you. See what you can find out about a woman calling herself Mrs. Crackenthorpe—Mrs. Martine Crackenthorpe—who was either living there or calling for letters there, between the dates of, say the fifteenth to the end of December."

"Right, sir."

Craddock busied himself with various other matters that were waiting attention on his desk. In the afternoon he went to see a theatrical agent who was a friend of his. His inquiries were not fruitful.

Later in the day when he returned to his office he found a wire from Paris on his desk.

PARTICULARS GIVEN BY YOU MIGHT APPLY TO ANNA STRAVINSKA OF BALLET MARITSKI. SUGGEST YOU COME OVER. DESSIN, PREFECTURE.

Craddock heaved a big sigh of relief and his brow cleared.

At last! So much, he thought, for the Martine Crackenthorpe hare. He decided to take the night ferry to Paris.

13

"It's so very kind of you to have asked me to take tea with you," said Miss Marple to Emma Crackenthorpe.

Miss Marple was looking particularly woolly and fluffy, a picture of a sweet old lady. She beamed as she looked round her: at Harold Crackenthorpe in his well-cut dark suit, at Alfred handing her sandwiches with a charming smile, at Cedric standing by the mantelpiece in a ragged tweed jacket, scowling at the rest of his family.

"We are very pleased that you could come," said Emma politely.

There was no hint of the scene which had taken place after lunch that day when Emma had exclaimed: "Dear me, I quite forgot. I told Miss Eyelesbarrow that she could bring her old aunt to tea today."

"Put her off," said Harold brusquely. "We've still got a lot to talk about. We don't want strangers here."

"Let her have tea in the kitchen or somewhere with the girl," said Alfred.

"Oh no, I couldn't do that," said Emma firmly. "That would be very rude."

"Oh, let her come," said Cedric. "We can draw her out a little about the wonderful Lucy. I should like to know more about that girl, I must say. I'm not sure that I trust her. Too smart by half."

"She's very well connected and quite genuine," said Harold. "I've made it my business to find out. One wanted to be sure. Poking about and finding the body the way she did . . ."

"If we only knew who this damned woman was," said Alfred.

Harold asked angrily, "I must say, Emma, that I think you were out of your senses, going and suggesting to the police that the dead woman might be Edmund's French girl friend. It will make them convinced that she came here, and that probably one or other of us killed her."

"Oh no, Harold. Don't exaggerate."

"Harold's quite right," said Alfred. "Whatever possessed you, I don't know. I've a feeling I'm being followed everywhere I go by plain-clothes men."

"I told her not to do it," said Cedric. "Then Quimper backed her up."

"It's no business of his," said Harold angrily. "Let him stick to pills and powders and national health."

"Oh, do stop quarreling," said Emma wearily. "I'm really glad this old Miss What's-her-name is coming to tea. It will do us all good to have a stranger here and be prevented from going over and over the same things again and again. I must go and tidy myself up a little."

She left the room.

"This Lucy Eyelesbarrow," said Harold and stopped. "As Cedric says, it is odd that she should nose about in the barn and go opening up a sarcophagus—really a Herculean task. Perhaps we ought to take steps. Her attitude, I thought, was rather antagonistic at lunch."

"Leave her to me," said Alfred. "I'll soon find out if she's up to anything."

"I mean, why open up that sarcophagus?"

"Perhaps she isn't really Lucy Eyelesbarrow at all," suggested Cedric.

"But what would be the point—" Harold looked thoroughly upset. "Oh damn!"

They looked at each other with worried faces.

"And here's this pestilential old woman coming to tea. Just when we want to think."

"We'll talk things over this evening," said Alfred. "In the meantime, we'll pump the old aunt about Lucy."

So Miss Marple had duly been fetched by Lucy and installed by the fire, and she was now smiling up at Alfred as he handed her sandwiches with the approval she always showed toward a good-looking man.

"Thank you so much. May I ask—? Oh, egg and sardine, yes that will be very nice. I'm afraid I'm always rather greedy over my tea. As one gets on, you know—and of course, at night only a very light meal—I have to be careful. I shall be ninety next year. Yes, indeed."

"Eighty-seven," said Lucy.

"No, dear, ninety. You young people don't know best about everything." Miss Marple spoke with a faint acidity. Then she turned to her hostess once more. "What a beautiful house you have. And so many beautiful things in it. Those bronzes, now, they remind me of some my father bought at the Paris Exhibition. Really, your grandfather did? In the classical style, aren't they? Very handsome. How delightful for you having your brothers with you. So often families are scattered—India, though I suppose that is all done with now, and Africa—the West Coast such a bad climate."

"Two of my brothers live in London."

"That is very nice for you."

"But my brother Cedric is a painter and lives in Iviza, one of the Balearic Islands."

"Painters are so fond of islands, are they not?" said Miss Marple. "Chopin—that was Majorca, was it not? but he was a musician. It is Gauguin I am thinking of. A sad life; misspent, one feels. I myself never really care for paintings of native women, and although I know he is very much admired, I have never cared for that lurid mustard color. One really feels quite bilious looking at his pictures."

She eyed Cedric with a slightly disapproving air.

"Tell us about Lucy as a child, Miss Marple," said Cedric.

She smiled up at him delightedly.

"Lucy was always so clever," she said. "Yes, you were, dear. Now don't interrupt. Quite remarkable at arithmetic. Why I remember when the butcher overcharged me for topside of beef—"

Miss Marple launched full steam ahead into reminiscences of Lucy's childhood and from there to experiences of her own in village life.

The stream of reminiscence was interrupted by the entry of Bryan and the boys, rather wet and dirty as a result of an enthusiastic search for clues. Tea was brought in and with it came Doctor Quimper who raised his eyebrows slightly as he looked round after acknowledging his introduction to the old lady.

"Hope your father's not under the weather, Emma?"

"Oh no—that is, he was just a little tired this afternoon."

"Avoiding visitors, I expect," said Miss Marple with a roguish smile. "How well I remember my own dear father. 'Got a lot of old pussies coming?' he would say to my mother. 'Send my tea into the study.' Very naughty about it, he was."

"Please don't think—" began Emma, but Cedric cut in.

"It's always tea in the study when his dear sons come down. Psychologically to be expected, eh, doctor?"

Doctor Quimper who was devouring sandwiches and coffee cake with the frank appreciation of a man who has usually too little time to spend on his meals, said:

"Psychology's all right if it's left to the psychologists. Trouble is, everyone is an amateur psychologist nowadays. My patients tell me exactly what complexes and neuroses they're suffering from, without giving me a chance to tell them. Thanks, Emma, I will have another cup. No time for lunch today."

"A doctor's life, I always think, is so noble and self-sacrificing," said Miss Marple.

"You can't know many doctors," said Doctor Quimper. "Leeches they used to be called and leeches they often are! At any rate we do get paid nowadays, the state sees to that. No sending in of bills that you know won't ever be met. Trouble is that all one's patients are determined to get everything they can 'out of the government,' and as a result if little Jenny coughs twice in the night, or little Tommy eats a couple of green apples, out the poor doctor has to come in the middle of the night. Oh well! Glorious cake, Emma. What a cook you are!"

"Not mine. Miss Eyelesbarrow's."

"You make 'em just as good," said Quimper loyally.

"Will you come and see Father?"

She rose and the doctor followed her. Miss Marple watched them leave the room.

"Miss Crackenthorpe is a very devoted daughter, I see," she said.

"Can't imagine how she sticks the old man, myself," said the outspoken Cedric.

"She has a very comfortable home here, and Father is very much attached to her," said Harold quickly.

"Em's all right," said Cedric. "Born to be an old maid."

There was a faint twinkle in Miss Marple's eye as she said:

"Oh, do you think so?"

Harold said quickly:

"My brother didn't use the term old maid in any derogatory sense, Miss Marple."

"Oh, I wasn't offended," said Miss Marple. "I just wondered if he was right. I shouldn't say myself that Miss Crackenthorpe would be an old maid. She's the type, I think, that's quite likely to marry late in life, and make a success of it."

"Not very likely living here," said Cedric. "Never sees anybody she could marry."

Miss Marple's twinkle became more pronounced than ever.

"There are always clergymen and doctors."

Her eyes, gentle and mischievous, went from one to another.

It was clear that she had suggested to them something that they had never thought of and which they did not find overpleasing.

Miss Marple rose to her feet, dropping as she did so, several little woolly scarves and her bag.

The three brothers were most attentive picking things up.

"So kind of you," fluted Miss Marple. "Oh yes, and my little blue muffler. Yes, as I say, so kind to ask me here. I've been picturing, you know, just what your home was like, so that I can visualize dear Lucy working here."

"Perfect home conditions, with murder thrown in," said Cedric.

"Cedric!" Harold's voice was angry.

Miss Marple smiled up at Cedric.

"Do you know who you remind me of? Young Thomas Eade, our bank manager's son. Always out to shock people. It didn't do in banking circles, of course, so he went to the West Indies. He came home when his father died and inherited quite a lot of money. So nice for him. He was always better at spending money than making it."

II

Lucy took Miss Marple home. On her way back a figure stepped out of the darkness and stood in the glare of the headlights just as she was about to turn into the back lane. He held up his hand and Lucy recognized Alfred Crackenthorpe.

"That's better," he observed, as he got in. "Brrr, it's cold! I fancied I'd like a nice bracing walk. I didn't. Taken the old lady home all right?"

"Yes. She enjoyed herself very much."

"One could see that. Funny what a taste old ladies have for any kind of society, however dull. And really, nothing could be duller than Rutherford Hall. Two days here is about as much as I can stand. How do you manage to stick it out, Lucy? Don't mind if I call you Lucy, do you?"

"Not at all. I don't find it dull. Of course with me it's not a permanency."

"I've been watching you. You're a smart girl, Lucy. Too smart to waste yourself cooking and cleaning."

"Thank you, but I prefer cooking and cleaning to the office desk."

"So would I. But there are other ways of living. You could be a free lance."

"I am."

"Not this way. I mean, working for yourself, pitting your wits against—"

"Against what?"

"The powers that be! All the silly pettifogging rules and regulations that hamper us all nowadays. The interesting thing is there's always a way round them if you're smart enough to find it. And you're smart. Come now, does the idea appeal to you?"

"Possibly."

Lucy maneuvered the car into the stable yard.

"Not going to commit yourself?"

"I'd have to hear more."

"Frankly, my dear girl, I could use you. You've got the sort of manner that's invaluable, creates confidence."

"Do you want me to help you sell gold bricks?"

"Nothing so risky. Just a little bypassing of the law—no more." His hand slipped up her arm. "You're a damned attractive girl, Lucy. I'd like you as a partner."

"I'm flattered."

"Meaning, nothing doing? Think about it. Think of the fun, the pleasure you'd get out of outwitting all the sobersides. The trouble is, one needs capital."

"I'm afraid I haven't got any."

"Oh, it wasn't a touch! I'll be laying my hands on some before long. My revered Papa can't live forever, mean old brute. When he pops off, I lay my hands on some real money. What about it, Lucy?"

"What are the terms?"

"Marriage if you fancy it. Women seem to, no matter how advanced and self-supporting they are. Besides, married women can't be made to give evidence against their husbands."

"Not so flattering!"

"Come off it, Lucy. Don't you realize I've fallen for you?"

Rather to her surprise Lucy was aware of a queer fascination. There was a quality of charm about Alfred, perhaps due to sheer animal magnetism. She laughed and slipped from his encircling arm.

"This is no time for dalliance. There's dinner to think about."

"So there is, Lucy, and you're a lovely cook. What's for dinner?"

"Wait and see! You're as bad as the boys!"

They entered the house and Lucy hurried to the kitchen. She was rather surprised to be interrupted in her preparations by Harold Crackenthorpe.

"Miss Eyelesbarrow, can I speak to you about something?"

"Would later do, Mr. Crackenthorpe? I'm rather behindhand."

"Certainly. Certainly. After dinner?"

"Yes, that will do."

Dinner was duly served and appreciated. Lucy finished washing up and came out into the hall to find Harold Crackenthorpe waiting for her.

"Yes, Mr. Crackenthorpe?"

"Shall we come in here?" He opened the door of the drawing room and led the way. He shut the door behind her.

"I shall be leaving early in the morning," he explained, "but I want to tell you how struck I have been by your ability."

"Thank you," said Lucy feeling a little surprised.

"I feel that your talents are wasted here—definitely wasted."

"Do you? I don't."

At any rate, he can't ask me to marry him, thought Lucy. He's got a wife already.

"I suggest that having very kindly seen us through this lamentable crisis, you call upon me in London. If you will ring up and make an appointment, I will leave instructions with my secretary. The truth is that we could use someone of your outstanding ability in the firm. We could discuss fully in what field your talents would be most ably employed. I can offer you, Miss Eyelesbarrow, a very good salary indeed with brilliant prospects. I think you will be agreeably surprised."

His smile was magnanimous.

Lucy said demurely, "Thank you, Mr. Crackenthorpe, I'll think about it."

"Don't wait too long. These opportunities should not be missed by a young woman anxious to make her way in the world."

Again his teeth flashed.

"Good night, Miss Eyelesbarrow, sleep well."

"Well," said Lucy to herself, "well. . . . This is all very interesting."

On her way up to bed, Lucy encountered Cedric on the stairs.

"Look here, Lucy, there's something I want to say to you."

"Do you want me to marry you and come to Iviza and look after you?"

Cedric looked very much taken aback and slightly alarmed.

"I never thought of such a thing."

"Sorry. My mistake."

"I just wanted to know if you've a timetable in the house?"

"Is that all? There's one on the hall table."

"You know," said Cedric, reprovingly, "you shouldn't go about thinking everyone wants to marry you. You're quite a good-looking girl but not as good-looking as all that. There's a name for that sort of thing. It grows on you and you get worse. Actually you're the last girl in the world I should care to marry. The last girl."

"Indeed?" said Lucy. "You needn't rub it in. Perhaps you'd prefer me as a stepmother?"

"What's that?" Cedric stared at her, stupefied.

"You heard me," said Lucy, and went into her room and shut the door.

14

DERMOT CRADDOCK was fraternizing with Armand Dessin of the Paris Prefecture. The two men had met on one or two occasions and got on well together. Since Craddock spoke French fluently, most of their conversation was conducted in that language.

"It is an idea only," Dessin warned him. "I have a picture here of the corps de ballet. That is she, the fourth from the left. It says anything to you, yes?"

Inspector Craddock said that actually it didn't. A strangled young woman is not easy to recognize, and in this picture all the young women concerned were heavily made up and were wearing extravagant bird headdresses.

"It could be," he said. "I can't go further than that. Who was she? What do you know about her?"

"Almost less than nothing," said the other cheerfully. "She was not important, you see. And the Ballet Maritski—it is not important, either. It plays in suburban theaters and goes on tour. It has no real names, no stars, no famous ballerinas. But I will take you to see Madame Joliet who runs it."

Madame Joliet was a brisk businesslike Frenchwoman with a shrewd eye, a small mustache, and a good deal of adipose tissue.

"Me, I do not like the police!" She scowled at them, without camouflaging her dislike of the visit. "Always, if they can, they make me embarrassments."

"No, no, madame, you must not say that," said Dessin who was a tall, thin, melancholy looking man. "When have I ever caused you embarrassments?"

"Over that little fool who drank the carbolic acid," said Madame Joliet promptly. "And all because she has fallen in love with the *chef d'orchestre*, who does not care for women and has other tastes.

Over that you made the big brou ha ha! Which is not good for my beautiful ballet."

"On the contrary, big box-office business," said Dessin. "And that was three years ago. You should not bear malice. Now about this girl, Anna Stravinska."

"Well, what about her?"

"Is she Russian?" asked Inspector Craddock.

"No, indeed. You mean, because of her name? But they all call themselves names like that, these girls. She was not important, she did not dance well, she was not particularly good-looking. *Elle etait assez bien, c'est tout.* She danced well enough for the corps de ballet, but no solos."

"Was she French?"

"Perhaps. She had a French passport. But she told me once that she had an English husband."

"She told you that she had an English husband? Alive or dead?"

Madame Joliet shrugged her shoulders.

"Dead, or he had left her. How should I know which? These girls—there is always some trouble with men."

"When did you last see her?"

"I take my company to London for six weeks. We play at Torquay, at Bournemouth, at Eastbourne, at somewhere else I forget and at Hammersmith. Then we come back to France, but Anna, she does not come. She sends a message only that she leaves the company, that she goes to live with her husband's family, some nonsense of that kind. I did not think it is true, myself. I think it more likely that she has met a man, you understand."

Inspector Craddock nodded. He perceived that that was what Madame Joliet would invariably think.

"And it is no loss to me. I do not care. I can get girls just as good and better to come and dance, so I shrug the shoulders and do not think of it any more. Why should I? They are all the same, these girls, mad about men."

"What date was this?"

"When we return to France? It was—yes—the Sunday before Christmas. And Anna she leaves two, or is it three, days before that? I cannot remember exactly. But the end of the week at Hammersmith we have to dance without her, and it means rearranging things. It was very naughty of her, but these girls—the moment they meet a man they are all the same. Only I say to everybody, 'Zut, I do not take her back, that one!'"

"Very annoying for you."

"Ah! me—I do not care. No doubt she passes the Christmas holiday with some man she has picked up. It is not my affair. I can find other girls—girls who will leap at the chance of dancing in the Ballet Maritski and who can dance as well or better than Anna."

Madame Joliet paused and then asked with a sudden gleam of interest, "Why do you want to find her? Has she come into money?"

"On the contrary," said Inspector Craddock politely. "We think she may have been murdered."

Madame Joliet relapsed into indifference.

"*Ça se peut!* It happens. Ah well! She was a good Catholic. She went to Mass on Sundays, and no doubt to confession."

"Did she ever speak to you, madame, of a son?"

"A son? Do you mean she had a child? That, now, I should consider most unlikely. These girls, all—all of them—know a useful address to which to go. M. Dessin knows that as well as I do."

"She may have had a child before she adopted a stage life," said Craddock. "During the war, for instance."

"*Ah! dans la guerre.* That is always possible. But if so, I know nothing about it."

"Who among the other girls were her closest friends?"

"I can give you two or three names, but she was not very intimate with anyone."

They could get nothing else useful from Madame Joliet.

Shown the compact, she said Anna had one of that kind, but so had most of the other girls. Anna had perhaps bought a fur coat in London, she did not know. "Me, I occupy myself with the rehearsals, with the stage lighting, with all the difficulties of my business. I have not time to notice what my artists wear."

After Madame Joliet, they interviewed the girls whose names she had given them. One or two of them had known Anna fairly well, but they all said that she had not been one to talk much about herself, and that when she did, it was, so one girl said, mostly lies.

"She liked to pretend things—stories about having been the mistress of a grand duke or of a great English financier or how she worked for the Resistance in the war, even a story about being a film star in Hollywood."

Another girl said:

"I think that really she had had a very tame bourgeoise existence. She liked to be in ballet because she thought it was romantic, but she was not a good dancer. You understand that if she were to say, 'My father was a draper in Amiens,' that would not be romantic! So instead she made up things."

"Even in London," said the first girl, "she threw out hints about a very rich man who was going to take her on a cruise round the world, because she reminded him of his dead daughter who had died in a car accident. *Quelle blague!*"

"She told me she was going to stay with a rich lord in Scotland," said the second girl. "She said she would shoot the deer there."

None of this was helpful. All that seemed to emerge from it was that Anna Stravinska was a proficient liar. She was certainly not shooting deer with a peer in Scotland, and it seemed equally unlikely that she was on the sundeck of a liner cruising round the world. But neither was there any real reason to believe that her body had been found in a sarcophagus at Rutherford Hall. The identification by the girls and Madame Joliet was very uncertain and hesitating. It looked something like Anna, they all agreed. But really! All swollen up—it might be anybody!

The only fact that was established was that, on December 19, Anna Stravinska had decided not to return to France, and that on the twentieth of December a woman resembling her in appearance had traveled to Brackhampton by the 4:54 train and had been strangled.

If the woman in the sarcophagus was not Anna Stravinska, where was Anna now?

To that, Madame Joliet's answer was simple and inevitable:

"With a man!"

And it was probably the correct answer, Craddock reflected ruefully.

One other possibility had to be considered, raised by the casual remark that Anna had once referred to having an English husband.

Had that husband been Edmund Crackenthorpe?

It seemed unlikely, considering the word picture of Anna that had been given him by those who knew her. What was much more probable was that Anna had at one time known the girl Martine sufficiently intimately to be acquainted with the necessary details. It might have been Anna who wrote that letter to Emma Crackenthorpe and, if so, Anna would have been quite likely to have taken fright at any question of an investigation. Perhaps she had even thought it prudent to sever her connection with the Ballet Maritski. Again, where was she now?

And again, inevitably, Madame Joliet's answer seemed the most likely.

With a man.

II

Before leaving Paris, Craddock discussed with Dessin the question of the woman named Martine. Dessin was inclined to agree with his English colleague that the matter had probably no connection with the woman found in the sarcophagus. All the same, he agreed, the matter ought to be investigated.

He assured Craddock that the Sûreté would do their best to discover if there actually was any record of a marriage between Lieutenant Edmund Crackenthorpe of the 4th Southshire Regiment and a French girl whose Christian name was Martine. Time: just prior to the fall of Dunkirk.

He warned Craddock, however, that a definite answer was doubtful. The area in question had not only been occupied by the Germans at almost exactly that time, but subsequently that part of France had suffered severe war damage at the time of the invasion. Many buildings and records had been destroyed.

"But rest assured, my dear colleague, we shall do our best."

With this, he and Craddock took leave of each other.

III

On Craddock's return Sergeant Wetherall was waiting to report with gloomy relish:

"Accommodation address, sir—that's what 126 Elvers Crescent is. Quite respectable and all that."

"Any identifications?"

"No. Nobody could recognize the photograph as that of a woman who had called for letters, but I don't think they would anyway. It's a month ago, very near, and a good many people use the place. It's actually a boardinghouse for students."

"She might have stayed there under another name."

"If so, they didn't recognize her as the original of the photograph."

He added:

"We circularized the hotels—nobody registering as Martine Crack-enthorpe anywhere. On receipt of your call from Paris, we checked up on Anna Stravinska. She was registered with other members of the company in a cheap hotel off Brook Green—mostly theatricals there. She cleared out on the night of Thursday the nineteenth after the show. No further record."

Craddock nodded. He suggested a line of further inquiries, though he had little hope of success from them.

After some thought, he rang up Wimborne, Henderson and Carstairs and asked for an appointment with Mr. Wimborne.

In due course, he was ushered into a particularly airless room where Mr. Wimborne was sitting behind a large old-fashioned desk covered with bundles of dusty-looking papers. Various deed boxes labeled *Sir John ffouldes, dec. Lady Derrin, George Rowbotham, Esq.*, ornamented the walls; whether as relics of a bygone era or as part of present-day legal affairs, the Inspector did not know.

Mr. Wimborne eyed his visitor with the polite wariness characteristic of a family lawyer toward the police.

"What can I do for you, Inspector?"

"This letter." Craddock pushed Martine's letter across the table. Mr. Wimborne touched it with a distasteful finger but did not pick it up. His color rose very slightly and his lips tightened.

"Quite so," he said, "quite so! I received a letter from Miss Emma Crackenthorpe yesterday morning, informing me of her visit to Scotland Yard and of—ah—all the circumstances. I may say that I am at a loss to understand—quite at a loss—why I was not consulted about this letter at the time of its arrival! Most extraordinary! I should have been informed immediately."

Inspector Craddock repeated soothingly such platitudes as seemed best calculated to reduce Mr. Wimborne to an amenable frame of mind.

"I'd no idea that there was ever any question of Edmund's having married," said Mr. Wimborne in an injured voice.

Inspector Craddock said that he supposed, in wartime . . . and left it to trail away vaguely.

"Wartime!" snapped Mr. Wimborne with waspish acerbity. "Yes, indeed, we were in Lincoln's Inn Fields at the outbreak of war and there was a direct hit on the house next door, and a great number of our records were destroyed. Not the really important documents, of course; they had been removed to the country for safety. But it caused a great deal of confusion. Of course, the Crackenthorpe business was in my father's hands at that time. He died six years ago. I dare say he may have been told about this so-called marriage of Edmund's, but on the face of it, it looks as though that marriage, even if contemplated, never took place, and so, no doubt my father did not consider the story of any importance. I must say, all this sounds very fishy to me. This coming forward, after all these years, and claiming a marriage and a legitimate son. Very fishy, indeed. What proofs had she got, I'd like to know?"

"Just so," said Craddock. "What would her position or her son's position be?"

"The idea was, I suppose, that she would get the Crackenthorpes to provide for her and for the boy."

"Yes, but I meant, what would she and the son be entitled to, legally speaking, if she could prove her claim?"

"Oh, I see." Mr. Wimborne picked up his spectacles which he had laid aside in his irritation, and put them on, staring through them at Inspector Craddock with shrewd attention. "Well, at the moment, nothing. But if she could prove that the boy was the son of Edmund Crackenthorpe, born in lawful wedlock, then the boy would be entitled to his share of Josiah Crackenthorpe's trust, on the death of Luther Crackenthorpe. More than that, he'd inherit Rutherford Hall, since he's the son of the eldest son."

"Would anyone want to inherit the house?"

"To live in? I should say, certainly not. But that estate, my dear Inspector, is worth a considerable amount of money. Very considerable. Land for industrial and building purposes. Land which is now in the heart of Brackhampton. Oh yes, a very considerable inheritance."

"If Luther Crackenthorpe dies, I believe you told me that Cedric gets it?"

"He inherits the real estate, yes, as the eldest surviving son."

"Cedric Crackenthorpe, I have been given to understand, is not interested in money?"

Mr. Wimborne gave Craddock a cold stare.

"Indeed? I am inclined, myself, to take statements of such a nature with what I might term a grain of salt. There are doubtless certain unworldly people who are indifferent to money. I myself have never met one."

Mr. Wimborne obviously derived a certain satisfaction from this remark.

Inspector Craddock hastened to take advantage of this ray of sunshine.

"Harold and Alfred Crackenthorpe," he ventured, "seem to have been a good deal upset by the arrival of this letter?"

"Well they might be," said Mr. Wimborne. "Well they might be."

"It would reduce their eventual inheritance?"

"Certainly. Edmund Crackenthorpe's son—always presuming there is a son—would be entitled to a fifth share of the trust money."

"That doesn't really seem a very serious loss?"

Mr. Wimborne gave him a shrewd glance.

"It is a totally inadequate motive for murder, if that is what you mean."

"But I suppose they're both pretty hard up," Craddock murmured.

He sustained Mr. Wimborne's sharp glance with perfect impassivity.

"Oh! So the police have been making inquiries? Yes, Alfred is almost incessantly in low water. Occasionally he is very flush of money for a short time, but it soon goes. Harold, as you seem to have discovered, is at present somewhat precariously situated."

"In spite of his appearance of financial prosperity?"

"Façade. All façade! Half these City concerns don't even know if they're solvent or not. Balance sheets can be made to look all right to the inexpert eye. But when the assets that are listed aren't really assets—when those assets are trembling on the brink of a crash—where are you?"

"Where, presumably, Harold Crackenthorpe is, in bad need of money."

"Well, he wouldn't have got it by strangling his late brother's widow," said Mr. Wimborne. "And nobody's murdered Luther Crackenthorpe which is the only murder that would do the family any good. So really, Inspector, I don't quite see where your ideas are leading you."

The worst of it was, Inspector Craddock thought, that he wasn't very sure himself.

15

INSPECTOR CRADDOCK had made an appointment with Harold Crackenthorpe at his office, and he and Sergeant Wetherall arrived there punctually. The office was on the fourth floor of a big block of City offices. Inside everything showed prosperity and the acme of modern business taste.

A neat young woman took his name, spoke in a discreet murmur through a telephone, and then rising, showed them into Harold Crackenthorpe's own private office.

Harold was sitting behind a large leather-topped desk and was looking as impeccable and self-confident as ever. If, as the Inspector's private knowledge led him to surmise, he was close upon Queer Street, no trace of it showed.

He looked up with a frank, welcoming interest.

"Good morning, Inspector Craddock. I hope this means that you have some definite news for us at last."

"Hardly that, I am afraid, Mr. Crackenthorpe. It's just a few more questions I'd like to ask."

"More questions? Surely by now we have answered everything imaginable."

"I dare say it feels like that to you, Mr. Crackenthorpe, but it's just a question of our regular routine."

"Well, what is it this time?" He spoke impatiently.

"I should be glad if you could tell me exactly what you were doing on the afternoon and evening of December the twentieth last, say between the hours of three p.m. and midnight."

Harold Crackenthorpe went an angry shade of plum red.

"That seems to be a most extraordinary question to ask me. What does it mean, I should like to know?"

Craddock smiled gently.

"It just means that I should like to know where you were between the hours of three p.m. and midnight on Friday, December the twentieth."

"Why?"

"It would help to narrow things down."

"Narrow them down? You have extra information, then?"

"We hope that we're getting a little closer, sir."

"I'm not at all sure that I ought to answer your question. Not, that is, without having my solicitor present."

"That, of course, is entirely up to you," said Craddock. "You are not bound to answer any questions and you have a perfect right to have a solicitor present before you do so."

"You are not—let me be quite clear—er—warning me in any way?"

"Oh no, sir." Inspector Craddock looked properly shocked. "Nothing of that kind. The questions I am asking you I am asking of several other people as well. There's nothing directly personal about this. It's just a matter of necessary eliminations."

"Well, of course, I'm anxious to assist in any way I can. Let me see now. Such a thing isn't easy to answer offhand, but we're very systematic here. Miss Ellis, I expect, can help."

He spoke briefly into one of the telephones on his desk and almost immediately a streamlined young woman in a well-cut black suit entered with a notebook.

"My secretary, Miss Ellis, Inspector Craddock. Now, Miss Ellis, the Inspector would like to know what I was doing on the afternoon and evening of—what was the date?"

"Friday, December the twentieth."

"Friday, December the twentieth. I expect you will have some record."

"Oh yes." Miss Ellis left the room, returned with an office memorandum calendar and turned the pages.

"You were in the office in the morning of December the twentieth. You had a conference with Mr. Goldie about the Cromartie merger, you lunched with Lord Forthville at the Berkeley—"

"Ah, it was that day, yes."

"You returned to the office at about three o'clock and dictated half a dozen letters. You then left to attend Sotheby's sale rooms where you were interested in some rare manuscripts which were coming up for sale that day. You did not return to the office again, but I have a note to remind you that you were attending the Catering Club dinner that evening." She looked up interrogatively.

"Thank you, Miss Ellis."

Miss Ellis glided from the room.

"That is all quite clear in my mind," said Harold. "I went to Sotheby's that afternoon but the items I wanted there went for far too high a price. I had tea in a small place in Jermyn Street—Russell's, I think it is called. I dropped into a News Theatre for about half an hour or so, then went home. I live at 43 Cardigan Gardens. The Catering Club dinner took place at seven-thirty at Caterers' Hall, and after it I returned home to bed. I think that should answer your questions?"

"That's all very clear, Mr. Crackenthorpe. What time was it when you returned home to dress?"

"I don't think I can remember exactly. Soon after six, I should think."

"And after the dinner?"

"It was, I think, half-past eleven when I got home."

"Did your manservant let you in? Or perhaps Lady Alice Crackenthorpe?"

"My wife, Lady Alice, is abroad in the South of France and has been since early in December. I let myself in with my latchkey."

"So there is no one who can vouch for your returning home when you say you did?"

Harold gave him a cold stare.

"I dare say the servants heard me come in. I have a man and wife. But really, Inspector—"

"Please, Mr. Crackenthorpe, I know these questions are annoying, but I have nearly finished. Do you own a car?"

"Yes, a Humber Hawk."

"You drive it yourself?"

"Yes. I don't use it much except at weekends. Driving in London is quite impossible nowadays."

"I presume you use it when you go down to see your father and sister at Brackhampton?"

"Not unless I am going to stay there for some length of time. If I just go down for the night, as, for instance, to the inquest the other day, I always go by train. There is an excellent train service and it is far quicker than going by car. The car my sister hires meets me at the station."

"Where do you keep your car?"

"I rent a garage in the mews behind Cardigan Gardens. Any more questions?"

"I think that's all for now," said Inspector Craddock smiling and rising. "I'm very sorry for having to bother you."

When they were outside, Sergeant Wetherall, a man who lived in a state of dark suspicion of all and sundry, remarked meaningly:

"He didn't like those questions—didn't like them at all. Put out, he was."

"If you have not committed a murder, it naturally annoys you if it seems someone thinks that you have," said Inspector Craddock mildly. "It would particularly annoy an ultrarespectable man like Harold Crackenthorpe. There's nothing in that. What we've got to find out now is if anyone actually saw Harold Crackenthorpe at the sale that afternoon, and the same applies to the teashop place. He could easily have traveled by the four fifty-four, pushed the woman out of the train and caught a train back to London in time to appear at the dinner. In the same way he could have driven his car down that night, moved the body to the sarcophagus and driven back again. Make inquiries in the mews."

"Yes, sir. Do you think that's what he did do?"

"How do I know?" asked Inspector Craddock. "He's a tall, dark man. He could have been on that train and he's got a connection with Rutherford Hall. He's a possible suspect in this case. Now for brother Alfred."

II

Alfred Crackenthorpe had a flat in West Hampstead, in a big modern building of slightly jerry-built type with a large courtyard in which the owners of flats parked their cars with a certain lack of consideration for others.

The flat was of the modern built-in type, evidently rented furnished. It had a long plywood table that let down from the wall, a divan bed, and various chairs of improbable proportions.

Alfred Crackenthorpe met them with engaging friendliness but was, the Inspector thought, nervous.

"I'm intrigued," he said. "Can I offer you a drink, Inspector Craddock?" He held up various bottles invitingly.

"No, thank you, Mister Crackenthorpe."

"As bad as that?" He laughed at his own little joke, then asked what it was all about.

Inspector Craddock said his little piece.

"What was I doing on the afternoon and evening of December the twentieth? How should I know? Why, that's—what?—over three weeks ago."

"Your brother Harold has been able to tell us very exactly."

"Brother Harold, perhaps. Not brother Alfred." He added with a touch of something, envious malice possibly: "Harold is the successful member of the family—busy, useful, fully employed, a time for everything and everything at that time. Even if he were to commit a murder, shall we say? it would be carefully timed and exact."

"Any particular reason for using that example?"

"Oh no—it just came into my mind as a supreme absurdity."

"Now about yourself."

Alfred spread out his hands.

"It's as I tell you, I've no memory for times or places. If you were to say Christmas Day now, then I should be able to answer you—there's a peg to hang it on. I know where I was Christmas Day. We spend that with my father at Brackhampton. I really don't know why. He grumbles at the expense of having us, and would grumble that we never came near him if we didn't come. We really do it to please my sister."

"And you did it this year?"

"Yes."

"But unfortunately your father was taken ill, was he not?"

Craddock was pursuing a side line deliberately, led by the kind of instinct that often came to him in his profession.

"He was taken ill. Living like a sparrow in the glorious cause of economy, sudden full eating and drinking had its effect."

"That was all it was, was it?"

"Of course. What else?"

"I gathered that his doctor was—worried."

"Oh, that old fool Quimper," Alfred spoke quickly and scornfully. "It's no use listening to him, Inspector. He's an alarmist of the worst kind."

"Indeed? He seemed a rather sensible kind of man to me."

"He's a complete fool. Father's not really an invalid, there's nothing wrong with his heart, but he takes in Quimper completely. Naturally, when father really felt ill, he made a terrific fuss, and had

Quimper going and coming, asking questions, going into everything he'd eaten and drunk. The whole thing was ridiculous!" Alfred spoke with unusual heat.

Craddock was silent for a moment or two, rather effectively. Alfred fidgeted, shot him a quick glance, and then said petulantly:

"Well, what is all this? Why do you want to know where I was on a particular Friday, three or four weeks ago?"

"So you do remember that it was a Friday?"

"I thought you said so."

"Perhaps I did," said Inspector Craddock. "At any rate, Friday the twentieth is the day I am asking about."

"Why?"

"A routine inquiry."

"That's nonsense. Have you found out something more about this woman? About where she came from?"

"Our information is not yet complete."

Alfred gave him a sharp glance.

"I hope you're not being led aside by this wild theory of Emma's that she might have been my brother Edmund's widow. That's complete nonsense."

"This Martine did not at any time apply to you?"

"To me? Good Lord, no. That would have been a laugh."

"She would be more likely, you think, to go to your brother Harold?"

"Much more likely. His name's frequently in the papers. He's well off. Trying a touch there wouldn't surprise me. Not that she'd have got anything. Harold's as tightfisted as the old man himself. Emma, of course, is the softhearted one of the family, and she was Edmund's favorite sister. All the same, Emma isn't credulous. She was quite alive to the possibility of this woman being phony. She had it all laid on for the entire family to be there—and a hardheaded solicitor as well."

"Very wise," said Craddock. "Was there a definite date fixed for this meeting?"

"It was to be soon after Christmas. The weekend of the twenty-seventh—" He stopped.

"Ah," said Craddock pleasantly. "So I see some dates have a meaning to you."

"I've told you no definite date was fixed."

"But you talked about it—when?"

"I really can't remember."

"And you can't tell me what you yourself were doing on Friday, December the twentieth?"

"Sorry, my mind's an absolute blank."

"You don't keep an engagement book?"

"Can't stand the things."

"The Friday before Christmas—it shouldn't be too difficult."

"I played golf one day with a likely prospect." Alfred shook his head. "No, that was the week before. I probably just mooched around. I spend a lot of my time doing that. I find one's business gets done in bars more than anywhere else."

"Perhaps the people here, or some of your friends, may be able to help?"

"Maybe. I'll ask them. Do what I can."

Alfred seemed more sure of himself now.

"I can't tell you what I was doing that day," he said, "but I can tell you what I wasn't doing. I wasn't murdering anyone in the Long Barn."

"Why should you say that, Mr. Crackenthorpe?"

"Come now, my dear Inspector. You're investigating this murder, aren't you? And when you begin to ask 'Where were you on such and such a day at such and such a time?' you're narrowing down things. I'd very much like to know why you've hit on Friday the twentieth between—what?—lunchtime and midnight? It couldn't be medical evidence, not after all this time. Did somebody see the deceased sneaking into the barn that afternoon? She went in and she never came out, etc.? Is that it?"

The sharp, black eyes were watching him narrowly, but Inspector Craddock was far too old a hand to react to that sort of thing.

"I'm afraid we'll have to let you guess about that," he said pleasantly.

"The police are so secretive."

"Not only the police. I think, Mr. Crackenthorpe, you could remember what you were doing on that Friday if you tried. Of course, you may have reasons for not wishing to remember—"

"You won't catch me that way, Inspector. It's very suspicious, of course, very suspicious, indeed, that I can't remember, but there it is! Wait a minute now! I went to Leeds that week, stayed at a hotel close to the town hall—can't remember its name, but you'd find it easily enough. That might have been on the Friday."

"We'll check up," said the Inspector unemotionally.

He rose: "I'm sorry you couldn't have been more co-operative, Mr. Crackenthorpe."

"Most unfortunate for me! There's Cedric with a safe alibi in Iviza, and Harold, no doubt, checked with business appointments and public dinners every hour, and here am I with no alibi at all. Very sad. And all so silly. I've already told you I don't murder people. And why should I murder an unknown woman anyway? What for? Even if the corpse is the corpse of Edmund's widow, why should any of us wish to do away with her? Now if she'd been married to Harold in the war and had suddenly reappeared, then it might have been awkward for the respectable Harold—bigamy and all that. But Edmund! Why, we'd all have enjoyed making Father stump up a bit to give her an allowance and send the boy to a decent school. Father would have been wild, but he couldn't in decency refuse to do something. Won't you have a drink before you go, Inspector? Sure? Too bad I haven't been able to help you."

III

"Sir, listen, do you know what?"

Inspector Craddock looked at his excited sergeant.

"Yes, Wetherall, what is it?"

"I've placed him, sir. That chap. All the time I was trying to fix it and suddenly it came. He was mixed up in that tinned-food business with Dicky Rogers. Never got anything on him—too cagey for that. And he's been in with one or more of the Soho lot. Watches and that Italian sovereign business."

Of course! Craddock realized now why Alfred's face had seemed vaguely familiar from the first. It had all been small-time stuff, never anything that could be proved. Alfred had always been on the outskirts of the racket with a plausible, innocent reason for having been mixed up in it at all. But the police had been quite sure that a small, steady profit came his way.

"That throws rather a light on things," Craddock said.

"Think he done it?"

"I shouldn't have said he was the type to do murder. But it explains other things—the reason why he couldn't come up with an alibi."

"Yes, that looks bad for him."

"Not really," said Craddock. "It's quite a clever line, just to say firmly you can't remember. Lots of people can't remember what they did and where they were even a week ago. It's especially useful if you don't particularly want to call attention to the way you spend your time—interesting rendezvous at lorry pullups with the Dicky Rogers crowd, for instance."

"So you think he's all right?"

"I'm not prepared to think anyone's all right just yet," said Inspector Craddock. "You've got to work on it, Wetherall."

Back at his desk, Craddock sat frowning, and making little notes on the pad in front of him.

Murderer (he wrote). . . . A tall, dark man!!!

Victim? . . . . Could have been Martine, Edmund Crackenthorpe's girl friend or widow.

> or

Could have been Anna Stravinska. Went out of circulation at appropriate time, right age and appearance, clothing, etc. No connection with Rutherford Hall as far as is known.

Could be Harold's first wife! Bigamy!

    "   "   "   mistress. Blackmail?!

If connection with Alfred, might be blackmail had knowledge that could have sent him to jail? If Cedric—might have had connection with him abroad—Paris? Balearics?

> or

Victim could be Anna S. posing as Martine

> or

Victim is unknown woman killed by unknown murderer!

"And most probably the latter," said Craddock aloud.

He reflected gloomily on the situation. You couldn't get far with a case until you had the motive. All the motives suggested so far seemed either inadequate or farfetched.

Now if only it had been the murder of old Mr. Crackenthorpe. Plenty of motive there.

Something stirred in his memory.
He made further notes on his pad.

> Ask Dr. Q. about Christmas illness.
> Cedric—alibi.
> Consult Miss M. for latest gossip.

16

WHEN CRADDOCK got to 4 Madison Road he found Lucy Eyelesbarrow with Miss Marple.

He hesitated for a moment on his plan of campaign and then decided that Lucy Eyelesbarrow might prove a valuable ally.

After greetings, he solemnly drew out his notecase, extracted three pound notes, added three shillings and pushed them across the table to Miss Marple.

"What's this, Inspector?"

"Consultation fee. You're a consultant—on murder! Pulse, temperature, local reactions, possible deep-seated cause of said murder. I'm just the poor harassed local G.P."

Miss Marple looked at him and twinkled. He grinned at her. Lucy Eyelesbarrow gave a faint gasp and then laughed.

"Why, Inspector Craddock, you're human after all."

"Oh well, I'm not strictly on duty this afternoon."

"I told you we had met before," said Miss Marple to Lucy. "Sir Henry Clithering is his godfather, a very old friend of mine."

"Would you like to hear, Miss Eyelesbarrow, what my godfather said about her, the first time we met? He described her as just the finest detective God ever made—natural genius cultivated in a suitable soil. He told me never to despise the"—Dermot Craddock paused for a moment to seek for a synonym for "old pussies"—"er—elderly ladies. He said they could usually tell you what might have happened, what ought to have happened and even what actually did happen! And," he said, "they can tell you why it happened!" He added "that this particular—er—elderly lady was at the top of the class."

"Well!" said Lucy, "that seems to be a testimonial all right."

Miss Marple was pink and confused and looked unusually dithery.

"Dear Sir Henry," she murmured. "Always so kind. Really I'm not at all clever, just, perhaps, a slight knowledge of human nature —living, you know, in a village."

She added, with more composure:

"Of course, I am somewhat handicapped, by not actually being on the spot. It is so helpful, I always feel, when people remind you of other people, because types are alike everywhere and that is such a valuable guide."

Lucy looked a little puzzled, but Craddock nodded comprehendingly.

"But you've been to tea there, haven't you?" he said.

"Yes, indeed. Most pleasant. I was a little disappointed that I didn't see old Mr. Crackenthorpe, but one can't have everything."

"Do you feel that if you saw the person who had done the murder, you'd know?" asked Lucy.

"Oh, I wouldn't say that, dear. One is always inclined to guess, and guessing would be very wrong when it is a question of anything as serious as murder. All one can do is to observe the people concerned, or who might have been concerned, and see of whom they remind you."

"Like Cedric and the bank manager?"

Miss Marple corrected her.

"The bank manager's son, dear. Mr. Eade himself was far more like Mr. Harold, a very conservative man, but perhaps a little too fond of money—the sort of man, too, who would go a long way to avoid scandal."

Craddock smiled and said:

"And Alfred?"

"Jenkins at the garage," Miss Marple replied promptly. "He didn't exactly appropriate tools, but he used to exchange a broken or inferior jack for a good one. And I believe he wasn't very honest over batteries, though I don't understand these things very well. I know Raymond left off dealing with him and went to the garage on the Milchester Road. As for Emma," continued Miss Marple thoughtfully, "she reminds me very much of Geraldine Webb—always very quiet, almost dowdy—and bullied a good deal by her elderly mother. Quite a surprise to everybody when the mother died unexpectedly and Geraldine came into a nice sum of money and went and had her hair cut and permed and went off on a cruise and came back married to a very nice barrister. They had two children."

The parallel was clear enough. Lucy said, rather uneasily: "Do you think you ought to have said what you did about Emma marrying? It seemed to upset the brothers."

Miss Marple nodded.

"Yes," she said. "So like men, quite unable to see what's going on under their eyes. I don't believe you noticed yourself."

"No," admitted Lucy. "I never thought of anything of that kind. They both seemed to me—"

"So old?" said Miss Marple smiling a little. "But Doctor Quimper isn't much over forty, I should say, though he's going gray on the temples, and it's obvious that he's longing for some kind of home life; and Emma Crackenthorpe is under forty, not too old to marry and have a family. The doctor's wife died quite young having a baby, so I have heard."

"I believe she did. Emma said something about it one day."

"He must be lonely," said Miss Marple. "A busy hard-working doctor needs a wife, someone sympathetic, not too young."

"Listen, darling," said Lucy. "Are we investigating crime, or are we matchmaking?"

Miss Marple twinkled.

"I'm afraid I am rather romantic. Because I am an old maid, perhaps. You know, dear Lucy, that as far as I am concerned, you have fulfilled your contract. If you really want a holiday abroad before taking up your next engagement, you would have time still for a short trip."

"And leave Rutherford Hall? Never! I'm the complete sleuth by now. Almost as bad as the boys. They spend their entire time looking for clues. They looked all through the dustbins yesterday. Most unsavory, and they hadn't really the faintest idea what they were looking for. If they come to you in triumph, Inspector Craddock, bearing a torn scrap of paper with *Martine—if you value your life keep away from the Long Barn!* on it, you'll know that I've taken pity on them and concealed it in the pigsty!"

"Why the pigsty, dear?" asked Miss Marple with interest. "Do they keep pigs?"

"Oh no, not nowadays. It's just that I go there sometimes."

For some reason Lucy blushed. Miss Marple looked at her with increased interest.

"Who's at the house now?" asked Craddock.

"Cedric's there, and Bryan's down for the weekend. Harold and

Alfred are coming down tomorrow. They rang up this morning. I somehow got the impression that you had been putting the cat among the pigeons, Inspector Craddock."

Craddock smiled.

"I shook them up a little. Asked them to account for their movements on Friday, December the twentieth."

"And could they?"

"Harold could. Alfred couldn't or wouldn't."

"I think alibis must be terribly difficult," said Lucy. "Times and places and dates. They must be hard to check up on, too."

"It takes time and patience, but we manage." He glanced at his watch. "I'll be coming along to Rutherford Hall presently to have a word with Cedric, but I want to get hold of Doctor Quimper first."

"You'll be just about right. He has his surgery at six and he's usually finished about half-past. I must get back and deal with dinner."

"I'd like your opinion on one thing, Miss Eyelesbarrow. What's the family view about this Martine business, among themselves?"

Lucy replied promptly.

"They're all furious with Emma for going to you about it, and with Doctor Quimper who, it seemed, encouraged her to do so. Harold and Alfred think it was a try on and not genuine. Emma isn't sure. Cedric thinks it was phony, too, but he doesn't take it as seriously as the other two. Bryan, on the other hand, seems quite sure that it's genuine."

"Why I wonder?"

"Well, Bryan's rather like that. Just accepts things at their face value. He thinks it was Edmund's wife, or rather widow, and that she had suddenly to go back to France, but that they'll hear from her again sometime. The fact that she hasn't written or anything up to now, seems to him to be quite natural because he never writes letters himself. Bryan's rather sweet. Just like a dog that wants to be taken for a walk."

"And do you take him for a walk, dear?" asked Miss Marple. "To the pigsties, perhaps?"

Lucy shot a keen glance at her.

"So many gentlemen in the house, coming and going," mused Miss Marple.

When Miss Marple uttered the word "gentlemen" she always gave it its full Victorian flavor—an echo from an era actually before her own time. You were conscious at once of dashing, full-blooded (and probably whiskered) males, sometimes wicked, but always gallant.

"You're such a handsome girl," pursued Miss Marple appraising Lucy. "I expect they pay you a good deal of attention, don't they?"

Lucy flushed slightly. Scrappy remembrances passed across her mind. Cedric leaning against the pigsty wall. Bryan sitting disconsolately on the kitchen table. Alfred's fingers touching hers as he helped her collect the coffee cups.

"Gentlemen," said Miss Marple, in the tone of one speaking of some alien and dangerous species, "are all very much alike in some ways—even if they are quite old . . ."

"Darling," cried Lucy. "A hundred years ago you would certainly have been burned as a witch!"

And she told her story of old Mr. Crackenthorpe's conditional proposal of marriage.

"In fact," said Lucy, "they've all made what you might call advances to me, in a way. Harold's was very correct; an advantageous financial position in the City. I don't think it's my attractive appearance; they must think I know something."

She laughed.

But Inspector Craddock did not laugh.

"Be careful," he said. "They might murder you instead of making advances to you."

"I suppose it might be simpler," Lucy agreed.

Then she gave a slight shiver.

"One forgets," she said. "The boys have been having such fun that one almost thought of it all as a game. But it's not a game."

"No," said Miss Marple. "Murder isn't a game."

She was silent for a moment or two before she said:

"Don't the boys go back to school soon?"

"Yes, next week. They go tomorrow to James Stoddart-West's home for the last few days of the holidays."

"I'm glad of that," said Miss Marple gravely. "I shouldn't like anything to happen while they're there."

"You mean to old Mr. Crackenthorpe. Do you think he's going to be murdered next?"

"Oh no!" said Miss Marple. "He'll be all right. I meant to the boys."

"To the boys?"

"Well, to Alexander."

"But surely—"

"Hunting about, you know, looking for clues. Boys love that sort of thing, but it might be very dangerous."

Craddock looked at her thoughtfully.

"You're not prepared to believe, are you, Miss Marple, that it's a case of an unknown woman murdered by an unknown man? You tie it up definitely with Rutherford Hall?"

"I think there's a definite connection, yes."

"All we know about the murderer is that he's a tall, dark man. That's what your friend says and all she can say. There are three tall, dark men at Rutherford Hall. On the day of the inquest, you know, I came out to see the three brothers standing waiting on the pavement for the car to drive up. They had their backs to me and it was astonishing how, in their heavy overcoats, they looked all alike. *Three tall, dark men.* And yet, actually, they're all three quite different types." He sighed. "It makes it very difficult."

"I wonder," murmured Miss Marple. "I have been wondering whether it might perhaps be all much simpler than we suppose. Murders so often are quite simple, with an obvious rather sordid motive . . ."

"Do you believe in the mysterious Martine, Miss Marple?"

"I'm quite ready to believe that Edmund Crackenthorpe either married, or meant to marry, a girl called Martine. Emma Crackenthorpe showed you his letter, I understand, and from what I've seen of her and from what Lucy tells me, I should say Emma Crackenthorpe is quite incapable of making up a thing of that kind. Indeed, why should she?"

"So granted Martine," said Craddock thoughtfully, "there is a motive of a kind. Martine's reappearance with a son would diminish the Crackenthorpe inheritance, though hardly to a point, one would think, to activate murder. They're all very hard up."

"Even Harold?" Lucy demanded incredulously.

"Even the prosperous-looking Harold Crackenthorpe is not the sober and conservative financier he appears to be. He's been plunging heavily and mixing himself up in some rather undesirable ventures. A large sum of money, soon, might avoid a crash."

"But if so—" said Lucy and stopped.

"Yes, Miss Eyelesbarrow—"

"I know, dear," said Miss Marple. "The wrong murder, that's what you mean."

"Yes. Martine's death wouldn't do Harold, or any of the others, any good. Not until—"

"Not until Luther Crackenthorpe died. Exactly. That occurred to me. And Mr. Crackenthorpe, senior, I gather from his doctor, is in much better life than any outsider would imagine."

"He'll last for years," said Lucy. Then she frowned.

"Yes?" Craddock spoke encouragingly.

"He was rather ill at Christmastime," said Lucy. "He said the doctor made a lot of fuss about it. 'Anyone would have thought I'd been poisoned by the fuss he made.' That's what he said."

She looked inquiringly at Craddock.

"Yes," said Craddock. "That's really what I want to ask Doctor Quimper about."

"Well, I must go," said Lucy. "Heavens, it's late."

Miss Marple put down her knitting and picked up the *Times* with a half-done crossword puzzle.

"I wish I had a dictionary here," she murmured. "Tontine and Tokay—I always mix those two words up. One, I believe, is a Hungarian wine."

"That's Tokay," said Lucy looking back from the door. "But one's a five-letter word and one's a seven. What's the clue?"

"Oh, it wasn't in the crossword," said Miss Marple vaguely. "It was in my head."

Inspector Craddock looked at her very hard. Then he said good-by and went.

17

CRADDOCK had to wait a few minutes while Quimper finished his evening surgery, and then the doctor came to him. He looked tired and depressed.

He offered Craddock a drink and when the latter accepted he mixed one for himself as well.

"Poor devils," he said as he sank down in a worn easy chair. "So scared and so stupid—no sense. Had a painful case this evening. Woman who ought to have come to me a year ago. If she'd come then, she might have been operated on successfully. Now it's too late. Makes me mad. The truth is people are an extraordinary mixture of heroism and cowardice. She's been suffering agony and borne it without a word, just because she was too scared to come and find out that what she feared might be true. At the other end of the scale are the people who come and waste my time because they've got a dangerous swelling causing them agony on their little finger which they think may be cancer and which turns out to be a common or garden chilblain! Well, don't mind me. I've blown off steam now. What did you want to see me about?"

"First, I've got you to thank, I believe, for advising Miss Crackenthorpe to come to me with the letter that purported to be from her brother's widow."

"Oh, that? Anything in it? I didn't exactly advise her to come. She wanted to. She was worried. All the dear little brothers were trying to hold her back, of course."

"Why should they?"

The doctor shrugged his shoulders.

"Afraid the lady might be proved genuine, I suppose."

"Do you think the letter was genuine?"

"No idea. Never actually saw it. I should say it was someone who knew the facts, just trying to make a touch. Hoping to work on Emma's feelings. They were dead wrong, there. Emma's no fool. She wouldn't take an unknown sister-in-law to her bosom without asking a few practical questions first."

He added with some curiosity, "But why ask my views? I've got nothing to do with it."

"I really came to ask you something quite different, but I don't quite know how to put it."

Doctor Quimper looked interested.

"I understand that not long ago—at Christmastime I think it was—Mr. Crackenthorpe had rather a bad turn of illness."

He saw a change at once in the doctor's face. It hardened.

"Yes."

"I gather a gastric disturbance of some kind?"

"Yes."

"This is difficult. Mr. Crackenthorpe was boasting of his health, saying he intended to outlive most of his family. He referred to you—you'll excuse me, Doctor—"

"Oh, don't mind me. I'm not sensitive as to what my patients say about me!"

"He spoke of you as an old fuss pot." Quimper smiled. "He said you had asked him all sorts of questions, not only as to what he had eaten, but as to who prepared it and served it."

The doctor was not smiling now. His face was hard again.

"Go on."

"He used some such phrase as 'talked as though he believed someone had poisoned me.'"

There was a pause.

"Had you any suspicion of that kind?"

Quimper did not answer at once. He got up and walked up and down. Finally he wheeled round on Craddock.

"What the devil do you expect me to say? Do you think a doctor can go about flinging accusations of poisoning here and there without any real evidence?"

"I'd just like to know, off the record, if that idea did enter your head?"

Doctor Quimper said evasively, "Old Crackenthorpe leads a fairly frugal life. When the family comes down, Emma steps up the food. Result—a nasty attack of gastroenteritis. The symptoms were consistent with that diagnosis."

Craddock persisted.

"I see. You were quite satisfied? You were not at all—shall we say—puzzled?"

"All right. All right. Yes, I was Yours Truly Puzzled! Does that please you?"

"It interests me," said Craddock. "What actually did you suspect, or fear?"

"Gastric cases vary, of course, but there were certain indications that would have been, shall we say, more consistent with arsenical poisoning than with plain gastroenteritis. Mind you, the two things are very much alike. Better men than myself have failed to recognize arsenical poisoning and have given a certificate in all good faith."

"And what was the result of your inquiries?"

"It seemed that what I suspected could not possibly be true. Mr. Crackenthorpe assured me that he had had similar attacks before I attended him, and from the same cause, he said. They had always taken place when there was too much rich food about."

"Which was when the house was full? With the family? Or guests?"

"Yes. That seemed reasonable enough. But frankly, Craddock, I wasn't happy. I went so far as to write to old Doctor Morris. He was my senior partner and retired soon after I joined him. Crackenthorpe was his patient originally. I asked about these earlier attacks that the old man had had."

"And what response did you get?"

Quimper grinned.

"I got a flea in the ear. I was more or less told not to be a damned fool. Well—" he shrugged his shoulders. "Presumably I was a damned fool."

"I wonder." Craddock was thoughtful.

Then he decided to speak frankly.

"Throwing discretion aside, Doctor, there are people who stand to benefit pretty considerably from Luther Crackenthorpe's death." The doctor nodded. "He's an old man and a hale and hearty one. He may live to be ninety-odd?"

"Easily. He spends his life taking care of himself, and his constitution is sound."

"And his sons and daughter are all getting on, and they are all feeling the pinch?"

"You leave Emma out of it. She's no poisoner. These attacks only happen when the others are there, not when she and he are alone."

"An elementary precaution if she's the one," the Inspector thought, but was careful not to say so aloud.

He paused, choosing his words carefully.

"Surely—I'm ignorant in these matters—but supposing just as a hypothesis that arsenic was administered, hasn't Crackenthorpe been very lucky not to succumb?"

"Now there," said the doctor, "you have got something odd. It is exactly that fact that leads me to believe that I have been, as old Morris puts it, a damned fool. You see, it's obviously not a case of small doses of arsenic administered regularly, which is what you might call the classic method of arsenic poisoning. Crackenthorpe has never had any chronic gastric trouble. In a way, that's what makes these sudden violent attacks seem unlikely. So, assuming they are not due to natural causes, it looks as though the poisoner is muffing it every time, which hardly makes sense."

"Giving an inadequate dose, you mean?"

"Yes. On the other hand, Crackenthorpe's got a strong constitution and what might do in another man doesn't do him in. There's always personal idiosyncrasy to be reckoned with. But you'd think that by now, the poisoner—unless he's unusually timid—would have stepped up the dose. Why hasn't he?

That is," he added, "if there is a poisoner which there probably isn't! Probably all my ruddy imagination from start to finish."

"It's an odd problem," the Inspector agreed. "It doesn't seem to make sense."

II

"Inspector Craddock!"

The eager whisper made the Inspector jump.

He had been just on the point of ringing the front-doorbell.

Alexander and his friend Stoddart-West emerged cautiously from the shadows.

"We heard your car and we wanted to get hold of you."

"Well, let's come inside." Craddock's hand went out to the doorbell again, but Alexander pulled at his coat with the eagerness of a pawing dog.

"We've found a clue," he breathed.

"Yes, we've found a clue," Stoddart-West echoed.

"Damn that girl," thought Craddock unamiably.

"Splendid," he said in perfunctory manner. "Let's go inside the house and look at it."

"No." Alexander was insistent. "Someone's sure to interrupt. Come to the harness room. We'll guide you."

Somewhat unwillingly, Craddock allowed himself to be guided round the corner of the house and along to the stable yard. Stoddart-West pushed open a heavy door, stretched up, and turned on a rather feeble electric light. The harness room, once the acme of Victorian spit and polish, was now the sad repository of everything that no one wanted. Broken garden chairs, rusted old garden implements, a vast decrepit mowing machine, rusted spring mattresses, hammocks and disintegrated tennis nets.

"We come here a good deal," said Alexander. "One can really be private here."

There were certain tokens of occupancy about. The decayed mattresses had been piled up to make a kind of divan, there was an old rusted table on which resposed a large tin of chocolate biscuits, there was a hoard of apples, a tin of toffee and a jigsaw puzzle.

"It really is a clue, sir," said Stoddart-West eagerly, his eyes gleaming behind his spectacles. "We found it this afternoon."

"We've been hunting for days. In the bushes—"

"And inside hollow trees."

"And we went all through the ashbins."

"There were some jolly interesting things there, as a matter of fact."

"And then we went into the boiler house—"

"Old Hillman keeps a great galvanized tub there full of waste paper."

"For when the boiler goes out and he wants to start it again."

"Any odd paper that's blowing about. He picks it up and shoves it in there."

"And that's where we found it."

"Found *what?*" Craddock interrupted the duet.

"The clue. Careful, Stodders, get your gloves on."

Importantly, Stoddart-West, in the best detective-story tradition, drew on a pair of rather dirty gloves and took from his pocket a Kodak photographic folder. From this he extracted in his gloved fingers with the utmost care a soiled and crumpled envelope which he handed importantly to the Inspector.

Both boys held their breath in excitement.

Craddock took it with due solemnity. He liked the boys and he was ready to enter into the spirit of the thing.

The letter had been through the post; there was no enclosure inside, it was just a torn envelope addressed to Mrs. Martine Crack-enthorpe, 126 Elvers Crescent, N. 10.

"You see?" said Alexander breathlessly. "It shows she was here —Uncle Edmund's French wife, I mean—the one there's all the fuss about. She must have actually been here and dropped it some-where. So it looks, doesn't it?"

Stoddart-West broke in, "It looks as though she was the one who got murdered—I mean, don't you think, sir, that it simply must have been her in the sarcophagus?"

They waited anxiously.

Craddock played up. "Possible, very possible," he said.

"This is important, isn't it?"

"You'll test it for fingerprints, won't you, sir?"

"Of course," said Craddock.

Stoddart-West gave a deep sigh.

"Smashing luck for us, wasn't it?" he said. "On our last day, too."

"Last day?"

"Yes," said Alexander. "I'm going to Stodders' place tomorrow for the last few days of the holidays. Stodders' people have got a smashing house—Queen Anne, isn't it?"

"William and Mary," said Stoddart-West.

"I thought your mother said—"

"Mum's French. She doesn't really know about English archi-tecture."

"But your father said it was built—"

Craddock was examining the envelope.

Clever of Lucy Eyelesbarrow. How had she managed to fake the postmark? He peered closely, but the light was too feeble. Great fun for the boys, of course, but rather awkward for him. Lucy, drat her, hadn't considered that angle. If this were genuine, it would enforce a course of action. There—

Beside him a learned architectural argument was being hotly pur-sued. He was deaf to it.

"Come on boys," he said, "we'll go into the house. You've been very helpful."

18

CRADDOCK was escorted by the boys through the back door into the house. This was, it seemed, their common mode of entrance. The kitchen was bright and cheerful. Lucy, in a large, white apron was rolling out pastry. Leaning against the dresser, watching her with a kind of doglike attention, was Bryan Eastley. With one hand he tugged at his large fair mustache.

"Hello, Dad," said Alexander kindly. "You out here again?"

"I like it out here," said Bryan, and added: "Miss Eyelesbarrow doesn't mind."

"Oh, I don't mind," said Lucy. "Good evening, Inspector Craddock."

"Coming to detect in the kitchen?" asked Bryan with interest.

"Not exactly. Mr. Cedric Crackenthorpe is still here, isn't he?"

"Oh yes, Cedric's here. Do you want him?"

"I'd like a word with him, yes, please."

"I'll go and see if he's in," said Bryan. "He may have gone round to the local pub."

He unpropped himself from the dresser.

"Thank you so much," said Lucy to him. "My hands are all over flour or I'd go."

"What are you making?" asked Stoddart-West anxiously.

"Peach flan."

"Good oh," said Stoddart-West.

"Is it nearly suppertime?" asked Alexander.

"No."

"Gosh! I'm terribly hungry."

"There's the end of the ginger cake in the larder."

The boys made a concerted rush and collided in the door.

"They're just like locusts," said Lucy.

"My congratulations to you," said Craddock.

"What on, exactly?"

"Your ingenuity, over this!"

"Over what?"

Craddock indicated the folder containing the letter.

"Very nicely done," he said.

"What are you talking about?"

"This, my dear girl, this." He half drew it out.

She stared at him uncomprehendingly.

Craddock felt suddenly dizzy.

"Didn't you fake this clue and put it in the boiler room for the boys to find? Quick—tell me."

"I haven't the faintest idea what you're talking about," said Lucy. "Do you mean that—"

Craddock slipped the folder quickly back in his pocket as Bryan returned.

"Cedric's in the library," he said. "Go on in."

He resumed his place on the dresser. Inspector Craddock went to the library.

II

Cedric Crackenthorpe seemed delighted to see the Inspector.

"Doing a spot more sleuthing down here?" he asked. "Got any farther."

"I think I can say we are a little farther on, Mr. Crackenthorpe."

"Found out who the corpse was?"

"We've not got a definite identification, but we have a fairly shrewd idea."

"Good for you."

"Arising out of our latest information, we want to get a few statements. I'm starting with you, Mr. Crackenthorpe, as you're on the spot."

"I shan't be much longer. I'm going back to Iviza in a day or two."

"Then I seem to be just in time."

"Go ahead."

"I should like a detailed account, please, of exactly where you were and what you were doing on Friday, December the twentieth."

Cedric shot a quick glance at him. Then he leaned back, yawned, assumed an air of great nonchalance, and appeared to be lost in the effort of remembrance.

"Well, as I've already told you, I was in Iviza. Trouble is, one day there is so like another. Painting in the morning, siesta from three p.m. to five. Perhaps a spot of sketching if the light's suitable. Then an *apéritif*, sometimes with the mayor, sometimes with the doctor, at the café in the plaza. After that some kind of a scratch meal. Most of the evening in Scotty's Bar with some of my lower-class friends. Will that do you?"

"I'd rather have the truth, Mr. Crackenthorpe."

Cedric sat up.

"That's a most offensive remark, Inspector."

"Do you think so? You told me, Mr. Crackenthorpe, that you left Iviza on December the twenty-first and arrived in England that same day?"

"So I did. Em! Hi, Em!"

Emma Crackenthorpe came through the adjoining door from the small morning room. She looked inquiringly from Cedric to the Inspector.

"Look here, Em. I arrived here for Christmas on the Saturday before, didn't I? Came straight from the airport?"

"Yes," said Emma wonderingly. "You got here about lunchtime."

"There you are," said Cedric to the Inspector.

"You must think us very foolish, Mr. Crackenthorpe," said Craddock pleasantly. "We can check on these things, you know. I think, if you'll show me your passport—"

He paused expectantly.

"Can't find the damned thing," said Cedric. "Was looking for it this morning. Wanted to send it to Cook's."

"I think you could find it, Mr. Crackenthorpe. But it's not actually necessary. The records show that you actually entered this country on the evening of December the nineteenth. Perhaps you will now account to me for your movements between that time until lunchtime on December the twenty-first when you arrived here."

Cedric looked very cross indeed.

"That's the hell of life nowadays," he said angrily. "All this red tape and form filling. That's what comes of a bureaucratic state. Can't go where you like and do as you please any more! Somebody's always asking questions. What's all this fuss about the twentieth, anyway? What's special about the twentieth?"

"It happens to be the day we believe the murder was committed. You can refuse to answer, of course, but—"

"Who says I refuse to answer? Give a chap time. And you were vague enough about the date of the murder at the inquest. What's turned up new since then?"

Craddock did not reply.

Cedric said, with a sidelong glance at Emma, "Shall we go into the other room?"

Emma said quickly: "I'll leave you." At the door, she paused and turned.

"This is serious, you know, Cedric. If the twentieth was the day of the murder, then you must tell Inspector Craddock exactly what you were doing."

She went through into the next room and closed the door behind her.

"Good old Em," said Cedric. "Well, here goes! Yes, I left Iviza on the nineteenth all right. Planned to break the journey in Paris and spend a couple of days routing up some old friends on the Left Bank. But as a matter of fact, there was a very attractive woman on the plane. Quite a dish. To put it plainly, she and I got off together. She was on her way to the States, had to spend a couple of nights in London to see about some business or other. We got to London on the nineteenth. We stayed at the Kingsway Palace in case your spies haven't found that out yet! Called myself John Brown —never does to use your own name on these occasions."

"And on the twentieth?"

Cedric made a grimace.

"Morning pretty well occupied by a terrific hangover."

"And the afternoon. From three o'clock onward?"

"Let me see. Well, I mooned about, as you might say. Went into the National Gallery—that's respectable enough. Saw a film. *Rowenna of the Range*. I've always had a passion for Westerns. This was a corker. . . . Then a drink or two in the bar and a bit of a sleep in my room, and out about ten o'clock with the girl friend and a round of various hot spots. Can't even remember most of their names—Jumping Frog was one, I think. She knew 'em all. Got pretty well plastered and, to tell you the truth, don't remember much more till I woke up the next morning with an even worse hangover. Girl friend hopped off to catch her plane and I poured cold water over my head, got a chemist to give me a devil's brew, and then started off for this place, pretending I'd just arrived at Heathrow. No need to upset Emma, I thought. You know what women are, always hurt if you don't come straight home. I had to borrow money from her to pay the taxi. I was completely cleaned out. No use asking the old man. He'd never cough up. Mean old brute. Well, Inspector, satisfied?"

"Can any of this be substantiated, Mr. Crackenthorpe? Say, between three p.m. and seven p.m."

"Most unlikely, I should think," said Cedric cheerfully. "National Gallery where the attendants look at you with lackluster eyes and a crowded picture house. No, not likely."

Emma re-entered. She held a small engagement book in her hand.

"You want to know what everyone was doing on December the twentieth, is that right, Inspector Craddock?"

"Well—er—yes, Miss Crackenthorpe."

"I have just been looking in my engagement book. On the twentieth I went into Brackhampton to attend a meeting of the Church Restoration Fund. That finished about a quarter to one and I lunched with Lady Adington and Miss Bartlett, who was also on the committee, at the Cadena Café. After lunch I did some shopping, stores for Christmas and also Christmas presents. I went to Greenford's and Lyall and Swift's, Boot's, and probably several other shops. I had tea about a quarter to five in the Shamrock Tea Rooms and then went to the station to meet Bryan who was coming by train. I got home about six o'clock and found my father in a very bad temper. I had left lunch ready for him, but Mrs. Hart who was to come in in the afternoon and give him his tea had not arrived. He was so angry that he had shut himself in his room and would not let me in or speak to me. He does not like my going out in the afternoon, but I make a point of doing so now and then."

"You're probably wise. Thank you, Miss Crackenthorpe."

He could hardly tell her that as she was a woman, height five-foot seven, her movements that afternoon were of no great importance. Instead he said: "Your other two brothers came down later, I understand?"

"Alfred came down late on Saturday evening. He tells me he tried to ring me on the telephone the afternoon I was out, but my father, if he is upset, will never answer the telephone. My brother Harold did not come down until Christmas Eve."

"Thank you, Miss Crackenthorpe."

"I suppose I mustn't ask"—she hesitated—"what has come up new that prompts these inquiries?"

Craddock took the folder from his pocket. Using the tips of his fingers, he extracted the envelope.

"Don't touch it, please, but do you recognize this?"

"But—" Emma stared at him, bewildered. "That's my handwriting. That's the letter I wrote to Martine."

"I thought it might be."

"But how did you get it? Did she—? Have you found her—?"

"It would seem possible that we have—found her. This empty envelope was found here."

"In the house?"

"In the grounds."

"Then, she did come here! She— You mean, it was Martine, there in the sarcophagus?"

"It would seem very likely, Miss Crackenthorpe," said Craddock gently.

It seemed even more likely when he got back to town. A message was awaiting him from Armand Dessin.

"One of the girl friends has had a postcard from Anna Stravinska. Apparently the cruise story was true! She has reached Jamaica and is having, in your phrase, a wonderful time!"

Craddock crumpled up the message and threw it into the waste-paper basket.

III

"I must say," said Alexander, sitting up in bed, thoughtfully consuming a chocolate bar, "that this has been the most smashing day ever. Actually finding a real clue!"

His voice was awed.

"In fact the whole holidays have been smashing," he added happily. "I don't suppose such a thing will ever happen again."

"I hope it won't happen again to me," said Lucy who was on her knees packing Alexander's clothes into a suitcase. "Do you want all this space fiction with you?"

"Not those two top ones. I've read them. The football and my football boots and the gum boots can go separately."

"What difficult things you boys do travel with."

"It won't matter. They're sending the Rolls for us. They've got a smashing Rolls. They've got one of the new Mercedes Benz, too."

"They must be rich."

"Rolling! Jolly nice, too. All the same, I rather wish we weren't leaving here. Another body might turn up."

"I sincerely hope not."

"Well, it often does in books. I mean somebody who's seen something or heard something gets done in, too. It might be you," he added, unrolling a second chocolate bar.

"Thank you!"

"I don't want it to be you," Alexander assured her. "I like you very much and so does Stodders. We think you're out of this world as a cook. Absolutely lovely grub. You're very sensible, too."

This last was clearly an expression of high approval. Lucy took it as such and said: "Thank you. But I don't intend to get killed just to please you."

"Well, you'd better be careful, then," Alexander told her.

He paused to consume more nourishment and then said in a slightly offhand voice,

"If Dad turns up from time to time, you'll look after him, won't you?"

"Yes, of course," said Lucy, a little surprised.

"The trouble with Dad is," Alexander informed her, "that London life doesn't suit him. He gets in, you know, with quite the wrong type of women." He shook his head in a worried manner.

"I'm very fond of him," he added, "but he needs someone to look after him. He drifts about and gets in with the wrong people. It's a great pity Mum died when she did. Bryan needs a proper home life."

He looked solemnly at Lucy and reached out for another chocolate bar.

"Not a fourth one, Alexander," Lucy pleaded. "You'll be sick."

"Oh, I don't think so. I ate six running once and I wasn't. I'm not the bilious type." He paused and then said, "Bryan likes you, you know."

"That's very nice of him."

"He's a bit of an ass in some ways," said Bryan's son, "but he was a jolly good fighter pilot. He's awfully brave. And he's awfully good-natured."

He paused. Then, averting his eyes to the ceiling, he said rather self-consciously:

"I think really, you know, it would be a good thing if he married again. Somebody decent. I shouldn't, myself, mind at all having a stepmother—not, I mean, if she was a decent sort. . . ."

With a sense of shock Lucy realized that there was a definite point in Alexander's conversation.

"All this stepmother bosh," went on Alexander, still addressing the ceiling, "is really quite out of date. Lots of chaps Stodders and I know have stepmothers—divorce and all that—and they get on quite well together. Depends on the stepmother, of course. And, of course, it does make a bit of confusion taking you out and on Sports Day and all that—I mean if there are two sets of parents, though again it helps if you want to cash in!" He paused, confronted with the problems of modern life. "It's nicest to have your own home and your own parents, but if your mother's dead—well, you see what I mean? If she's a decent sort," said Alexander for the third time.

Lucy felt touched.

"I think you're very sensible, Alexander," she said. "We must try and find a nice wife for your father."

"Yes," said Alexander noncommittally.

He added in an offhand manner, "I thought I'd just mention it. Bryan likes you very much. He told me so."

"Really," thought Lucy to herself. "There's too much matchmaking round here. First Miss Marple and now Alexander!"

For some reason or other, pigsties came into her mind. . . .

She stood up.

"Good night, Alexander. There will be only your washing things and pajamas to put in in the morning. Good night."

"Good night," said Alexander. He slid down in bed, laid his head on the pillow, closed his eyes, giving a perfect picture of a sleeping angel, and was immediately asleep.

19

"Nor what you'd call conclusive," said Sergeant Wetherall with his usual gloom.

Craddock was reading through the report on Harold Crackenthorpe's alibi for December 20th.

He had been noticed at Sotheby's about 3:30, but was thought to have left shortly after that. His photograph had not been recognized at Russell's teashop, but as they did a busy trade there at teatime and he was not a habitué, that was hardly surprising. His manservant confirmed that he had returned to Cardigan Gardens to dress for his dinner party at a quarter to seven—rather late, since the dinner was at 7:30, and Mr. Crackenthorpe had been somewhat irritable in consequence. Did not remember hearing him come in that evening, but as it was some time ago could not remember accurately and, in any case, he frequently did not hear Mr. Crackenthorpe come in. He and his wife liked to retire early whenever they could. The garage in the mews where Harold kept his car was a private lockup that he rented and there was no one to notice who came or went or any reason to remember one evening in particular.

"All negative," said Craddock, with a sigh.

"He was at the Caterers' dinner all right, but left rather early before the end of the speeches."

"What about the railway stations?"

But there was nothing there, either at Brackhampton or at Paddington. It was nearly four weeks ago, and it was highly unlikely that anything would have been remembered.

Craddock sighed and stretched out his hand for the data on Cedric. That again was negative, though a taxi driver had made a doubtful recognition of having taken a fare to Paddington that day some time in the afternoon "what looked something like that bloke.

Dirty trousers and a shock of hair. Cussed and swore a bit because fares had gone up since he was last in England." He identified the day because a horse called Crawler had won the 2:30 and he'd had a tidy bit on. Just after dropping the gent, he'd heard it on the radio in his cab and had gone home forthwith to celebrate.

"Thank God for racing," said Craddock, and put the report aside.

"And here's Alfred," said Sergeant Wetherall.

Some nuance in his voice made Craddock look up sharply. Wetherall had the pleased appearance of a man who has kept a tidbit until the end.

In the main the check was unsatisfactory. Alfred lived alone in his flat and came and went at unspecified times. His neighbors were not the inquisitive kind and were in any case office workers who were out all day. But toward the end of the report, Wetherall's large finger indicated the final paragraph.

Sergeant Leakie, assigned to a case of thefts from lorries had been at the Load of Bricks, a lorry pullup on the Waddington-Brackhampton Road, keeping certain lorry drivers under observation. He had noticed, at an adjoining table, Chick Evans, one of the Dicky Rogers mob. With him had been Alfred Crackenthorpe whom he knew by sight, having seen him give evidence in the Dicky Rogers case. He'd wondered what they were cooking up together. Time: 9:30 P.M., Friday, December 20th. Alfred Crackenthorpe had boarded a bus a few minutes later, going in the direction of Brackhampton. William Baker, ticket collector at Brackhampton Station, had clipped ticket of gentleman whom he recognized by sight as one of Miss Crackenthorpe's brothers, just before departure of 11:55 train for Paddington. Remembers day as there had been story of some batty old lady who swore she had seen somebody murdered in a train that afternoon.

"Alfred?" said Craddock as he laid the report down. "Alfred? I wonder."

"Puts him right on the spot, there," Wetherall pointed out.

Craddock nodded. Yes, Alfred could have traveled down by the 4:33 to Brackhampton, committing murder on the way. Then he could have gone out by bus to the Load of Bricks. He could have left there at 9:30 and would have had plenty of time to go to Rutherford Hall, move the body from the embankment to the sarcophagus and get into Brackhampton in time to catch the 11:55 back to London. One of the Dicky Rogers gang might even have helped him move the body, though Craddock doubted this. An unpleasant lot, but not killers.

"Alfred?" he repeated speculatively.

II

At Rutherford Hall there had been a gathering of the Crackenthorpe family. Harold and Alfred had come down from London and very soon voices were raised and tempers were running high.

On her own initiative, Lucy mixed cocktails in a jug with ice and took them toward the library. The voices sounded clearly in the hall, and indicated that a good deal of acrimony was being directed toward Emma.

"Entirely your fault, Emma." Harold's deep-bass voice rang out angrily. "How you could be so shortsighted and foolish beats me. If you hadn't taken that letter to Scotland Yard and started all this—"

Alfred's higher-pitched voice said: "You must have been out of your senses!"

"Now don't bully her," said Cedric. "What's done is done. Much more fishy if they'd identified the woman as the missing Martine and we'd all kept mum about having heard from her."

"It's all very well for you, Cedric," said Harold angrily. "You were out of the country on the twentieth which seems to be the day they are inquiring about. But it's very embarrassing for Alfred and myself. Fortunately I can remember where I was that afternoon and what I was doing."

"I bet you can," said Alfred. "If you'd arranged a murder, Harold, you'd arrange your alibi very carefully, I'm sure."

"I gather you are not so fortunate," said Harold coldly.

"That depends," said Alfred. "Anything's better than presenting a cast-iron alibi to the police if it isn't really cast iron. They're so clever at breaking these things down."

"If you are insinuating that I killed the woman—"

"Oh, do stop, all of you," cried Emma. "Of course none of you killed the woman."

"And just for your information, I wasn't out of England on the twentieth," said Cedric. "And the police are wise to it! So we're all under suspicion."

"If it hadn't been for Emma—"

"Oh, don't begin again, Harold," cried Emma.

Doctor Quimper came out of the study where he had been closeted with old Mr. Crackenthorpe. His eye fell on the jug in Lucy's hand.

"What's this? A celebration?"

"More in the nature of oil on troubled waters. They're at it hammer and tongs in there."

"Recriminations?"

"Mostly abusing Emma."

Doctor Quimper's eyebrows rose.

"Indeed?" He took the jug from Lucy's hand, opened the library door and went in.

"Good evening."

"Ah, Doctor Quimper, I should like a word with you." It was Harold's voice, raised and irritable. "I should like to know what you meant by interfering in a private and family matter, and telling my sister to go to Scotland Yard about it."

Doctor Quimper said calmly, "Miss Crackenthorpe asked my advice. I gave it to her. In my opinion she did perfectly right."

"You dare to say—"

"Girl!"

It was old Mr. Crackenthorpe's familiar salutation. He was peering out of the study door just behind Lucy.

Lucy turned rather reluctantly.

"Yes, Mr. Crackenthorpe?"

"What are you giving us for dinner tonight? I want curry. You make a very good curry. It's ages since we've had curry."

"The boys don't care much for curry, you see."

"The boys, the boys—what do the boys matter? I'm the one who matters. And anyway, the boys have gone—good riddance. I want a nice hot curry, do you hear?"

"All right, Mr. Crackenthorpe, you shall have it."

"That's right. You're a good girl, Lucy. You look after me, and I'll look after you."

Lucy went back to the kitchen. Abandoning the fricassee of chicken which she had planned, she began to assemble the preparations for curry. The front door banged and from the window she saw Doctor Quimper stride angrily from the house to his car and drive away.

Lucy sighed. She missed the boys. And in a way she missed Bryan, too.

Oh well! She sat down and began to peel mushrooms.
At any rate she'd give the family a rattling good dinner.
Feed the brutes!

III

It was 3:00 A.M. when Doctor Quimper drove his car into the garage, closed the doors and came in pulling the front door behind him rather wearily. Well, Mrs. Josh Simpkins had a fine, healthy pair of twins to add to her present family of eight. Mr. Simpkins had expressed no elation over the arrival. "Twins," he had said gloomily. "What's the good of them? Quads now, they're good for something. All sorts of things you get sent, and the press comes round and there's pictures in the paper, and they do say as Her Majesty sends you a telegram. But what's twins except two mouths to feed instead of one? Never been twins in our family, nor in the missus's either. Don't seem fair, somehow."

Doctor Quimper walked upstairs to his bedroom and started throwing off his clothes. He glanced at his watch. Five minutes past three. It had proved an unexpectedly tricky business bringing those twins into the world, but all had gone well. He yawned. He was tired, very tired. He looked appreciatively at his bed.

Then the telephone rang.

Doctor Quimper swore and picked up the receiver.

"Doctor Quimper?"

"Speaking."

"This is Lucy Eyelesbarrow from Rutherford Hall. I think you'd better come over. Everybody seems to have been taken ill."

"Taken ill? How? What symptoms?"

Lucy detailed them.

"I'll be over straightaway. In the meantime—" He gave her short, sharp instructions.

Then he quickly resumed his clothes, flung a few extra things into his emergency bag, and hurried down to his car.

IV

It was some three hours later when the doctor and Lucy, both of them somewhat exhausted, sat down by the kitchen table to drink large cups of black coffee.

"Ha." Doctor Quimper drained his cup, set it down with a clatter on the saucer. "I needed that. Now, Miss Eyelesbarrow, let's get down to brass tacks."

Lucy looked at him. The lines of fatigue showed clearly on his face, making him look older than his forty-four years; the dark hair on his temples was flecked with gray; and there were lines under his eyes.

"As far as I can judge," said the doctor, "they'll be all right now. But how come? That's what I want to know. Who cooked the dinner?"

"I did," said Lucy.

"And what was it? In detail."

"Mushroom soup. Curried chicken and rice. Sillabubs. A savory of chicken livers in bacon."

"*Canapés Diane,*" said Doctor Quimper unexpectedly.

Lucy smiled faintly.

"Yes, *Canapés Diane.*"

"All right, let's go through it. Mushroom soup, out of a tin, I suppose?"

"Certainly not. I made it."

"You made it. Out of what?"

"Half a pound of mushrooms, chicken stock, milk, a *roux* of butter and flour, and lemon juice."

"Ah. And one's supposed to say 'It must have been the mushrooms.'"

"It wasn't the mushrooms. I had some of the soup myself and I'm quite all right."

"Yes, you're quite all right. I hadn't forgotten that."

Lucy flushed.

"If you mean—"

"I don't mean. You're a highly intelligent girl. You'd be groaning upstairs, too, if I'd meant what you thought I meant. Anyway, I know all about you. I've taken the trouble to find out."

"Why on earth did you do that?"

Doctor Quimper's lips were set in a grim line.

"Because I'm making it my business to find out about the people who come here and settle themselves in. You're a bona fide young woman who does this particular job for a livelihood, and you seem never to have had any contact with the Crackenthorpe family previous to coming here. So you're not a girl friend of either Cedric, Harold or Alfred, helping them to do a bit of dirty work."

"Do you really think?"

"I think quite a lot of things," said Quimper. "But I have to be careful. That's the worst of being a doctor. Now, let's get on. Curried chicken. Did you have some of that?"

"No. When you've cooked a curry, you've dined off the smell, I find. I tasted it, of course. I had soup and some sillabub."

"How did you serve the sillabub?"

"In individual glasses."

"Now then, how much of all this is cleared up?"

"If you mean washing up, everything was washed up and put away."

Doctor Quimper groaned.

"There's such a thing as being overzealous," he said.

"Yes, I can see that as things have turned out, but there it is, I'm afraid."

"What do you have still?"

"There's some of the curry left in a bowl in the larder. I was planning to use it as a basis for mulligatawny soup this evening. There's some mushroom soup left, too. No sillabub and none of the savory."

"I'll take the curry and the soup. What about chutney? Did they have chutney with it?"

"Yes. In one of those stone jars."

"I'll have some of that, too."

He rose: "I'll go up and have a look at them again. After that, can you hold the fort until morning? Keep an eye on them all? I can have a nurse round, with full instructions, by eight o'clock."

"I wish you'd tell me straight out. Do you think it's food poisoning—or—or, well, poisoning."

"I've told you already. Doctors can't think, they have to be sure. If there's a positive result from these food specimens I can go ahead. Otherwise—"

"Otherwise?" Lucy repeated.

Doctor Quimper laid a hand on her shoulder.

"Look after two people in particular," he said. "Look after Emma. I'm not going to have anything happen to Emma . . ."

There was emotion in his voice that could not be disguised. "She's not even begun to live yet," he said. "And you know, people like Emma Crackenthorpe are the salt of the earth. Emma—well, Emma means a lot to me. I've never told her so but I shall. Look after Emma."

"You bet I will," said Lucy.

"And look after the old man. I can't say that he's ever been my favorite patient but he is my patient and I'm damned if I'm going to let him be hustled out of the world because one or other of his unpleasant sons—or all three of them, maybe—want him out of the way so that they can handle his money."

He threw her a sudden quizzical glance.

"There," he said. "I've opened my mouth too wide. But keep your eyes skinned, there's a good girl and, incidentally, keep your mouth shut."

V

Inspector Bacon was looking upset.

"Arsenic?" he said. "Arsenic?"

"Yes. It was in the curry. Here's the rest of the curry, for your fellow to have a go at. I've only done a very rough test on a little of it, but the result was quite definite."

"So there's a poisoner at work?"

"It would seem so," said Doctor Quimper dryly.

"And they're all affected, you say, except that Miss Eyelesbarrow."

"Except Miss Eyelesbarrow."

"Looks a bit fishy for her."

"What motive could she possibly have?"

"Might be barmy," suggested Bacon. "Seem all right, they do, sometimes, and yet all the time they're right off their rocker, so to speak."

"Miss Eyelesbarrow isn't off her rocker. Speaking as a medical man, Miss Eyelesbarrow is as sane as you or I. If Miss Eyelesbarrow is feeding the family arsenic in their curry, she's doing it for a reason. Moreover, being a highly intelligent young woman, she'd be careful not to be the only one unaffected. What she'd do, what any intelligent poisoner would do, would be to eat a very little of the poisoned curry, and then exaggerate the symptoms."

"And then you wouldn't be able to tell?"

"That she'd had less than the others? Probably not. People don't all react alike to poisons anyway; the same amount will upset some people more than others. Of course," added Doctor Quimper cheerfully, "once the patient's dead, you can estimate fairly closely how much was taken."

"Then it might be—" Inspector Bacon paused to consolidate his ideas. "It might be that there's one of the family now who's making more fuss than he need, someone who you might say is mucking in with the rest so as to avoid arousing suspicion? How's that?"

"The idea has already occurred to me. That's why I'm reporting to you. It's in your hands now. I've got a nurse on the job that I can trust, but she can't be everywhere at once. In my opinion, nobody's had enough to cause death."

"Made a mistake, the poisoner did?"

"No. It seems to me more likely that the idea was to put enough in the curry to cause signs of food poisoning, for which probably the mushrooms would be blamed. People are always obsessed with the idea of mushroom poisoning. Then one person would probably take a turn for the worse and die."

"Because he'd been given a second dose?"

The doctor nodded.

"That's why I'm reporting to you at once, and why I've put a special nurse on the job."

"She knows about the arsenic?"

"Of course. She knows and so does Miss Eyelesbarrow. You know your own job best, of course, but if I were you, I'd get out there and make it quite clear to them all that they're suffering from arsenic poisoning. That will probably put the fear of the Lord into our murderer and he won't dare to carry out his plan. He's probably been banking on the food-poisoning theory."

The telephone rang on the Inspector's desk. He picked it up and said:

"O.K. Put her through." He said to Quimper, "It's your nurse on the phone. Yes, hullo—speaking . . . What's that? Serious relapse . . . Yes . . . Doctor Quimper's with me now . . . If you'd like a word with him—"

He handed the receiver to the doctor.

"Quimper speaking . . . I see . . . Yes . . . Quite right. . . . Yes, carry on with that. We'll be along."

He put the receiver down and turned to Bacon.

"Who is it?"

"It's Alfred," said Doctor Quimper. "And he's dead."

20

OVER THE TELEPHONE, Craddock's voice came in sharp disbelief.

"Alfred?" he said. "Alfred?"

Inspector Bacon, shifting the telephone receiver a little, said: "You didn't expect that?"

"No, indeed. As a matter of fact, I'd just got him taped for the murderer!"

"I heard about him being spotted by the ticket collector. Looked bad for him all right. Yes, looked as though we'd got our man."

"Well," said Craddock flatly, "we were wrong."

There was a moment's silence. Then Craddock asked:

"There was a nurse in charge. How did she come to slip up?"

"Can't blame her. Miss Eyelesbarrow was all in and went to get a bit of sleep. The nurse had got five patients on her hands: the old man, Emma, Cedric, Harold and Alfred. She couldn't be everywhere at once. It seems old Mr. Crackenthorpe started creating in a big way. Said he was dying. She went in, got him soothed down, came back again and took Alfred in some tea with glucose. He drank it and that was that."

"Arsenic again?"

"Seems so. Of course it could have been a relapse, but Quimper doesn't think so and Johnson agrees."

"I suppose," said Craddock, doubtfully, "that Alfred was meant to be the victim?"

Bacon sounded interested. "You mean that whereas Alfred's death wouldn't do anyone a penn'orth of good, the old man's death would benefit the lot of them? I suppose it might have been a mistake; somebody *might* have thought the tea was intended for the old man."

"Are they sure that that's the way the stuff was administered?"

"No, of course they aren't sure. The nurse, like a good nurse, washed up the whole contraption. Cups, spoons, teapot—everything. But it seems the only feasible method."

"Meaning?" said Craddock thoughtfully, "that one of the patients wasn't as ill as the others. Saw his chance and doped the cup."

"Well, there won't be any more funny business," said Inspector Bacon grimly. "We've got two nurses on the job now, to say nothing of Miss Eyelesbarrow, and I've got a couple of men there, too. You coming down?"

"As fast as I can make it!"

II

Lucy Eyelesbarrow came across the hall to meet Inspector Craddock. She looked pale and drawn.

"You've been having a bad time of it," said Craddock.

"It's been like one long ghastly nightmare," said Lucy. "I really thought last night that they were all dying."

"About this curry—"

"It was the curry?"

"Yes, very nicely laced with arsenic. Quite the Borgia touch."

"If that's true," said Lucy, "it must—it's got to be—one of the family."

"No other possibility?"

"No, you see I only started making that damned curry quite late, after six o'clock, because Mr. Crackenthorpe specially asked for curry. And I had to open a new tin of curry powder, so that couldn't have been tampered with. I suppose curry would disguise the taste?"

"Arsenic hasn't any taste," said Craddock absently. "Now—opportunity. Which of them had the chance to tamper with the curry while it was cooking?"

Lucy considered.

"Actually," she said, "anyone could have sneaked into the kitchen while I was laying the table in the dining room."

"I see. Now who was there in the house? Old Mr. Crackenthorpe, Emma, Cedric—"

"Harold and Alfred. They'd come down from London in the afternoon. Oh, and Bryan, Bryan Eastley. But he left just before dinner. He had to meet a man in Brackhampton."

Craddock said thoughtfully, "It ties up with the old man's illness at Christmas. Quimper suspected that that was arsenic. Did they all seem equally ill last night?"

Lucy considered. "I think old Mr. Crackenthorpe seemed the worst. Doctor Quimper had to work like a maniac on him. He's a jolly good doctor, I will say. Cedric made far the most fuss. Of course, strong, healthy people always do."

"What about Emma?"

"She has been pretty bad."

"Why Alfred I wonder?" said Craddock.

"I know," said Lucy. "I suppose it was meant to be Alfred?"

"Funny, I asked that too!"

"It seems, somehow, so pointless."

"If I could only get at the motive for all this business," said Craddock. "It doesn't seem to tie up. The strangled woman in the sarcophagus was Edmund Crackenthorpe's widow, Martine. Let's assume that. It's pretty well proved by now. There must be a connection between that and the deliberate poisoning of Alfred. It's all here, in the family somewhere. Even saying one of them's mad doesn't help."

"Not really," Lucy agreed.

"Well, look after yourself," said Craddock warningly. "There's a poisoner in this house, remember, and one of your patients upstairs probably isn't as ill as he pretends to be."

Lucy went upstairs again slowly after Craddock's departure. An imperious voice, somewhat weakened by illness, called to her as she passed old Mr. Crackenthorpe's room.

"Girl, girl, is that you? Come here."

Lucy entered the room. Mr. Crackenthorpe was lying in bed well propped up with pillows. For a sick man he was looking, Lucy thought, remarkably cheerful.

"The house is full of damned hospital nurses," complained Mr. Crackenthorpe. "Rustling about, making themselves important, taking my temperature, not giving me what I want to eat—a pretty penny all that must be costing. Tell Emma to send 'em away. You could look after me quite well."

"Everybody's been taken ill, Mr. Crackenthorpe," said Lucy. "I can't look after everybody, you know."

"Mushrooms," said Mr. Crackenthorpe. "Damned dangerous things, mushrooms. It was that soup we had last night. You made it," he added accusingly.

"The mushrooms were quite all right, Mr. Crackenthorpe."

"I'm not blaming you, girl, I'm not blaming you. It's happened before. One blasted fungus slips in and does it. Nobody can tell. I know you're a good girl. You wouldn't do it on purpose. How's Emma?"

"Feeling rather better this afternoon."

"Ah. And Harold?"

"He's better too."

"What's this about Alfred having kicked the bucket?"

"Nobody's supposed to have told you that, Mr. Crackenthorpe."

Mr. Crackenthorpe laughed, a high, whinnying laugh of intense amusement. "I hear things," he said. "Can't keep things from the old man. They try to. So Alfred's dead, is he? He won't sponge on me any more, and he won't get any of the money either. They've all been waiting for me to die, you know; Alfred in particular. Now he's dead. I call that rather a good joke."

"That's not very kind of you, Mr. Crackenthorpe," said Lucy severely.

Mr. Crackenthorpe laughed again. "I'll outlive them all," he crowed. "You see if I don't, my girl. You see if I don't."

Lucy went to her room, took out her dictionary and looked up the word *tontine*. She closed the book thoughtfully and stared ahead of her.

III

"Don't see why you want to come to me," said Doctor Morris, irritably.

"You've known the Crackenthorpe family a long time," said Inspector Craddock.

"Yes, yes, I knew all the Crackenthorpes. I remember old Josiah Crackenthorpe. He was a hard nut—shrewd man, though. Made a lot of money." He shifted his aged form in his chair and peered under bushy eyebrows at Inspector Craddock. "So you've been listening to that young fool, Quimper," he said. "These zealous young doctors! Always getting ideas in their heads. Got it into his head that somebody was trying to poison Luther Crackenthorpe. Nonsense! Melodrama! Of course, he had gastric attacks. I treated him for them. Didn't happen very often, nothing peculiar about them."

"Doctor Quimper," said Craddock, "seemed to think there was."

"Doesn't do for a doctor to go thinking. After all, I should hope I could recognize arsenical poisoning when I saw it."

"Quite a lot of well-known doctors haven't noticed it," Craddock pointed out. "There was"—he drew upon his memory—"the Greenbarrow case, Mrs. Reney, Charles Leeds, three people in the Westbury family, all buried nicely and tidily without the doctors who attended them having the least suspicion. Those doctors were all good, reputable men."

"All right, all right," said Doctor Morris, "you're saying that I could have made a mistake. Well, I don't think I did." He paused a minute and then said, "Who did Quimper think was doing it, if it was being done?"

"He didn't know," said Craddock. "He was worried. After all, you know," he added, "there's a great deal of money there."

"Yes, yes, I know, which they'll get when Luther Crackenthorpe dies. And they want it pretty badly. That is true enough, but it doesn't follow that they'd kill the old man to get it."

"Not necessarily," agreed Inspector Craddock.

"Anyway," said Doctor Morris, "my principle is not to go about suspecting things without due cause. Due cause," he repeated. "I'll admit that what you've just told me has shaken me up a bit. Arsenic on a big scale, apparently, but I still don't see why you come to me. All I can tell you is that I didn't suspect it. Maybe I should have. Maybe I should have taken those gastric attacks of Luther Crackenthorpe's much more seriously. But you've got a long way beyond that now."

Craddock agreed. "What I really need," he said, "is to know a little more about the Crackenthorpe family. Is there any queer mental strain in them, a kink of any kind?"

The eyes under the bushy eyebrows looked at him sharply. "Yes, I can see your thoughts might run that way. Well, old Josiah was sane enough. Hard as nails, very much all there. His wife was neurotic, had a tendency to melancholia. Came of an inbred family. She died soon after Luther was born. I'd say, you know, that Luther inherited a certain—well—instability from her. He was commonplace enough as a young man, but he was always at loggerheads with his father. His father was disappointed in him and I think he resented that and brooded on it, and in the end got a kind of obsession about it. He carried that on into his own married life. You'll notice, if you talk to him at all, that he's got a hearty dislike for all his own sons. His daughters he was fond of. Both Emma and Edie, the one who died."

"Why does he dislike the sons so much?" asked Craddock.

"You'll have to go to one of these new-fashioned psychiatrists to find that out. I'd just say that Luther has never felt very adequate as a man himself, and that he bitterly resents his financial position. He has possession of an income but no power of appointment of capital. If he had the power to disinherit his sons he probably wouldn't dislike them as much. Being powerless in that respect gives him a feeling of humiliation."

"That's why he's so pleased at the idea of outliving them all?" said Inspector Craddock.

"Possibly. It is the root, too, of his parsimony, I think. I should say that he's managed to save a considerable sum out of his large income, mostly, of course, before taxation rose to its present giddy heights."

A new idea struck Inspector Craddock. "I suppose he's left his savings by will to someone? That he can do."

"Oh, yes, though God knows who he has left it to. Maybe to Emma, but I should rather doubt it. She'll get her share of the old man's money. Maybe to Alexander, the grandson."

"He's fond of him, is he?" said Craddock.

"Used to be. Of course he was his daughter's child, not a son's child. That may have made a difference. And he had quite an affection for Bryan Eastley, Edie's husband. Of course I don't know Bryan well; it's some years since I've seen any of the family. But it struck me that he was going to be very much at a loose end after the war. He's got those qualities that you need in wartime: courage, dash and a tendency to let the future take care of itself. But I don't think he's got any stability. He'll probably turn into a drifter."

"As far as you know there's no peculiar kink in any of the younger generation?"

"Cedric's an eccentric type, one of those natural rebels. I wouldn't say he was perfectly normal, but you might say, who is? Harold's fairly orthodox, not what I call a very pleasant character, cold-hearted, eye to the main chance. Alfred's got a touch of the delinquent about him. He's a wrong 'un, always was. Saw him taking money out of a missionary box once that they used to keep in the hall. That type of thing. Ah well, the poor fellow's dead, I suppose I shouldn't be talking against him."

"What about—" Craddock hesitated. "Emma Crackenthorpe?"

"Nice girl, quiet, one doesn't always know what she's thinking. Has her own plans and her own ideas but she keeps them to herself. She's more character than you might think from her general manner and appearance."

"You knew Edmund, I suppose, the son who was killed in France?"

"Yes. He was the best of the bunch, I'd say. Goodhearted, gay, a nice boy."

"Did you ever hear that he was going to marry or had married a French girl just before he was killed?"

Doctor Morris frowned. "It seems as though I remember something about it," he said, "but it's a long time ago."

"Quite early on in the war, wasn't it?"

"Yes. Ah well, I daresay he'd have lived to regret it if he had married a foreign wife."

"There's some reason to believe that he did do just that," said Craddock.

In a few brief sentences he gave an account of recent happenings.

"I remember seeing something in the papers about a woman found in a sarcophagus. So it was at Rutherford Hall."

"And there's reason to believe that the woman was Edmund Crackenthorpe's widow."

"Well, well, that seems extraordinary. More like a novel than real life. But who'd want to kill the poor thing—I mean, how does it tie up with arsenical poisoning in the Crackenthorpe family?"

"In one of two ways," said Craddock, "but they are both very farfetched. Somebody perhaps is greedy and wants the whole of Josiah Crackenthorpe's fortune."

"Damn fool if he does," said Doctor Morris. "He'll only have to pay the most stupendous taxes on the income from it."

21

"NASTY THINGS, mushrooms," said Mrs. Kidder.

Mrs. Kidder had made the same remark about ten times in the last few days. Lucy did not reply.

"Never touch 'em myself," said Mrs. Kidder, "much too dangerous. It's a merciful Providence as there's only been one death. The whole lot might have gone and you too, Miss. A wonderful escape you've had."

"It wasn't the mushrooms," said Lucy. "They were perfectly all right."

"Don't you believe it," said Mrs. Kidder. "Dangerous they are, mushrooms. One toadstool in among the lot and you've had it.

"Funny," went on Mrs. Kidder, among the rattle of plates and dishes in the sink, "how things seem to come all together, as it were. My sister's eldest had measles and our Ernie fell down and broke 'is arm, and my 'usband came out all over with boils. All in the same week! You'd hardly believe it, would you. It's been the same thing here," went on Mrs. Kidder. "First that nasty murder and now Mr. Alfred dead with mushroom poisoning. Who'll be the next, I'd like to know?"

Lucy felt rather uncomfortably that she would like to know, too.

"My husband, he doesn't like me coming here now," said Mrs. Kidder, "thinks it's unlucky, but what I say is I've known Miss Crackenthorpe a long time now and she's a nice lady and she depends on me. And I couldn't leave poor Miss Eyelesbarrow, I said, not to do everything herself in the house. Pretty hard it is on you, Miss, all these trays."

Lucy was forced to agree that life did seem to consist very largely of trays at the moment. She was at the moment arranging trays to take to the various invalids.

"As for them nurses, they never do a hand's turn," said Mrs. Kidder. "All they want is pots and pots of tea made strong. And meals prepared. Wore out, that's what I am." She spoke in a tone of great satisfaction, though actually she had done very little more than her normal morning's work.

Lucy said solemnly, "You never spare yourself, Mrs. Kidder."

Mrs. Kidder looked pleased. Lucy picked up the first of the trays and started off up the stairs.

"What's this?" said Mr. Crackenthorpe disapprovingly.

"Beef tea and baked custard," said Lucy.

"Take it away," said Mr. Crackenthorpe. "I won't touch that sort of stuff. I told that nurse I wanted a beefsteak."

"Doctor Quimper thinks you ought not to have beefsteak just yet," said Lucy.

Mr. Crackenthorpe snorted. "I'm practically well again. I'm getting up tomorrow. How are the others?"

"Mr. Harold's much better," said Lucy. "He's going back to London tomorrow."

"Good riddance," said Mr. Crackenthorpe. "What about Cedric? Any hope that he's going back to his island tomorrow?"

"He won't be going just yet."

"Pity. What's Emma doing? Why doesn't she come and see me?"

"She's still in bed, Mr. Crackenthorpe."

"Women always coddle themselves," said Mr. Crackenthorpe, "but you're a good, strong girl," he added approvingly. "Run about all day, don't you?"

"I get plenty of exercise," said Lucy.

Old Mr. Crackenthorpe nodded his head approvingly. "You're a good strong girl," he said, "and don't think I've forgotten what I talked to you about before. One of these days you'll see what you'll see. Emma isn't always going to have things her own way. And don't listen to the others when they tell you I'm a mean old man. I'm careful of my money. I've got a nice little packet put by and I know who I'm going to spend it on when the time comes." He leered at her affectionately.

Lucy went rather quickly out of the room, avoiding his clutching hand.

The next tray was taken into Emma.

"Oh, thank you, Lucy. I'm really feeling quite myself again by now. I'm hungry, and that's a good sign, isn't it? My dear," went on

Emma as Lucy settled the tray on her knees, "I'm really feeling very upset about your aunt. You haven't had any time to go and see her, I suppose?"

"No, I haven't, as a matter of fact."

"I'm afraid she must be missing you."

"Oh, don't worry, Miss Crackenthorpe. She understands what a terrible time we've been through."

"Have you rung her up?"

"No, I haven't just lately."

"Well, do. Ring her up every day. It makes such a difference to old people to get news."

"You're very kind," said Lucy. Her conscience smote her a little as she went down to fetch the next tray. The complications of illness in the house had kept her thoroughly absorbed and she had had no time to think of anything else. She decided that she would ring Miss Marple up as soon as she had taken Cedric his meal.

There was only one nurse in the house now and she passed Lucy on the landing, exchanging greetings.

Cedric, looking incredibly tidied up and neat, was sitting up in bed writing busily on sheets of paper.

"Hullo, Lucy," he said, "what hell brew have you got for me to-day? I wish you'd get rid of that god-awful nurse, she's simply too arch for words. Calls me 'we' for some reason. 'And how are we this morning? Have we slept well? Oh dear, we're very naughty, throwing off the bedclothes like that.'" He imitated the refined accents of the nurse in a high falsetto voice.

"You seem very cheerful," said Lucy. "What are you busy with?"

"Plans," said Cedric. "Plans for what to do with this place when the old man pops off. It's a jolly good bit of land here, you know. I can't make up my mind whether I'd like to develop some of it myself, or whether I'll sell it in lots all in one go. Very valuable for industrial purposes. The house will do for a nursing home or a school. I'm not sure I shan't sell half the land and use the money to do something rather outrageous with the other half. What do you think?"

"You haven't got it yet," said Lucy, dryly.

"I shall have it, though," said Cedric. "It's not divided up like the other stuff. I get it outright. And if I sell it for a good fat price the money will be capital, not income, so I shan't have to pay taxes on it. Money to burn. Think of it."

"I always understood you rather despised money," said Lucy.

"Of course I despise money when I haven't got any," said Cedric. "It's the only dignified thing to do. What a lovely girl you are, Lucy, or do I just think so because I haven't seen any good-looking women for a long time?"

"I expect that's it," said Lucy.

"Still busy tidying everyone and everything up?"

"Somebody seems to have been tidying you up," said Lucy, looking at him.

"That's that damned nurse," said Cedric with feeling. "Have they had the inquest on Alfred yet? What happened?"

"It was adjourned," said Lucy.

"Police being cagey. This mass poisoning does give one a bit of a turn, doesn't it? Mentally, I mean. I'm not referring to more obvious aspects," he added. "Better look after yourself, my girl."

"I do," said Lucy.

"Has young Alexander gone back to school yet?"

"I think he's still with the Stoddart-Wests. I think it's the day after tomorrow that school begins."

Before getting her own lunch Lucy went to the telephone and rang up Miss Marple.

"I'm so terribly sorry I haven't been able to come over, but I've really been very busy."

"Of course, my dear, of course. Besides there's nothing that can be done just now. We just have to wait."

"Yes, but what are we waiting for?"

"Elspeth McGillicuddy ought to be home very soon now," said Miss Marple. "I wrote to her to fly home at once. I said it was her duty. So don't worry too much, my dear." Her voice was kindly and reassuring.

"You don't think—" Lucy began, but stopped.

"That there will be any more deaths? Oh, I hope not, my dear. But one never knows, does one? When anyone is really wicked, I mean. And I think there is great wickedness here."

"Or madness," said Lucy.

"Of course I know that is the modern way of looking at things. I don't agree myself."

Lucy rang off, went into the kitchen and picked up her tray of lunch. Mrs. Kidder had divested herself of her apron and was about to leave.

"You'll be all right, Miss, I hope?" she asked solicitously.

"Of course I shall be all right," snapped Lucy.

She took her tray not into the big, gloomy dining room but into the small study. She was just finishing the meal when the door opened and Bryan Eastley came in.

"Hello," said Lucy, "this is very unexpected."

"I suppose it is," said Bryan. "How is everybody?"

"Oh, much better. Harold's going back to London tomorrow."

"What do you think about it all? Was it really arsenic?"

"It was arsenic all right," said Lucy.

"It hasn't been in the papers yet."

"No, I think the police are keeping it up their sleeves for the moment."

"Somebody must have a pretty good down on the family," said Bryan. "Who's likely to have sneaked in and tampered with the food?"

"I suppose I'm the most likely person, really," said Lucy.

Bryan looked at her anxiously. "But you didn't, did you?" he asked. He sounded slightly shocked.

"No. I didn't," said Lucy.

Nobody could have tampered with the curry. She had made it alone in the kitchen and brought it to table, and the only person who could have tampered with it was one of the five people who sat down to the meal.

"I mean, why should you?" said Bryan. "They're nothing to you, are they? I say," he added, "I hope you don't mind my coming back here like this?"

"No, no, of course I don't. Have you come to stay?"

"Well, I'd like to, if it wouldn't be an awful bore to you."

"No. No, we can manage."

"You see, I'm out of a job at the moment and I—well, I get rather fed up. Are you really sure you don't mind?"

"Oh, I'm not the person to mind, anyway. It's Emma."

"Oh, Emma's all right," said Bryan. "Emma's always been very nice to me. In her own way, you know. She keeps things to herself a lot, in fact she's rather a dark horse, old Emma. This living here and looking after the old man would get most people down. Pity she never married. Too late now, I suppose."

"I don't think it's too late at all," said Lucy.

"Well—" Bryan considered. "A clergyman perhaps," he said hopefully. "She'd be useful in the parish and tactful with the Mothers'

Union. I do mean the Mothers' Union, don't I? Not that I know what it really is, but you come across it sometimes in books. And she'd wear a hat in church on Sundays," he added.

"Doesn't sound much of a prospect to me," said Lucy, rising and picking up the tray.

"I'll do that," said Bryan, taking the tray from her. They went into the kitchen together. "Shall I help you wash up? I do like this kitchen," he added. "In fact, I know it isn't the sort of thing that people do like nowadays, but I like this whole house. Shocking taste, I suppose, but there it is. You could land a plane quite easily in the park," he added with enthusiasm.

He picked up a glass cloth and began to wipe the spoons and forks.

"Seems a waste, it coming to Cedric," he remarked. "First thing he'll do is to sell the whole thing and go beaking off abroad again. Can't see, myself, why England isn't good enough for anybody. Harold wouldn't want this house either, and of course it's much too big for Emma. Now if only it came to Alexander, he and I would be as happy together here as a couple of sandboys. Of course it would be nice to have a woman about the house." He looked thoughtfully at Lucy. "Oh, well, what's the good of talking? If Alexander were to get this place it would mean a whole lot of them would have to die first, and that's not really likely, is it? Though from what I've seen of the old boy he might easily live to be a hundred, just to annoy them all. I don't suppose he was much cut up by Alfred's death, was he?"

Lucy said shortly, "No, he wasn't."

"Cantankerous old devil," said Bryan Eastley cheerfully.

22

"DREADFUL, the things people go about saying," said Mrs. Kidder. "I don't listen, mind you, more than I can help. But you'd hardly believe it." She waited hopefully.

"Yes, I suppose so," said Lucy.

"About that body that was found in the Long Barn," went on Mrs. Kidder, moving crablike backward on her hands and knees, as she scrubbed the kitchen floor, "saying as how she'd been Mr. Edmund's fancy piece during the war, and how she come over here and a jealous husband followed her and did her in. It is a likely thing as a foreigner would do, but it wouldn't be likely after all these years, would it?"

"It sounds most unlikely to me."

"But there's worse things than that, they say," said Mrs. Kidder. "Say anything, people will. You'd be surprised. There's those that say Mr. Harold married somewhere abroad and that she come over and found out he'd committed bigamy with that Lady Alice, and that she was going to bring 'im to court and that he met her down here and did her in and hid her body in the sarcoffus. Did you ever!"

"Shocking," said Lucy vaguely, her mind elsewhere.

"Of course I don't listen," said Mrs. Kidder virtuously, "I wouldn't put no stock in such tales myself. It beats me how people think up such things, let alone say them. All I hope is none of it gets to Miss Emma's ears. It might upset her and I shouldn't like that. She's a very nice lady, Miss Emma is, and I've not heard a word against her, not a word. And of course Mr. Alfred being dead nobody says anything against him now. Not even that it's a judgment, which they well might do. But it's awful, Miss, isn't it, the wicked talk there is."

Mrs. Kidder spoke with immense enjoyment.

"It must be quite painful for you to listen to it," said Lucy.

"Oh, it is," said Mrs. Kidder. "It is, indeed. I says to my husband, I says, 'However can they?'"

The bell rang.

"There's the doctor, Miss. Will you let 'im in, or shall I?"

"I'll go," said Lucy.

But it was not the doctor. On the doorstep stood a tall, elegant woman in a mink coat. Drawn up to the gravel sweep was a purring Rolls with a chauffeur at the wheel.

"Can I see Miss Emma Crackenthorpe, please?"

It was an attractive voice, the R's slightly blurred. The woman was attractive, too. About thirty-five, with dark hair and expensively and beautifully made up.

"I'm sorry," said Lucy, "Miss Crackenthorpe is ill in bed and can't see anyone."

"I know she has been ill, yes, but it is very important that I should see her."

"I'm afraid," Lucy began.

The visitor interrupted her. "I think you are Miss Eyelesbarrow, are you not?" She smiled, an attractive smile. "My son has spoken of you, so I know. I am Lady Stoddart-West and Alexander is staying with me now."

"Oh, I see," said Lucy.

"And it is really important that I should see Miss Crackenthorpe," continued the other. "I know all about her illness and I assure you this is not just a social call. It is because of something that the boys have said to me—that my son has said to me. It is, I think, a matter of grave importance and I would like to speak to Miss Crackenthorpe about it. Please, will you ask her?"

"Come in." Lucy ushered her visitor into the hall and into the drawing room. Then she said, "I'll go up and ask Miss Crackenthorpe."

She went upstairs, knocked on Emma's door and entered.

"Lady Stoddart-West is here," she said. "She wants to see you very particularly."

"Lady Stoddart-West?" Emma looked surprised. A look of alarm came into her face. "There's nothing wrong, is there, with the boys —with Alexander?"

"No, no," Lucy reassured her. "I'm sure the boys are all right. It seems to be something the boys have told her or said to her."

"Oh. Well—" Emma hesitated. "Perhaps I ought to see her. Do I look all right, Lucy?"

"You look very nice," said Lucy.

Emma was sitting up in bed, a soft, pink shawl was round her shoulders and brought out the faint rose-pink of her cheeks. Her dark hair had been neatly brushed and combed by the nurse. Lucy had placed a bowl of autumn leaves on the dressing table the day before. Her room looked attractive and quite unlike a sickroom.

"I'm really quite well enough to get up," said Emma. "Doctor Quimper said I could tomorrow."

"You look really quite yourself again," said Lucy. "Shall I bring Lady Stoddart-West up?"

"Yes, do."

Lucy went downstairs again. "Will you come up to Miss Crackenthorpe's room?"

She escorted the visitor upstairs, opened the door for her to pass in and then shut it. Lady Stoddart-West approached the bed with outstretched hand.

"Miss Crackenthorpe? I really do apologize for breaking in on you like this. I have seen you, I think, at the sports at the school."

"Yes," said Emma, "I remember you quite well. Do sit down."

In the chair conveniently placed by the bed, Lady Stoddart-West sat down. She said in a quiet low voice,

"You must think it very strange of me coming here like this, but I have a reason. I think it is an important reason. You see, the boys have been telling me things. You can understand that they were very excited about the murder that happened here. I confess I did not like it at the time. I was nervous. I wanted to bring James home at once. But my husband laughed. He said that obviously it was a murder that had nothing to do with the house and the family and he said that from what he remembered from his boyhood, and from James's letters, both he and Alexander were enjoying themselves so wildly that it would be sheer cruelty to bring them back. So I gave in and agreed that they should stay on until the time arranged for James to bring Alexander back with him."

Emma said: "You think we ought to have sent your son home earlier?"

"No, no, that is not what I mean at all. Oh, it is difficult for me, this! But what I have to say must be said. You see, they have picked up a good deal, the boys. They told me that this woman—the murdered woman—that the police have an idea that she may be a French girl whom your eldest brother, who was killed in the war, knew in France. That is so?"

"It is a possibility," said Emma, her voice breaking slightly, "that we are forced to consider. It may have been so."

"There is some reason for believing that the body is that of this girl, this Martine?"

"I have told you, it is a possibility."

"But why—why should they think that she was this Martine? Did she have letters on her—papers?"

"No. Nothing of that kind. But you see I had had a letter from this Martine."

"You had had a letter from *Martine?*"

"Yes. A letter telling me she was in England and would like to come and see me. I invited her down here, but got a telegram saying she was going back to France. Perhaps she did go back to France. We do not know. But since then an envelope was found here addressed to her. That seems to show that she had come down here. But I really don't see—" She broke off.

Lady Stoddart-West broke in quickly,

"You really do not see what concern it is of mine? That is very true. I should not, in your place. But when I heard this, or rather, a garbled account of this, I had to come to make sure it was really so, because, if it is—"

"Yes?" said Emma.

"Then I must tell you something that I had never intended to tell you. You see, *I am Martine.*"

Emma stared at her guest as though she could hardly take in the sense of her words.

"You!" she said. "You are Martine?"

The other nodded vigorously. "But yes. It surprises you, I am sure, but it is true. I met your brother Edmund in the first days of the war. He was indeed billeted at our house. Well, you know the rest. We fell in love. We intended to be married, and then there was the retreat to Dunkirk, Edmund was reported missing. Later he was reported killed. I will not speak to you of that time. It was long ago and it is over. But I will say to you that I loved your brother very much.

"Then came the grim realities of war. The Germans occupied France. I became a worker for the Resistance. I was one of those who was assigned to pass Englishmen through France to England. It was in that way that I met my present husband. He was an Air Force officer, parachuted into France to do special work. When the war ended we were married. I considered once or twice whether I should write to you or come and see you but I decided against it. It could do no good, I thought, to rake up old memories. I had a new life and I had no wish to recall the old." She paused and then said, "But it gave me, I will tell you, a strange pleasure when I found that my son James's greatest friend at his school was a boy whom I found to be Edmund's nephew. Alexander, I may say, is very like Edmund, as I dare say you yourself appreciate. It seemed to me a very happy state of affairs that James and Alexander should be such friends."

She leaned forward and placed her hand on Emma's arm. "But you see, dear Emma, do you not, that when I heard this story about the murder, about this dead woman being suspected to be the Martine that Edmund had known, that I had to come and tell you the truth. Either you or I must inform the police of the fact. Whoever the dead woman is, she is not Martine."

"I can hardly take it in," said Emma, "that you, you should be the Martine that dear Edmund wrote to me about." She sighed, shaking her head, then she frowned perplexedly. "But I don't understand. Was it you, then, who wrote to me?"

Lady Stoddart-West shook a vigorous head. "No, no, of course I did not write to you."

"Then—" Emma stopped.

"Then there was someone pretending to be Martine who wanted perhaps to get money out of you? That is what it must have been. But who can it be?"

Emma said slowly: "I suppose there were people at the time who knew?"

The other shrugged her shoulders. "Probably, yes. But there was no one intimate with me, no one very close to me. I have never spoken of it since I came to England. And why wait all this time? It is curious, very curious."

Emma said, "I don't understand it. We will have to see what Inspector Craddock has to say." She looked with suddenly softened eyes at her visitor. "I'm so glad to know you at last, my dear."

"And I you. Edmund spoke of you very often. He was very fond of you. I am happy in my new life, but all the same, I do not quite forget."

Emma leaned back and heaved a deep sigh. "It's a terrible relief," she said. "As long as we feared that the dead woman might be Martine, it seemed to be tied up with the family. But now, oh, it's an absolute load off my back. I don't know who the poor soul was but she can't have had anything to do with us!"

23

THE streamlined secretary brought Harold Crackenthorpe his usual afternoon cup of tea.

"Thanks, Miss Ellis, I shall be going home early today."

"I'm sure you ought really not to have come at all, Mr. Crackenthorpe," said Miss Ellis. "You look quite pulled down still."

"I'm all right," said Harold Crackenthorpe, but he did feel pulled down. No doubt about it, he'd had a very nasty turn. Ah well, that was over.

Extraordinary, he thought broodingly, that Alfred should have succumbed and the old man should have come through. After all, what was he?—seventy-three, seventy-four? Been an invalid for years. If there was one person you'd have thought would have been taken off, it would have been the old man. But no. It had to be Alfred. Alfred who, as far as Harold knew, was a healthy, wiry sort of chap. Nothing much the matter with him.

He leaned back in his chair sighing. That girl was right. He didn't feel up to things yet, but he had wanted to come down to the office. Wanted to get the hang of how affairs were going. Touch and go, that's what it was! Touch and go. All this—he looked round him —the richly appointed office, the pale gleaming wood, the expensive modern chairs, it all looked prosperous enough, and a good thing, too! That's where Alfred had always gone wrong. If you looked prosperous, people thought you were prosperous. There were no rumors going around as yet about his financial stability. All the same, the crash couldn't be delayed very long. Now if only his father had passed out instead of Alfred, as surely, surely he ought to have done. Practically seemed to thrive on arsenic! Yes, if his father had succumbed: well, there wouldn't have been anything to worry about.

Still, the great thing was not to seem worried. A prosperous appearance. Not like poor old Alfred who always looked seedy and shiftless, who looked in fact exactly what he was. One of those small-time speculators, never going all out boldly for the big money. In with a shady crowd here, doing a doubtful deal there, never quite rendering himself liable to prosecution but going very near the edge. And where had it got him? Short periods of affluence and then back to seediness and shabbiness once more. No broad outlook about Alfred. Taken all in all, you couldn't say Alfred was much loss. He'd never been particularly fond of Alfred and with Alfred out of the way the money that was coming to him from that old curmudgeon, his grandfather, would be sensibly increased, divided not into five shares but into four shares. Very much better.

Harold's face brightened a little. He rose, took his hat and coat and left the office. Better take it easy for a day or two. He wasn't feeling too strong yet. His car was waiting below and very soon he was weaving through the London traffic to his house.

Darwin, his manservant, opened the door.

"Her Ladyship has just arrived, sir," he said.

For a moment Harold stared at him. Alice! Good Heavens, was it today that Alice was coming home? He'd forgotten all about it. Good thing Darwin had warned him. It wouldn't have looked so good if he'd gone upstairs and looked too astonished at seeing her. Not that it really mattered, he supposed. Neither Alice nor he had many illusions about the feeling they had for each other. Perhaps Alice was fond of him; he didn't know.

All in all Alice was a great disappointment to him. He hadn't been in love with her, of course, but though a plain woman she was quite a pleasant one. And her family and connections had undoubtedly been useful. Not perhaps as useful as they might have been, because in marrying Alice he had been considering the position of hypothetical children. Nice relations for his boys to have. But there hadn't been any boys, or girls either, and all that had remained had been him and Alice growing older together without much to say to each other and with no particular pleasure in each other's company.

She stayed away a good deal with relations and usually went to the Riviera in the winter. It suited her and it didn't worry him.

He went upstairs now into the drawing room and greeted her punctiliously.

"So you're back, my dear. Sorry I couldn't meet you, but I was held up in the City. I got back as early as I could. How was San Raphael?"

Alice told him how San Raphael was. She was a thin woman with sandy-colored hair, a well-arched nose and vague, hazel eyes. She talked in a well-bred, monotonous and rather depressing voice. It had been a good journey back, the Channel a little rough. The customs, as usual, very trying at Dover.

"You should come by air," said Harold, as he always did. "So much simpler."

"I dare say, but I don't really like air travel. I never have. Makes me nervous."

"Saves a lot of time," said Harold.

Lady Alice Crackenthorpe did not answer. It was possible that her problem in life was not to save time but to occupy it. She inquired politely after her husband's health.

"Emma's telegram quite alarmed me," she said. "You were all taken ill, I understand."

"Yes, yes," said Harold.

"I read in the paper the other day," said Alice, "of forty people in a hotel going down with food poisoning at the same time. All this refrigeration is dangerous, I think. People keep things too long in them."

"Possibly," said Harold. Should he, or should he not mention arsenic? Somehow, looking at Alice, he felt himself quite unable to do so. In Alice's world, he felt, there was no place for poisoning by arsenic. It was a thing you read about in the papers. It didn't happen to you or your own family. But it had happened in the Crackenthorpe family. . . .

He went up to his room and lay down for an hour or two before dressing for dinner. At dinner, tête-à-tête with his wife, the conversation ran on much the same lines. Desultory, polite. The mention of acquaintances and friends at San Raphael.

"There's a parcel for you on the hall table, a small one," Alice said.

"Is there? I didn't notice it."

"It's an extraordinary thing but somebody was telling me about a murdered woman having been found in a barn or something like that. She said it was at Rutherford Hall. I suppose it must be some other Rutherford Hall."

"No," said Harold, "no, it isn't. It was in our barn, as a matter of fact."

"Really, Harold! A murdered woman in the barn at Rutherford Hall, and you never told me anything about it."

"Well, there hasn't been much time, really," said Harold, "and it was all rather unpleasant. Nothing to do with us, of course. The press milled round a good deal. Of course we had to deal with the police and all that sort of thing."

"Very unpleasant," said Alice. "Did they find out who did it?" she added, with rather perfunctory interest.

"Not yet," said Harold.

"What sort of a woman was she?"

"Nobody knows. French apparently."

"Oh, French," said Alice, and allowing for the difference in class, her tone was not unlike that of Inspector Bacon. "Very annoying for you all," she agreed.

They went out from the dining room and crossed into the small study where they usually sat when they were alone. Harold was feeling quite exhausted by now. I'll go up to bed early, he thought.

He picked up the small parcel from the hall table, about which his wife had spoken to him. It was a small neatly waxed parcel, done up with meticulous exactness. Harold ripped it open as he came to sit down in his usual chair by the fire.

Inside was a small tablet box bearing the label, *"Two to be taken nightly."* With it was a small piece of paper with the chemist's heading in Brackhampton. *"Sent by request of Doctor Quimper"* was written on it.

Harold Crackenthorpe frowned. He opened the box and looked at the tablets. Yes, they seemed to be the same tablets he had been having. But surely, surely Quimper had said that he needn't take any more? "You won't want them now." That's what Quimper had said.

"What is it, dear?" said Alice. "You look worried."

"Oh, it's just some tablets. I've been taking them at night. But I rather thought the doctor said don't take any more."

His wife said placidly, "He probably said don't forget to take them."

"He may have done, I suppose," said Harold doubtfully.

He looked across at her. She was watching him. Just for a moment or two he wondered—he didn't often wonder about Alice—exactly what she was thinking. That mild gaze of hers told him nothing. Her eyes were like windows in an empty house. What did Alice think about him, feel about him? Had she been in love with him once? He supposed she had. Or did she marry him because she thought he was doing well in the City and she was tired of her own impecunious existence? Well, on the whole, she'd done quite well out of it. She'd got a car and a house in London, she could travel abroad when she felt like it and get herself expensive clothes, though goodness knows they never looked like anything on Alice. Yes, on the whole, she'd done pretty well. He wondered if she thought so. She wasn't really fond of him, of course, but then he wasn't really fond of her. They had nothing in common, nothing to talk about, no memories to share. If there had been children, but there hadn't been any children. Odd that there were no children in the family except young Edie's boy. Young Edie. She'd been a silly girl, making that foolish, hasty wartime marriage. Well, he'd given her good advice.

He'd said, "It's all very well, these dashing young pilots, glamor, courage, all that, but he'll be no good in peacetime, you know. Probably be barely able to support you."

And Edie had said, what did it matter? She loved Bryan and Bryan loved her, and he'd probably be killed quite soon. Why shouldn't they have some happiness? What was the good of looking to the future when they might all be bombed any minute. And after all, Edie had said, the future doesn't really matter because some day there'll be all grandfather's money.

Harold squirmed uneasily in his chair. Really, that will of his grandfather's had been iniquitous! Keeping them all dangling on a string. The will hadn't pleased anybody. It didn't please the grandchildren and it made their father quite livid. The old boy was absolutely determined not to die. That's what made him take so much care of himself. But he'd have to die soon. Surely, surely he'd have to die soon. Otherwise— All Harold's worries swept over him once more, making him feel sick and tired and giddy.

Alice was still watching him, he noticed. Those pale, thoughtful eyes, they made him uneasy somehow.

"I think I shall go to bed," he said. "It's been my first day out in the City."

"Yes," said Alice, "I think that's a good idea. I'm sure the doctor told you to take things easy at first."

"Doctors always tell you that," said Harold.

"And don't forget to take your tablets, dear," said Alice. She picked up the box and handed it to him.

He said good night and went upstairs. Yes, he needed the tablets. It would have been a mistake to leave them off too soon. He took two of them and swallowed them with a glass of water.

24

"NOBODY could have made more of a muck of it than I seem to have done," said Dermot Craddock gloomily.

He sat, his long legs stretched out, looking somehow incongruous in faithful Florence's somewhat overfurnished parlor. He was thoroughly tired, upset and dispirited.

Miss Marple made soft, soothing noises of dissent. "No, no, you've done very good work, my dear boy. Very good work, indeed."

"I've done very good work, have I? I've let a whole family be poisoned, Alfred Crackenthorpe's dead and now Harold's dead, too. What the hell's going on there? That's what I should like to know."

"Poisoned tablets," said Miss Marple thoughtfully.

"Yes. Devilishly cunning, really. They looked just like the tablets that he'd been having. There was a printed slip sent in with them *'by Doctor Quimper's instructions.'* Well, Quimper never ordered them. There were chemist's labels used. The chemist knew nothing about it, either. No. That box of tablets came from Rutherford Hall."

"Do you actually know it came from Rutherford Hall?"

"Yes. We've had a thorough checkup. Actually it's the box that held the sedative tablets prescribed for Emma."

"Oh, I see. For Emma . . ."

"Yes. It's got her fingerprints on it and the fingerprints of both the nurses and the fingerprint of the chemist who made it up. Nobody else's, naturally. The person who sent them was careful."

"And the sedative tablets were removed and something else substituted?"

"Yes. That of course is the devil with tablets. One tablet looks exactly like another."

"You are so right," agreed Miss Marple. "I remember so very well in my young days, the black mixture and the brown mixture—the cough mixture that was—and the white mixture, and Doctor So-and-So's pink mixture. People didn't mix those up nearly as much. In fact, you know, in my village in St. Mary Mead we still like that kind of medicine. It's a bottle they always want, not tablets. What were the tablets?" she asked.

"Aconite. They were the kind of tablets that are usually kept in a poison bottle, diluted one in a hundred for outside application."

"And so Harold took them and died," Miss Marple said thoughtfully. Dermot Craddock uttered something like a groan.

"You mustn't mind my letting off steam to you," he said. "Tell it all to Aunt Jane; that's how I feel!"

"That's very, very nice of you," said Miss Marple, "and I do appreciate it. As Sir Henry's godson I feel toward you quite differently from the way I should feel to any ordinary detective inspector."

Dermot Craddock gave her a fleeting grin. "But the fact remains that I've made the most ghastly mess of things all along the line," he said. "The Chief Constable down here calls in Scotland Yard, and what do they get? They get me making a prize ass of myself!"

"No, no," said Miss Marple.

"Yes, yes. I don't know who poisoned Alfred, I don't know who poisoned Harold, and to cap it all I haven't the least idea now who the original murdered woman was! This Martine business seemed a perfectly safe bet. The whole thing seemed to tie up. And now what happens? The real Martine shows up and turns out, most improbably, to be the wife of Sir Robert Stoddart-West. So who's the woman in the barn now? Goodness knows. First I go all out on the idea she's Anna Stravinska, and then she's out of it."

He was arrested by Miss Marple giving one of her small, peculiarly significant coughs.

"But is she?" she murmured.

Craddock stared at her. "Well, that postcard from Jamaica."

"Yes," said Miss Marple, "but that isn't really evidence, is it? I mean, anyone can get a postcard sent from almost anywhere, I suppose. I remember Mrs. Brierly, such a very bad nervous breakdown. Finally they said she ought to go to the mental hospital for observation, and she was so worried about the children knowing about it and so she wrote about fourteen postcards and arranged that they should be posted from different places abroad, and told them that

Mummie was going abroad on a holiday." She added, looking at Dermot Craddock, "You see what I mean."

"Yes, of course," said Craddock, staring at her. "Naturally we'd have checked that postcard if it hadn't been for the Martine business fitting the bill so well."

"So convenient," murmured Miss Marple.

"It tied up," said Craddock. "After all there's the letter Emma received signed Martine Crackenthorpe. Lady Stoddart-West didn't send that, but somebody did. Somebody who was going to pretend to be Martine, and who was going to cash in, if possible, on being Martine. You can't deny that."

"No, no."

"And then, the envelope of the letter Emma wrote to her with the London address on it. Found at Rutherford Hall, showing she'd actually been there."

"But the murdered woman hadn't been there!" Miss Marple pointed out. "Not in the sense you mean. She only came to Rutherford Hall after she was dead. Pushed out of a train on to the railway embankment."

"Oh—yes."

"What the envelope really proves is that the murderer was there. Presumably he took that envelope off her with her other papers and things, and then dropped it by mistake—or—I wonder now, was it a mistake? Surely Inspector Bacon, and your men too, made a thorough search of the place, didn't they, and didn't find it. It only turned up later in the boiler house."

"That's understandable," said Craddock. "The old gardener chap used to spear up any odd stuff that was blowing about and shove it in there."

"Where it was very convenient for the boys to find," said Miss Marple thoughtfully.

"You think we were meant to find it?"

"Well, I just wonder. After all it would be fairly easy to know where the boys were going to look next, or even to suggest to them . . . Yes, I do wonder. It stopped you thinking about Anna Stravinska any more, didn't it?"

Craddock said, "And you think it really may be her all the time?"

"I think someone may have got alarmed when you started making inquiries about her, that's all. I think somebody didn't want those inquiries made."

"Let's hold on to the basic fact that someone was going to impersonate Martine," said Craddock. "And then for some reason didn't.
Why?"

"That's a very interesting question," said Miss Marple.

"Somebody sent a wire saying Martine was going back to France,
then arranged to travel down with the girl and kill her on the way.
You agree so far?"

"Not exactly," said Miss Marple. "I don't think, really, you're
making it simple enough."

"Simple!" exclaimed Craddock. "You're mixing me up," he complained.

Miss Marple said in a distressed voice that she wouldn't think of
doing anything like that.

"Come, tell me," said Craddock, "do you or do you not think you
know who the murdered woman was?"

Miss Marple sighed. "It's so difficult," she said, "to put it the right
way. I mean, I don't know *who* she was, but at the same time I'm
fairly sure who she *was*, if you know what I mean."

Craddock threw up his head. "Know what you mean? I haven't
the faintest idea." He looked out through the window. "There's your
Lucy Eyelesbarrow coming to see you," he said. "Well, I'll be off.
My *amour propre* is very low this afternoon and having a young
woman coming in, radiant with efficiency and success, is more than
I can bear."

25

"I LOOKED up tontine in the dictionary," said Lucy.

The first greetings were over and now Lucy was wandering rather aimlessly round the room, touching a china dog here, an antimacassar there, the plastic work box in the window.

"I thought you probably would," said Miss Marple equably.

Lucy spoke slowly, quoting the words. "Lorenzo Tonti, Italian banker, originator, 1653, of a form of annuity in which the shares of subscribers who die are added to the profit shares of the survivors." She paused. "That's it, isn't it? That fits well enough, and you were thinking of it even then before the last two deaths."

She took up once more her restless, almost aimless prowl round the room. Miss Marple sat watching her. This was a very different Lucy Eyelesbarrow from the one she knew.

"I suppose it was asking for it really," said Lucy. "A will of that kind, ending so that if there was only one survivor left he'd get the lot. And yet, there was quite a lot of money, wasn't there? You'd think it would be enough shared out—" She paused, the words tailing off.

"The trouble is," said Miss Marple, "that people are greedy. Some people. That's so often, you know, how things start. You don't start with murder, with wanting to do murder or even thinking of it. You just start by being greedy, by wanting more than you're going to have." She laid her knitting down on her knee and stared ahead of her into space. "That's how I came across Inspector Craddock first, you know. A case in the country. Near Medenham Spa. That began the same way, just a weak amiable character who wanted a great deal of money. Money that that person wasn't entitled to, but there seemed an easy way to get it. Not murder then. Just something so easy and simple that it hardly seemed wrong. That's how things begin. But it ended with three murders."

"Just like this," said Lucy. "We've had three murders now. The woman who impersonated Martine and who would have been able to claim a share for her son, and then Alfred, and then Harold. And now it only leaves two, doesn't it?"

"You mean," said Miss Marple, "there are only Cedric and Emma left?"

"Not Emma. Emma isn't a tall, dark man. No. I mean Cedric and Bryan Eastley. I never thought of Bryan because he's fair. He's got a great, fair mustache and blue eyes, but you see—the other day—" She paused.

"Yes, go on," said Miss Marple. "Tell me. Something has upset you very badly, hasn't it?"

"It was when Lady Stoddart-West was going away. She had said good-by and then suddenly turned to me just as she was getting into the car and asked: 'Who was that tall, dark man who was standing on the terrace as I came in?'

"I couldn't imagine who she meant at first, because Cedric was still laid up. So I said, rather puzzled, 'You don't mean Bryan Eastley?' and she said, 'Of course, that's who it was, Squadron Leader Eastley. He was hidden in our loft once in France during the Resistance. I remembered the way he stood, and the set of his shoulders,' and she said, 'I should like to meet him again,' but we couldn't find him."

Miss Marple said nothing, just waited.

"And then," said Lucy, "later I looked at him . . . He was standing with his back to me and I saw what I ought to have seen before. That even when a man's fair, his hair looks dark because he plasters it down with stuff. Bryan's hair is a sort of medium brown, I suppose, but it can look dark. So, you see, it might have been Bryan that your friend saw in the train. It might. . . ."

"Yes," said Miss Marple. "I had thought of that."

"I suppose you think of everything!" said Lucy bitterly.

"Well, dear, one has to really."

"But I can't see what Bryan would get out of it. I mean, the money would come to Alexander, not to him. I suppose it would make an easier life, they could have a bit more luxury, but he wouldn't be able to tap the capital for his schemes, or anything like that."

"But if anything happened to Alexander before he was twenty-one, then Bryan would get the money as his father and next of kin," Miss Marple pointed out.

. Lucy cast a look of horror at her.

"He'd never do that. No father would ever do that just—just to get the money."

Miss Marple sighed. "People do, my dear. It's very sad and very terrible, but they do.

"People do very terrible things," Miss Marple continued. "I know a woman who poisoned three of her children just for a little bit of insurance money. And then there was an old woman, quite a nice old woman apparently, who poisoned her son when he came home on leave. Then there was that old Mrs. Stanwich. That case was in the paper. I dare say you read about it. Her daughter died and her son, and then she said she was poisoned herself. There was poison in some gruel, but it came out, you know, that she'd put it there herself. She was just planning to poison the last daughter. That wasn't exactly for money. She was jealous of them for being younger than she was and alive, and she was afraid—it's a terrible thing to say but it's true—they would enjoy themselves after she was gone. She'd always kept a very tight hold on the purse strings. Yes, of course she was a little peculiar, as they say, but I never see myself that that's any real excuse. I mean you can be a little peculiar in so many different ways. Sometimes you just go about giving all your possessions away and writing checks on bank accounts that don't exist, just so as to benefit people. It shows, you see, that behind being peculiar you have quite a nice disposition. But of course if you're peculiar and behind it you have a bad disposition, well, there you are. Now, does that help you at all, my dear Lucy?"

"Does what help me?" asked Lucy bewildered.

"What I've been telling you," said Miss Marple. She added gently, "You mustn't worry, you know. You really mustn't worry. Elspeth McGillicuddy will be here any day now."

"I don't see what that has to do with it."

"No, dear, perhaps not. But I think it's important myself."

"I can't help worrying," said Lucy. "You see I've got interested in the family."

"I know, dear, it's very difficult for you because you are quite strongly attracted to both of them, aren't you, in very different ways."

"What do you mean?" said Lucy. Her tone was sharp.

"I was talking about the two sons of the house," said Miss Marple. "Or rather the son and the son-in-law. It's fortunate that the two more unpleasant members of the family have died and the two more attractive ones are left. I can see that Cedric Crackenthorpe is very attractive. He is inclined to make himself out worse than he is and has a provocative way with him."

"He makes me fighting mad sometimes," said Lucy.

"Yes," said Miss Marple, "and you enjoy that, don't you? You're a girl with a lot of spirit and you enjoy a battle. Yes, I can see where that attraction lies. And then Mr. Eastley is a rather plaintive type, rather like an unhappy little boy. That of course is attractive, too."

"And one of them's a murderer," said Lucy bitterly, "and it may be either of them. There's nothing to choose between them really. There's Cedric, not caring a bit about his brother Alfred's death or about Harold's. He just sits back looking thoroughly pleased making plans for what he'll do with Rutherford Hall, and he keeps saying that it'll need a lot of money to develop it in the way he wants to do. Of course I know he's the sort of person who exaggerates his own callousness and all that. But that could be a cover, too. I mean everyone says that you're more callous than you really are. But you mightn't be. You might be even more callous than you seem!"

"Dear, dear Lucy, I'm so sorry about all this."

"And then Bryan," went on Lucy. "It's extraordinary, but Bryan really seems to want to live there. He thinks he and Alexander would find it awfully jolly and he's full of schemes."

"He's always full of schemes of one kind or another, isn't he?"

"Yes, I think he is. They all sound rather wonderful, but I've got an uneasy feeling that they'd never really work. I mean, they're not practical. The idea sounds all right, but I don't think he ever considers the actual working difficulties."

"They are up in the air, so to speak?"

"Yes, in more ways than one. I mean they are usually literally up in the air. They are all air schemes. Perhaps a really good fighter pilot never does quite come down to earth again. . . ."

She added: "And he likes Rutherford Hall so much because it reminds him of the big rambling Victorian house he lived in when he was a child."

"I see," said Miss Marple thoughtfully. "Yes, I see."

Then, with a quick sideways glance at Lucy, she said with a kind of verbal pounce, "But that isn't all of it, is it, dear? There's something else."

"Oh yes, there's something else. Just something that I didn't realize until just a couple of days ago. Bryan was actually on that train."

"On the four thirty-three from Paddington?"

"Yes. You see Emma thought she was required to account for her movements on December the twentieth and she went over it all very carefully—a committee meeting in the morning and then shopping in the afternoon and tea at the Green Shamrock, and then, she said, she went to meet Bryan at the station. I worked out when she'd had tea and the time, and the train she met must have been the four thirty-three. So I asked Bryan, quite casually, and he said, Yes, it was, and added that his car had had a bump and was being repaired and so he had to come down by train—an awful bore, he said, he hates trains. He seemed quite natural about it all. It may be quite all right, but I wish, somehow, he hadn't been on that train. . . ."

"Actually on the train," said Miss Marple thoughtfully.

"It doesn't really prove anything. The awful thing is all this suspicion. Not to know. And perhaps we never shall know!"

"Of course we shall know, dear," said Miss Marple briskly. "I mean, all this isn't going to stop just at this point. The one thing I do know about murderers is that they can never let well alone. Or perhaps one should say, ill alone. At any rate," said Miss Marple with finality, "they can't once they've done a second murder. Now don't get too upset, Lucy. The police are doing all they can, and looking after everybody, and the great thing is that Elspeth McGillicuddy will be here very soon now!"

26

"Now, Elspeth, you're quite clear as to what I want you to do?"

"I'm clear enough," said Mrs. McGillicuddy, "but what I say to you is, Jane, that it seems very odd."

"It's not odd at all," said Miss Marple.

"Well, I think so. To arrive at the house and to ask almost immediately whether I can—er—go upstairs."

"It's very cold weather," Miss Marple pointed out, "and after all, you might have eaten something that disagreed with you and—er—have to ask to go upstairs. I mean, these things happen. I remember poor Louisa Felby came to see me once and she had to ask to go upstairs five times during one little half hour. That," added Miss Marple parenthetically, "was a bad Cornish pasty."

"If you'd just tell me what you're driving at, Jane," said Mrs. McGillicuddy.

"That's just what I don't want to do," said Miss Marple.

"How irritating you are, Jane. First you make me come all the way back to England before I need—"

"I'm sorry about that," said Miss Marple, "but I couldn't do anything else. Someone, you see, may be killed at any moment. Oh, I know they're all on their guard and the police are taking all the precautions they can, but there's always the outside chance that the murderer might be too clever for them. So you see, Elspeth, it was your duty to come back. After all, you and I were brought up to do our duty, weren't we?"

"We certainly were," said Mrs. McGillicuddy, "no laxness in our young days."

"So that's quite all right," said Miss Marple. "And that's the taxi now," she added, as a faint hoot was heard outside the house.

Mrs. McGillicuddy donned her heavy pepper-and-salt coat and

Miss Marple wrapped herself up with a good many shawls and scarves. Then the two ladies got into the taxi and were driven to Rutherford Hall.

II

"Who can this be driving up?" Emma asked, looking out of the window, as the taxi swept past it. "I do believe it's Lucy's old aunt."

"What a bore," said Cedric.

He was lying back in a long chair looking at *Country Life* with his feet reposing on the side of the mantelpiece.

"Tell her you're not at home."

"When you say tell her I'm not at home, do you mean that I should go out and say so? Or that I should tell Lucy to tell her aunt so?"

"Hadn't thought of that," said Cedric. "I suppose I was thinking of our butler-and-footman days, if we ever had them. I seem to remember a footman before the war. He had an affair with the kitchen maid and there was a terrific rumpus about it. Isn't there one of those old hags about the place cleaning?"

But at that moment the door was opened by Mrs. Hart, whose afternoon it was for cleaning the brasses, and Miss Marple came in, very fluttery, in a whirl of shawls and scarves, with a tall, uncompromising figure behind her.

"I do hope," said Miss Marple, taking Emma's hand, "that we are not intruding. But you see, I'm going home the day after tomorrow, and I couldn't bear not to come over and see you and say good-by and thank you again for your goodness to Lucy. Oh, I forgot. May I introduce my friend, Mrs. McGillicuddy, who is staying with me?"

"How d'you do," said Mrs. McGillicuddy, looking at Emma with complete attention and then shifting her gaze to Cedric, who had now risen to his feet. Lucy entered the room at this moment.

"Aunt Jane, I had no idea . . ."

"I had to come and say good-by to Miss Crackenthorpe," said Miss Marple, turning to her, "who has been so very, very kind to you, Lucy."

"It's Lucy who's been very kind to us," said Emma.

"Yes, indeed," said Cedric. "We've worked her like a galley slave.

Waiting on the sick room, running up and down the stairs, cooking little invalid messes . . ."

Miss Marple broke in. "I was so very, very sorry to hear of your illness. I do hope you're quite recovered now, Miss Crackenthorpe?"

"Oh, we're quite well again now," said Emma.

"Lucy told me you were all very ill. So dangerous, isn't it, food poisoning? Mushrooms, I understand."

"The cause remains rather mysterious," said Emma.

"Don't you believe it," said Cedric. "I bet you've heard the rumors that are flying round, Miss—er—"

"Marple," said Miss Marple.

"Well, as I say, I bet you've heard the rumors that are flying round. Nothing like arsenic for raising a little flutter in the neighborhood."

"Cedric," said Emma, "I wish you wouldn't. You know Inspector Craddock said . . ."

"Bah," said Cedric, "everybody knows. Even you've heard something, haven't you?" He turned to Miss Marple and Mrs. McGillicuddy.

"I myself," said Mrs. McGillicuddy, "have only just returned from abroad. The day before yesterday," she added.

"Ah, well, you're not up in our local scandal then," said Cedric. "Arsenic in the curry, that's what it was. Lucy's aunt knows all about it, I bet."

"Well," said Miss Marple, "I did just hear—I mean, it was just a hint, but of course I didn't want to embarrass you in any way, Miss Crackenthorpe."

"You must pay no attention to my brother," said Emma. "He just likes making people uncomfortable." She gave him an affectionate smile as she spoke.

The door opened and Mr. Crackenthorpe came in, tapping angrily with his stick.

"Where's tea?" he said. "Why isn't tea ready? You! Girl!" he addressed Lucy, "why haven't you brought tea in?"

"It's just ready, Mr. Crackenthorpe. I'm bringing it in now. I was just setting the table ready."

Lucy went out of the room again and Mr. Crackenthorpe was introduced to Miss Marple and Mrs. McGillicuddy.

"Like my meals on time," said Mr. Crackenthorpe. "Punctuality and economy. Those are my watchwords."

"Very necessary, I'm sure," said Miss Marple, "especially in these times with taxation and everything."

Mr. Crackenthorpe snorted. "Taxation! Don't talk to me of those robbers. A miserable pauper, that's what I am. And it's going to get worse, not better. You wait, my boy," he addressed Cedric, "when you get this place ten to one the Socialists will have it off you and turn it into a Welfare Center or something. And take all your income to keep it up with!"

Lucy reappeared with a tea tray, Bryan Eastley following her carrying a tray of sandwiches, bread and butter and cake.

"What's this? What's this?" Mr. Crackenthorpe inspected the tray. "Frosted cake? We having a party today? Nobody told me about it."

A faint flush came into Emma's face.

"Doctor Quimper's coming to tea, Father. It's his birthday today and—"

"Birthday?" snorted the old man, "what's he doing with a birthday? Birthdays are only for children. I never count my birthdays and I won't let anyone else celebrate them either."

"Much cheaper," agreed Cedric. "You save the price of candles on your cake."

"That's enough from you, boy," said Mr. Crackenthorpe.

Miss Marple was shaking hands with Bryan Eastley. "I've heard about you, of course," she said, "from Lucy. Dear me, you remind me so much of someone I used to know at St. Mary Mead. That's the village where I've lived for so many years, you know. Ronnie Wells, the solicitor's son. Couldn't seem to settle somehow when he went into his father's business. He went out to East Africa and started a series of cargo boats on the lakes out there. Victoria Nyanza, or is it Albert I mean? Anyway, I'm sorry to say that it wasn't a success, and he lost all his capital. Most unfortunate! Not any relation of yours, I suppose? The likeness is so great."

"No," said Bryan, "I don't think I've any relations called Wells."

"He was engaged to a very nice girl," said Miss Marple. "Very sensible. She tried to dissuade him, but he wouldn't listen to her. He was wrong of course. Women have a lot of sense, you know, when it comes to money matters. Not high finance, of course. No woman can hope to understand that, my dear father said. But every day matters. . . . What a delightful view you have from this window," she added, making her way across and looking out.

Emma joined her.

"Such an expanse of parkland! How picturesque the cattle look against the trees. One would never dream that one was in the middle of a town."

"We're rather an anachronism, I think," said Emma. "If the windows were open now you'd hear far off the noise of the traffic."

"Oh, of course," said Miss Marple, "there's noise everywhere, isn't there? Even in St. Mary Mead. We're now quite close to an airfield, you know, and really the way those jet planes fly over. Most frightening. Two panes in my little greenhouse broken the other day. Going through the sound barrier, or so I understand, though what it means I never have known."

"It's quite simple, really," said Bryan, approaching amiably. "You see, it's like this."

Miss Marple dropped her handbag and Bryan politely picked it up. At the same moment Mrs. McGillicuddy approached Emma and murmured, in an anguished voice, and the anguish was quite genuine, since Mrs. McGillicuddy deeply disliked the task which she was now performing:

"I wonder, could I go upstairs for a moment?"

"Of course," said Emma.

"I'll take you," said Lucy.

Lucy and Mrs. McGillicuddy left the room together.

"Very cold, driving today," said Miss Marple in a vaguely explanatory manner.

"About the sound barrier," said Bryan, "you see, it's like this— Oh, hello, there's Quimper."

The doctor drove up in his car. He came in rubbing his hands and looking very cold.

"Going to snow," he said, "that's my guess. Hello, Emma, how are you? Good Lord, what's all this?"

"We made you a birthday cake," said Emma. "D'you remember? You told me today was your birthday."

"I didn't expect all this," said Quimper. "You know it's years—why, it must be, yes, sixteen years—since anyone's remembered my birthday." He looked almost uncomfortably touched.

"Do you know Miss Marple?" Emma introduced him.

"Oh yes," said Miss Marple, "I met Doctor Quimper here before and he came and saw me when I had a very nasty chill the other day and he was most kind."

"All right again now, I hope?" said the doctor.

Miss Marple assured him that she was quite all right now.

"You haven't been to see me lately, Quimper," said Mr. Crackenthorpe. "I might be dying for all the notice you take of me!"

"I don't see you dying yet awhile," said Doctor Quimper.

"I don't mean to," said Mr. Crackenthorpe. "Come on, let's have tea. What're we waiting for?"

"Oh, please," said Miss Marple, "don't wait for my friend. She would be most upset if you did."

They sat down and started tea. Miss Marple accepted a piece of bread and butter first, and then went on to a sandwich.

"Are they—?" She hesitated.

"Fish," said Bryan. "I helped make 'em."

Mr. Crackenthorpe gave a cackle of laughter.

"Poisoned fishpaste," he said. "That's what they are. Eat 'em at your peril."

"Please, Father!"

"You've got to be careful what you eat in this house," said Mr. Crackenthorpe to Miss Marple. "Two of my sons have been murdered like flies. Who's doing it—that's what I want to know."

"Don't let him put you off," said Cedric, handing the plate once more to Miss Marple. "A touch of arsenic improves the complexion, they say, so long as you don't have too much."

"Eat one yourself, boy," said old Mr. Crackenthorpe.

"Want me to be official taster?" said Cedric. "Here goes."

He took a sandwich and put it whole into his mouth. Miss Marple gave a gentle, ladylike little laugh and took a sandwich. She took a bite and said:

"I do think it's so brave of you all to make these jokes. Yes, really, I think it's very brave indeed. I do admire bravery so much."

She gave a sudden gasp and began to choke. "A fish bone," she gasped out, "in my throat."

Quimper rose quickly. He went across to her, moved her backwards toward the window and told her to open her mouth. He pulled out a case from his pocket, selecting some forceps from it. With quick professional skill he peered down the old lady's throat. At that moment the door opened and Mrs. McGillicuddy, followed by Lucy, came in. Mrs. McGillicuddy gave a sudden gasp as her eyes fell on the tableau in front of her: Miss Marple leaning back and the doctor holding her throat and tilting up her head.

"But that's him," cried Mrs. McGillicuddy. "That's the man in the train. . . ."

With incredible swiftness Miss Marple slipped from the doctor's grasp and came toward her friend.

"I thought you'd recognize him, Elspeth!" she said. "No. Don't say another word." She turned triumphantly round to Doctor Quimper. "You didn't know, did you, Doctor, when you strangled that woman in the train, that somebody actually saw you do it? It was my friend here. Mrs. McGillicuddy. She saw you. Do you understand? *Saw you with her own eyes.* She was in another train that was running parallel with yours."

"What the hell—" Doctor Quimper made a quick step toward Mrs. McGillicuddy but again, swiftly, Miss Marple was between him and her.

"Yes," said Miss Marple. "She saw you, and she recognizes you, and she'll swear to it in court. It's not often, I believe," went on Miss Marple in her gentle plaintive voice, "that anyone actually sees a murder committed. It's usually circumstantial evidence of course. But in this case the conditions were very unusual. There was actually an eye witness to murder."

"You devilish old hag," said Doctor Quimper. He lunged forward at Miss Marple but this time it was Cedric who caught him by the shoulder.

"So you're the murdering devil, are you?" said Cedric as he swung him round. "I never liked you and I always thought you were a wrong 'un, but Lord knows, I never suspected you."

Bryan Eastley came quickly to Cedric's assistance. Inspector Craddock and Inspector Bacon entered the room from the farther door.

"Doctor Quimper," said Bacon, "I must caution you that . . ."

"You can take your caution to hell," said Doctor Quimper. "Do you think anyone's going to believe what a couple of batty old women say? Who's ever heard of all this rigmarole about a train!"

Miss Marple said, "Elspeth McGillicuddy reported the murder to the police at once on the twentieth of December and gave a description of the man."

Doctor Quimper gave a sudden heave of the shoulders. "If ever a man had the devil's own luck," said Doctor Quimper.

"But—" said Mrs. McGillicuddy.

"Be quiet, Elspeth," said Miss Marple.

"Why should I want to murder a perfectly strange woman?" said Doctor Quimper.

"She wasn't a strange woman," said Inspector Craddock. "She was your wife."

27

"So you see," said Miss Marple, "it really turned out to be, as I began to suspect, very, very simple. The simplest kind of crime. So many men seem to murder their wives."

Mrs. McGillicuddy looked at Miss Marple and Inspector Craddock. "I'd be obliged," she said, "if you'd put me a little more up to date."

"He saw a chance, you see," said Miss Marple, "of marrying a rich wife, Emma Crackenthorpe. Only he couldn't marry her because he had a wife already. They'd been separated for years but she wouldn't divorce him. That fitted in very well with what Inspector Craddock told me of this girl who called herself Anna Stravinska. She had an English husband, so she told one of her friends, and it was also said she was a very devout Catholic. Doctor Quimper couldn't risk marrying Emma bigamously, so he decided, being a very ruthless and cold-blooded man, that he would get rid of his wife. The idea of murdering her in the train and later putting her body in the sarcophagus in the barn was really rather a clever one. He meant it to tie up, you see, with the Crackenthorpe family. Before that he'd written a letter to Emma which purported to be from the girl Martine whom Edmund Crackenthorpe had talked of marrying. Emma had told Doctor Quimper all about her brother, you see. Then, when the moment arose he encouraged her to go to the police with the story. He wanted the dead woman identified as Martine. I think he may have heard that inquiries were being made by the Paris police about Anna Stravinska, and so he arranged to have a postcard come from her from Jamaica.

"It was easy for him to arrange to meet his wife in London, to tell her that he hoped to be reconciled with her and that he would like her to come down and 'meet his family.' We won't talk about the next part of it, which is very unpleasant to think about. Of course he was a greedy man. When he thought about taxation, and how much it cuts into income, he began thinking that it would be nice to have a good deal more capital. Perhaps he'd already thought of that before he decided to murder his wife. Anyway he started spreading rumors that someone was trying to poison old Mr. Crackenthorpe so as to get the ground prepared, and then he ended by administering arsenic to the family. Not too much, of course, for he didn't want old Mr. Crackenthorpe to die."

"But I still don't see how he managed," said Craddock. "He wasn't in the house when the curry was being prepared."

"Oh, but there wasn't any arsenic in the curry then," said Miss Marple. "He added it to the curry afterward when he took it away to be tested. He probably put the arsenic in the cocktail jug earlier. Then of course it was quite easy for him in his role of medical attendant, to poison off Alfred Crackenthorpe and also to send the tablets to Harold in London, having safeguarded himself by telling Harold that he wouldn't need any more tablets. Everything he did was bold and audacious and cruel and greedy, and I am really very, very glad," finished Miss Marple, looking as fierce as a fluffy old lady can look, "that they haven't abolished capital punishment yet because I do feel that if there is anyone who ought to hang, it's Doctor Quimper."

"Hear, hear," said Inspector Craddock.

"It occurred to me, you know," continued Miss Marple, "that even if you only see anybody from the back view, so to speak, nevertheless a back view is characteristic. I thought that if Elspeth were to see Doctor Quimper in exactly the same position as she'd seen the man in the train, that is, with his back to her bent over a woman whom he was holding by the throat, then I was almost sure she would recognize him, or would make some kind of startled exclamation. That is why I had to lay my little plan with Lucy's kind assistance."

"I must say," said Mrs. McGillicuddy, "it gave me quite a turn. I said 'That's him' before I could stop myself. And yet, you know, I hadn't actually seen the man's face and . . ."

"I was terribly afraid that you were going to say so, Elspeth," said Miss Marple.

"I was," said Mrs. McGillicuddy. "I was going to say that of course I hadn't seen his face."

"That," said Miss Marple, "would have been quite fatal! You see, dear, he thought you really did recognize him. I mean, he couldn't know that you hadn't seen his face."

"A good thing I held my tongue then," said Mrs. McGillicuddy.

"I wasn't going to let you say another word," said Miss Marple.

Craddock laughed suddenly. "You two!" he said. "You're a marvelous pair. What next, Miss Marple? What's the happy ending? What happens to poor Emma Crackenthorpe, for instance?"

"She'll get over the doctor, of course," said Miss Marple, "and I dare say if her father were to die—and I don't think he's quite so robust as he thinks he is—that she'd go on a cruise or perhaps stay abroad like Geraldine Webb, and I dare say something might come of it. A nicer man than Doctor Quimper, I hope."

"What about Lucy Eyelesbarrow? Wedding bells there, too?"

"Perhaps," said Miss Marple. "I shouldn't wonder."

"Which of 'em is she going to choose?" said Dermot Craddock.

"Don't you know?" said Miss Marple.

"No, I don't," said Craddock. "Do you?"

"Oh yes, I think so," said Miss Marple.

And she twinkled at him.

Death in the Air

To
ORMOND BEADLE

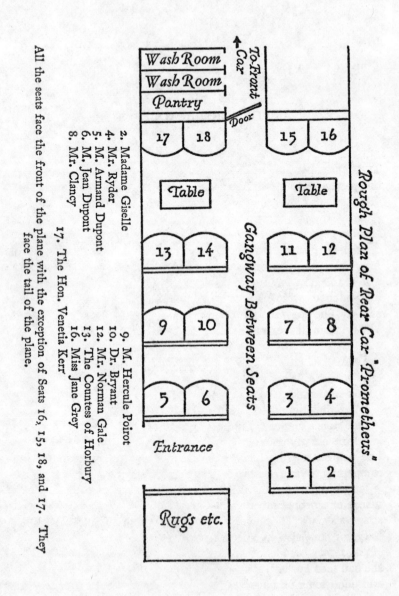

Rough Plan of Rear Car "Prometheus"

To Front Car

Wash Room

Wash Room

Pantry

Door

17 18

15 16

Table

Table

13 14

11 12

9 10

7 8

5 6

3 4

Gangway Between Seats

Entrance

1 2

Rugs etc.

2. Madame Giselle
4. Mr. Ryder
5. M. Armand Dupont
6. M. Jean Dupont
8. Mr. Clancy

9. M. Hercule Poirot
10. Dr. Bryant
12. Mr. Norman Gale
13. The Countess of Horbury
16. Miss Jane Grey

17. The Hon. Venetia Kerr

All the seats face the front of the plane with the exception of Seats 16, 15, 18, and 17. They face the tail of the plane.

1

THE September sun beat down hotly on Le Bourget aerodrome as the passengers crossed the ground and climbed into the air liner "Prometheus," due to depart for Croydon in a few minutes' time.

Jane Grey was among the last to enter and take her seat, Number 16. Some of the passengers had already passed on through the center door past the tiny pantry kitchen and the two washrooms to the front car. Most people were already seated. On the opposite side of the gangway there was a good deal of chatter—a rather shrill, high-pitched woman's voice dominating it. Jane's lips twisted slightly. She knew that particular type of voice so well.

"My dear, it's extraordinary—no idea. . . . Where do you say? . . . Juan les Pins? . . . Oh, yes. . . . No, Le Pinet. . . . Yes, just the same old crowd. . . . But of course let's sit together. . . . Oh, can't we? . . . Who? . . . Oh, I see."

And then a man's voice, foreign, polite:

"With the greatest of pleasure, madame."

Jane stole a glance out of the corner of her eye.

A little elderly man with large mustaches and an egg-shaped head was politely moving himself and his belongings from the seat corresponding to Jane's on the opposite side of the gangway.

Jane turned her head slightly and got a view of the two women whose unexpected meeting had occasioned this polite action on the stranger's part. The mention of Le Pinet had stimulated her curiosity, for Jane, also, had been at Le Pinet.

She remembered one of the women perfectly—remembered how she had seen her last, at the baccarat table, her little hands clenching and unclenching themselves; her delicately made-up, Dresden-china face flushing and paling alternately. With a little effort, Jane thought, she could have remembered her name. A friend had mentioned it;

had said, "She's a peeress, she is. But not one of the proper ones; she was only some chorus girl or other."

Deep scorn in the friend's voice. That had been Maisie, who had a first-class job as a masseuse, taking off flesh.

The other woman, Jane thought in passing, was the real thing. "The horsey county type," thought Jane, and forthwith forgot the two women and interested herself in the view obtainable through the window of Le Bourget aerodrome. Various other machines were standing about. One of them looked like a big metallic centipede.

The one place she was obstinately determined not to look was straight in front of her, where, on the seat opposite, sat a young man.

He was wearing a rather bright periwinkle-blue pullover. Above the pullover, Jane was determined not to look. If she did, she might catch his eye. And that would never do!

Mechanics shouted in French; the engine roared, relaxed, roared again; obstructions were pulled away; the plane started.

Jane caught her breath. It was only her second flight. She was still capable of being thrilled. It looked—it looked as though they must run into that fence thing—no, they were off the ground, rising, rising, sweeping round; there was Le Bourget beneath them.

The midday service to Croydon had started. It contained twenty-one passengers—ten in the forward carriage, eleven in the rear one. It had two pilots and two stewards. The noise of the engines was very skillfully deadened. There was no need to put cotton wool in the ears. Nevertheless, there was enough noise to discourage conversation and encourage thought.

As the plane roared above France on its way to the Channel, the passengers in the rear compartment thought their various thoughts.

Jane Grey thought: "I won't look at him—I won't. It's much better not. I'll go on looking out of the window and thinking. I'll choose a definite thing to think about; that's always the best way. That will keep my mind steady. I'll begin at the beginning and go all over it."

Resolutely she switched her mind back to what she called the beginning—that purchase of a ticket in the Irish Sweep. It had been an extravagance, but an exciting extravagance.

A lot of laughter and teasing chatter in the hairdressing establishment in which Jane and five other young ladies were employed:

"What'll you do if you win it, dear?"

"I know what I'd do."

Plans, castles in the air, a lot of chaff.

Well, she hadn't won it—*it* being the big prize. But she *had* won a hundred pounds.

A hundred pounds!

"You spend half of it, dear, and keep the other half for a rainy day. You never know."

"I'd buy a fur coat, if I was you—a real tip-top one."

"What about a cruise?"

Jane had wavered at the thought of a cruise, but in the end she had remained faithful to her first idea. A week at Le Pinet. So many of her ladies had been going to Le Pinet or just come back from Le Pinet. Jane—her clever fingers patting and manipulating the waves, her tongue uttering mechanically the usual clichés, "Let me see. How long is it since you had your perm, madam? . . . Your hair's such an uncommon color, madam. . . . What a wonderful summer it has been, hasn't it, madam?"—had thought to herself, "Why the devil can't I go to Le Pinet?" Well, now she could!

Clothes presented small difficulty. Jane, like most London girls employed in smart places, could produce a miraculous effect of fashion for a ridiculously small outlay. Nails, make-up and hair were beyond reproach.

Jane went to Le Pinet.

Was it possible that now, in her thoughts, ten days at Le Pinet had dwindled down to one incident?

An incident at the roulette table. Jane allowed herself a certain amount each evening for the pleasures of gambling. That sum she was determined not to exceed. Contrary to the prevalent superstition, Jane's beginner's luck had been bad. This was her fourth evening and the last stake of that evening. So far she had staked prudently on color or on one of the dozens; she had won a little, but lost more. Now she waited, her stake in her hand.

There were two numbers on which nobody had staked. Five and six. Should she put this, her last stake, on one of those numbers? If so, which of them? Five or six? Which did she feel?

Five—five was going to turn up. The ball was spun. Jane stretched out her hand. Six—she'd put it on six.

Just in time. She and another player opposite staked simultaneously. She on six, he on five.

"*Rien ne va plus*," said the croupier.

The ball clicked, settled.

"*Le numéro cinq, rouge, impair, manque.*"

Jane could have cried with vexation. The croupier swept away the stakes, paid out. The man opposite said: "Aren't you going to take up your winnings?"

"Mine?"

"Yes."

"But I put on six."

"Indeed you didn't. I put on six and you put on five."

He smiled—a very attractive smile. White teeth in a very brown face. Blue eyes. Crisp short hair.

Half unbelievingly, Jane picked up her gains. Was it true? She felt a little muddled herself. Perhaps she had put her counters on five. She looked doubtingly at the stranger and he smiled easily back.

"That's right," he said. "Leave a thing lying there and somebody else will grab it who has got no right to it. That's an old trick."

Then, with a friendly little nod of the head, he had moved away. That, too, had been nice of him. She might have suspected otherwise that he had let her take his winnings in order to scrape acquaintance with her. But he wasn't that kind of man. He was nice. And here he was, sitting opposite to her.

And now it was all over, the money spent, a last two days—rather disappointing days—in Paris, and now home on her return air ticket. "And what next?"

"Stop," said Jane to her mind. "Don't think of what's going to happen next. It'll only make you nervous."

The two women had stopped talking.

She looked across the gangway. The Dresden-china woman exclaimed petulantly, examining a broken fingernail. She rang the bell, and when the white-coated steward appeared she said:

"Send my maid to me. She's in the other compartment."

"Yes, my lady."

The steward, very deferential, very quick and efficient, disappeared again. A dark-haired French girl dressed in black appeared. She carried a small jewel case.

Lady Horbury spoke to her in French:

"Madeleine, I want my red morocco case."

The maid passed along the gangway. At the extreme end of the car were some piled-up rugs and cases.

The girl returned with a small red dressing case.

Cicely Horbury took it and dismissed the maid.

"That's all right, Madeleine. I'll keep it here."

The maid went out again. Lady Horbury opened the case and from the beautifully fitted interior she extracted a nail file. Then she looked long and earnestly at her face in a small mirror and touched it up here and there—a little powder, more lip salve.

Jane's lips curled scornfully; her glance traveled farther down the car.

Behind the two women was the little foreigner who had yielded his seat to the county woman. Heavily muffled up in unnecessary mufflers, he appeared to be fast asleep. Perhaps made uneasy by Jane's scrutiny, his eyes opened, looked at her for a moment, then closed again.

Beside him sat a tall, gray-haired man with an authoritative face. He had a flute case open in front of him and was polishing the flute with loving care. Funny, Jane thought, he didn't look like a musician—more like a lawyer or a doctor.

Behind those two were a couple of Frenchmen, one with a beard and one much younger—perhaps his son. They were talking and gesticulating in an excited manner.

On her own side of the car, Jane's view was blocked by the man in the blue pullover—the man at whom, for some absurd reason, she was determined not to look.

"Absurd to feel so—so excited. I might be seventeen," thought Jane disgustedly.

Opposite her, Norman Gale was thinking:

"She's pretty—really pretty. She remembers me all right. She looked so disappointed when her stakes were swept away. It was worth a lot more than that to see her pleasure when she won. I did that rather well. She's very attractive when she smiles—no pyorrhoea there—healthy gums and sound teeth. . . . Damn it, I feel quite excited. Steady, my boy."

He said to the steward, who hovered at his side with the menu, "I'll have cold tongue."

The Countess of Horbury thought: "What shall I do? It's the hell of a mess. The hell of a mess. There's only one way out that I can see. If only I had the nerve— Can I do it? Can I bluff it out? My nerves are all to pieces. That's the Coke. Why did I ever take to Coke? My face looks awful—simply awful. That cat, Venetia Kerr, being here makes it worse. She always looks at me as though I were dirt. Wanted Stephen herself. Well, she didn't get him! That long face of hers gets on my nerves. It's exactly like a horse. I hate these county women. What shall I do? I've got to make up my mind. The old hag meant what she said."

She fumbled in her vanity bag for her cigarette case and fitted a cigarette into a long holder. Her hands shook slightly.

The Honorable Venetia Kerr thought: "Little tart! That's what she is. Poor old Stephen! If he could only get rid of her!"

She, in turn, felt for her cigarette case. She accepted Cicely Horbury's match.

The steward said: "Excuse me, ladies; no smoking."

Cicely Horbury said, "Hell!"

Monsieur Hercule Poirot thought: "She is pretty, that little one over there. There is determination in that chin. Why is she so worried over something? Why is she so determined not to look at the handsome young man opposite her? She is very much aware of him and he of her." The plane dropped slightly. "*Mon estomac!*" thought Hercule Poirot, and closed his eyes determinedly.

Beside him, Doctor Bryant, caressing his flute with nervous hands, thought: "I can't decide. I simply cannot decide. This is the turning point of my career."

Nervously he drew out his flute from its case, caressingly, lovingly. Music—in music there was an escape from all your cares. Half smiling, he raised the flute to his lips; then put it down again. The little man with the mustaches beside him was fast asleep. There had been a moment, when the plane had bumped a little, when he had looked distinctly green. Doctor Bryant was glad that he himself became neither train-sick nor sea-sick nor air-sick.

Monsieur Dupont *père* turned excitedly in his seat and shouted at Monsieur Dupont *fils*, sitting beside him:

"There is no doubt about it! They are *all* wrong—the Germans, the Americans, the English! They date the prehistoric pottery all wrong! Take the Samarra ware—"

Jean Dupont, tall, fair, with a false air of indolence, said:

"You must take the evidences from all sources. There is Tall Halaf, and Sakje Geuze—"

They prolonged the discussion.

Armand Dupont wrenched open a battered attaché case.

"Take these Kurdish pipes, such as they make today. The decoration on them is almost exactly similar to that on the pottery of five thousand B.C."

An eloquent gesture almost swept away the plate that a steward was placing in front of him.

Mr. Clancy, writer of detective stories, rose from his seat behind Norman Gale and padded to the end of the car, extracted a Continental Bradshaw from his raincoat pocket and returned with it to work out a complicated alibi for professional purposes.

Mr. Ryder, in the seat behind him, thought: "I'll have to keep my end up, but it's not going to be easy. I don't see how I'm going to raise the dibs for the next dividend. If we pass the dividend, the fat's in the fire. . . . Oh, hell!"

Norman Gale rose and went to the washroom. As soon as he had gone, Jane drew out a mirror and surveyed her face anxiously. She also applied powder and lipstick.

A steward placed coffee in front of her.

Jane looked out of the window. The Channel showed blue and shining below.

A wasp buzzed round Mr. Clancy's head just as he was dealing with 19:55 at Tsaribrod, and he struck at it absently. The wasp flew off to investigate the Duponts' coffee cups.

Jean Dupont slew it neatly.

Peace settled down on the car. Conversation ceased, but thoughts pursued their way.

Right at the end of the car, in Seat Number 2, Madame Giselle's head lolled forward a little. One might have taken her to be asleep. But she was not asleep. She neither spoke nor thought.

Madame Giselle was dead.

2

HENRY MITCHELL, the senior of the two stewards, passed swiftly from table to table, depositing bills. In half an hour's time they would be at Croydon. He gathered up notes and silver, bowed, said, "Thank you, sir. . . . Thank you, madam." At the table where the two Frenchmen sat, he had to wait a minute or two; they were so busy discussing and gesticulating. And there wouldn't be much of a tip, anyway, from them, he thought gloomily. Two of the passengers were asleep—the little man with the mustaches and the old woman down at the end. She was a good tipper, though; he remembered her crossing several times. He refrained, therefore, from awaking her.

The little man with the mustaches woke up and paid for the bottle of mineral water and the thin captain's biscuits, which was all he had had.

Mitchell left the other passenger as long as possible. About five minutes before they reached Croydon, he stood by her side and leaned over her.

"Pardon, madam; your bill."

He laid a deferential hand on her shoulder. She did not wake. He increased the pressure, shaking her gently, but the only result was an unexpected slumping of the body down in the seat. Mitchell bent over her; then straightened up with a white face.

Albert Davis, second steward, said:
"Cool You don't mean it."
"I tell you it's true."
Mitchell was white and shaking.
"You sure, Henry?"
"Dead sure. At least—well, I suppose it might be a fit."

"We'll be at Croydon in a few minutes."

"If she's just taken bad—"

They remained a minute or two undecided; then arranged their course of action. Mitchell returned to the rear car. He went from table to table, bending his head and murmuring confidentially:

"Excuse me, sir; you don't happen to be a doctor?"

Norman Gale said, "I'm a dentist. But if there's anything I can do—" He half rose from his seat.

"I'm a doctor," said Doctor Bryant. "What's the matter?"

"There's a lady at the end there—I don't like the look of her."

Bryant rose to his feet and accompanied the steward. Unnoticed, the little man with the mustaches followed them.

Doctor Bryant bent over the huddled figure in Seat Number 2— the figure of a stoutish middle-aged woman dressed in heavy black.

The doctor's examination was brief.

He said: "She's dead."

Mitchell said: "What do you think it was? Kind of fit?"

"That I can't possibly say without a detailed examination. When did you last see her—alive, I mean?"

Mitchell reflected.

"She was all right when I brought her coffee along."

"When was that?"

"Well, it might have been three-quarters of an hour ago—about that. Then, when I brought the bill along, I thought she was asleep."

Bryant said: "She's been dead at least half an hour."

Their consultation was beginning to cause interest; heads were craned round, looking at them. Necks were stretched to listen.

"I suppose it might have been a kind of fit like?" suggested Mitchell hopefully.

He clung to the theory of a fit. His wife's sister had fits. He felt that fits were homely things that any man might understand.

Doctor Bryant had no intention of committing himself. He merely shook his head with a puzzled expression.

A voice spoke at his elbow—the voice of the muffled-up man with the mustaches.

"There is," he said, "a mark on her neck."

He spoke apologetically, with a due sense of speaking to superior knowledge.

"True," said Doctor Bryant.

The woman's head lolled over sideways. There was a minute

puncture mark on the side of her throat, with a circle of red round it.

"Pardon," the two Duponts joined in. They had been listening for the last few minutes. "The lady is dead, you say, and there is a mark on the neck?"

It was Jean, the younger Dupont, who spoke:

"May I make a suggestion? There was a wasp flying about. I killed it." He exhibited the corpse in his coffee saucer. "Is it not possible that the poor lady has died of a wasp sting? I have heard such things happen."

"It is possible," agreed Bryant. "I have known of such cases. Yes, that is certainly quite a possible explanation. Especially if there were any cardiac weakness."

"Anything I'd better do, sir?" asked the steward. "We'll be at Croydon in a minute."

"Quite, quite," said Doctor Bryant as he moved away a little. "There's nothing to be done. The—er—body must not be moved, steward."

"Yes, sir, I quite understand."

Doctor Bryant prepared to resume his seat and looked in some surprise at the small, muffled-up foreigner who was standing his ground.

"My dear sir," he said, "the best thing to do is to go back to your seat. We shall be at Croydon almost immediately."

"That's right, sir," said the steward. He raised his voice: "Please resume your seats, everybody."

"*Pardon*," said the little man. "There is something—"

"Something?"

"*Mais oui*, something that has been overlooked."

With the tip of a pointed patent-leather shoe, he made his meaning clear. The steward and Doctor Bryant followed the action with their eyes. They caught the glint of orange and black on the floor, half concealed by the edge of the black skirt.

"Another wasp?" said the doctor, surprised.

Hercule Poirot went down on his knees. He took a small pair of tweezers from his pocket and used them delicately. He stood up with his prize.

"Yes," he said, "it is very like a wasp, but it is not a wasp."

He turned the object about this way and that, so that both the doctor and the steward could see it clearly—a little knot of teased fluffy silk, orange and black, attached to a long peculiar-looking thorn with a discolored tip.

"Good gracious! Good gracious me!" The exclamation came from little Mr. Clancy, who had left his seat and was poking his head desperately over the steward's shoulder. "Remarkable—really very remarkable—absolutely the most remarkable thing I have ever come across in my life. Well, upon my soul, I should never have believed it."

"Could you make yourself just a little clearer, sir?" asked the steward. "Do you recognize this?"

"Recognize it? Certainly I recognize it." Mr. Clancy swelled with passionate pride and gratification. "This object, gentlemen, is the native thorn shot from a blowpipe by certain tribes—er—I cannot be exactly certain now if it is South American tribes or whether it is the inhabitants of Borneo which I have in mind. But that is undoubtedly a native dart that has been aimed by a blowpipe, and I strongly suspect that on the tip—"

"—is the famous arrow poison of the South American Indians," finished Hercule Poirot. And he added, *"Mais enfin! Est-ce que c'est possible?"*

"It is certainly very extraordinary," said Mr. Clancy, still full of blissful excitement. "As I say, most extraordinary. I am myself a writer of detective fiction, but actually to meet, in real life—"

Words failed him.

The aeroplane heeled slowly over, and those people who were standing up staggered a little. The plane was circling round in its descent to Croydon aerodrome.

3

THE steward and the doctor were no longer in charge of the situation. Their place was usurped by the rather absurd-looking little man in the muffler. He spoke with an authority and a certainty of being obeyed that no one thought of questioning.

He whispered to Mitchell and the latter nodded, and—pushing his way through the passengers—he took up his stand in the doorway leading past the washrooms to the front car.

The plane was running along the ground now. When it finally came to a stop, Mitchell raised his voice:

"I must ask you, ladies and gentlemen, to keep your seats and remain here until somebody in authority takes charge. I hope you will not be detained long."

The reasonableness of this order was appreciated by most of the occupants of the car, but one person protested shrilly.

"Nonsense!" cried Lady Horbury angrily. "Don't you know who I am? I insist on being allowed to leave at once!"

"Very sorry, my lady. Can't make exceptions."

"But it's absurd—absolutely absurd." Cicely tapped her foot angrily. "I shall report you to the company. It's outrageous that we should be shut up here with a dead body."

"Really, my dear," Venetia Kerr spoke with her well-bred drawl, "too devastating, but I fancy we'll have to put up with it." She herself sat down and drew out a cigarette case. "Can I smoke now, steward?"

The harassed Mitchell said: "I don't suppose it matters now, miss."

He glanced over his shoulder. Davis had disembarked the passengers from the front car by the emergency door and had now gone in search of orders.

The wait was not a long one, but it seemed to the passengers as though half an hour, at least, had passed before an erect, soldierly figure in plain clothes, accompanied by a uniformed policeman, came hurriedly across the aerodrome and climbed into the plane by the door that Mitchell held open.

"Now, then, what's all this?" demanded the newcomer in brisk official tones.

He listened to Mitchell and then to Doctor Bryant, and he flung a quick glance over the crumpled figure of the dead woman.

He gave an order to the constable and then addressed the passengers:

"Will you please follow me, ladies and gentlemen?"

He escorted them out of the plane and across the aerodrome, but he did not enter the usual customs department. Instead, he brought them to a small private room.

"I hope not to keep you waiting any longer than is unavoidable, ladies and gentlemen."

"Look here, inspector," said Mr. James Ryder. "I have an important business engagement in London."

"Sorry, sir."

"I am Lady Horbury. I consider it absolutely outrageous that I should be detained in this manner!"

"I'm sincerely sorry, Lady Horbury. But, you see, this is a very serious matter. It looks like a case of murder."

"The arrow poison of the South American Indians," murmured Mr. Clancy deliriously, a happy smile on his face.

The inspector looked at him suspiciously.

The French archæologist spoke excitedly in French, and the inspector replied to him slowly and carefully in the same language.

Venetia Kerr said: "All this is a most crashing bore, but I suppose you have your duty to do, inspector," to which that worthy replied, "Thank you, madam," in accents of some gratitude.

He went on:

"If you ladies and gentlemen will remain here, I want a few words with Doctor—er—Doctor—"

"Bryant, my name is."

"Thank you. Just come this way with me, doctor."

"May I assist at your interview?"

It was the little man with the mustaches who spoke.

The inspector turned on him, a sharp retort on his lips. Then his face changed suddenly.

"Sorry, Monsieur Poirot," he said. "You're so muffled up I didn't recognize you. Come along by all means."

He held the door open and Bryant and Poirot passed through, followed by the suspicious glances of the rest of the company.

"And why should he be allowed out and we made to stay here?" cried Cicely Horbury.

Venetia Kerr sat down resignedly on a bench.

"Probably one of the French police," she said. "Or a customs spy." She lit a cigarette.

Norman Gale said rather diffidently to Jane:

"I think I saw you at—er—Le Pinet."

"I was at Le Pinet."

Norman Gale said: "It's an awfully attractive place. I like the pine trees."

Jane said: "Yes, they smell so nice."

And then they both paused for a minute or two, uncertain what to say next.

Finally Gale said:

"I—er—recognized you at once in the plane."

Jane expressed great surprise.

"Did you?"

Gale said: "Do you think that woman was really murdered?"

"I suppose so," said Jane. "It's rather thrilling, in a way, but it's rather nasty too"—and she shuddered a little, and Norman Gale moved just a little nearer in a protective manner.

The Duponts were talking French to each other. Mr. Ryder was making calculations in a little notebook and looking at his watch from time to time. Cicely Horbury sat with her foot tapping impatiently on the floor. She lit a cigarette with a shaking hand.

Against the door on the inside leaned a very large, blue-clad, impassive-looking policeman.

In a room near by, Inspector Japp was talking to Doctor Bryant and Hercule Poirot.

"You've got a knack of turning up in the most unexpected places, Monsieur Poirot."

"Isn't Croydon aerodrome a little out of your beat, my friend?" asked Poirot.

"Ah! I'm after rather a big bug in the smuggling line. A bit of luck, my being on the spot. This is the most amazing business I've come across for years. Now, then, let's get down to it. . . . First of all, doctor, perhaps you'll give me your full name and address."

"Roger James Bryant. I am a specialist on diseases of the ear and throat. My address is 329 Harley Street."

A stolid constable sitting at a table took down these particulars.

"Our own surgeon will, of course, examine the body," said Japp, "but we shall want you at the inquest, doctor."

"Quite so, quite so."

"Can you give us any idea of the time of death?"

"The woman must have been dead at least half an hour when I examined her—that was a few minutes before we arrived at Croydon. I can't go nearer than that, but I understand from the steward that he had spoken to her about an hour before."

"Well, that narrows it down for all practical purposes. I suppose it's no good asking you if you observed anything of a suspicious nature?"

The doctor shook his head.

"And me, I was asleep," said Poirot with deep chagrin. "I suffer almost as badly in the air as on the sea. Always I wrap myself up well and try to sleep."

"Any idea as to the cause of death, doctor?"

"I should not like to say anything definite at this stage. This is a case for post-mortem examination and analysis."

Japp nodded comprehendingly.

"Well, doctor," he said, "I don't think we need detain you now. I'm afraid you'll—er—have to go through certain formalities—all the passengers will. We can't make exceptions."

Doctor Bryant smiled.

"I should prefer you to make sure that I have no—er—blowpipes or other lethal weapons concealed upon my person," he said gravely.

"Rogers will see to that." Japp nodded to his subordinate. "By the way, doctor, have you any idea what would be likely to be on this—"

He indicated the discolored thorn, which was lying in a small box on the table in front of him.

Doctor Bryant shook his head.

"Difficult to say without an analysis. Curare is the usual poison employed by the South American natives, I believe."

"Would that do the trick?"

"It is a very swift and rapid poison."

"But not very easy to obtain, eh?"

"Not at all easy for a layman."

"Then we'll have to search you extra carefully," said Japp, who was always fond of his joke. . . . "Rogers!"

The doctor and the constable left the room together.

Japp tilted back his chair and looked at Poirot.

"Rum business, this," he said. "Bit too sensational to be true. I mean, blowpipes and poisoned darts in an aeroplane—well, it insults one's intelligence."

"That, my friend, is a very profound remark," said Poirot.

"A couple of my men are searching the plane," said Japp. "We've got a fingerprint man and a photographer coming along. I think we'd better see the stewards next."

He strode to the door and gave an order. The two stewards were ushered in. The younger steward had recovered his balance. He looked more excited than anything else. The other steward still looked white and frightened.

"That's all right, my lads," said Japp. "Sit down. Got the passports there? . . . Good."

He sorted through them quickly.

"Ah, here we are. Marie Morisot, French passport. Know anything about her?"

"I've seen her before. She crossed to and fro from England fairly often," said Mitchell.

"Ah, in business of some kind. You don't know what her business was?"

Mitchell shook his head. The younger steward said: "I remember her too. I saw her on the early service—the eight o'clock from Paris."

"Which of you was the last to see her alive?"

"Him." The younger steward indicated his companion.

"That's right," said Mitchell. "That's when I took her her coffee."

"How was she looking then?"

"Can't say I noticed. I just handed her the sugar and offered her milk, which she refused."

"What time was that?"

"Well, I couldn't say exactly. We were over the Channel at the time. Might have been somewhere about two o'clock."

"Thereabouts," said Albert Davis, the other steward.

"When did you see her next?"

"When I took the bills round."

"What time was that?"

"About a quarter of an hour later. I thought she was asleep. . . . Crikey! She must have been dead then!" The steward's voice sounded awed.

"You didn't see any signs of this—" Japp indicated the little wasp-like dart.

"No, sir, I didn't."

"What about you, Davis?"

"The last time I saw her was when I was handing the biscuits to go with the cheese. She was all right then."

"What is your system of serving meals?" asked Poirot. "Do each of you serve separate cars?"

"No, sir, we work it together. The soup, then the meat and vegetables and salad, then the sweet, and so on. We usually serve the rear car first, and then go out with a fresh lot of dishes to the front car."

Poirot nodded.

"Did this Morisot woman speak to anyone on the plane, or show any signs of recognition?" asked Japp.

"Not that I saw, sir."

"You, Davis?"

"No, sir."

"Did she leave her seat at all during the journey?"

"I don't think so, sir."

"There's nothing you can think of that throws any light on this business—either of you?"

Both the men thought, then shook their heads.

"Well, that will be all for now, then. I'll see you again later."

Henry Mitchell said soberly:

"It's a nasty thing to happen, sir. I don't like it—me having been in charge, so to speak."

"Well, I can't see that you're to blame in any way," said Japp. "Still, I agree, it's a nasty thing to happen."

He made a gesture of dismissal. Poirot leaned forward.

"Permit me one little question."

"Go ahead, Monsieur Poirot."

"Did either of you two notice a wasp flying about the plane?"

Both men shook their heads.

"There was no wasp that I know of," said Mitchell.

"There was a wasp," said Poirot. "We have its dead body on the plate of one of the passengers."

"Well, I didn't see it, sir," said Mitchell.

"No more did I," said Davis.

"No matter."

The two stewards left the room. Japp was running his eye rapidly over the passports.

"Got a countess on board," he said. "She's the one who's throwing her weight about, I suppose. Better see her first before she goes right off the handle and gets a question asked in the House about the brutal methods of the police."

"You will, I suppose, search very carefully all the baggage—the hand baggage—of the passengers in the rear car of the plane?"

Japp winked cheerfully.

"Why, what do you think, Monsieur Poirot? We've got to find that blowpipe—if there is a blowpipe and we're not all dreaming! Seems like a kind of nightmare to me. I suppose that little writer chap hasn't suddenly gone off his onion and decided to do one of his crimes in the flesh instead of on paper? This poisoned-dart business sounds like him."

Poirot shook his head doubtfully.

"Yes," continued Japp, "everybody's got to be searched, whether they kick up rough or not, and every bit of truck they had with them has got to be searched, too—and that's flat."

"A very exact list might be made, perhaps," suggested Poirot. "A list of everything in these people's possession."

Japp looked at him curiously.

"That can be done if you say so, Monsieur Poirot. I don't quite see what you're driving at, though. We know what we're looking for."

"*You* may, perhaps, *mon ami*. But *I* am not so sure. I look for something, but I know not what it is."

"At it again, Monsieur Poirot! You do like making things difficult, don't you? Now for her ladyship, before she's quite ready to scratch my eyes out."

Lady Horbury, however, was noticeably calmer in her manner. She accepted a chair and answered Japp's questions without the least hesitation. She described herself as the wife of the Earl of Horbury, gave her address as Horbury Chase, Sussex, and Grosvenor

Square, London. She was returning to London from Le Pinet and Paris. The deceased woman was quite unknown to her. She had noticed nothing suspicious during the flight over. In any case, she was facing the other way—towards the front of the plane—so had had no opportunity of seeing anything that was going on behind her. She had not left her seat during the journey. As far as she remembered, no one had entered the rear car from the front one, with the exception of the stewards. She could not remember exactly, but she thought that two of the men passengers had left the rear car to go to the washrooms, but she was not sure of this. She had not observed anyone handling anything that could be likened to a blowpipe. No—in answer to Poirot—she had not noticed a wasp in the car.

Lady Horbury was dismissed. She was succeeded by the Honorable Venetia Kerr.

Miss Kerr's evidence was much the same as that of her friend. She gave her name as Venetia Anne Kerr, and her address as Little Paddocks, Horbury, Sussex. She herself was returning from the south of France. As far as she was aware, she had never seen the deceased before. She had noticed nothing suspicious during the journey. Yes, she had seen some of the passengers farther down the car striking at a wasp. One of them, she thought, had killed it. That was after luncheon had been served.

Exit Miss Kerr.

"You seem very much interested in that wasp, Monsieur Poirot."

"The wasp is not so much interesting as suggestive, eh?"

"If you ask me," said Japp, changing the subject, "those two Frenchmen are the ones in this! They were just across the gangway from the Morisot woman, they're a seedy-looking couple, and that battered old suitcase of theirs is fairly plastered with outlandish foreign labels. Shouldn't be surprised if they'd been to Borneo or South America or wherever it is. Of course we can't get a line on the motive, but I dare say we can get that from Paris. We'll have to get the Sûreté to collaborate over this. It's their job more than ours. But if you ask me, those two toughs are our meat."

Poirot's eyes twinkled a little.

"What you say is possible, certainly; but as regards some of your points, you are in error, my friend. Those two men are not toughs or cutthroats, as you suggest. They are, on the contrary, two very distinguished and learned archæologists."

"Go on! You're pulling my leg!"

"Not at all. I know them by sight perfectly. They are Monsieur Armand Dupont and his son, Monsieur Jean Dupont. They have returned not long ago from conducting some very interesting excavations in Persia at a site not far from Susa."

"Go on!"

Japp made a grab at a passport.

"You're right, Monsieur Poirot," he said, "but you must admit they don't look up to much, do they?"

"The world's famous men seldom do! I myself—*moi, qui vous parle* —I have before now been taken for a hairdresser!"

"You don't say so," said Japp with a grin. "Well, let's have a look at your distinguished archæologists."

Monsieur Dupont *père* declared that the deceased was quite unknown to him. He had noticed nothing of what had happened on the journey over, as he had been discussing a very interesting point with his son. He had not left his seat at all. Yes, he had noticed a wasp towards the end of lunch. His son had killed it.

Monsieur Jean Dupont confirmed this evidence. He had noticed nothing of what went on round about him. The wasp had annoyed him and he had killed it. What had been the subject of the discussion? The prehistoric pottery of the Near East.

Mr. Clancy, who came next, came in for rather a bad time. Mr. Clancy, so felt Inspector Japp, knew altogether too much about blowpipes and poisoned darts.

"Have you ever owned a blowpipe yourself?"

"Well, I—er—well, yes, as a matter of fact, I have."

"Indeed!" Inspector Japp pounced on the statement.

Little Mr. Clancy fairly squeaked with agitation:

"You mustn't—er—misunderstand. My motives are quite innocent. I can explain—"

"Yes, sir, perhaps you will explain."

"Well, you see, I was writing a book in which the murder was committed that way."

"Indeed."

Again that threatening intonation. Mr. Clancy hurried on:

"It was all a question of fingerprints—if you understand me. It was necessary to have an illustration illustrating the point I meant —I mean, the fingerprints—the position of them—the position of them on the blowpipe, if you understand me, and having noticed such a thing—in the Charing Cross Road it was—at least two years ago now—and so I bought the blowpipe, and an artist friend of mine very kindly drew it for me, with the fingerprints, to illustrate my point. I can refer you to the book—*The Clue of the Scarlet Petal*—and my friend too."

"Did you keep the blowpipe?"

"Why, yes—why, yes, I think so—I mean, yes, I did."

"And where is it now?"

"Well, I suppose—well, it must be somewhere about."

"What, exactly, do you mean by somewhere about, Mr. Clancy?"

"I mean—well, somewhere—I can't say where. I—I am not a very tidy man."

"It isn't with you now, for instance?"

"Certainly not. Why, I haven't seen the thing for nearly six months."

Inspector Japp bent a glance of cold suspicion on him and continued his questions:

"Did you leave your seat at all in the plane?"

"No, certainly not—at least—well, yes, I did."

"Oh, you *did*. Where did you go?"

"I went to get a Continental Bradshaw out of my raincoat pocket. The raincoat was piled with some rugs and suitcases by the entrance at the end."

"So you passed close by the deceased's seat?"

"No—at least—well, yes, I must have done so. But this was long before anything could have happened. I'd only just drunk my soup."

Further questions drew negative answers. Mr. Clancy had noticed nothing suspicious. He had been absorbed in the perfecting of his cross-Europe alibi.

"Alibi, eh?" said the inspector darkly.

Poirot intervened with a question about wasps.

Yes, Mr. Clancy had noticed a wasp. It had attacked him. He was afraid of wasps. . . . When was this? . . . Just after the steward had brought him his coffee. He struck at it and it went away.

Mr. Clancy's name and address were taken and he was allowed to depart, which he did with relief on his face.

"Looks a bit fishy to me," said Japp. "He actually *had* a blowpipe, and look at his manner. All to pieces."

"That is the severity of your official demeanor, my good Japp."

"There's nothing for anyone to be afraid of if they're only telling the truth," said the Scotland Yard man austerely.

Poirot looked at him pityingly.

"In verity, I believe that you yourself honestly believe that."

"Of course I do. It's true. Now, then, let's have Norman Gale."

Norman Gale gave his address as Shepherd's Avenue, Muswell Hill. By profession he was a dentist. He was returning from a holiday spent at Le Pinet on the French coast. He had spent a day in Paris, looking at various new types of dental instruments.

He had never seen the deceased and had noticed nothing suspicious during the journey. In any case, he had been facing the other way—towards the front car. He had left his seat once during the journey—to go to the washroom. He had returned straight to his seat and had never been near the rear end of the car. He had not noticed any wasp.

After him came James Ryder, somewhat on edge and brusque in manner. He was returning from a business visit to Paris. He did not know the deceased. Yes, he had occupied the seat immediately in front of hers. But he could not have seen her without rising and looking over the back of his seat. He had heard nothing—no cry or exclamation. No one had come down the car except the stewards. Yes, the two Frenchmen had occupied the seats across the gangway from his. They had talked practically the whole journey. The younger of the two had killed a wasp at the conclusion of the meal. No, he hadn't noticed the wasp previously. He didn't know what a blowpipe was like, as he'd never seen one, so he couldn't say if he'd seen one on the journey or not.

Just at this point there was a tap on the door. A police constable entered, subdued triumph in his bearing.

"The sergeant's just found this, sir," he said. "Thought you'd like to have it at once."

He laid his prize on the table, unwrapping it with care from the handkerchief in which it was folded.

"No fingerprints, sir, so far as the sergeant can see, but he told me to be careful."

The object thus displayed was an undoubted blowpipe of native manufacture.

Japp drew his breath in sharply.

"Good Lord, then it *is* true! Upon my soul, I didn't believe it!"

Mr. Ryder leaned forward interestedly.

"So that's what the South Americans use, is it? Read about such things, but never seen one. Well, I can answer your question now. I didn't see anyone handling anything of this type."

"Where was it found?" asked Japp sharply.

"Pushed down out of sight behind one of the seats, sir."

"Which seat?"

"Number Nine."

"Very entertaining," said Poirot.

Japp turned to him.

"What's entertaining about it?"

"Only that Number Nine was *my* seat."

"Well, that looks a bit odd for you, I must say," said Mr. Ryder. Japp frowned.

"Thank you, Mr. Ryder; that will do."

When Ryder had gone, he turned to Poirot with a grin.

"This *your* work, old bird?"

"*Mon ami,*" said Poirot with dignity, "when I commit a murder, it will not be with the arrow poison of the South American Indians."

"It is a bit low," agreed Japp. "But it seems to have worked."

"That is what gives one so furiously to think."

"Whoever it was must have taken the most stupendous chances. Yes, by Jove, they must! Lord, the fellow must have been an absolute lunatic. Who have we got left? Only one girl. Let's have her in and get it over. Jane Grey—sounds like a history book."

"She is a pretty girl," said Poirot.

"Is she, you old dog? So you weren't asleep all the time, eh?"

"She was pretty—and nervous," said Poirot.

"Nervous, eh?" said Japp alertly.

"Oh, my dear friend, when a girl is nervous it usually means a young man, not crime."

"Oh, well, I suppose you're right. . . . Here she is."

Jane answered the questions put to her clearly enough. Her name was Jane Grey and she was employed at Messrs. Antoine's hairdressing establishment in Bruton Street. Her home address was 10 Harrogate Street, N.W. 5. She was returning to England from Le Pinet.

"Le Pinet, h'm!"

Further questions drew the story of the sweep ticket.

"Ought to be made illegal, those Irish Sweeps," growled Japp.

"I think they're marvelous," said Jane. "Haven't you ever put half a crown on a horse?"

Japp blushed and looked confused.

The questions were resumed. Shown the blowpipe, Jane denied having seen it at any time. She did not know the deceased, but had noticed her at Le Bourget.

"What made you notice her particularly?"

"Because she was so frightfully ugly," said Jane truthfully.

Nothing else of any value was elicited from her, and she was allowed to go.

Japp fell back into contemplation of the blowpipe.

"It beats me," he said. "The crudest detective-story dodge coming out trumps! What have we got to look for now? A man who's traveled in the part of the world this thing comes from? And where exactly does it come from? Have to get an expert on to that. It may be Malayan or South American or African."

"Originally, yes," said Poirot. "But if you observe closely, my friend, you will notice a microscopic piece of paper adhering to the pipe. It looks to me very much like the remains of a torn-off price ticket. I fancy that this particular specimen has journeyed from the wilds via some curio dealer's shop. That will possibly make our search more easy. Just one little question."

"Ask away."

"You will still have that list made—the list of the passengers' belongings?"

"Well, it isn't quite so vital now, but it might as well be done. You're very set on that?"

"*Mais oui,* I am puzzled—very puzzled. If I could find something to help me—"

Japp was not listening. He was examining the torn price ticket.

"Clancy let out that he bought a blowpipe. These detective-story writers, always making the police out to be fools, and getting their procedure all wrong. Why, if I were to say the things to my super that their inspectors say to superintendents, I should be thrown out of the force tomorrow on my ear. Set of ignorant scribblers! This is just the sort of fool murder that a scribbler of rubbish would think he could get away with."

4

THE inquest on Marie Morisot was held four days later. The sensational manner of her death had aroused great public interest, and the coroner's court was crowded.

The first witness called was a tall, elderly Frenchman with a gray beard—Maître Alexandre Thibault. He spoke English slowly and precisely, with a slight accent but quite idiomatically.

After the preliminary questions the coroner asked, "You have viewed the body of the deceased. Do you recognize it?"

"I do. It is that of my client, Marie Angélique Morisot."

"That is the name on the deceased's passport. Was she known to the public by another name?"

"Yes, that of Madame Giselle."

A stir of excitement went round. Reporters sat with pencils poised. The coroner said: "Will you tell us exactly who this Madame Morisot, or Madame Giselle, was?"

"Madame Giselle—to give her her professional name; the name under which she did business—was one of the best-known moneylenders in Paris."

"She carried on her business—where?"

"At the Rue Joliette. That was also her private residence."

"I understand that she journeyed to England fairly frequently. Did her business extend to this country?"

"Yes. Many of her clients were English people. She was very well known amongst a certain section of English society."

"How would you describe that section of society?"

"Her clientele was mostly among the upper and professional classes—in cases where it was important that the utmost discretion should be observed."

"She had the reputation of being discreet?"

"Extremely discreet."

"May I ask if you have an intimate knowledge of—er—her various business transactions?"

"No. I dealt with her legal business, but Madame Giselle was a first-class woman of business, thoroughly capable of attending to her own affairs in the most competent manner. She kept the control of her business entirely in her own hands. She was, if I may say so, a woman of very original character and a well-known public figure."

"To the best of your knowledge, was she a rich woman at the time of her death?"

"She was an extremely wealthy woman."

"Had she, to your knowledge, any enemies?"

"Not to my knowledge."

Maître Thibault then stepped down and Henry Mitchell was called.

The coroner said: "Your name is Henry Charles Mitchell and you reside at 11 Shoeblack Lane, Wandsworth?"

"Yes, sir."

"You are in the employment of Universal Air Lines?"

"Yes, sir."

"You are the senior steward on the air liner 'Prometheus'?"

"Yes, sir."

"On Tuesday last, the eighteenth, you were on duty on the 'Prometheus' on the twelve-o'clock service from Paris to Croydon. The deceased traveled by that service. Had you ever seen the deceased before?"

"Yes, sir. I was on the eight forty-five A.M. service six months ago, and I noticed her traveling by that once or twice."

"Did you know her name?"

"Well, it must have been on my list, sir, but I didn't notice it specially, so to speak."

"Have you ever heard the name of Madame Giselle?"

"No, sir."

"Please describe the occurrences of Tuesday last in your own way."

"I'd served the luncheons, sir, and was coming round with the bills. The deceased was, as I thought, asleep. I decided not to wake her until about five minutes before we got in. When I tried to do so, I discovered that she was dead or seriously ill. I discovered that there was a doctor on board. He said—"

"We shall have Doctor Bryant's evidence presently. Will you take a look at this?"

The blowpipe was handed to Mitchell, who took it gingerly.

"Have you ever seen that before?"

"No, sir."

"You are certain that you did not see it in the hands of any of the passengers?"

"Yes, sir."

"Albert Davis."

The younger steward took the stand.

"You are Albert Davis, of 23 Barcome Street, Croydon? You are employed by Universal Air Lines?"

"Yes, sir."

"You were on duty on the 'Prometheus' as second steward on Tuesday last?"

"Yes, sir."

"What was the first that you knew of the tragedy?"

"Mr. Mitchell, sir, told me that he was afraid something had happened to one of the passengers."

"Have you ever seen this before?"

The blowpipe was handed to Davis.

"No, sir."

"You did not observe it in the hands of any of the passengers?"

"No, sir."

"Did anything at all happen on the journey that you think might throw light on this affair?"

"No, sir."

"Very good. You may stand down."

"Doctor Roger Bryant."

Doctor Bryant gave his name and address and described himself as a specialist in ear and throat diseases.

"Will you tell us in your own words, Doctor Bryant, exactly what happened on Tuesday last, the eighteenth?"

"Just before getting into Croydon I was approached by the chief steward. He asked me if I was a doctor. On my replying in the affirmative, he told me that one of the passengers had been taken ill. I rose and went with him. The woman in question was lying slumped down in her seat. She had been dead some time."

"What length of time in your opinion, Doctor Bryant?"

"I should say at least half an hour. Between half an hour and an hour would be my estimate."

"Did you form any theory as to the cause of death?"

"No. It would have been impossible to say without a detailed examination."

"But you noticed a small puncture on the side of the neck?"

"Yes."

"Thank you. . . . Doctor James Whistler."

Doctor Whistler was a thin, scraggy little man.

"You are the police surgeon for this district?"

"I am."

"Will you give your evidence in your own words?"

"Shortly after three o'clock on Tuesday last, the eighteenth, I received a summons to Croydon aerodrome. There I was shown the body of a middle-aged woman in one of the seats of the air liner 'Prometheus.' She was dead, and death had occurred, I should say, about an hour previously. I noticed a circular puncture on the side of the neck, directly on the jugular vein. This mark was quite consistent with having been caused by the sting of a wasp or by the insertion of a thorn which was shown to me. The body was removed to the mortuary, where I was able to make a detailed examination."

"What conclusions did you come to?"

"I came to the conclusion that death was caused by the introduction of a powerful toxin into the blood stream. Death was due to acute paralysis of the heart and must have been practically instantaneous."

"Can you tell us what that toxin was?"

"It was a toxin I had never come across before."

The reporters, listening attentively, wrote down: "Unknown poison."

"Thank you. . . . Mr. Henry Winterspoon."

Mr. Winterspoon was a large, dreamy-looking man with a benignant expression. He looked kindly but stupid. It came as something of a shock to learn that he was chief government analyst and an authority on rare poisons.

The coroner held up the fatal thorn and asked Mr. Winterspoon if he recognized it.

"I do. It was sent to me for analysis."

"Will you tell us the result of that analysis?"

"Certainly. I should say that originally the dart had been dipped in a preparation of native curare—an arrow poison used by certain tribes."

The reporters wrote with gusto.

"You consider, then, that death may have been due to curare?"

"Oh, no," said Mr. Winterspoon. "There was only the faintest trace of the original preparation. According to my analysis, the dart had recently been dipped in the venom of Dispholidus Typus, better known as the Boomslang, or Tree Snake."

"A boomslang? What is a boomslang?"

"It is a South African snake—one of the most deadly and poisonous in existence. Its effect on a human being is not known, but some idea of the intense virulence of the venom can be realized when I tell you that on injecting the venom into a hyena, the hyena died before the needle could be withdrawn. A jackal died as though shot by a gun. The poison causes acute hemorrhage under the skin and also acts on the heart, paralyzing its action."

The reporters wrote: "Extraordinary story. Snake poison in air drama. Deadlier than the cobra."

"Have you ever known the venom to be used in a case of deliberate poisoning?"

"Never. It is most interesting."

"Thank you, Mr. Winterspoon."

Detective Sergeant Wilson deposed to the finding of the blowpipe behind the cushion of one of the seats. There were no fingerprints on it. Experiments had been made with the dart and the blowpipe. What you might call the range of it was fairly accurate up to about ten yards.

"Monsieur Hercule Poirot."

There was a little stir of interest, but Monsieur Poirot's evidence was very restrained. He had noticed nothing out of the way. Yes, it was he who had found the tiny dart on the floor of the car. It was in such a position as it would naturally have occupied if it had fallen from the neck of the dead woman.

"The Countess of Horbury."

The reporters wrote: "Peer's wife gives evidence in air-death mystery." Some of them put: "in snake-poison mystery."

Those who wrote for women's papers put: "Lady Horbury wore one of the new collegian hats and fox furs" or "Lady Horbury, who is one of the smartest women in town, wore black with one of the new collegian hats" or "Lady Horbury, who before her marriage was

Miss Cicely Bland, was smartly dressed in black, with one of the new hats."

Everyone enjoyed looking at the smart and lovely young woman, though her evidence was of the briefest. She had noticed nothing; she had never seen the deceased before.

Venetia Kerr succeeded her, but was definitely less of a thrill.

The indefatigable purveyors of news for women wrote: "Lord Cottesmore's daughter wore a well-cut coat and skirt with one of the new stocks." And noted down the phrase: "Society women at inquest."

"James Ryder."

"You are James Bell Ryder and your address is 17 Blainberry Avenue, N.W.?"

"Yes."

"What is your business or profession?"

"I am managing director of the Ellis Vale Cement Company."

"Will you kindly examine this blowpipe?" A pause. "Have you ever seen this before?"

"No."

"You did not see any such thing in anybody's hand on board the 'Prometheus'?"

"No."

"You were sitting in Seat Number Four, immediately in front of the deceased."

"What if I was?"

"Please do not take that tone with me. You were sitting in Seat Number Four. From that seat you had a view of practically everyone in the compartment."

"No, I hadn't. I couldn't see any of the people on my side of the thing. The seats have got high backs."

"But if one of those people had stepped out into the gangway, into such a position as to be able to aim the blowpipe at the deceased, you would have seen them then?"

"Certainly."

"And you saw no such thing?"

"No."

"Did any of the people in front of you move from their seats?"

"Well, the man two seats ahead of me got up and went to the washroom compartment."

"That was in a direction away from you and from the deceased?"

"Yes."

"Did he come down the car towards you at all?"

"No, he went straight back to his seat."

"Was he carrying anything in his hand?"

"Nothing at all."

"You're sure of that?"

"Quite."

"Did anyone else move from his seat?"

"The chap in front of me. He came the other way—past me to the back of the car."

"I protest," squeaked Mr. Clancy, springing up from his seat in court. "That was earlier—much earlier—about one o'clock."

"Kindly sit down," said the coroner. "You will be heard presently. . . . Proceed, Mr. Ryder. Did you notice if this gentleman had anything in his hands?"

"I think he had a fountain pen. When he came back he had an orange-colored book in his hand."

"Is he the only person who came down the car in your direction? Did you yourself leave your seat?"

"Yes, I went to the washroom compartment—and I didn't have any blowpipe in my hand either."

"You are adopting a highly improper tone. Stand down."

Mr. Norman Gale, dentist, gave evidence of a negative character. Then the indignant Mr. Clancy took the stand.

Mr. Clancy was news of a minor kind, several degrees inferior to a peeress.

"Mystery-story writer gives evidence. Well-known author admits purchase of deadly weapon. Sensation in court."

But the sensation was, perhaps, a little premature.

"Yes, sir," said Mr. Clancy shrilly. "I did purchase a blowpipe, and what is more, I have brought it with me today. I protest strongly against the inference that the blowpipe with which the crime was committed was my blowpipe. Here is my blowpipe."

And he produced the blowpipe with a triumphant flourish.

The reporters wrote: "Second blowpipe in court."

The coroner dealt severely with Mr. Clancy. He was told that he was here to assist justice, not to rebut totally imaginary charges against himself. Then he was questioned about the occurrences on the "Prometheus," but with very little result. Mr. Clancy, as he explained at totally unnecessary length, had been too bemused with the eccentricities of foreign train services and the difficulties of the twenty-four-hour times to have noticed anything at all going on round about him. The whole car might have been shooting snake-venomed darts out of blowpipes, for all Mr. Clancy would have noticed of the matter.

Miss Jane Grey, hairdresser's assistant, created no flutter among journalistic pens.

The two Frenchmen followed.

Monsieur Armand Dupont deposed that he was on his way to London, where he was to deliver a lecture before the Royal Asiatic Society. He and his son had been very interested in a technical discussion and had noticed very little of what went on round them. He had not noticed the deceased until his attention had been attracted by the stir of excitement caused by the discovery of her death.

"Did you know this Madame Morisot, or Madame Giselle, by sight?"

"No, monsieur, I had never seen her before."

"But she is a well-known figure in Paris, is she not?"

Old Monsieur Dupont shrugged his shoulders.

"Not to me. In any case, I am not very much in Paris these days."

"You have lately returned from the East, I understand?"

"That is so, monsieur. From Persia."

"You and your son have traveled a good deal in out-of-the-way parts of the world?"

"Pardon?"

"You have journeyed in wild places?"

"That, yes."

"Have you ever come across a race of people that used snake venom as an arrow poison?"

This had to be translated; and when Monsieur Dupont understood the question, he shook his head vigorously.

"Never—never have I come across anything like that."

His son followed him. His evidence was a repetition of his father's. He had noticed nothing. He had thought it possible that the deceased had been stung by a wasp, because he had himself been annoyed by one and had finally killed it.

The Duponts were the last witnesses.

The coroner cleared his throat and addressed the jury.

This, he said, was without doubt the most astonishing and incredible case with which he had ever dealt in this court. A woman had been murdered—they could rule out any question of suicide or accident—in mid-air, in a small inclosed space. There was no question of any outside person having committed the crime. The murderer or murderess must be of necessity one of the witnesses they had heard this morning. There was no getting away from that fact, and a very terrible and awful one it was. One of the persons present had been lying in a desperate and abandoned manner.

The manner of the crime was one of unparalleled audacity. In the full view of ten—or twelve, counting the stewards—witnesses, the murderer had placed a blowpipe to his lips and sent the fatal dart on its murderous course through the air, and no one had observed the act. It seemed frankly incredible, but there was the evidence of the blowpipe, of the dart found on the floor, of the mark on the deceased's neck and of the medical evidence to show that, incredible or not, it had happened.

In the absence of further evidence incriminating some particular person, he could only direct the jury to return a verdict of murder against a person or persons unknown. Everyone present had denied any knowledge of the deceased woman. It would be the work of the police to find out how and where a connection lay. In the absence of any motive for the crime, he could only advise the verdict he had just mentioned. The jury would now consider the verdict.

A square-faced member of the jury with suspicious eyes leaned forward, breathing heavily.

"Can I ask a question, sir?"

"Certainly."

"You say as how the blowpipe was found down a seat? Whose seat was it?"

The coroner consulted his notes. Sergeant Wilson stepped to his side and murmured.

"Ah, yes. The seat in question was Number Nine—a seat occupied by Monsieur Hercule Poirot. Monsieur Poirot, I may say, is a very well-known and respected private detective who has—er—collaborated several times with Scotland Yard."

The square-faced man transferred his gaze to the face of Monsieur Hercule Poirot. It rested with a far from satisfied expression on the little Belgian's long mustaches.

"Foreigners," said the eyes of the square-faced man—"you can't trust foreigners, not even if they are hand and glove with the police."

Out loud he said:

"It was this Mr. Porrott who picked up the dart, wasn't it?"

"Yes."

The jury retired. They returned after five minutes and the foreman handed a piece of paper to the coroner.

"What's all this?" The coroner frowned. "Nonsense. I can't accept this verdict."

A few minutes later the amended verdict was returned: "We find that the deceased came to her death by poison, there being insufficient evidence to show by whom the poison was administered."

5

As Jane left the court after the verdict, she found Norman Gale beside her.

He said:

"I wonder what was on that paper that the coroner wouldn't have at any price."

"I can tell you, I think," said a voice behind him.

The couple turned, to look into the twinkling eyes of Monsieur Hercule Poirot.

"It was a verdict," said the little man, "of willful murder against me."

"Oh, surely—" cried Jane.

Poirot nodded happily.

"*Mais oui.* As I came out I heard one man say to the other: 'That little foreigner—mark my words—he done it!' The jury thought the same."

Jane was uncertain whether to condole or to laugh. She decided on the latter. Poirot laughed in sympathy.

"But, see you," he said, "definitely I must set to work and clear my character."

With a smile and a bow, he moved away.

Jane and Norman stared after his retreating figure.

"What an extraordinarily rum little beggar," said Gale. "Calls himself a detective. I don't see how he could do much detecting. Any criminal could spot him a mile off. I don't see how he could disguise himself."

"Haven't you got a very old-fashioned idea of detectives?" asked Jane. "All the false-beard stuff is very out of date. Nowadays detectives just sit and think out a case psychologically."

"Rather less strenuous."

"Physically, perhaps. But of course you need a cool clear brain."

"I see. A hot muddled one won't do."

They both laughed.

"Look here," said Gale. A slight flush rose in his cheeks and he spoke rather fast: "Would you mind—I mean, it would be frightfully nice of you—it's a bit late—but how about having some tea with me? I feel—comrades in misfortune and—"

He stopped. To himself he said:

"What is the matter with you, you fool? Can't you ask a girl to have a cup of tea without stammering and blushing and making an utter ass of yourself? What will the girl think of you?"

Gale's confusion served to accentuate Jane's coolness and self-possession.

"Thank you very much," she said. "I would like some tea."

They found a tea shop, and a disdainful waitress with a gloomy manner took their order with an air of doubt as of one who might say: "Don't blame me if you're disappointed. They say we serve teas here, but I never heard of it."

The tea shop was nearly empty. Its emptiness served to emphasize the intimacy of tea drinking together. Jane peeled off her gloves and looked across the table at her companion. He was attractive—those blue eyes and that smile. And he was nice too.

"It's a queer show, this murder business," said Gale, plunging hastily into talk. He was still not quite free from an absurd feeling of embarrassment.

"I know," said Jane. "I'm rather worried about it—from the point of view of my job, I mean. I don't know how they'll take it."

"Ye-es. I hadn't thought of that."

"Antoine's mayn't like to employ a girl who's been mixed up in a murder case and had to give evidence and all that."

"People are queer," said Norman Gale thoughtfully. "Life's so—so unfair. A thing like this that isn't your fault at all." He frowned angrily. "It's damnable!"

"Well, it hasn't happened yet," Jane reminded him. "No good getting hot and bothered about something that hasn't happened. After all, I suppose there is some point in it; I might be the person who murdered her! And when you've murdered one person, they say you usually murder a lot more; and it wouldn't be very comfortable having your hair done by a person of that kind."

"Anyone's only got to look at you to know you couldn't murder anybody," said Norman, gazing at her earnestly.

"I'm not so sure about that," said Jane. "I'd like to murder some of my ladies sometimes—if I could be sure I'd get away with it! There's one in particular—she's got a voice like a corn crake and she grumbles at everything. I really think sometimes that murdering her would be a good deed and not a crime at all. So you see I'm quite criminally minded."

"Well, you didn't do this particular murder, anyway," said Gale. "I can swear to that."

"And I can swear you didn't do it," said Jane. "But that won't help you if your patients think you have."

"My patients, yes." Gale looked rather thoughtful. "I suppose you're right; I hadn't really thought of that. A dentist who might be a homicidal maniac—no, it's not a very alluring prospect."

He added suddenly and impulsively:

"I say, you don't mind my being a dentist, do you?"

Jane raised her eyebrows.

"I? Mind?"

"What I mean is, there's always something rather—well, comic about a dentist. Somehow, it's not a romantic profession. Now, a doctor everyone takes seriously."

"Cheer up," said Jane. "A dentist is decidedly a cut above a hairdresser's assistant."

They laughed and Gale said: "I feel we're going to be friends. Do you?"

"Yes. I think I do."

"Perhaps you'll dine with me one night and we might do a show?"

"Thank you."

There was a pause, and then Gale said:

"How did you like Le Pinet?"

"It was great fun."

"Had you ever been there before?"

"No, you see—"

Jane, suddenly confidential, came out with the story of the winning sweep ticket. They agreed together on the general romance and desirability of sweeps and deplored the attitude of an unsympathetic English government.

Their conversation was interrupted by a young man in a brown suit who had been hovering uncertainly near by for some minutes before they noticed him.

Now, however, he lifted his hat and addressed Jane with a certain glib assurance.

"Miss Jane Grey?" he said.

"Yes."

"I represent the *Weekly Howl*, Miss Grey. I wondered if you would care to do us a short article on this air-death murder. Point of view of one of the passengers."

"I think I'd rather not, thanks."

"Oh, come now, Miss Grey. We'd pay well for it."

"How much?" asked Jane.

"Fifty pounds, or—well, perhaps we'd make it a bit more. Say sixty."

"No," said Jane. "I don't think I could. I shouldn't know what to say."

"That's all right," said the young man easily. "You needn't actually write the article, you know. One of our fellows will just ask you for a few suggestions and work the whole thing up for you. It won't be the least trouble to you."

"All the same," said Jane, "I'd rather not."

"What about a hundred quid? Look here; I really will make it a hundred. And give us a photograph."

"No," said Jane. "I don't like the idea."

"So you may as well clear out," said Norman Gale. "Miss Grey doesn't want to be worried."

The young man turned to him hopefully.

"Mr. Gale, isn't it?" he said. "Now look here, Mr. Gale. If Miss Grey feels a bit squeamish about it, what about your having a shot? Five hundred words. And we'll pay you the same as I offered Miss Grey—and that's a good bargain, because a woman's account of another woman's murder is better news value. I'm offering you a good chance."

"I don't want it. I shan't write a word for you."

"It'll be good publicity apart from the pay. Rising professional man—brilliant career ahead of you—all your patients will read it."

"That," said Norman Gale, "is mostly what I'm afraid of!"

"Well, you can't get anywhere without publicity in these days."

"Possibly, but it depends on the kind of publicity. I'm hoping that just one or two of my patients may not read the papers and may continue in ignorance of the fact that I've been mixed up in a murder case. Now you've had your answer from both of us. Are you going quietly, or have I got to kick you out of here?"

"Nothing to get annoyed about," said the young man, quite undisturbed by this threat of violence. "Good evening, and ring me up at the office if you change your mind. Here's my card."

He made his way cheerfully out of the tea shop, thinking to himself as he did so: "Not too bad. Made quite a decent interview."

And, in truth, the next issue of the *Weekly Howl* had an important column on the views of two of the witnesses in the air-murder mystery. Miss Jane Grey had declared herself too distressed to talk about the matter. It had been a terrible shock to her and she hated to think about it. Mr. Norman Gale had expressed himself at great length on the effect upon a professional man's career of being mixed up in a criminal case, however innocently. Mr. Gale had humorously expressed the hope that some of his patients only read the fashion columns and so might not suspect the worst when they came for the ordeal of the "chair."

When the young man had departed, Jane said:

"I wonder why he didn't go for the more important people."

"Leaves that to his betters, probably," said Gale grimly. "He's probably tried there and failed."

He sat frowning for a minute or two. Then he said:

"Jane—I'm going to call you Jane; you don't mind, do you?—Jane, who do you think really murdered this Giselle woman?"

"I haven't the faintest idea."

"Have you thought about it? Really thought about it?"

"Well, no, I don't suppose I have. I've been thinking about my own part in it, and worrying a little. I haven't really wondered seriously which—which of the others did it. I don't think I'd realized until today that one of them must have done it."

"Yes, the coroner put it very plainly. I know I didn't do it and I know you didn't do it because—well, because I was watching you most of the time."

"Yes," said Jane. "I know you didn't do it—for the same reason. And of course I know I didn't do it myself! So it must have been one of the others—but I don't know which. I haven't the slightest idea. Have you?"

"No."

Norman Gale looked very thoughtful. He seemed to be puzzling out some train of thought. Jane went on:

"I don't see how we can have the least idea, either. I mean we didn't see anything—at least I didn't. Did you?"

Gale shook his head.

"Not a thing."

"That's what seems so frightfully odd. I dare say you wouldn't have seen anything. You weren't facing that way. But I was. I was looking right along the middle. I mean, I could have been—"

Jane stopped and flushed. She was remembering that her eyes had been mostly fixed on a periwinkle-blue pullover, and that her mind, far from being receptive to what was going on around her, had been mainly concerned with the personality of the human being inside the periwinkle-blue pullover.

Norman Gale thought:

"I wonder what makes her blush like that. . . . She's wonderful. . . . I'm going to marry her. Yes, I am. . . . But it's no good looking too far ahead. I've got to have some good excuse for seeing her often. This murder business will do as well as anything else. . . . Besides, I really think it would be as well to do something—that whippersnapper of a reporter and his publicity—"

Aloud he said:

"Let's think about it now. Who killed her? Let's go over all the people. The stewards?"

"No," said Jane.

"I agree. The women across the aisle from us?"

"I don't suppose anyone like Lady Horbury would go killing people. And the other one—Miss Kerr—well, she's far too county. She wouldn't kill an old Frenchwoman, I'm sure."

"Only an unpopular M.F.H. I expect you're not far wrong, Jane. Then there's mustachios, but he seems, according to the coroner's jury, to be the most likely person; so that washes him out. The doctor? That doesn't seem very likely either."

"If he'd wanted to kill her, he could have used something quite untraceable and nobody would ever have known."

"Ye-es," said Norman doubtfully. "These untraceable, tasteless, odorless poisons are very convenient, but I'm a bit doubtful if they really exist. What about the little man who owned up to having a blowpipe?"

"That's rather suspicious. But he seemed a very nice little man, and he needn't have said he had a blowpipe; so that looks as though he were all right."

"Then there's Jameson—no, what's his name?—Ryder."

"Yes, it might be him."

"And the two Frenchmen."

"That's the most likely of all. They've been to queer places. And of course they may have had some reason we know nothing about. I thought the younger one looked very unhappy and worried."

"You probably would be worried if you'd committed a murder," said Norman Gale grimly.

"He looked nice, though," said Jane. "And the old father was rather a dear. I hope it isn't them."

"We don't seem to be getting on very fast," said Norman Gale.

"I don't see how we can get on without knowing a lot of things about the old woman who was murdered. Enemies, and who inherits her money and all that."

Norman Gale said thoughtfully:

"You think this is mere idle speculation?"

Jane said coolly, "Isn't it?"

"Not quite." Gale hesitated, then went on slowly, "I have a feeling it may be useful."

Jane looked at him inquiringly.

"Murder," said Norman Gale, "doesn't concern the victim and the guilty only. It affects the innocent too. You and I are innocent, but the shadow of murder has touched us. We don't know how that shadow is going to affect our lives."

Jane was a person of cool common sense, but she shivered suddenly.

"Don't," she said. "You make me feel afraid."

"I'm a little afraid myself," said Gale.

6

HERCULE POIROT rejoined his friend, Inspector Japp. The latter had a grin on his face.

"Hullo, old boy," he said. "You've had a pretty near squeak of being locked up in a police cell."

"I fear," said Poirot gravely, "that such an occurrence might have damaged me professionally."

"Well," said Japp with a grin, "detectives do turn out to be criminals sometimes—in storybooks."

A tall thin man with an intelligent melancholy face joined them, and Japp introduced him.

"This is Monsieur Fournier, of the Sûreté. He has come over to collaborate with us about this business."

"I think I have had the pleasure of meeting you once some years ago, Monsieur Poirot," said Fournier, bowing and shaking hands. "I have also heard of you from Monsieur Giraud."

A very faint smile seemed to hover on his lips. And Poirot, who could well imagine the terms in which Giraud—whom he himself had been in the habit of referring to disparagingly as the "human foxhound"—had spoken of him, permitted himself a small discreet smile in reply.

"I suggest," said Poirot, "that both you gentlemen should dine with me at my rooms. I have already invited Maître Thibault. That is, if you and my friend Japp do not object to my collaboration."

"That's all right, old cock," said Japp, slapping him heartily on the back. "You're in on this on the ground floor."

"We shall be indeed honored," murmured the Frenchman ceremoniously.

"You see," said Poirot, "as I said to a very charming young lady just now, I am anxious to clear my character."

"That jury certainly didn't like the look of you," agreed Japp, with a renewal of his grin. "Best joke I've heard for a long time."

By common consent, no mention of the case was made during the very excellent meal which the little Belgian provided for his friends.

"After all, it is possible to eat well in England," murmured Fournier appreciatively, as he made delicate use of a thoughtfully provided toothpick.

"A delicious meal, Monsieur Poirot," said Thibault.

"Bit Frenchified, but damn good," pronounced Japp.

"A meal should always lie lightly on the *estomac*," said Poirot. "It should not be so heavy as to paralyze thought."

"I can't say my stomach ever gives me much trouble," said Japp. "But I won't argue the point. Well, we'd better get down to business. I know that Monsieur Thibault has got an appointment this evening, so I suggest that we should start by consulting him on any point that seems likely to be useful."

"I am at your service, gentlemen. Naturally, I can speak more freely here than in a coroner's court. I had a hurried conversation with Inspector Japp before the inquest and he indicated a policy of reticence—the bare necessary facts."

"Quite right," said Japp. "Don't ever spill the beans too soon. But now let's hear all you can tell us of this Giselle woman."

"To speak the truth, I know very little. I know her as the world knew her—as a public character. Of her private life as an individual I know very little. Probably Monsieur Fournier here can tell you more than I can. But I will say to you this: Madame Giselle was what you call in this country 'a character.' She was unique. Of her antecedents nothing is known. I have an idea that as a young woman she was good-looking. I believe that as a result of smallpox she lost her looks. She was—I am giving you my impressions—a woman who enjoyed power—she had power. She was a keen woman of business. She was the type of hard-headed Frenchwoman who would never allow sentiment to affect her business interests, but she had the reputation of carrying on her profession with scrupulous honesty."

He looked for assent to Fournier. That gentleman nodded his dark melancholic head.

"Yes," he said, "she was honest, according to her lights. Yet the law could have called her to account if only evidence had been forthcoming; but that—" He shrugged his shoulders despondently. "It is too much to ask—with human nature what it is."

"You mean?"

"*Chantage.*"

"Blackmail?" echoed Japp.

"Yes, blackmail of a peculiar and specialized kind. It was Madame Giselle's custom to lend money on what I think you call in this country 'note of hand alone.' She used her discretion as to the sums she lent and the methods of repayment, but I may tell you that she had her own methods of getting paid."

Poirot leaned forward interestedly.

"As Maître Thibault said today, Madame Giselle's clientele lay amongst the upper and professional classes. Those classes are particularly vulnerable to the force of public opinion. Madame Giselle had her own intelligence service. It was her custom, before lending money—that is, in the case of a large sum—to collect as many facts as possible about the client in question, and her intelligence system, I may say, was an extraordinarily good one. I will echo what our friend has said—according to her lights, Madame Giselle was scrupulously honest. She kept faith with those who kept faith with her. I honestly believe that she has never made use of her secret knowledge to obtain money from anyone, unless that money was already owed to her."

"You mean," said Poirot, "that this secret knowledge was her form of security?"

"Exactly. And in using it she was perfectly ruthless and deaf to any finer shades of feeling. And I will tell you this, gentlemen: Her system paid! Very, very rarely did she have to write off a bad debt. A man or woman in a prominent position would go to desperate lengths to obtain the money which would obviate a public scandal. As I say, we knew of her activities, but as for prosecution"—he shrugged his shoulders—"that is a more difficult matter. Human nature is human nature."

"And supposing," said Poirot, "that she did, as you say happened occasionally, have to write off a bad debt? What then?"

"In that case," said Fournier slowly, "the information she held was published, or was given to the person concerned in the matter."

There was a moment's silence. Then Poirot said:

"Financially, that did not benefit her?"

"No," said Fournier. "Not directly, that is."

"But indirectly?"

"Indirectly," said Japp, "it made the others pay up, eh?"

"Exactly," said Fournier. "It was valuable for what you call the moral effect."

"Immoral effect, I should call it," said Japp. "Well"—he rubbed his nose thoughtfully—"it opens up a very pretty line in motives for murder—a very pretty line. Then there's the question of who is going to come into her money." He appealed to Thibault. "Can you help us there at all?"

"There was a daughter," said the lawyer. "She did not live with her mother; indeed, I fancy that her mother has never seen her since she was a tiny child. But she made a will many years ago now, leaving everything, with the exception of a small legacy to her maid, to her daughter, Anne Morisot. As far as I know, she has never made another."

"And her fortune is large?" asked Poirot.

The lawyer shrugged his shoulders.

"At a guess, eight or nine million francs."

Poirot pursed his lips to a whistle. Japp said, "Lord, she didn't look it! Let me see. What's the exchange?—that's—why, that must be well over a hundred thousand pounds! Whew!"

"Mademoiselle Anne Morisot will be a very wealthy young woman," said Poirot.

"Just as well she wasn't on that plane," said Japp dryly. "She might have been suspected of bumping off her mother to get the dibs. How old would she be?"

"I really cannot say. I should imagine about twenty-four or five."

"Well, there doesn't seem anything to connect her with the crime. We'll have to get down to this blackmailing business. Everyone on that plane denies knowing Madame Giselle. One of them is lying. We've got to find out which. An examination of her private papers might help, eh, Fournier?"

"My friend," said the Frenchman, "immediately the news came through, after I had conversed with Scotland Yard on the telephone, I went straight to her house. There was a safe there containing papers. All those papers had been burned."

"Burned? Who by? Why?"

"Madame Giselle had a confidential maid, Élise. Élise had instructions, in the event of anything happening to her mistress, to open the safe, the combination of which she knew, and burn the contents."

"What? But that's amazing!" Japp stared.

"You see," said Fournier, "Madame Giselle had her own code. She kept faith with those who kept faith with her. She gave her promise to her clients that she would deal honestly with them. She was ruthless, but she was also a woman of her word."

Japp shook his head dumbly. The four men were silent, ruminating on the strange character of the dead woman.

Maître Thibault rose.

"I must leave you, messieurs. I have to keep an appointment. If there is any further information I can give you at any time, you know my address."

He shook hands with them ceremoniously and left the apartment.

7

With the departure of Maître Thibault, the three men drew their chairs a little closer to the table.

"Now then," said Japp, "let's get down to it." He unscrewed the cap of his fountain pen. "There were eleven passengers in that plane —in the rear car, I mean—the other doesn't come into it—eleven passengers and two stewards—that's thirteen people we've got. One of those thirteen did the old woman in. Some of the passengers were English, some were French. The latter I shall hand over to Monsieur Fournier. The English ones I'll take on. Then there are inquiries to be made in Paris—that's your job, too, Fournier."

"And not only in Paris," said Fournier. "In the summer Giselle did a lot of business at the French watering places—Deauville, Le Pinet, Wimereux. She went down south, too, to Antibes and Nice and all those places."

"A good point—one or two of the people in the 'Prometheus' mentioned Le Pinet, I remember. Well, that's one line. Then we've got to get down to the actual murder itself—prove who could possibly be in a position to use that blowpipe." He unrolled a large sketch plan of the car of the aeroplane and placed it in the center of the table. "Now then, we're ready for the preliminary work. And to begin with, let's go through the people one by one, and decide on the probabilities and—even more important—the possibilities."

"To begin with, we can eliminate Monsieur Poirot here. That brings the number down to eleven."

Poirot shook his head sadly.

"You are of too trustful a nature, my friend. You should trust nobody—nobody at all."

"Well, we'll leave you in, if you like," said Japp good-temperedly. "Then there are the stewards. Seems to me very unlikely it should be either of them from the probability point of view. They're not likely to have borrowed money on a grand scale, and they've both got a good record—decent sober men, both of them. It would surprise me very much if either of them had anything to do with this. On the other hand, from the possibility point of view we've got to include them. They were up and down the car. They could actually have taken up a position from which they could have used that blowpipe—from the right angle, I mean—though I don't believe that a steward could shoot a poisoned dart out of a blowpipe in a car full of people without someone noticing him do it. I know by experience that most people are blind as bats, but there are limits. Of course, in a way, the same thing applies to every blessed person. It was madness—absolute madness—to commit a crime that way. Only about a chance in a hundred that it would come off without being spotted. The fellow that did it must have had the luck of the devil. Of all the damn fool ways to commit a murder—"

Poirot, who had been sitting with his eyes down, smoking quietly, interposed a question:

"You think it was a foolish way of committing a murder, yes?"

"Of course it was. It was absolute madness."

"And yet it succeeded. We sit here, we three, we talk about it, but we have no knowledge of who committed the crime! That is success!"

"That's pure luck," argued Japp. "The murderer ought to have been spotted five or six times over."

Poirot shook his head in a dissatisfied manner.

Fournier looked at him curiously.

"What is it that is in your mind, Monsieur Poirot?"

"*Mon ami,*" said Poirot, "my point is this: An affair must be judged by its results. This affair has succeeded. That is my point."

"And yet," said the Frenchman thoughtfully, "it seems almost a miracle."

"Miracle or no miracle, there it is," said Japp. "We've got the medical evidence, we've got the weapon—and if anyone had told me a week ago that I should be investigating a crime where a woman was killed with a poisoned dart with snake venom on it—well, I'd have laughed in his face! It's an insult—that's what this murder is—an insult."

He breathed deeply. Poirot smiled.

"It is, perhaps, a murder committed by a person with a perverted sense of humor," said Fournier thoughtfully. "It is most important in a crime to get an idea of the psychology of the murderer."

Japp snorted slightly at the word "psychology," which he disliked and mistrusted.

"That's the sort of stuff Monsieur Poirot likes to hear," he said.

"I am very interested, yes, in what you both say."

"You don't doubt that she was killed that way, I suppose?" Japp asked him suspiciously. "I know your tortuous mind."

"No, no, my friend. My mind is quite at ease on that point. The poisoned thorn that I picked up was the cause of death—that is quite certain. But, nevertheless, there are points about this case—"

He paused, shaking his head perplexedly.

Japp went on:

"Well, to get back to our Irish stew, we can't wash out the stewards absolutely, but I think myself it's very unlikely that either of them had anything to do with it. Do you agree, Monsieur Poirot?"

"Oh, you remember what I said. Me, I would not wash out—what a term, *mon Dieu!*—anybody at this stage."

"Have it your own way. Now, the passengers. Let's start up at the end by the stewards' pantry and the washrooms. Seat Number Sixteen." He jabbed a pencil on the plan. "That's the hairdressing girl, Jane Grey. Got a ticket in the Irish Sweep—blewed it at Le Pinet. That means the girl's a gambler. She might have been hard up and borrowed from the old dame; doesn't seem likely either that she borrowed a large sum, or that Giselle could have a hold over her. Seems rather too small a fish for what we're looking for. And I don't think a hairdresser's assistant has the remotest chance of laying her hands on snake venom. They don't use it as a hair dye or for face massage.

"In a way, it was rather a mistake to use snake venom; it narrows things down a lot. Only about two people in a hundred would be likely to have any knowledge of it and be able to lay hands on the stuff."

"Which makes one thing, at least, perfectly clear," said Poirot.

It was Fournier who shot a quick glance of inquiry at him.

Japp was busy with his own ideas.

"I look at it like this," he said: "The murderer has got to fall into one of two categories. Either he's a man who's knocked about the world in queer places—a man who knows something of snakes, and of the more deadly varieties, and of the habits of the native tribes who use the venom to dispose of their enemies. That's Category Number One."

"And the other?"

"The scientific line. Research. This boomslang stuff is the kind of thing they experiment with in high-class laboratories. I had a talk with Winterspoon. Apparently, snake venom—cobra venom, to be exact—is sometimes used in medicine. It's used in the treatment of epilepsy with a fair amount of success. There's a lot being done in the way of scientific investigation into snake bite."

"Interesting and suggestive," said Fournier.

"Yes. But let's get on. Neither of those categories fits the Grey girl. As far as she's concerned, motive seems unlikely; chances of getting the poison, poor. Actual possibility of doing the blowpipe act very doubtful indeed—almost impossible. See here."

The three men bent over the plan.

"Here's Number Sixteen," said Japp. "And here's Number Two where Giselle was sitting, with a lot of people and seats intervening. If the girl didn't move from her seat—and everybody says she didn't —she couldn't possibly have aimed the thorn to catch Giselle on the side of the neck. I think we can take it she's pretty well out of it.

"Now then, Number Twelve, opposite. That's the dentist, Norman Gale. Very much the same applies to him. Small fry. I suppose he'd have a slightly better chance of getting hold of snake venom."

"It is not an injection usually favored by dentists," murmured Poirot gently. "It would be a case of kill rather than cure."

"A dentist has enough fun with his patients as it is," said Japp, grinning. "Still, I suppose he might move in circles where you could get access to some funny business in drugs. He might have a scientific friend. But as regards possibility, he's pretty well out of it. He did leave his seat, but only to go to the washroom—that's in the opposite direction. On his way back to his seat he couldn't be farther than the gangway here, and to shoot off a thorn from a blowpipe so as to catch the old lady in the neck, he'd have to have a kind of pet thorn that would do tricks and make a right-angle turn. So he's pretty well out of it."

"I agree," said Fournier. "Let us proceed."

"We'll cross the gangway now. Number Seventeen."

"That was my seat originally," said Poirot. "I yielded it to one of the ladies, since she desired to be near her friend."

"That's the Honorable Venetia. Well, what about her? She's a big bug. She might have borrowed from Giselle. Doesn't look as though she had any guilty secrets in her life, but perhaps she pulled a horse in a point to point, or whatever they call it. We'll have to pay a little attention to her. The position's possible. If Giselle had got her head turned a little, looking out of the window, the Honorable Venetia could take a sporting shot—or do you call it a sporting puff? —diagonally across down the car. It would be a bit of a fluke, though. I rather think she'd have to stand up to do it. She's the sort of woman who goes out with the guns in the autumn. I don't know whether shooting with a gun is any help to you with a native blow-pipe. I suppose it's a question of eye just the same. Eye and practice. And she's probably got friends—men—who've been big-game hunting in odd parts of the globe. She might have got hold of some queer native stuff that way. What balderdash it all sounds, though! It doesn't make sense."

"It does indeed seem unlikely," said Fournier. "Mademoiselle Kerr —I saw her at the inquest today." He shook his head. "One does not readily connect her with murder."

"Seat Thirteen," said Japp. "Lady Horbury. She's a bit of a dark horse. I know something about her I'll tell you presently. I shouldn't be surprised if she had a guilty secret or two."

"I happen to know," said Fournier, "that the lady in question has been losing very heavily at the baccarat table at Le Pinet."

"That's smart of you. Yes, she's the type of pigeon to be mixed up with Giselle."

"I agree absolutely."

"Very well, then; so far, so good. But how did she do it? She didn't leave her seat either, you remember. She'd have had to have knelt up in her seat and leaned over the top—with eleven people looking at her. Oh, hell, let's get on."

"Numbers Nine and Ten," said Fournier, moving his finger on the plan.

"Monsieur Hercule Poirot and Doctor Bryant," said Japp. "What has Monsieur Poirot to say for himself?"

Poirot shook his head sadly.

"*Mon estomac*," he said pathetically. "Alas, that the brain should be the servant of the stomach."

"I, too," said Fournier with sympathy. "In the air, I do not feel well."

He closed his eyes and shook his head expressively.

"Now then, Doctor Bryant. What about Doctor Bryant? Big bug in Harley Street. Not very likely to go to a Frenchwoman money-lender, but you never know. And if any funny business crops up with a doctor, he's done for life! Here's where my scientific theory comes in. A man like Bryant, at the top of the tree, is in with all the medical-research people. He could pinch a test tube of snake venom as easy as winking when he happens to be in some swell laboratory."

"They check these things, my friend," objected Poirot. "It would not be just like plucking a buttercup in a meadow."

"Even if they do check 'em. A clever man could substitute something harmless—it could be done. Simply because a man like Bryant would be above suspicion."

"There is much in what you say," agreed Fournier.

"The only thing is: Why did he draw attention to the thing? Why not say the woman died from heart failure—natural death?"

Poirot coughed. The other two looked at him inquiringly.

"I fancy," he said, "that that was the doctor's first—well, shall we say, impression? After all, it looked very like natural death—possibly as the result of a wasp sting. There was a wasp, remember."

"Not likely to forget that wasp," put in Japp. "You're always harping on it."

"However," continued Poirot, "I happened to notice the fatal thorn on the ground and picked it up. Once we had found that, everything pointed to murder."

"The thorn would be bound to be found anyway."

Poirot shook his head.

"There is just a chance that the murderer might have been able to pick it up unobserved."

"Bryant?"

"Bryant or another."

"H'm, rather risky."

Fournier disagreed.

"You think so now," he said, "because you know that it is murder. But when a lady dies suddenly of heart failure, if a man is to drop his handkerchief and stoop to pick it up, who will notice the action or think twice about it?"

"That's true," agreed Japp. "Well, I fancy Bryant is definitely on the list of suspects. He could lean his head round the corner of his seat and do the blowpipe act—again diagonally across the car. But why nobody saw him— However, I won't go into that again. Who-ever did it wasn't seen!"

"And for that, I fancy, there must be a reason," said Fournier. "A reason that, by all I have heard"—he smiled—"will appeal to Monsieur Poirot. I mean a psychological reason."

"Continue, my friend," said Poirot. "It is interesting, what you say there."

"Supposing," said Fournier, "that when traveling in a train you were to pass a house in flames. Everyone's eyes would at once be drawn to the window. Everyone would have his attention fixed on a certain point. A man in such a moment might whip out a dagger and stab a man, and nobody would see him do it."

"That is true," said Poirot. "I remember a case in which I was concerned—a case of poison where that very point arose. There was, as you call it, a psychological moment. If we discover that there was such a moment during the journey of the 'Prometheus'—"

"We ought to find that out by questioning the stewards and the passengers," said Japp.

"True. But if there was such a psychological moment, it must follow logically that the cause of that moment must have originated with the murderer. He must have been able to produce the particular effect that caused that moment."

"Perfectly, perfectly," said the Frenchman.

"Well, we'll note down that as a point for questions," said Japp. "I'm coming now to Seat Number Eight—Daniel Michael Clancy."

Japp spoke the name with a certain amount of relish.

"In my opinion, he's the most likely suspect we've got. What's easier than for a mystery author to fake up an interest in snake venom and get some unsuspecting scientific chemist to let him handle the stuff? Don't forget he went down past Giselle's seat—the only one of the passengers who did."

"I assure you, my friend," said Poirot, "that I have not forgotten that point."

He spoke with emphasis.

Japp went on:

"He could have used that blowpipe from fairly close quarters without any need of a psychological moment, as you call it. And he stood quite a respectable chance of getting away with it. Remember, he knows all about blowpipes; he said so."

"Which makes one pause, perhaps."

"Sheer artfulness," said Japp. "And as to this blowpipe he produced today—who is to say that it's the one he bought two years ago? The whole thing looks very fishy to me. I don't think it's healthy for a man to be always brooding over crime and detective stories. Reading up all sorts of cases. It puts ideas into his head."

"It is certainly necessary for a writer to have ideas in his head," agreed Poirot.

Japp returned to his plan of the plane.

"Number Four was Ryder—the seat slap in front of the dead woman. Don't think he did it. But we can't leave him out. He went to the washroom, he could have taken a pot shot on the way back from fairly close quarters. The only thing is, he'd be right up against the archæologist fellows when he did so. They'd notice it —couldn't help it."

Poirot shook his head thoughtfully.

"You are not, perhaps, acquainted with many archæologists? If these two were having a really absorbing discussion on some point at issue—*eh bien,* my friend, their concentration would be such that they would be quite blind and deaf to the outside world. They would be existing, you see, in five thousand or so B.C. Nineteen hundred and thirty-four A.D. would have been nonexistent for them."

Japp looked a little skeptical.

"Well, we'll pass on to them. What can you tell us about the Duponts, Fournier?"

"Monsieur Armand Dupont is one of the most distinguished archæologists in France."

"Then that doesn't get us anywhere much. Their position in the car is pretty good from my point of view—across the gangway, but slightly farther forward than Giselle. And I suppose that they've knocked about the world and dug things up in a lot of queer places; they might easily have got hold of some native snake poison."

"It is possible, yes," said Fournier.

"But you don't believe it's likely?"

Fournier shook his head doubtfully.

"Monsieur Dupont lives for his profession. He is an enthusiast. He was formerly an antique dealer. He gave up a flourishing business to devote himself to excavation. Both he and his son are devoted heart and soul to their profession. It seems to me unlikely—I will not say impossible; since the ramifications of the Stavisky business, I will believe anything!—unlikely that they are mixed up in this business."

"All right," said Japp.

He picked up the sheet of paper on which he had been making notes and cleared his throat.

"This is where we stand: Jane Grey. Probability, poor. Possibility, practically nil. Gale. Probability, poor. Possibility, again practically nil. Miss Kerr. Very improbable. Possibility, doubtful. Lady Horbury. Probability, good. Possibility, practically nil. Monsieur Poirot, almost certainly the criminal; the only man on board who could create a psychological moment."

Japp enjoyed a good laugh over his little joke and Poirot smiled indulgently and Fournier a trifle diffidently. Then the detective resumed:

"Bryant. Probability and possibility, both good. Clancy. Motive doubtful, probability and possibility very good indeed. Ryder. Probability uncertain, possibility quite fair. The two Duponts. Probability poor as regards motive, good as to means of obtaining poison. Possibility, good.

"That's a pretty fair summary, I think, as far as we can go. We'll have to do a lot of routine inquiry. I shall take on Clancy and Bryant first; find out what they've been up to; if they've been hard up at any time in the past; if they've seemed worried or upset lately; their movements in the last year—all that sort of stuff. I'll do the same for Ryder. Then it won't do to neglect the others entirely. I'll get Wilson to nose round there. Monsieur Fournier, here, will undertake the Duponts."

The man from the Sûreté nodded.

"Be well assured, that will be attended to. I shall return to Paris tonight. There may be something to be got out of Élise, Giselle's maid, now that we know a little more about the case. Also, I will check up Giselle's movements very carefully. It will be well to know where she has been during the summer. She was, I know, at Le Pinet once or twice. We may get information as to her contacts with some of the English people involved. Ah, yes, there is much to do."

They both looked at Poirot, who was absorbed in thought.

"You going to take a hand at all, Monsieur Poirot?" asked Japp.

Poirot roused himself.

"Yes, I think I should like to accompany Monsieur Fournier to Paris."

"Enchanté," said the Frenchman.

"What are you up to, I wonder?" said Japp. He looked at Poirot curiously. "You've been very quiet over all this. Got some of your little ideas, eh?"

"One or two—one or two—but it is very difficult."

"Let's hear about it."

"One thing that worries me," said Poirot slowly, "is the place where the blowpipe was found."

"Naturally! It nearly got you locked up."

Poirot shook his head.

"I do not mean that. It is not because it was found pushed down beside my seat that it worries me—it was its being pushed down behind any seat."

"I don't see anything in that," said Japp. "Whoever did it had got to hide the thing somewhere. He couldn't risk its being found on him."

"*Évidemment*. But you may have noticed, my friend, when you examined the plane, that although the windows cannot be opened, there is in each of them a ventilator—a circle of small, round holes in the glass which can be opened or closed by turning a fan of glass. These holes are of a sufficient circumference to admit of the passage of our blowpipe. What could be simpler than to get rid of the blowpipe that way? It falls to the earth beneath and it is extremely unlikely that it will ever be found."

"I can think of an objection to that—the murderer was afraid of being seen. If he pushed the blowpipe through the ventilator, someone might have noticed."

"I see," said Poirot. "He was not afraid of being seen placing the blowpipe to his lips and dispatching the fatal dart, but he was afraid of being seen trying to push the blowpipe through the window!"

"Sounds absurd, I admit," said Japp, "but there it is. He did hide the blowpipe behind the cushion of a seat. We can't get away from that."

Poirot did not answer, and Fournier asked curiously:

"It gives you an idea, that?"

Poirot bowed his head assentingly.

"It gives rise to, say, a speculation in my mind."

With absent-minded fingers he straightened the unused inkstand that Japp's impatient hand had set a little askew.

Then lifting his head sharply, he asked:

"À *propos*, have you that detailed list of the belongings of the passengers that I asked you to get me?"

8

"I'M a man of my word, I am," said Japp.

He grinned and dived his hand into his pocket, bringing out a mass of closely typewritten paper.

"Here you are. It's all here, down to the minutest detail! And I'll admit that there is one rather curious thing in it. I'll talk to you about it when you've finished reading the stuff."

Poirot spread out the sheets on the table and began to read. Fournier moved up and read them over his shoulder.

JAMES RYDER

Pockets. Linen handkerchief marked J. Pigskin note case—seven £1 notes, three business cards. Letter from partner, George Elbermann, hoping "loan has been successfully negotiated . . . otherwise we're in Queer Street." Letter signed Maudie making appointment Trocadéro following evening. Cheap paper, illiterate handwriting. Silver cigarette case. Match folder. Fountain pen. Bunch of keys. Yale door key. Loose change in French and English money.

Attaché Case. Mass of papers concerning dealings in cement. Copy of "Bootless Cup" (banned in this country). A box of Immediate Cold Cures.

DOCTOR BRYANT

Pockets. Two linen handkerchiefs. Note case containing £20 and 500 francs. Loose change in French and English money. Engagement book. Cigarette case. Lighter. Fountain pen. Yale door key. Bunch of keys.

Flute in case. Carrying "Memoirs of Benvenuto Cellini" and "Les Maux de l'Oreille."

NORMAN GALE

Pockets. Silk handkerchief. Wallet containing £1 in English money and 600 francs. Loose change. Business cards of two French firms, makers of dental instruments. Bryant & May match box, empty. Silver lighter. Briar pipe. Rubber tobacco pouch. Yale door key.

Attaché Case. White-linen coat. Two small dental mirrors. Dental rolls of cotton wool. *La Vie Parisienne. The Strand Magazine. The Autocar.*

ARMAND DUPONT

Pockets. Wallet containing 1000 francs and £10 in English. Spectacles in case. Loose change in French money. Cotton handkerchief. Packet of cigarettes, match folder. Cards in case. Toothpick.

Attaché Case. Manuscript of proposed address to Royal Asiatic Society. Two German archæological publications. Two sheets of rough sketches of pottery. Ornamented hollow tubes—said to be Kurdish pipe stems. Small basketwork tray. Nine unmounted photographs—all of pottery.

JEAN DUPONT

Pockets. Note case containing £5 in English and 300 francs. Cigarette case. Cigarette holder—ivory. Lighter. Fountain pen. Two pencils. Small notebook full of scribbled notes. Letter in English from L. Marriner, giving invitation to lunch at restaurant near Tottenham Court Road. Loose change in French.

DANIEL CLANCY

Pockets. Handkerchief—ink-stained. Fountain pen—leaking. Note case containing £4 and 100 francs. Three newspaper cuttings dealing with recent crimes. One poisoning by arsenic, and two embezzlement. Two letters from house agents with details of country properties. Engagement book. Four pencils. Penknife. Three receipted and four unpaid bills. Letter from "Gordon" headed "S. S. Minotaur." Half-done crossword puzzle cut from *Times.* Notebook containing suggestions for plots. Loose change in Italian, French, Swiss and English money. Receipted hotel bill, Naples. Large bunch of keys.

In overcoat pocket. Manuscript notes of "Murder on Vesuvius." Continental Bradshaw. Golf ball. Pair of socks. Toothbrush. Receipted hotel bill, Paris.

MISS KERR

Vanity bag. Compact. Two cigarette holders—one ivory, one jade. Cigarette case. Match folder. Handkerchief. £2 English money. Loose change. One half letter of credit. Keys.

Dressing Case. Shagreen fitted. Bottles, brushes, combs, and so on. Manicure outfit. Washing bag containing toothbrush, sponge, tooth powder, soap. Two pairs of scissors. Five letters from family and friends in England. Two Tauchnitz novels. Photograph of two spaniels.

Carried *Vogue* and *Good Housekeeping.*

MISS GREY

Hand bag. Lipstick, rouge, compact. Yale key and one trunk key. Pencil. Cigarette case. Holder. Match folder. Two handkerchiefs. Receipted hotel bill Le Pinet. Small book French Phrases. Note case 100 francs and 10 shillings. Loose French and English change. One casino counter, value 5 francs.

In pocket of traveling coat. Six post cards of Paris, two handkerchiefs and silk scarf. Letter signed "Gladys." Tube of aspirin.

LADY HORBURY

Vanity bag. Two lipsticks, rouge, compact. Handkerchief. Three *mille* notes. £6 English money. Loose change—French. A diamond ring. Five French stamps. Two cigarette holders. Lighter with case.

Dressing Case. Complete make-up outfit. Elaborate manicure set—gold. Small bottle labeled in ink "Boracic Powder."

As Poirot came to the end of the list, Japp laid his finger on the last item.

"Rather smart of our man. He thought that didn't seem quite in keeping with the rest. Boracic powder, my eye! The white powder in that bottle was cocaine."

Poirot's eyes opened a little. He nodded his head slowly.

"Nothing much to do with our case, perhaps," said Japp. "But you don't need me to tell you that a woman who's got the cocaine habit hasn't got much moral restraint. I've an idea, anyway, that her ladyship wouldn't stick at much to get what she wanted, in spite of all that helpless-feminine business. All the same, I doubt if she'd have the nerve to carry a thing like this through. And frankly, I can't see that it was possible for her to do it. The whole thing is a bit of a teaser."

Poirot gathered up the loose typewritten sheets and read them through once again. Then he laid them down with a sigh.

"On the face of it," he said, "it seems to point very plainly to one person as having committed the crime. And yet, I cannot see why, or even how."

Japp stared at him.

"Are you pretending that by reading all this stuff you've got an idea who did it?"

"I think so."

Japp seized the papers from him and read them through, handing each sheet over to Fournier when he had finished with it. Then he slapped them down on the table and stared at Poirot.

"Are you pulling my leg, Moosior Poirot?"

"No, no. *Quelle idée!*"

The Frenchman in his turn laid down the sheets.

"What about you, Fournier?"

The Frenchman shook his head.

"I may be stupid," he said, "but I cannot see that this list advances us much."

"Not by itself," said Poirot, "but taken in conjunction with certain features of the case. . . . No? Well, it may be that I am wrong —quite wrong."

"Well, come out with your theory," said Japp. "I'll be interested to hear it, at all events."

Poirot shook his head.

"No, as you say, it is a theory—a theory only. I hoped to find a certain object on that list. *Eh bien,* I have found it. It is there. But it seems to point in the wrong direction. The right clue on the wrong person. That means there is much work to be done, and truly, there is much that is still obscure to me. I cannot see my way. Only, certain facts seem to stand out, to arrange themselves in a significant pattern. You do not find it so? No, I see you do not. Let us, then, each work to his own idea. I have no certainty, I tell you; only a certain suspicion."

"I believe you're just talking through your hat," said Japp. He rose. "Well, let's call it a day. I work the London end, you return to Paris, Fournier—and what about our Monsieur Poirot?"

"I still wish to accompany Monsieur Fournier to Paris—more than ever now."

"More than ever? I'd like to know just what kind of maggot you've got in your brain."

"Maggot? *Ce n'est pas joli, ça!*"

Fournier shook hands ceremoniously.

"I wish you good evening, with many thanks for your delightful hospitality. We will meet, then, at Croydon tomorrow morning?"

"Exactly. *À demain.*"

"Let us hope," said Fournier, "that nobody will murder us en route."

The two detectives departed.

Poirot remained for a time as in a dream. Then he rose, cleared away any traces of disorder, emptied the ash trays and straightened the chairs.

He went to a side table and picked up a copy of the *Sketch*. He turned the pages until he came to the one he sought.

"Two Sun Worshipers," it was headed. "The Countess of Horbury and Mr. Raymond Barraclough at Le Pinet." He looked at the two laughing figures in bathing suits, their arms entwined.

"I wonder," said Hercule Poirot. "One might do something along those lines. Yes, one might."

9

THE weather on the following day was of so perfect a nature that even Hercule Poirot had to admit that his *estomac* was perfectly peaceful.

On this occasion they were traveling by the 8:45 air service to Paris.

There were seven or eight travelers besides Poirot and Fournier in the compartment and the Frenchman utilized the journey to make some experiments. He took from his pocket a small piece of bamboo, and three times during the journey he raised this to his lips, pointing it in a certain direction. Once he did it bending himself round the corner of his seat. Once with his head slightly turned sideways. Once when he was returning from the washroom. And on each occasion he caught the eye of some passenger or other eying him with mild astonishment. On the last occasion, indeed, every eye in the car seemed to be fixed upon him.

Fournier sank in his seat discouraged, and was but little cheered by observing Poirot's open amusement.

"You are amused, my friend? But you agree, one must try the experiments?"

Évidemment! In truth, I admire your thoroughness. There is nothing like ocular demonstration. You play the part of the murderer with blowpipe. The result is perfectly clear. Everybody sees you!"

"Not everybody."

"In a sense, no. On each occasion there is somebody who does not see you. But for a successful murder that is not enough. You must be reasonably sure that nobody will see you."

"And that is impossible, given ordinary conditions," said Fournier. "I hold then to my theory that there must have been extraordinary conditions. The psychological moment! There must have been a psychological moment when everyone's attention was mathematically centered elsewhere."

"Our friend Inspector Japp is going to make minute inquiries on that point."

"Do you not agree with me, Monsieur Poirot?"

Poirot hesitated a minute, then he said slowly:

"I agree that there was—that there must have been a psychological reason why nobody saw the murderer. But my ideas are running in a slightly different channel from yours. I feel that in this case mere ocular facts may be deceptive. Close your eyes, my friend, instead of opening them wide. Use the eyes of the brain, not of the body. Let the little gray cells of the mind function. Let it be their task to show you what actually happened."

Fournier stared at him curiously.

"I do not follow you, Monsieur Poirot."

"Because you are deducing from things that you have seen. Nothing can be so misleading as observation."

Fournier shook his head again and spread out his hands.

"I give it up. I cannot catch your meanings."

"Our friend Giraud would urge you to pay no attention to my vagaries. 'Be up and doing,' he would say. 'To sit still in an armchair and think—that is the method of an old man past his prime.' But I say that a young hound is often so eager upon the scent that he overruns it. For him is the trail of the red herring. There, it is a very good hint I have given you there."

And leaning back, Poirot closed his eyes, it may have been to think, but it is quite certain that five minutes later he was fast asleep.

On arrival in Paris they went straight to Number 3, Rue Joliette.

The Rue Joliette is on the south side of the Seine. There was nothing to distinguish Number 3 from the other houses. An aged concierge admitted them and greeted Fournier in a surly fashion.

"So, we have the police here again! Nothing but trouble. This will give the house a bad name."

He retreated grumbling into his apartment.

"We will go to Giselle's office," said Fournier. "It is on the first floor."

He drew a key from his pocket as he spoke and explained that the French police had taken the precaution of locking and sealing the door whilst awaiting the result of the English inquest.

"Not, I fear," said Fournier, "that there is anything here to help us."

He detached the seals, unlocked the door, and they entered. Madame Giselle's office was a small stuffy apartment. It had a somewhat old-fashioned type of safe in a corner, a writing desk of businesslike appearance and several shabbily upholstered chairs. The one window was dirty, and it seemed highly probable that it had never been opened.

Fournier shrugged his shoulders as he looked round.

"You see?" he said. "Nothing. Nothing at all."

Poirot passed round behind the desk. He sat down in the chair and looked across the desk at Fournier. He passed his hand gently across the surface of the wood, then down underneath it.

"There is a bell here," he said.

"Yes, it rings down to the concierge."

"Ah, a wise precaution. Madame's clients might sometimes become obstreperous."

He opened one or two of the drawers. They contained stationery, a calendar, pens and pencils, but no papers and nothing of a personal nature.

Poirot merely glanced into them in a cursory manner.

"I will not insult you, my friend, by a close search. If there were anything to find, you would have found it, I am sure." He looked across at the safe. "Not a very efficacious pattern, that."

"Somewhat out of date," agreed Fournier.

"It was empty?"

"Yes. That cursed maid had destroyed everything."

"Ah, yes, the maid. The confidential maid. We must see her. This room, as you say, has nothing to tell us. It is significant, that; do you not think so?"

"What do you mean by significant, Monsieur Poirot?"

"I mean that there is in this room no personal touch. I find that interesting."

"She was hardly a woman of sentiment," said Fournier dryly.

Poirot rose.

"Come," he said. "Let us see this maid—this highly confidential maid."

Élise Grandier was a short, stout woman of middle age with a florid face and small shrewd eyes that darted quickly from Fournier's face to that of his companion and then back again.

"Sit down, Mademoiselle Grandier," said Fournier.

"Thank you, monsieur."

She sat down composedly.

"Monsieur Poirot and I have returned today from London. The inquest—the inquiry, that is, into the death of Madame—took place yesterday. There is no doubt whatsoever. Madame was poisoned."

The Frenchwoman shook her head gravely.

"It is terrible, what you say there, monsieur. Madame poisoned. Who would ever have dreamed of such a thing?"

"That is, perhaps, where you can help us, mademoiselle."

"Certainly, monsieur, I will, naturally, do all I can to aid the police. But I know nothing—nothing at all."

"You know that Madame had enemies?" said Fournier sharply.

"That is not true. Why should Madame have enemies?"

"Come, come, Mademoiselle Grandier," said Fournier dryly. "The profession of a moneylender—it entails certain unpleasantnesses."

"It is true that sometimes the clients of Madame were not very reasonable," agreed Élise.

"They made scenes, eh? They threatened her?"

The maid shook her head.

"No, no, you are wrong there. It was not they who threatened. They whined, they complained, they protested they could not pay —all that, yes." Her voice held a very lively contempt.

"Sometimes, perhaps, mademoiselle," said Poirot, "they could not pay."

Élise Grandier shrugged her shoulders.

"Possibly. That is their affair! They usually paid in the end."

Her tone held a certain amount of satisfaction.

"Madame Giselle was a hard woman," said Fournier.

"Madame was justified."

"You have no pity for the victims?"

"Victims—victims." Élise spoke with impatience. "You do not understand. Is it necessary to run into debt? To live beyond your means? To run and borrow, and then expect to keep the money as a gift? It is not reasonable, that! Madame was always fair and just. She lent, and she expected repayment. That is only fair. She herself had no debts. Always she paid honorably what she owed. Never, never were there any bills outstanding. And when you say that Madame was a hard woman, it is not the truth! Madame was kind.

She gave to the Little Sisters of the Poor when they came. She gave money to charitable institutions. When the wife of Georges, the concierge, was ill, Madame paid for her to go to a hospital in the country."

She stopped, her face flushed and angry.

She repeated, "You do not understand. No, you do not understand Madame at all."

Fournier waited a moment for her indignation to subside, and then said:

"You made the observation that Madame's clients usually managed to pay in the end. Were you aware of the means Madame used to compel them?"

She shrugged her shoulders.

"I know nothing, monsieur—nothing at all."

"You knew enough to burn Madame's papers."

"I was following her instructions. If ever, she said, she were to meet with an accident, or if she were taken ill and died somewhere away from home, I was to destroy her business papers."

"The papers in the safe downstairs?" asked Poirot.

"That is right. Her business papers."

"And they were in the safe downstairs?"

His persistence brought the red up in Élise's cheeks.

"I obeyed Madame's instructions," she said.

"I know that," said Poirot, smiling. "But the papers were not in the safe. That is so, is it not? That safe, it is far too old-fashioned; quite an amateur might have opened it. The papers were kept elsewhere. In Madame's bedroom, perhaps?"

Élise paused a moment, and then answered:

"Yes, that is so. Madame always pretended to clients that papers were kept in the safe, but in reality the safe was a blind. Everything was in Madame's bedroom."

"Will you show us where?"

Élise rose and the two men followed her. The bedroom was a fair-sized room, but was so full of ornate heavy furniture that it was hard to move about freely in it. In one corner was a large old-fashioned trunk. Élise lifted the lid and took out an old-fashioned alpaca dress with a silk underskirt. On the inside of the dress was a deep pocket.

"The papers were in this, monsieur," she said. "They were kept in a large sealed envelope."

"You told me nothing of this," said Fournier sharply, "when I questioned you three days ago?"

"I ask pardon, monsieur. You asked me where were the papers that should be in the safe? I told you I had burned them. That was true. Exactly where the papers were kept seemed unimportant."

"True," said Fournier. "You understand, Mademoiselle Grandier, that those papers should not have been burned."

"I obeyed Madame's orders," said Élise sullenly.

"You acted, I know, for the best," said Fournier soothingly. "Now I want you to listen to me very closely, mademoiselle. Madame was murdered. It is possible that she was murdered by a person or persons about whom she held certain damaging knowledge. That knowledge was in those papers you burned. I am going to ask you a question, mademoiselle, and do not reply too quickly without reflection. It is possible—indeed, in my view, it is probable and quite understandable—that you glanced through those papers before committing them to the flames. If that is the case, no blame will be attached to you for so doing. On the contrary, any information you have acquired may be of the greatest service to the police, and may be of material service in bringing the murderer to justice. Therefore, mademoiselle, have no fear in answering truthfully. Did you, before burning the papers, glance over them?"

Élise breathed hard. She leaned forward and spoke emphatically.

"No, monsieur," she said, "I looked at nothing. I read nothing. I burned the envelope without undoing the seal."

10

FOURNIER stared hard at her for a moment or two. Then, satisfied that she was speaking the truth, he turned away with a gesture of discouragement.

"It is a pity," he said. "You acted honorably, mademoiselle, but it is a pity."

"I cannot help it, monsieur. I am sorry."

Fournier sat down and drew a notebook from his pocket.

"When I questioned you before, you told me, mademoiselle, that you did not know the names of Madame's clients. Yet, just now, you speak of them whining and asking for mercy. You did, therefore, know something about these clients of Madame Giselle's?"

"Let me explain, monsieur. Madame never mentioned a name. She never discussed her business. But all the same, one is human, is one not? There are ejaculations, comments. Madame spoke to me sometimes as she would to herself."

Poirot leaned forward.

"If you would give us an instance, mademoiselle—" he said.

"Let me see—ah, yes—say a letter comes. Madame opens it. She laughs—a short dry laugh. She says, 'You whine and you snivel, my fine lady. All the same, you must pay.' Or she would say to me, 'What fools! What fools! To think I would lend large sums without proper security. Knowledge is security, Élise. Knowledge is power.' Something like that she would say."

"Madame's clients who came to the house—did you ever see any of them?"

"No, monsieur—at least hardly ever. They came to the first floor only, you understand. And very often they came after dark."

"Had Madame Giselle been in Paris before her journey to England?"

"She returned to Paris only the afternoon before."

"Where had she been?"

"She had been away for a fortnight—to Deauville, Le Pinet, Paris —Plage and Wimereux—her usual September round."

"Now think, mademoiselle. Did she say anything—anything at all —that might be of use?"

Élise considered for some moments. Then she shook her head.

"No, monsieur," she said, "I cannot remember anything. Madame was in good spirits. Business was going well, she said. Her tour had been profitable. Then she directed me to ring up Universal Air Lines and book a passage to England for the following day. The early-morning service was booked, but she obtained a seat on the twelve-o'clock service."

"Did she say what took her to England? Was there any urgency about it?"

"Oh, no, monsieur. Madame journeyed to England fairly frequently. She usually told me the day before."

"Did any clients come to see Madame that evening?"

"I believe there was one client, monsieur, but I am not sure. Georges, perhaps, would know. Madame said nothing to me."

Fournier took from his pockets various photographs—mostly snapshots, taken by reporters, of various witnesses leaving the coroner's court.

"Can you recognize any of these, mademoiselle?"

Élise took them and gazed at each in turn. Then she shook her head.

"No, monsieur."

"We must try Georges then."

"Yes, monsieur. Unfortunately, Georges has not very good eyesight. It is a pity."

Fournier rose.

"Well, mademoiselle, we will take our leave. That is, if you are quite sure that there is nothing—nothing at all—that you have omitted to mention?"

"I? What—what could there be?"

Élise looked distressed.

"It is understood then. . . . Come, Monsieur Poirot. . . . I beg your pardon. You are looking for something?"

Poirot was indeed wandering round the room in a vague searching way.

"It is true," said Poirot. "I am looking for something I do not see."

"What is that?"

"Photographs. Photographs of Madame Giselle's relations—of her family."

Élise shook her head.

"She had no family, Madame. She was alone in the world."

"She had a daughter," said Poirot sharply.

"Yes, that is so. Yes, she had a daughter."

Élise sighed.

"But there is no picture of that daughter?" Poirot persisted.

"Oh, Monsieur does not understand. It is true that Madame had a daughter, but that was long ago, you comprehend. It is my belief that Madame had never seen that daughter since she was a tiny baby."

"How was that?" demanded Fournier sharply.

Élise's hands flew out in an expressive gesture.

"I do not know. It was in the days when Madame was young. I have heard that she was pretty then. Pretty and poor. She may have been married. She may not. Myself, I think not. Doubtless some arrangement was made about the child. As for Madame, she had the smallpox, she was very ill, she nearly died. When she got well, her beauty was gone. There were no more follies, no more romance. Madame became a woman of business."

"But she left her money to this daughter?"

"That is only right," said Élise. "Who should one leave one's money to except one's own flesh and blood? Blood is thicker than water. And Madame had no friends. She was always alone. Money was her passion. To make more and more money. She spent very little. She had no love for luxury."

"She left you a legacy. You know that?"

"But yes, I have been informed. Madame was always generous. She gave me a good sum every year as well as my wages. I am very grateful to Madame."

"Well," said Fournier, "we will take our leave. On the way out I will have another word with old Georges."

"Permit me to follow you in a little minute, my friend," said Poirot.

"As you wish."

Fournier departed.

Poirot roamed once more round the room, then sat down and fixed his eyes on Élise.

Under his scrutiny the Frenchwoman got slightly restive.

"Is there anything more Monsieur requires to know?"

"Mademoiselle Grandier," said Poirot, "do you know who murdered your mistress?"

"No, monsieur. Before the good God, I swear it."

She spoke very earnestly. Poirot looked at her searchingly, then bent his head.

"*Bien,*" he said. "I accept that. But knowledge is one thing, suspicion is another. Have you any idea—an idea only—who might have done such a thing?"

"I have no idea, monsieur. I have already said so to the agent of police."

"You might say one thing to him and another thing to me."

"Why do you say that, monsieur? Why should I do such a thing?"

"Because it is one thing to give information to the police and another thing to give it to a private individual."

"Yes," admitted Élise, "that is true."

A look of indecision came over her face. She seemed to be thinking. Watching her very closely, Poirot leaned forward and spoke:

"Shall I tell you something, Mademoiselle Grandier? It is part of my business to believe nothing I am told—nothing, that is, that is not proved. I do not suspect first this person and then that person; I suspect everybody. Anybody connected with a crime is regarded by me as a criminal until that person is proved innocent."

Élise Grandier scowled at him angrily.

"Are you saying that you suspect me—me—of having murdered Madame? It is too strong, that! Such a thought is of a wickedness unbelievable!"

Her large bosom rose and fell tumultuously.

"No, Élise," said Poirot, "I do not suspect you of having murdered Madame. Whoever murdered Madame was a passenger in the aeroplane. Therefore, it was not your hand that did the deed. But you might have been an accomplice before the act. You might have passed on to someone the details of Madame's journey."

"I did not. I swear I did not."

Poirot looked at her again for some minutes in silence. Then he nodded his head.

"I believe you," he said. "But, nevertheless, there is something that you conceal. . . . Oh, yes, there is! Listen, I will tell you something. In every case of a criminal nature one comes across the same phenomena when questioning witnesses. Everyone keeps something back. Sometimes—often, indeed—it is something quite harmless, something, perhaps, quite unconnected with the crime, but—I say it again—there is always something. That is so with you. Oh, do not deny! I am Hercule Poirot and I know. When my friend Monsieur Fournier asked you if you were sure there was nothing you had omitted to mention, you were troubled. You answered, unconsciously, with an evasion. Again just now when I suggested that you might tell me something which you would not care to tell the police, you very obviously turned the suggestion over in your mind. There is, then, something. I want to know what that something is."

"It is nothing of importance."

"Possibly not. But all the same, will you not tell me what it is? Remember," he went on as she hesitated, "I am not of the police."

"That is true," said Élise Grandier. She hesitated, and went on: "Monsieur, I am in a difficulty. I do not know what Madame herself would have wanted me to do."

"There is a saying that two heads are better than one. Will you not consult me? Let us examine the question together."

The woman still looked at him doubtfully. He said with a smile:

"You are a good watch dog, Élise. It is a question, I see, of loyalty to your dead mistress?"

"That is quite right, monsieur. Madame trusted me. Ever since I entered her service I have carried out her instructions faithfully."

"You were grateful, were you not, for some great service she had rendered you?"

"Monsieur is very quick. Yes, that is true. I do not mind admitting it. I had been deceived, monsieur, my savings stolen, and there was a child. Madame was good to me. She arranged for the baby to be brought up by some good people on a farm—a good farm, monsieur, and honest people. It was then, at that time, that she mentioned to me that she, too, was a mother."

"Did she tell you the age of her child, where it was, any details?"

"No, monsieur; she spoke as of a part of her life that was over and done with. It was best so, she said. The little girl was well provided for and would be brought up to a trade or profession. It would also inherit her money when she died."

"She told you nothing further about this child or about its father?"

"No, monsieur, but I have an idea—"

"Speak, Mademoiselle Élise."

"It is an idea only, you understand."

"Perfectly, perfectly."

"I have an idea that the father of the child was an Englishman."

"What, exactly, do you think gave you that impression?"

"Nothing definite. It is just that there was a bitterness in Madame's voice when she spoke of the English. I think, too, that in her business transactions she enjoyed having anyone English in her power. It is an impression only."

"Yes, but it may be a very valuable one. It opens up possibilities. . . . Your own child, Mademoiselle Élise? Was it a girl or a boy?"

"A girl, monsieur. But she is dead—dead these five years now."

"Ah, all my sympathy."

There was a pause.

"And now, Mademoiselle Élise," said Poirot, "what is this something that you have hitherto refrained from mentioning?"

Élise rose and left the room. She returned a few minutes later with a small shabby black notebook in her hand.

"This little book was Madame's. It went with her everywhere. When she was about to depart for England, she could not find it. It was mislaid. After she had gone, I found it. It had dropped down behind the head of the bed. I put it in my room to keep until Madame should return. I burned the papers as soon as I heard of Madame's death, but I did not burn the book. There were no instructions as to that."

"When did you hear of Madame's death?"

Élise hesitated a minute.

"You heard it from the police, did you not?" said Poirot. "They came here and examined Madame's papers. They found the safe empty and you told them that you had burned the papers, but actually you did not burn the papers until afterwards."

"It is true, monsieur," admitted Élise. "Whilst they were looking in the safe, I removed the papers from the trunk. I said they were burned, yes. After all, it was very nearly the truth. I burned them at the first opportunity. I had to carry out Madame's orders. You see my difficulty, monsieur? You will not inform the police? It might be a very serious matter for me."

"I believe, Mademoiselle Élise, that you acted with the best intentions. All the same, you understand, it is a pity—a great pity. But it does no good to regret what is done and I see no necessity for communicating the exact hour of the destruction to the excellent Monsieur Fournier. Now let me see if there is anything in this little book to aid us."

"I do not think there will be, monsieur," said Élise, shaking her head. "It is Madame's private memorandums, yes, but there are numbers only. Without the documents and files, these entries are meaningless."

Unwillingly, she held out the book to Poirot. He took it and turned the pages. There were penciled entries in a sloping foreign writing. They seemed to be all of the same kind. A number followed by a few descriptive details such as:

CX 265. Colonel's wife. Stationed Syria. Regimental funds.
GF 342. French Deputy, Stavisky connection.

There were perhaps twenty entries in all. At the end of the book were penciled memoranda of dates or places such as:

Le Pinet, Monday. Casino, 10:30. Savoy Hotel, 5 o'clock. A. B. C. Fleet Street 11 o'clock.

None of these were complete in themselves, and seemed to have been put down less as actual appointments than as aids to Giselle's memory.

Élise was watching Poirot anxiously.

"It means nothing, monsieur, or so it seems to me. It was comprehensible to Madame, but not to a mere reader."

Poirot closed the book and put it in his pocket.

"This may be very valuable, mademoiselle. You did wisely to give it to me. And your conscience may be quite at rest. Madame never asked you to burn this book."

"That is true," said Élise, her face brightening a little.

"Therefore, having no instructions, it is your duty to hand this over to the police. I will arrange matters with Monsieur Fournier so that you shall not be blamed for not having done so sooner."

"Monsieur is very kind."

Poirot rose.

"I will go now and join my colleague. Just one last question: When you reserved a seat in the aeroplane for Madame Giselle, did you ring up the aerodrome at Le Bourget or the office of the company?"

"I rang up the office of Universal Air Lines, monsieur."

"And that, I think, is in the Boulevard des Capucines?"

"That is right, monsieur; Boulevard des Capucines."

Poirot made a note in his little book; then, with a friendly nod, he left the room.

11

FOURNIER was deep in conversation with old Georges. The detective was looking hot and annoyed.

"Just like the police," the old man was grumbling in his deep, hoarse voice. "Ask one the same question over and over again! What do they hope for? That sooner or later one will give over speaking the truth and take to lies instead? Agreeable lies, naturally; lies that suit the book of *ces messieurs.*"

"It is not lies I want but the truth."

"Very well, it is the truth that I have been telling you. Yes, a woman did come to see Madame the night before she left for England. You show me those photographs, you ask me if I recognize the woman among them. I tell you what I have told you all along—my eyesight is not good, it was growing dark, I did not look closely. I did not recognize the lady. If I saw her face to face I should probably not recognize her. There! You have it plainly for the fourth or fifth time."

"And you cannot even remember if she was tall or short, dark or fair, young or old? It is hardly to be believed, that."

Fournier spoke with irritable sarcasm.

"Then do not believe it. What do I care? A nice thing—to be mixed up with the police! I am ashamed. If Madame had not been killed high up in the air, you would probably pretend that I, Georges, had poisoned her. The police are like that."

Poirot forestalled an angry retort on Fournier's part by slipping a tactful arm through that of his friend.

"Come, *mon vieux*," he said. "The stomach calls. A simple but satisfying meal, that is what I prescribe. Let us say *omelette aux champignons, Sole à la Normande*, a cheese of Port Salut. And with it red wine. What wine exactly?"

Fournier glanced at his watch.

"True," he said. "It is one o'clock. Talking to this animal here—" He glared at Georges.

Poirot smiled encouragingly at the old man.

"It is understood," he said. "The nameless lady was neither tall nor short, fair nor dark, thin nor fat; but this at least you can tell us: Was she chic?"

"Chic?" said Georges, rather taken aback.

"I am answered," said Poirot. "She was chic. And I have a little idea, my friend, that she would look well in a bathing dress."

Georges stared at him.

"A bathing dress? What is this about a bathing dress?"

"A little idea of mine. A charming woman looks still more charming in a bathing dress. Do you not agree? See here?"

He passed to the old man a page torn from the *Sketch*.

There was a moment's pause. The old man gave a very slight start.

"You agree, do you not?" asked Poirot.

"They look well enough, those two," said the old man, handing the sheet back. "To wear nothing at all would be very nearly the same thing."

"Ah," said Poirot. "That is because nowadays we have discovered the beneficial action of sun on the skin. It is very convenient, that."

Georges condescended to give a hoarse chuckle and moved away as Poirot and Fournier stepped out into the sunlit street.

Over the meal as outlined by Poirot, the little Belgian produced the little black memorandum book.

Fournier was much excited, though distinctly irate with Élise. Poirot argued the point:

"It is natural—very natural. The police—it is always a word frightening to that class. It embroils them in they know not what. It is the same everywhere, in every country."

"That is where you score," said Fournier. "The private investigator gets more out of witnesses than you ever get through official channels. However, there is the other side of the picture. We have official records, the whole system of a big organization at our command."

"So let us work together amicably," said Poirot, smiling. . . . "This omelet is delicious."

In the interval between the omelet and the sole, Fournier turned the pages of the black book. Then he made a penciled entry in his notebook.

He looked across at Poirot.

"You have read through this? Yes?"

"No, I have only glanced at it. You permit?"

He took the book from Fournier.

When the cheese was placed before them, Poirot laid down the book on the table and the eyes of the two men met.

"There are certain entries," began Fournier.

"Five," said Poirot.

"I agree. Five."

He read out from the notebook:

"CL 52. English Peeress. Husband.

"RT 362. Doctor. Harley Street.

"MR 24. Forged Antiquities.

"XVB 724. English. Embezzlement.

"GF 45. Attempted Murder. English."

"Excellent, my friend," said Poirot. "Our minds march together to a marvel. Of all the entries in that little book, those five seem to me to be the only ones that can in any way bear a relation to the persons traveling in the aeroplane. Let us take them one by one."

"'English Peeress. Husband,'" said Fournier. "That may conceivably apply to Lady Horbury. She is, I understand, a confirmed gambler. Nothing could be more likely than that she should borrow money from Giselle. Giselle's clients are usually of that type. The word 'husband' may have one of two meanings. Either Giselle expected the husband to pay up his wife's debts or she had some hold over Lady Horbury, a secret which she threatened to reveal to the lady's husband."

"Precisely," said Poirot. "Either of those two alternatives might apply. I favor the second one myself, especially as I would be prepared to bet that the woman who visited Giselle the night before the aeroplane journey was Lady Horbury."

"Ah, you think that, do you?"

"Yes, and I fancy you think the same. There is a touch of chivalry, I think, in our concierge's disposition. His persistence in remembering nothing at all about the visitor seems rather significant. Lady Horbury is an extremely pretty woman. Moreover, I observed his start—oh, a very slight one—when I handed him a reproduction of her in bathing costume from the *Sketch*. Yes, it was Lady Horbury who went to Giselle's that night."

"She followed her to Paris from Le Pinet," said Fournier slowly. "It looks as though she were pretty desperate."

"Yes, yes, I fancy that may be true."

Fournier looked at him curiously.

"But it does not square with your private ideas, eh?"

"My friend, as I tell you, I have what I am convinced is the right clue pointing to the wrong person. I am very much in the dark. My clue cannot be wrong, and yet—"

"You wouldn't like to tell me what it is?" suggested Fournier.

"No, because I may, you see, be wrong. Totally and utterly wrong. And in that case I might lead you, too, astray. No, let us each work according to our own ideas. To continue with our selected items from the little book."

"'RT 362. Doctor. Harley Street,'" read out Fournier.

"A possible clue to Doctor Bryant. There is nothing much to go on, but we must not neglect that line of investigation."

"That, of course, will be the task of Inspector Japp."

"And mine," said Poirot. "I, too, have my finger in this pie."

"'MR 24. Forged Antiquities,'" read Fournier. "Far-fetched, perhaps, but it is just possible that that might apply to the Duponts. I can hardly credit it. Monsieur Dupont is an archæologist of world-wide reputation. He bears the highest character."

"Which would facilitate matters very much for him," said Poirot. "Consider, my dear Fournier, how high has been the character, how lofty the sentiments, and how worthy of admiration the life of most swindlers of note—before they are found out!"

"True—only too true," agreed the Frenchman with a sigh.

"A high reputation," said Poirot, "is the first necessity of a swindler's stock in trade. An interesting thought. But let us return to our list."

"'XVB 724' is very ambiguous. 'English. Embezzlement.'"

"Not very helpful," agreed Poirot. "Who embezzles? A solicitor? A bank clerk? Anyone in a position of trust in a commercial firm. Hardly an author, a dentist or a doctor. Mr. James Ryder is the only representative of commerce. He may have embezzled money, he may have borrowed from Giselle to enable his theft to remain undetected. As to the last entry. 'GF 45. Attempted Murder. English.' That gives us a very wide field. Author, dentist, doctor, business man, steward, hairdresser's assistant, lady of birth and breeding—

any one of those might be GF 45. In fact, only the Duponts are exempt by reason of their nationality."

With a gesture he summoned the waiter and asked for the bill.

"And where next, my friend?" he inquired.

"To the Sûreté. They may have some news for me."

"Good. I will accompany you. Afterwards, I have a little investigation of my own to make in which, perhaps, you will assist me."

At the Sûreté, Poirot renewed acquaintance with the chief of the detective force, whom he had met some years previously in the course of one of his cases. Monsieur Gilles was very affable and polite.

"Enchanted to learn that you are interesting yourself in this case, Monsieur Poirot."

"My faith, my dear Monsieur Gilles, it happened under my nose. It is an insult, that, you agree? Hercule Poirot, to sleep while murder is committed!"

Monsieur Gilles shook his head tactfully.

"These machines! On a day of bad weather, they are far from steady—far from steady. I myself have felt seriously incommoded once or twice."

"They say that an army marches on its stomach," said Poirot. "But how much are the delicate convolutions of the brain influenced by the digestive apparatus? When the *mal de mer* seizes me, I, Hercule Poirot, am a creature with no gray cells, no order, no method—a mere member of the human race somewhat below average intelligence! It is deplorable, but there it is! And talking of these matters, how is my excellent friend Giraud?"

Prudently ignoring the significance of the words "these matters," Monsieur Gilles replied that Giraud continued to advance in his career.

"He is most zealous. His energy is untiring."

"It always was," said Poirot. "He ran to and fro. He crawled on all fours. He was here, there and everywhere. Not for one moment did he ever pause and reflect."

"Ah, Monsieur Poirot, that is your little foible. A man like Fournier will be more to your mind. He is of the newest school—all for the psychology. That should please you."

"It does. It does."

"He has a very good knowledge of English. That is why we sent him to Croydon to assist in this case. A very interesting case, Monsieur Poirot. Madame Giselle was one of the best-known characters in Paris. And the manner of her death, extraordinary! A poisoned dart from a blowpipe in an aeroplane. I ask you! Is it possible that such a thing could happen?"

"Exactly!" cried Poirot. "Exactly! You hit the nail upon the head. You place a finger unerringly— Ah, here is our good Fournier. You have news, I see."

The melancholy-faced Fournier was looking quite eager and excited.

"Yes, indeed. A Greek antique dealer, Zeropoulos, has reported the sale of a blowpipe and darts three days before the murder. I propose now, monsieur"—he bowed respectfully to his chief—"to interview this man."

"By all means," said Gilles. "Does Monsieur Poirot accompany you?"

"If you please," said Poirot. "This is interesting. Very interesting."

The shop of Monsieur Zeropoulos was in the Rue St. Honoré. It was by way of being a high-class antique dealer's shop. There was a good deal of Rhages ware and other Persian pottery. There were one or two bronzes from Luristan, a good deal of inferior Indian jewelry, shelves of silks and embroideries from many countries, and a large proportion of perfectly worthless beads and cheap Egyptian goods. It was the kind of establishment in which you could spend a million francs on an object worth half a million, or ten francs on an object worth fifty centimes. It was patronized chiefly by tourists and knowledgeable connoisseurs.

Monsieur Zeropoulos himself was a short stout little man with beady black eyes. He talked volubly and at great length.

The gentlemen were from the police? He was delighted to see them. Perhaps they would step into his private office. Yes, he had sold a blowpipe and darts—a South American curio. "You comprehend, gentlemen, me, I sell a little of everything! I have my specialties. Persia is my specialty. Monsieur Dupont—the esteemed Monsieur Dupont—he will answer for me. He himself comes always to see my collection, to see what new purchases I have made, to give his judgment on the genuineness of certain doubtful pieces. What a man! So learned! Such an eye! Such a feel! But I wander from the point. I have my collection—my valuable collection that all connoisseurs know—and also I have— Well, frankly, messieurs, let us call it junk! Foreign junk, that is understood; a little bit of everything—from the South Seas, from India, from Japan, from Borneo. No matter! Usually I have no fixed price for these things. If anyone takes an interest, I make my estimate and I ask a price, and naturally I am beaten down and in the end I take only half. And even then—I will admit it—the profit is good! These articles, I buy them from sailors, usually at a very low price."

Monsieur Zeropoulos took a breath and went on happily, delighted with himself, his importance and the easy flow of his narration.

"This blowpipe and darts, I have had it for a long time—two years perhaps. It was in that tray there, with a cowrie necklace and a red Indian headdress and one or two crude wooden idols and some inferior jade beads. Nobody remarks it, nobody notices it, till there comes this American and asks me what it is."

"An American?" said Fournier sharply.

"Yes, yes, an American—unmistakably an American—not the best type of American either. The kind that knows nothing about anything and just wants a curio to take home. He is of the type that makes the fortune of bead sellers in Egypt—that buys the most preposterous scarabs ever made in Czechoslovakia. Well, very quickly I size him up. I tell him about the habits of certain tribes, the deadly poisons they use. I explain how very rare and unusual it is that anything of this kind comes into the market. He asks the price and I tell him. It is my American price, not quite so high as formerly. . . . Alas! They have had the depression over there! . . . I wait for him to bargain, but straightaway he pays my price. I am stupefied. It is a pity. I might have asked more! I give him the blowpipe and the darts wrapped up in a parcel and he takes them away. It is finished. But afterwards, when I read in the paper of this astounding murder, I wonder—yes, I wonder very much. And I communicate with the police."

"We are much obliged to you, Monsieur Zeropoulos," said Fournier politely. "This blowpipe and dart—you think you would be able to identify them? At the moment they are in London, you understand, but an opportunity will be given you of identifying them."

"The blowpipe was about so long"—Monsieur Zeropoulos measured a space on his desk. "And so thick—you see, like this pen of mine. It was of a light color. There were four darts. They were long pointed thorns, slightly discolored at the tips, with a little fluff of red silk on them."

"Red silk?" asked Poirot keenly.

"Yes, monsieur. A cerise red, somewhat faded."

"That is curious," said Fournier. "You are sure that there was not one of them with a black-and-orange fluff of silk?"

"Black and orange? No, monsieur."

The dealer shook his head.

Fournier glanced at Poirot. There was a curious satisfied smile on the little man's face.

Fournier wondered why. Was it because Zeropoulos was lying? Or was it for some other reason?

Fournier said doubtfully: "It is very possible that this blowpipe and dart have nothing whatever to do with the case. It is just one chance in fifty, perhaps. Nevertheless, I should like as full a description as possible of this American."

Zeropoulos spread out a pair of Oriental hands.

"He was just an American. His voice was in his nose. He could not speak French. He was chewing the gum. He had tortoise-shell glasses. He was tall and, I think, not very old."

"Fair or dark?"

"I could hardly say. He had his hat on."

"Would you know him again if you saw him?"

Zeropoulos seemed doubtful.

"I could not say. So many Americans come and go. He was not remarkable in any way."

Fournier showed him the collection of snapshots, but without avail. None of them, Zeropoulos thought, was the man.

"Probably a wild-goose chase," said Fournier as they left the shop.

"It is possible, yes," agreed Poirot. "But I do not think so. The price tickets were of the same shape and there are one or two points of interest about the story and about Monsieur Zeropoulos' remarks. And now, my friend, having been upon one wild-goose chase, indulge me and come upon another."

"Where to?"

"To the Boulevard des Capucines."

"Let me see. That is—"

"The office of Universal Air Lines."

"Of course. But we have already made perfunctory inquiries there. They could tell us nothing of interest."

Poirot tapped him kindly on the shoulder.

"Ah, but, you see, an answer depends on the questions. You did not know what questions to ask."

"And you do?"

"Well, I have a certain little idea."

He would say no more and in due course they arrived at the Boulevard des Capucines.

The office of Universal Air Lines was quite small. A smart-looking dark man was behind a highly polished wooden counter and a boy of about fifteen was sitting at a typewriter.

Fournier produced his credentials and the man, whose name was Jules Perrot, declared himself to be entirely at their service.

At Poirot's suggestion, the typewriting boy was dispatched to the farthest corner.

"It is very confidential, what we have to say," he explained.

Jules Perrot looked pleasantly excited.

"Yes, messieurs?"

"It is this matter of the murder of Madame Giselle."

"Ah, yes, I recollect. I think I have already answered some questions on the subject."

"Precisely. Precisely. But it is necessary to have the facts very exactly. Now, Madame Giselle reserved her place—when?"

"I think that point has already been settled. She booked her seat by telephone on the seventeenth."

"That was for the twelve-o'clock service on the following day?"

"Yes, monsieur."

"But I understand from her maid that it was on the eight forty-five A.M. service that Madame reserved a seat?"

"No, no; at least this is what happened. Madame's maid asked for the eight forty-five service, but that service was already booked up, so we gave her a seat on the twelve o'clock instead."

"Ah, I see. I see."

"Yes, monsieur."

"I see. I see. But all the same, it is curious. Decidedly, it is curious."

The clerk looked at him inquiringly.

"It is only that a friend of mine, deciding to go to England at a moment's notice, went to England on the eight forty-five service that morning, and the plane was half empty."

Monsieur Perrot turned over some papers. He blew his nose.

"Possibly, your friend has mistaken the day. The day before or the day after—"

"Not at all. It was the day of the murder, because my friend said that if he had missed that plane, as he nearly did, he would have actually been one of the passengers in the 'Prometheus.'"

"Ah, indeed. Yes, very curious. Of course, sometimes people do not arrive at the last minute, and then, naturally, there are vacant places. And then sometimes there are mistakes. I have to get in touch with Le Bourget; they are not always accurate."

The mild inquiring gaze of Hercule Poirot seemed to be upsetting to Jules Perrot. He came to a stop. His eyes shifted. A little bead of perspiration came out on his forehead.

"Two quite possible explanations," said Poirot. "But somehow, I fancy, not the true explanation. Don't you think it might perhaps be better to make a clean breast of the matter?"

"A clean breast of what? I don't understand you."

"Come, come. You understand me very well. This is a case of murder—murder, Monsieur Perrot. Remember that, if you please. If you withhold information, it may be very serious for you—very serious indeed. The police will take a very grave view. You are obstructing the ends of justice."

Jules Perrot stared at him. His mouth fell open. His hands shook.

"Come," said Poirot. His voice was authoritative, autocratic. "We want precise information, if you please. How much were you paid, and who paid you?"

"I meant no harm—I had no idea—I never guessed—"

"How much? And who by?"

"F-five thousand francs. I never saw the man before. I—this will ruin me."

"What will ruin you is not to speak out. Come now, we know the worst. Tell us exactly how it happened."

The perspiration rolling down his forehead, Jules Perrot spoke rapidly, in little jerks:

"I meant no harm. Upon my honor, I meant no harm. A man came in. He said he was going to England on the following day. He wanted to negotiate a loan from—from Madame Giselle. But he wanted their meeting to be unpremeditated. He said it would give him a better chance. He said that he knew she was going to England on the following day. All I had to do was to tell her the early service was full up and to give her Seat Number Two in the 'Prometheus.' I swear, messieurs, that I saw nothing very wrong in that. What difference could it make?—that is what I thought. Americans are like that—they do business in unconventional ways."

"Americans?" said Fournier sharply.

"Yes, this monsieur was an American."

"Describe him."

"He was tall, stooped, had gray hair, horn-rimmed glasses and a little goatee beard."

"Did he book a seat himself?"

"Yes, monsieur. Seat Number One. Next to—to the one I was to keep for Madame Giselle."

"In what name?"

"Silas—Silas Harper."

Poirot shook his head gently.

"There was no one of that name traveling, and no one occupied Seat Number One."

"I saw by the paper that there was no one of that name. That is why I thought there was no need to mention the matter. Since this man did not go by the plane—"

Fournier shot him a cold glance.

"You have withheld valuable information from the police," he said. "This is a very serious matter."

Together, he and Poirot left the office, leaving Jules Perrot staring after them with a frightened face.

On the pavement outside, Fournier removed his hat and bowed.

"I salute you, Monsieur Poirot. What gave you this idea?"

"Two separate sentences. One this morning when I heard a man in our plane say that he had crossed on the morning of the murder in a nearly empty plane. The second sentence was that uttered by Élise when she said that she had rung up the office of Universal Air Lines and that there was no room on the early-morning service. Now, those two statements did not agree. I remembered the steward on the 'Prometheus' saying that he had seen Madame Giselle before on the early service; so it was clearly her custom to go by the eight forty-five A.M. plane.

"But somebody wanted her to go on the twelve o'clock—somebody was already traveling by the 'Prometheus.' Why did the clerk say that the early service was booked up? A mistake? Or a deliberate lie? I fancied the latter. I was right."

"Every minute this case gets more puzzling!" cried Fournier. "First we seem to be on the track of a woman. Now it is a man. This American—"

He stopped and looked at Poirot.

The latter nodded gently.

"Yes, my friend," he said. "It is so easy to be an American here in Paris! A nasal voice, the chewing gum, the little goatee, the horn-rimmed spectacles—all the appurtenances of the stage American."

He took from his pocket the page he had torn from the *Sketch.*

"What are you looking at?"

"At a countess in her bathing suit."

"You think— But no, she is petite, charming, fragile; she could not impersonate a tall stooping American. She has been an actress, yes, but to act such a part is out of the question. No, my friend, that idea will not do."

"I never said it would," said Hercule Poirot.

And still he looked earnestly at the printed page.

12

LORD HORBURY stood by the sideboard and helped himself absent-mindedly to kidneys.

Stephen Horbury was twenty-seven years of age. He had a narrow head and a long chin. He looked very much what he was—a sporting, out-of-door kind of man without anything very spectacular in the way of brains. He was kind-hearted, slightly priggish, intensely loyal and invincibly obstinate.

He took his heaped plate back to the table and began to eat. Presently he opened a newspaper, but immediately, with a frown, he cast it aside. He thrust aside his unfinished plate, drank some coffee and rose to his feet. He paused uncertainly for a minute, then, with a slight nod of the head, he left the dining room, crossed the wide hall and went upstairs. He tapped at a door and waited for a minute. From inside the room a clear high voice cried out, "Come in!"

Lord Horbury went in.

It was a wide beautiful bedroom facing south. Cicely Horbury was in bed—a great carved-oak Elizabethan bed. Very lovely she looked, too, in her rose-chiffon draperies, with the curling gold of her hair. A breakfast tray with the remains of orange juice and coffee on it was on a table beside her. She was opening her letters. Her maid was moving about the room.

Any man might be excused if his breath came a little faster when confronted by so much loveliness, but the charming picture his wife presented affected Lord Horbury not at all.

There had been a time, three years ago, when the breath-taking loveliness of his Cicely had set the young man's senses reeling. He had been madly, wildly, passionately in love. All that was over. He had been mad. He was now sane.

Lady Horbury said in some surprise:

"Why, Stephen?"

He said abruptly, "I'd like to talk to you alone."

"Madeleine," Lady Horbury spoke to her maid. "Leave all that. Get out."

The French girl murmured: "*Très bien*, m'lady," shot a quick interested look out of the corner of her eye at Lord Horbury and left the room.

Lord Horbury waited till she had shut the door, then he said:

"I'd like to know, Cicely, just exactly what is behind this idea of coming down here?"

Lady Horbury shrugged her slender beautiful shoulders.

"After all, why not?"

"Why not? It seems to me there are a good many reasons."

His wife murmured: "Oh, reasons."

"Yes, reasons. You'll remember that we agreed that as things were between us, it would be as well to give up this farce of living together. You were to have the town house and a generous—an extremely generous—allowance. Within certain limits, you were to go your own way. Why this sudden return?"

Again Cicely shrugged her shoulders.

"I thought it better."

"You mean, I suppose, that it's money?"

Lady Horbury said: "How I hate you! You're the meanest man alive."

"Mean! Mean, you say, when it's because of you and your senseless extravagance that there's a mortgage on Horbury."

"Horbury—Horbury—that's all you care for! Horses and hunting and shooting and crops and tiresome old farmers. What a life for a woman!"

"Some women enjoy it."

"Yes, women like Venetia Kerr, who's half a horse herself. You ought to have married a woman like that."

Lord Horbury walked over to the window.

"It's a little late to say that. I married you."

"And you can't get out of it," said Cicely. Her laugh was malicious, triumphant. "You'd like to get rid of me, but you can't."

He said, "Need we go into all this?"

"Very much God and the old school, aren't you? Most of my friends fairly laugh their heads off when I tell them the kind of things you say."

"They are quite welcome to do so. Shall we get back to our original subject of discussion? Your reason for coming here."

But his wife would not follow his lead. She said:

"You advertised in the papers that you wouldn't be responsible for my debts. Do you call that a gentlemanly thing to do?"

"I regret having had to take that step. I warned you, you will remember. Twice I paid up. But there are limits. Your insensate passion for gambling—well, why discuss it? But I do want to know what prompted you to come down to Horbury? You've always hated the place, been bored to death here."

Cicely Horbury, her small face sullen, said, "I thought it better just now."

"Better just now?" He repeated the words thoughtfully. Then he asked a question sharply: "Cicely, had you been borrowing from that old French moneylender?"

"Which one? I don't know what you mean."

"You know perfectly what I mean. I mean the woman who was murdered on the plane from Paris—the plane on which you traveled home. Had you borrowed money from her?"

"No, of course not. What an idea!"

"Now don't be a little fool over this, Cicely. If that woman did lend you money, you'd better tell me about it. Remember, the business isn't over and finished with. The verdict at the inquest was willful murder by a person or persons unknown. The police of both countries are at work. It's only a matter of time before they come on the truth. The woman's sure to have left records of her dealings. If anything crops up to connect you with her, we should be prepared beforehand. We must have Ffoulkes' advice on the matter."

Ffoulkes, Ffoulkes, Wilbraham & Ffoulkes were the family solicitors, who, for generations, had dealt with the Horbury estate.

"Didn't I give evidence in that damned court and say I had never heard of the woman?"

"I don't think that proves very much," said her husband dryly. "If you did have dealings with this Giselle, you can be sure the police will find it out."

Cicely sat up angrily in bed.

"Perhaps you think I killed her. Stood up there in that plane and puffed darts at her from a blowpipe. Of all the crazy businesses!"

"The whole thing sounds mad," Stephen agreed thoughtfully. "But I do want you to realize your position."

"What position? There isn't any position. You don't believe a word I say. It's damnable. And why be so anxious about me all of a sudden? A lot you care about what happens to me. You dislike me. You hate me. You'd be glad if I died tomorrow. Why pretend?"

"Aren't you exaggerating a little? In any case, old-fashioned though you think me, I do happen to care about my family name. An out-of-date sentiment which you will probably despise. But there it is."

Turning abruptly on his heel, he left the room.

A pulse was beating in his temple. Thoughts followed each other rapidly through his head:

"Dislike? Hate? Yes, that's true enough. Should I be glad if she died tomorrow? I'd feel like a man who's been let out of prison. . . . What a queer beastly business life is! When I first saw her—in *Do It Now*—what a child, what an adorable child she looked! So fair and so lovely. . . . Young fool! I was mad about her—crazy. She seemed everything that was adorable and sweet. And all the time she was what she is now—vulgar, vicious, spiteful, empty-headed. . . . I can't even see her loveliness now."

He whistled and a spaniel came running to him, looking up at him with adoring sentimental eyes.

He said, "Good old Betsy," and fondled the long fringed ears.

Cramming an old fishing hat on his head, he left the house accompanied by the dog.

This aimless saunter of his round the estate began gradually to soothe his jangled nerves. He stroked the neck of his favorite hunter, had a word with the groom, then he went to the home farm and had a chat with the farmer's wife. He was walking along a narrow lane, Betsy at his heels, when he met Venetia Kerr on her bay mare.

Venetia looked her best upon a horse. Lord Horbury looked up at her with admiration, fondness and a queer sense of home-coming.

He said, "Hullo, Venetia."

"Hullo, Stephen."

"Where've you been? Out in the five acre?"

"Yes, she's coming along nicely, isn't she?"

"First rate. Have you seen that two-year-old of mine I bought at Chattisley's sale?"

They talked horses for some minutes. Then he said:

"By the way, Cicely's here."

"Here, at Horbury?"

It was against Venetia's code to show surprise, but she could not quite keep the undertone of it out of her voice.

"Yes. Turned up last night."

There was a silence between them. Then Stephen said:

"You were at that inquest, Venetia. How—how—er—did it go?"

She considered a moment.

"Well, nobody was saying very much, if you know what I mean."

"Police weren't giving anything away?"

"No."

Stephen said, "Must have been rather an unpleasant business for you."

"Well, I didn't exactly enjoy it. But it wasn't too devastating. The coroner was quite decent."

Stephen slashed absent-mindedly at the hedge.

"I say, Venetia, any idea—have you, I mean—as to who did it?"

Venetia Kerr shook her head slowly.

"No." She paused a minute, seeking how best and most tactfully to put into words what she wanted to say. She achieved it at last with a little laugh: "Anyway, it wasn't Cicely or me. That I do know. She'd have spotted me and I'd have spotted her."

Stephen laughed too.

"That's all right then," he said cheerfully.

He passed it off as a joke, but she heard the relief in his voice. So he had been thinking—

She switched her thoughts away.

"Venetia," said Stephen, "I've known you a long time, haven't I?"

"H'm, yes. Do you remember those awful dancing classes we used to go to as children?"

"Do I not? I feel I can say things to you—"

"Of course you can." She hesitated, then went on in a calm matter-of-fact tone: "It's Cicely, I suppose?"

"Yes. Look here, Venetia. Was Cicely mixed up with this woman Giselle in any way?"

Venetia answered slowly, "I don't know. I've been in the south of France, remember. I haven't heard the Le Pinet gossip yet."

"What do you think?"

"Well, candidly, I shouldn't be surprised."

Stephen nodded thoughtfully. Venetia said gently:

"Need it worry you? I mean, you live pretty semi-detached lives, don't you? This business is her affair, not yours."

"As long as she's my wife it's bound to be my business too."

"Can you—er—agree to a divorce?"

"A trumped-up business, you mean? I doubt if she'd accept it."

"Would you divorce her if you had the chance?"

"If I had cause I certainly would." He spoke grimly.

"I suppose," said Venetia thoughtfully, "she knows that."

"Yes."

They were both silent. Venetia thought: "She has the morals of a cat! I know that well enough. But she's careful. She's shrewd as they make 'em." Aloud she said: "So there's nothing doing?"

He shook his head. Then he said:

"If I were free, Venetia, would you marry me?"

Looking very straight between her horse's ears, Venetia said in a voice carefully devoid of emotion:

"I suppose I would."

Stephen! She'd always loved Stephen—always since the old days of dancing classes and cubbing and bird's-nesting. And Stephen had been fond of her, but not fond enough to prevent him from falling desperately, wildly, madly in love with a clever calculating cat of a chorus girl.

Stephen said, "We could have a marvelous life together."

Pictures floated before his eyes—hunting, tea and muffins, the smell of wet earth and leaves, children. All the things that Cicely could never share with him, that Cicely would never give him. A kind of mist came over his eyes. Then he heard Venetia speaking, still in that flat, emotionless voice:

"Stephen, if you care, what about it? If we went off together, Cicely would have to divorce you."

He interrupted her fiercely:

"Do you think I'd let you do a thing like that?"

"I shouldn't care."

"I should."

He spoke with finality.

Venetia thought: "That's that. It's a pity, really. He's hopelessly prejudiced, but rather a dear. I wouldn't like him to be different."

Aloud she said: "Well, Stephen, I'll be getting along."

She touched her horse gently with her heel. As she turned to wave a good-by to Stephen, their eyes met, and in that glance was all the feeling that their careful words had avoided.

As she rounded the corner of the lane, Venetia dropped her whip.

A man walking picked it up and returned it to her with an exaggerated bow.

"A foreigner," she thought as she thanked him. "I seem to remember his face." Half of her mind searched through the summer days at Juan les Pins while the other half thought of Stephen.

Only just as she reached home did memory suddenly pull her half-dreaming brain up with a jerk:

"The little man who gave me his seat in the aeroplane. They said at the inquest he was a detective."

And hard on that came another thought:

"What is he doing down here?"

13

JANE presented herself at Antoine's on the morning after the inquest with some trepidation of spirit.

The person who was usually regarded as Monsieur Antoine himself, and whose real name was Andrew Leech, greeted her with an ominous frown.

It was by now second nature to him to speak in broken English once within the portals of Bruton Street.

He upbraided Jane as a complete *imbécile*. Why did she wish to travel by air, anyway? What an idea! Her escapade would do his establishment infinite harm. Having vented his spleen to the full, Jane was permitted to escape, receiving as she did so a large-sized wink from her friend, Gladys.

Gladys was an ethereal blonde with a haughty demeanor and a faint, far-away professional voice. In private, her voice was hoarse and jocular.

"Don't you worry, dear," she said to Jane. "The old brute's sitting on the fence watching which way the cat will jump. And it's my belief it isn't going to jump the way he thinks it is. Ta-ta, dearie, here's my old devil coming in, damn her eyes. I suppose she'll be in seventeen tantrums, as usual. I hope she hasn't brought that lap dog with her."

A moment later Gladys' voice could be heard with its faint far-away notes:

"Good morning, madam. Not brought your sweet little Pekingese with you? Shall we get on with the shampoo, and then we'll be all ready for Monsieur Henri."

Jane had just entered the adjoining cubicle, where a henna-haired woman was sitting waiting, examining her face in the glass and saying to a friend:

"Darling, my face is really too frightful this morning; it really is."

The friend, who, in a bored manner, was turning over the pages of a three weeks' old *Sketch*, replied uninterestedly:

"Do you think so, my sweet? It seems to me much the same as usual."

On the entrance of Jane, the bored friend stopped her languid survey of the *Sketch* and subjected Jane to a piercing stare instead.

Then she said, "It is, darling. I'm sure of it."

"Good morning, madam," said Jane, with that airy brightness expected of her and which she could now produce quite mechanically and without any effort whatsoever. "It's quite a long time since we've seen you here. I expect you've been abroad."

"Antibes," said the henna-haired woman, who in her turn was staring at Jane with the frankest interest.

"How lovely," said Jane with false enthusiasm. "Let me see. Is it a shampoo and set, or are you having a tint today?"

Momentarily diverted from her scrutiny, the henna-haired woman leaned forward and examined her hair attentively.

"I think I could go another week. Heavens, what a fright I look!"

The friend said, "Well, darling, what can you expect at this time of the morning?"

Jane said: "Ah, wait until Monsieur Georges has finished with you."

"Tell me"—the woman resumed her stare—"are you the girl who gave evidence at the inquest yesterday? The girl who was in the aeroplane?"

"Yes, madam."

"How too terribly thrilling! Tell me about it."

Jane did her best to please:

"Well, madam, it was all rather dreadful, really." She plunged into narration, answering questions as they came. What had the old woman looked like? Was it true that there were two French detectives aboard and that the whole thing was mixed up with the French government scandals? Was Lady Horbury on board? Was she really as good-looking as everyone said? Who did she, Jane, think had actually done the murder? They said the whole thing was being hushed up for government reasons, and so on and so on.

This first ordeal was only a forerunner of many others, all on the same lines. Everyone wanted to be done by "the girl who was on the plane." Everyone was able to say to her friends, "My dear, positively too marvelous. The girl at my hairdresser's is the girl. . . . Yes, I should go there if I were you; they do your hair very well. . . . Jeanne, her name is—rather a little thing—big eyes. She'll tell you all about it if you ask her nicely."

By the end of the week Jane felt her nerves giving way under the strain. Sometimes she felt that if she had to go through the recital once again she would scream or attack her questioner with the dryer.

However, in the end she hit upon a better way of relieving her feelings. She approached Monsieur Antoine and boldly demanded a raise of salary.

"You ask that? You have the impudence? When it is only out of kindness of heart that I keep you here, after you have been mixed up in a murder case. Many men less kind-hearted than I would have dismissed you immediately."

"That's nonsense," said Jane coolly. "I'm a draw in this place, and you know it. If you want me to go, I'll go. I'll easily get what I want from Henri's or the Maison Richet."

"And who is to know you have gone there? Of what importance are you anyway?"

"I met one or two reporters at that inquest," said Jane. "One of them would give my change of establishment any publicity needed."

Because he feared that this was indeed so, grumblingly Monsieur Antoine agreed to Jane's demands. Gladys applauded her friend heartily.

"Good for you, dear," she said. "Old Andrew was no match for you that time. If a girl couldn't fend for herself a bit, I don't know where we'd all be. Grit, dear, that's what you've got, and I admire you for it."

"I can fight for my own hand all right," said Jane, her small chin lifting itself pugnaciously. "I've had to all my life."

"Hard lines, dear," said Gladys. "But keep your end up with old Andrew. He likes you all the better for it, really. Meekness doesn't pay in this life, but I don't think we're either of us troubled by too much of that."

Thereafter Jane's narrative, repeated daily with little variation, sank into the equivalent of a part played on the stage.

The promised dinner and theater with Norman Gale had duly come off. It was one of those enchanting evenings when every word and confidence exchanged seemed to reveal a bond of sympathy and shared tastes.

They liked dogs and disliked cats. They both hated oysters and loved smoked salmon. They liked Greta Garbo and disliked Katharine Hepburn. They didn't like fat women and admired really jet-black hair. They disliked very red nails. They disliked loud voices and noisy restaurants. They preferred busses to tubes.

It seemed almost miraculous that two people should have so many points of agreement.

One day at Antoine's, opening her bag, Jane let a letter from Norman fall out. As she picked it up with a slightly heightened color, Gladys pounced upon her:

"Who's your boy friend, dear?"

"I don't know what you mean," retorted Jane, her color rising.

"Don't tell me! I know that letter isn't from your mother's great-uncle. I wasn't born yesterday. Who is he, Jane?"

"It's someone—a man—that I met at Le Pinet. He's a dentist."

"A dentist," said Gladys with lively distaste. "I suppose he's got very white teeth and a smile."

Jane was forced to admit that this was indeed the case.

"He's got a very brown face and very blue eyes."

"Anyone can have a brown face," said Gladys. "It may be the seaside or it may be out of a bottle—two and eleven pence at the chemist's. Handsome Men are Slightly Bronzed. The eyes sound all right. But a dentist! Why, if he was going to kiss you, you'd feel he was going to say, 'Open a little wider, please.'"

"Don't be an idiot, Gladys."

"You needn't be so touchy, my dear. I see you've got it badly. . . . Yes, Mr. Henry, I'm just coming. . . . Drat Henry. Thinks he's God Almighty, the way he orders us girls about!"

The letter had been to suggest dinner on Saturday evening. At lunchtime on Saturday, when Jane received her augmented pay, she felt full of high spirits.

"And to think," said Jane to herself, "that I was worrying so that day coming over in the aeroplane. Everything's turned out beautifully. Life is really too marvelous."

So full of exuberance did she feel that she decided to be extravagant and lunch at the Corner House and enjoy the accompaniment of music to her food.

She seated herself at a table for four where there were already a middle-aged woman and a young man sitting. The middle-aged woman was just finishing her lunch. Presently she called for her bill, picked up a large collection of parcels and departed.

Jane, as was her custom, read a book as she ate. Looking up as she turned a page, she noticed the young man opposite her staring at her very intently, and at the same moment realized that his face was vaguely familiar to her.

Just as she made these discoveries, the young man caught her eye and bowed.

"Excuse me, mademoiselle. You do not recognize me?"

Jane looked at him more attentively. He had a fair boyish-looking face, attractive more by reason of its extreme mobility than because of any actual claim to good looks.

"We have not been introduced, it is true," went on the young man. "Unless you call murder an introduction and the fact that we both gave evidence in the coroner's court."

"Of course," said Jane. "How stupid of me! I thought I knew your face. You are—"

"Jean Dupont," said the man, and gave a funny, rather engaging little bow.

A remembrance flashed into Jane's mind of a dictum of Gladys', expressed perhaps without undue delicacy:

"If there's one fellow after you, there's sure to be another. Seems to be a law of Nature. Sometimes it's three or four."

Now, Jane had always led an austere hard-working life—rather like the description, after the disappearance, of girls who were missing—"She was a bright cheerful girl, with no men friends," and so on. Jane had been "a bright cheerful girl, with no men friends." Now it seemed that men friends were rolling up all round. There was no doubt about it; Jean Dupont's face as he leaned across the table held more than mere interested politeness. He was pleased to be sitting opposite Jane. He was more than pleased, he was delighted.

Jane thought to herself, with a touch of misgiving:

"He's French, though. You've got to look out with the French; they always say so."

"You're still in England, then," said Jane, and silently cursed herself for the extreme inanity of her remark.

"Yes. My father has been to Edinburgh to give a lecture there, and we have stayed with friends also. But now—tomorrow—we return to France."

"I see."

"The police, they have not made an arrest yet?" said Jean Dupont.

"No. There's not even been anything about it in the papers lately. Perhaps they've given it up."

Jean Dupont shook his head.

"No, no, they will not have given it up. They work silently"—he made an expressive gesture—"in the dark."

"Don't," said Jane uneasily. "You give me the creeps."

"Yes, it is not a very nice feeling—to have been so close when a murder was committed." He added: "And I was closer than you were. I was very close indeed. Sometimes I do not like to think of that."

"Who do you think did it?" asked Jane. "I've wondered and wondered."

Jean Dupont shrugged his shoulders.

"It was not I. She was far too ugly!"

"Well," said Jane, "I suppose you would rather kill an ugly woman than a good-looking one?"

"Not at all. If a woman is good-looking, you are fond of her; she treats you badly; she makes you jealous, mad with jealousy. 'Good,' you say, 'I will kill her. It will be a satisfaction.'"

"And is it a satisfaction?"

"That, mademoiselle, I do not know. Because I have not yet tried." He laughed, then shook his head. "But an ugly old woman like Giselle—who would want to bother to kill her?"

"Well, that's one way of looking at it," said Jane. She frowned. "It seems rather terrible, somehow, to think that perhaps she was young and pretty once."

"I know, I know." He became suddenly grave. "It is the great tragedy of life—that women grow old."

"You seem to think a lot about women and their looks," said Jane.

"Naturally. It is the most interesting subject possible. That seems strange to you because you are English. An Englishman thinks first of his work—his job, he calls it—and then of his sport, and last—a good way last—of his wife. Yes, yes, it is really so. Why, imagine, in a little hotel in Syria was an Englishman whose wife had been taken ill. He himself had to be somewhere in Iraq by a certain date. *Eh bien,* would you believe it, he left his wife and went on so as to be on duty in time? And both he and his wife thought that quite natural; they thought him noble, unselfish. But the doctor, who was not English, thought him a barbarian. A wife, a human being—that should come first. To do one's job—that is something much less important."

"I don't know," said Jane. "One's work has to come first, I suppose."

"But why? You see, you, too, have the same point of view. By doing one's work one obtains money; by indulging and looking after a woman one spends it; so the last is much more noble and ideal than the first."

Jane laughed.

"Oh, well," she said, "I think I'd rather be regarded as a mere luxury and self-indulgence than be regarded sternly as a first duty. I'd rather a man felt that he was enjoying himself looking after me than that he should feel I was a duty to be attended to."

"No one, mademoiselle, would be likely to feel that with you."

Jane blushed slightly at the earnestness of the young man's tone. He went on talking quickly:

"I have only been in England once before. It was very interesting to me the other day at the—inquest, you call it?—to study three young and charming women, all so different from one another."

"What did you think of us all?" asked Jane, amused.

"That Lady Horbury—bah, I know her type well. It is very exotic, very, very expensive—you see it sitting round the baccarat table— the soft face, the hard expression—and you know—you know so well what it will be like in, say, fifteen years. She lives for sensation, that one. For high play, perhaps for drugs. *Au fond*, she is uninteresting!"

"And Miss Kerr?"

"Ah, she is very, very English. She is the kind that any shopkeeper on the Riviera will give credit to—they are very discerning, our shop-keepers. Her clothes are very well cut, but rather like a man's. She walks about as though she owns the earth; she is not conceited about it; she is just an Englishwoman. She knows which department of England different people come from. It is true; I have heard ones like her in Egypt. 'What? The Etceteras are here? The Yorkshire Etceteras? Oh, the Shropshire Etceteras.'"

His mimicry was good. Jane laughed at the drawling, well-bred tones.

"And then, me," she said.

"And then you. And I say to myself, 'How nice, how very nice it would be if I were to see her again one day.' And here I am sitting opposite you. The gods arrange things very well sometimes."

Jane said: "You're an archæologist, aren't you? You dig up things."

And she listened with keen attention while Jean Dupont talked of his work.

Jane gave a little sigh at last.

"You've been in so many countries. You've seen so much. It all sounds so fascinating. And I shall never go anywhere or see anything."

"You would like that? To go abroad? To see wild parts of the earth? You would not be able to get your hair waved, remember."

"It waves by itself," said Jane, laughing.

She looked up at the clock and hastily summoned the waitress for her bill.

Jean Dupont said with a little embarrassment:

"Mademoiselle, I wonder if you would permit—as I have told you, I return to France tomorrow—if you would dine with me tonight."

"I'm so sorry. I can't. I'm dining with someone."

"Ah! I am sorry—very sorry. You will come again to Paris, soon?"

"I don't expect so."

"And me, I do not know when I shall be in London again! It is sad!"

He stood a moment, holding Jane's hand in his.

"I shall hope to see you again, very much," he said, and sounded as though he meant it.

14

AT about the time that Jane was leaving Antoine's, Norman Gale was saying in a hearty professional tone:

"Just a little tender, I'm afraid. Tell me if I hurt you."

His expert hand guided the electric drill.

"There. That's all over. . . . Miss Ross."

Miss Ross was immediately at his elbow, stirring a minute white concoction on a slab.

Norman Gale completed his filling and said:

"Let me see, it's next Tuesday you're coming for those others?"

His patient, rinsing her mouth ardently, burst into a fluent explanation: She was going away—so sorry—would have to cancel the next appointment. Yes, she would let him know when she got back.

And she escaped hurriedly from the room.

"Well," said Gale, "that's all for today."

Miss Ross said: "Lady Higginson rang up to say she must give up her appointment next week. She wouldn't make another. Oh, and Colonel Blunt can't come on Thursday."

Norman Gale nodded. His face hardened.

Every day was the same. People ringing up. Canceled appointments. All varieties of excuses—going away, going abroad, got a cold, may not be here.

It didn't matter what reason they gave. The real reason Norman had just seen quite unmistakably in his last patient's eye as he reached for the drill. A look of sudden panic.

He could have written down the woman's thoughts on paper:

"Oh, dear. Of course, he was in that aeroplane when that woman was murdered. . . . I wonder. . . . You do hear of people going off their heads and doing the most senseless crimes. It really isn't safe. The man might be a homicidal lunatic. They look the same as other people, I've always heard. I believe I always felt there was rather a peculiar look in his eye."

"Well," said Gale, "it looks like being a quiet week next week, Miss Ross."

"Yes, a lot of people have dropped out. Oh, well, you can do with a rest. You worked so hard earlier in the summer."

"It doesn't look as though I were going to have a chance of working very hard in the autumn, does it?"

Miss Ross did not reply. She was saved from having to do so by the telephone ringing. She went out of the room to answer it.

Norman dropped some instruments into the sterilizer, thinking hard.

"Let's see how we stand. No beating about the bush. This business has about done for me professionally. Funny. It's done well for Jane. People come on purpose to gape at her. Come to think of it, that's what's wrong here. They have to gape at me, and they don't like it! Nasty, helpless feeling you have in a dentist's chair. If the dentist were to run amuck—

"What a strange business murder is! You'd think it was a perfectly straight-forward issue, and it isn't. It affects all sorts of queer things you'd never think of. . . . Come back to facts. As a dentist, I seem to be about done for. . . . What would happen, I wonder, if they arrested the Horbury woman? Would my patients come trooping back? Hard to say. Once the rot's set in. . . . Oh, well, what does it matter? I don't care. Yes, I do, because of Jane. . . . Jane's adorable. I want her. And I can't have her yet. . . . A damnable nuisance."

He smiled.

"I feel it's going to be all right. She cares. She'll wait. . . . Damn it, I shall go to Canada—yes, that's it—and make money there."

He laughed to himself.

Miss Ross came back into the room.

"That was Mrs. Lorrie. She's sorry—"

"—but she may be going to Timbuctoo," finished Norman. *"Vive les rats!* You'd better look out for another post, Miss Ross. This seems to be a sinking ship."

"Oh, Mr. Gale, I shouldn't think of deserting you."

"Good girl. You're not a rat, anyway. But seriously, I mean it. If something doesn't happen to clear up this mess, I'm done for."

"Something ought to be done about it!" said Miss Ross with energy. "I think the police are disgraceful. They're not trying."

Norman laughed.

"I expect they're trying all right."

"Somebody ought to do something."

"Quite right. I've rather thought of trying to do something myself; though I don't quite know what."

"Oh, Mr. Gale, I should. You're so clever."

"I'm a hero to that girl all right," thought Norman Gale. "She'd like to help me in my sleuth stuff, but I've got another partner in view."

It was that same evening that he dined with Jane.

Half unconsciously he pretended to be in very high spirits, but Jane was too astute to be deceived. She noted his sudden moments of absent-mindedness, the little frown that showed between his brows, the sudden strained line of his mouth.

She said at last:

"Norman, are things going badly?"

He shot a quick glance at her, then looked away.

"Well, not too frightfully well. It's a bad time of year."

"Don't be idiotic," said Jane sharply.

"Jane!"

"I mean it. Don't you think I can see that you're worried to death?"

"I'm not worried to death. I'm just annoyed."

"You mean people are fighting shy—"

"Of having their teeth attended to by a possible murderer. Yes."

"How cruelly unfair!"

"It is, rather. Because, frankly, Jane, I'm a jolly good dentist. And I'm not a murderer."

"It's wicked. Somebody ought to do something."

"That's what my secretary, Miss Ross, said this morning."

"What's she like?"

"Miss Ross?"

"Yes."

"Oh, I don't know. Big, lots of bones, nose rather like a rocking horse, frightfully competent."

"She sounds quite nice," said Jane graciously.

Norman rightly took this as a tribute to his diplomacy. Miss Ross's bones were not really quite as formidable as stated and she had an extremely attractive head of red hair, but he felt, and rightly, that it was just as well not to dwell on the latter point to Jane.

"I'd like to do something," he said. "If I was a young man in a book, I'd find a clue or I'd shadow somebody."

Jane tugged suddenly at his sleeve.

"Look, there's Mr. Clancy—you know, the author. Sitting over there by the wall by himself. We might shadow him."

"But we were going to the flicks!"

"Never mind the flicks. I feel somehow this might be meant. You said you wanted to shadow somebody and here's somebody to shadow. You never know. We might find out something."

Jane's enthusiasm was infectious. Norman fell in with the plan readily enough.

"As you say, one never knows," he said. "Whereabouts has he got to in his dinner? I can't see properly without turning my head, and I don't want to stare."

"He's about level with us," said Jane. "We'd better hurry a bit and get ahead, and then we can pay the bill and be ready to leave when he does."

They adopted this plan. When at last little Mr. Clancy rose and passed out into Dean Street, Norman and Jane were fairly close on his heels.

"In case he takes a taxi," Jane explained.

But Mr. Clancy did not take a taxi. Carrying an overcoat over one arm, and occasionally allowing it to trail on the ground, he ambled gently through the London streets. His progress was somewhat erratic. Sometimes he moved forward at a brisk trot; sometimes he slowed down till he almost came to a stop. Once, on the very brink of crossing a road, he did come to a standstill, standing there with one foot hanging out over the curb and looking exactly like a slow-motion picture.

His direction, too, was erratic. Once he actually took so many right-angle turns that he traversed the same streets twice over.

Jane felt her spirits rise.

"You see?" she said excitedly. "He's afraid of being followed. He's trying to put us off the scent."

"Do you think so?"

"Of course. Nobody would go round in circles, otherwise."

"Oh!"

They had turned a corner rather quickly and had almost cannoned into their quarry. He was standing staring up at a butcher's shop. The shop itself was naturally closed, but it seemed to be something about the level of the first floor that was riveting Mr. Clancy's attention.

He said aloud:

"Perfect. The very thing. What a piece of luck!"

He took out a little book and wrote something down very carefully. Then he started off again at a brisk pace, humming a little tune.

He was now heading definitely for Bloomsbury. Sometimes, when he turned his head, the two behind could see his lips moving.

"There is something up," said Jane. "He's in great distress of mind. He's talking to himself and he doesn't know it."

As he waited to cross by some traffic lights, Norman and Jane drew abreast.

It was quite true: Mr. Clancy was talking to himself. His face looked white and strained. Norman and Jane caught a few muttered words:

"Why doesn't she speak? Why? There must be a reason."

The lights went green. As they reached the opposite pavement, Mr. Clancy said:

"I see now. Of course. That's why she's got to be silenced!"

Jane pinched Norman ferociously.

Mr. Clancy set off at a great pace now. The overcoat dragged hopelessly. With great strides the little author covered the ground, apparently oblivious of the two people on his track.

Finally, with disconcerting abruptness, he stopped at a house, opened the door with a key and went in.

Norman and Jane looked at each other.

"It's his own house," said Norman. "Forty-seven Cardington Square. That's the address he gave at the inquest."

"Oh, well," said Jane. "Perhaps he'll come out again by and by. And anyway, we have heard something. Somebody—a woman—is going to be silenced. And some other woman won't speak. Oh, dear, it sounds dreadfully like a detective story."

A voice came out of the darkness.

"Good evening," it said.

The owner of the voice stepped forward. A pair of magnificent mustaches showed in the lamplight.

"*Eh bien*," said Hercule Poirot. "A fine evening for the chase, is it not?"

15

Of the two startled young people, it was Norman Gale who recovered himself first.

"Of course," he said. "It's Monsieur—Monsieur Poirot. Are you still trying to clear your character, Monsieur Poirot?"

"Ah, you remember our little conversation? And it is the poor Mr. Clancy you suspect?"

"So do you," said Jane acutely, "or you wouldn't be here."

He looked at her thoughtfully for a moment.

"Have you ever thought about murder, mademoiselle? Thought about it, I mean, in the abstract—cold-bloodedly and dispassionately?"

"I don't think I've ever thought about it at all until just lately," said Jane.

Hercule Poirot nodded.

"Yes, you think about it now because a murder has touched you personally. But me, I have dealt with crime for many years now. I have my own way of regarding things. What should you say the most important thing was to bear in mind when you are trying to solve a murder?"

"Finding the murderer," said Jane.

Norman Gale said: "Justice."

Poirot shook his head.

"There are more important things than finding the murderer. And justice is a fine word, but it is sometimes difficult to say exactly what one means by it. In my opinion, the important thing is to clear the innocent."

"Oh, naturally," said Jane. "That goes without saying. If anyone is falsely accused—"

"Not even that. There may be no accusation. But until one person is proved guilty beyond any possible doubt, everyone else who is associated with the crime is liable to suffer in varying degrees."

Norman Gale said with emphasis:

"How true that is."

Jane said:

"Don't we know it!"

Poirot looked from one to the other.

"I see. Already you have been finding that out for yourselves."

He became suddenly brisk:

"Come now, I have affairs to see to. Since our aims are the same, we three, let us combine together? I am about to call upon our ingenious friend, Mr. Clancy. I would suggest that Mademoiselle accompanies me in the guise of my secretary. Here, mademoiselle, is a notebook and a pencil for the shorthand."

"I can't write shorthand," gasped Jane.

"But naturally not. But you have the quick wits, the intelligence. You can make plausible signs in pencil in the book, can you not? Good. As for Mr. Gale, I suggest that he meets us in, say, an hour's time. Shall we say upstairs at Monseigneur's? *Bon!* We will compare notes then."

And forthwith he advanced to the bell and pressed it.

Slightly dazed, Jane followed him, clutching the notebook.

Gale opened his mouth as though to protest, then seemed to think better of it.

"Right," he said. "In an hour. At Monseigneur's."

The door was opened by a rather forbidding-looking elderly woman attired in severe black.

Poirot said, "Mr. Clancy?"

She drew back and Poirot and Jane entered.

"What name, sir?"

"Mr. Hercule Poirot."

The severe woman led them upstairs and into a room on the first floor.

"Mr. Air Kule Prott," she announced.

Poirot realized at once the force of Mr. Clancy's announcement at Croydon to the effect that he was not a tidy man. The room, a long one with three windows along its length and shelves and bookcases on the other walls, was in a state of chaos. There were papers strewn about, cardboard files, bananas, bottles of beer, open books, sofa cushions, a trombone, miscellaneous china, etchings, and a bewildering assortment of fountain pens.

In the middle of this confusion, Mr. Clancy was struggling with a camera and a roll of films.

"Dear me," said Mr. Clancy, looking up as the visitors were announced. He put the camera down and the roll of films promptly fell on the floor and unwound itself. He came forward with outstretched hand. "Very glad to see you, I'm sure."

"You remember me, I hope," said Poirot. "This is my secretary, Miss Grey."

"How d'you do, Miss Grey." He shook her by the hand and then turned back to Poirot. "Yes, of course I remember you—at least—now, where was it exactly? Was it at the Skull and Crossbones Club?"

"We were fellow passengers on an aeroplane from Paris on a certain fatal occasion."

"Why, of course," said Mr. Clancy. "And Miss Grey too! Only I hadn't realized she was your secretary. In fact, I had some idea that she was in a beauty parlor—something of that kind."

Jane looked anxiously at Poirot.

The latter was quite equal to the situation.

"Perfectly correct," he said. "As an efficient secretary, Miss Grey has at times to undertake certain work of a temporary nature; you understand?"

"Of course," said Mr. Clancy. "I was forgetting. You're a detective —the real thing. Not Scotland Yard. Private investigation. . . . Do sit down, Miss Grey. . . . No, not there; I think there's orange juice on that chair. . . . If I shift this file. . . . Oh, dear, now everything's tumbled out. Never mind. . . . You sit here, Monsieur Poirot. . . . That's right, isn't it? Poirot? . . . The back's not really broken. It only creaks a little as you lean against it. Well, perhaps it's best not to lean too hard. . . . Yes, a private investigator like my Wilbraham Rice. The public have taken very strongly to Wilbraham Rice. He bites his nails and eats a lot of bananas. I don't know why I made him bite his nails, to start with; it's really rather disgusting, but there it is. He started by biting his nails and now he has to do it in every single book. So monotonous. The bananas aren't so bad; you get a bit of fun out of them—criminals slipping on the skin. I eat bananas myself—that's what put it into my head. But I don't bite my nails. . . . Have some beer?"

"I thank you, no."

Mr. Clancy sighed, sat down himself, and gazed earnestly at Poirot.

"I can guess what you've come about. The murder of Giselle. I've thought and thought about that case. You can say what you like; it's amazing—poisoned darts and a blowpipe in an aeroplane. An idea I have used myself, as I told you, both in book and short-story form. Of course it was a very shocking occurrence, but I must confess, Monsieur Poirot, that I was thrilled—positively thrilled."

"I can quite see," said Poirot, "that the crime must have appealed to you professionally, Mr. Clancy."

Mr. Clancy beamed.

"Exactly. You would think that anyone, even the official police, could have understood that! But not at all. Suspicion—that is all I got. Both from the inspector and at the inquest. I go out of my way to assist the course of justice and all I get for my pains is palpable thick-headed suspicion!"

"All the same," said Poirot, smiling, "it does not seem to affect you very much."

"Ah," said Mr. Clancy. "But, you see, I have my methods, Watson. If you'll excuse my calling you Watson. No offense intended. Interesting, by the way, how the technic of the idiot friend has hung on. Personally, I myself think the Sherlock Holmes stories greatly overrated. The fallacies—the really amazing fallacies—that there are in those stories— But what was I saying?"

"You said that you had your methods."

"Ah, yes." Mr. Clancy leaned forward. "I'm putting that inspector—what is his name? Japp? Yes, I'm putting him in my next book. You should see the way Wilbraham Rice deals with him."

"In between bananas, as one might say."

"In between bananas—that's very good, that." Mr. Clancy chuckled.

"You have a great advantage as a writer, monsieur," said Poirot. "You can relieve your feelings by the expedient of the printed word. You have the power of the pen over your enemies."

Mr. Clancy rocked gently back in his chair.

"You know," he said, "I begin to think this murder is going to be a really fortunate thing for me. I'm writing the whole thing exactly as it happened—only as fiction, of course, and I shall call it *The Air*

Mail Mystery. Perfect pen portraits of all the passengers. It ought to sell like wild fire, if only I can get it out in time."

"Won't you be had up for libel, or something?" asked Jane.

Mr. Clancy turned a beaming face upon her.

"No, no, my dear lady. Of course, if I were to make one of the passengers the murderer—well, then, I might be liable for damages. But that is the strong part of it all—an entirely unexpected solution is revealed in the last chapter."

Poirot leaned forward eagerly.

"And that solution is?"

Again Mr. Clancy chuckled.

"Ingenious," he said. "Ingenious and sensational. Disguised as the pilot, a girl gets into the plane at Le Bourget and successfully stows herself away under Madame Giselle's seat. She has with her an ampul of the newest gas. She releases this, everybody becomes unconscious for three minutes, she squirms out, fires the poisoned dart, and makes a parachute descent from the rear door of the car."

Both Jane and Poirot blinked.

Jane said: "Why doesn't she become unconscious from the gas too?"

"Respirator," said Mr. Clancy.

"And she descends into the Channel?"

"It needn't be the Channel. I shall make it the French coast."

"And anyway, nobody could hide under a seat; there wouldn't be room."

"There will be room in my aeroplane," said Mr. Clancy firmly.

"*Épatant*," said Poirot. "And the motive of the lady?"

"I haven't quite decided," said Mr. Clancy meditatively. "Probably Giselle ruined the girl's lover, who killed himself."

"And how did she get hold of the poison?"

"That's the really clever part," said Mr. Clancy. "The girl's a snake charmer. She extracts the stuff from her favorite python."

"*Mon Dieu!*" said Hercule Poirot.

He said:

"You don't think, perhaps, it is just a little sensational?"

"You can't write anything too sensational," said Mr. Clancy firmly. "Especially when you're dealing with the arrow poison of the South American Indians. I know it was snake juice really, but the principle is the same. After all, you don't want a detective story to be like real life? Look at the things in the papers—dull as ditch water."

"Come now, monsieur, would you say this little affair of ours is dull as ditch water?"

"No," admitted Mr. Clancy. "Sometimes, you know, I can't believe it really happened."

Poirot drew the creaking chair a little nearer to his host. His voice lowered itself confidentially:

"Mr. Clancy, you are a man of brains and imagination. The police, as you say, have regarded you with suspicion; they have not sought your advice. But I, Hercule Poirot, desire to consult you."

Mr. Clancy flushed with pleasure.

"I'm sure that's very nice of you."

He looked flustered and pleased.

"You have studied the criminology. Your ideas will be of value. It would be of great interest to me to know who, in your opinion, committed the crime."

"Well—" Mr. Clancy hesitated, reached automatically for a banana and began to eat it. Then, the animation dying out of his face, he shook his head. "You see, Monsieur Poirot, it's an entirely different thing. When you're writing you can make it anyone you like, but of course in real life there is a real person. You haven't any command over the facts. I'm afraid, you know, that I'd be absolutely no good as a real detective."

He shook his head sadly and threw the banana skin into the grate.

"It might be amusing, however, to consider the case together," suggested Poirot.

"Oh, that, yes."

"To begin with, supposing you had to make a sporting guess, who would you choose?"

"Oh, well, I suppose one of the two Frenchmen."

"Now, why?"

"Well, she was French. It seems more likely somehow. And they were sitting on the opposite side not too far away from her. But really I don't know."

"It depends," said Poirot thoughtfully, "so much on motive."

"Of course, of course. I suppose you tabulate all the motives very scientifically?"

"I am old-fashioned in my methods. I follow the old adage, 'Seek whom the crime benefits.'"

"That's all very well," said Mr. Clancy. "But I take it that's a little difficult in a case like this. There's a daughter who comes into money, so I've heard. But a lot of the people on board might benefit, for all we know—that is, if they owed her money and haven't got to pay it back."

"True," said Poirot. "And I can think of other solutions. Let us suppose that Madame Giselle knew of something—attempted murder, shall we say—on the part of one of those people."

"Attempted murder?" said Mr. Clancy. "Now why attempted murder? What a very curious suggestion."

"In cases such as these," said Poirot, "one must think of everything."

"Ah!" said Mr. Clancy. "But it's no good thinking. You've got to know."

"You have reason—you have reason. A very just observation."

Then he said:

"I ask your pardon, but this blowpipe that you bought—"

"Damn that blowpipe," said Mr. Clancy. "I wish I'd never mentioned it."

"You bought it, you say, at a shop in the Charing Cross Road? Do you, by any chance, remember the name of that shop?"

"Well," said Mr. Clancy, "it might have been Absolom's—or there's Mitchell & Smith. I don't know. But I've already told all this to that pestilential inspector. He must have checked up on it by this time."

"Ah!" said Poirot. "But I ask for quite another reason. I desire to purchase such a thing and make a little experiment."

"Oh, I see. But I don't know that you'll find one all the same. They don't keep sets of them, you know."

"All the same, I can try. . . . Perhaps, Miss Grey, you would be so obliging as to take down those two names?"

Jane opened her notebook and rapidly performed a series of—she hoped—professional-looking squiggles. Then she surreptitiously wrote the names in longhand on the reverse side of the sheet, in case these instructions of Poirot's should be genuine.

"And now," said Poirot, "I have trespassed on your time too long. I will take my departure with a thousand thanks for your amiability."

"Not at all. Not at all," said Mr. Clancy. "I wish you would have had a banana."

"You are most amiable."

"Not at all. As a matter of fact, I'm feeling rather happy tonight. I'd been held up in a short story I was writing—the thing wouldn't pan out properly, and I couldn't get a good name for the criminal. I wanted something with a flavor. Well, just a bit of luck I saw just the name I wanted over a butcher's shop. Pargiter. Just the name I was looking for. There's a sort of genuine sound to it—and about five minutes later I got the other thing. There's always the same snag in stories. Why won't the girl speak? The young man tries to make her and she says her lips are sealed. There's never any real reason, of course, why she shouldn't blurt out the whole thing at once, but you have to try and think of something that's not too definitely idiotic. Unfortunately, it has to be a different thing every time!"

He smiled gently at Jane.

"The trials of an author!"

He darted past her to a bookcase.

"One thing you must allow me to give you."

He came back with a book in his hand.

"*The Clue of the Scarlet Petal*. I think I mentioned at Croydon that that book of mine dealt with arrow poison and native darts."

"A thousand thanks. You are too amiable."

"Not at all. I see," said Mr. Clancy suddenly to Jane, "that you don't use the Pitman system of shorthand."

Jane flushed scarlet. Poirot came to her rescue:

"Miss Grey is very up-to-date. She uses the most recent system invented by a Czechoslovakian."

"You don't say so? What an amazing place Czechoslovakia must be. Everything seems to come from there—shoes, glass, gloves, and now a shorthand system. Quite amazing."

He shook hands with them both.

"I wish I could have been more helpful."

They left him in the littered room smiling wistfully after them.

16

FROM Mr. Clancy's house they took a taxi to the Monseigneur, where they found Norman Gale awaiting them.

Poirot ordered some consommé and a *chaud-froid* of chicken.

"Well," said Norman, "how did you get on?"

"Miss Grey," said Poirot, "has proved herself the super-secretary."

"I don't think I did so very well," said Jane. "He spotted my stuff when he passed behind me. You know, he must be very observant."

"Ah, you noticed that? This good Mr. Clancy is not quite so absent-minded as one might imagine."

"Did you really want those addresses?" asked Jane.

"I think they might be useful, yes."

"But if the police—"

"Ah, the police! I should not ask the same questions as the police have asked. Though, as a matter of fact, I doubt whether the police have asked any questions at all. You see, they know that the blow-pipe found in the plane was purchased in Paris by an American."

"In Paris? An American? But there wasn't any American in the aeroplane."

Poirot smiled kindly on her.

"Precisely. We have here an American just to make it more difficult. *Voilà tout.*"

"But it was bought by a man?" said Norman.

Poirot looked at him with rather an odd expression.

"Yes," he said, "it was bought by a man."

Norman looked puzzled.

"Anyway," said Jane, "it wasn't Mr. Clancy. He'd got one blowpipe already, so he wouldn't want to go about buying another."

Poirot nodded his head.

"That is how one must proceed. Suspect everyone in turn and then wipe him or her off the list."

"How many have you wiped off so far?" asked Jane.

"Not so many as you might think, mademoiselle," said Poirot with a twinkle. "It depends, you see, on the motive."

"Has there been—" Norman Gale stopped, and then added apologetically: "I don't want to butt in on official secrets, but is there no record of this woman's dealings?"

Poirot shook his head.

"All the records are burned."

"That's unfortunate."

"*Évidemment!* But it seems that Madame Giselle combined a little blackmailing with her profession of moneylending, and that opens up a wider field. Supposing, for instance, that Madame Giselle had knowledge of a certain criminal offense—say, attempted murder on the part of someone."

"Is there any reason to suppose such a thing?"

"Why, yes," said Poirot slowly, "there is. One of the few pieces of documentary evidence that we have in this case."

He looked from one to the other of their interested faces and gave a little sigh.

"Ah, well," he said. "That is that. Let us talk of other matters—for instance, of how this tragedy has affected the lives of you two young people."

"It sounds horrible to say so, but I've done well out of it," said Jane.

She related her rise of salary.

"As you say, mademoiselle, you have done well, but probably only for the time being. Even a nine days' wonder does not last longer than nine days, remember."

Jane laughed.

"That's very true."

"I'm afraid it's going to last more than nine days in my case," said Norman.

He explained the position. Poirot listened sympathetically.

"As you say," he observed thoughtfully, "it will take more than nine days, or nine weeks, or nine months. Sensationalism dies quickly, fear is long-lived."

"Do you think I ought to stick it out?"

"Have you any other plan?"

"Yes. Chuck up the whole thing. Go out to Canada or somewhere and start again."

"I'm sure that would be a pity," said Jane firmly.

Norman looked at her.

Poirot tactfully became engrossed with his chicken.

"I don't want to go," said Norman.

"If I discover who killed Madame Giselle, you will not have to go," said Poirot cheerfully.

"Do you really think you will?" asked Jane.

Poirot looked at her reproachfully.

"If one approaches a problem with order and method, there should be no difficulty in solving it; none whatever," said Poirot severely.

"Oh, I see," said Jane, who didn't.

"But I should solve this problem quicker if I had help," said Poirot.

"What kind of help?"

Poirot did not speak for a moment or two. Then he said:

"Help from Mr. Gale. And perhaps, later, help from you also."

"What can I do?" asked Norman.

Poirot shot a sideways glance at him.

"You will not like it," he said warningly.

"What is it?" repeated the young man impatiently.

Very delicately, so as not to offend English susceptibilities, Poirot used a toothpick. Then he said:

"Frankly, what I need is a blackmailer."

"A blackmailer?" exclaimed Norman. He stared at Poirot as a man does who cannot believe his ears.

Poirot nodded.

"Precisely," he said. "A blackmailer."

"But what for?"

"*Parbleu!* To blackmail."

"Yes, but I mean, who? Why?"

"Why," said Poirot, "is my business. As to who—" He paused for a moment, then went on in a calm businesslike tone:

"Here is the plan I will outline for you. You will write a note—that is to say, I will write a note and you will copy it—to the Countess of Horbury. You will mark it Personal. In the note you will ask for an interview. You will recall yourself to her memory as having traveled to England by air on a certain occasion. You will also refer to certain business dealings of Madame Giselle's having passed into your hands."

"And then?"

"And then you will be accorded an interview. You will go and you will say certain things—in which I will instruct you. You will ask for—let me see—ten thousand pounds."

"You're mad!"

"Not at all," said Poirot. "I am eccentric, possibly, but mad, no."

"And suppose Lady Horbury sends for the police. I shall go to prison."

"She will not send for the police."

"You can't know that."

"*Mon cher*, practically speaking, I know everything!"

"And anyway I don't like it."

"You will not get the ten thousand pounds—if that makes your conscience any clearer," said Poirot with a twinkle.

"Yes, but look here, Monsieur Poirot; this is the sort of wildcat scheme that might ruin me for life."

"Ta-ta-ta. The lady will not go to the police—that I assure you."

"She may tell her husband."

"She will not tell her husband."

"I don't like it."

"Do you like losing your patients and ruining your career?"

"No, but—"

Poirot smiled at him kindly.

"You have the natural repugnance, yes? That is very natural. You have, too, the chivalrous spirit. But I can assure you that Lady Horbury is not worth all this fine feeling; to use your idiom, she is a very nasty piece of goods."

"All the same, she can't be a murderess."

"Why?"

"Why? Because we should have seen her. Jane and I were sitting just opposite."

"You have too many preconceived ideas. Me, I desire to straighten things out, and to do that, I must know."

"I don't like the idea of blackmailing a woman."

"Ah, *mon Dieu,* what there is in a word! There will be no blackmail. You have only to produce a certain effect. After that, when the ground is prepared, I will step in."

Norman said:

"If you land me in prison—"

"No, no, no. I am very well known at Scotland Yard. If anything should occur, I will take the blame. But nothing will occur other than what I have prophesied."

Norman surrendered with a sigh.

"All right. I'll do it. But I don't half like it."

"Good. This is what you will write. Take a pencil."

He dictated slowly.

"*Voilà*," he said. "Later I will instruct you as to what you are to say. . . . Tell me, mademoiselle, do you ever go to the theater?"

"Yes, fairly often," said Jane.

"Good. Have you seen, for instance, a play called *Down Under?*"

"Yes. I saw it about a month ago. It's rather good."

"An American play, is it not?"

"Yes."

"Do you remember the part of Harry, played by Mr. Raymond Barraclough?"

"Yes. He was very good."

"You thought him attractive? Yes?"

"Frightfully attractive."

"Ah, *il est sex appeal?*"

"Decidedly," said Jane, laughing.

"Just that, or is he a good actor as well?"

"Oh, I think he acts well too."

"I must go and see him," said Poirot.

Jane stared at him, puzzled.

What an odd little man he was, hopping from subject to subject like a bird from one branch to another.

Perhaps he read her thoughts. He smiled.

"You do not approve of me, mademoiselle? Of my methods?"

"You jump about a good deal."

"Not really. I pursue my course logically, with order and method. One must not jump wildly to a conclusion. One must eliminate."

"Eliminate?" said Jane. "Is that what you're doing?" She thought a moment. "I see. You've eliminated Mr. Clancy."

"Perhaps," said Poirot.

"And you've eliminated us, and now you're going, perhaps, to eliminate Lady Horbury. . . . Oh!"

She stopped as a sudden thought struck her.

"What is it, mademoiselle?"

"That talk of attempted murder? Was that a test?"

"You are very quick, mademoiselle. Yes, that was part of the course I pursue. I mention attempted murder and I watch Mr. Clancy, I watch you, I watch Mr. Gale—and in neither of you three is there any sign, not so much as the flicker of an eyelash. And let me tell you that I could not be deceived on that point. A murderer can be ready to meet any attack that he foresees. But that entry in a little note-book could not have been known to any of you. So, you see, I am satisfied."

"What a horrible tricky sort of person you are, Monsieur Poirot," said Jane. "I shall never know why you are saying things."

"That is quite simple. I want to find out things."

"I suppose you've got very clever ways of finding out things?"

"There is only one really simple way."

"What is that?"

"To let people tell you."

Jane laughed. "Suppose they don't want to?"

"Everyone likes talking about themselves."

"I suppose they do," admitted Jane.

"That is how many a quack makes a fortune. He encourages pa-tients to come and sit and tell him things—how they fell out of the perambulator when they were two, and how their mother ate a pear and the juice fell on her orange dress, and how, when they were one and a half, they pulled their father's beard; and then he tells them that now they will not suffer from the insomnia any longer, and he takes two guineas, and they go away, having enjoyed them-selves, oh, so much—and perhaps they do sleep."

"How ridiculous," said Jane.

"No, it is not so ridiculous as you think. It is based on a funda-mental need of human nature—the need to talk, to reveal oneself. You yourself, mademoiselle, do you not like to dwell on your child-hood memories? On your mother and your father?"

"That doesn't apply in my case. I was brought up in an orphan-age."

"Ah, that is different. It is not gay, that."

"I don't mean that we were the kind of charity orphans who go out in scarlet bonnets and cloaks. It was quite fun, really."

"It was in England?"

"No, in Ireland, near Dublin."

"So you are Irish. That is why you have the dark hair and the blue-gray eyes with the look—"

"—as though they had been put in with a smutty finger," Norman finished with amusement.

"*Comment?* What is that you say?"

"That is a saying about Irish eyes—that they have been put in with a smutty finger."

"Really? It is not elegant, that. And yet, it expresses it well." He bowed to Jane. "The effect is very good, mademoiselle."

Jane laughed as she got up.

"You'll turn my head, Monsieur Poirot. Good night and thank you for supper. You'll have to stand me another if Norman is sent to prison for blackmail."

A frown came over Norman's face at the reminder.

Poirot bade the two young people good night.

When he got home he unlocked a drawer and took out a list of eleven names.

Against four of these names he put a light tick. Then he nodded his head thoughtfully.

"I think I know," he murmured to himself, "but I have got to be sure. *Il faut continuer.*"

17

MR. HENRY MITCHELL was just sitting down to a supper of sausage and mash when a visitor called to see him.

Somewhat to the steward's astonishment, the visitor in question was the full-mustachioed gentleman who had been one of the passengers on the fatal plane.

Monsieur Poirot was very affable, very agreeable in his manner. He insisted on Mr. Mitchell's getting on with his supper, paid a graceful compliment to Mrs. Mitchell, who was standing staring at him open-mouthed.

He accepted a chair, remarked that it was very warm for the time of year and then gently came round to the purpose of his call.

"Scotland Yard, I fear, is not making much progress with the case," he said.

Mitchell shook his head.

"It was an amazing business, sir—amazing. I don't see what they've got to go on. Why, if none of the people on the plane saw anything, it's going to be difficult for anyone afterwards."

"Truly, as you say."

"Terribly worried, Henry's been, over it," put in his wife. "Not able to sleep of nights."

The steward explained:

"It's lain on my mind, sir, something terrible. The company have been very fair about it. I must say I was afraid at first I might lose my job."

"Henry, they couldn't. It would have been cruelly unfair."

His wife sounded highly indignant. She was a buxom highly complexioned woman with snapping dark eyes.

"Things don't always happen fairly, Ruth. Still, it turned out better than I thought. They absolved me from blame. But I felt it, if you understand me. I was in charge, as it were."

"I understand your feelings," said Poirot sympathetically. "But I assure you that you are overconscientious. Nothing that happened was your fault."

"That's what I say, sir," put in Mrs. Mitchell.

Mitchell shook his head.

"I ought to have noticed that the lady was dead sooner. If I'd tried to wake her up when I first took round the bills—"

"It would have made little difference. Death, they think, was very nearly instantaneous."

"He worries so," said Mrs. Mitchell. "I tell him not to bother his head so. Who's to know what reason foreigners have for murdering each other, and if you ask me, I think it's a dirty trick to have done it in a British aeroplane."

She finished her sentence with an indignant and patriotic snort.

Mitchell shook his head in a puzzled way.

"It weighs on me, so to speak. Every time I go on duty I'm in a state. And then the gentleman from Scotland Yard asking me again and again if nothing unusual or sudden occurred on the way over. Makes me feel as though I must have forgotten something, and yet I know I haven't. It was a most uneventful voyage in every way until —until it happened."

"Blowpipes and darts—heathen, I call it," said Mrs. Mitchell.

"You are right," said Poirot, addressing her with a flattering air of being struck by her remarks. "Not so is an English murder committed."

"You're right, sir."

"You know, Mrs. Mitchell, I can almost guess what part of England you come from?"

"Dorset, sir. Not far from Bridport. That's my home."

"Exactly," said Poirot. "A lovely part of the world."

"It is that. London isn't a patch on Dorset. My folk have been settled at Dorset for over two hundred years, and I've got Dorset in the blood, as you might say."

"Yes, indeed." He turned to the steward again. "There's one thing I'd like to ask you, Mitchell."

The man's brow contracted.

"I've told all that I know; indeed I have, sir."

"Yes, yes, this is a very trifling matter. I only wondered if anything on the table—Madame Giselle's table, I mean—was disarranged?"

"You mean when—when I found her?"

"Yes. The spoons and forks, the saltcellar—anything like that?" The man shook his head.

"There wasn't anything of that kind on the tables. Everything was cleared away, bar the coffee cups. I didn't notice anything myself. I shouldn't, though. I was much too flustered. But the police would know that, sir; they searched the plane through and through."

"Ah, well," said Poirot, "it is no matter. Sometime I must have a word with your colleague Davis."

"He's on the early eight forty-five A.M. service now, sir."

"Has this business upset him much?"

"Oh, well, sir, you see, he's only a young fellow. If you ask me, he's almost enjoyed it all. The excitement! And everyone standing him drinks and wanting to hear about it."

"Has he, perhaps, a young lady?" asked Poirot. "Doubtless his connection with the crime would be very thrilling to her."

"He's courting old Johnson's daughter at the Crown and Feathers," said Mrs. Mitchell. "But she's a sensible girl; got her head screwed on the right way. She doesn't approve of being mixed up with a murder."

"A very sound point of view," said Poirot, rising. "Well, thank you, Mr. Mitchell—and you, Mrs. Mitchell—and I beg of you, my friend, do not let this weigh upon your mind."

When he had departed, Mitchell said: "The thick heads in the jury at the inquest thought he'd done it. But if you ask me, he's secret service."

"If you ask me," said Mrs. Mitchell, "there's Bolshies at the back of it."

Poirot had said that he must have a word with the other steward, Davis, sometime. As a matter of fact, he had it not many hours later, in the bar of the Crown and Feathers.

He asked Davis the same question he had asked Mitchell.

"Nothing disarranged, no, sir. You mean upset? That kind of thing?"

"I mean—well, shall we say something missing from the table, or something that would not usually be there?"

Davis said slowly:

"There was something. I noticed it when I was clearing up after the police had done with the place. But I don't suppose that it's the sort of thing you mean. It's only that the dead lady had two coffee spoons in her saucer. It does sometimes happen when we're serving in a hurry. I noticed it because there's a superstition about that; they say two spoons in a saucer means a wedding."

"Was there a spoon missing from anyone else's saucer?"

"No, sir, not that I noticed. Mitchell or I must have taken the cup and saucer along that way—as I say, one does sometimes, what with the hurry and all. I laid two sets of fish knives and forks only a week ago. On the whole, it's better than laying the table short, for then you have to interrupt yourself and go and fetch the extra knife or whatever it is you've forgotten."

Poirot asked one more question—a somewhat jocular one:

"What do you think of French girls, Davis?"

"English is good enough for me, sir."

And he grinned at a plump fair-haired girl behind the bar.

18

MR. JAMES RYDER was rather surprised when a card bearing the name of Monsieur Hercule Poirot was brought to him.

He knew that the name was familiar but for the moment he could not remember why. Then he said to himself:

"Oh, that fellow!" And told the clerk to show the visitor in.

Monsieur Hercule Poirot was looking very jaunty. In one hand he carried a cane. He had a flower in his buttonhole.

"You will forgive my troubling you, I trust," said Poirot. "It is this affair of the death of Madame Giselle."

"Yes?" said Mr. Ryder. "Well, what about it? Sit down, won't you? Have a cigar?"

"I thank you, no. I smoke always my own cigarettes. Perhaps you will accept one?"

Ryder regarded Poirot's tiny cigarettes with a somewhat dubious eye.

"Think I'll have one of my own, if it's all the same to you. Might swallow one of those by mistake." He laughed heartily.

"The inspector was round here a few days ago," said Mr. Ryder, when he had induced his lighter to work. "Nosey, that's what those fellows are. Can't mind their own business."

"They have, I suppose, to get information," said Poirot mildly.

"They needn't be so offensive about it," said Mr. Ryder bitterly. "A man's got his feelings and his business reputation to think about."

"You are, perhaps, a little oversensitive."

"I'm in a delicate position, I am," said Mr. Ryder. "Sitting where I did—just in front of her—well, it looks fishy, I suppose. I can't help where I sat. If I'd known that woman was going to be murdered, I wouldn't have come by that plane at all. I don't know, though, perhaps I would."

He looked thoughtful for a moment.

"Has good come out of evil?" asked Poirot, smiling.

"It's funny, your saying that. It has and it hasn't, in a manner of speaking. I mean I've had a lot of worry. I've been badgered. Things have been insinuated. And why me—that's what I say. Why don't they go and worry that Doctor Hubbard—Bryant, I mean. Doctors are the people who can get hold of highfaluting undetectable poisons. How'd I get hold of snake juice? I ask you!"

"You were saying," said Poirot, "that although you had been put to a lot of inconvenience—"

"Ah, yes, there was a bright side to the picture. I don't mind telling you I cleaned up a tidy little sum from the papers. Eyewitness stuff—though there was more of the reporter's imagination than of my eyesight; but that's neither here nor there."

"It is interesting," said Poirot, "how a crime affects the lives of people who are quite outside it. Take yourself, for example; you make suddenly a quite unexpected sum of money—a sum of money perhaps particularly welcome at the moment."

"Money's always welcome," said Mr. Ryder.

He eyed Poirot sharply.

"Sometimes the need of it is imperative. For that reason men embezzle, they make fraudulent entries"—he waved his hands—"all sorts of complications arise."

"Well, don't let's get gloomy about it," said Mr. Ryder.

"True. Why dwell on the dark side of the picture? This money was grateful to you, since you failed to raise a loan in Paris."

"How the devil did you know that?" asked Mr. Ryder angrily.

Hercule Poirot smiled.

"At any rate, it is true."

"It's true enough. But I don't particularly want it to get about."

"I will be discretion itself, I assure you."

"It's odd," mused Mr. Ryder, "how small a sum will sometimes put a man in Queer Street. Just a small sum of ready money to tide him over a crisis. And if he can't get hold of that infinitesimal sum, to hell with his credit. Yes, it's odd. Money's odd. Credit's odd. Come to that, life is odd!"

"Very true."

"By the way, what was it you wanted to see me about?"

"It is a little delicate. It has come to my ears—in the course of my profession, you understand—that in spite of your denials, you did have dealings with this woman Giselle."

"Who says so? It's a lie—a damned lie—I never saw the woman!"

"Dear me, that is very curious!"

"Curious! It's a damned libel."

Poirot looked at him thoughtfully.

"Ah," he said. "I must look into the matter."

"What do you mean? What are you getting at?"

Poirot shook his head.

"Do not enrage yourself. There must be a mistake."

"I should think there was. Catch me getting myself mixed up with these high-toned society moneylenders. Society women with gambling debts—that's their sort."

Poirot rose.

"I must apologize for having been misinformed." He paused at the door. "By the way, just as a matter of curiosity, what made you call Doctor Bryant, Doctor Hubbard just now?"

"Blessed if I know. Let me see. Oh, yes, I think it must have been the flute. The nursery rime, you know. Old Mother Hubbard's dog: 'But when she came back he was playing the flute.' Odd thing, how you mix up names."

"Ah, yes, the flute. These things interest me, you understand, psychologically."

Mr. Ryder snorted at the word "psychologically." It savored to him of what he called that tom-fool business, psychoanalysis.

He looked at Poirot with suspicion.

19

THE Countess of Horbury sat in her bedroom at 115 Grosvenor Square in front of her toilet table. Gold brushes and boxes, jars of face cream, boxes of powder, dainty luxury all around her. But in the midst of the luxury, Cicely Horbury sat with dry lips and a face on which the rouge showed up in unbecoming patches on her cheeks.

She read the letter for the fourth time.

THE COUNTESS OF HORBURY,
    Dear Madam: Re Madame Giselle, deceased.
    I am the holder of certain documents formerly in the possession of the deceased lady. If you or Mr. Raymond Barraclough are interested in the matter, I should be happy to call upon you with a view to discussing the affair.
    Or perhaps you would prefer me to deal with your husband in the matter?

                                        Yours truly,
                                                JOHN ROBINSON.

Stupid, to read the same thing over and over again. As though the words might alter their meaning.

She picked up the envelope—two envelopes—the first with Personal on it. The second with Private and Very Confidential.

Private and Very Confidential.

The beast—the beast.

And that lying old Frenchwoman who had sworn that "All arrangements were made" to protect clients in case of her own sudden demise.

Damn her.

Life was hell—hell!

"Oh, God, my nerves," thought Cicely. "It isn't fair. It isn't fair."

Her shaking hand went out to a gold-topped bottle.

"It will steady me. Pull me together."

She snuffed the stuff up her nose.

There. Now she could think!

What to do?

See the man, of course. Though where she could raise any money
—perhaps a lucky flutter at that place in Carlos Street—

But time enough to think of that later. See the man; find out what
he knows.

She went over to the writing table, dashed off in her big unformed
handwriting:

The Countess of Horbury presents her compliments to Mr. John
Robinson and will see him if he calls at eleven o'clock tomorrow
morning.

"Will I do?" asked Norman.

He flushed a little under Poirot's startled gaze.

"Name of a name," said Hercule Poirot, "what kind of a comedy is
it that you are playing?"

Norman Gale flushed even more deeply.

He mumbled, "You said a slight disguise would be as well."

Poirot sighed. Then he took the young man by the arm and
marched him to the looking-glass.

"Regard yourself," he said. "That is all I ask of you—regard yourself! What do you think you are? A Santa Claus dressed up to amuse
the children? I agree that your beard is not white—no, it is black;
the color for villains. But what a beard—a beard that screams to
heaven! A cheap beard, my friend, and most imperfectly and ama-
teurishly attached! Then there are your eyebrows—but it is that
you have the mania for false hair? The spirit gum, one smells it several yards away, and if you think that anyone will fail to perceive
that you have a piece of sticking plaster attached to a tooth, you are
mistaken. My friend, it is not your métier—decidedly not—to play
the part."

"I acted in amateur theatricals a good deal at one time," said Norman Gale stiffly.

"I can hardly believe it. At any rate, I presume they did not let
you indulge in your own ideas of make-up. Even behind the foot-

lights your appearance would be singularly unconvincing. In Grosvenor Square in broad daylight—"

Poirot gave an eloquent shrug of the shoulders by way of finishing the sentence.

"No, *mon ami*," he said. "You are a blackmailer, not a comedian. I want her ladyship to fear you, not to die of laughing when she sees you. I observe that I wound you by what I am saying. I regret, but it is a moment when only the truth will serve. Take this, and this—" he pressed various jars upon him. "Go into the bathroom and let us have an end of what you call in this country the fooltommery."

Crushed, Norman Gale obeyed. When he emerged a quarter of an hour later, his face a vivid shade of brick red, Poirot gave him a nod of approval.

"*Très bien.* The farce is over. The serious business begins. I will permit you to have a small mustache. But I will, if you please, attach it to you myself. . . . There. . . . And now we will part the hair differently. . . . So. That is quite enough. Now let me see if you at least know your lines."

He listened with attention, then nodded.

"That is good. *En avant* and good luck to you."

"I devoutly hope so. I shall probably find an enraged husband and a couple of policemen."

Poirot reassured him:

"Have no anxiety. All will march to a marvel."

"So you say," muttered Norman rebelliously.

With his spirits at zero, he departed on his distasteful mission.

At Grosvenor Square he was shown into a small room on the first floor. There, after a minute or two, Lady Horbury came to him.

Norman braced himself. He must not—positively must not—show that he was new to this business.

"Mr. Robinson?" said Cicely.

"At your service," said Norman, and bowed.

"Damn it all! Just like a shopwalker," he thought disgustedly. "That's fright."

"I had your letter," said Cicely.

Norman pulled himself together. "The old fool said I couldn't act," he said to himself with a mental grin.

Aloud he said rather insolently:

"Quite so. Well, what about it, Lady Horbury?"

"I don't know what you mean."

"Come, come. Must we really go into details? Everyone knows how pleasant a—well, call it a weekend at the seaside—can be, but husbands seldom agree. I think you know, Lady Horbury, just exactly what the evidence consists of. Wonderful woman, old Giselle. Always had the goods. Hotel evidence, and so on, is quite first class. Now the question is who wants it most—you or Lord Horbury? That's the question."

She stood there quivering.

"I'm a seller," said Norman, his voice growing commoner as he threw himself more whole-heartedly into the part of Mr. Robinson. "Are you a buyer? That's the question."

"How did you get hold of this evidence?"

"Now really, Lady Horbury, that's rather beside the point. I've got it—that's the main thing."

"I don't believe you. Show it to me."

"Oh, no." Norman shook his head with a cunning leer. "I didn't bring anything with me. I'm not so green as that. If we agree to do business, that's another matter. I'll show you the stuff before you hand the money over. All fair and aboveboard."

"How—how much?"

"Ten thousand of the best—pounds, not dollars."

"Impossible. I could never lay my hands on anything like that amount."

"It's wonderful what you can do if you try. Jewels aren't fetching what they did, but pearls are still pearls. Look here, to oblige a lady, I'll make it eight thousand. That's my last word. And I'll give you two days to think it over."

"I can't get the money, I tell you."

Norman sighed and shook his head.

"Well, perhaps it's only right Lord Horbury should know what's been going on. I believe I'm correct in saying that a divorced woman gets no alimony, and Mr. Barraclough's a very promising young actor, but he's not touching big money yet. Now not another word. I'll leave you to think it over, and mind what I say—I mean it."

He paused, and then added:

"I mean it just as Giselle meant it."

Then quickly, before the wretched woman could reply, he had left the room.

"Ouch!" said Norman as he reached the street. He wiped his brow. "Thank goodness that's over."

It was a bare hour later when a card was brought to Lady Horbury.

"Monsieur Hercule Poirot."

She thrust it aside.

"Who is he? I can't see him!"

"He said, m'lady, that he was here at the request of Mr. Raymond Barraclough."

"Oh." She paused. "Very well, show him in."

The butler departed, reappeared.

"Monsieur Hercule Poirot."

Exquisitely dressed in the most dandiacal style, Monsieur Poirot entered, bowed.

The butler closed the door. Cicely took a step forward.

"Mr. Barraclough sent you?"

"Sit down, madame." His tone was kindly but authoritative.

Mechanically she sat. He took a chair near her. His manner was fatherly and reassuring.

"Madame, I entreat you, look upon me as a friend. I come to advise you. You are, I know, in grave trouble."

She murmured faintly: "I don't—"

"*Écoutez,* madame. I do not ask you to give away your secrets. It is unnecessary. I know them beforehand. That is the essence of being a good detective—to know."

"A detective." Her eyes widened. "I remember. You were on the plane; it was you—"

"Precisely. It was me. Now, madame, let us get to business. As I said just now, I do not press you to confide in me. You shall not start by telling me things; I will tell them to you. This morning, not an hour ago, you had a visitor. That visitor—his name was Brown, perhaps."

"Robinson," said Cicely faintly.

"It is the same thing—Brown, Smith, Robinson—he uses them in turn. He came here to blackmail you, madame. He has in his possession certain proofs of, shall we say, indiscretion? Those proofs were once in the keeping of Madame Giselle. Now this man has them. He offers them to you for, perhaps, seven thousand pounds."

"Eight."

"Eight, then. And you, madame, will not find it easy to get that sum very quickly?"

"I can't do it—I simply can't do it. I'm in debt already. I don't know what to do."

"Calm yourself, madame. I come to assist you."

She stared at him.

"How do you know all this?"

"Simply, madame, because I am Hercule Poirot. *Eh bien*, have no fears. Place yourself in my hands; I will deal with this Mr. Robinson."

"Yes," said Cicely sharply. "And how much will you want?"

Hercule Poirot bowed.

"I shall ask only a photograph, signed, of a very beautiful lady."

She cried out: "Oh, dear, I don't know what to do! My nerves! I'm going mad!"

"No, no, all is well. Trust Hercule Poirot. Only, madame, I must have the truth—the whole truth. Do not keep anything back or my hands will be tied."

"And you'll get me out of this mess?"

"I swear to you solemnly that you will never hear of Mr. Robinson again."

She said, "All right. I'll tell you everything."

"Good. Now then, you borrowed money from this woman Giselle?"

Lady Horbury nodded.

"When was that? When did it begin, I mean?"

"Eighteen months ago. I was in a hole."

"Gambling?"

"Yes, I had an appalling run of luck."

"And she lent you as much as you wanted?"

"Not at first. Only a small sum to begin with."

"Who sent you to her?"

"Raymond—Mr. Barraclough told me that he had heard she lent money to society women."

"But later she lent you more?"

"Yes, as much as I wanted. It seemed like a miracle at the time."

"It was Madame Giselle's special kind of miracle," said Poirot dryly. "I gather that before then you and Mr. Barraclough had become—er—friends?"

"Yes."

"But you were very anxious that your husband should not know about it?"

Cicely cried angrily:

"Stephen's a prig! He's tired of me! He wants to marry someone else. He'd have jumped at the thought of divorcing me."

"And you did not want divorce?"

"No. I—I—"

"You liked your position, and also you enjoyed the use of a very ample income. Quite so. *Les femmes,* naturally, they must look after themselves. To proceed, there arose the question of repayment?"

"Yes. And I—I couldn't pay back the money. And then the old devil turned nasty. She knew about me and Raymond. She'd found out places and dates and everything. I can't think how."

"She had her methods," said Poirot dryly. "And she threatened, I suppose, to send all this evidence to Lord Horbury."

"Yes, unless I paid up."

"And you couldn't pay?"

"No."

"So her death was quite providential?"

Cicely Horbury said earnestly:

"It seemed too, too wonderful."

"Ah, precisely—too, too wonderful. But it made you a little nervous, perhaps?"

"Nervous?"

"Well, after all, madame, you alone of anyone on the plane had a motive for desiring her death."

She drew in her breath sharply.

"I know. It was awful. I was in an absolute state about it."

"Especially since you had been to see her in Paris the night before and had had something of a scene with her?"

"The old devil! She wouldn't budge an inch. I think she actually enjoyed it. Oh, she was a beast through and through! I came away like a rag."

"And yet you said at the inquest that you had never seen the woman before?"

"Well, naturally, what else could I say?"

Poirot looked at her thoughtfully.

"You, madame, could say nothing else."

"It's been too ghastly—nothing but lies, lies, lies. That dreadful inspector man has been here again and again badgering me with questions. But I felt pretty safe. I could see he was only trying it on. He didn't know anything."

"If one does guess, one should guess with assurance."

"And then," continued Cicely, pursuing her own line of thought, "I couldn't help feeling that if anything were to leak out, it would have leaked out at once. I felt safe till that awful letter yesterday."

"You have not been afraid all this time?"

"Of course I've been afraid!"

"But of what? Of exposure? Or of being arrested for murder?"

The color ebbed away from her cheeks.

"Murder! But I didn't— Oh, you don't believe that! I didn't kill her. I didn't!"

"You wanted her dead."

"Yes, but I didn't kill her! . . . Oh, you must believe me—you must. I never moved from my seat. I—"

She broke off. Her beautiful blue eyes were fixed on him imploringly.

Hercule Poirot nodded soothingly.

"I believe you, madame, for two reasons—first, because of your sex, and, secondly, because of a wasp."

She stared at him.

"A wasp?"

"Exactly. That does not make sense to you, I see. Now then, let us attend to the matter in hand. I will deal with this Mr. Robinson. I pledge you my word that you shall never see or hear of him again. I will settle his—his—I have forgotten the word—his bacon? No, his goat. Now, in return for my services, I will ask you two little questions. Was Mr. Barraclough in Paris the day before the murder?"

"Yes, we dined together. But he thought it better I should go and see the woman alone."

"Ah, he did, did he? Now, madame, one further question: Your stage name before you were married was Cicely Bland. Was that your real name?"

"No, my real name is Martha Jebb. But the other—"

"—made a better professional name. And you were born—where?"

"Doncaster; but why—"

"Mere curiosity. Forgive me. And now, Lady Horbury, will you permit me to give you some advice? Why not arrange with your husband a discreet divorce?"

"And let him marry that woman?"

"And let him marry that woman. You have a generous heart, madame. And besides, you will be safe—oh, so safe—and your husband he will pay you an income."

"Not a very large one."

"*Eh bien,* once you are free, you will marry a millionaire."

"There aren't any nowadays."

"Ah, do not believe that, madame. The man who had three millions, perhaps now he has two millions—*eh bien,* it is still enough."

Cicely laughed.

"You're very persuasive, Monsieur Poirot. And are you really sure that dreadful man will never bother me again?"

"On the word of Hercule Poirot," said that gentleman solemnly.

20

DETECTIVE INSPECTOR JAPP walked briskly up Harley Street, stopped at a certain door, and asked for Doctor Bryant.

"Have you an appointment, sir?"

"No, I'll just write a few words," and on an official card he wrote:

> Should be much obliged if you could spare me a few moments. I won't keep you long.

He sealed up the card in an envelope and gave it to the butler.

He was shown into a waiting room. There were two women there and a man. Japp settled down with an elderly copy of *Punch*.

The butler reappeared, and crossing the floor, said in a discreet voice:

"If you wouldn't mind waiting a short time, sir, the doctor will see you, but he's very busy this morning."

Japp nodded. He did not in the least mind waiting—in fact, he rather welcomed it. The two women had begun to talk. They had, obviously, a very high opinion of Doctor Bryant's abilities. More patients came in. Evidently Doctor Bryant was doing well in his profession.

"Fairly coining money," thought Japp to himself. "That doesn't look like needing to borrow, but of course the loan may have taken place a long time ago. Anyway, he's got a fine practice; a breath of scandal would bust it to bits. That's the worst of being a doctor."

A quarter of an hour later, the butler reappeared and said:

"The doctor will see you now, sir."

Japp was shown into Doctor Bryant's consulting room—a room at the back of the house with a big window. The doctor was sitting at his desk. He rose and shook hands with the detective.

His fine-lined face showed fatigue, but he seemed in no way disturbed by the inspector's visit.

"What can I do for you, inspector?" he said as he resumed his seat and motioned Japp to a chair opposite.

"I must apologize first for calling in your consulting hours, but I shan't keep you long, sir."

"That is all right. I suppose it is about the aeroplane death?"

"Quite right, sir. We're still working on it."

"With any result?"

"We're not so far on as we'd like to be. I really came to ask you some questions about the method employed. It's this snake-venom business that I can't get the hang of."

"I'm not a toxicologist, you know," said Doctor Bryant, smiling. "Such things aren't in my line. Winterspoon's your man."

"Ah, but you see, it's like this, doctor: Winterspoon's an expert —and you know what experts are. They talk so that the ordinary man can't understand them. But as far as I can make out, there's a medical side to this business. Is it true that snake venom is sometimes injected for epilepsy?"

"I'm not a specialist in epilepsy either," said Doctor Bryant. "But I believe that injections of cobra venom have been used in the treatment of epilepsy with excellent results. But, as I say, that's not really my line of country."

"I know—I know. What it really amounts to is this: I felt that you'd take an interest, having been on the aeroplane yourself. I thought it possible that you'd have some ideas on the subject yourself that might be useful to me. It's not much good my going to an expert if I don't know what to ask him."

Doctor Bryant smiled.

"There is something in what you say, inspector. There is probably no man living who can remain entirely unaffected by having come in close contact with murder. I am interested, I admit. I have speculated a good deal about the case in my quiet way."

"And what do you think, sir?"

Bryant shook his head slowly.

"It amazes me. The whole thing seems almost unreal, if I might put it that way. An astounding way of committing a crime. It seems a chance in a hundred that the murderer was not seen. He must be a person with a reckless disregard of risks."

"Very true, sir."

"The choice of poison is equally amazing. How could a would-be murderer possibly get hold of such a thing?"

"I know. It seems incredible. Why, I don't suppose one man in a thousand has ever heard of such a thing as a boomslang, much less actually handled the venom. You yourself, sir—now, you're a doctor, but I don't suppose you've ever handled the stuff."

"There are certainly not many opportunities of doing so. I have a friend who works at tropical research. In his laboratory there are various specimens of dried snake venoms—that of the cobra, for instance—but I cannot remember any specimen of the boomslang."

"Perhaps you can help me." Japp took out a piece of paper and handed it to the doctor. "Winterspoon wrote down these three names; said I might get information there. Do you know any of these men?"

"I know Professor Kennedy slightly, Heidler I know well; mention my name and I'm sure he'll do all he can for you. Carmichael's an Edinburgh man; I don't know him personally, but I believe they've done some good work up there."

"Thank you, sir; I'm much obliged. Well, I won't keep you any longer."

When Japp emerged into Harley Street, he was smiling to himself in a pleased fashion.

"Nothing like tact," he said to himself. "Tact does it. I'll be bound he never saw what I was after. Well, that's that."

21

WHEN Japp got back to Scotland Yard, he was told that Monsieur Hercule Poirot was waiting to see him.

Japp greeted his friend heartily.

"Well, Monsieur Poirot, and what brings you along? Any news?"

"I came to ask you for news, my good Japp."

"If that isn't just like you. Well, there isn't much and that's the truth. The dealer fellow in Paris has identified the blowpipe all right. Fournier's been worrying the life out of me from Paris about his *moment psychologique*. I've questioned those stewards till I'm blue in the face and they stick to it that there wasn't a *moment psychologique*. Nothing startling or out of the way happened on the voyage."

"It might have occurred when they were both in the front car."

"I've questioned the passengers too. Everyone can't be lying."

"In one case I investigated everyone was!"

"You and your cases! To tell the truth, Monsieur Poirot, I'm not very happy. The more I look into things the less I get. The chief's inclined to look on me rather coldly. But what can I do? Luckily, it's one of those semiforeign cases. We can put it on the Frenchmen over here, and in Paris they say it was done by an Englishman and that it's our business."

"Do you really believe the Frenchman did it?"

"Well, frankly, I don't. As I look at it, an archæologist is a poor kind of fish. Always burrowing in the ground and talking through his hat about what happened thousands of years ago, and how do they know, I should like to know? Who's to contradict them? They say some rotten string of beads is five thousand three hundred and twenty-two years old, and who's to say it isn't? Well, there they are, liars perhaps—though they seem to believe it themselves—but harmless. I had an old chap in here the other day who'd had a scarab pinched. Terrible state he was in—nice old boy, but helpless as a baby in arms. No, between you and me, I don't think for a minute that pair of French archæologists did it."

"Who do you think did it?"

"Well, there's Clancy, of course. He's in a queer way. Goes about muttering to himself. He's got something on his mind."

"The plot of a new book, perhaps."

"It may be that—and it may be something else. But try as I may, I can't get a line on motive. I still think CL 52 in the black book is Lady Horbury, but I can't get anything out of her. She's pretty hard-boiled, I can tell you."

Poirot smiled to himself. Japp went on:

"The stewards—well, I can't find a thing to connect them with Giselle."

"Doctor Bryant?"

"I think I'm on to something there. Rumors about him and a patient. Pretty woman—nasty husband—takes drugs or something. If he's not careful he'll be struck off by the medical council. That fits in with RT 362 well enough, and I don't mind telling you that I've got a pretty shrewd idea where he could have got the snake venom from. I went to see him and he gave himself away rather badly over that. Still, so far it is all surmise, no facts. Facts aren't any too easy to get at in this case. Ryder seems all square and aboveboard; says he went to raise a loan in Paris and couldn't get it, gave names and addresses, all checked up. I've found out that the firm was nearly in Queer Street about a week or two ago, but they seem to be just pulling through. There you are again, unsatisfactory. The whole thing is a muddle."

"There is no such thing as muddle—obscurity, yes, but muddle can exist only in a disorderly brain."

"Use any word you choose. The result's the same. Fournier's stumped too. I suppose you've got it all taped out, but you'd rather not tell!"

"You mock yourself at me. I have not got it all taped out. I proceed, a step at a time, with order and method, but there is still far to go."

"I can't help feeling glad to hear that. Let's hear about these orderly steps."

Poirot smiled.

"I make a little table, so." He took a paper from his pocket. "My idea is this: A murder is an action performed to bring about a certain result."

"Say that again slowly."

"It is not difficult."

"Probably not, but you make it sound so."

"No, no, it is very simple. Say you want money; you get it when an aunt dies. *Bien.* You perform an action—this is to kill the aunt—and get the result—inherit the money."

"I wish I had some aunts like that," sighed Japp. "Go ahead. I see your idea. You mean there's got to be a motive."

"I prefer my own way of putting it. An action is performed—the action being murder. What now are the results of that action? By studying the different results, we should get the answer to our conundrum. The results of a single action may be very varied; that particular action affects a lot of different people. *Eh bien,* I study today—three weeks after the crime—the result in eleven different cases."

He spread out the paper.

Japp leaned forward with some interest and read over Poirot's shoulder.

Miss Grey. Result—temporary improvement. Increased salary.

Mr. Gale. Result—bad. Loss of practice.

Lady Horbury. Result—good, if she's CL 52.

Miss Kerr. Result—bad, since Giselle's death makes it more unlikely Lord Horbury will get the evidence to divorce his wife.

"H'm." Japp interrupted his scrutiny. "So you think she's keen on his lordship? You are a one for nosing out love affairs."

Poirot smiled. Japp bent over the chart once more.

Mr. Clancy. Result—good. Expects to make money by book dealing with the murder.

Doctor Bryant. Result—good if RT 362.

Mr. Ryder. Result—good, owing to small amount of cash obtained through articles on murder which tided firm over delicate time. Also good if Ryder is XVB 724.

M. Dupont. Result—unaffected.

M. Jean Dupont. Result—the same.

Mitchell. Result—unaffected.

Davis. Result—unaffected.

"And you think that's going to help you?" asked Japp skeptically. "I can't see that writing down 'I don't know. I don't know. I can't tell,' makes it any better."

"It gives one a clear classification," explained Poirot. "In four cases —Mr. Clancy, Miss Grey, Mr. Ryder and, I think I may say, Lady Horbury—there is a result on the credit side. In the cases of Mr. Gale and Miss Kerr there is a result on the debit side; in four cases there is no result at all, so far as we know, and in one—Doctor Bryant— there is either no result or a distinct gain."

"And so?" asked Japp.

"And so," said Poirot, "we must go on seeking."

"With precious little to go upon," said Japp gloomily. "The truth of it is that we're hung up until we can get what we want from Paris. It's the Giselle side that wants going into. I bet I could have got more out of that maid than Fournier did."

"I doubt it, my friend. The most interesting thing about this case is the personality of the dead woman. A woman without friends, without relations—without, as one might say, any personal life. A woman who was once young, who once loved and suffered, and then with a firm hand pulled down the shutter—all that was over! Not a photograph, not a souvenir, not a knickknack. Marie Morisot became Madame Giselle, moneylender."

"Do you think there is a clue in her past?"

"Perhaps."

"Well, we could do with it! There aren't any clues in this case."

"Oh, yes, my friend, there are."

"The blowpipe, of course."

"No, no, not the blowpipe."

"Well, let's hear your ideas of the clues in the case."

Poirot smiled.

"I will give them titles, like the names of Mr. Clancy's stories! The Clue of the Wasp. The Clue in the Passenger's Baggage. The Clue of the Extra Coffee Spoon."

"You're potty," said Japp kindly. And added:

"What's this about a coffee spoon?"

"Madame Giselle had two spoons in her saucer."

"That's supposed to mean a wedding."

"In this case," said Poirot, "it meant a funeral."

22

WHEN Norman Gale, Jane and Poirot met for dinner on the night after the blackmailing incident, Norman was relieved to hear that his services as Mr. Robinson were no longer required.

"He is dead, the good Mr. Robinson," said Poirot. He raised his glass. "Let us drink to his memory."

"R. I. P.," said Norman with a laugh.

"What happened?" asked Jane of Poirot.

He smiled at her.

"I found out what I wanted to know."

"Was she mixed up with Giselle?"

"Yes."

"That was pretty clear from my interview with her," said Norman.

"Quite so," said Poirot. "But I wanted a full and detailed story."

"And you got it?"

"I got it."

They both looked at him inquiringly, but Poirot, in a provoking manner, began to discuss the relationship between a career and a life.

"There are not so many round pegs in square holes as one might think. Most people, in spite of what they tell you, choose the occupations that they secretly desire. You will hear a man say who works in an office, 'I should like to explore, to rough it in far countries.' But you will find that he likes reading the fiction that deals with that subject, but that he himself prefers the safety and moderate comfort of an office stool."

"According to you," said Jane, "my desire for foreign travel isn't genuine. Messing about with women's heads is my true vocation. Well, that isn't true."

Poirot smiled at her.

"You are young still. Naturally, one tries this, that and the other, but what one eventually settles down into is the life one prefers."

"And suppose I prefer being rich?"

"Ah, that, it is more difficult!"

"I don't agree with you," said Gale. "I'm a dentist by chance, not choice. My uncle was a dentist; he wanted me to come in with him, but I was all for adventure and seeing the world. I chucked dentistry and went off to farm in South Africa. However, that wasn't much good; I hadn't got enough experience. I had to accept the old man's offer and come and set up business with him."

"And now you are thinking of chucking dentistry again and going off to Canada. You have a Dominion complex!"

"This time I shall be forced to do it."

"Ah, but it is incredible how often things force one to do the thing one would like to do."

"Nothing's forcing me to travel," said Jane wistfully. "I wish it would."

"*Eh bien,* I make you an offer here and now. I go to Paris next week. If you like, you can take the job of my secretary. I will give you a good salary."

Jane shook her head.

"I mustn't give up Antoine's. It's a good job."

"So is mine a good job."

"Yes, but it's only temporary."

"I will obtain you another post of the same kind."

"Thanks, but I don't think I'll risk it."

Poirot looked at her and smiled enigmatically.

Three days later he was rung up.

"Monsieur Poirot," said Jane, "is that job still open?"

"But, yes. I go to Paris on Monday."

"You really mean it? I can come?"

"Yes, but what has happened to make you change your mind?"

"I've had a row with Antoine. As a matter of fact, I lost my temper with a customer. She was an—an absolute— Well, I can't say just what she was through the telephone. I was feeling nervy, and instead of doing my soothing-sirup stuff, I just let rip and told her exactly what I thought of her."

"Ah, the thought of the great wide-open spaces."

"What's that you say?"

"I say that your mind was dwelling on a certain subject."

"It wasn't my mind, it was my tongue that slipped. I enjoyed it. Her eyes looked just like her beastly Pekingese's—as though they were going to drop out—but here I am, thrown out on my ear, as you might say. I must get another job sometime, I suppose, but I'd like to come to Paris first."

"Good; it is arranged. On the way over, I will give you your instructions."

Poirot and his new secretary did not travel by air, for which Jane was secretly thankful. The unpleasant experience of her last trip had shaken her nerve. She did not want to be reminded of that lolling figure in rusty black.

On their way from Calais to Paris they had the compartment to themselves and Poirot gave Jane some idea of his plans.

"There are several people in Paris that I have to see. There is the lawyer—Maître Thibault. There is also Monsieur Fournier, of the Sûreté—a melancholy man, but intelligent. And there are Monsieur Dupont *père* and Monsieur Dupont *fils*. Now, Mademoiselle Jane, while I am taking on the father, I shall leave the son to you. You are very charming, very attractive. I fancy that Monsieur Dupont will remember you from the inquest."

"I've seen him since then," said Jane, her color rising slightly.

"Indeed? And how was that?"

Jane, her color rising a little more, described their meeting in the Corner House.

"Excellent; better and better. Ah, it was a famous idea of mine to bring you to Paris with me. Now listen carefully, Mademoiselle Jane. As far as possible do not discuss the Giselle affair, but do not avoid the subject if Jean Dupont introduces it. It might be well if, without actually saying so, you could convey the impression that Lady Horbury is suspected of the crime. My reason for coming to Paris, you can say, is to confer with Monsieur Fournier and to inquire particularly into any dealings Lady Horbury may have had with the dead woman."

"Poor Lady Horbury. You do make her a stalking horse!"

"She is not the type I admire. *Eh bien,* let her be useful for once."

Jane hesitated for a minute, then said:

"You don't suspect young Monsieur Dupont of the crime, do you?"

"No, no, no. I desire information merely." He looked at her sharply. "He attracts you, eh, this young man? *Il est sex appeal?*"

Jane laughed at the phrase.

"No, that's not how I would describe him. He's very simple, but rather a dear."

"So that is how you describe him—very simple?"

"He is simple. I think it's because he's led a nice unworldly life."

"True," said Poirot. "He has not, for instance, dealt with teeth. He has not been disillusioned by the sight of a public hero shivering with fright in the dentist's chair."

Jane laughed.

"I don't think Norman's roped in any public heroes yet as patients."

"It would have been a waste, since he is going to Canada."

"He's talking of New Zealand now. He thinks I'd like the climate better."

"At all events he is patriotic. He sticks to the British Dominions."

"I'm hoping," said Jane, "that it won't be necessary."

She fixed Poirot with an inquiring eye.

"Meaning that you put your trust in Papa Poirot? Ah, well, I will do the best I can; that I promise you. But I have the feeling very strongly, mademoiselle, that there is a figure who has not yet come into the limelight—a part as yet unplayed."

He shook his head, frowning.

"There is, mademoiselle, an unknown factor in this case. Everything points to that."

Two days after their arrival in Paris, Monsieur Hercule Poirot and his secretary dined in a small restaurant, and the two Duponts, father and son, were Poirot's guests.

Old Monsieur Dupont Jane found as charming as his son, but she got little chance of talking to him. Poirot monopolized him severely from the start. Jane found Jean no less easy to get on with than she had done in London. His attractive boyish personality pleased her now as it had then. He was such a simple friendly soul.

All the same, even while she laughed and talked with him, her ear was alert to catch snatches of the two older men's conversation. She wondered precisely what information it was that Poirot wanted. So far as she could hear, the conversation had never touched once on the murder. Poirot was skillfully drawing out his companion on the subject of the past. His interest in archæological research in Persia seemed both deep and sincere. Monsieur Dupont was enjoying his evening enormously. Seldom did he get such an intelligent and sympathetic listener.

Whose suggestion it was that the two young people should go to a cinema was not quite clear, but when they had gone, Poirot drew his chair a little closer to the table and seemed prepared to take a still more practical interest in archæological research.

"I comprehend," he said. "Naturally, it is a great anxiety in these difficult days to raise sufficient funds. You accept private donations?"

Monsieur Dupont laughed.

"My dear friend, we sue for them practically on bended knees! But our particular type of dig does not attract the great mass of humanity. They demand spectacular results! Above all, they like gold—large quantities of gold! It is amazing how little the average person cares for pottery. Pottery—the whole romance of humanity can be expressed in terms of pottery. Design, texture—"

Monsieur Dupont was well away. He besought Poirot not to be led astray by the specious publications of B——, the really criminal misdating of L——, and the hopelessly unscientific stratification of G——. Poirot promised solemnly not to be led astray by any of the publications of these learned personages.

Then he said:

"Would a donation, for instance, of five hundred pounds—"

Monsieur Dupont nearly fell across the table in his excitement:

"You—you are offering that? To me? To aid our researches! But it is magnificent! Stupendous! The biggest private donation we have had!"

Poirot coughed.

"I will admit, there is a favor—"

"Ah, yes, a souvenir—some specimen of pottery."

"No, no, you misunderstand me," said Poirot quickly, before Monsieur Dupont could get well away again. "It is my secretary—that charming young girl you saw tonight—if she could accompany you on your expedition?"

Monsieur Dupont seemed slightly taken aback for a moment.

"Well," he said, pulling his mustache, "it might possibly be arranged. I should have to consult my son. My nephew and his wife are to accompany us. It was to have been a family party. However, I will speak to Jean."

"Mademoiselle Grey is passionately interested in pottery. The past has for her an immense fascination. It is the dream of her life to dig. Also she mends socks and sews on buttons in a manner truly admirable."

"A useful accomplishment."

"Is it not? And now you were telling me about the pottery of Susa."

Monsieur Dupont resumed a happy monologue on his own particular theories of Susa I and Susa II.

Poirot reached his hotel, to find Jane saying good night to Jean Dupont in the hall.

As they went up in the lift, Poirot said: "I have obtained for you a job of great interest. You are to accompany the Duponts to Persia in the spring."

Jane stared at him.

"Are you quite mad?"

"When the offer is made to you, you will accept with every manifestation of delight."

"I am certainly not going to Persia. I shall be in Muswell Hill or New Zealand with Norman."

Poirot twinkled at her gently.

"My dear child," he said, "it is some months to next March. To express delight is not to buy a ticket. In the same way I have talked about a donation, but I have not actually signed a check! By the way, I must obtain for you in the morning a handbook on prehistoric pottery of the Near East. I have said that you are passionately interested in the subject."

Jane sighed.

"Being secretary to you is no sinecure, is it? Anything else?"

"Yes. I have said that you sew on buttons and darn socks to perfection."

"Do I have to give a demonstration of that tomorrow too?"

"It would be as well, perhaps," said Poirot, "if they took my word for it."

23

At half past ten on the following morning the melancholy Monsieur Fournier walked in to Poirot's sitting room and shook the little Belgian warmly by the hand.

His own manner was far more animated than usual.

"Monsieur," he said, "there is something I want to tell you. I have, I think, at last seen the point of what you said in London about the finding of the blowpipe."

"Ah!" Poirot's face lighted up.

"Yes," said Fournier, taking a chair. "I pondered much over what you had said. Again and again I say to myself: 'Impossible that the crime should have been committed as we believe.' And at last—at last I see a connection between that repetition of mine and what you said about the finding of the blowpipe."

Poirot listened attentively, but said nothing.

"That day in London you said: 'Why was the blowpipe found when it might so easily have been passed out through the ventilator?' And I think now that I have the answer: The blowpipe was found because the murderer wanted it to be found."

"Bravo!" said Poirot.

"That was your meaning, then? Good. I thought so. And I went on a step further. I ask myself, 'Why did the murderer want the blowpipe to be found?' And to that I got the answer: 'Because the blowpipe was not used.'"

"Bravo! Bravo! My reasoning exactly."

"I say to myself: 'The poisoned dart, yes, but not the blowpipe.' Then something else was used to send that dart through the air— something that a man or woman might put to their lips in a normal manner, and which would cause no remark. And I remembered your insistence on a complete list of all that was found in the passengers' luggage and upon their persons. There were two things that especially attracted my attention—Lady Horbury had two cigarette holders, and on the table in front of the Duponts were a number of Kurdish pipes."

Monsieur Fournier paused. He looked at Poirot. Poirot did not speak.

"Both those things could have been put to the lips naturally without anyone remarking on it. I am right, am I not?"

Poirot hesitated, then he said:

"You are on the right track, yes, but go a little further. And do not forget the wasp."

"The wasp?" Fournier stared. "No, there I do not follow you. I cannot see where the wasp comes in."

"You cannot see? But it is there that I—"

He broke off as the telephone rang.

He took up the receiver.

"Allô. Allô. . . . Ah, good morning. . . . Yes, it is I myself, Hercule Poirot." In an aside to Fournier, he said, "It is Thibault. . . .

"Yes, yes, indeed. . . . Very well. And you? . . . Monsieur Fournier? . . . Quite right. . . . Yes; he has arrived. He is here at this moment."

Lowering the receiver, he said to Fournier:

"He tried to get you at the Sûreté. They told him that you had come to see me here. You had better speak to him. He sounds excited."

Fournier took the telephone.

"Allô. Allô. . . . Yes, it is Fournier speaking. . . . What? . . . What? . . . In verity, is that so? . . . Yes, indeed. . . . Yes. . . . Yes, I am sure he will. We will come round at once."

He replaced the telephone on its hook and looked across at Poirot.

"It is the daughter. The daughter of Madame Giselle."

"What?"

"Yes, she has arrived to claim her heritage."

"Where has she come from?"

"America, I understand. Thibault has asked her to return at half past eleven. He suggests we should go round and see him."

"Most certainly. We will go immediately. I will leave a note for Mademoiselle Grey."

He wrote:

Some developments have occurred which force me to go out. If Monsieur Jean Dupont should ring up or call, be amiable to him. Talk of buttons and socks, but not as yet of prehistoric pottery. He admires you, but he is intelligent!

Au revoir.

HERCULE POIROT.

"And now let us come, my friend," he said, rising. "This is what I have been waiting for—the entry on the scene of the shadowy figure of whose presence I have been conscious all along. Now, soon, I ought to understand everything."

Maître Thibault received Poirot and Fournier with great affability. After an interchange of compliments and polite questions and answers, the lawyer settled down to the discussion of Madame Giselle's heiress.

"I received a letter yesterday," he said. "And this morning the young lady herself called upon me."

"What age is Mademoiselle Morisot?"

"Mademoiselle Morisot—or rather Mrs. Richards; for she is married—is exactly twenty-four years of age."

"She brought documents to prove her identity?" asked Fournier.

"Certainly. Certainly."

He opened a file at his elbow.

"To begin with, there is this."

It was a copy of a marriage certificate between George Leman, bachelor, and Marie Morisot, both of Quebec. Its date was 1910. There was also the birth certificate of Anne Morisot Leman. There were various other documents and papers.

"This throws a certain light on the early life of Madame Giselle," said Fournier.

Thibault nodded.

"As far as I can piece it out," he said, "Marie Morisot was nursery governess or sewing maid when she met this man Leman.

"He was, I gather, a bad lot who deserted her soon after the marriage, and she resumed her maiden name.

"The child was received in the Institut de Marie at Quebec and was brought up there. Marie Morisot, or Leman, left Quebec shortly afterwards—I imagine with a man—and came to France. She remitted sums of money from time to time and finally dispatched a lump sum of ready money to be given to the child on attaining the age of twenty-one. At that time, Marie Morisot, or Leman, was no doubt living an irregular life, and considered it better to sunder any personal relations."

"How did the girl realize that she was the heiress to a fortune?"

"We have inserted discreet advertisements in various journals. It seems one of these came to the notice of the principal of the Institut de Marie and she wrote or telegraphed to Mrs. Richards, who was then in Europe, but on the point of returning to the States."

"Who is Richards?"

"I gather he is an American or Canadian from Detroit; by profession a maker of surgical instruments."

"He did not accompany his wife?"

"No, he is still in America."

"Is Mrs. Richards able to throw any light upon a possible reason for her mother's murder?"

The lawyer shook his head.

"She knows nothing about her. In fact, although she had once heard the principal mention it, she did not even remember what her mother's maiden name was."

"It looks," said Fournier, "as though her appearance on the scene is not going to be of any help in solving the murder problem. Not, I must admit, that I ever thought it would. I am on quite another tack at present. My inquiries have narrowed down to a choice of three persons."

"Four," said Poirot.

"You think four?"

"It is not I who say four. But on the theory that you advanced to me you cannot confine yourself to three persons." He made a sudden rapid motion with his hands. "The two cigarette holders, the Kurdish pipes and a flute. Remember the flute, my friend."

Fournier gave an exclamation, but at that moment the door opened and an aged clerk mumbled:

"The lady has returned."

"Ah," said Thibault. "Now you will be able to see the heiress for yourself. . . . Come in, madame. Let me present to you Monsieur Fournier, of the Sûreté, who is in charge in this country of the inquiries into your mother's death. This is Monsieur Hercule Poirot, whose name may be familiar to you and who is kindly giving us his assistance. Madame Richards."

Giselle's daughter was a dark chic-looking young woman. She was very smartly, though plainly, dressed.

She held out her hand to each of the men in turn, murmuring a few appreciative words.

"Though I fear, messieurs, that I have hardly the feeling of a daughter in the matter. I have been to all intents and purposes an orphan all my life."

In answer to Fournier's questions, she spoke warmly and gratefully of Mère Angélique, the head of the Institut de Marie.

"She has always been kindness itself to me."

"You left the Institut—when, madame?"

"When I was eighteen, monsieur. I started to earn my living. I was, for a time, a manicurist. I have also been in a dressmaker's establishment. I met my husband in Nice. He was then just returning to the States. He came over again on business to Holland and we were married in Rotterdam a month ago. Unfortunately, he had to return to Canada. I was detained, but I am now about to rejoin him."

Anne Richards' French was fluent and easy. She was clearly more French than English.

"You heard of the tragedy—how?"

"Naturally, I read of it in the papers. But I did not know—that is, I did not realize—that the victim in the case was my mother. Then I received a telegram here in Paris from Mère Angélique giving me the address of Maître Thibault and reminding me of my mother's maiden name."

Fournier nodded thoughtfully.

They talked a little further, but it seemed clear that Mrs. Richards could be of little assistance to them in their search for the murderer. She knew nothing at all of her mother's life or business relations.

Having elicited the name of the hotel at which she was staying, Poirot and Fournier took leave of her.

"You are disappointed, *mon vieux*," said Fournier. "You had some idea in your brain about this girl? Did you suspect that she might be an impostor? Or do you, in fact, still suspect that she is an impostor?"

Poirot shook his head in a discouraged manner.

"No, I do not think she is an impostor. Her proofs of identity sound genuine enough. It is odd, though; I feel that I have either seen her before, or that she reminds me of someone."

"A likeness to the dead woman?" suggested Fournier doubtfully. "Surely not."

"No, it is not that. I wish I could remember what it was. I am sure her face reminds me of someone."

Fournier looked at him curiously.

"You have always, I think, been intrigued by the missing daughter."

"Naturally," said Poirot, his eyebrows rising a little. "Of all the people who may or may not benefit by Giselle's death, this young woman does benefit very definitely in hard cash."

"True, but does that get us anywhere?"

Poirot did not answer for a minute or two. He was following the train of his own thoughts. He said at last:

"My friend, a very large fortune passes to this girl. Do you wonder that, from the beginning, I speculated as to her being implicated? There were three women on that plane. One of them, Miss Venetia Kerr, was of well-known and authenticated family. But the other two? Ever since Élise Grandier advanced the theory that the father of Madame Giselle's child was an Englishman, I have kept it in my mind that one of the two other women might conceivably be this daughter. They were both of approximately the right age. Lady Horbury was a chorus girl whose antecedents were somewhat obscure and who acted under a stage name. Miss Jane Grey, as she once told me, had been brought up in an orphanage."

"Ah-ha!" said the Frenchman. "So that is the way your mind has been running? Our friend Japp would say that you were being over-ingenious."

"It is true that he always accuses me of preferring to make things difficult."

"You see?"

"But as a matter of fact, it is not true. I proceed always in the simplest manner imaginable! And I never refuse to accept facts."

"But you are disappointed? You expected more from this Anne Morisot?"

They were just entering Poirot's hotel. An object lying on the reception desk recalled Fournier's mind to something Poirot had said earlier in the morning.

"I have not thanked you," he said, "for drawing my attention to the error I had committed. I noted the two cigarette holders of Lady Horbury and the Kurdish pipes of the Duponts. It was unpardonable on my part to have forgotten the flute of Doctor Bryant. Though I do not seriously suspect him."

"You do not?"

"No. He does not strike me as the kind of man to—"

He stopped. The man standing at the reception desk talking to the clerk turned, his hand on the flute case. His glance fell on Poirot and his face lit up in grave recognition.

Poirot went forward; Fournier discreetly withdrew into the background. As well that Bryant should not see him.

"Doctor Bryant," said Poirot, bowing.

"Monsieur Poirot."

They shook hands. A woman who had been standing near Bryant moved away toward the lift. Poirot sent just a fleeting glance after her.

He said: "Well, *Monsieur le docteur,* are your patients managing to do without you for a little?"

Doctor Bryant smiled—that melancholy attractive smile that the other remembered so well. He looked tired, but strangely peaceful.

"I have no patients now," he said.

Then, moving toward a little table, he said:

"A glass of sherry, Monsieur Poirot? Or some other *apéritif?*"

"I thank you."

They sat down and the doctor gave the order. Then he said slowly:

"No, I have no patients now. I have retired."

"A sudden decision?"

"Not so very sudden."

He was silent as the drinks were set before them. Then, raising his glass, he said:

"It is a necessary decision. I resign of my own free will before I am struck off the register." He went on speaking in a gentle faraway voice: "There comes to everyone a turning point in their lives, Monsieur Poirot. They stand at the crossroads and have to decide. My profession interests me enormously; it is a sorrow—a very great sorrow—to abandon it. But there are other claims. There is, Monsieur Poirot, the happiness of a human being."

Poirot did not speak. He waited.

"There is a lady—a patient of mine—I love her very dearly. She has a husband who causes her infinite misery. He takes drugs. If you were a doctor you would know what that meant. She has no money of her own, so she cannot leave him.

"For some time I have been undecided, but now I have made up my mind. She and I are now on our way to Konya to begin a new life. I hope that at last she may know a little happiness. She has suffered so long."

Again he was silent. Then he said in a brisker tone:

"I tell you this, Monsieur Poirot, because it will soon be public property, and the sooner you know, the better."

"I understand," said Poirot. After a minute, he said, "You take your flute, I see."

Doctor Bryant smiled.

"My flute, Monsieur Poirot, is my oldest companion. When everything else fails, music remains."

His hand ran lovingly over the flute case; then, with a bow, he rose.

Poirot rose also.

"My best wishes for your future, *Monsieur le docteur*, and for that of Madame," said Poirot.

When Fournier rejoined his friend, Poirot was at the desk making arrangements for a trunk call to Quebec.

24

"WHAT now?" cried Fournier. "You are still preoccupied with this girl who inherits? Decidedly, it is the *idée fixe* you have there."

"Not at all—not at all," said Poirot. "But there must be in all things order and method. One must finish with one thing before proceeding to the next."

He looked round.

"Here is Mademoiselle Jane. Suppose that you commence *déjeuner*. I will join you as soon as I can."

Fournier acquiesced and he and Jane went into the dining room.

"Well?" said Jane with curiosity. "What is she like?"

"She is a little over medium height, dark with a matte complexion, a pointed chin—"

"You're talking exactly like a passport," said Jane. "My passport description is simply insulting, I think. It's composed of mediums and ordinary. Nose, medium; mouth, ordinary. How do they expect you to describe a mouth? Forehead, ordinary; chin, ordinary."

"But not ordinary eyes," said Fournier.

"Even they are gray, which is not a very exciting color."

"And who has told you, mademoiselle, that it is not an exciting color?" said the Frenchman, leaning across the table.

Jane laughed. "Your command of the English language," she said, "is highly efficient. Tell me more about Anne Morisot. Is she pretty?"

"*Assez bien*," said Fournier cautiously. "And she is not Anne Morisot. She is Anne Richards. She is married."

"Was the husband there too?"

"No."

"Why not, I wonder?"

"Because he is in Canada or America."

He explained some of the circumstances of Anne's life. Just as he was drawing his narrative to a close, Poirot joined them.

He looked a little dejected.

"Well, *mon cher?*" inquired Fournier.

"I spoke to the principal—to Mère Angélique herself. It is romantic, you know, the transatlantic telephone. To speak so easily to someone nearly halfway across the globe."

"The telegraphed photograph—that, too, is romantic. Science is the greatest romance there is. But you were saying?"

"I talked with Mère Angélique. She confirmed exactly what Mrs. Richards told us of the circumstances of her having been brought up at the Institut de Marie. She spoke quite frankly about the mother who left Quebec with a Frenchman interested in the wine trade. She was relieved at the time that the child would not come under her mother's influence. From her point of view, Giselle was on the downward path. Money was sent regularly, but Giselle never suggested a meeting."

"In fact, your conversation was a repetition of what we heard this morning."

"Practically, except that it was more detailed. Anne Morisot left the Institut de Marie six years ago to become a manicurist, afterwards she had a job as a lady's maid, and finally left Quebec for Europe in that capacity. Her letters were not frequent, but Mère Angélique usually heard from her about twice a year. When she saw an account of the inquest in the paper, she realized that this Marie Morisot was in all probability the Marie Morisot who had lived in Quebec."

"What about the husband?" asked Fournier. "Now that we know definitely that Giselle was married, the husband might become a factor?"

"I thought of that. It was one of the reasons for my telephone call. George Leman, Giselle's blackguard of a husband, was killed in the early days of the war."

He paused and then remarked abruptly:

"What was it that I just said—not my last remark, the one before? I have an idea that, without knowing it, I said something of significance."

Fournier repeated as well as he could the substance of Poirot's remarks, but the little man shook his head in a dissatisfied manner.

"No, no, it was not that. Well, no matter."

He turned to Jane and engaged her in conversation.

At the close of the meal he suggested that they should have coffee in the lounge.

Jane agreed and stretched out her hand for her bag and gloves, which were on the table. As she picked them up she winced slightly.

"What is it, mademoiselle?"

"Oh, it's nothing," laughed Jane. "It's only a jagged nail. I must file it."

Poirot sat down again very suddenly.

"*Nom d'un nom d'un nom,*" he said quietly.

The other two stared at him in surprise.

"Monsieur Poirot!" cried Jane. "What is it?"

"It is," said Poirot, "that I remember now why the face of Anne Morisot is familiar to me. I have seen her before. In the aeroplane on the day of the murder. Lady Horbury sent for her to get a nail file. Anne Morisot was Lady Horbury's maid."

25

This sudden revelation had an almost stunning effect on the three people sitting round the luncheon table. It opened up an entirely new aspect of the case.

Instead of being a person wholly remote from the tragedy, Anne Morisot was now shown to have been actually present on the scene of the crime. It took a minute or two for everyone to readjust his ideas.

Poirot made a frantic gesture with his hands; his eyes were closed; his face contorted in agony.

"A little minute—a little minute," he implored them. "I have got to think, to see, to realize how this affects my ideas of the case. I must go back in mind. I must remember. A thousand maledictions on my unfortunate stomach. I was preoccupied only with my internal sensations!"

"She was actually on the plane, then," said Fournier. "I see. I begin to see."

"I remember," said Jane. "A tall dark girl." Her eyes half closed in an effort of memory. "Madeleine, Lady Horbury called her."

"That is it—Madeleine," said Poirot.

"Lady Horbury sent her along to the end of the plane to fetch a case—a scarlet dressing case."

"You mean," said Fournier, "that this girl went right past the seat where her mother was sitting?"

"That is right."

"The motive," said Fournier. He gave a great sigh. "And the opportunity. Yes, it is all there."

Then, with a sudden vehemence most unlike his usual melancholy manner, he brought down his hand with a bang on the table.

"But *parbleu!*" he cried. "Why did no one mention this before? Why was she not included amongst the suspected persons?"

"I have told you, my friend—I have told you," said Poirot wearily. "My unfortunate stomach."

"Yes, yes, that is understandable. But there were other stomachs unaffected. The stewards, the other passengers."

"I think," said Jane, "that perhaps it was because it was so very early this happened. The plane had only just left Le Bourget. And Giselle was alive and well an hour or so after that. It seemed as though she must have been killed much later."

"That is curious," said Fournier thoughtfully. "Can there have been a delayed action of the poison? Such things happen."

Poirot groaned and dropped his head into his hands.

"I must think. I must think. Can it be possible that all along my ideas have been entirely wrong?"

"*Mon vieux,*" said Fournier, "such things happen. They happen to me; it is possible that they have happened to you. One has occasionally to pocket one's pride and readjust one's ideas."

"That is true," agreed Poirot. "It is possible that all along I have attached too much importance to one particular thing. I expected to find a certain clue. I found it, and I built up my case from it. But if I have been wrong from the beginning—if that particular article was where it was merely as the result of an accident—why, then—yes, I will admit that I have been wrong—completely wrong."

"You cannot shut your eyes to the importance of this turn of events," said Fournier. "Motive and opportunity—what more can you want?"

"Nothing. It must be as you say. The delayed action of the poison is indeed extraordinary—practically speaking, one would say impossible. But where poisons are concerned, the impossible does happen. One has to reckon with idiosyncrasy."

His voice tailed off.

"We must discuss a plan of campaign," said Fournier. "For the moment, it would, I think, be unwise to arouse Anne Morisot's suspicions. She is completely unaware that you have recognized her. Her bona fides have been accepted. We know the hotel at which she is staying and we can keep in touch with her through Thibault. Legal formalities can always be delayed. We have two points established—opportunity and motive. We have still to prove that Anne Morisot had snake venom in her possession. There is also the question of the American who bought the blowpipe and bribed Jules Perrot. It might certainly be the husband, Richards. We have only her word for it that he is in Canada."

"As you say, the husband—yes, the husband. Ah! wait—wait."

Poirot pressed his hands upon his temples.

"It is all wrong," he murmured. "I do not employ the little gray cells of the brain in an orderly and methodical way. No, I leap to conclusions. I think, perhaps, what I am meant to think. No, that is wrong again. If my original idea were right, I could not be meant to think—"

He broke off.

"I beg your pardon," said Jane.

Poirot did not answer for a moment or two. Then he took his hands from his temples, sat very upright and straightened two forks and a saltcellar which offended his sense of symmetry.

"Let us reason," he said. "Anne Morisot is either guilty or innocent of the crime. If she is innocent, why has she lied? Why has she concealed the fact that she was lady's maid to Lady Horbury?"

"Why, indeed?" said Fournier.

"So we say Anne Morisot is guilty because she has lied. But wait. Suppose my first supposition was correct. Will that supposition fit in with Anne Morisot's guilt or with Anne Morisot's lie? Yes, yes, it might—given one premise. But in that case, and if that premise is correct, then Anne Morisot should not have been on the plane at all."

The others looked at him politely, if with, perhaps, a rather perfunctory interest.

Fournier thought:

"I see now what the Englishman, Japp, meant. He makes difficulties, this old one. He tries to make an affair which is now simple sound complicated. He cannot accept a straightforward solution without pretending that it squares with his preconceived ideas."

Jane thought:

"I don't see in the least what he means. Why couldn't the girl be in the plane? She had to go wherever Lady Horbury wanted her to go. I think he's rather a mountebank, really."

Suddenly Poirot drew in his breath with a hiss.

"Of course," he said. "It is a possibility! And it ought to be very simple to find out."

He rose.

"What now, my friend?" asked Fournier.

"Again the telephone," said Poirot.

"The transatlantic to Quebec?"

"This time it is merely a call to London."

"To Scotland Yard?"

"No, to Lord Horbury's house in Grosvenor Square. If only I have the good fortune to find Lady Horbury at home."

"Be careful, my friend, if any suspicion gets round to Anne Morisot that we have been making inquiries about her, it would not suit our affair. Above all, we must not put her upon her guard."

"Have no fears. I will be discreet. I ask only one little question. A question of a most harmless nature." He smiled. "You shall come with me if you like."

"No, no."

"But, yes. I insist."

The two men went off, leaving Jane in the lounge.

It took some little time to put the call through. But Poirot's luck was in. Lady Horbury was lunching at home.

"Good. Will you tell Lady Horbury that it is Monsieur Hercule Poirot speaking from Paris." There was a pause. "That is you, Lady Horbury? . . . No, no, all is well. I assure you all is well. It is not that matter at all. I want you to answer me a question. . . . Yes. . . . When you go from Paris to England by air, does your maid usually go with you, or does she go by train? . . . By train. And so on that particular occasion? . . . I see. . . . You are sure? . . . Ah, she has left you. . . . I see. She left you very suddenly, at a moment's notice. . . . *Mais oui*, base ingratitude. It is too true. A most ungrateful class! . . . Yes, yes, exactly. . . . No, no, you need not worry. *Au revoir*. Thank you."

He replaced the receiver and turned to Fournier, his eyes green and shining.

"Listen, my friend; Lady Horbury's maid usually traveled by train and boat. On the occasion of Giselle's murder, Lady Horbury decided at the last moment that Madeleine had better go by air too."

He took the Frenchman by the arm.

"Quick, my friend," he said. "We must go to her hotel. If my little idea is correct—and I think it is—there is no time to be lost."

Fournier stared at him. But before he could frame a question, Poirot had turned away and was heading for the revolving doors leading out of the hotel.

Fournier hastened after him.

"But I do not understand? What is all this?"

The commissionaire was holding open the door of a taxi. Poirot jumped in and gave the address of Anne Morisot's hotel.

"And drive quickly, but quickly!"

Fournier jumped in after him.

"What fly is this that has bitten you? Why this mad rush, this haste?"

"Because, my friend, if, as I say, my little idea is correct, Anne Morisot is in imminent danger."

"You think so?"

Fournier could not help a skeptical tone creeping into his voice.

"I am afraid," said Poirot. "Afraid. *Bon Dieu,* how this taxi crawls!"

The taxi at the moment was doing a good forty miles an hour and cutting in and out of traffic with a miraculous immunity due to the excellent eye of the driver.

"It crawls to such an extent that we shall have an accident in a minute," said Fournier dryly. "And Mademoiselle Grey, we have left her planted there awaiting our return from the telephone, and instead we leave the hotel without a word. It is not very polite, that!"

"Politeness or impoliteness, what does it matter in an affair of life and death?"

"Life or death?" Fournier shrugged his shoulders.

He thought to himself:

"It is all very well, but this obstinate madman may endanger the whole business. Once the girl knows that we are on her track—"

He said in a persuasive voice:

"See now, Monsieur Poirot; be reasonable. We must go carefully."

"You do not understand," said Poirot. "I am afraid—afraid."

The taxi drew up with a jerk at the quiet hotel where Anne Morisot was staying.

Poirot sprang out and nearly collided with a young man just leaving the hotel.

Poirot stopped dead for a moment, looking after him.

"Another face that I know. But where? . . . Ah! I remember. It is the actor, Raymond Barraclough."

As he stepped forward to enter the hotel, Fournier placed a restraining hand on his arm.

"Monsieur Poirot, I have the utmost respect, the utmost admiration for your methods, but I feel very strongly that no precipitate action must be taken. I am responsible here in France for the conduct of this case."

Poirot interrupted him:

"I comprehend your anxiety. But do not fear any precipitate action on my part. Let us make inquiries at the desk. If Madame Richards is here and all is well, then no harm is done and we can discuss together our future action. You do not object to that?"

"No, no, of course not."

"Good."

Poirot passed through the revolving door and went up to the reception desk. Fournier followed him.

"You have a Mrs. Richards staying here, I believe," said Poirot.

"No, monsieur. She was staying here, but she left today."

"She has left?" demanded Fournier.

"Yes, monsieur."

"When did she leave?"

The clerk glanced up at the clock.

"A little over half an hour ago."

"Was her departure unexpected? Where has she gone?"

The clerk stiffened at the questions and was disposed to refuse to answer. But when Fournier's credentials were produced, the clerk changed his tone and was eager to give any assistance in his power.

No, the lady had not left an address. He thought her departure was the result of a sudden change of plans. She had formerly said she was making a stay of about a week.

More questions. The concierge was summoned, the luggage porters, the lift boys.

According to the concierge, a gentleman had called to see the lady. He had come while she was out, but had awaited her return and they had lunched together. What kind of gentleman? An American gentleman. Very American. She had seemed surprised to see him. After lunch, the lady gave orders for her luggage to be brought down and put on a taxi.

Where had she driven to? She had driven to the Gare du Nord— at least that was the order she had given to the taximan. Did the American gentleman go with her? No, she had gone alone.

"The Gare du Nord," said Fournier. "That means England on the face of it. The two-o'clock service. But it may be a blind. We must telephone to Boulogne and also try and get hold of that taxi."

It was as though Poirot's fears had communicated themselves to Fournier.

The Frenchman's face was anxious.

Rapidly and efficiently he set the machinery of the law in motion.

It was five o'clock when Jane, sitting in the lounge of the hotel with a book, looked up to see Poirot coming toward her.

She opened her mouth reproachfully, but the words remained unspoken. Something in his face stopped her.

"What is it?" she said. "Has anything happened?"

Poirot took both her hands in his.

"Life is very terrible, mademoiselle," he said.

Something in his tone made Jane feel frightened.

"What is it?" she said again.

Poirot said slowly:

"When the boat train reached Boulogne, they found a woman in a first-class carriage, dead."

The color ebbed from Jane's face.

"Anne Morisot?"

"Anne Morisot. In her hand was a little blue glass bottle which had contained prussic acid."

"Oh!" said Jane. "Suicide?"

Poirot did not answer for a moment or two. Then he said, with the air of one who chooses his words carefully:

"Yes, the police think it was suicide."

"And you?"

Poirot slowly spread out his hands in an expressive gesture.

"What else is there to think?"

"She killed herself? Why? Because of remorse or because she was afraid of being found out?"

Poirot shook his head.

"Life can be very terrible," he said. "One needs much courage."

"To kill oneself? Yes, I suppose one does."

"Also to live," said Poirot, "one needs courage."

26

THE next day Poirot left Paris. Jane stayed behind with a list of duties to perform. Most of these seemed singularly meaningless to her, but she carried them out to the best of her powers. She saw Jean Dupont twice. He mentioned the expedition which she was to join, and Jane did not dare to undeceive him without orders from Poirot, so she hedged as best she could and turned the conversation to other matters.

Five days later she was recalled to England by a telegram.

Norman met her at Victoria and they discussed recent events.

Very little publicity had been given to the suicide. There had been a paragraph in the papers stating that a Canadian lady, a Mrs. Richards, had committed suicide in the Paris-Boulogne express, but that was all. There had been no mention of any connection with the aeroplane murder.

Both Norman and Jane were inclined to be jubilant. Their troubles, they hoped, were at an end. Norman was not so sanguine as Jane.

"They may suspect her of doing her mother in, but now that she's taken this way out, they probably won't bother to go on with the case. And unless it is proved publicly, I don't see what good it is going to be to all of us poor devils. From the point of view of the public, we shall remain under suspicion just as much as ever."

He said as much to Poirot, whom he met a few days later in Piccadilly.

Poirot smiled.

"You are like all the rest. You think I am an old man who accomplishes nothing! Listen, you shall come tonight to dine with me. Japp is coming, and also our friend, Mr. Clancy. I have some things to say that may be interesting."

The dinner passed off pleasantly. Japp was patronizing and good-humored, Norman was interested, and little Mr. Clancy was nearly as thrilled as when he had recognized the fatal thorn.

It seemed clear that Poirot was not above trying to impress the little author.

After dinner, when coffee had been drunk, Poirot cleared his throat in a slightly embarrassed manner not free from self-importance.

"My friends," he said, "Mr. Clancy here has expressed interest in what he would call 'my methods, Watson,' *C'est ça, n'est-ce pas?* I propose, if it will not bore you all—"

He paused significantly, and Norman and Japp said quickly, "No, no," and "Most interesting."

"—to give you a little résumé of my methods in dealing with this case."

He paused and consulted some notes. Japp whispered to Norman: "Fancies himself, doesn't he? Conceit's that little man's middle name."

Poirot looked at him reproachfully and said, "Ahem!"

Three politely interested faces were turned to him and he began:

"I will start at the beginning, my friends. I will go back to the air liner 'Prometheus' on its ill-fated journey from Paris to Croydon. I am going to tell you my precise ideas and impressions at the time; passing on to how I came to confirm or modify them in the light of future events.

"When, just before we reached Croydon, Doctor Bryant was approached by the steward and went with him to examine the body, I accompanied him. I had a feeling that it might—who knows?—be something in my line. I have, perhaps, too professional a point of view where deaths are concerned. They are divided, in my mind, into two classes—deaths which are my affair and deaths which are not my affair—and though the latter class is infinitely more numerous, nevertheless, whenever I come in contact with death, I am like the dog who lifts his head and sniffs the scent.

"Doctor Bryant confirmed the steward's fear that the woman was dead. As to the cause of death, naturally, he could not pronounce on that without a detailed examination. It was at this point that a suggestion was made—by Mr. Jean Dupont—that death was due to shock following on a wasp sting. In furtherance of this hypothesis, he drew attention to a wasp that he himself had slaughtered shortly before.

"Now, that was a perfectly plausible theory, and one quite likely to be accepted. There was the mark on the dead woman's neck, closely resembling the mark of a sting, and there was the fact that a wasp had been in the plane.

"But at that moment I was fortunate enough to look down and espy what might at first have been taken for the body of yet another wasp. In actuality it was a native thorn with a little teased orange-and-black silk on it.

"At this point Mr. Clancy came forward and made the statement that it was a thorn shot from a blowpipe after the manner of some native tribe. Later, as you all know, the blowpipe itself was discovered.

"By the time we reached Croydon, several ideas were working in my mind. Once I was definitely on the firm ground, my brain began to work once more with its normal brilliance."

"Go it, Monsieur Poirot," said Japp, with a grin. "Don't have any false modesty."

Poirot threw him a look and went on:

"One idea presented itself very strongly to me—as it did to everyone else—and that was the audacity of a crime being committed in such a manner, and the astonishing fact that nobody noticed its being done!

"There were two other points that interested me. One was the convenient presence of the wasp. The other was the discovery of the blowpipe. As I remarked after the inquest to my friend Japp, why on earth did the murderer not get rid of it by passing it out through the ventilating hole in the window? The thorn itself might be difficult to trace or identify, but a blowpipe which still retained a portion of its price label was a very different matter.

"What was the solution? Obviously, that the murderer wanted the blowpipe to be found.

"But why? Only one answer seemed logical. If a poisoned dart and a blowpipe were found, it would naturally be assumed that the murder had been committed by a thorn shot from a blowpipe. Therefore, in reality the murder had not been committed that way.

"On the other hand, as medical evidence was to show, the cause of death was undoubtedly the poisoned thorn. I shut my eyes and asked myself: 'What is the surest and most reliable way of placing a poisoned thorn in the jugular vein?' And the answer came immediately: 'By hand.'

"And that immediately threw light on the necessity for the finding of the blowpipe. The blowpipe inevitably conveyed the suggestion of distance. If my theory was right, the person who killed Madame Giselle was a person who went right up to her table and bent over her.

"Was there such a person? Yes, there were two people. The two stewards. Either of them could go up to Madame Giselle, lean toward her, and nobody would notice anything unusual.

"Was there anyone else?

"Well, there was Mr. Clancy. He was the only person in the car who had passed immediately by Madame Giselle's seat—and I remembered that it was he who had first drawn attention to the blowpipe-and-thorn theory."

Mr. Clancy sprang to his feet.

"I protest!" he cried. "I protest! This is an outrage!"

"Sit down," said Poirot. "I have not finished yet. I have to show you all the steps by which I arrived at my conclusion.

"I had now three persons as possible suspects. Mitchell, Davis and Mr. Clancy. None of them at first sight appeared likely murderers, but there was much investigation to be done.

"I next turned my mind to the possibilities of the wasp. It was suggestive, that wasp. To begin with, no one had noticed it until about the time coffee was served. That in itself was rather curious. I constructed a certain theory of the crime. The murderer presented to the world two separate solutions of the tragedy. On the first or simplest, Madame Giselle was stung by a wasp and had succumbed to heart failure. The success of that solution depended on whether or no the murderer was in a position to retrieve the thorn. Japp and I agreed that that could be done easily enough—so long as no suspicion of foul play had arisen. There was the particular coloring of the silk which I had no doubt was deliberately substituted for the original cerise so as to simulate the appearance of a wasp.

"Our murderer, then, approaches the victim's table, inserts the thorn and releases the wasp! The poison is so powerful that death would occur almost immediately. If Giselle cried out, it would probably not be heard, owing to the noise of the plane. If it was just noticed, well, there was a wasp buzzing about to explain the cry. The poor woman had been stung.

"That, as I say, was Plan Number One. But supposing that, as actually happened, the poisoned thorn was discovered before the murderer could retrieve it. In that case, the fat is in the fire. The theory of natural death is impossible. Instead of getting rid of the blowpipe through the window, it is put in a place where it is bound to be discovered when the plane is searched. And at once it will be assumed that the blowpipe was the instrument of the crime. The proper atmosphere of distance will be created, and when the blowpipe is traced it will focus suspicion in a definite and prearranged direction.

"I had now my theory of the crime, and I had three suspects, with a barely possible fourth—Monsieur Jean Dupont, who had outlined the death-by-a-wasp-sting theory, and who was sitting on the gangway so near Giselle that he might just possibly have moved from his seat without being noticed. On the other hand, I did not really think he would have dared to take such a risk.

"I concentrated on the problem of the wasp. If the murderer had brought the wasp onto the plane and released it at the psychological moment, he must have had something in the nature of a small box in which to keep it.

"Hence my interest in the contents of the passengers' pockets and hand luggage.

"And here I came up against a totally unexpected development. I found what I was looking for—but, as it seemed to me, on the wrong person. There was an empty small-sized Bryant and May's match box in Mr. Norman Gale's pocket. But by everybody's evidence, Mr. Gale had never passed down the gangway of the car. He had only visited the washroom compartment and returned to his own seat.

"Nevertheless, although it seems impossible, there was a method by which Mr. Gale could have committed the crime—as the contents of his attaché case showed."

"My attaché case?" said Norman Gale. He looked amused and puzzled. "Why, I don't even remember now what was in it."

Poirot smiled at him amiably.

"Wait a little minute. I will come to that. I am telling you my first ideas.

"To proceed, I had four persons who could have done the crime—from the point of view of possibility. The two stewards, Clancy and Gale.

"I now looked at the case from the opposite angle—that of motive; if a motive were to coincide with a possibility—well, I had my murderer! But alas, I could find nothing of the kind. My friend Japp has accused me of liking to make things difficult. On the contrary, I approached this question of motive with all the simplicity in the world. To whose benefit would it be if Madame Giselle were removed? Clearly, to her unknown daughter's benefit, since that unknown daughter would inherit a fortune. There were also certain persons who were in Madame Giselle's power—or shall we say, who might be in Giselle's power for aught we knew? That, then, was a task of elimination. Of the passengers in the plane I could only be certain of one who was undoubtedly mixed up with Giselle. That one was Lady Horbury.

"In Lady Horbury's case the motive was very clear. She had visited Giselle at her house in Paris the night before. She was desperate and she had a friend, a young actor, who might easily have impersonated the American who bought the blowpipe, and might also have bribed the clerk in Universal Air Lines to insure that Giselle traveled by the twelve-o'clock service.

"I had, as it were, a problem in two halves. I did not see how it was possible for Lady Horbury to commit the crime. And I could not see for what motive the stewards, Mr. Clancy or Mr. Gale should want to commit it.

"Always, in the back of my mind, I considered the problem of Giselle's unknown daughter and heiress. Were any of my four suspects married, and if so, could one of the wives be this Anne Morisot? If her father was English, the girl might have been brought up in England. Mitchell's wife I soon dismissed—she was of good old Dorset country stock. Davis was courting a girl whose father and mother were alive. Mr. Clancy was not married. Mr. Gale was obviously head over ears in love with Miss Jane Grey.

"I may say that I investigated the antecedents of Miss Grey very carefully, having learned from her in casual conversation that she had been brought up in an orphanage near Dublin. But I soon satisfied myself that Miss Grey was not Madame Giselle's daughter.

"I made out a table of results. The stewards had neither gained nor lost by Madame Giselle's death, except that Mitchell was obviously suffering from shock. Mr. Clancy was planning a book on the subject by which he hoped to make money. Mr. Gale was fast losing his practice. Nothing very helpful there.

"And yet, at that time I was convinced that Mr. Gale was the murderer—there was the empty match box, the contents of his attaché case. Apparently he lost, not gained, by the death of Giselle. But those appearances might be false appearances.

"I determined to cultivate his acquaintance. It is my experience that no one, in the course of conversation, can fail to give themselves away sooner or later. Everyone has an irresistible urge to talk about themselves.

"I tried to gain Mr. Gale's confidence. I pretended to confide in him, and I even enlisted his help. I persuaded him to aid me in the fake blackmailing of Lady Horbury. And it was then that he made his first mistake.

"I had suggested a slight disguise. He arrived to play his part with a ridiculous and impossible outfit! The whole thing was a farce. No one, I felt sure, could play a part as badly as he was proposing to play one. What, then, was the reason for this? Because his knowledge of his own guilt made him chary of showing himself to be a good actor. When, however, I had adjusted his ridiculous make-up, his artistic skill showed itself. He played his part perfectly and Lady Horbury did not recognize him. I was convinced then that he could have disguised himself as an American in Paris and could also have played the necessary part in the 'Prometheus.'

"By this time I was getting seriously worried about Mademoiselle Jane. Either she was in this business with him, or else she was entirely innocent; and in the latter case she was a victim. She might wake up one day to find herself married to a murderer.

"With the object of preventing a precipitate marriage, I took Mademoiselle Jane to Paris as my secretary.

"It was while we were there that the missing heiress appeared to claim her fortune. I was haunted by a resemblance that I could not place. I did place it in the end, but too late.

"At first, the discovery that she had actually been in the plane and had lied about it seemed to overthrow all my theories. Here, overwhelmingly, was the guilty person.

"But if she were guilty, she had an accomplice—the man who bought the blowpipe and bribed Jules Perrot.

"Who was that man? Was it conceivably her husband?

"And then, suddenly, I saw the true solution. True, that is, if one point could be verified.

"For my solution to be correct, Anne Morisot ought not to have been on the plane.

"I rang up Lady Horbury and got my answer. The maid, Madeleine, traveled in the plane by a last-minute whim of her mistress."

He stopped.

Mr. Clancy said:

"Ahem—but I'm afraid I'm not quite clear."

"When did you stop pitching on me as the murderer?" asked Norman.

Poirot wheeled round on him.

"I never stopped. You are the murderer. . . . Wait. I will tell you everything. For the last week Japp and I have been busy. It is true that you became a dentist to please your uncle, John Gale. You took his name when you came into partnership with him, but you were his sister's son, not his brother's. Your real name is Richards. It was as Richards that you met the girl Anne Morisot at Nice last winter when she was there with her mistress. The story she told us was true as to the facts of her childhood, but the later part was edited carefully by you. She did know her mother's maiden name. Giselle was at Monte Carlo; she was pointed out and her real name was mentioned. You realized that there might be a large fortune to be got. It appealed to your gambler's nature. It was from Anne Morisot that you learned of Lady Horbury's connection with Giselle. The plan of the crime formed itself in your head. Giselle was to be murdered in such a way that suspicion would fall on Lady Horbury. Your plans matured and finally fructified. You bribed the clerk in Universal Air Lines so that Giselle should travel on the same plane as Lady Horbury. Anne Morisot had told you that she herself was going to England by train; you never expected her to be on the plane, and it seriously jeopardized your plans. If it was once known that Giselle's daughter and heiress had been on the plane, suspicion would naturally have fallen upon her. Your original idea was that she should claim the inheritance with a perfect alibi, since she would have been on a train or a boat at the time of the crime! And then you would have married her.

"The girl was by this time infatuated with you. But it was money you were after, not the girl herself.

"There was another complication to your plans. At Le Pinet you saw Mademoiselle Jane Grey and fell madly in love with her. Your passion for her drove you on to play a much more dangerous game.

"You intended to have both the money and the girl you loved. You were committing a murder for the sake of money and you were in no mind to relinquish the fruits of the crime. You frightened Anne Morisot by telling her that if she came forward at once to proclaim her identity, she would certainly be suspected of the murder. Instead you induced her to ask for a few days' leave and you went together to Rotterdam, where you were married.

"In due course you primed her how to claim the money. She was to say nothing of her employment as lady's maid and it was very clearly to be made plain that she and her husband had been abroad at the time of the murder.

"Unfortunately, the date planned for Anne Morisot to go to Paris and claim her inheritance coincided with my arrival in Paris, where Miss Grey had accompanied me. That did not suit your book at all. Either Mademoiselle Jane or myself might recognize in Anne Morisot the Madeleine who had been Lady Horbury's maid.

"You tried to get in touch with her in time, but failed. You finally arrived in Paris yourself and found she had already gone to the lawyer. When she returned, she told you of her meeting with me. Things were becoming dangerous and you made up your mind to act quickly.

"It had been your intention that your new-made wife should not survive her accession to wealth very long. Immediately after the marriage ceremony, you had both made wills leaving all you had one to the other! A very touching business.

"You intended, I fancy, to follow a fairly leisurely course. You would have gone to Canada—ostensibly because of the failure of your practice. There you would have resumed the name of Richards and your wife would have rejoined you. All the same, I do not fancy it would have been very long before Mrs. Richards regrettably died, leaving a fortune to a seemingly inconsolable widower. You would then have returned to England as Norman Gale, having had the good fortune to make a lucky speculation in Canada! But now you decided that no time must be lost."

Poirot paused and Norman Gale threw back his head and laughed.

"You are very clever at knowing what people intend to do! You ought to adopt Mr. Clancy's profession!" His tone deepened to one of anger: "I never heard such a farrago of nonsense. What you imagined, Monsieur Poirot, is hardly evidence!"

Poirot did not seem put out. He said:

"Perhaps not. But then I have some evidence."

"Really?" sneered Norman. "Perhaps you have evidence as to how I killed old Giselle when everyone in the aeroplane knows perfectly well I never went near her?"

"I will tell you exactly how you committed the crime," said Poirot. "What about the contents of your dispatch case? You were on a holiday. Why take a dentist's linen coat? That is what I asked myself. And the answer is this: Because it resembled so closely a steward's coat.

"This is what you did: When coffee was served and the stewards had gone to the other compartment, you went to the washroom, put on your linen coat, padded your cheeks with cotton-wool rolls, came out, seized a coffee spoon from the box in the pantry opposite, hurried down the gangway with the steward's quick run, spoon in hand, to Giselle's table. You thrust the thorn into her neck, opened the match box and let the wasp escape, hurried back into the washroom, changed your coat and emerged leisurely to return to your table. The whole thing took only a couple of minutes.

"Nobody notices a steward particularly. The only person who might have recognized you was Mademoiselle Jane, but you know women! As soon as a woman is left alone—particularly when she is traveling with an attractive young man—she seizes the opportunity to have a good look in her hand mirror, powder her nose and adjust her make-up."

"Really," sneered Gale, "a most interesting theory, but it didn't happen. Anything else?"

"Quite a lot," said Poirot. "As I have just said, in the course of conversation a man gives himself away. You were imprudent enough to mention that for a while you were on a farm in South Africa. What you did not say, but what I have since found out, is that it was a snake farm."

For the first time, Norman Gale showed fear. He tried to speak, but the words would not come.

Poirot continued:

"You were there under your own name of Richards; a photograph of you transmitted by telephone has been recognized. That same photograph has been identified in Rotterdam as the man Richards who married Anne Morisot."

Again Norman Gale tried to speak and failed. His whole personality seemed to change. The handsome vigorous young man turned into a rat-like creature with furtive eyes looking for a way of escape and finding none.

"It was haste ruined your plan," said Poirot. "The superior of the Institut de Marie hurried things on by wiring to Anne Morisot. It would have looked suspicious to ignore that wire. You had impressed it upon your wife that unless she suppressed certain facts either she or you might be suspected of murder, since you had both, unfortunately, been in the plane when Giselle was killed. When you met her afterwards and you learned that I had been present at the interview, you hurried things on. You were afraid I might get the truth out of Anne. Perhaps she herself was beginning to suspect you. You hustled her away out of the hotel and into the boat train. You administered prussic acid to her by force and you left the empty bottle in her hand."

"A lot of damned lies!"

"Oh, no. There was a bruise on her neck."

"Damned lies, I tell you!"

"You even left your fingerprints on the bottle."

"You lie! I wore—"

"Ah, you wore gloves? I think, monsieur, that little admission cooks your gander."

"You damned interfering little mountebank!" Livid with passion, his face unrecognizable, Gale made a spring at Poirot. Japp, however, was too quick for him. Holding him in a capable unemotional grip, Japp said:

"James Richards alias Norman Gale, I hold a warrant for your arrest on the charge of willful murder. I must warn you that anything you say will be taken down and used in evidence."

A terrible shudder shook the man. He seemed on the point of collapse.

A couple of plainclothes men were waiting outside. Norman Gale was taken away.

Left alone with Poirot, little Mr. Clancy drew a deep breath of ecstasy.

"Monsieur Poirot," he said, "that has been absolutely the most thrilling experience of my life. You have been wonderful!"

Poirot smiled modestly.

"No, no. Japp deserves as much credit as I do. He has done wonders in identifying Gale as Richards. The Canadian police want Richards. A girl he was mixed up with there is supposed to have committed suicide, but facts have come to light which seem to point to murder."

"Terrible," Mr. Clancy chirped.

"A killer," said Poirot. "And like many killers, attractive to women."

Mr. Clancy coughed.

"That poor girl. Jane Grey."

Poirot shook his head sadly.

"Yes, as I said to her, life can be very terrible. But she has courage. She will come through."

With an absent-minded hand, he arranged a pile of picture papers that Norman Gale had disarranged in his wild spring.

Something arrested his attention—a snapshot of Venetia Kerr at a race meeting "talking to Lord Horbury and a friend."

He handed it to Mr. Clancy.

"You see that? In a year's time there will be an announcement: 'A marriage is arranged and will shortly take place between Lord Horbury and the Honorable Venetia Kerr.' And do you know who will have arranged that marriage? Hercule Poirot! There is another marriage that I have arranged too."

"Lady Horbury and Mr. Barraclough?"

"Ah, no, in that matter I take no interest." He leaned forward. "No, I refer to a marriage between Monsieur Jean Dupont and Miss Jane Grey. You will see."

It was a month later that Jane came to Poirot.

"I ought to hate you, Monsieur Poirot."

She looked pale and fine-drawn, with dark circles round her eyes.

Poirot said gently:

"Hate me a little if you will. But I think you are one of those who would rather look truth in the face than live in a fool's paradise. And you might not have lived in it so very long. Getting rid of women is a vice that grows."

"He was so terribly attractive," said Jane.

She added:

"I shall never fall in love again."

"Naturally," agreed Poirot. "That side of life is finished for you."

Jane nodded.

"But what I must do is to have work—something interesting that I could lose myself in."

Poirot tilted back his chair and looked at the ceiling.

"I should advise you to go to Persia with the Duponts. That is interesting work, if you like."

"But—but I thought that was only camouflage on your part?"

Poirot shook his head.

"On the contrary, I have become so interested in archæology and prehistoric pottery that I sent the check for the donation I had promised. I heard this morning that they were expecting you to join the expedition. Can you draw at all?"

"Yes, I was rather good at drawing at school."

"Excellent. I think you will enjoy your season."

"Do they really want me to come?"

"They are counting on it."

"It would be wonderful," said Jane, "to get right away."

A little color rose in her face.

"Monsieur Poirot"—she looked at him suspiciously—"you're not—you're not being kind?"

"Kind?" said Poirot, with a lively horror at the idea. "I can assure you, mademoiselle, that where money is concerned I am strictly a man of business."

He seemed so offended that Jane quickly begged his pardon.

"I think," she said, "that I'd better go to some museums and look at some prehistoric pottery."

"A very good idea."

At the doorway, Jane paused and then came back.

"You mayn't have been kind in that particular way, but you have been kind to me."

She dropped a kiss on the top of his head and went out again.

"*Ça, c'est trés gentil!*" said Hercule Poirot.